contents

MICKY SPILLANE SPECIAL

ARTICLES

INTERVIEWS

REGULAR FEATURES

COLUMNS

crime time 2.6

FICTION

publisher
CT Publishing
PO Box 5880
Birmingham B16 8JF
Phone: 0121 689 4466,
Fax: 01582 712244, e-mail:
ct@crimetime.demon.co.uk
distribution
Turnaround
printing
Caledonian International Book
Publishing, Glasgow
editor:
Barry Forshaw
fiction/design:
Peter Dillon-Parkin
film editor:
Michael Carlson
advertising
Please phone for rates, or write to the
editorial address.
subscriptions:
£20 for four issues to
Crime Time Subscriptions, 18
Coleswood Rd, Harpenden, Herts
AL5 1EQ
legal stuff
Crime Time is © 1999
CT Publishing
ISBN 1-902002-20-2

tirade

DISAGREE WITH US. Go ahead – what are you waiting for? We're trying our hardest to ruffle our reader's feathers, and we may have found a way of making sure you don't confuse us with *Hello* magazine. From now on, throughout the magazine, you'll find some diametrically opposite views of selected new books, on the assumption that at least one of them will upset fans of writer X (the corollary, of course, is that you're likely to agree with the opposing review twenty pages on). The best magazines are always a hothouse of dissenting opinions (who wants a cosy uniformity of view?), and now that so many top crime writers have taken time out from their criminal endeavours to write for us, we can offer a genuine panoply of views. Mark Timlin may lose his lunch while reading a particular writer, but the same writer will have Gwendolyn Butler ascending the slopes of Mount Parnassus. And while Lawrence Block may love the novels of writer Y, it's a good bet that Natasha Cooper will be nodding off by chapter three. We've also inaugurated a crime panel, so that our reviewers can really go head-to-head over favourites and bêtes-noirs (Brian Ritterspak and Judith Gray are only just getting back on speaking terms after our last meeting). But what good is an opinion you aren't prepared to tread on toes for?

of course, we're hoping this will add to the indefinable appeal of CT – as will (we trust) our other innovations this month: beefing up our media sections (Charles Waring joins film editor Michael Carlson to keep you au fait with TV crime – look for Charles' piece on the unmissable *Sopranos* – and if you haven't been watching the latter, why not, for God's sake?).

Speaking of giving offence, we offer an in-depth look this month at one of the most famous (and reviled)writers in the crime genre – Mickey Spillane (Steve Holland looks at the books, Michael Carlson talks to the man, and Woody Haut interviews AL Bezzerides about the screenplay for the classic Aldrich film of *Kiss Me Deadly*. I asked Mickey about the latter movie, which he dislikes, and was stonewalled – Mike Carlson gets much more penetrating results in his interview).

Finally: The Crime Time website. (www.crimetime.co.uk) Rather than extol its virtues here, let me send you to our man in cyberspace, Steven Kelly (editor of the Richmond Review). Elsewhere in this issue, he'll tell you why you should be at the Crime Time site rather than spending your evening downloading images of questionable legality.

Barry Forshaw

adrian muller

DEAD ON DEANSGATE

Britain's biggest crime fiction conference—held during the weekend of the 22nd-24th of October—has finally revealed their Guest Author line-up. Visiting from the US are Michael Connelly and Elizabeth George, and representing Britain is Val McDermid. Just over ninety authors have registered to date, and fans will be able to get their favourite writers to sign old and new books, as well as being able to ask them questions during a wide range of panels. .Depending on when you read this – it may be too late, given CT's erratic schedule! - For more information contact: Dead on Deansgate, Waterstone's Booksellers, 91 Deansgate, Manchester M3 2BW. Tel: 0161-837-3000, fax: 0161-835-1534, email: crime@waterstones-manchester-deansgate.co.uk

TELLY SLEUTHS

Fans of the BBC's *The Mrs. Bradley Mysteries* will be glad to hear that Dame Diana Rigg is set to return as the Renaissance sleuth. Knowledgeable about anything from psycho-analysis—she studied with Freud—to poisons, Mrs. Bradley will find herself teamed up with a policeman played by former Dr. Who, Peter Davidson.

Poirot will also be back on our screens later this year. Christmastime will see David Suchet solve mysteries in feature length adaptations of *The Murder of Roger Ackroyd* and *Lord Edgware Dies*.

Presumably the publication of a new Colin Dexter novel, *The Remorseful Day*, means that it is only a question of time

before Endeavour Morse is back on our screens again also...

AGATHA CHRISTIE

Charles Osborne has adapted another play by the Queen of Crime. The novelisation of *The Unexpected Guest* will be HarperCollins' new 'Christie for Christmas'. Also look out for Osborne's *The Life and Crimes of Agatha Christie*. Subtitled 'A biographical companion to the works of Agatha Christie' the book is the first to analyse Dame Agatha's books *and* film and television adaptations.

CRIMEWAVE

New to news-stands is a crime fiction magazine called *Crimewave*. This quarterly magazine distinguishes itself from publications like *Crime Time* and *Shots* because its content is solely made up out of short stories. The current issue *Crimewave 2* includes contributions from Martin Edwards, Michael Z. Lewin, and Ian Rankin. Free copies will be sent to the first ten *Crime Time* readers to send their name and address to:

Crime Time/Crimewave Offer
TTA Press
5 Martins Lane
Witcham
Ely
Cambs CB6 2LB

JANET LAURENCE

Fans and collectors will presumably be on the lookout for *Caneletto and the Case of the Privy Garden*, Laurence's second

Canaletto mystery. The first in this historical series, *Caneletto and the Case of Westminster Bridge*, sold out almost as soon as it appeared in bookstores, thereby making it a collector's item. This second outing for the Italian painter is published in September. Janet Laurence is currently working on a new instalment in her other series featuring cookery expert Darina Lisle.

PETER LOVESEY

Readers who only know of Peter Lovesey through his Peter Diamond books are in for a treat as publisher Allison & Busby reissue the author's Sargeant Cribb series. Lovesey's first novel, *Wobble to Death,* was first published in 1970 after it won first prize in a competition for unpublished crimewriters. The mystery, set during a Victorian endurance race, was supposed to be a one-off featuring Sergeant Cribb and his sidekick, Constable Thackery. However, demand was such that the sergeant appeared in a further seven instalments as well as a highly successful television series. *Wobble to Death* appeared in July, *The Detective Wore Silk Drawers*, follows in October, and *Abracadaver* is due in March. Hopefully the remaining five will also follow.

CLASSIC CRIME

Pan is following up it's successful reissue of classic out- of-print mysteries with a further five titles with introductions by best-selling authors. The foreword to Eric Ambler's *Epitaph for a Spy* was written by Robert Harris, *Before the Fact* by Francis Iles—the source for Hitchcock's film *Suspicion*—has an introduction by Colin Dexter, and Frances Fyfield and Reginald Hill praise Cyril Law's *Tragedy at Law*, and Hillary Waugh's *Last Seen Wearing* respectively. Fans of Golden Age espionage and mystery writing should take this opportunity to snap up these rare and groundbreaking titles.

ANABEL DONALD

This August, after a gap of more than a year, Macmillan published a new instalment in Anabel Donald's Alex Tanner series. *Destroy Unopened* is the fifth novel to feature female PI Alex Tanner, and the good news is that Macmillan have reissued the whole series, some of which have been out of print for some time. Those readers fresh to the series do well to read them in order, starting with *An Uncommon Murder*, the book that introduced Alex, who at the time was a freelance researcher with sleuthing dreams.

MAGNA CUM MURDER INTERNATIONAL

After five successful Magna cum Murder conventions in the United States, the organisers are teaming up with the Bibliotheque des Litteratures Policiere, The Sorbonne and the Ville de Paris to bring the festival to Paris, France. With events scheduled for November 24 - 27, 1999, the panels will cover such diverse subjects as the influence of U.S. literature French polar, criminality and terrorism, crime fiction in film, and humour. Additionally, extra activities and events including tours and museum visits are being planned, and a welcome cocktail party hosted by Ville de Paris on Wednesday evening. Guest of Honour is Donald E. Westlake, and further authors include John Harvey, Jeremiah Healy, Peter Lovesey, Val McDermid, and James Sallis. For further information or to request registration materials please contact:

Kathryn Kennison, Magna cum Murder
The E.B. and Bertha C. Ball Center
Ball State University, Muncie, IN 47303
Phone: 00-1-765-285-8975
Fax: 00-1-765-747-9566
email: Kennisonk@aol.com or
ksbs828@aol.com

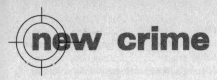

new crime

JULY

Jane Adams - *Final Frame* (Mike Croft). Macmillan, £16.99.

Jake Arnott - *The Long Firm*. Sceptre, £10.00.

Janet Bettle - *Unnatural Causes* (Geri Lander - new series). Piatkus, £17.99.

Alice Blanchard - *Darkness Peering*. Bantam, £9.99.

Lawrence Block - *Tanner on Ice* (Evan Tanner). No Exit Press, £5.99.

Christopher Brookmyre - *One Fine Day in the Middle of the Night*. Little Brown, £9.99.

John Burns - *Nark* (Max Chard). Macmillan, £16.99.

Patrick Conrad - *Limousine*. Jonathan Cape, £9.99.

Thomas H. Cook - *Instruments of Night*. Gollancz, £16.99.

Natasha Cooper - *Fault Lines* (Trish McGuire). Simon & Schuster, £16.99.

Robert Crais - *L.A. Requiem* (Elvis Cole). Orion, £9.99/£16.99.

Paul Doherty - *The Field of Blood* (Brother Athelstan). Headline, £16.99.

Reg Gadney - *Mother, Son and Holy Ghost*. Faber & Faber, £5.99.

Elizabeth George - *In Pursuit of the Proper Sinner* (Lynley & Havers). Hodder & Stoughton, £16.99.

Ed Gorman - *The Poker Club*, CT Publishing, £16.99.

Ed Gorman - *The Long Midnight*, CT Publishing, £4.99.

Ed Gorman - *Serpent's Kiss*, CT Publishing, £4.99.

Anne Granger - *Beneath These Stones* (Mitchell & Markby). Headline, £16.99.

Lesley Grant-Adamson - *Undertow*. Hodder & Stoughton, £16.99.

D.M. Greenwood - *Foolish Ways* (Theodora Braithwaite). Headline, £16.99.

Martha Grimes - *Biting the Moon*. Headline, £16.99.

Andrea Hart - *The Return*. Corgi, £5.99.

Humphrey Hawksley - *Absolute Measures*. Headline, £9.99/£16.99.

Shaun Hutson - *Warhol's Prophecy*. Macmillan, £16.99.

Judith Jones - *After Melissa* (Kerry Lake). Constable, £16.99.

Andrew Klavan - *Hunting Down Amanda*. Little Brown, £12.99.

Bill Knox - *The Taste of Proof* (Colin Thane). Constable, £16.99.

Richard Laymon - *Come Out Tonight*. Headline, £16.99.

John Lescroart - *Nothing But the Truth*. Headline, £16.99.

Samuel Lock - *Nothing But the Truth*. Vintage, £5.99.

Kevin Logan - *Survival of the Fittest* (debut crime novel). HarperCollins, £7.99.

Judy Mercer - *Split Image* (Ariel Gold). No Exit Press, £5.99.

Charles Osborne - *The Life and Crimes of Agatha Christie: A Biographical Companion*. HarperCollins, £16.99.

David Pascoe - *Fox on the Run* (debut crime novel). Orion, £9.99.

Dianne Pugh - *Pushover*. Headline, £16.99.

Danuta Reah - *Only Darkness* (debut crime novel). HarperCollins, £16.99.

Lisa Scottoline - *Mistaken Identity*. HarperCollins, £16.99.

Peter Straub - *Pork Pie Hat*. Orion, £6.99.

Alison Taylor - *Unsafe Convictions*. Heinemann, £15.99.

Jim Williams - *Recherche*. Simon & Schuster, £16.99.

Robert Wilson - *A Small Death in Lisbon*. HarperCollins, £9.99.

Don Winslow - *California Fire and Life*. Century, £10.00.

AUGUST

Andrea Badenoch - *Driven*. Macmillan, £16.99.

Robert Barnard - *Touched by the Dead*. HarperCollins, £16.99.

Paul Bennett - *The Money Race* (Nick Shannon). Warner, £5.99.

Peter Brighton - *The Death of a Smile* (debut crime novel). Simon & Schuster, £5.99.

Dougie Brimson - *The Crew* (debut crime novel). Headline, £9.99.

James Lee Burke - *Heartwood* (Billy Bob Holland). Orion, £16.99.

Harlan Coben - *The Final Detail*. Hodder & Stoughton, £16.99.

Mark B. Cohen - *Butcher's Ball*. Hodder & Stoughton, £16.99.

Christopher Dardon & Dick Lochte - *The Trials of Nicky Hill*. Piatkus, £5.99.

John Gordon Davis - *Unofficial and Deniable*. HarperCollins, £16.99.

Anabel Donald - *Destroy Unopened* (Alex Tanner). Macmillan, £5.99.

Brendan DuBois - *Resurrection Day*. Little Brown, £10.00.

Marjorie Eccles - *Cast a Cold Eye* (Gil Mayo). Constable, £16.99.

Janet Evanovich - *High Five* (Stephanie Plum). Macmillan, £14.99.

Colin Falconer - *Rough Justice* (Madeleine Fox - new series). Hodder & Stoughton, £16.99.

Robert Ferrigno - *Heartbreaker*. Hutchinson, £10.00.

Dan Fesperman - *Lie in the Dark*. No Exit Press, £9.99/£16.99.

Emer Gillespie - *Blow Down*. Headline, £16.99.

Jo-Ann Goodwin - *Danny Boy*. Bantam, £9.99.

Sue Grafton - *O is for Outlaw* (Kinsey Millhone). Macmillan, £9.99.

Chrisine Green - *Fatal Cut*. Severn House, £17.99.

J.M. Gregson - *Malice Aforethought* (Lambert & Hook). Severn House, £16.99.

Mary Higgins Clark - *We'll Meet Again*. Simon & Schuster, £16.99.

Lynn Hightower - *The Debt Collector* (Sonora Blair). Hodder & Stoughton, £16.99.

Joyce Holmes - *Thin Ice* (Fizz & Buchanan). Headline, £16.99.

Alan Hunter - *Gently Through the Mill* (George Gently). Constable, £16.99.

Quintin Jardine - *Gallery of Whispers* (Bob Skinner). Headline, £16.99.

Faye Kellerman - *Jupiter's Bones* (Peter Decker). Headline, £9.99/£16.99.

Linda LaPlante - Trial and Retribution. Macmillan, £5.99/£17.99.

Janet Laurence - *Canaletto and the Case of the Privy Garden* (Canaletto). Macmillan, £16.99.

Michael Ledwidge - *The Narrowback* (debut crime novel). Warner, £9.99.

Frederic Lindsay - *Idle Hands*. Hodder & Stoughton, £16.99.

Sam Llewellyn - *Under the Sea Garden*. Headline, £16.99.

Sara MacDonald - *The Sleep of Birds*. Headline, £16.99.

Alistair MacNeill - *Counterplot*. Gollancz, £16.99.

Hannah March - *The Devil's Highway* (Robert Fairfax). Headline, £16.99.

Edward Marston - *The King's Evil*. Headline, £16.99.

M.R.D. Meek - *A House to Die For*. Severn House, £16.99.

John Milne - *Alive and Kicking* (Jimmy Jenner). No Exit Press, £6.99.

John Milne - *Daddy's Girl* (Jimmy Jenner). No Exit Press, £6.99

David Mitchell - *Ghostwritten* (debut crime novel). Sceptre, £10.00.

Gemma O'Connor - *Sins of Omission*. Bantam, £5.99.

Chuck Palahniuk - *Survivor*. Jonathan Cape, £10.00

Robert B. Parker - *Small Vices* (Spenser). No Exit Press, £5.99.

David Peace - *Nineteenseventyfour*. Serpent's Tail, £8.99.

Michael Pearce - *Death of an Effendi* (Mamur Zapt). HarperCollins, £16.99.

George P. Pelecanos - *The Sweet Forever*. Serpent's Tail, £9.99.

Otto Penzler (editor) - *Murder for Revenge* (short stories). Orion, £16.99.

Gary Phillips - *Bad Night is Falling* (Ivan Monk). No Exit Press, £6.99.

Denise Ryan - *The Hit*. Piatkus, £5.99.

Carol Smith - *Family Reunion*. Little Brown, £17.99.

Shamus Smyth - *Quinn*. Flame, £10.00.

Michelle Spring - *Nights in White Satin* (Laura Principal). Orion, £9.99/£16.99.

John Straley - *The Angels Will Not Care* (Cecil Younger). Gollancz, £9.99/£16.99.

Aline Templeton - *Night and Silence*. Hodder & Stoughton, £16.99.

SEPTEMBER

Gilbert Adair - *A Closed Book*. Faber & Faber, £9.99.

Paul Adam - *Unholy Trinity*. Little Brown, £9.99.

Jeffrey Ashford - *An Honest Betrayal*. Severn House, £17.99.

Francis Bennet - *Secret Kingdom*. Gollancz, £9.99/£16.99.

Agatha Christie (adapted Charles Osborn) - *The Unexpected Guest*. HarperCollins, £15.99.

Judith Cook - *Kill the Witch*. Headline, £16.99.

Michael Cordy - *Crime Zero*. Bantam, £9.99.

Patricia Cornwell - *Black Notice* (Kay Scarpetta). Little Brown, £16.99.

Frank Delaney - *Pearl* (Nicholas Newman). Harper-Collins, £16.99.

Colin Dexter - *The Remorseful Day* (Endeavour Morse). Macmillan, £16.99.

Michael Dibdin - *Blood Rain* (Aurelio Zen). Faber & Faber, £16.99.

Dick Francis - *Second Wind* (short stories). Michael Joseph, £16.99.

Philip Friedman - *No Higher Law*. Headline, £16.99.

Kinky Friedman - *Spanking Watson* (Kinky Friedman). Faber & Faber, £5.99.

John Harvey - *Now's the Time* (Charlie Resnick – short stories). Slow Dancer Press.

Jack Higgins - *The Whitehouse Connection*. Michael Joseph, £16.99.

Linda Howard - *Now You See Her.* Pocket Fiction, £5.99/£16.99.

James H. Jackson - *Cold Cut*. Headline, £9.99/£16.99.

H.R.F. Keating - *Jack, the Lady Killer*. Flambard.

Douglas Kennedy - *The Job*. Abacus, £5.99.

Joe R. Lansdale - *Freezer Burn*. Gollancz, £9.99/£16.99

Gavin Lyall - *Honourable Intentions*. Hodder & Stoughton, £16.99.

Gwen Moffat - *Running Dogs*. Severn House, £17.99.

Margaret Murphy - *Past Reason*. Macmillan, £16.99.

Jack O'Connell - *Wireless* (Quinsigmond series). No Exit Press, £6.99.

Gemma O'Connor - *Falls the Shadow*. Bantam, £5.99.

Sara Paretsky - *Hardtime* (V.I. Warshawski). Hamish Hamilton, £15.99.

Ruth Rendell - *Harm Done*. Hutchinson, £16.99.

Mike Ripley - *Bootlegged Angel* (Fitzroy Maclean Angel). Constable, £16.99.

James Russell - *Oh No, Not My Baby*. Do Not Press, £7.50.

Emma Sinclair - *The Path Through the Woods*. Piatkus, £17.99.

William Smethurst - *Woken's Eye*. Headline, £16.99.

Julie Smith - *The Axeman's Jazz* (Sip Langdon). Slow Dancer Press.

John B. Spencer - *Stitch*. Do Not Press, £7.50.

Veronica Stallwood - *Oxford Shift* (Kate Ivory). Headline, £16.99.

Susan Sussman (with Sarajane Avidon) - *Audition for Murder*. Piatkus, £9.99/£16.99.

Peter Tasker - *Samurai Boogie*. Orion, £16.99.

Peter Turnbull - *Fear of Drowning* (first in a new series). HarperCollins, £16.99.

William Wolfe - *Wacking Jimmy*. No Exit Press, £6.99.

Daniel Woodrell - *Tomato Red*. No Exit Press, £6.99.

Margaret Yorke - *The Price of Guilt*. Little Brown, £15.99.

FOR FURTHER INFORMATION ON THE ABOVE TITLES, OR TO ORDER BOOKS, CONTACT:

Crime in Store, 14 Bedford Street, Covent Garden, London WC2E 9HE.
Tel: +44-171-379-3795, fax: +44-171-379-8988.
Email: CrimeBks@aol.com
Website: http://www.ndirect.co.uk/~ecorrigan/cis/crimeinstore.htm

Murder One, 71-73 Charing Cross Road, London WC2H 0AA.
Tel: 0171-734-3483, fax: +44-171-734-3429.
Email: 106562.2021@compuserve.com
Website: http://www.murderone.co.uk

Post Mortem Books, 58 Stanford Avenue, Hassocks, Sussex BN6 8JH.
Tel: 01273-843066, fax: 00-44-1273-845090.
Email: ralph@pmbooks.demon.co.uk
Website: http://www.postmortembooks.co.uk

writers on writing

sparkle hayter
a good man is hard to find

sparkle hayter

the last manly man

Tips Bridget Jones off the scales and steals her fags!

*We don't need an excuse to catch up with Sparkle Hayter. But (if we did) her new novel from No Exit Press, **The Last Manly Man** is excuse enough...over to you, Sparkle...*

In *The Last Manly Man*, my heroine Robin is trying to take the high road and be a better person. She tries to do a good deed for a strange man in a hat and finds once again that no good deed goes unpunished. Nevertheless, some misguided sense of goodness leads her into a mystery involving radical feminists, macho moguls, econuts, and horny chimps called bonobos.

In *TLMM*, Robin stands back a bit and tries to see things from a more male POV, the sexism perpetrated on men and the effect it has had. She finds herself in a traditional male role, as a boss responsible for the welfare of her employees, and through it finds a lot of sympathy for men. At the same time, she develops some behaviours traditionally considered male, i.e., she is busy trying to save the world and finds it kind of annoying that her boyfriends want to talk about their problems when there are bigger things going on. She just wants to have sex with her guys, release some tension, and get back to her important work. Hee. Turnabout is fair play, right?

I love doing that with Robin, having her own actions turn around and bite her in the ass. At one time she was the screw-up who gossipped about the higher-ups. Now she's one of the higher-ups being gossiped about. She was angry and had a big chip on her shoulder in the first book. By TLMM, she has to deal with angry employees with big chips on their shoulders. She has complained about men's sexism and cursed them for running out on her, and now she finds herself being sexist and running out on the men who care about her.

In *TLMM*, she finds ways to use different kinds of weaponry too. In one case, she uses the happiness of other people to defend herself, and in another, she uses truth in an off-beat way. Gee, I wish I was more like her... sometimes.

I have a long way to go before I completely assimilate my influences. I always feel funny talking about influences, like I'm implying a comparison to them. BUT.. I got into mystery after falling in love with Simon Brett's actor-sleuth Charles Paris. On the comedy side, Lenny Bruce's drive to speak what he believed was true despite enormous opposition is an inspiration to writers everywhere — or should be. Ernie Kovacs' loopy view of the world and Steve Martin's erudite silliness are two things I admire and aspire to.

My earliest unpublished novel goes back to age ten and the string of unpublished novels goes right up to the late 1980s and what I like to call my "Bad Hemingway" novels. I destroyed a couple of those books and if there are any remaining copies somewhere, they'll remain stuffed away. But I do look on it with affection, because each of those books was another step on this nutty journey.

Some mystery writers I never miss are: Lawrence Block, who is either a genius or an alien from outer space (or both); Janet Evanovich, because she's light-hearted and has crazy plots and makes me laugh (and we'd probably be great friends if she hadn't stolen my husband); Lauren Henderson, because I'd follow her detective Sam Jones anywhere; Joan Hess, who just always cracks me up, and who isn't too PC; and Richard Barre, who has such a clean but textured style. When I'm writing, I don't read other mysteries, so that unfortunately limits the number of books I read within the genre.

Outside mystery, I like picaresque novels, Marukami and Andrew Miller are two new faves. I read a lot of science and history books. I especially like history books that are lively and readable and look at the lives of the regular folks, not just the kings, queens and other celebs. Eleanor Duckett's book, *Death and Life in the Tenth Century* is one of my favourites. It's full of insight and information and really well-written. The names of people in the tenth century alone are worth the price of the book, Pandulf Ironhead, Egbert the One-eyed, Notker the Stammerer, Harald Bluetooth, and lots of popes named Sylvester (a name I'd like to see come back into vogue for Popes, wouldn't you?). This book is especially interesting for Monty Python fans, because you'll be reading about some horrible battle, about people losing legs and arms and fighting on, and you can't help but flash to the Holy Grail. I didn't realise how historically accurate Holy Grail was until I read the Duckett book. Holy Grail was funny on a whole other level after reading that book.

Not long ago, there was a lively discussion on one of the mystery listservs about whether mysteries contribute to this sudden violent streak in mankind. Maybe. I have it on very good authority that North Korea was inspired to pursue nuclear weapons after its runt leader indulged in a marathon reading of English vicar mysteries. So you never know.

My detective Robin Hudson is against violence except in self-defence. She much prefers nonlethal weaponry and surviving by resourcefulness, wit and happy accident. There isn't much graphic violence in these books, usually one fight scene, occasionally two, per book, and the approach is always the same: violence is bad but if you have to fight your way out of a situation, don't hesitate to defend yourself. Use whatever is at hand, be it poison ivy, a glue gun, or a comatose Mafia granny.

Candour in erotic scenes? I guess that depends on the writer. There are no actual sex scenes described in my books, but sexuality is one of the things the detective, Robin Hudson, discusses very frankly, and it is at the root of a couple of the murders in these books. It's a pretty big driving force in life so books without any mention of it strike me as a tad odd in a way. In general, Robin is for MORE safe, dirty, consensual fucking, and less violence.

Some crime novels happen in a kind of never-neverland, but my detective is in the news media — she sees and has seen too much not to stand up and say, "Hey, this world is really fucked up. Stop pretending it isn't!" My narrator is very flawed and fairly honest about it, often to her own detriment.

My methods of working are kind of serendipitous. I never know when I'm going to be sent a story about a heroic chicken, or find a clipping about an 18-lb turtle, or a cosmic cabdriver is going to utter the one line that pulls the story together for me.

I listen to a lot of music when I write. I have CNN with the sound off and the closed-captioning on, and I listen to music at the same time. For *The Last Manly Man*, I listened a lot to a two-CD world music sampler, *And the World's All Yours*, compiled by Charlie Gillett. I listened to that so much the CDs wore out. Anyone who sends me a new copy will receive an advance copy of *Chelsea Girls*. I haven't been able to find it here in the US.

The plot sidelining in my books usually twists back into the story in a surprising way I think. Very little is wasted. I like to hide clues in jokes. So when you read one of these books, you don't really know if Robin is digressing, or if there's some clue contained in an anecdote. That's very useful to me.

I adore my UK publisher, Ion Mills at No Exit. My U.S. editor Claire Wachtel is an angel. I love her. I loved my previous editor, at Viking Penguin too, Caroline White. I landed at my first publisher at a time when I was going through a great deal of personal turmoil in my life, and the publisher was grieving over a personal tragedy, and we were all messed up and didn't get along. I am grateful to them for giving me my big break though. I learned a lot from them. *What's a Girl Gotta Do* was rejected over 30 times, but most of the rejections came with good writing tips and advice and that was very encouraging.

I want to give the reader a funny, interesting story. I feel an obligation to the reader to make Robin be very honest about herself and her failings AND her strengths (I think the latter is harder for people, especially women, oftentimes). I want to present her not as some ideal who makes other people feel crummy about themselves, but as a very human character. I want her to appear as someone who is flawed, fucks up sometimes, gets in her own way sometimes, behaves badly on occasion, but always keeps going, takes her knocks, and retains some kind of hope of better things. I write for me too. I'm seeking my own answers when I write a book, and trying to make myself laugh.

I've heard books referred to as "product" one too many times. My series was just dropped when Rupert Murdoch and HarperCollins took over my US publisher, William Morrow, so I view this very personally. On the other hand, the pressure to produce a book a year come hell or high water and to SELL SELL SELL myself was driving me nuts, and it turns out being booted by the kindly Lord Murdoch is the best thing that happened to me. It's bad for books and a lot of other writers though I think. It could produce a lot more clone books that seem machine-made, it curbs a writer's urge to be adventurous and risk failure, and the push to promote and become popular is turning too many writers into banal sociopaths, afraid to say anything real lest they offend someone and hurt their sales. On a larger level, it's worrisome how control of the popular culture is being concentrated into fewer and fewer wealthy hands. That's one of the themes of the Robin Hudson series, the power of the media, and of the people who own the media.

My next one is called *The Chelsea Girl Murders*. It's a kind of retort to the 'Finding Mr. Right' novels and man-trapping books. It's about love and getting along with other people. It may well be the last in the Robin Hudson mystery series. I was going to take Robin to one of two other U.S., publishers but given the current climate and the tightening of the mystery market that didn't make long term sense. I figured, fuck it — time to take another leap into the unknown. Hee. Robin will return, but probably in a book that is more of a comic caper and even less of a murder mystery. In the meantime, I'm trying some different things.

writers on writing

the best books are crime stories
andrew klavan

Andrew Klavan talks about his new book from Little, Brown, and why you should slap your kids if you find them reading Andrew Klavan...

HUNTING DOWN AMANDA is a chase thriller. A bereaved jazzman gets a mysterious prostitute to pretend she's his dead wife for one night. Then he becomes obsessed with her and follows her—only to bring the wrath of both the law and a high-tech band of killers down on his head. It's fast, hard modern stuff but it's got echoes of legend in it—of Orpheus and Eurydice mainly; and Demeter and Persephone. I think of it sort of as noir mythology.

I sort of stumbled on the whole world of literature and to be perfectly honest the guy who really taught me to write was William Shakespeare. Sword fights, ghosts, battles—and all the time, a searching look into human character—that's exactly the sort of thing I want in my thrillers. And look, I may not be as good as he is yet, but I dress a lot of better. Because I had

no real role models in the trade—Shakespeare, I was disappointed to learn, was dead—I think I wasted a lot of time trying to be *"literary,"* trying to live up to some standard of experimentation and off-beat-itude that had nothing to do with the sort of books I like to read. I wouldn't want to re-read that stuff now and most of it I've thrown away. But really, one way or another, sometimes through small presses, sometimes through countless rewrites, I've managed to work most of what I've written into print. For good or ill.

85 percent of just about everyone isn't very good at his job. Doctors, lawyers, whatever. Writers too—whether they work in genre fiction or not. Still, for me, the best books of the last ten years have almost all been crime stories. *The Secret History* by Donna Tartt; *A Simple Plan* by Scott Smith; *The Death and Life of Bobby Z* by Don Winslow; *A Dark Adapted Eye* by Barbara Vine. In other fields—Gabriel Marquez and Saul Bellow are great.

Martin Amis can be very good. I used to read everything Stephen King did—he was just so creative with storytelling and language, such a natural. And I've read all the Aubrey-Maturin sea stories by Patrick O'Brian: I think he's one of the two or three best writers working in English.

I write what the story calls for. If it's a violent story, I write it violent; if not, not. *True Crime* hardly had a drop of blood in it. *The Animal Hour* has a severed head in a toilet. Every time there's some shocking piece of real-life violence—the Jamie Bulger case, that horrible school massacre that just went down in Colorado—the pundits turn to two causes: guns and violent films or videos. Now I'm no big fan of guns, but it seems to me we turn to those two causes because they're the only ones that won't disturb our liberal verities, that won't force us to take a good hard look at ourselves and the low value we put on children and parenthood, despite all our sentiment about them. I mean, guess what? I'm not here to instil values in your children; that's your job. You want your kids not to grow up to be sociopaths, try spending some time with them, try keeping your marriage together. If they're watching stuff they shouldn't on TV, be there to stop them—sorry, Charlie, but that's the only way it works. And if you ever, ever catch them reading one of my books, slap their bloody faces off. Then shoot em where they lie.

Learning from Shakespeare again, I believe in letting each character speak for himself and not judging them—unless the narrator is judging them. I have very close friends who are far more conservative than I and very close friends who are far more liberal. I've even had several friends whose opinions appalled me—who were bigots, say—and yet their humanity somehow connected with mine—a scary experience, but there you are. In the end, the truth is, nobody knows what's right. My liberal friends are always so self-righteous—they think they've got it down pat—but half of what they say is patent nonsense. And my conservative friends are always so angry at the liberals—but they haven't got the answers either. We're all in the dark, acting out of some unknowable mixture of selfishness and whatever it is we call conscience. When you feel that way, as I do, it's pretty hard to pontificate. You just let each character have his say.

The great baseball player Willie Mays, when asked how he stayed cheerful under all the pressure, used to say of baseball, *"Hey, it ain't my life and it ain't my wife."* Well, art is like that too. First and foremost, it's a diversion: it ain't your life, it ain't your wife. Writers—all sorts of artists—are always blowing the Pomposity Tuba about what they're trying to accomplish, what they're trying to say. But a thriller writer—he's got to entertain you. I mean, no matter how deep my insights into the human condition, no matter how brilliant my cultural understanding or my spiritual speculation, I've got to make you gasp, laugh, widen your eyes with terror and surprise. That's my first priority. So people come to genre writers because they know we still feel a responsibility to amuse them. We understand that this is something they're doing during their *leisure* time, for crying out loud. It aint their life, it ain't their wife.

Some writers say you gotta have experience, some say you gotta keep up with the trends. Emily Dickinson spent most of her time in her room but managed to knock out a decent poem or two for all that. But me, I like the movies and they've affected my sense of narrative as they have most people's. Alfred Hitchcock was an early influence, of course. And one of the things I love about Patrick O'Brian is the way he's adapted cinematic techniques to some of the least cinematic novels ever written. I've tried to do that too. A couple of times my books have been bought for film—and then they find they can't make them because they're too internal: I've used apparently cinematic techniques but the important action really took place inside the mind. As for music—ah well, that's a little different. You've got to have some kind of music in your life, don't you. *Hunting Down Amanda* is awash in my love of American swing and jazz—even the chapter titles come from old songs. A man that hath no music in himself… is fit for treasons, stratagems and spoils… It's almost literally true, isn't it, since language can describe our hate, our reason, our greed—but not our love, our faith, our devotion. For those, there's no words, only that sort of hymnal rhythm that rises up in

you, that feeling only music can imitate. That's where the poetry in language comes in, trying to convey those feelings.

He was just the guy with the torch, the guy who showed the way. And finally—this is beginning to sound like an Oscar speech—but there's my wife, Ellen. Not a teacher or mentor exactly, but an incredibly dishy babe for all that, and the absolute light of my life.

The John Grisham school has a credo: forget the characters, they get in the way of the story. But, I mean, what *is* a story if it's not a bunch of stuff that happens to people or stuff that people do? Not anyone can be in every story. Think of Othello being asked to avenge his father's death— or Hamlet being asked to believe his wife was unfaithful on the evidence of a handkerchief. It just wouldn't work. The story'd be over in ten minutes. So, sure, I come up with a plotline first, but what makes the plotline work for me, what gets me into it, is the people involved, the characters. That's what my books are about.

My father was a radio disc jockey and he was always very nice to people. Not to me, you understand, but I mean to other people. And I remember once asking him how come he was always so nice to everyone and he said, *"Because that's the audience."* So yeah, I keep my reader in mind—that's the audience. I mean, writing's a form of communication after all. Novels are meant to be read. Keeping the reader in mind keeps you honest, keeps you from showing off your brilliance for its own sake.

I read somewhere once that in the later days of the Roman empire, the city of Rome was so multi-cultural that the only form of theatre that could survive was pantomime—not enough people spoke Latin. Likewise, the simplistic world of imagery that you get in the movies and TV is easier, more literal, less challenging—and so more democratic, I suppose. Already, it seems to me, we've begun to let imagery rule our lives, to think in imagery when only language forces the honesty you need to have hard, realistic insights. I don't think reading will vanish but it might well return to being what it was at first—the preserve of the intellectual elite. It's a scary thought, but I don't make the rules.

And we look at Anrdew Klavan's **Hunting Down Amanda,** *(Little, Brown, £9.99)*

Klavan is a writer's writer – which is not to say that the ordinary reader will not be comprehensively pinned to his seat by the Hitchcockian suspense on offer here. Dark and atmospheric, this new thriller echoes such earlier Klavan winners as *The Uncanny* and *Corruption* in its unblinking view of human nature and blisteringly effective storytelling. On a cold night in New York, jazz musician Lonnie Blake tries to forget the pain of his wife's death by consoling himself with a beautiful young woman, Carol, who has been escaping from an unknown attacker. She vanishes, leaving no trace – and Blake's attempts to track her down soon involve him in a lethal chase. Carol's daughter (the eponymous Amanda) is part of a secret that people are prepared to kill and die for. Blake is serviceably characterised, and perhaps we need to know a little more about him than Klavan tells us. But such is the panache with which the author keeps his narrative on the move, any reservations such as this seem unimportant.

shakespearian whodunnits

whydunnit?

mike ashley

YOU CAN THANK Mark Crean, if you like.

When I did my first volume of 'historical whodunnits', there was no idea that at some time in the future I'd compile two volumes of Shakespearean mysteries. Yet now, looking back on these books, I have a certain pride and satisfaction about them. It's partly because of the challenge, but also because, so far as I am aware, no one else, in any genre, has tackled the entirety of Shakespeare's output and attempted to translate it into a different idiom.

It all came about at a fairly impromptu meeting that I had at the offices of Robinson Publishing with Nick Robinson and editor Mark Crean in August 1996. Nick was pleased with the sales of both *The Mammoth Book of Historical Whodunnits* and *The Mammoth Book of Historical Detectives*, but didn't want to do a third such 'Mammoth'. Yet he felt there was still a lot of mileage in anthologies of historical mysteries and we were knocking ideas about.

I had already compiled *Classical Whodunnits*. That had come about rather indirectly. The Past Times chain were keen to publish a book of historical fiction set in ancient Greece and Rome --one of the buyers at Past Times was apparently a keen fan of Mary Renault's work. So am I, and I was only too happy to do such a volume. Nick was less sure how this book would sell through the book stores and suggested that, as a companion to *Classical Stories*, I did a *Classical Whodunnits* volume, so that the two could be sold as a set.

I love the world of ancient Greece and Rome, and I like the mystery stories set there, but it wouldn't have been my first choice of a tour of historical periods. If I'd been starting from scratch my first choice would have been *Medieval Whodunnits*, because that was the period at which Ellis Peters had been so successful and where the public's mind seemed attuned.

So, at our meeting, Nick, Mark and I knocked around ideas. I had three or four that I was keen to try – Elizabethan, Regency, Medieval and Gaslight. These were four very recognisable periods with a lot going for them. However, I had signed up to *The Mammoth Book of New Sherlock Holmes Adventures*, which was already ploughing the Gaslight furrow. Nick felt the Regency period was played out, and was less convinced about the general appeal of the medieval period, regardless of Brother Cadfael. We seemed to be coming round to Elizabethan, but Nick's mind, as mercurial as ever, was trying to think of a hook to hang it on.

I happened to comment about the number of characters in the Elizabethan period who people know and who would be of interest – Drake, Raleigh, Spenser, Marlowe, Shakespeare ....

It was Mark Crean who jumped onto that. *"Why not Shakespearean Whodunnits?"*

Nick's mind shot off like a rocket. *"Ah-ha – was Gloucester guilty or framed? What about Richard III? And just how did Falstaff die?"* Ideas sparked. Nick was instantly convinced this would sell. Once the idea took hold there was no point in trying to explore others. Nick was keen to talk about it to Herman Graf of Carroll & Graf in the States. With the Frankfurt Book Fair looming he also wanted to get something more tangible together. He left me to explore the idea and come up with a firm proposal.

I left enthused and a little boggled. I have to confess that I am not a great fan of Shakespeare's work. The man himself – whoever he was – fascinates me, but apart from *A Midsummer Night's Dream, Julius Caesar, The Tempest* and *The Merchant of Venice*, I had little interest in his plays. Like many, I suspect, I was suffocated on Shakespeare by the inept education system and had not had much desire to return to him. Although I'd seen some of the plays on television, especially the series BBC-2 did in the early days (I did <u>try</u> to like Shakespeare) I remained uninspired. But I could see the potential. I knew enough about the plays to know they were full of murder and intrigue. And then there was the man himself, and his world. Clearly, though, I needed to do a crash course in Shakespeare to remind myself what was what.

I was surprised how easy that was. Over thirty years since I had last read any Shakespeare, I found I could revisit his plays with a wholly different attitude. I still didn't like them all, but I found a fascination with them I hadn't noticed before. Of course, I was now reading them with a purpose (something which never arises at school!) – looking for plots for mystery stories. These hit me from every angle. Before long I had ideas from just about all of his plays and I put some of these together in an outline proposal. There were some obvious ones. Falstaff struck me as an obvious character to be a detective, let alone any investigation into his own death. In the historical plays there were all the real mysteries such as the Princes in the Tower, the murder of Julius Caesar, the death of Henry VI. But I also wanted to look at things from a new angle. For instance – were the deaths of Romeo and Juliet just as Shakespeare revealed, or was it a cover up? And what became of Shylock after the trial in *Merchant of Venice*? Was that the end of the story?

There were some plays where I was less sure. I couldn't see much in *Love's Labour's Lost*, although the character of Holofernes suggested he might have some potential. I couldn't think of anything for *Troilus and Cressida*. *Two Gentlemen of Verona* and *The Comedy of Errors* hinged so much on mistaken identity, and twins, that I felt they might be too transparent. And as for all those women disguised as men ....

Coming up with ideas was one thing, but would anyone be interested in contributing? Although I'd become very enthused about the project, I feared others might find it a bit esoteric. So I e-mailed round and wrote to a few contacts to see who was interested.

I was amazed at the response. Everyone seemed interested. Ed Hoch e-mailed back at the speed of light and instantly bagged *Macbeth*, claiming he could do something with the Three Witches. Needless to say there were several claimants for *Richard III* and *Hamlet*. It wasn't long before I knew I had enough interest to make this project workable. While this had been going on, Nick Robinson and I had exchanged a few letters and we both had similar feelings about the project. The characters had to be kept in period – we did not want Shylock or Fal-

staff turning up in the twentieth century, or medieval characters using mobile phones. At the same time some of the anachronisms of the plays should be kept. In other words the stories had to be true to the original. Nick was also keen to cover as many of the plays as we could. I felt that should be possible. Depending on which ones you include, Shakespeare wrote between 35 and 40 plays, though there are a number of apocrypha and there are also the poems. The budget allowed to me to acquire around 160,000 words, so provided the stories averaged about 4,000 words, we could do it.

I finalised my proposal, sent it in and, before I could say Nick Robinson, the contract appeared. We were on our way.

Now I had to allocate plays! There were two problems. Although I had asked people to prioritise there were several who had claimed the same plays as first priority. And there remained several unallocated plays. To some extent the second problem helped solve the first. Where writers had suggested an as yet unallocated play as a second or even third choice I persuaded them to explore that. In fact I had been surprised from the start how quickly people had plumped for some of the more obscure plays. I hadn't expected *Coriolanus*, *Two Gentlemen of Verona*, *Timon of Athens* or *Cymbeline*, for example, to be snapped up so quickly. On the other hand I had expected *The Merry Wives of Windsor* and *Antony and Cleopatra* to go quite quickly, and these were lingering. The contract called for delivery of the stories in April 1997 and it was in late October that the book was confirmed, so I had to move quickly.

During this time, thanks to Amy Myers, a notice about the book appeared in *Red Herrings*, the newsletter of the Crime Writers Association. This brought in a few more contributors and a surprise. Susan Kelly sent me a copy of her story, *"Much Ado About Something"*, which had appeared in Maxim Jakubowski's anthology *Crime Yellow*. I'd missed this anthology, and so had no idea that someone had already tried a Shakespearean mystery, and a very clever one at that.

Things continued to move remarkably well. By November I had only two plays unallocated: *All's Well That Ends Well*, which I had thought someone would take, and *Titus Andronicus*. This is such a bloodthirsty play that I wasn't too surprised no one wanted it. It was difficult to get any angle on it. Nevertheless, I thought that was good going to have allocated all but two of the entire corpus. In fact by then two stories had already come in. Stephen Baxter was the first on the scene with his version of *A Midsummer Night's Dream*. Since this is my favourite of Shakespeare's plays I was delighted with the way Stephen had treated the subject, and this seemed to bode well. Soon after Peter Tremayne delivered *"An Ensuing Evil"*, which used as its base the first performance of *Henry VIII*. These two stories were a perfect start. One was set entirely within the world of the play, and looking at the conse-

quences of the actions. The other was set in Shakespeare's world but looking at a mystery in which the first performance of a play had a key part.

Over the next few months, apart from knocking ideas to and fro with authors, I waited. By January stories were filtering in, but not as quickly as I would like. By February I started chasing. Two factors were now emerging. Firstly many of the stories that had come in were averaging over 4,000 words. In fact some were up to 8,000 words. I could see I was rapidly running out of budget. That ought to be helped by the second factor. Some authors had found it difficult to do the story they had planned, either through other commitments or difficulty with the plot, and either couldn't do it at all, or couldn't finish in time.

It became apparent by early March that I was not, after all, going to cover every play. And although I had over half of the plays covered, it was not quite as simple as drawing the line there. Once having decided not to try and cover every play I was determined then to ensure a degree of balance in the collection. I could have forced the anthology to cover just the historical plays, but that would have meant not including some of the excellent stories I had received based on *Romeo and Juliet*, *Two Gentlemen of Verona* and, of course, *A Midsummer Night's Dream*. In fact, to do an anthology and leave out the plays that people know best, such as *Romeo and Juliet*, would have been wrong. There had to be enough well known plays in there for people to have an initial rapport with the book.

That led to another problem. The authors assigned with *Julius Caesar* and *Hamlet* had become heavily committed on other projects and could not now meet my deadline. These were certainly two of the plays I felt people knew and I had to have at least one of them in. So here I was on the one hand with potentially too many plays, but on the other hand not all of the ones I wanted. Moreover a couple of stories had come in with plots bearing too much similarity with other stories. And, if that weren't enough, I had ended up with two stories based on *As You Like It*. I still don't know how that happened.

In the end I cajoled Steve Lockley until he found time to complete *Hamlet*. I contacted Tom Holt and asked if he'd mind attempting a story based on *Julius Caesar* at such short notice. Tom is an expert on the classical world and he was only too keen to give it a go. His story came in at lightning pace. And I worked with one or two other writers to look for more original ways of reconfiguring their stories.

Once I knew I could not cover all of the plays I was then prepared to drop some stories, though I didn't like doing this. There was no prospect, at that time, of doing a companion volume, and I felt awkward about having commissioned stories that were rather specialist and wouldn't automatically have a home elsewhere.

But such are the decisions editors have to make and in the end I drew the line. I felt I had a good balance of plays, plots and settings. I did the final polish and submitted it. I was pleased with it, but also slightly disappointed that I hadn't managed to cover all of the plays.

In the meantime Robinson's had had something of a breakthrough. Originally Past Times were not interested in this book. But then Nick Robinson decided to try a different, more light-hearted cover, and somehow this clicked. With their order, in addition to the standard outlets, Nick felt happy with the outcome. The book was published in September 1997.

I'm sure you all have those same mixed feelings when a book appears. I thought it was good, but also knew what might have been. It received a range of reviews. The Shakespearean academics were a bit dismissive, but generally there was a good response. One or two stories were singled out for especial praise, which always pleases me. I was sorry when Darrell Schweitzer informed me that a whole page was missing from his story, "The Death of Falstaff". By one of those strange quirks the text actually carries on and you don't immediately notice something's missing. It's only the later references back to comments on that page that cause some puzzlement. It was, thankfully, restored for the second printing.

Although I'd spoken with Robinson's editors about a companion volume, I was not convinced that they would run with it. It was one of those one-off ideas that doesn't necessarily work a second time around. What I didn't know was that Past Times were very interested in a boxed set. What could I match *Shakespearean Whodunnits* with? Well, *More Shakespearean Whodunnits* seemed the obvious answer.

The idea remained with Robinson's for a few months and then, in mid-January 1998, I had a surprise phone call. *"We've got you down for delivering the second Shakespearean volume at the end of February. Is that right?"*

"What, this February?" was my astonished response. *"Uhm .... no."*

It seems that Past Times had agreed to take the two volumes and needed them in readiness for their new catalogue that July. The book had to be compiled and published in less than six months!

I tried not to panic. I knew I had a few of the stories from the first volume that I had not been able to use, and I hoped that the authors who were previously interested but had time constraints might now be able to deliver. Over a very busy two days I e-mailed, phoned and faxed everyone that I could. I'd said to Robinson's I could get them final copy by the end of May. Even that was pushing it. They agreed, provided they could receive some of the stories in advance to speed up the copy editing.

I knew the second volume couldn't be like the first. The first had used up just over half of the major plays, including most of the well known ones. If I was going to get a companion volume of similar size then I needed to vary the approach. In any case, a second volume exactly the same as the first would be too repetitive. So this time, in my hastily drafted proposal-come-guidelines, I suggested that we also explore the apocryphal plays attributed to Shakespeare and we looked more at Shakespeare's world. I was happy to entertain some stories with Shakespeare either as the detective, or as the victim of a crime or even as the villain of the piece. And, I thought there was scope to revisit maybe one or two of the plays covered in the first volume, provided the stories were sufficiently different.

Once again I was astonished at the response. The plays were grabbed up readily and thirstily. Even *Titus Andronicus* had two candidates this time! I was delighted with the interest in the apocrypha. I hadn't really taken much notice of these plays before, knowing I was entering sensitive territory. For the first book they had clearly been unnecessary, but now they had some relevance. Since there was a mystery attached to their authorship, anyway, there was scope for exploring them. Both *Arden of Feversham* and *A Yorkshire Tragedy* are based on actual murders, so there was no way of leaving those out. In the end apart from *Cardenio*, which is debatable anyway, I think we covered all of the main apocryphal plays.

I was also delighted that authors who had been unable to complete the first time round, because of pressure of work, could now deliver. I had been intrigued by Chaz Brenchley's idea for *"Master Eld, His Wayzgoose"* ever since he had mentioned the title at the very outset. And thankfully David Langford could now deliver his story based on *The Tempest* and Robert Weinberg his on *Julius Caesar*, though he drafted in Lois Gresh to help him.

Some of you may wonder why Gail-Nina Anderson appears twice in the book. When I was compiling the first volume, Gail had suggested she do *The Merry Wives of Windsor*. However, she also began collaborating with Simon Clark on his story based on *Measure for Measure*. Unfortunately Simon had other commitments, so Gail decided to do the story herself. Her draft manuscript had turned up on the day I had drawn the line on the first volume. But I loved the story. So, when the second volume came along, this was one I immediately wanted to use, but I also wanted to honour Gail's original request to do a Falstaff story. If she could do that one as well, it was hers.

The second volume was real knife-edge stuff. With such limited time and with Robinson wanting a first batch of stories as soon as possible, I didn't have the 'luxury' of the first volume. I knew I was going to be restricted. Once I'd committed myself to the first batch of stories, if any later ones arrived which duplicated ideas, I was going to be stuck. Thankfully that did not happen. But it was a race to the line. On the last weekend I was still exchanging e-mails with Stan Nicholls over the draft of his story. The final version came over at about midnight, and I was up till about 2.00am reconfiguring it on the computer and printing out the final version.

I was also delighted that Edward Marston had agreed to contribute an introduction as well as a new story. I had written all I wanted to say about Shakespeare in my introduction to the first volume. It was good to have a fresh set of views on the subject.

I still don't quite know how we all met that deadline. I think that's another reason why I have such a liking for these two books. Not only are they different, but they were written under very exacting conditions, especially the second volume, and yet somehow it all came together. At least, I think so. It's down to the reader to judge in the end. We must have done something right, though. The book got some good reviews and Chaz Brenchley's story was short-listed for an award.

When it was all over I felt a real sense of achievement. Here was the entire Shakespearean corpus (well, virtually all of it) reworked into a mystery medium. I felt that the authors had made some remarkable insights into the plays and I found that reading the stories threw new light on the plays for me and encouraged me to re-read them yet again. I needed to do this anyway when writing my interlinking blurbs in the book, but at least now I could do it from a fresh angle. I rather hope that these stories will have made others reconsider Shakespeare's work afresh.

It was a challenge I'm not sure I'd want to repeat. At one time, Robinson's did suggest *Chaucerian Whodunnits*, but I think that's pushing things a bit too far. The idea of *Dickensian Whodunnits* still appeals to me. So maybe ... just maybe. I'm a sucker for punishment!

crime (through) time
a perspective: part one
dan staines

ARGUABLY, the real essence of a detective novel is the investigation of a puzzle by someone determined to get to the truth, and this approach might also be taken by a historian, whether investigating the motives behind a major historical event, or how people lived and behaved in societies past. That said, its not surprising that the two have been blended to great effect, producing one of the most striking crime fiction phenomena of recent years. Though having no especially strong background in history, since I read and more importantly, enjoy, the fruits of this recent publishing boom, I'd like to examine why this type of crime novel has become so popular, what kinds of novels are being written at the moment and what characteristics blend to produce a really satisfying novel.

The ultimate mix of historical and criminal investigation might be a novel like Josephine Tey's *The Daughter of Time* or Colin Dexter's *The Wench Is Dead*, where a modern detective becomes curious about and begins investigates

events of the past. However, the type of historical crime novel that has really come into its own is really just that, a detective or mystery novel set in the past. Since the success of Ellis Peters' Brother Cadfael stories, the historical crime novel has gained steadily in popularity. Now, glancing through the pages of a recent copy of this very magazine, one can read novels set anywhere from 19th century Lombardy or fourteenth century York, to seventh century Ireland or Republican Rome. Given that historical crime novels have rapidly become extremely popular, the question remains—just why are they so popular? Perhaps the main reason why writers like Davis, Saylor, Doherty and Peters are so popular is the sheer quality and entertainment value of their writing. How skilfully, or how enjoyably, a writer creates their novel is always a major factor in why a particular writer becomes popular for any genre or setting; however, historical novels deserve more exploration in their own right.

Besides the quality of novels in their own right, readers often remark that they enjoy the setting as something different, or more interesting than contemporary ones, or that they enjoy reading about how people lived and acted in times past. If you've ever read any history books or watched a documentary about a particular period, the added dimension of reading a crime novel set in that time is a distinct attraction, and when historical crime novels are written well, they often give an added insight into the world in which they are set, and even provide a detailed 'history lesson' in their own right.

A counter-argument is that a badly researched novel can give a false or misleading picture of the time, but historical crime novels are probably no more guilty of this than other novels with a situation unfamiliar to the reader, and reading historical novels might well lead the reader explore more widely periods like fourteenth century England or Imperial Rome. One might compare the attraction of historical crime to that of the 'Golden Age' whodunnits; both can offer a slightly nostalgic view of the past, even romantic at times, and sometimes use their settings for similar puzzle-based mysteries. Historical novels can also be less violent and graphic than their modern counterparts, and can offer a degree of detachment for the reader; it might be more comfortable to view a murder in medieval Southwark as less close to home than a murder in inner-city Nottingham.

Interestingly, several notable historical crime writers, Lindsey Davis amongst them, defected from writing historical romances, reflecting a shift in the fiction market, and that their own outlook and style of writing might reflect this. This is a little unfair, and unjustified considering how many historical crime writers depict life in, say medieval England, as being at times squalid and violent, and other readers have often assured me that they in no way view such times through rose-tinted glasses. Given their obvious popularity, it seems appropriate to take a look at some of the more notable authors and novels, on a brief trip forward through time. Although there are numerous writers currently producing historical mysteries, I'd like to share some of the writers that I've found both enjoyable and informative.

An appropriate starting point for this particular review is ancient Rome, and Lindsey Davis, who I've mentioned rather more than most authors, could be credited with pioneering crime fiction from this period with her hugely successful Marcus Didius Falco novels. Although some of her detractors often remark that her characters seem little more twentieth than first century, many including myself have found these witty and captivating novels a delight to read, not least for the engaging characters of Falco, private informer and occasional spy, and his aristocratic girlfriend, Helena Justina.

Davis's main 'rival' is Steven Saylor, creator of the 'Roma Sub Rosa' novels, set in Republican Rome. Saylor writes very different novels from Davis, dealing with the complex and often violent politics of the time, using his detective, Gordianus the Finder, to explore pivotal events in the history of Rome, and in doing has created a series of richly textured and engrossing crime novels.

However, fans of the classical age can also explore the Greece of Alexander the Great through Anna Apostlou (a pseudonym for Paul Doherty), who examines murders including that of Philip of Macedon. Doherty has also taken the plunge into writing about Ancient Egypt with *The Mask of Ra*, joining writers including Lynda Robinson and Anton Gill.

Shifting sharply forward in time, barring Peter Tremayne's Sister Fidelma novels set in seventh century Ireland, the Dark Ages seem equally dark as far as historical crime goes in Europe. This certainly isn't the case for seventh century Tang Dynasty China, setting for Robert van Gulik's classic Judge Dee series. van Gulik follows the exploits of Judge Dee, a magistrate based on the historical judge and statesman Ti Jenciheh, through a number of beautifully-crafted mysteries and locked-room puzzles based on actual historical cases from the period or contemporary tales. van Gulik doesn't try as hard as more recent historical crime writers to emphasise the atmosphere of the time, but his deft, concise style conveys a wealth of historical detail and complexity.

Back in Europe, the reader can more or less follow English and British history from the Norman Conquest to the present-day, such is the huge range of novels set in this time. Medieval England is particularly popular as a setting, and several authors in particular are worth a second look. Edward Marston kicks off the period with his popular and skilfully executed series of novels concerning two Domesday commissioners conducting their business around England in the years following the Norman Conquest. Susannah Gregory, follows the trials and tribulations in fourteenth century Cambridge of Matthew Bartholemew, physician, Fellow of Michaelhouse College, and reluctant investigator. Her first novel, *A Plague Upon Both Your Houses*, is in many ways her strongest, painting a vivid picture of Cambridge's ordeal with the Black Death, but the series continues strongly, particularly when dealing with the often violent conflict between Town and Gown.

However, perhaps the most significant writer from this period is the late Ellis Peters, creator of Brother Cadfael, the gentle, inquisitive Welsh monk, who investigates both mundane domestic murders and politically-fraught cases amid civil war and political upheaval in twelfth century Shrewsbury. Peters has her detractors, not least for the similarity in plot between some of her later novels, but her work includes some wonderful books, with Cadfael a memorable and likeable detective.

Although Peters occupies a unique place in the pantheon of historical crime writers, another writer, Paul Doherty, is perhaps the most prolific of all, having written over forty novels in a bewildering range of settings and times under at least seven different pseudonyms. His novels include the successful and hugely enjoyable Hugh Corbett series, concerning Edward I's clerk, engaged on secret espionage and 'political' activities but invariably ending up trying to resolve cases of murder. As Paul Harding, he writes the equally acclaimed Brother Athelstan novels, the eponymous friar acting as secretarius to the Falstaffian Sir John Cranston, coroner of fourteenth century London during the turbulent reign of the young Richard II, and aiding him in his investigation into a number of cleverly devised 'locked-room' puzzles. Lately, Doherty has been drawn towards the supernatural, an approach which allows him to display a remarkable talent for creating a chilling, brooding atmosphere, particularly in the Canterbury Tales novels, a set of tales of mystery and terror told by Chaucer's pilgrims in the dark evenings. The supernatural as rational explanation for events is also rather refreshing when one considers the frequent imposition of modern attitudes on historical characters.

Doherty also writes as Michael Clynes, taking as narrator the Flashman-like Roger Shallot, a former rogue and thief who looks back with fond nostalgia on his bawdy exploits in the court of Henry VIII, as C.L. Grace, telling the stories of Kathryn Swinbrooke, a Canterbury physician, as Anna Apostolou on murders in Alexander's Greece, as Ann Dukthas on Nicholas Segalla, immortal scholar and detective, and as himself in a wide-range of non-series novels investigating historical crimes throughout the ages. Although his undoubted knowledge of medieval England serves him well in the majority of his novels, his few attempts to move beyond this period show lapses in research which undermine his writing. Doherty's main weakness is his often poorly realised characterisation, notably the use of the straight-arrow, rational investigator with his roguish, worldly-wise assistant in all too many of his novels, but his obvious authority on all manner of historical fact and detail and his deft creation of a rich, 'believable' atmosphere blends to create some

notably engrossing and entertaining historical crime novels.

Elizabethan England provides the setting for an excellent series of novels, written by P.F. Chisholm, based on the journals and letters of Sir Robert Carey, Deputy Warden of one of the Border Marches. Chisholm uses this detailed source material and created a superb and darkly humorous series of novels which capture superbly the atmosphere and events of daily life in the border city of Carlisle, dominated by corrupt or inept officials and the eternally feuding and downright larcenous Borderer 'names', set against the political rivalry between England and Scotland. Carey is a likeable mixture of effete courtier and political realist, but the admirably drawn supporting cast are surely one of the secrets of Chisholm's success. Chisholm also writes as Patricia Finney, creating an acclaimed series set in the murky world of Elizabeth's secret service, that have been likened to Le Carre in their feel and perspective.

Oddly, one of the most fascinating and influential periods of English history, the Civil War, is sadly deficient in historical crime, which seems a great shame, unlike Restoration England, which provides a rich, bawdy setting for writers like the much-acclaimed Iain Pears, author of *An Instance of the Fingerpost*, and Molly Brown, whose *Invitation to a Funeral* stands out as an especially memorable and exciting historical crime novels.

The man credited with founding the modern police force, magistrate Sir John Fielding, is also a popular choice for a character in novels set in Georgian England, including those by Deryn Lake and Bruce Alexander. Alexander takes 'The

Blind Beak' as his detective, endowing him with phenomenal powers of deduction and a suitably innocent assistant, to act as his eyes in solving a series of baffling murders, which owes somewhat more to Holmes and Nero Wolfe than the historical Fielding.

The legacy of Conan Doyle continues to inspire many writers to create their own novels based around the Holmes canon, including M.J. Trow's novels with Inspector Lestrade as an unlikely hero, but Victorian Britain has also been the setting for many other successful series. Amongst the best known are Anne Perry's Thomas and Charlotte Pitt novels, concerning a lowly police inspector and his upper-class wife, and the distinctly superior William Monk series, following the struggle of a police inspector, suffering from amnesia, to maintain his position within the police force. The Monk novels capture brilliantly the dark, claustrophobic world in which Monk tries desperately to find himself in the truest sense.

Peter Lovesey has also written a series of original and beautifully-realised novels about policeman Sergeant Cribb, and yet another series featuring as detective none other than Bertie, Prince of Wales and amateur sleuth. Although not set in Britain, the Age of Empire finds its own niche within Michael Pearce's hugely entertaining Mamur Zapt series, where Captain Gareth Owen finds himself beset by all manner of political and criminal problems as head of the secret police, the 'Mamur Zapt', in colonial Egypt. Pearce creates complex and multiply-stranded plots, and his superb handling of dialogue and a sense of place blends to create a particularly satisfying and frequently hilarious sequence of novels.

Although so many historical crime novels are set in Britain, there are many other writers who use equally intriguing and vividly drawn settings, from the seventeenth century Japan of Laura Joh Rowlands to the New England small town life in the newly-born United States described by Margaret Lawrence.

With his debut, The Alienist, Caleb Carr offered a ground-breaking combination of historical novel, police procedural and psychological thriller set nineteenth century New York. Another increasingly popular themes is the historical crime novel in the twentieth century; Walter Mosely follows social change in post-war America from the viewpoint of Easy Rawlins, a black investigator finding his way through the starkly different worlds of black and white society. James Ellroy also explores similar ground in his series of novels set in the corrupt underworld of US politics and organised crime.

The birthplace of the 'Golden Age' whodunnits has also become a setting for historical novels in their own right, with writers like Charles Todd and Rennie Airth looking at police investigation between-the-wars Britain. Fittingly, this last time period brings us full-circle, and also suggests that historical crime novels are certainly never going to be limited to tales of medieval monks and Roman senators, but offer all manner of styles and settings for the discerning reader bored with modern-day mundanity. In the final part of this discussion, we'll take a look at what qualities can make the historical crime novel the success it is today, and the problems and pitfalls that can face a historical crime novelist.

writers block

Time for an expanded section on one of CT's favourite writers, the inimitable Lawrence Block. First, an in-depth interview by Mark Campbell, followed by Larry's regular column. And finally, news of The Man's new novels…what more could Blockians ask?

Allegedly, Lawrence Block does not know how many books he has written. And having met him, I can well believe it. There he sits on a comfortable reclining chair in the quiet confines of High Stakes, London's premier betting bookshop (surely London's only betting

bookshop?), relaxed to the point of somnolence. He is sixty, although he doesn't look it, and he is clearly happy with his lot. He is nearly bald, wears tinted glasses and a black sports jacket, and speaks with a deep mid-West drawl that brings to mind gravel being sloshed with a bucket of water. He looks like he'd be unfazed by anything the world might throw at him – you sense he's seen it all before, be it in real life or in the pages of one of his many, many escapist novels.

Right now, though, he is on a publicity tour of the British Isles for his latest Tanner novel, Tanner on Ice, together with Last Manly Man author Sparkle Hayter. He admits to being exhausted by a hectic schedule, and is clearly grateful for the chance to rest between engagements. During our brief chat, he's the model of urbanity, leaning back in the chair and taking time to answer my questions, only raising his voice to laugh, which he does frequently. In short, Block gives flesh to the phrase 'laid back'.

Glad to see you in the UK – do you enjoy it over here?

Very much.

Why?

They speak English!

You can't cope with different languages?

Not really. I can read a tiny bit of French and a little Spanish, though. I can speak in Spanish, but when people respond I don't have a clue what they're saying, so the conversation's very one-sided.

What motivates you to write? Having written books on the writing process, do you have an expert answer?

No, I don't. I've been writing so long that there comes a point where the original reason why you did it is long lost in time, and I suppose I write now because that's what it is that I do. It's been a lot of years and a lot of books. It's not always been enjoyable doing it, but when it's going well, it's wonderful.

At this stage in your life, could you imagine yourself doing anything other than writing?

Sometimes I can with great joy imagine myself doing almost anything except writing; but it's been so long since I've done any other kind of work, and I never did any for any great length of time. And the work that I do is somewhat writing-related anyway – I have one job in a literary agency and one job in a magazine – and occasionally I get hired to give a talk somewhere. I generally tend to take those bookings because the idea of getting paid and not having to write is so appealing. And then

I remember when I started out, the idea of getting paid for writing something was so enormously appealing. And I figured out the common denominator, and I think it's the fact that I like getting paid! (Laughs)

Do you enjoy publicising your books?

Well, I find the mini-performance that's involved in a book tour is extremely exhausting. It doesn't require anything that you'd call acting, it's just meeting people and responding to audience questions – but you have to handle a lot of human energy back and forth, and it can be draining.

How do you write? Do you plan to the hilt, or just go straight into it?

I just sit down and write. I think about it for a couple of months or more before I start work, but that

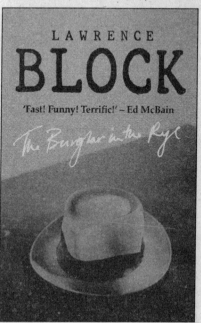

LAWRENCE
BLOCK

'Fast! Funny! Terrific!' – Ed McBain

The Burglar in the Rye

doesn't have the effect of working out the plot for me. That's something I can only seem to do while I'm doing it, and I just try and write my way through it.

Some writers have it all set before they sit down and start work. There's a writer – I don't know if he's still working – called Richard S. Prather who wrote a batch of detective stories, mostly for Gold Medal in the 50s and 60s, and they were the lightest, frothiest, bubbliest things in the world – you'd think they just tumbled out effortlessly. But what he did was he would start off by writing an outline, a two-page outline, then he would expand that into a chapter outline, then he would expand that into a detailed scene-by-scene outline, round about half the length of the finished book, and then he would expand that – from 30,000 words to 60,000 – and that was the book. He made it sound as formulaic as baking a cake, and it came out looking utterly spontaneous. So every writer invents his own way of doing it and there's no way to tell from the finished product how it was done. There's no right way, just a great number of wrong ways.

Do you find you gravitate towards reading crime books?

I don't either seek out or avoid the genre. People tend to think that you must want to read the same sort of thing that you write, and that's usually not true. It's only true for me if the stuff is really good and accomplished enough. I get an awful lot of first novels sent for quotes and I'm usually not going to like them because I've been this for too long and I'm too much aware of technique and it gets in the way. Even though the story and the writing may be excellent, in a lot of ways I can get putt off. Also if it's too much like what I write, it's too much like what I write…

How do you find a voice for your characters? Is it directly from your own personality?

The voice of your character and how that happens is mysterious, it's a mystery. I don't think there's a way to do it, I think it just happens. I have several different narrators in different series, with very different voices, and one think I know and just don't have to think about is how they sound. That just happens, and I just let it happen. Even with tanner, where I hadn't written in that voice for over 25 years, it was like turning on a tap and letting it all flow. I can't even take credit for that, it was just effortless. Other things about the book were not effortless, but that was.

As you say, *Tanner On Ice* resurrects a hero last seen in action in the Seventies – how did you avoid straying into Austin Powers mode?

Well, I never saw that film, so it made it easier.

Okay, let's change the subject – what's your favourite TV programme?

Oh, that would be Law and Order, which I watch fairly religiously. It's fiction, but very much based on reality, often spinning off one way or another from something that's actually happened. It's a cop show essentially. But an increasing number of them are more and more character-orientated, like soap operas with cop backgrounds, and this is very story-driven – it's about the case and they generally keep the personal crap about the characters to a minimum. And it's an intricately plotted show – I like that a lot.

You've probably been interviewed into the ground recently, but what question do you really get sick of being asked?

Probably that one! (Laughs) Ask me where I get my ideas from, that's a good one.

Okay, where do you get your ideas from?

I get them from a little man in Cleveland.

That's good, yes. But let me ask you about your critics – do you take any notice of them?

I'm always suspicious of the people who say they don't, because I think it's hard to block out any kind of input that way. On the other hand, I'm so contrary that probably if a critic doesn't like something, that's precisely what I'll set out to do. But I try not to think what people want – I've come to believe that the worst disservice I can do readers is to try and give them what I think they want. Some editor in New York, I don't know his name, once said: *"Your job is not to give people what they want, it's to take them places they didn't know they wanted to go."* He probably doesn't have a future in the business, at least not the way publishers think!

So why do you think the crime genre is so popular?

I think part of it is a wee bit by default, in that so much contemporary mainstream fiction, the popular bestseller sort, is usually just flat bad, it's real lowest common denominator stuff, and literary fiction has lost touch with story, so that it's not about anything, it's about itself all too often. A lot of people who a generation ago would have thought crime fiction was not something that would interest them, have picked it up and found that it has – they get the story value they used to get elsewhere. And also I think stories in crime fiction have gotten better. There's a lot more characterisation in contemporary work than there was in the so-called Golden Age.

And why so many women crime writers?

Well, some women crime writers have said that they wrote their first book in order to kill in print someone they would have liked to have killed in real life. I've heard that from several different people.

Last question. The big trend at the moment is historical crime. If you had a choice, in what period of history would you set one?

(Long pause.) I don't know, maybe 18th Century. I say that purely in the realm of fantasy because as to actually writing anything period I wouldn't be inclined to do that at all – I would feel very unequal to the task. I enjoy reading things set a other times, but I would feel very, very diffident about doing it myself.

And now, from the horse's mouth…

**THE BLOCK UPDATE
LAWRENCE BLOCK**
Hello there! I write these lines

from my desk in New York, where I've been spending precious little time lately. But the UK has my new Matt Scudder in September from Orion – it's called *Everybody Dies* – and as I've just returned from the first half of the most ambitious book tour since that of Paul the Apostle, (and I've just about time to catch my breath before I'm off again) – I thought I'd better get something down.

The tour for the *Burglar in the Rye* (which No Exit Press will be publishing in the UK), I'm delighted to report, has gone swimmingly so far. If it's done nothing else, it's brought my writer friends to a rare meeting of the minds. When the most recent newsletter went out, folks everywhere weighed in with their views on what I'd scheduled for myself, and writers who have never agreed on anything before were suddenly in accord. Being writers, of course, they showed some individuality in expressing themselves, even if they were all saying essentially the same thing. "Insane," several wrote. "Out of your mind" was another popular response. Joan Hess chose "Demented, seriously demented." Well, you get the idea.

What took me aback, I must admit, is that they said this as if it were news. Here I thought these people knew me, and yet they seemed surprised. . .Never mind. As it turned out, the July session was a great success. I did more driving than I might have preferred—there were days on end, actually, when I drove all day, did my gig, drove a few hours more, slept, and got up only to get behind the wheel again. I'm afraid I was a tad ambitious when it came to working out distances. See, when you look at the map, Rapid City and Missoula are just mere inches apart. Same goes for Albuquerque and Wichita.

But the events themselves made it all worthwhile. If I had to pick a high point, I suppose it would be the afternoon session when a woman asked me how I'd learned all the tricks burglars use, and how I managed to be so on-the-nose accurate about their methods. "Ha," some one said. "*How would you know if he got it right or not?*" "Well," she replied, "*fifteen years ago, that's what I did for a living.*" When the people in the business tell you you're getting it right...

Now what else did I want to tell you? Let me see. Well, I think I know what the next book'll be, although it's not completed yet. I'm halfway through a sequel to *Hit Man,* which will most likely be published sometime in late 2000. After that, well, I'm not sure. Speaking of Tanner, which I wasn't, the third book in the series, *Tanner's Twelve Swingers* will be out soon. On the film front, Keller, the film version of *Hit Man,* is very much a go project, with Jeff Bridges signed to star. And Scott Frank, the Oscar-nominated screenwriter who did such thoughtful and effective adaptations of Elmore Leonard's *Get Shorty* and *Out of Sight*, is at work on a screenplay for the Jersey Films production of *A Walk Among the Tombstones*. I feel my work's in good hands, and have high hopes for both pictures—that they'll actually be made, and that they'll make everybody happy.

short is beautiful
martin edwards

EDITING THE CWA's annual anthology of crime fiction is one of the most pleasurable literary tasks that, as a lifelong fan of the genre, I can imagine. When the manuscripts flood in from CWA members, as they do each autumn, I feel rather like a small boy left to mind a sweet-

shop. Quite apart from the fun of receiving manuscripts from household name authors, there is in addition the special delight of finding a gem written by a new writer or, perhaps, one who has seldom tried short stories, or even fiction, in the past. The enthusiastic response from CWA members to my annual request for submissions convinces me that my love of the crime short story is widely shared. Notoriously, though, crime anthologies on both sides of the Atlantic seldom if ever achieve bestseller status. It seems as though book buyers prefer novels rather than story collections. Yet the latter can offer the reader, as well as the compiler, a wealth of enjoyable discoveries. Anthologies may occasionally be uneven in content, but the variety of the best of them surely offers more than adequate compensation.

It is, I think, generally true that the best crime writers are also apt to be gifted short story writers. Take Ruth Rendell, for instance. Arguably, she is the finest British crime novelist to have emerged in the past 40 years; one could also make out a good case for the proposition that she is our outstanding writer of short crime stories as well. Reginald Hill is another master of the genre who is as comfortable with the short form as with the novel. Indeed, Joe Sixsmith, now a well-established series character, first saw the light of day in a short story, *Bring Back The Cat!* Ian Rankin, too, is as skilful an exponent of the short story as he is of the police novel and thriller. As one would expect, Dalziel and Pascoe, and also Inspector Rebus, feature in short stories by Hill and Rankin respectively, but it is significant that both authors use the form to experiment with fresh ideas, characters, settings and even styles of writing. This gives a clue, perhaps, to one of the particular attraction of the short story for the crime writer. After coming at last to the end of a novel, for instance, what better way to unwind, in literary terms, than to write something completely different—a short story which is a break from one's usual work not merely in length, but also subject and mood?

There is another factor which makes the short story an appealing proposition for many professional writers. Few of us, and certainly not those who have no other day job to pay the rent, can ignore commercial realities altogether. Those who write series are usually expected by their publishers to produce a new title every year or so. To write a very different type of book may,

to many authors, simply seem to be too much of a risk. To invest perhaps a year of one's life in an experiment that has no guarantee of success requires quite a leap of faith. To spend, say, a fortnight in writing a short story is a gamble that a writer may be much more willing to take. It follows, therefore, that some of the most interesting and innovative work in the crime fields from established authors may come when they let their hair down and put together a short story which is a real change from the novels with which their readers associate them. Or, quite simply, the short form may open possibilities which are not otherwise available. In my own case, for example, I have never felt that urge to write a historical novel. If I am to write a manuscript of eighty thousand words or more, I am much happier setting it in the present day. But short stories are a different matter. As well as a Sherlockian pastiche, I have experimented with tales set in ancient Britain, the eighteenth and nineteenth centuries, and the Second World War. Tackling those periods at novel length would have felt burdensome; writing the short stories was, in contrast, a joy (well, I am not quite so sure about Britain in the time of King Lear, but you get the idea ...) Similarly, whilst successful comic crime novels are rare, humorous short mysteries can be enormous fun to write.

There are also plenty of story ideas which particularly suit the short form: these include, to my mind, the impossible crime story. Again, I cannot easily imagine myself writing a locked room mystery novel, but trying to pull off the conjuring trick in the space of six or seven thousand words is a much more attractive proposition; I dreamed up a 'miracle problem' for Harry Devlin to solve in a story for an American magazine some time ago and relished the challenge so much that I am about to embark on another. Short stories also offer writers the chance to supplement their full-length series. A story might deal with a particular incident in a series detective's past or, perhaps, flesh out our understanding of a member of the supporting cast. It is through a short story, for example, that we learn that Lord Peter Wimsey finished up as a father of three. Just occasionally, a short story may prove so compelling that it can be re-worked into a novel. One of the most famous examples of this is Anthony Berkeley's masterly story *The Avenging Chance*, which he turned into *The Poisoned Chocolates Case*, again featuring Roger Sheringham—but boasting an entirely different solution. Clever stuff.

Then there are the writers who specialise in short stories rather than novels. The outstanding example is the legendary American, Edward D. Hoch. Hoch has written novels, but his deserved fame rests upon his extraordinary flair for the short form: remarkably, he has proved as ingenious as he is prolific. He is also, as I can testify from

personal experience, an editor's dream: the complete professional who can turn his hand to almost any mystery theme and setting and produce a compulsively readable tale. Hoch is in a class of his own, of course, but in this country we have a young writer who has established a considerable speciality in the short story. I have never met Mat Coward, but I have included a story of his in each of the four CWA anthologies I have edited so far, because his versatility is matched by his understanding of what is required for success in this demanding form.

Yet despite all these positive features, people have been predicting the death of the short crime story in Britain for decades. When I was first asked to edit the CWA anthology, I decided to check out the work of my predecessors. In the very first collection, *Butcher's Dozen*, published in 1956, I found this comment from the joint editors, Josephine Bell, Michael Gilbert and Julian Symons:

"It is not possible to have a hand in the selection of such an anthology, without being led into some thoughts about the market for crime stories in this country. It must be said that, upon the whole, the outlook is bleak."

One could be forgiven for thinking that, the more things change, the more they stay the same. I was invited to edit the anthology in 1995. In that year, no CWA collection had appeared—the first time this had happened for thirty years. The three year contract for the attractively (and, no doubt, very expensively) produced Culprit series had expired and, despite great efforts, the existing editorial team were unable to find a publisher enthusiastic enough to take the book on. This struck me as a pity, not least because I first heard of the CWA when as a teenager I received, for a Christmas present, the latest annual anthology, then entitled *John Creasey's Mystery Bedside Book*. Certainly, I little realised all those years ago that I would one day be given the exciting job of trying to get the anthology back on its feet.

The temporary demise of the CWA anthology at that time was all the more disappointing because, a few years earlier, prospects for crime anthologies in the UK had looked very bright. Macmillan published the long running *Winter's Crimes* series, Little, Brown brought out several editions of *Midwinter Mysteries* and Maxim Jakabowski's *New Crimes* books catered with verve for hard-boiled tastes as well as offering more traditional stories. By 1995, however, all these series had come to an end. One can only assume that disappointing sales were the explanation; certainly, the editors could not be faulted for their choice of material, which was almost invariably of a high standard.

I had previously been involved in compiling a number of collections of regional crime fiction. There have now been three volumes of *Northern Blood*, the first of which came out in 1992, and I also co-edited Anglian Blood with Robert Church.

The experience was immensely satisfying and led me to the conclusion that themed anthologies, if carefully put together, are apt to be very well received by crime readers as well as by critics. I therefore decided that, as with the Mystery Writers of America anthologies, the CWA collection should have a different theme (and appropriate title) each year. The idea found favour with both publishers and contributors and *Perfectly Criminal*, *Whydunit?* and *Past Crimes* attracted many more submissions than I could possibly include. When one receives stories from Harry Keating, Peter Lovesey, Reginald Hill, Margaret Yorke, Ruth Rendell, Ian Rankin, Val McDermid and company, one is genuinely spoiled for choice. I have often said—and I mean it—that by far the hardest part of the job lies in rejecting each year a number of high quality stories simply because space does not permit their inclusion. I am, I must admit, no fan of either Alex Ferguson or Manchester United, but I can at least empathise with his dilemma in choosing between, say, Yorke, Cole and Sheringham (Teddy, not Roger) when only two strikers' places are available...

This year's collection, *Missing Persons* (published by Constable), has a theme which I believe brought out the best in the contributors. It was, of course, a pleasure to include stories by Rendell and Hoch, but perhaps even better was the excitement of reading some of the stories submitted by writers with whose work I was not previously familiar; one wonderful example that springs to mind is the gripping tale written by Bill Kirton.

The favourable response on both sides of the Atlantic to the CWA anthologies convinces me that there is at least as much interest today in crime short stories as at any point in my lifetime. There are heartening signs in the anthology field: Mike Ashley's hefty collections of historical mysteries, for instance, have earned many well-deserved accolades and that great talent spotter Maxim Jakubowski has recently put together a couple of historical crime anthologies as well. There are, moreover, very encouraging signs in the magazine field. *Crime Time, Shots* and *Sherlock Holmes: The Detective Magazine* regularly feature short stories of distinction, while Mat Coward has now edited a couple of issues of *Crimewave*, a new magazine which features nothing but short fiction. Even *The Strand* has been revived. The enthusiasm shown by the various editors is a significant contribution to the health of the genre. The availability of high quality markets means, I believe, that an increasing number of writers will be attracted to the short form, while the existence of the CWA Macallan Dagger, awarded for the best short story of the year, offers a further incentive to writers of talent.

So these are exciting times for lovers of short crime fiction. And I wonder whether, perhaps, we may even begin to see a sharp rise in interest from the paying customer. After all, we are constantly told that attention spans are shortening and that the public taste nowadays demands instant gratification. The best short stories in the genre provide not only that, but lasting pleasure as well.

Martin Edwards' latest Harry Devlin novel, First Cut Is The Deepest, *is published by Hodder and Stoughton,*

interview

crimewriting, necrophilia and radiohead
carol anne davis

Safe As Houses

CAROL ANNE DAVIS

BLOOD LINES

"Dark in ways that Ruth Rendell and Minette Walters can only dream of." – IAN RANKIN

PRESS

MY NEW BOOK is called *Safe As Houses* and it follows a sociopath as he sets up a safe house and commits his first and subsequent lust murders. As his work and home life disintegrate he commits increasingly sadistic acts. His wife eventually realises that he's leading a dual existence but she completely misconstrues the signs. I once took part in a series of 'Women Tackling Crime' classes in which most of the women present feared the stranger lurking in the bushes—yet statistics show that we're most at risk from people we already know.

I suspect my earliest influences stem from my childhood—I'm sure that's true of most writers. I didn't so much invent an imaginary friend as an imaginary life. I don't think I read any dark fiction in those days but I was fascinated by the prospect of Enid Blyton's magical *The Faraway Tree* where you climbed up the trunk and disappeared into a different land. I also remember stories about ordinary houses which had hidden panels. The characters would touch the wallpaper and a secret tunnel would open up that led them to underground treasure or a wonderful attic den. I was this impressionable little bastard who went around determinedly tapping the walls and shouting 'open sesame.' Luckily they didn't have child psychologists in these days.

I threw out my early novel manuscripts years ago. They helped me learn about structure and content, so I don't regret writing them. But even if | returned to the same material, I'd write about it very differently now. The first novel was the inevitable biographical one, about a working class girl at university. The second was a more heavily politicised feminist tract in which the selfsame girl encounters work, men and vodka and survives. I think it was a bit of a wish fulfilment tale, as working girl was terminally bewildered and almost unemployable and it was more of a pamphlet than a novel as it only ran to fifty thousand words.

I try to read most true crime books by Ann Rule, John Douglas and anyone else who has, say, spent time in a prison establishing a rapport with serial killers. Fiction is more awkward, as like most writers I tend not to read other people's novels whilst writing my own. When I do buy books it's by independent outfits who need the money more than the big publishing houses. And I subscribe to various small press magazines. I stopped reading Stephen King for a while after *Misery* because I thought it was unnecessary for him to show the axe severing the victim's leg. If I'd been writing that same scene I would have ended one chapter with the mad woman raising the axe—and opened the next chapter several days later when the victim is trying to come to terms with the loss of the limb. You can set up a scene so that it's horrifyingly clear what's going to happen—you don't need the crunch of bone too. But discretion can go too far—Some of the worst writing in the world takes place when people like Alan Titchmarsh try to write about sex coyly. I wrote about necrophilia in *Shrouded*, so obviously I'm not afraid to open the coffin lid or the bedroom door. And there are masturbation scenes in *Safe As Houses* where David phones pornographic telephone lines. I see nothing wrong with showing strong sexual content as long as it's connected to the character's development or to the plot. The book that I've just finished writing (the successor to *Safe As Houses*) has some scenes in which the couple experiment with sexual role play. I thought it was important to show their lively, provocative side as a foil to the not-of-their-making darkness that increasingly envelops them.

I'm sure some writers are apolitical—just look at some of the cosies. They aren't written by people who are in touch with many aspects of the world. I'm not having a go at these writers or their readers as I'd rather people read something rather than nothing—but it's clear that some of them are living in a parallel universe. I'm not a political animal in that I haven't found a party I can believe in enough to vote for. But I sign petitions against whale slaughter and against genetically-modified foods and try to highlight the work of charities which seek to end child abuse.

I love the cinema but I don't think that a writer has to be a film fan in order to write contemporary prose.

You'd certainly be wasting your time following cinematic trends as Hollywood does a subject to death and then renounces it completely. For example, we've just had a teen horror revival with *Buffy The Vampire Slayer*, *Scream 2*, *I Still Know What You Did Last Summer* and so on. But if a writer wrote such a novel now it would be pitifully dated by the time they'd finished it. Trends are so mercurial that you have to write about the issues which seize your imagination, whether or not they are currently fashionable. As for music being a source of inspiration? Well, I've used it when necessary to depress my mood. I listened to Radiohead extensively when writing my parasuicide-themed chapbook *Expiry Date*. (A limited edition mini-novella that was published in The States by Dark Raptor Press.) And I played Chris Isaacs *Wicked Game* over and over before starting to write *Safe As Houses*, as the record has a really psychopathic edge.

Usually I start off with a pivotal incident in mind—for example the childhood beating and sexual trauma that turns Douglas in *Shrouded* into a potential necrophile. I'll then ask myself how a child might progress after an incident like that, how he'd relate to people (or not) as he became a man. What would his ideal lust object be? And how we achieve this ideal? The same is true in *Safe As Houses* where I have this man who hasn't dealt with the demons of his past— but when his child gets ill his own hellish vulnerability comes back to haunt him. Rather than deal with this

he subjugates women in order to make himself appear especially strong. These are incidents in the plot, albeit character-driven ones. They take the story down a logical—or at least logical to a damaged protagonist—route. Plot is important as it keeps the reader involved in the book. I've read literary novels where the characterisation is beautifully drawn and the prose is so perfect that I'm emerald with envy. But so little happens plot-wise that I feel slightly cheated at the end.

My third crime novel looks at a balanced professional couple whose lives are devastated by an external destructiveness. In order to survive they have to start acting in increasingly macabre and murderous ways. Both *Shrouded* and *Safe As Houses* explored outsider figures so I wanted to concentrate on integrated people this time, to show the cataclysmic wrath of the normally quiet man.

Safe As Houses, a paperback original which The Guardian *described as 'unputdownable', costs £7.50 and is published by The Do-Not Press.*

multicultural murder
sujata massey
adrian muller

Some years ago the American crime fiction convention Malice Domestic started awarding writing grants to unpublished authors. One of the first recipients to win this prize was Sujata Massey. She began writing The Salaryman's Wife *whilst teaching English in Japan, and with the financial aid Massey was able to complete the manuscript. When it appeared in 1997 it made Sujata Massey the first published Malice Domestic grant winner. Rei Shimura, the Japanese-American heroine of this paperback original, has gone on to appear in two further instalments, the latest of which,* The Flower Master, *was the first to be published in hardback format earlier this year. In the following interview Sujata Massey talks about her writing career to date.*

SUJATA MASSEY has a multi-cultural background. Born to an Indian father and a German mother in England, the family moved to the United States when Sujata was a young child. They temporarily stayed in California, then Pennsylvania, and finally settled in St.

Paul, Minnesota, where her father became a professor of geology and geophysics at the state university. *"It was also in St. Paul,"* says Sujata, *"where I finally lost my Northumbrian accent."*

It seems very strange that this casually elegant woman with attractive, dusky features would ever have spoken with a thick, northern, British inflection. Was it difficult being from a 'strange' country and mixed parentage? *"I'm aware that, because of my skin colour, most people who meet me like to* pigeon-hole me as Indian," Sujata says. "I never tried to be American, which made life hard for me at elementary school in the Midwest. Composed mostly of blond Lutherans and Catholics I never fit into school life in the United States.

My lifelong citizenship status has been as a United Kingdom subject, so I felt lucky to have not one but three countries to belong to, and I found a great deal of comfort when I travelled to my parents' homelands." However, in her teen years Sujata began experiencing difficulties there too. "With the German and Indian cultures being so diverse I would often say or do the wrong thing." This sense of "cultural schizophrenia" as Massey calls it, is a feature she would later give to her fictional heroine Rei Shimura.

Recently, having now lived most of her life in the United States, Sujata Massey applied for American citizenship.

As a child Sujata Massey first came into contact with crime fiction through Enid Blyton's Famous Five. "Blyton probably helped shape my affection for mysteries that are solved by groups of friends together," Massey says. "I then went on to read others, like Sir Arthur Conan Doyle, Wilkie Collins, and Agatha Christie."

Whilst she was an undergraduate of Johns Hopkins University she took a writing workshop by Martha Grimes whose novels bridged the way for Sujata to start reading modern day crime writers. "My favourite North American authors include S.J. Rozan, Barbara D'Amato, Harlan Coben, Marcia Muller, Sue Grafton, Laura Lippman, Sparkle Hayter...", and to prove she hasn't forgotten her British roots she also mentions she is a fan of Michael Dibdin, Lauren Henderson, and Paul Mann.

After college Sujata Massey went on to become a journalist for the Baltimore Evening Sun. It was during this period that she met her future husband Anthony Massey. The marriage was to be instrumental in the setting of the mysteries she would later come to write.

"Tony had taken a US Navy scholarship to pay for part of his medical school expenses," Sujata explains. "Once he had his MD he was asked to pay back the Navy by working as a general medical officer in the Navy fleet. I encouraged him to join a group of ships based out of Yokosuka, Japan, because I wanted live in Asia."

With her husband away at sea for fourteen out of the twenty-four months she was to spend in Japan, Sujata began writing fiction, taught English, and studied the Japanese language, flower-arranging and cooking. "It all sounds like very traditional female stuff," she says, "but in fact these activities taught me details about domestic life in Japan that have been invaluable to my writing."

Sujata would have quite happily stayed in Japan longer, but they returned on the completion of her husband's contract with the Navy. "Coming back gave me a chance to take writers' workshops, join Sisters in Crime, and start attending mystery conventions. The networking helped me refine my manuscript and taught me how to get published."

From her interest in crime fiction it always seemed clear that if Sujata Massey was going to write a novel it would be one featuring a sleuth. Before she began, she carefully took stock of her options. "I didn't have the background to write a book that was strong on police procedure or gory details, so I used the classic, slightly comic English mysteries of manners as my blueprint. Of course I updated the characters so they were young and funky and living in Japan."

So she always envisaged Japan as the setting for her first novel? "Yes. I was captivated by the world I had entered when I moved to Japan, so I decided to use it as the background. Mind you," she laughs, "when I started writing in Japan I thought I would only write one book, and I would be lucky to finish it, let alone see it published." Now she is tied to a multi-book series featuring Rei she has become aware of the down-side. "Since I don't live there anymore it doesn't seem the most practical idea," she says still laughing. "However, I enjoy travelling to Japan every year to fact-check the books. What's special about the series is that most of the neighbourhoods, shops, restaurants, media and personalities I mention are real. I wanted to write a book that somebody could take to Japan and walk around with. Also, if you write about places as you've seen them, it makes the book feel more authentic. The only things that are fictional in the books are the characters themselves and, of course, all those murders: Japan is a very safe country for everyone except Rei Shimura."

Rei Shimura came into being after Sujata Massey decided that the central character of The Salaryman's Wife should be a young person with a strong motivation to be in Japan. "I spent a long time worrying about whether it was ethically right for me to write in the voice of someone who had partial Japanese heritage," the author says, "and in the end, I decided it was all right. After all, men write in the voices of women characters, and vice versa. Also," she adds, "by the time I started writing The Salaryman's Wife I knew about life in Japan more intimately than about life in the countries of my parents."

Taking into account her own cultural identity, Sujata Massey focused on the similar expectations Indian and Japanese societies have from their women and used this in establishing conflicts for Rei. The result is a woman proud of her Asian heritage, but with American feminist expectations for her own lifestyle. When readers meet Rei Shimura she is 27, and a teacher of English to Japanese businessmen. Born in the USA to a mother from Maryland and a father from Japan, she has moved to Tokyo because she loves the culture and wants to try and make the country her homeland. In The Salaryman's Wife Rei is drawn into solving a murder when she is the first to find the body of a rich Japanese businessman, or salaryman as they are referred to in that country.

Reccurring characters introduced in this first instalment are Richard, her gay flatmate; her Japanese aunt Norie; and her cousin Tom, a doctor. Hugh Glendinning, a Scott working in Japan, also returns in later books, if only to make his presence felt off-stage. He is one of the people present at the scene of the death of his boss' wife, and soon becomes romantically involved with Rei.

Since Sujata Massey shares the multi-cultural background with her heroine, as well as having taught English in Japan, are their any more similarities she has in common with Rei?

"Many people think Rei is my alter ego, but actually," she says smiling, *"I'm a lot closer to Hugh Glendinning in terms of loving fun and luxury!"* More seriously she continues, *"However, like Rei, I believe strongly that when a foreigner lives abroad, it's important to pay attention to cultural cues and contribute to the society instead of holding oneself above the natives. It's pretty easy to put a foot in one's mouth while trying to go native, which Rei does about as much as I did while I lived in Japan. Also, in Zen Attitude, my second book, Rei struggles with the issue of her independence as a woman in a relationship where the man earns more money. This was something that was shocking for me to deal with in my own life when I first married."*

So what is it that draws Rei to Hugh? Smiling the author replies, *"If I saw Martha Grimes' Melrose Plant or Dorothy L. Sayers' Lord Peter Wimsey alone in a bar, I'd send over a drink immediately and hope for future contact!"* Like these writers, Sujata herself seems not unattracted to one of her own creations, and she agrees this is partially true. *"Hugh came about because I've always adored sexy, cool British men in mysteries. However, Rei and I both know that dashing rakes are fun to play around with, but are not good marriage material."*

So it would seem that Mr. Glendinning will have to start respecting his girlfriend's independence more. *"I really am not sure what's going to happen with him,"* says Massey. *"Marcia Muller's Sharon McCone has gone through several lovers in her series before getting to the right one. I'd like to see Rei try a relationship with a Japanese man."*

In the second book, *Zen Attitude*, Rei has moved into Hugh's luxury apartment, and the heroine's love of Japanese antiques, a sub-plot in *The Salaryman's Wife*, has now taken centre stage. A potentially lucrative deal has gone wrong and Rei again finds herself caught up in a murder investigation. On top of that she has Hugh's brother Angus to deal with. Backpacking his way across the world he invades Hugh's flat during his stay in Japan, paying little attention to anyone else's comforts but his own. What he does bring is an influx of very contemporary music, something Sujata Massey already carefully introduced in her first novel. *"While many writers don't mention bands because they are afraid that they will go out of fashion and thus date their books, I love to weave in music as a background element. My goal is to present a perfect snapshot of a particular year in Japan, and I can do that by mentioning songs, trendy toys, clothing fads, and political and economic events. These days I'm getting into a newer kind of British music which I'm not sure how to classify: Massive Attack, Garbage, Sneaker Pimps and Cornershop are some of my favourites."* Laughing she confesses, *"I don't care for Nine Inch Nails, Revolting Cocks, and most of Angus' collection."*

Naturally Sujata also includes references to Japanese acts. *"Akiko Yano is a jazz singer with a really lovely voice. I also enjoy a band called Dreams Come True and Cibo Matto, so I try to give them plugs when I can."* She plans to delve deeper into Japan's pop culture and world of animation in the fourth of the Shimura series, tentatively titled *The Floating Girl*.

Since Sujuta Massey writes mysteries set in Japan, is she familiar with any of their crime writers? "Yes, yes!" she says enthusiastically. "The Japanese crime writing tradition began in the 1920s with a man who took the name "Edogawa Rampo" as a salute to Edgar Allen Poe. In the 1930s and 1940s the premier Japanese mystery authors were Seichi Matsumoto and Akimitsu Takagi, both of whom have works published in English in the US." On a roll now she continues, "There are two contemporary women authors I enjoy, Shizuko Natsuki and Miyuki Miyabe, whose works are also translated into English."

Though Sujata Massey's books are sold in international bookstores in Japan and other Asian countries—with positive reviews appearing in the Japan Times newspaper—they have not yet appeared in Japanese translations. "At this point," the authors says, "the majority of my readers in Japan are expatriate Europeans and Americans." This is set to change when publishing house Kodansha brings out the translated version of The Salaryman's Wife next year. "So we have to see what the Japanese think of it then!" she says brightly.

Not that Massey hasn't had feed back already. With some pride she says, "I've heard from Japanese-, Chinese-, and Korean-American readers who have felt that Rei was a character similar to them. These readers have parents and relatives who expect them to behave in a traditional Eastern cultural manner, which is sometimes difficult for a young person who has been socialised in the West." Smiling she adds, "It's ironic how many readers see themselves in Rei because the Japanese think of themselves as a very different race from others."

Though Rei Shimura was off to the United States at the close of Zen Attitude, Sujata Massey has no intention of keeping her there. At the opening of The Flower Master, which appeared earlier this year, Rei is back in Tokyo up to her arms in murder and, this time, Japanese flower arranging, also known as ikebana. At the suggestion that it might be interesting to see how her heroine responds in a US setting the author firmly replies, "Her life will remain based in Asia. Perhaps she might venture from Japan occasionally to another country such as Malaysia or Singapore, but the collapse of the Asian economy is bound to impact on Rei's life and travel patterns. I think readers would be interested in seeing Rei in other parts of the world, but for her to move to the United States would just be boring. Well," she admits, "at least for me, as the writer, it would be boring."

When working on a book Sujata Massey writes from eight in the morning until she has written at least one thousand words. She usually ends up writing four to six hours with a break for an exercise session—"Running or walking," she says.

The author makes frequent use of fellow scribe Sue Grafton's writing tip to keep an electronic journal on the computer. "In it I write down all kinds of ideas for the book ranging from titles and character names to possible plot complications. If I have trouble composing a scene, I go to my journal and mess around and, more often than not, come back to the manuscript with an idea on how to proceed."

Massey also attends two writing groups. "I like having the group go over my manuscript with their suggestions for improving characters or clarifying the writing," she says, adding that it has also taught her how to offer criticism tempered with honest praise in return.

"Even though I write full time at home, it takes me about 11 months to complete a novel, which means at least four drafts before my editor sees it." She smiles as she says, "I envy the skill of my author-friend Laura Lippman, who works two day jobs and writes only two hours in the morning, yet manages to finish a book faster than I do!"

Meeting fans, friends and colleagues like Laura Lipman are some of the things Sujata likes best about her work. "Authors of literary fiction rarely get the chance to share and learn from their readers and colleagues, so I feel very lucky to have landed in the mystery genre."

The downside comes with the snobbery many writers of genre fiction encounter. "Mystery authors very rarely see their books reviewed outside of mystery magazines or crime columns in newspapers." Massey laughs, "As you can tell, I like to have my cake and eat it, too."

Yet she hardly grins and bares the situation. She credits her editor Carolyn Marino for the stroke of brilliance of mailing a thousand bound advance reading copies of The Salaryman's Wife to booksellers and reviewers. Sujata also received a hundred copies for her own use. "This was a wonderful opportunity for me to share my book with people whom I thought might talk about the it," she says. "I mailed them to die-hard mystery fans and booksellers I learned about through the DorothyL internet list-server, as well as my own lists of reviewers and booksellers. I called up booksellers myself to express my interest in signing at their stores. I attended many mystery conventions and funded my own book tour, staying with friends in cities that I knew had good independent mystery bookstores. You cannot do too much to promote your first book."

It paid off because it is almost unheard of for a first time author to get mentions in mainstream publications such as People magazine the USA Today newspaper, but between them the Marino and Massey managed to do exactly that.

Sujata Massey has "a very spicy idea" for a stand-alone suspense novel set in India, but at the moment she is finding it hard to fit in into her schedule of writing the Rei Shimura series. She is contracted to write the fourth instalment for a year 2000 publication, and depending on the continuing success of the series she'll consider writing more. "I'm deeply attached to the characters I've created and can see the series continuing as long as others feel the same way," the author concludes.

The Salaryman's Wife, Zen Attitude, and The Flower Master are available as American imports from your local (crime fiction) bookstore.

my pen is deadly
mickey spillane
michael carlson

Michael Carlson takes a deep breath and talks to Mickey Spillane on a rare visit to London (his first since he played his own distinctly non-PC protagonist Mike Hammer in the film of The Girl Hunters *all those years ago) Check out his piece on Spillane at the National Film Theatre in our film section...*

The best part about interviewing Mickey Spillane is the fun he appears to be having...I likened it to a cowboy trying to saddle a wily old mustang that refuses to be broken and knows all the cowboy tricks. Mickey holds little back, and he is so animated with stories you soon realise that one of the keys to his success is his genuine interest in people. He's the kind of person who would fit in anywhere.

There are a number of stories he asked be off the record, and a couple of them then popped up a few nights later during his Guardian Lecture, but I've kept to his request. I've also had to leave out Mickey's instructions on how to kiss a duck's tail without ruffling the feathers, mostly because there's no way I can describe it in prose. Mickey's persona is that of a tough guy who doesn't really care about his art, but as this

interview makes clear, good story telling grows from understanding people, and Spillane has a PhD in people...

I'll brown nose you right from the start...

Oh I'm an old pro, you won't get away with that...

...I told my mother I was interviewing Mickey Spillane and she said *"you make sure you tell him I named you after Mike Hammer,"* **because she was 19 and reading I the jury while she was pregnant and decided she liked the**

name Michael

I got a kid named Mike…jeez, the names they gave ME. My father was Catholic, my mother was Protestant, and because of that I got Christened in both churches, so I've got all these names…but my Dad always called me Mick. My mother called me Babe, and Babe is not a nice name for a guy, unless you're Babe Ruth

A lot of writers don't write under their given names

Yeah most of them. People are always surprised to find out my name is Spillane!

I was the first one probably in writing to use a nickname, Mickey, and it stuck. You see, in all my titles I used to use the personal pronoun: *I The Jury*, *Kiss Me,Deadly*, *My Gun Is Quick*, *Vengence Is Mine*…I ran out of pronouns! THEY stuck, they were important to use…it gives you a personal introduction. Now I'm not an author, I'm a writer, that's all I am. Authors want their names down in history; I want to keep the smoke coming out of the chimney.

(We discuss the failed attempt by Robinson Publishers to bring out a Spillane omnibus to coincide with his visit…the first he's heard of it…)

I like British publishers…when we were making a movie over here, Corgi books wanted to reprint…I did a lot of novelettes for magazines, and they put two novelettes together and you've almost got a novel, so they did that, and then my US publishers bought them from England. It's like a lot of movie stars, they never made in the US, they came to Europe and they made it big.

Why are your books out of print in the states

I'll tell you why. They have these corporate turnovers and they say *"I think he's old and passé,"* but they never look at the sales! On top of that they never look at all the other things that're going on…I'm 82 years old, wherever I go everybody knows me, but here's why…I'm a merchandiser, I'm not just a writer, I stay in every avenue you can think of. For 19 years I was doing the Miller Beer ads, in front of the public every day, we made Miller Lite the second largest selling beer in the world and everybody said *"no one'll drink that stuff."* We had a group of great sports guys, who were better known now, from the ads, than they were in the sports world. Then there's a corporate takeover, and we're not part of their group, so they discontinue the ads and wheee (makes noise of bomb falling) sales crash…

With all the young, pulp fictions about has the market passed by Mike Hammer?

No, no one's forgotten him, he's still on TV. Now we made the Guinness book of records, Mike Hammer has been on three different times with the same actor Stacy Keach, playing the same role. Now they're getting ready to go back for movies, and he's saying, 'I'm too old,' and he is! You think John Wayne had hair?

I saw Keach do Hamlet, oh, it must be 30 years ago…

Sir Cedric Hardwicke, remember him? I met him with Victor Saville and he says, (imitating posh English accent) *"I always wanted to play Mike Hammer"* and I say *"You can't, cause you have no hair"* and he says *"hair? You can buy hair anywhere!"*

This is true, you know. But the way he says it!

How many writers get to play their own characters in the movies?

I had a better time playing my own character in the beer ads, I'm with 'the Doll,' Lee Meredith. We're the same size, but I made her wear high heels so she'd be taller than me. Every time I'm walking through the airport people go 'where's the Doll?' We haven't done that for 12 years, but people still know the characters. I was with Lee walking down Broadway and the big crowds are gathering, and we can't cross the street, and finally a cop comes up and gets us across the street and on the other side it's the same thing again *"hey, it's the Doll!"* and I says *"Lee, we're not out of it yet, we're still in there..."* And on top of this, I wrote another book...let me tell you what this feels like, you'll be the only one who knows. You get an old guy working for Ford Motor Company, he was there when they made the Model T and Model A and big V8s and he's still there, and he's a real smart guy, and finally, he's up in the front of the thing. Henry Ford, you know, and all these guys are saying *"Get rid of the old guy, give him the watch, get him out of here,"* so he goes out and he starts his own motor company and they can't get rid of him... And it's funny, cause now I'm getting all these crazy awards...I got this Grand Master Award from the Crime Writers and I said, *"You know, the only reason you guys never gave me this before is I never belonged to your club, that's why."* Then they gave me this Brasher Doubloon in Europe...Hurricane Hugo hit me, and took away all my stuff, wheee...I don't need more stuff...

I'm going to write my last Mike Hammer novel...I used to write fast, but I can't now, my rear end gets tired...I can't put in 12 hours a day sitting in a chair

You wrote *I, The Jury* very quickly.

In 9 days. It was either 9 or 19...

You knew it was going to be a huge hit?

I knew a couple of things...during the war years they came out with reprints of all the Dumas novels, *Moby Dick*, for the servicemen, and I saw this and believe me I'm a very sharp merchandiser, and I say this is the new marketplace for writing, original paperback books. Now at that time you had to go through hardback. So I wrote *I The Jury* and turned it in to EP Dutton, it had been rejected by four different publishers, saying no no this is too violent, too dirty...and it was picked up by Roscoe Fawcett, Fawcett Publications, and he was a distributor, doing comic books, but he saw the potential and he went to New American Library, which was Signet Books, and he said *"If you print this book I'll distribute it."* Now they can't get distribution, so it's a win-win thing for them, but they have to get it published in hardback. So they go to Dutton and say if you print this, we'll do the paperback, so now it's win-win-win, and they offer me $250 and I say no, I need a thousand dollars to build a house in Newburgh, so I get a $1,000 advance, which was unheard of. So Roscoe ordered a million copies, and *that* was unheard of! So somebody in his outfit says, oh that wasn't what he meant, he must've meant a quarter million. So they bring out a quarter of a million at the wrong time, cause books sell great at Christmas time, but my book came out between Christmas and New Year, which is death, and it went straight to the top, because it was word of mouth. And it's sold out and Fawcett says get the rest of them out, and the guy says there aren't any more and Roscoe says whaddaya mean, I ordered a million, and a guy got fired!

And then you took a long time on your next book and that was rejected…

The Twisted Thing, yeah, that was rejected…editors are funny, they were still old time editors and they didn't like this new-style stuff…there's too much sex, too much violence…but actually, it's a true story, the story it was based on was true…and when I finally turned it in…wow, it went right to the top. I held it for 18 years, they were desperate for something new…finally I said, yeah, how about this one. (Laughs) I got one like that now. I turned a book into Dutton, not a Mike Hammer, and they're holding because the editor doesn't like it. I don't care what the editor likes or dislikes, I care what the people like. I don't want that editor to tell me what the people want.

Before that you'd written comic books for Martin Goodman.

Oh yeah, I was one of the first guys writing comic books, I wrote *Captain America,* with guys like Stan Lee, who became famous later on with Marvel Comics. Stan could write on three typewriters at once! I wrote the *Human Torch, Submariner.* I worked my way down. I started off at the high level, in the slick magazines, but they didn't use my name, they used house names. Anyway, then I went downhill to the pulps, then downhill further to the comics. I went

downhill class-wise, but I went uphill, money-wise! I was making more money in the comics. I wrote the original Mike Hammer as a comic, Mike Danger.

(After the first boom in Hammer novels, Spillane wrote one story for Manhunt, *a men's magazine.)*

Lemme tell you how that happened. I had this story I'd written for *Colliers,* but the editor there was a woman, and she said, *"As long as I'm editor here there'll never be a story by Mickey Spillane here."* So I turned in a short-short, which they bought, and St. John, the editor of *Manhunt,* came up on day and asked me about the story I wrote for *Colliers* and he said *"I'd be interested in buying that from you."* Now I wasn't thinking fast enough, cause they've always got more than one check already written in their pockets, but that story didn't take me long to write, and he said, *"would you accept $25,000 for it"* and I said sure, and he pulls this check out.

That was a lot of money then…

Sure…but he published it in four instalments, and that made *Manhunt* magazine.

I saw this photo of you signing a contract with Victor Saville and…

Victor Saville was bad news because he wanted money just to do one big picture. I'd sold millions but he wanted to make *The Chalice,* which fell on its face with a deadly thud, and he could've made the biggest hit in the world with *I, The Jury.* Instead he gets this slob writer called Harry Essex, who last I heard was making porno films, and he ruined everything, I mean, everything's stupid. Imagine this guy hits Mike Hammer over the head with a wooden coathanger and knocks him out. You hit Mike Hammer over the head with a wooden coathanger, he'll beat the crap out of you.

You went to see it and…

Yeah, I hadda walk out of it…

And the audience reaction was…

Awful. Biff Elliott walks out and says 'I'm Mike Hammer' and someone goes *"Dat's Mike Hammah?"* He was a good actor, a good friend, but he's left-handed with a Boston accent. Saville's lawyer saw him do live TV in New York, he won a prize, says, *"aw I got the right guy to play Hammer."* I had the right guy, Jack Stang, a real cop, only he couldn't act.

When I saw that picture of you, with Saville, you look like a young Ted Williams signing his first baseball contract with the Red Sox…there's an image of the way American men used to want to be…but is that all gone now?

Yeah, it's strange. It's not all gone, certain things keep cropping up in our business. Stephen King. Now I'm not crazy about him, but he's a great a writer.

He's got a market, he fulfils that market, no one says Henry Ford's a bad car maker, he was a great car maker. Cadillacs are different than Fords, but you don't say people are bad…Hemingway hated me. I sold 200 million books, and he didn't. Of course most of mine sold for 25 cents, but still…you look at all this stuff with a grain of salt. You say, why all this nonsense? I know an awful lot of Hollywood people, who are so self-important, I can't understand it. My father was a good Irish saloon-keeper, my mother always said to him, *"Jack, how come you know everybody here?"* and he'd say, *"be-cause I say hello."* I'm just like that, I've always been that way. I'm at a party once, with Hy Gardner, the columnist, and I wind up sitting between Salvador Dali and Jimmy Durante, and they're talking to each other in something like English, and neither one understands a word the other's saying, so I'm in the middle, interpreting…I was an only child…my Dad was the easiest guy in the world to retire, me, I can't retire, I've got no money (laughs) I've gotta keep writing. But where's the next step, where do you go? But at my age, you start to get tired. You're not full of piss and vinegar. The vinegar's all gone (laughs) It's a strange thing, it happens to me…they make up these easy schedules and I say, don't take it easy, I'm here to work.

What about writing another children's book?

I wrote those books as an exercise, they sold, they won the Junior Literary Guild Award, which made all the guys who write kids books very aggravated, *"how can you win that award?"* but you know what that does, it gets you into all the school libraries, which is a lot of sales. I've got one more kids book which I haven't sold yet, I've got it at home, it's all finished, maybe I'll sell it over here…

The biggest book in Britain right now is a children's book…

Really? Do you read those things? No? Well, *The Day The Sea Rolled Back*, now where I live on the beach they've got this strange thing, every five, ten years, a combination of wind, tide, rotation of the earth, whatever it is, but at low tide it goes way offshore. So the kids can go under the fishing piers and find lead, and whatever's dropped off. They're all excited. So what I did was take a thing that really happens, and extend it, so it goes back, like ten miles...and this could possibly happen it like that big tide in Nova Scotia, you can't run fast enough.

It seems like you collect a lot of facts in case they might come in handy.

But I don't research anything. If I need something, I'll invent it.

Mike Hammer was sort of a one-man cold war...

Yeah...

And when the cold war ended...

Yeah, I got out...

...did you get the feeling Mike Hammer was right all the time?

See, heroes never die. John Wayne isn't dead, Elvis isn't dead. Otherwise you don't have a hero. You can't kill a hero. That's why I never let him get older.

He doesn't get older, but does he change with the world?

Remember the elephant says, *"If only I knew then what I know now."* So now when I write about Mike Hammer, he looks at a girl, he *knows* now...you know what, he's got all this information about age, that would be me, but he's still a young guy, he can use that.

Would he still put Velda on a pedestal?

Oh yeah. People still come up to me and say *"She walked towards me, her hips waving a happy hello,"* things I wrote. They remember this stuff. *"On some people skin is skin, on you it's an opportunity to dine."*

Opportunity to dine. Have you read the Hannibal Lecter books?

I liked *Hannibal*, but I don't know how they're gonna make a movie out of it.

They oughta leave it right like it is. But violence isn't like it used to be. Sex isn't like it used to be either...I've got a great line I use. I get asked it all the time, someone comes up and says *"How could Mike Hammer have possibly shot that naked broad right in the belly button"? I say "He missed."* (Laughs)

He shot high?

No, I just said he missed. I didn't say one thing wrong, there's nothing dirty about that...*they* were the dirty ones. There was another there, this girl is giving Mike information, and he's opening a suitcase, and she wants him to look at her. She's just given him this big piece of information and she says 'Mike!' and she's taken this housecoat and spread it open and she's naked and he says *"My beautiful blonde had a brunette base."* Interesting. Only place you see a beautiful blonde is you go to Sweden or someplace. She might've had her roots showing, but everybody's got another thought. But these are the little things that work their way into a story.

Speaking of opening boxes, *Kiss Me Deadly* is the best regarded of the hammer films, but you've said before you don't like it

I don't like any of them, because they don't read the books. In *Kiss Me Deadly* my story is better than his story. Anthony Quinn played in *The Long Wait* and he didn't read the book either. I said, 'Read the book,' and he did and he came back and said *"Why'd they make it that way?"* They did because it's Hollywood. Everybody wants their name on the screen. I played in a movie called *Ring Of Fear* with Clyde Beatty and Pat

O'Brien. I'd watched Clyde Beatty since I was a kid, he was a great act, and you know, *Devil Dogs Of The Air*, O'Brien and Cagney, great things. And now, in the middle of the shooting the agents came to me and asked who's gonna be first in the credits, and I said I don't care, put me last, and that took me right out of the way. It put me in the middle, so I said, we should leave Clyde on top cause it's his picture. That was some movie. This was where I got the Jag. The guy wrote and directed the picture had problems, but John Wayne who produced it, never gave up on his friends. Duke was having a bad time, going through a divorce, and they needed to fix the script. So they're thinking who could do it, and someone says, Spillane's a writer, he could do it. Now I'm playing *me* in the picture, for pete's sake. They called me up in Newburgh on Wednesday, I'm already back home across the country, and said come back and fix it. So I took my Wagner records, flew West, and worked Friday, Saturday, Sunday. They set me up in a beautiful hotel suite, and I worked. So I'm sitting there Sunday, all done, having a cold beer and listening to *The Ring* and in comes Andy McLaughlan, Victor's son. He says, 'How you doing?' and I tell him I'm all done and he thinks I mean I'm done for the day because it's Sunday, and I say 'I'm finished,' and he says *"whaddaya mean you're finished, you just got here!"* So I hand him the pages, and he's reading and going 'Wow, wow, wow' and he calls Duke and Bob Fellows and says we got it. He goes out in the street and says to this woman *"You wanna make a hundred bucks?"* and the guy she's with nearly slugs him, but he

was looking for typists! So they type up their pages, and they left me alone. So I go home. A few days later, they're going to go to Phoenix to shoot, and they can't find me. They call all the bars, the police stations, the whore houses, nothing. So they say try him at home and Bob says, *"He wouldn't be at home."* But I was. So they get me out there to Phoenix and make the picture. And they wanta pay me for the script but I won't take nothing for that, it was a favour. But Duke says, *"He was looking at those Jags in the lot next to the Cock and Bull."* One night, I'm back in Newburgh, it's snowing, and out in front of my house is this beautiful Jag with a red ribbon around it, and a note that says 'Thanks, Duke.' People see that car now, I had a guy saying 'Who makes those?' I said, *"That car's older than you are!"*

let's talk about your influences. I know Carroll John Daly must've been a big one

Oh he was a great writer for the pulps...Tyne Daly from Cagney and Lacey, she's his niece you know, but Daly was a great story writer, but he couldn't write long books. He was my favourite, and after I was a big writer I wrote a fan letter to John, saying how much I admired him when I was young, and wanted to write like him, and how I thought of Race Williams when I created Mike Hammer, and I got a letter back from his agent saying they were gonna sue me for stealing his character! So I got in touch with John and he was angry, this was his first fan letter in years! And he fired his agent!

What about Chandler? there's that famous scene where Marlowe throws what's pretty obviously a Mike Ham-

mer book into the garbage

I know. I think it's pretty stupid. Did I tell you the Hemingway story?

No.

Hemingway hated me. I outsell him and he was steamed. One day he wrote a story for *Bluebook* berating me. So I'm going on a big TV show in Chicago and I don't get it, that's sour grapes…I mean if you can't say something nice about someone why say anything at all? So I go on this show and the host says *"Did you see what Hemingway said about you in Bluebook?"* and I say 'Hemingway who?'

That killed him.

Not literally?

Oh boy no. Every summer I went down to Florida on treasure hunts, and there's this great restaurant called the Chesapeake and they had a picture of Hemingway behind the bar. So one day the owner asks if she could have a picture of me to put up there, and she puts one there. One day Hemingway comes in and sees my picture and says *"What's he doing next to me? Either take his down or take mine down!"* So they took his down and he never came back to that restaurant. (Laughs) I don't like to tell that story cause you're talking about a dead guy can't defend himself… he was a great reporter, but he got carried away with all the other stuff, the bullfighting…I'm always on the side of the bull, I hope the bull blows the hell out of that crazy guy in the clown suit out there. I don't like to see animals hurt, not deliberately. If they're putting the bull out there, don't stick the things in him first.

But you can kill off lots of people…

That's different, it's a fair fight…I saw a bull once, charge a bison eating in a field. And the bison just drops his head, the bull hits in and BOOM, he's out, and the bison goes back to eating. I went to college out there, in Fort Hayes, Kansas, where they filmed *Dancing With Wolves*. I used to love to watch the bison. One day an old male died, and the rest, they stood around him, and they did this for two, three days, no one could get to the body out. Finally it's was as if they decided, OK, you people can come get the body out. It was amazing. It always surprises me, how animals seem to have an instinctive knowledge…now what am I talking about dead bulls for?

You were raised a Catholic right?

No I wasn't raised either one (Catholic or Protestant). I'm one of the Jehovah's Witnesses.

You joined in the fifties?

Fifty-one. You don't join that, you have to be a witness. Witnessing is an active word.

The word 'apocalyptic' keeps coming up in criticism of your work. Do you believe in a Second Coming?

The word coming is a misnomer. The word used is *parousia* in Greek, and it means 'presence'. Take President Clinton. Do you know him? No. But you feel his presence, all the taxes he lays on you. We feel his presence because we have to live under his direction. So when these things were asked of Jesus they asked *"What will be the sign of your presence, and the end of the system of things…"* Now that was translated in the King James Bible as the end of the world. Now the word 'world,' and the word 'earth,' are two different things…the Bible says the earth abides forever. It's the simplicity of it, religion has turned everything inside out! Someone says *"how'd you like to be able to live forever?"* You say, *"oh boy would I liketa live forever, there's so many things I'd like to do."* I used to be able to pass a football with either hand, now I can't throw from here to the wall...there's so many things...I think the best time for me was around thirty-five...but if you're not a wise guy you can put up with those things... I know too many guys my age, they walk around, like they're crippled. I try to stay in good physical shape, I don't smoke, I don't drink...I'll have a beer once in a while. People say," *you have a beer, you're a Jehovah's Witness..."* But the Bible doesn't proclaim against drinking, it proclaims against drunkenness...anyway, someone says *"How'd you like to live forever..."* We know what death is, you can kick a dead dog, it won't bite you...but Jesus makes the greatest remark—I think it's so funny nobody pays any attention—he says *"This means everlasting life,"* and they say *"What? You gotta stand on your head, you gotta pay knowledge, what?"* and he says it's taking in knowledge of you, the only true God, and that's so easy...I get so excited about this, I'll keep talking to you like this if you don't say that's enough, but this is why people think you're a nut, they say, *"Don't people turn you down?"* I say *"They don't turn me down, they turn God down."* That's why people can't stop drinking, do drugs, that's why the world's the way it is...do you know a stable country in the world?

Iceland?

Where I live in South Carolina, it's stable, but it's so crooked...the local sheriff, he says *"You're the only guy I trust, cause you don't vote for anybody..."*

Was it simpler back when you were writing *I The Jury*, was it different then?

No, the field changes. When I started the paperback market, there were only a few good writers, now the market's loaded...you don't know which one to take.

The women have a great thing going for them now, and they're making use of things, like there's a bunch of gay women who write great stuff, very masculine stuff, and I like their work, but you can see where they put in their petitions towards being gay, which is all right but it doesn't make for a great role model...

Mike Hammer is always putting his petition forward for what we used to call the American Way.

It's a black and white painting

Everything's black and white, commies are bad!

Now hear this!

But what if it were today, and the American Way is a series of crooked Presidents...what happens to Mike Hammer then

That's demoralising...then how can you do this...there was a piece in our local paper the other day about girls, 12, 13, in school, they're practising oral sex. And when someone tells them to stop they say, *"What's wrong? The President does it!"*

This comes out in the paper, a big deal. This guy has no sense of shame. I can't get over how many of the vets voted for him, he's a draft dodger. You understand the Kennedys, everybody says *"They're good Irish boys,"* but the phoniness of it all.

And that poor Kennedy boy who crashed... I'm a pilot, I got 11,000 hours,

I was a big fighter pilot during the war, I just passed my physical…they hate it, I'm over 80, they don't want guys over 80 flying, anyway, he had what, less than 100 hours? All the pilots I know knew what happened to him, he spun out, and he couldn't drop his stick…you what we say about this guy, *"He ruined a damn good airplane."* And took people with him.

Maybe the difference is Mike Hammer's been in a war?

You remember Audie Murphy, the most decorated American solider, became an actor in Westerns? A cop told me, he stopped a car on 101 in California, and Audie comes out of his car, dark, middle of the night, with a rifle. The cop saw his eyes, he looked nuts, and before Audie could do anything he said *"Hey Audie, how're you doing?"* and stuck out his hand. Audie stopped, and then stuck out his hand. He said it was like looking into death's eyes, and Audie was a sweet looking guy, like a little kid. But Audie'd been shot so many times

Coming out of the war were there more guys like that than people think, they'd all faced that.

Yeah, I was like that. In foryt-five when we got out it was a different scene. We weren't the same people. I'm a pussy cat. I write about that stuff, but I don't want to mess around with all that nonsense. You change as you get older, but, how much older am I gonna get? I buy a new dog, I gotta make sure I live to be 100. It sounds silly, but it's true. I talk to you about these things, these are only little incidents, actually they're little anecdotes

You've got a million of them, I bet?

Yeah but I don't ever think about them You ask me a question, they pop in my mind

Did you ever write anything in the Hammer books to specifically answer criticisms

I don't pay any attention to them. Those guys, they get free books and then they try to tear you down. Critics themselves, they used to tear me up. One time I had the whole New York Times bestseller list, then the Godfather came along, pushed me out…here's something funny, Hy Gardner gave me this…at one point I was the fifth most translated writer in world. Ahead of me were Lenin, Gorky, Tolstoy, and Jules Verne. (Laughs) It doesn't mean anything, but it's a funny thing to bring up. One day this little prissy guy, I'm at a tea party, if you can picture me at a tea party, and this guy comes up to me and says *"What a horrible commentary on the reading habits of Americans to think that you have seven of the top ten bestsellers of all time"* and I looked at him at I said *"You're lucky I don't write three more books."*

Do you do a lot of reading?

I read all the time…I read a lot of history books.

Who do you like in crime writing?

I really like Max Allan Collins…he's a great researcher…his Nate Heller books on the Lindbergh story, and on the Cermak assassination are both excellent, and the new one, on Amelia Earhardt is great. I say *"Max, you're writing is so good, but you research too much! You could write more if you just invented it!"* But I like the guy…we're strange buddies (Laughs)

Why strange?

I'll tell ya, when I worked with

Shirley Eaton (in *The Girl Hunters*) or with Lee Meredith, these were two girls who gave everything, they made things look good for you. Why, for the sake of making yourself look good, destroy a picture. And that's how Max is, he doesn't try to take anybody down, and it's nice to know that people like that are still around. It's like when you're doing an interview and you say this is off the record…well, if you wanta go off the record, you shouldn't say it, but sometimes it fits in with what you're trying to tell the guy…now I don't care anymore. That interview in *The Guardian*, he did it tongue in cheek and the headline, (*The Hardest Jehovah's Witness In The World*) he wouldn't know what he was fooling with…

Well, he wouldn't have written the headline.

I don't give a lot of crappy stuff out, they want to know something, hey, I'll tell you. I don't know of anything I hold back (laughs)

Well, you're tough to pin down.

I'll tell you, I've been the *National Enquirer* four times and they've never said anything bad about me yet (laughs)

But you must know exactly what interviewers will be asking?

Oh sure, I give them leading answers so they'll ask me questions I want to answer. I'll tell you what gets people aggravated. I've done literally thousands of TV shows, and you get on a show with people, with actors, and they're terrible, unless they've got a script in their hand they don't know what to do, they don't know how to sit still, and all of a sudden you're walking away with the show and they don't know what to do! They don't understand, if they'd only stop the nonsense and just talk! You know who the nicest guy I ever met in the acting field was? Basil Rathbone. He was the neatest fellow around, nice, kind, considerate…he always played villains, except for Sherlock Holmes. He had the perfect sneer.

Who would've been the best guy to play Mike Hammer?

Jack Stang, if he could act. He was a tough Marine. He went into one Japanese island in the Pacific, with 240 men, he was one of four came out. ((We look at pictures of Stang's screen test, which Mickey wrote)) That's Jonathan Winters, the comedian, playing the corpse. And that's me…jeez, did I ever look like that!

I always wanted to have Mike Mazurki play Hammer…too bad he couldn't act. Remember when Dick Powell played Marlowe? Well Mike Mazurki is playing Moose Malloy, a big guy, he's six-six, and Chandler said he wore this outlandish plaid jacket, *"It was so big it had golf balls for buttons."* Comes time to make the movie, they didn't use that line! He was big enough. It was like hitting Hammer over the head with a coathanger.

Sometimes things that mean so much in a book get lost on the screen.

When Harry Essex wrote *I The Jury*, there's a shot from a .38, hits a brick wall.

Biff Elliott picks it up, it's in perfect condition, he says 'It's a .38,' I say *"Biff, you were in the Army, you know that bullet'd be flat!"* He says *"It didn't make any difference."*

It's like the magic bullet.

Yeah, exactly. I remember when I'm playing Hammer. I'm 46 years old, I'm in good shape, the director says to me "Can you run?" I say "Yeah, what's happened?"

He says "Can you run?" I say "Sure." So we do the scene, and I ran away from the camera. Roy Rowland says "What're you doing!" I said "Tell me what you want, don't say 'Can you run.'" We made that picture in Britain. Did you know Billy Hill?

No, I haven't been here that long.

Well, this is going back 35 years. Billy Hill was the Al Capone of London. The other guy was Jack Spot, actually his name was Jack Comma, he changed it to a period. Billy Hill had a big war record, he terrorised Europe! Second day I was here Jack Spot comes into the Rembrandt Hotel where I was staying, and they had all these hall porters, and they're all going crazy, and we're telling stories.

Anyway, he left, and up comes this guy in a bowler hat and raincoat, and he says, sucking a pencil tip, "Tell me sir, did you recently entertain a guest named Mr. Jack Spot?" And I say 'Yes' and he sucks the pencil again, makes a note, and says "Would you mind giving me the gist of the conversation, sir?" I said, "Sure, he wanted to know about all the hoods in New York." So he left, and all the hall porters are saying "He's from Scotland Yard, this like out of the movies."

Now next day, I'm the only guy who drinks water, and I'm drinking ice water and this guy walks up, Billy Hill, and he comes up and says "Hey Mick, how ya doing, my name is Billy Hill." Now this is before Benny Hill, even, and the hall porters are shaking, no one will look him in the eye. And we know a couple of guys in common in New York,

and he says "I'd like to go out and watch a movie being made," and I say "Sure, come out, be my guest." Next day he comes out to the old set in Elstree, and I didn't tell the assistant director, who was a fuss-budget, and I'm showing Billy around, introducing him to Shirley Eaton, and the AD says "Who's that on my set, I'm going to throw him off," and someone says to him, "That's Billy Hill," and he melted, aaagh, because he knew Billy heard him. So he disappeared. So he's trying to hide, and finally Billy turns around and glares at him, and he almost dies!

Now Billy asked if there was anything he could do for me, and we had this awful Spanish gun for Mike Hammer, so I asked him if he knew where we could find a .45, and next day he shows up on the set with a gunny sack, and he says "I got your pieces for you, where should I put them?" and he dumps about two dozen .45s there, and ammo, and the prop boy nearly hit the roof, "Those are REAL GUNS,." Bob Fellows the producer, knew this, but he didn't pay any attention, he just got them registered. The paperwork was incredible.

A .45's important isn't it?

That's what I carry. I'm licensed to carry it. (Reaches into his back pocket).

I know you don't have a .45 back there.

No, here's the licence. See my birthday, March 9th, the anniversary of the battle between the Monitor and the Merrimac, Hampton Virginia, 1862. It's a South Carolina licence. It's a nice place, but too many Yankees coming down there. It was OK when I was the only one! You'd think the South won the Civil War

But it agrees with you.

I'm a country boy. I hate New York. But that's where things happen, so I use it as a base for stories, I know enough about it. But I have to keep going back there.

Things change. The Blue Ribbon, that I thought'd be there forever, that's gone. The face of the city changes. The city's almost alive, you can see the movement of people from one section to another. When they took all the Els down on the East Side and let the sunlight in, everything changed. But it's too crowded, jammed up, I can't be happy there.

But if we ever have another hurricane in South Carolina, the evacuation will be jam packed. In a hurricane three things kill you, water, trees and poles falling down on you, and traffic.

Carl Hiaasen says people are arrogant, millions of them build in the path of hurricanes in Florida and then they're surprised when nature doesn't detour to avoid them.

Where I am they can smell out a hurricane. My house survived Hurricane Hazel, but it didn't get past Hugo.

Tell me a little about Max's film (*Mike Hammer's Mickey Spillane*, see film section).

It's very embarrassing, because everybody's saying nice things about me. These are people in the writing business, I watch it, I want to put my head down...

You expect people not to say nice things?

One day a guy from the *National Enquirer* comes up to do a story in Myrtle Beach, and they say, do a story about Spillane and he tells them he can't, be-

cause I don't do anything! You know, most guys get in trouble through drinking, look that that guy Willis, with Demi Moore, they're looking to get into the papers. I don't want that. What I got married, they wrote *"Mickey Spillane marries daughter's girlhood chum!"* Jane was a divorcee with two kids when I married her...I used to throw her out of the house when she was a little girl, now I'm saying 'I do!' How do I do this? Oh, and they said I had a secret wedding! I only had 200 people there. That's what they do to you. But I didn't do anything. I'm not gonna sue them.

Your second wife helped promote your books by posing naked on the covers.

She wanted to do that. I fondly refer to her as 'the snake.' She liked the publicity, the big time. She went Hollywood, in a bad way.

You never went Hollywood?

Me? Shoot.

Can I translate that as 'shit?'

If you want! I go into Hollywood, do my business, and get out. That's not my lifestyle. And their lifestyle is terrible. They don't live too long. You know how old Hitler was when he died? 59?

But that wasn't natural causes!

He would've died younger in Hollywood! Erroll Flynn, 53 he was. Gee. You look at him and you say, *"What happened?"* I don't want to be like that. But I don't care about posterity. I say "Now!"

mickey spillane

you, the jury

steve holland

He's been slated for his use of sex and violence, condemned for his right-wing politics... What is it about this guy that critics so loath and Joe Q. Citizen loves? Judge Steve Holland presides over the case of the most vilified author ever to sell 200 million copies of his books around God's green earth. Would the clerk of the court please read out the charges...

MICKEY SPILLANE
Hard-boiled's most extreme stylist or cynical exploiter of Machismo?

FRANK SPILLANE has the unusual distinction of being named twice. His father, bartender John Joseph Spillane was a Catholic and his son was baptised with the middle name Michael; at the Protestant church of his mother Catherine Anne he was christened Frank Morrison Spillane. To his father he was always 'Mickey', and that's the name that stuck and the way his fans have always known him.[1]

Growing up in Elizabeth, New Jersey, young Mickey showed a flair for sports and telling stories; the latter

earned him a little extra money when he began selling yarns soon after graduating high school while the former got him a place at Kansas State Teachers College, albeit briefly. He was soon back in New York, and in

1939 found work with Funnies, Inc., a comic strip production-line run by Lloyd V. Jacquet who supplied strips, written and drawn in house, to the majority of the leading comic publishers of the time; Spillane found himself working on characters such as The Human Torch, Sub-Mariner, Captain America, Blue Bolt, Batman, Captain Marvel and Plastic Man for the next few years before seeing war service with the Air Force, training pilots at Greenwood, Mississippi. He returned to New York in 1946 where he supported himself and new bride Mary Ann Spillane by writing back-up strips like *Jackie the Slick Chick* and *Smarty Pants*.

Using what money he had, Spillane bought a few acres of land near Newburgh, an hour's drive out of New York City, but needed to raise $1000 for materials to build his new home. He'd been touting around a new comic strip character to publishers: Mike Danger was a tougher version of the *"Mike Lancer"* detective strip he had penned for Harvey back in 1942. No-one was biting — this was post-war and the heroes who had seen the country through the bad times had no more campaigns to fight and were on the slide. Rather than waste the concept, Spillane turned Danger into Mike Hammer (named after the local Hammer's Bar and Grill), and pounded out a novel in a matter of days[2].

Spillane passed the pages around a few close buddies like Ray and Joe Gill, friends from the Jacquet shop, and Dave Gerrity who lived nearby; the consensus was that it would nev-er sell. But another friend, Jack McKenna, took the manuscript to publishers E.P. Dutton. It's said that at Dutton, vice president John Edmondson took the book to pay back a favour to McKenna, believing that if it bombed, they'd make their money back selling reprint rights to the (then new) paperback reprint market.

I, the Jury was published in July 1947.

WITNESSES FOR THE PROSECUTION

"I shook the rain from my hat and walked into the room."—Mickey Spillane, *I, the Jury*.

"The dialogue and action leave little to be imagined."—New York Times, 3 August 1947.

"Able, if painfully derivative, writing and plotting, in so vicious a glorification of force, cruelty and extra-legal methods that the novel might be made required reading in a Gestapo training school."—Anthony Boucher, *San Francisco Chronicle*, 3 August 1947.

"Lurid action, lurid characters, lurid writing, lurid plot, lurid finish. Verdict: Lurid"—Saturday Review of Literature, 9 August 1947.

"His novel is a shabby and rather nasty little venture from the indefensible logic of its opening scene to the drooling titillation of its final striptease."—James Sandoe, *Chicago Sun Book Week*, 17 August 1947.

CROSS-EXAMINATION BY THE DEFENCE

"I said [to John Edmondson at Dutton] 'I'd like to reprint I, the Jury.' He said, 'Two thousand dollars; send along a

contract.' I said, 'Who the hell has ever heard of Mickey Spillane — let's take a chance. Five hundred dollars.' He said, 'A thousand.' I said, 'Seven-fifty.' He said, 'Boy, you've got a book.'"—Victor Weybright, editor, New American Library, 1958.

To fans, hard-boiled meant the two-fisted tales of gumshoes and G-Men that had appeared in pulps like *Dime Detective* since the 1920s; to the critics it was still a slowly emerging literature led by Dashiell Hammett and Raymond Chandler, both ex-*Black Mask* writers who had surfaced in hardcover. The Private Eye was Sam Spade or Philip Marlowe, portrayed on the screen by Humphrey Bogart; *film noir* had yet to be recognised in America as a style and had only just been thus named in France. The critics ripped into Spillane's novel, and only a little over half the 7,000 print run sold.

Mike Hammer was not the wise-cracking Bogart. He did not wise-crack. He got angry and threatened. Chandler's novels were relatively bloodless; although he started slowly, Hammer was to average ten killings per novel. Spillane wasn't a new Chandler. *I, the Jury* had echoes of *The Maltese Falcon*, especially the downbeat ending of the latter where Spade hands Brigid O'Shaughnessy over to the cops, but Spillane wasn't even a new Hammett. He was a new Carroll John Daly, and Mike Hammer was Race Williams for the post-war audience.

Williams, like Hammer, laid his cards on the table: "*People—especially the police—don't understand me. And*

what we don't understand we don't appreciate. The police look upon me as being so close to the criminal that you can't tell the difference... Every cop in the great city has my reputation hammered into him as a gun and a killer. No use to go into detail on that point. I carry a gun— two of them, for that matter. As to being a killer, well—I'm not a target, if you get what I mean. I've killed in my time, and I daresay I'll kill again. There—let the critics of my methods paste that in their hats."[3]

"*I'm a Private Investigator who doesn't believe in red tape. I never did object to a little gun play. I shoot fast and I hit what I shoot at.*"[4]

"*That's my racket, Meet lead with lead, violence with violence, and death with death. This working on the side of the law may have its advantages, but it has its disadvantages, too. The law is always looking for evidence; legal evidence, when a few corpses decorating the scenery would be much more effective and certainly quicker."*[5]

It's the same personal code Spillane gave to Mike Hammer. But ten years had gone by since Daly's heyday when a Race Williams story could raise the circulation of a magazine by 20-25%. The War had acclimatised the American public to brutality and, whilst critic Christopher La Farge argues[6] that *"Some men were toughened by combat but the huge majority of them came off from the experience with a desire to put that side of war — and the brutal methods self-preservation taught them — as far back in their minds as possible,"* the notion that danger could be faced and won by force was ingrained, not only in GIs who had fought through hell and survived, but in the wider population who had waited back home, imagining the worst.

Awareness of widespread crime in America was growing and it had none of the glamour of Prohibition era gangsters: the Senate Investigation headed by Estes Kefauver broadcast on television in 1950-51 revealed that organised crime formed a shadow government with its own laws, business practises and law enforcement (Murder, Inc.) that would require new legislation to combat.

Juvenile delinquency was on the rise; one spark that really lit a flame was the invasion of Hollister, California, on July 4th, 1947, by 4,000 motorcyclists: a small number of arrests led to a riot in which the police station was attacked, the main thoroughfare was blocked off and turned into a dragstrip, and it took State Police intervention to diffuse the situation. It made headline news nationwide and it showed America how powerless the legal system was against these thuggish outlaws, a large mobile force who could descend on any town they chose. Maybe your town was next.

Mickey Spillane gave readers a hero for those troubled times when the law seemed unable to cope, one who did not act with frustrating slowness or sit around simply debating the problem: meet violence with violence, and when the bad guy is down, kick him in the teeth. If Hammett (in Chandler's words) gave murder back to the people who committed it, Spillane offered a sword of justice to people who dreamed of vengeance but felt powerless. Hammer was a fantasy.

Nowhere else in fiction will you find a character who so openly reveals his hand as Mike Hammer: in the opening two pages of *I, the Jury*, Hammer is confronted with the body of his closest friend and, looking down at the corpse, knowing that the killer had cold-bloodedly tormented his friend as he lay dying, he swears an oath that he will find and wipe out his murderer. *"He won't sit on the chair. He won't hang. He will die exactly as you died, with a .45 slug in the gut, just a little below the belly button. No matter who it is, Jack, I'll get the one. Remember, no matter who it is, I promise."*

As he makes this vow, Mike Hammer is still a cipher to his readers, the "*I*" of the title — he *is* his readers. We have no idea who this first person narrator is, only that he seems to command respect from the police the moment he walks in the room; he is kind, thinking first to offer some words of comfort to the girl crying her heart out on the studio couch, but focused. Pat Chambers tells us its a nasty wound but we look anyway without feeling nauseous; we calmly examine the room, smartly summarise what has happened, and coldly tell the police that their system will not serve our needs, that we will take the law into our own hands:

"You're a cop, Pat. You're tied down by rules and regulations. There's someone over you. I'm alone. I can slap someone in the puss and they can't do a damn thing. No one can kick me out of my job. Maybe there's nobody to put up a huge fuss if I get gunned down, but then I still have a private cop's licence with the privilege to pack a rod, and they're afraid of me. I hate hard, Pat. When I latch on to the one behind this they're going to wish they hadn't started it. Some day, before long, I'm going to have my rod in my mitt and the killer in front of me. I'm going to watch the killer's face. I'm going to plunk one right in his gut, and when he's dying on the floor I may kick his teeth out."[7]

Hammer speaks with control over his emotions, directly and forcibly, as we would all like to. And what makes Mickey Spillane a page-turner is not whether Mike Hammer will shoot the killer in the guts — that was his mission statement and even in those few pages you know he'll do it — but will he follow through? Will he really kick the killer's teeth out as he lays there, dying?

WITNESSES FOR THE
PROSECUTION

"*I picked a paperback off the table and made a pretence of reading it. It was about some private eye whose idea of a hot scene was a dead, naked woman hanging from the shower rail with the marks of torture on her...I threw the paperback into the wastebasket, not having a garbage can handy at the moment.*"—Raymond Chandler, *Playback.*

In one novel alone — *Vengeance is Mine* — Spillane is guilty of:

Blasphemy—the title.

Racism—"*If we had both been in the jungle and some slimy Jap had picked him off I would have rammed the butt of a rifle down the brown bastard's throat for it.*" (p28)

Violence—"*I leaned back against the wall and kicked out and up with a slashing toe that nearly tore him in half. He tried to scream. All I heard was a bubbling sound. The billy hit the floor and he doubled over, hands clawing at his groin. This time I measured it right. I took a short half-step and kicked his face in.*" (p60)

Casual violence to women—"*I reached up and smacked her across the mouth as hard as I could. Her head rocked, but she still stood there, and now her eyes were more vicious than ever. "Still want me to make you?"*

"*Make me,*" she said. (p50)

Homophobia—"*There was a*

852

SIGNET

Mickey Spillane

VENGEANCE IS MINE

A Sensational New MIKE HAMMER Mystery by the Author of

I, THE JURY and MY GUN IS QUICK

A SIGNET BOOK
Complete and Unabridged

"THERE WAS A TIME WHEN WILD, GORY SCENES OF VIOLENCE WERE STOCK ITEMS IN A STORY OR SCRIPT. I CERTAINLY WENT ALL OUT MYSELF WHEN THAT WAS THE TREND."—MICKEY SPILLANE, TV GUIDE, 1961.

Individual scenes are difficult to defend, if indeed they are defendable. The violence and sexual magnetism are part of the Mike Hammer power fantasy. Hammer's racism (especially against the then recently defeated Japanese) and homophobia simply reflected American society of the time; and since Hammer is, in the eyes of his critics, a testosterone-driven he man, his rejection of homosexual advances is at least in character.

Physically, Mike Hammer is a six-foot New Yorker, 190 pounds, not especially good-looking. He can rough house it with the best, take a licking and hand one out. If he needs it, his .45 can be in his hand faster than you can blink. He fights for the underdog, and sometimes that's himself. He makes promises and he keeps them. He is a loyal friend.

Hammer is, however, the archetypal *homme fatale*. Women fall for him in a moment, attracted to, and turned on by, his toughness. Hammer, in his own way, places them on pedestals: Charlotte Manning in *I, the Jury*, Juno Reeves in *Vengeance is Mine*, and others, have lit Hammer's heart and soul. The women he feels he has fallen in love with, he rejects sexually, asking

pansy down at the end of the bar trying to make a guy who was too drunk to notice and was about to give it up as a bad job. I got a smile from the guy and he came close to getting knocked on his neck. The bartender was one of them, too, and he looked put out because I came in with a dame." (p86)

Sexism—All women want Mike Hammer: Juno Reeves (*"Make it up to me now"*), Connie Wales (*"Make me"*), the secretary/mistress of a businessman (*"She danced close enough to almost get behind me and had a hell of an annoying habit of sticking her tongue out to touch the tip of my ear"*), Marion Lester (*"I hope next time it's under more pleasant circumstances"*).

them to wait: he tends to have opportunistic sex with call girls and nymphomaniacs who plead with him to stay overnight. Ultimately, Hammer is in love with his secretary, the curvaceous Velda with her long dark hair kept in a page-boy cut, but *"I never made a pass at her. Not that I didn't want to, but it would be striking too close to home."* [8] She is Hammer's equal — she holds a private investigator's license and isn't afraid to use the .32 automatic she carries.

Being a friend to Mike Hammer is a dangerous business: we tend to meet his best friends over their corpses, and even police officer Pat Chambers was put on Spillane's earth to occasionally pull his pal out of the fire, but mostly to do his legwork and remind him (and the reader) why Mike has to operate outside the law.

Hammer is only able to forge lasting relationships with ex-Army veterans, those he fought alongside, like *Jury*'s Jack Williams, or casual acquaintances like *Vengeance*'s Chester Wheeler. The only thing we learn about Hammer's past is that he fought *"in the muck and the slime of the jungle, there in the stink that hung over the beaches rising from the bodies of the dead, there in the half-light of too many dusks and dawns laced together with the criss-crossed patterns of bullets,"* and it has so traumatised him that *"I had gotten a taste of death and found it palatable to the extent that I could never again eat the fruits of normal civilisation."* [9]

This is Hammer's dilemma and the cause of much interior monologue: although he fights for the forces of right, he has to keep himself a man apart because he does not want to taint the few good things in his life. This is especially noticeable in *One Lonely Night* where Hammer becomes almost suicidal: *"I was looking at myself the same way those people did back there. I was looking at a big guy with an ugly reputation, a guy who had no earthly reason for existing in a decent, normal society."* [10]

At the end of the book, Hammer finds his answer: *"I lived to kill because my soul was a hardened thing that revelled in the thought of taking the blood of the bastards who made murder their business. I lived because I could laugh it off and others couldn't. I was the evil that opposed other evil, leaving the good and the meek in the middle to live and inherit the earth!"* [11]

The biblical imagery, which peaks in the line *"I lived to kill so that others could live,"* infuriated Spillane's critics even more; this was his answer to their constant sniping at Hammer's sadistic motives. Mike is, literally, the Hammer of God.

WITNESSES FOR THE PROSECUTION

"They can't kill me. I still got potential."—Mickey Spillane, 1984.

"As ammunition for the various bodies crying for the suppression or control of crime writing, this new Spillane novel could hardly be surpassed; as a detective story, it is in inferior to his I THE JURY in plot (which is both strained and obvious) and writing (which often approaches parody), but fully equal to it in its attempt to see how far uncensored publishing can go."—Anthony Boucher, *New York Times*, 12 February 1950, re-

viewing *My Gun is Quick*.

"*The mixture even more repellent than before… As rife with sexuality and sadism as any of his novels, based on a complete misunderstanding of law and on the wildest coincidence in detective fiction, it still can boast the absence of the hypocritical 'crusading' sentiments of Mike Hammer. For that reason, and for some slight ingenuity in its denouement, it may rank as the best Spillane—which is the faintest praise this department has ever bestowed.*"—Anthony Boucher, *New York Times*, 5 August 1951, reviewing *The Big Kill*.

CROSS-EXAMINATION BY THE DEFENCE

"*I don't care what they say about me, as long as they don't rip up my dollar bills.*"—Mickey Spillane.

Critics were given a voice in both the D.A. in *Vengeance is Mine* ("*You let yourself get out of hand once too often…it's my opinion that the city is better off without you*") and the Judge in *One Lonely Night* ("*Goddamn, he wouldn't let me alone! He went on and on cutting me down until I was nothing but scum in the gutter*"). Neither were sympathetically drawn characters.

Spillane's style was often the target of critics, who typically found his writing painfully bad. Certainly he had none of the eloquence of Raymond Chandler, but who did? "*I'm not an author, I'm a writer,*" Spillane told Julie Baumgold in an *Esquire* interview[12]. "*I can write a book in a few weeks, never rewrite, never read galleys. Bad reviews don't matter.*" Elsewhere, he has said, "*I'm writing for the public. An

author would never do that. They write one book, they think they're set. I'll tell you when you're a good writer. When you're successful. I'd write like Thomas Wolfe if I thought it would sell.*"[13]

His writing was stylish enough for Anthony Boucher, one of Spillane's harshest critics, to comment that the release of *Kiss Me, Deadly* "*Comes almost as a relief after the interim flood of Spillane imitators. Chief difference, I think, is that Spillane really believes (God help him) in what he's writing, while the imitators are just trying to turn a fast buck.*"[14]

Spillane's writing style is best described as hard-boiled easy reading in which the text was written to make the reader want to turn the pages; Spillane drops in the very occasional literary or mythological allusion, but for the most part sticks to driving the plot along efficiently from problem to solution, occasionally having Mike reflect on the case so that nobody forgets the plot. He sticks to the well-rehearsed puzzle formula: the murder in the opening chapter is solved in the final chapter, but rather than gathering the suspects, it's a one-on-one meeting between Mike and the villain he needs to smite.

It has always been presumed that Spillane's audience was mostly male since there are no statistics available to say who was buying his books, but to say they only sold to "*horny ex-GIs looking for a hot read*"[15] is a simplification: he was, for instance, Ayn Rand's favourite novelist because Hammer "*meets out justice immediately, lethally and illegally*"; Janis Joplin read his novels; his fan base ranged from school campuses to the Supreme Court.

It was the paperback buying audience that put Spillane on the map. In hardcover, he made a reasonable impact, selling 25,000 copies of his first six novels; *Kiss Me, Deadly*, released in 1952, sold an astonishing 75,000 copies and found its way onto the best-seller lists of the *New York Herald Tribune* and the *New York Times*. In paperback, Signet Books (a division of New American Library) had already sold 15 million copies by then, doubled that figure by 1958 (during which time no new Spillane titles had appeared) and were piling on two million sales a year. The substantial printings produced by Corgi in the UK in the early 1960s helped worldwide sales leap to 70 million (half of them in the USA). By 1988 that figure had nearly doubled again at 130 million; nowadays the quoted figure tends to be around the 200 million mark.

Statistically, Spillane was a phenomenon in a class of his own: his first seven novels still rank in the top fifteen sellers of the past fifty years. At one point, when they were all in the top ten, Spillane joked that it was a good thing he hadn't written three more.

He is the fifth most translated author in the world behind Lenin, Tolstoy, Gorky and Jules Verne. *"I have no fans,"* he told Art Harris of the *Washington Post*[16]. *"You know what I got? Customers."*

His ability to draw his customers back book-after-book speaks volumes about his abilities, proving that he has a natural talent for writing to a market. But, more than that, his work is translated all over the world and audiences other than *"horny GIs"* lap up his novels: his influence can be seen in the work of Dutch author Jan Cremer, Swedish novelist Lars Goerling and even Kenyan Meja Mwangi. The *"Sons of Spillane"* are a recognisable breed who followed in Hammer's heavy-treading, gut-kicking footsteps.

Even the critics started to soften to Spillane's smack-in-the-face style when he returned to writing novels in the 1960s, and even more-so in the 1990s when he was welcomed back like an old friend who had been away too long. His 1979 children's novel *The Day the Sea Rolled Back* won a Junior Literary Guild Award. The notion that he wrote tough because that's all he was capable of, that he lacks intelligence and cynically exploits his audience (ignore the contradiction) are unproven. His only tip of the hat to marketing has been to give the audience what they want.

WITNESS FOR THE PROSECUTION

"I had one good, efficient, enjoyable way of getting rid of cancerous Commies. I killed them."—Mickey Spillane, *One Lonely Night.*

"Mike Hammer is the logical conclusion, almost a sort of brutal apotheosis, of McCarthyism; when things seem wrong, let one man cure the wrong by whatever means he, as a privileged saviour, chooses... he operates, as has Senator McCarthy, on the final philosophy that the end can justify the means; in this Hammerism and McCarthyism are similar."—

Christopher La Farge, *"Mickey Spillane and His Bloody Hammer"*, *The Saturday Review*, 1954.

CROSS-EXAMINATION BY THE DEFENCE

"There is no shame in killing a killer. David did it when he knocked off Goliath. Saul did it when he slew his tens of thousands. There's no shame to killing an evil thing."—Mickey Spillane, *One Lonely Night*.

Hammer is a more complex character than many give him credit for and the notion that Hammer is Spillane and Spillane is Hammer has been given credence because Spillane has so often played the role of his creation, on book covers, in films, on adverts and in interviews.

Spillane himself has been described as *"a moral, quietly religious person,"*[17] who became a Jehovah's Witness in 1951; it was rumoured that he quit writing in 1952 because his religious beliefs no longer allowed him to pen the sex and violence he was famous for. His editor, Victor Weybright, believed he had a psychological block; he and others felt that the criticism of his work had finally taken its toll.

In fact, Spillane had not quit writing at all, providing magazines and comics with a slow but steady output of stories and articles, acting on a record and working on film scripts over the next few years. The enormous success of *Kiss Me, Deadly* allowed him to sit back and take a break from the character who had taken over his life. During his break,

he moved from Newburgh to a beach home on Murrells Inlet in Myrtle Beach, South Carolina, where he indulged himself stock car racing, diving and generally enjoying the comforts of wealth.

But before that, Spillane penned two of his most famous books, *One Lonely Night* and *Kiss Me, Deadly*, which rounded out the first phase of Mike Hammer's life. *The Big Kill* (the fifth Hammer novel) was a more atypical revenge story, and Spillane had even experimented with a second character in *The Long Wait*, which featured Johnny McBride in a yarn about amnesia and vengeance, although McBride was summarily dismissed by critics as Hammer under another name.

One Lonely Night was the novel that earned — or confirmed in many eyes — Spillane his reputation as a right-wing fanatic. The character of Mike Hammer raised the notion from his very first appearance: Would a nation give its problems over to one man to be solved? Part of Hammer's attraction was, after all, that one man could — by force and determination — make a difference and this one-man army was more effective than the combined strength of the police force at solving crime.

Perhaps the concept of Hammer as God's Tool was too uncomfortable. Instead, critics turned him into a witch-hunting McCarthyite, out to destroy godless Commies by any means possible, burning to death those he can't machine gun down. The book seems an implicit political statement from Spillane... except that

Hammer's actions are so over the top that they read like a parody, and the fanatical anti-Communist Joe McCarthy figure, here named Lee Deamer, turns out to be the real Russian agent sent to steal government plans. The snake in the grass. The danger that lurks within.

People who are not what they seem is a favourite theme for Hammer novels: Charlotte Manning, the psychiatrist, turns out to be the psycho; businessman Arthur Berin-Grotin's business turns out to be prostitution; Juno Reeves turns out to be a man!; actress Marsha Lee is not who she seems; nor is Lily Carver. Even the straightforward murder-revenge motivation that draws Mike Hammer into a situation masks a bigger plot, be it blackmail, destroying Communist cells, or chasing Mafia heroine.

Hammer is always working to a deadline (an apt phrase remembering his regular shoot out finales) and under duress, usually from authority who have taken away his license or have an APB out for his arrest for murder. If Mike wasn't in immediate danger, Velda would be. This simplifies motivation but does not remove all complexities. Hammer is eternally tortured by his memories of shooting Charlotte Manning that resurface in dreams and sometimes in the faces of those he finds intimacy with. The ongoing almost-romance between Hammer and Velda develops slowly over a number of titles until, in *The Girl Hunters*, it seems that he has left it too late. After a ten year hiatus, Spillane returned to Mike Hammer and, as Collins and Taylor

put it, *"the themes of the first six Hammer stories are resolved in a satisfying manner rare to series fiction."*[18] Even Anthony Boucher now recognised the *"genuine vigour and conviction lacking in his imitators."*[19] *"For almost twenty years I have been one of the leaders in the attacks on Spillane; but of late I begin to wonder whether we reviewers, understandably offended by Spillane's excesses of brutality and his outrageously antidemocratic doctrines, may not have underestimated his virtues."*[20]

JUDGE'S SUMMING UP

The majority of Mickey Spillane's novels were produced in two distinct periods: 1947-52 and 1961-73, with the occasional brief resurgence; the latest two Hammer novels were published in 1989 and 1996. Although his later books have sold nowhere near as many copies as the first seven, they have been more welcomed by reviewers, who — late in the day — have noticed the narrative grip Spillane can hold and saw him prove his ability to alter his style for a different market in his two children's novels.

That said, his latest Hammer yarns have been described as limp, *"softened with time"* and the stories tread familiar territory, especially *Black Alley* which even begins with the murder of another army buddy.

Does this imply an inability to dream up new plots for an outmoded hero past his sell-by date, or a continuing tradition to give his readers what they want? Has Hammer's machismo grown tired through Spillane's own writings or have his followers dulled the readers to tough-guy heroics? In retrospect, should we consider Spillane a unique stylist in the hard-boiled genre or a cynical exploiter of sex and violence to market his novels?

That, ladies and gentlemen of the jury, is for you to decide. You may now retire to consider your verdict.

NOTES

With thanks to expert witness Denny Lien.

1. Biographical details are mostly derived from *One Lonely Knight: Mickey Spillane's Mike Hammer* by Max Allan Collins & James L. Taylor, Bowling Green, OH, Popular Press, 1984, *"Night of the Guns"* by Lynn F. Meyers Jr., *Paperback Parade #46*, Aug 1996, and *Contemporary Authors*. Since the publication of the former, all biographical features about Spillane *must* begin with the 'named twice' sequence or the writer will have his authors license revoked.

2. A feature in *Life* magazine in 1952 said he'd taken 19 days to write his first novel, although in his article *"Night of the Guns"*, *op cit*, p68) Lynn Myers relates that Spillane later claimed it took only nine days.

3. Carroll John Daly, *The Hidden Hand* (serialised in *Black Mask*, Jun-Oct 1928), New York, Clode, 1929 (HarperCollins, 1992, p[1]-2).

4. Carroll John Daly, *Murder From the East* (serialised in *Black Mask*, May-Jun, Aug 1934), New York, Clode, Stokes, 1935 (International Polygonics, 1978, p8).

5. Carroll John Daly, *"The Death Drop"*, in *Black Mask*, May 1933 (quoted in *Yesterday's Faces Volume 4: The*

Solvers by Robert Sampson, Ohio, Bowling Green State University Popular Press, 1987, p201).

6. Christopher La Farge, *"Mickey Spillane and His Bloody Hammer"*, *The Saturday Review*, 6 November 1954.

7. Spillane, *I, the Jury* (Corgi, 1967 printing, p9-10).

8. Spillane, *ibid* (p14).

9. Spillane, *One Lonely Night* (Corgi, 1970 printing, p8).

10. Spillane, *ibid* (p9)(19.

11. Spillane, *ibid* (p148).

12. Spillane, interview by Julie Baumgold, *Esquire*, August 1995 (quoted in *Contemporary Authors*).

13. Spillane, interview by Margaret Kirk, *Chicago Tribune*, [?18 Apr 1986] (quoted in *Contemporary Authors*).

14. Anthony Boucher, review, *New York Times*, 26 Oct 1952.

15. Collins & Taylor, *op cit*, p7.

16. Spillane, interview by Art Harris, *Washington Post*, 24 October 1984 (quoted in *Contemporary Authors*).

17. Collins & Taylor, *op cit*, p7.

18. Collins & Taylor, *op cit*, p87.

19. Anthony Boucher, *New York Times Review of Books*, 14 October 1962.

20. Anthony Boucher, *New York Times Review of Books*, 27 February 1966.

LIST OF EXHIBITS

THE MIKE HAMMER NOVELS
I, the Jury. New York, Dutton, Jul 1947; London, Barker, 1952.

My Gun Is Quick. New York, Dutton, Feb 1950; London, Barker, 1951.

Vengeance Is Mine. New York, Dutton, 1950; London, Barker, 1951.

One Lonely Night. New York, Dutton, 1951; London, Barker, 1952.

The Big Kill. New York, Dutton, Aug 1951; London, Barker, 1952.

Kiss Me, Deadly. New York, Dutton, Oct 1952; London, Barker, 1953.

The Girl Hunters. New York, Dutton, 1962; London, Barker, 1962.

The Snake. New York, Dutton, 1964; London, Barker, 1964.

The Twisted Thing. New York, Dutton, 1966; London, Barker, 1966.

The Body Lovers. New York, Dutton, 1967; London, Barker, 1967.

Survival...Zero!. New York, Dutton, 1970; London, Corgi, 1970.

The Killing Man. New York, Dutton, 1989.

Black Alley. New York, Dutton, 1996.

OTHER NOVELS BY SPILLANE

The Long Wait. New York, Dutton, 1951; London, Barker, 1953.

The Deep. New York, Dutton, 1961; London, Barker, 1961.

The Day of the Guns (Mann). New York, Dutton, 1964; London, Barker, 1965.

Bloody Sunrise (Mann). New York, Dutton, 1965; London, Barker, 1965.

The Death Dealers (Mann). New York, Dutton, 1965; London, Barker, 1966.

The By-Pass Control (Mann). New York, Dutton, 1966; London, Barker, 1967.

The Delta Factor. New York, Dutton, 1969; London, Corgi, 1969.

The Erection Set. New York, Dutton, 1972; London, W.H. Allen, 1972.

The Last Cop Out. New York, Dutton, 1973; London, W.H. Allen, 1973.

The Day the Sea Rolled Back (for children). New York, Dutton, 1979; London, Methuen, 1980.

The Ship That Never Was (for children). New York, Bantam, 1982.

SHORT STORY COLLECTIONS

Me, Hood!. London, Corgi, 1963.

Return of the Hood. London, Corgi, 1964.

The Flier. London, Corgi, 1964.

Killer Mine. London, Corgi, 1965; New York, Signet, 1968.

Me, Hood!. New York, Signet, 1969.

The Tough Guys. New York, Signet, 1969.

Tomorrow I Die, edited by Max Allan Collins. New York, Mysterious Press, 1984.

mickey spillane

spillane at the nft
michael carlson

THE BRIEF SEASON of Spillane films at the NFT ran as part of the B Reels series, which brought us, among other things, another look at John Flynn's excellent Parker movie, *The Outfit*. Adrian Wootton's programming at the NFT is fast becoming a key for fans of detective fiction as well as detective film.

Of course the Mick satisfies on both counts (sort of like his old Miller Lite ads: tastes great, less filling). The book on Spillane's celluloid is that the books might taste great, but the movies were simply less filling. Seeing them in quick succession proved that was most definitely not the case.

The biggest coup, besides Spillane's own presence, was the two showings of *I, The Jury* in its original 3D format, and with the 20 minutes of cuts made by the British censor restored. What the censor was looking at must have been Spillane's reputation, or Orwell's essay on 'Yank mags', because even by the standards of 1953, it's not overwhelmingly violent.

Produced by Victor Saville, written and directed by Harry Essex (of whom Spillane has little good to say, see interview), *I, The Jury*'s biggest failing it that it is excessively wordy. You hurtle through a typical Spillane plot at top speed, not so much cogitating over it as crashing through it. The plots make sense, but they don't need the explication which Essex, who must've seen too many parlour detectives at work, seems to favour.

It's also tough to accept Biff Elliott as Mike Hammer. He tries to hard to look tough, but comes off as someone trying to be Marlon Brando, rather than Hammer. He's young and innocent seeming, too worried about his scarf, to be Hammer, and this is made even more evident by the casting of Preston Foster as Pat Chambers. Pat and Mike are contemporaries, here Foster is excellent in the cliched role of the veteran cop warning off the young hothead.

On the positive side, Peggie Castle does well with a role that requires her to be brainy psychiatrist and blonde fatale at the same time, and Margaret Sheridan is absolutely wonderful as Velda, Hammer's faithful secretary and aide de camp. Sheridan brings a combination of looks, class, and nous to the role that would do a Howard Hawk's heroine proud. If I hadn't been an infant when this film came out I could've fallen for her big.

What makes I, The Jury remarkable is the 3D photography by John Alton. I'M no expert in 3D, but Alton's work takes advantage of the depth without ever making you aware of it. Unlike most 3D movies, nothing jumps out at you, neither literally nor figuratively. Instead, Alton is able to create a film noir mood in an extra dimension, even foreshadowing scenes with shots that suggest what they will be used for later. Bob Furmanek, of the 3D Film Archive, should be commended for restoring and providing this film: let's just hope British audiences

don't have to wait another 46 years to see it again!

Another film that has been unjustly ignored is *The Girl Hunters*, made in 1963 with Spillane himself starring as Hammer. First off, Mickey's not a bad actor, and he never appears to be straining credulity as his own hero. He's a little short, and you notice it when he stands cheek to cheek with Shirley Eaton and her head is far bigger than his (the saying goes that actors are small people with big heads, literally and figuratively). What he does do well is fit in the locations. This movie was shot in Britain, with location shooting done in New York, and you can see the way Spillane becomes a part of joints like the Blue Ribbon bar. The joining is seamless, and director Roy Rowland does a nice job with atmosphere and pacing. Scott Peters may not quite work as Chambers, but Eaton is wonderful in her role, just a year before she would be painted gold by James Bond (the British Mike Hammer) and, like so many Bond girls, see her career stalled afterwards.

Unfortunately the NFT showing of *Kiss Me Deadly* didn't contain the recently discovered alternate ending, so you weren't able to compare the effects of total destruction of the world with mere destruction of a house and a dame who plays Pandora. No one can accuse Robert Aldrich of pandora-ing to Spillane's tastes: his take on Hammer's violence gives the movie a fierce apocalyptic drive which in its way is truer to the spirit of the books in their time than any of the other adaptations. Mickey says, *"they didn't even read the book!"* but the deal is really that Aldrich read into it much. His interpretation may or may not be correct, it may offend Hammer purists, but it is the only Spillane adaptation that can fairly be called a classic.

Highlight of the series, of course, was Spillane's Guardian lecture, played to a packed house in NFT1. Having interviewing Mickey myself, I recognised many of the anecdotes: he has a million of them, all entertaining and all told well. He uses them to deflect questions he doesn't feel like answering, but they are also the accumulated history of someone who likes people, and is genuinely interested in them. It's also part of what Max Allan Collins described as Spillane's combination entertainer and pitchman persona, which he believes Mickey developed to insulate himself from the critics. For whatever reason, it's a good show, particularly as one watched Mickey go wherever he wanted to with Wootton's questions. When it got to audience questions it was more of the same.

Spillane's take on Hollywood was simple: when he played Hammer they thought he needed to look more unkempt. *"They're the kind of people who want you to look unkempt, so they take you to Rodeo Drive and spend $4,000 buying you new clothes to make you look messier."*

Spillane says he doesn't care about posterity. *"Now,"* he says, *"is all that matters"*. But it's unquestionable that he will go down in posterity as one of the greats of detective fiction, and as he said himself, *"hang around long enough and you become respectable."*

Another step toward his respectability was a special showing of Collins' 48 minute documentary *Mike Hammer's Mickey Spillane*. This was made doubly special by the showing of a long-long pilot for a Mike Hammer television

show, done in 1954 and starring Brian Keith. This was written and directed by Blake Edwards, who would go on to make the Peter Gunn TV series, and of course to a long and successful career in feature films. You can see quite clearly where the Peter Gunn character came from, and what Edwards was planning to do with it.

The pilot became the basis of the syndicated Mike Hammer TV show starring Darren McGavin a couple of years later (McGavin was also starring in *Riverboat* on network TV: no other star has ever done two series simultaneously). Keith's Hammer is excellent, right mix of violence and affability, where McGavin's was played, like most of his roles, with more tongue in cheek. A real find, and a real pleasure to see.

The documentary is done in the style of the US *Biography* series, which airs on the A&E network, and hopefully Collins will be able to sell it in to them. It means it's long on detail and appreciation, and not necessarily as full of critical analysis as you might have got from the old days of the *South Bank Show* or *Omnibus*, for example.

That's not a complaint, just a stylistic analysis. In fact, in a series of interviews with leading crime writers, Spillane's place within the field becomes clear, as does the remarkable strength of his influence. Only Michael Collins, author of the one-armed detective who puts his hands behind his head, Dan Fortune, has anything bad to say about Spillane, but what is more revealing comes from the biographical detail of his life: you realise that it's not Mike Hammer, but Mickey Spillane himself, who is Frank Michael Morrison Spillane's greatest creation.

in the thieves' market:
the life and times
of a.i. bezzerides
woody haut

The end of Kiss Me Deadly - thanks to The Unofficial Mike Hammer site at http://www.interlog.com/~roco/hammer.html for these and other images

WITH ITS HARDBOILED DIALOGUE, tough-guy violence and helter-skelter ambience, Robert Aldrich's 1955 adaptation of Mickey Spillane novel *Kiss Me Deadly* has been called 'the apotheosis' of the classic noir style by film encyclopaedist Steven H. Scheuer. While Nicholas Christopher, author of *Somewhere in the Night*, believes it to be *"perhaps the most perfectly realised film noir ever made."* However highly critics rate it, most would agree that the real genius behind the film is not Spillane, but writer A.I. Bezzerides, whose screenplay, combined with Aldrich's oeuvre, drags Spillane's novel and film noir as a genre kicking and screaming into the post-McCarthy era.

Spillane has gone on record regarding just how much he dislikes Bezzerides' script. And no wonder. For Bezzerides, trained as a communications engineer, disassembles the novel, only to put it back together, this time as an instrument of subversion rather than, as

Spillane intended, a reductionist artefact supporting a the dubious values of 1950s America.

After Aldrich had him read the novel, Bezzerides told the director, "This is lousy. Let me see what I can do with it." Three weeks later the script was finished. As Bezzerides told Lee Server in the mid 1980s, "You give me a piece of junk, I can't write it. I have to write something else. So I went to work on it. I wrote it fast because I had contempt for it. It was automatic writing. You get into a kind of stream and you can't stop." Obviously he enjoyed the task. For Bezzerides puts Spillane's macho tough-guy Mike Hammer through the wringer, making him chase the Great Whatsit- not money or drugs as in the novel, but an atomic Pandora's Box- and, in doing so, turns Spillane's novel into a warped quest that ends in nuclear oblivion.

Yet Bezzerides makes no great claim regarding the film's relationship to McCarthyism and the atomic bomb. As he told Server, "I didn't think about it when I wrote it. These things were in the air at the time and I put them in...I was having fun with it. I wanted to make every scene, every character, interesting." Accordingly, Bezzerides populates his adaptation with an assortment of corrupt and crazy characters, including a dim-witted murderess, a scientist who cannot stop talking about ancient myths, a thieving autopsy surgeon, an escaped lunatic and a nymphomaniac ("Whatever it is, the answer's yes."). So tight and well-organised is Bezzerides'script that Aldrich was able to shoot the film in three weeks. When the director was on his deathbed, he told Bezzerides that he had recently reread the script. When Bezzerides asked what

could have possibly prompted the director to do something like that, Aldrich said he wanted to figure out how he could possibly have filmed Kiss Me Deadly in so short a time. 'You know what?' said Aldrich. 'It was all there.'

So who is A.I. Bezzerides? Born in 1908 in Turkey, his parents- an Armenian mother and a Turkish-speaking Greek father- moved to Fresno, California while Albert Issok- later to be known as Al or 'Buzz'- was an infant. Influenced by Chekhov, Dostoevsky, Babel and, later, Sherwood Anderson, Bezzerides began writing while studying communications engineering at the University of California, Berkeley. Like that other Armenian-American and childhood friend, William Saroyan, a writer in whose shadow Buzz was fated to walk (prompting a humorous letter- "pardon the tone...but I am a little perturbed"- on the subject to Story magazine in 1941), Bezzerides, the more hard-edged and less sentimental of the two, concentrated on describing the people he knew best; namely, first-generation families eking out a living in the fields and towns of Central California.

After a string of odd jobs in the communications industry, Bezzerides landed a job as a researcher at the Department of Water and Power in Los Angeles. While employed there he wrote and published his first novel, The Long Haul, now better known as They Drive by Night. Eventually, Bezzerides would go on to publish two other excellent novels: There Is a Happy Land and Thieves Market. The former, the story of an Okie who, along with his family, attempts to make it as a farmer in the San Joaquin Valley, might well be Bezzerides most accomplished novel. Published by Henry Holt in 1942, after Bezzerides' career as a screenwriter was well established, and for many years out of print- a copy will currently set you back something like $450- it, like Kromer's Waiting *for Nothing* and Anderson's *Thieves Like Us*, has become another forgotten classic of the Depression.

Better known are Bezzerides' two trucker-noir novels, *The Long Haul,* first published in 1938 by Carrick and Evans, and *Thieves Market*, published in 1949 by Scribners. Both are semi-autobiographical, based on personal experience and stories heard from his father about independent truckers, and their life on the road, in the fields and packing houses, or in the markets of Stockton, Oakland and San Francisco, where, according to Bezzerides, cheating and brutality were a regular occurrence. A number of these sites are marked out on the back cover of a 1950 Dell paperback edition of *They Drive by Night*. Below the heading *"WHERE WILDCAT TRUCKERS FIGHT THE LONG HIGHWAYS"* is a map- typical of Dell paperbacks during the era- on which the journey of the book's protagonist along Highway 99, from Holland's Summit Cafe in the Tejon Pass to Red Bluff in Northern California, can be traced. Four decades later, Bezzerides would link those early experiences to *Kiss Me Deadly's* hardboiled perspective, saying, *"When I saw what the produce dealers did, and what the engineers with their swindle sheets were doing, I knew that the world was going to end."*

Both novels would be snatched up and, according to Bezzerides, ruined by Hollywood. *The Long Haul* would be adapted for the screen by Warner Brothers in 1940 under the title *They Drive by Night*. Directed by Raoul Walsh, it stars

George Raft and Humphrey Bogart. At least Bezzerides was allowed to write the screenplay for *Thieves Market,* which would be purchased by Twentieth Century in 1949 and renamed *Thieves Highway*. Directed by Jules Dassin, the film stars Richard Conte and Lee J. Cobb.

Bezzerides is right, neither films do their respective novels justice. Yet, however flawed, both have much to offer and, like a handful of other films made during the 1940s, come as close as Hollywood would dare to a cinema with mild proletariat overtones. This in an era just prior to the hysteria engendered by McCarthyism, an ear that would affect Bezzerides as it did so many others. Though a member of the leftwing Writers Guild, Bezzerides, unlike many of his friends, never joined the Communist Party. Probably for the simple reason that he was too independent to follow a party line. Nevertheless, he taught writing at the Little Red Schoolhouse where many Communists worked, and, because of this, his name was placed on the blacklist.

With a low opinion of producers- *"the goddmanedest crooks you ever saw. And they think writing is shit."*- Bezzerides is a veritable catalogue of movie rip-offs. For example, shortly after publishing his first novel, *The Long Haul,* an agent phoned and asked if he'd be interested in selling his novel to Warner Brothers, saying he'd be able to get $1,500 for it. When Bezzerides balked at the figure, the agent said, *"We'll see if we can get more."* He phoned back and said the studio was willing to go up to $2,500. Bezzerides reluctantly agreed to the offer. When he went to the studio he noticed on Jack Warner's desk a copy of a script adapted from his novel by Jerry Wald. The story goes that George Raft had gained too much weight to make his next film, which was to be a boxing movie, and, to keep him at the studio, Warners decided that *The Long Haul* would be the perfect vehicle him. Later, when Bezzerides told another studio writer about what had happened, the latter said, *"You could have asked for $100,000 and they would have given it to you."* In the end, Bezzerides received $2,000, while George Raft got $55,000, Bogart $11,200, screenwriter Jerry Wald $11,167, and director Raoul Walsh's $17,500.

By the time *Thieves Market* was published in 1949, Bezzerides was already a highly paid freelance scriptwriter who had worked for every major Hollywood studio, including five years as a contract writer at Warners. After *Thieves Market* was published, Warners offered Bezzerides $100,000 for the rights, but his agent had agreed to sell it to Fox for $80,000, still a substantial amount of money in 1949.

Nevertheless, Bezzerides was less than satisfied with the film version of *Thieves Market*. For one thing, Fox decided not to use the original title because *"San Francisco objects to it"*- whether that means San Francisco's city fathers or the Teamsters union is unclear. Then Dassin insisted on casting his then girlfriend Valentina Cortesa as the prostitute, a role that Bezzerides felt would be perfect for an actress like Shelly Winters. Worst of all, the studio severely altered the story. In the novel, the father is dead from the beginning of the book. To validate his father's life, the kid decides to take up trucking. But in the film, Zanuck insisted that the father should be alive, and the protagonist's motivation a result of his father's inability to work due to his crippled condition.

Foregoing a career as a novelist, Bezzerides ended up writing some fifteen screenplays and numerous television dramas. His first screen credit was for Curtis Bernhardt's 1942 *Juke Girl* starring Ronald Reagan, in which the latter, still a real life liberal. plays a trucker who sides with striking workers. Bezzerides went on to write such films as Nicholas Ray's 1951 noir classic- and another example of Bezzerides' fascination with the psychology of male violence- *On Dangerous Ground*, Bernhardt's 1951 *Sirocco* at Columbia, John Houseman's 1952 *Holiday for Sinners* at Metro, William Wellman's 1954 *Track of the Cat* at Warners, Lewis Allen's 1955 *Bullet for Joey* at United Artists, Robert Aldrich's 1959 The *Angry Hills* at MGM, and Melvin Frank's 1959 *The Jayhawkers* at Paramount. His television work included episodes of *Sunset Strip, Wells Fargo, The Virginian, Rawhide, Bonanza*, and *DuPont Theater*.

In the mid 1960s he was responsible for creating *The Big Valley*, a series about immigrant families in Central Valley which was intended as an antidote to *Bonanza*. It proved one of the most popular syndicated programmes of the era, yet those producing it made sure it never showed a profit on paper, thus denying Bezzerides a share in its four year run. While its star, Barbara Stanwyck, sued for her portion of the profits, Bezzerides wasn't in a position to do the same, and had to settle out of court for a fraction of that which was due him.

It was while working at the studios during the war that he met and befriended William Faulkner (*"The screenplay form was alien to him."*). Fifty years later anecdotes about their relationship would figure in the Coen brothers' film *Barton Fink.* Though one might be excused for thinking that the film's portrayal of the relationship between John Turturro character and the Faulkner-like southern writer might have been based on John Fante's friendship with that notorious southerner. In fact, Fante and Bezzerides were something of a double act, their friendship having been established in 1939 when the young wannabe-writer Fante walked by Stanley Rose's Hollywood bookstore and saw Bezzerides staring at his newly published book, *The Long Haul,* which was on display in the window. Fante noticed Bezzerides' photograph on the book jacket and asked how much of an advance he received. When Bezzerides told him, Fante asked if would give him the money as a loan. Always a generous person, Bezzerides no doubt surprised Fante by handing him the money. A year or so after the incident in front of Stanley Rose's bookstore, Fante, in a letter to his mother, writes that he and Bezzerides are working on a story together which they hoped to sell to one of the studios.

As of this writing, of Bezzerides' three novels, only *Thieves Market* remains in print. The present edition, published by University of California, contains an engaging afterword by Bezzerides and a forward written by Garrett White which nicely summarises Bezzerides' career. However, *The Long Haul* has been unavailable for some time. And *There Was a Happy Land* for even longer. Unfortunately, the exigencies of scriptwriting cut short Bezzerides' promising career as a novelist. For Hollywood, more often than not, is a life sentence; once caught within its clutches, it's difficult to escape.

In the early 1950s Bezzerides met Silvia Richards, who had worked alongside King Vidor and Fritz Lang and written such screenplays as *Ruby Gentry, Possessed* and *Rancho Notorious.* They were soon married and living in Woodland Hills. Presently, Buzz Bezzerides is still alive, cantankerous as ever, and planning to write a book on the various swindles he has, over the years, witnessed, a book *"that will point like a long finger toward the sky-scratching high-rises that cluster in the hearts of all big cities...in the world, towers destined to metamorphose into tombstones that will mark the end of MAN-CONCOCTED CIVILISATION."* An interesting prospect from a formidable writer whose career as a novelist was sacrificed to the glitter and gold of Hollywood.

SOURCES:

Lee Server, 'A.I. Bezzerides,' *Screenwriter: Words Become Pictures,* Main Street, 1987.

Garrett White, 'Foreword,' *Thieves Market,* University of California, 1997.

A.I. Bezzerides, 'Afterword,'*Thieves Market,* University of California, 1997.

Philippe Garnier, *Honni Soit Qui Malibu,* Grasset, France, 1996.

Woody Haut is the author of Neon Noir *, published by Serpent's Tail at £9.99*

violence in venice
donna leon
barry forshaw

Donna Leon talks to Barry Forshaw about her recent book for Heinemann, Fatal Remedies, *and how music is her muse, in an interview not calculated to endear her to the anorak members of the community...*

Fatal Remedies, opens with the arrest of Paola Brunetti, wife of the chief character, police Commissario Guido Brunetti. She's tossed a rock through the window of a travel agency in Venice which arranges sex tours to Third World countries. This leads, as one might imagine, to marital discord and prompts many arguments between them about justice, law, the rights of the rich and poor. The owner of the travel agency is subsequently murdered, and this leads Brunetti off to investigate other depredations against the Third World, though these are committed in a different manner.

The writers I most admire are Jane Austen, Henry James, Emily Dickinson, and Charles Dickens. None of them inspired me, if that means made me want to write, for their genius would stop anyone from daring to presume to do so. But they did show me what a sentence was.

Three years of reviewing nothing but crime fiction has addled my wits, probably shortened by life, and certainly put my IQ below room temperature *[Tell us about it!—Ed]*. The general quality of the prose and thought is so low that, when books by Ruth Rendell, Barbara Vine, or Reginald Hill arrive, I am tempted to fall to my knees and remain there while I read them. I am sick with envy of their talents. Another writer for whom I have complete respect and for whose books I give daily thanks is Patrick O'Brian. The Aubrey/Maurtin books have been the greatest source of reading pleasure of the last decade. I find that I prefer, now, to read non-fiction, almost exclusively history. A day in bed with Gibbon or Josephus is bliss.

I think of the Martians: what must they think of us, circling us up there in their little UFO's, tuning in and observing a species the chief entertainment of which seems to be the depiction of the physical suffering and violent death of other members of the same species. I admit here that my own hands aren't clean, as I've written two scenes of violence in nine books. But one of them I refused to proof read, and the other bores me. I'd like to stay clear of it in future.

I think it is best for writers to keep our characters fully clothed at all times. Just as I would shy away from a dinner guest who gave explicit details of his or her sexual life while I was trying to eat, so too do I shy away from anyone who tries to do the same to me in my own bed, which is where I do most of my reading.

I think crime novels appeal to some sort of deep-seated, one might almost say atavistic, desire that justice be done. Since we see precious little of that around us, at least these books supply the lack.

Music...I love books and have always made my living with them, either teaching or writing, but my real passion is music, and specifically opera, and more specifically Baroque opera. I'm not sure that it's a factor in my inspiration so much as it is a constant source of joy. Becoming rich and famous is a great lark, but the best part of it is now being able to go see and hear any opera I choose to. Also, since the German-language public associates my name with opera, I'm often asked to write about it for the German press. Recently I interviewed Celicia Bartoli in Zurich and thought I wouldn't survive the experience, sAo great is my admiration for her talent and so inadequate did I believe myself for the task of talking about music with her. Aside from that glorious voice, one of the gifts of the age, she's also a fiercely intelligent woman who seems, quite wonderfully, devoid of spite or malice of any sort.

All I need to get going is an opening scene or a powerful scene that will take place somewhere in the book, that and a general sense of some political evil I'd like to deal with. That's enough to get me going, and then the books pretty much take over. Like the writers who have ongoing characters, I've got the cast in place, so I've just got to worry about plot. All of the books are set in Venice, but I'd love to take Brunetti to Naples, a city I love, if only because the chaos and corruption are so visible, not hidden, the way they are in the north. I'd lived in Venice for more than a decade when I wrote the first book, so the choice of Venice was not calculated to capitalize on its beauty or allure: it was the only place I'd ever lived for long enough to know about. Because I've been here for decades and because most of my friends are Venetian, I had access to their vision as well as that of an Anglo-Saxon with all of our prejudices.

I had the misfortune to be published by HarperCollins in the States, where my own editor referred to the paperback cover of one of the books as "shit." Beat me to it, he did. Hopeless incompetents, the whole lot of them, with the single exception of Larry Ashmead, who should be made the Pope of Publishing. He'd love the miter. If he's allowed a female Bishop, it should be Maria Rejt, now again at Macmillan. In Switzerland, and here I'll fall to my knees again, I had the tremendous good fortune to be published by Diogenes Verlag of Zurich. They now own my copyright, my absolute loyalty, and my heart.

Since I've read so many mysteries, I guess my mind has been fashioned into something resembling the sort of Everyman Mind of the Mystery Reader. So I write for that mind and sensibility. But I suppose I should add here that it is a mind that wrote a doctoral dissertation and a sensibility that chose to write it about Jane Austen. I attribute my failure to have an American publisher to those two last facts.

I don't know about reading or its future. I'd like to think it does have a future, but when I look at what most people actually read, the junk that gets printed and praised, I despair. I think things are better in England than in the States, and I know they are better in Germany, where a writer can still count on a common cultural background between the text and the reader. Many young American university students, and I've been teaching them for decades, simply do not read, and many of the stupid classes they take don't require them to do so, at least not at any serious level. The sad thing about most of what is popular today is that it is so undemanding: morally, intellectually, even syntactically. It's sitcom or shoot 'em up cop shows between hard, or soft, covers.

I think the success of most of the megastars of popular fiction has nothing whatsoever to do with literature: instead, it has to do with books, and the two are hardly the same. Writers like Margaret Atwood and Doris Lessing soar above the rest of us who make our living by writing books, for they are in the business of producing literature. Twenty years from now, who's going to read anyone on today's best seller list? I think Gore Vidal wrote an essay that took a retrospective look at a best seller list from the fifties. Enough to make one pray not to appear on the list. I look at them occasionally and they make me shudder, they do. I realize that having this sort of aloof disdain for people who do the same job I do must sound like the worst sort of professional jealousy. But you can't love books, grow dizzy from the joy of language, the glory of a well-turned phrase, and not want to cringe at the way so much rubbish gets printed and praised. In the face of the genius of writers like James or Trollope, the least those of us who are dashing to the bank could do is bow our heads in humility.

I'm amazed at the conspiracy of silence, which seems to have grown up around crime fiction, almost as if critics feared they'd lose their jobs if they told the truth about these books and thus caused fewer to be printed. I sometimes read other reviewers' reviews of the same books I've read and wonder if perhaps the Italian postal system is removing pages from the ones that get to me, for it often sounds as though we hadn't read the same text. Further, people tell me about all these conferences and meetings, where mystery fans and writers get together and talk about these books as though they were discussing literature. Have they no shame? I even had a student from a German university ask if I'd help him write a master's thesis about my books. I told him he was mad and suggested he go home and reread Jane Austen. Problem is he's probably never even read Jane Austen. The whole thing is sad, isn't it? But what do I know about all this stuff? My mind was corrupted at an early age by reading too many books.

michael dibdin
barry forshaw

*He's the favourite crime writer of
so many of our contributors, we decided that a chat with the creator of the
immortal Aurelio Zen was in order. A
new title from Faber,* **Blood Rain,** *was
the catalyst...(and see the generous
offer elsewhere in this issue!)*

WHAT I REMEMBER MOST about *Blood
Rain* is finishing it in Rome, in a rented
apartment, during the coldest winter
since 1986 – it even snowed for several
days. Heating in the apartment was
minimal, so I went around wearing two
pairs of socks, all my street clothes, a
dressing-gown, an overcoat, a scarf, a
woolly hat, and those gloves with the
fingertips cut off which street traders
use. I was working 12 to 14 hours a
day and went slightly mad. My wife
joined me a week before I finished and
claims that I started haranguing her in
Italian, which she doesn't speak. Casting an eye over the stacked dishes in
the sink, the overflowing ashtrays and

the empty wine bottles, she remarked, *"So, is this method writing, or what?"* As for the book, it's set in Sicily, and brings Aurelio Zen face to face with the Mafia. It's a project I'd been thinking about for years without quite daring to tackle. It's quite a challenge to deal with the realities of the very complex situation in Sicily in an adequate way, and yet write something which works as a crime novel in its own right. Fortunately, everyone who's read it seems to think that I've succeeded, so maybe method writing is the way to go.

I read voraciously as a teenager, and I think that everyone I read and enjoyed must have influenced me in some way, if only by giving me some sense of what's achievable in fiction. Within the specific limits of the genre, my primary influences were undoubtedly Conan Doyle, Simenon and Chandler, but I was also helped on my way by relatively minor figures such as John Buchan and Erskine Childers – *The Riddle of the Sands* is still unsurpassed as a broodingly atmospheric thriller. I also much enjoyed the early Len Deightons: The Ipcress File and Funeral in Berlin. It's interesting to note how short all these books were, like Fleming's Bond novels. None of them would stand a chance of getting published in today's steroid-pumped thriller market.

I look back at my own early work with the same mixture of affection and repulsion with which I regard the 20-year-old self who wrote it. It certainly won't be published, but I'll probably keep a copy in case one of my children should be interested in reading it once I'm safely dead. As for my current MO, I wish I had one! Basically I stare at the screen or the page – I work both ways, depending – until total panic sets in, and hope that something happens. I try to get something down, then go back and look at it, at which point I'm usually so revolted that I plunge straight into a massive rewrite out of sheer disgust. And so it goes, by fits and starts of always more or less unsatisfactory activity. The only enjoyable bit is watching minor characters turn into major players, and seeing how the plot could work more efficiently and elegantly with just a few minor changes. Then one day there's a novel there, and I think, *"Where did that come from?"* And the following year, when I do a promotional tour, I'll be reading from it and think, *"You know, this isn't all that bad, but of course that was last year, when I still had talent."*

I mentioned Fleming : his erotic sections were considered very strong in their day. But today...as for explicit sex and violence – like day-trips to Venice – are two of the things we can do which were not possible for earlier generations, so there's an understandable tendency to want to take it to the max. Hey, okay, maybe we can't write as good as those old guys, but they couldn't show split-beaver shots or pigs eating someone's face off, so let's go for it. The problem is that these freedoms come with a built-in penalty of diminishing returns.

Read the humungous horrors in the latest bestseller! Okay, I've read them. Yes, they're humungous. Now what? Patricia Highsmith could create more genuine tension with a raised eyebrow or an evaded question than most of her successors with a chainsaw-wielding maniac on the rampage. And a day-return from Gatwick isn't necessarily the best way to visit Venice, either.

Am I a political writer? Well, it all depends what you mean by political, as Professor Joad used to say. If you mean party politics, or any kind of identifiable ideology that is implicitly supported by the narrative, then I think the result is as deadly for crime fiction as for any other kind. But if you mean political in the broader sense, meaning the sum of the choices or decisions which create the society in which we live, then I'd say that it was absolutely essential and unavoidable. You can see the distinction very clearly in the work of Chandler and Hammett. Both were left-leaning and disturbed by the corruption and abuses they saw in the society they wrote about, but there is no overt political agenda in their books. They exposed problems; they didn't propose solutions.

Most of my readers seem to love some of my books and loathe others, but the titles concerned are always different. I wouldn't really want to know, anyway. Once you understand your *"appeal"*, or think you do, next thing you'll be deliberately trying to pander to it. A writer's appeal is like a person's charm: the moment it's identified and described, it turns into a stilted mockery of its former self.

Films are a poisoned chalice for writers, particularly for crime writers. It's hard not to want to get your stuff filmed; there's simply too much money and increased sales at stake. But it's a short and slippery slope from that position to starting to write books that are clearly designed specifically to be filmed, and which therefore don't work as books. Because despite their superficial similarities, the two media are actually quite different. The things that books do most effectively – interior monologue or POV , to take one example – are clumsy and lumbering on screen, while a fictional description can never match the unselective density of the simplest cinematic shot. I love movies for their own sake, in their own terms. I don't want them to be books, and I wish fewer people wanted books to be movies, and regarded the text version as a kind of low-tech substitute for the real thing.

There were two teachers I had at school who were very important. One was my French teacher, George Craig, now Reader in French at Sussex University, who passed on a sense of intellectual rigour and also of the wider world outside the little Ulster town where I was growing up. The other was James Simmons, the poet, who taught English at my school, but also jazz, blues, beat poetry, enthusiasm, drunkenness and general anarchy at late night gatherings at his house. Finally, and perhaps most important, was a woman called Eileen Coleman, the mother of my best friend at school, an extraordinary person who had been – among many other things – a lover of Oliver St John Gogarty (the model for Blazes Boylan in Joyce's Ulysses). She had an endless fund of good stories, as well as the ability to smoke an unfiltered Woodbine until it had almost two inches of ash hanging off the end but not dropping until she tapped it. She later drowned in a boating accident off the Donegal coast. I loved her dearly, and dedicated *The Dying of the Light* to her memory.

Plot...what is plot, if not the series of events put in motion by the things characters do or don't do? And what is character, if not the personality resulting from a series of formative events in the past or present? The two elements seem to me as inextricably connected as melody and harmony in music. When I'm writing, one or the other may temporarily assume more importance for a brief moment, but ultimately they are two sides of the same coin.

At the risk of making colleagues and rivals envious, I have to say that for the most part I've had a very smooth ride in regard to publishers. Both Faber and Faber in London, and Pantheon Books in New York, have seemed to understand what I have tried to do, and been happy to let me do it without

editorial interference. I realise how rare this is, particularly now, and how lucky I have been. There was one minor incident involving an earlier editor in New York who returned one of the Zen books with a long letter saying things like *"I feel he should weep at this point"* and *"There's no one in this chapter who I'm rooting for"*. I simply held on to the MSS until two weeks after the return date, then sent it in unchanged with a note saying *"Thanks for your valuable suggestions—hope you agree this is a big improvement"*. I never heard another word.

Writing, like reading, is by its nature a solitary activity. This has always made it both suspect and sexy, both of which are good. The problem today is that the writer is both the person who writes and the person who impersonates the writer for the purposes of marketing the book, and the two are not the same. The I giving this interview is not the I who writes my books. There is no duplicity involved here, just an irreducible fact of life. The solitary I writes the books but can't talk or even think about them coherently, while the worldly I can comment on them ad nauseam but couldn't write one to save his life.

To me, the religious experience is, above and beyond anything else, an act of surrender. As such, it is potentially a salutary corrective for writers, who are, after all, playing at being God, and if sufficiently successful may actually come to believe that they are. At the same time, religion – like booze and drugs – offers instant solutions or palliatives for the intractable problems that writing is supposed to address. So, once again, it's a question of balance. And religion is a saleable commodity...like writers. And here, the analogy I'd use here is the rock scene back in the 60s, when none of the record companies had quite figured out what was going on and who these Beatles and Stones and Yardbirds were. It was hit and miss marketing, and so a lot of weird and wonderful stuff got played and recorded and released. Most of it was crap, of course – most of all art at any moment is crap – but there was a spirit of adventure and excitement in the air. You never quite knew what was going to happen next. What depresses me about the crime genre at the moment, like pop music , is not that it's mostly crap, but that it's been published and promoted (and in many cases written) because some suit somewhere thought that he or she could second-guess the market and make X or Y into an instant best-seller on the basis that they have their finger on the public pulse, or that similar stuff had done well in the past. This is not only intellectual, aesthetic and moral suicide, but commercial suicide as well, because publishers don't know what's going to sell. If they did, they wouldn't be publishers, they'd be bond traders.

My next book is an Aurelio Zen and it's set in Iceland. So there!

bloody material
kim newman
barry forshaw

One of the brightest and most imaginative writers in Britain today, Kim Newman is a novelist beyond category. Horror, crime, noirish fantasy: all commingle in the heady brew that is his remarkable body of work. A CT encounter was overdue – and his much-acclaimed new novel, from Simon & Schuster, Life's Lottery, was the catalyst.

Crime happens in *Life's Lottery* – but is it a crime novel?

Hmmm....well, I'm less interested in categories than the notion of dealing in a new way with the subject matter of the so-called realist novel—the minutiae of everyday life. It's in the second person, which is one of those things you're not supposed to do, and you the reader get to live the life of a fairly ordinary bloke, following the various choices he makes or doesn't make. I suppose it's an experimental book, but I hope it's accessible to mainstream readers. There are strands of mystery, horror and science fiction, depending on whether you make realistic choices, but the heart of it is just the ordinary stuff.

What do you unwind with? What genres of fiction?

I'm quite widely read, not to mention being pretty well up on a great deal of cinema (which has certainly influenced my fiction as much as prose literature). As a teenager, I read a lot of H.P. Lovecraft and that style of horror; but I think the antidote to that was Raymond Chandler. Writers I especially admire include H.G. Wells, Stanley Ellin, Cornell Woolrich, Richard Condon, Philip Dick, Richard Matheson; and, from today, Ramsey Campbell, James Ellroy, Joe Lansdale, Paul McAuley, Dennis Etchison, Jonathan Coe, Tim Powers.

Any interesting juvenilia that's likely to see the light?

Aside from a few things written as a schoolboy which I probably don't have any more, there isn't any unpublished work. I started selling in my early 20s, and even the stories and novels that got initial rejections were eventually reworked and sold.

You're a pretty extreme writer...

Some people find some of my work extreme in violence and sex, but I think of myself as fairly trailing edge as far as these things go. Of my early works, *Bad Dreams* and *Jago* probably have more grue and explicit sex than I tend to do these days. I try to write what the story needs. I did do a novel called *Orgy of the Blood Parasites*, which

As normal as you or I, that's our Kim...

was pretty much non-stop luridness; since then, the urge hasn't struck so often. I try to portray violence and sex in a realistic context, with as much emphasis on the emotional consequences as the acts themselves, which have all been overdescribed by so many writers that it's hard to think of a new way of getting them over. Sex scenes, especially, are hard to write, though I'm not especially afraid of tackling them.

Politics is certainly a presence in your work...left-of-centre?

Sometimes you have to stand back from your own opinions to write. Having been formed as a writer in the 80s, it's hard to get away from Margaret Thatcher; but that may well be the country's problem as much as mine.

Tell me a little about your working methods.

When I'm first-drafting a book, I try to get about 2000 words a day done, usually in the morning. I then have to fit in all the freelance stuff around that.

Your work is quite unlike anyone else's...

I don't really write the sort of thing everyone else does. I recognise others who work in similar fields to mine, but I do a lot of different things. People have said I'm an original writer, but this may just be perversity. I often reverse-think things: when tackling a subject, I imagine what the standard way of doing it would be and then go in another direction.

Your position as an influential writer on film – doesn't that get in the way of your fiction?

I'm certainly as influenced by film as literature, and I have an eclectic taste in music, which does indeed feed into the work. When writing stories or novels set within the last century, I dig out music appropriate to the time and place and play it while I work, whether it be the Velvet Underground for a story about New York and Andy Warhol, or Nino Rota for a story about Rome in 1959. Popular music is often associational, which helps. The manager of the shop where I buy CDs has remarked on the breadth of my interests.

Did you have a personal literary guru?

I had good teachers at school, college and university. I did a course called 'Late Victorian Revolt' at the University of Sussex which was taught by the poet Laurence Lerner and Wells' biographer Norman Mackenzie, and that has resonated in several novels—*Jago, Anno Dracula, The Bloody Red Baron*—and a non-fiction book, *Millennium Movies*.

How do you create a novel?

Usually the idea first (narrative hook, gimmick, premise, location), then the characters (in some of my books, the process is a lot like casting a movie as you think of who you need), then the plot.

You've stayed with the same publisher for your novels, if not for your film books.

As a novelist, I'm still with my first publisher (Simon & Schuster), though I've done other types of books for other houses. I'm happier with them than many of my writer friends are with their publishers. I did have the typical first-book nightmare, with a house that went out of business just after publishing the book, my non-fiction study *Nightmare Movies*.

How important is solitude to a writer?

I live alone, but in the middle of a city. I appreciate both solitude (writing really is something you have to do yourself) and society (without which, after all, there would be nothing to write about).

What can you tell me about your next book?

I'm currently writing a book called *An English Ghost Story*. Most of my recent books have been very complex, so I just want to do something about four people in a house.

not so rancid
james hawes
martin hughes

James Hawes has managed to cram Kafka's mordant introspection into the 90's Nick Hornby/Men Behaving Badly crap bloke shtick and then poured all of that into the modern crime novel. It's no mean feat. A White Merc with Fins *(Random House) was very well received,* Rancid Aluminium *a little less so. But it's some measure of his success that both are now going to be seen in movie form. Hawes is here for a reading and Q & A, so there's the usual pile of books to sign at the back of the room, but his enthusiasm seems reserved for the movie.*

Merc *having spent far too long in development hell apparently drove Hawes into production for* Rancid Aluminium*...*

White Merc was such a bad experience, trying to get that to move. Over eighteen months trying to nudge that into existence. After the rights being bought and sold, all the re-writes it's now being made by the *Shooting Fish* guy. So we decided to produce *Rancid Aluminium*.

How did you find film production?

Incredibly stressful - approaching a financier saying, *"Give us a million pounds."*

He'd say, *"How can I give you a million pounds if I don't know who's playing these parts ?"* We couldn't sign people up if we didn't have the money. Two days before filming commenced we were all personally bankrupt, all our personal cheques were bouncing.

Tell us about the *Rancid Aluminium* movie.

We've got Rhys Iffans playing the lead - he's brilliant, he's going to be bigger than Ewan McGregor in a year's time. Massive. The Russian girl will be played by Tara Fitzgerald, on screen these two are like *(makes noise like cats fighting).* She told us that the part she liked best in the book was the bit about the spunk dripping down the character's leg. We told her Rhys was the lead and asked if he'd shagged her, she said, *"No, not yet."* We asked Rhys about Tara and he said if she was the lead he'd do it for a gram a day!

They're fabulous, they're both great actors, just keep the camera on them. We've got a great long shot, just forty five seconds of them kissing.

We've got Steven Berkoff to play Mr Kant - a difficult man to work with,

Joseph Ffiennes - excellent, fabulous depth, Keith Allen as Dr Jones and Sadie Frost as Pete's girlfriend. A huge amount of talent.

How did you go about adapting the novel for a screenplay?

There are different demands, especially from a book that's written in the first person. An entire film script, you've got 4 - 5,000 words max, the whole thing. You can't have that so you've got to change things, which means we have to do things rather than say them.

This must have presented a few problems.

We found that the first draft was very similar to the book. It just felt so much like *telling.* We had a big sit down and decided to go for broke - the director sat me down and told me what he liked about it, *"There's a Jungian heart to it. There's this guy - where's his father? He hasn't got a father, has he ? Where's his mother ? Why does he have to get everyone pregnant ? Who is this Mr Kant ? Why does he have to cross the ocean to get there ? Why does he die and get re-born ?"*

He persuaded me what we should go for in the film. That films have this strong and really quite simple building block drive and relationships that have to power it through. I was really convinced - so much so that after finishing the screenplay and finishing filming in January, I wanted to rewrite the novel. So the novel is now entirely rewritten (to be republished to tie in with the movie).

The other, purely technical fact is that Rhys Iffans was playing second lead to Hugh Grant in *Notting Hill* and he's younger, not at all fat and bald, he's a young person, lean and spiky. He isn't married, he has a girlfriend. We built up the accountant's part and they're now both in their thirties, on movie cameras they're like brothers.

Doesn't this upset the chemistry of the existing characters ?

There's a dark side and a light side, so then you get that sort of conflict. You realise that he has to knock out his dark side. It all becomes much simpler in terms of plotting but also much more complex. It's all powered by characters and individual antagonism.

You have a keen eye for this uneasy blend of aspiration/cynicism - you've picked up very strongly on the times we're living in, the current mentality of the thirty something male....

Yes, where are we all going, are we going to have children, are we going to make financial arrangements for them, are we going to have sheds and houses ?

Look at the pubs in North London. I never realised where the people who read Nick Hornby lived, they're all there, people who are forty or older acting like they're eighteen, like the party never stopped. It's a huge, burning, fascinating issue of the time. We have no sense of the ceremonies that mark certain periods of life anymore.

We'll wake up and find tanks in the street with young men festooned with cigarettes and burning eyes saying, *"What have you done with your freedom ? You've just partied and shopped and fucked it all away, and now we're coming."*

What defence will we have against some new moralism ? Nothing. We've done nothing with it, we've spent it all on crap holidays, designer goods, crap meals.

Ah, the crying shame of those wasted years !

I think that's what I'm writing about now. *Dead Long Enough,* I'm about two thirds of the way through.

rules are the deathblow
jack o'connell
eve tan gee

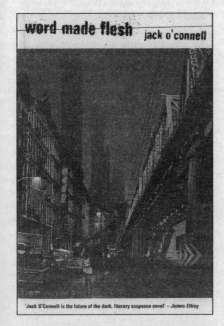

word made flesh jack o'connell

'Jack O'Connell is the future of the dark, literary suspense novel' – James Ellroy

*Send us a picture of the author?
Why on earth would any publisher
want to do that?*

Word Made Flesh is the best crime novel I've read since...the last Jack O'Connell. So I decided to pin him down...

Loved *Word Made Flesh* – let's talk about it.
Sure we can, but I warn you up front to take everything I say with a grain of salt.
Why is that?
Because I genuinely believe I'm one of the least qualified people to talk about my work. And because the nature of my relationship with my book changes at the moment of its publication. I see my books as transcriptions of what I call the dream-life. Books are visions, even when they're banal visions. They come into the world by way of an obsessive process wherein compulsive individuals spend inordinate amounts of time in self-imposed solitary confinement, hearing voices and transcrib-

ing those voices. At the moment of publication, that vision, for better or worse, is mutated, instantaneously, into a commodity. The book severs the umbilical and departs the monastery and goes off into the world where it's received, harshly or warmly, by others, by readers who understand the book, very often, in a way that's quite different from the writer's understanding.

How did *Word Made Flesh* come about?

Originally, it came about in the most cynical way imaginable. I began the book on January 1, 1995. My wife was pregnant with our second child. I sat down with a calendar and flipped forward to her due date and understood that once there was a toddler and an infant in the house, my writing time would be somewhat curtailed. So first I made a moronic, bone-dumb writing schedule. I was punching the calculator, scratching with the pencil, thinking *If I write x-pages each day for x-days, I'll have a first draft manuscript by the time James makes his arrival in the world.* An "ass-backward" way of working as my father used to say. Then all I needed was a plot. So I rooted around in my notebooks and pulled a couple items from "*column A*" and a couple from "*column B*" and applied the Elmore Leonard theorem, you know (all you need is a weary good guy, some bad-ass killers, a few guns and a bag-o'-money. The writing process on my previous book (*The Skin Palace*) had been, to put it kindly, a bit unwieldy. It was a long haul and there were a lot of characters and a lot of subplots. I wanted to strip things down, including the language. I wanted to go raw and fast, like an old Gold Medal fable. I remember saying to my wife, "*I want this one to be the novel-equivalent of Springsteen's Nebraska.*" Well, obviously, if you've read *Word*, things didn't work out that way.

What happened?

My son arrived ten days early. I had one chapter left to write to finish the first draft. It was a Friday night and we were beat and watching the season finale of the *X Files*, okay? Mulder's old man gets whacked and my wife lets out a yell from the couch. Her water had broken. About twenty-six hours later, James D is born. I didn't get back to work on the book for months. When I read what I had, I came close to burning it all. But here's a curious thing, and it reinforces my notion that some books want very much to be written into the world. *Word* ended up being a novel concerned with the meaning of books, of writing, of reading. And the reading I did in the year or two that followed my son's birth began to coalesce, to all come together and form a kind of metabook, and the metabook began to inform my thoughts about my manuscript. And those thoughts, slowly but persistently, radiated my manuscript and evolved it into what it ultimately became.

Which begs the question, what were you reading?

Over the course of that period, I read Ernst Pawel's magnificent biography of Kafka, *The Nightmare of Reason*, over and over. I couldn't leave it alone. It was like the bloody socket

BOX NINE jack o'connell

'a surrealistic noir epic' – GQ

left in the wake of the pulled tooth. I couldn't keep my tongue from roaming through it. The book became, for a time, a touchstone. I had two copies of it. Kept one in the house and one in the car. I'd wake up and read snatches of it. I'd read sentences at traffic lights. Pawel's book intertwined with David Lehman's *Signs of the Times: Deconstruction and the Fall of Paul de Man*, they bounced off one another and then they bounced off my sleepless brain. Maybe one time too many, eh? And, of course, I went back and reread Anne Frank's diary in the midst of all this rethinking. And slowly, I began to make notes about how a book I'd hoped would be a stripped-to-the-bone joy ride might be transformed into something else. Listen, I've been on an anti-irony kick

for a while, but it strikes me that the single book I consciously tried to assemble for speed and purity became, over time, my most dense work so far.

Looking back, was it a difficult book to write?

When I hear writers use the word *"grueling"* in relation to their writing life I want to roll my eyes. On my bad days, I want to reach for my grandfather's billy club. That said, it was the toughest book I've written. It was a reckless undertaking, maybe moronic, to write about the holocaust and language theory and the intersection of those two subjects using a genre format.

Do you think you were successful?

Honestly, that's never for me to judge. To step back and broaden your question, we're never successful. There's a story about writer Lorrie Moore that may or may not be apocryphal, but which sums up the nature of the compulsion beautifully. The story goes that she takes a pencil into the bookstore and makes changes to the published book as it sits on the shelf waiting to be purchased. The only thing better would be to get the name of each buyer and mail them successive drafts, changes, betterments until one or the other, writer or reader, dies. Were it possible to do this, I'd send different versions of the book to different readers.

Why?

Why not? The acts of reading and writing are connected in immensely complicated ways, I think. I'm old fashioned enough to genuinely believe each act is sacramental. That every reader remakes every book in the act of reading. The reader takes the raw material the writer provides and invents her own book. If I supplied a slew of differing raw materials to each inventor, we'd fabricate more and more stories, we'd up the ante geometrically.

That makes me want to ask you about your own reading habits.

Influence is a tricky and fascinating subject, I think. I recall in my early twenties trying to work my way through Luis Zufoksy's *A* and, in the midst of my reading, hearing he was an *"influence"* on Robert Creeley. This floored me, but at the time my conception of influence was extremely literal. Evidence of influence may not exist in the work itself, as a force that helped shape style and voice. Sometimes I think the most profound influences are those writers who jar our worldview, alter our personal cosmology.

As a kid, I spent every found dime at the corner drug store on paperbacks. The day the cost of paperback rose from 60 to 75 cents was a bitch of a day for me. I read whatever was stocked in the little black wire spin rack next to the cash register. I sometimes say that the traveling paperback salesman that supplied Rexall drugstores throughout New England was my first writing teacher. As a kid, I just read everything – the Hardy Boys series and Jack London and Ray Bradbury. I had a period in my midteens when I devoured a lot of Harlan Ellison stories. But the biggest bolt of lightening hit at 16, on that day in Spanish class, when a kid turned around and asked if I'd read Jack Kerouac. *On the Road* was the first book that changed me as a person. This is a cliché at this point, I know. But nothing was the same for me after that reading experience. Nothing's been the same since. More than any other, that one book made me want to beat myself into a writer. A few years later, Pynchon's *Crying of Lot 49* worked the same kind of spell on me. Just disassembled my identity and my sense of the world. A few years after that I immersed myself in *Ulysses* and became fairly enamored of the idea of the book as universe. When I was writing my first journeyman short stories, in my early twenties, a friend, a teacher, pointed me to Raymond Carver's *What We Talk About When We Talk About Love* when it was first published. Carver's voice seduced me and, ultimately, took over for a time and I wrote imitation-Carver stories for about a year.

As a reader, I've always been fond of obsessing over a newly discovered writer who rings the bell for you. I remember going on an extended John Barth binge at one point, just tearing through Barth. They almost lost me forever in *LETTERS*. That's just a stunning book. My sister, who's a professor of Spanish, turned me on fairly early to all the Latin American Boom writers, Borges and Garcia Marquez and Cortazar. Some of Cortzar's stories had a big impact on me and I think you can still see some of the lasting effects in my stuff.

All of these writers and all of these books helped shape me to varying degrees. But so did a lot of other things. Hearing Springsteen's *"Jungleland"* at 15 was an important moment, you know? That song was a book. It was pop, but it had this scope and this density. It was a noir epic. It had characters and plot progression, metaphor and a tragic view. It sounded like the city, all these interweaving dramas unspooling through the night. As a teen, I wanted to just radiate myself with that vision and atmosphere and melodramatic intensity and spew it out in a big fat book. Tramping downtown with my friends during that same year, paying a buck for a rerelease double-feature at the Paris Cinema, watching *Assault on Precinct 13* and *Mean Street*, *Dirty Harry* and *It's Alive*, all this weird pop jive, it went into me and took root. And it mixed with all of the sundry media mentioned above and came to build the platform, both conscious and subconscious, I write from.

Like most writers, I've got an abundance of early, dreadful, unpublished work, which calls out to be destroyed. I think about such things, probably, too much. But since I don't know when the bus will jump the road and run me down, why don't I take precautions tonight and feed the fire with my juvenilia? This year's debate about what Hemingway *"would have wanted"* should be instructive, as should the endless and, to me, endlessly fascinating Kerouac estate war. You can't trust friends to do the job after you're gone. Max Brod, bless him, ignored his buddy's last request. But I can understand the desire to get the job done by putting it on someone else. It's a little like suicide, isn't it? You're erasing some part of your existence. Jim Crumley once told me about a moment in his life when he walked to his fireplace and heaved in 1000 pages of a novel he'd been working on for a decade. Because he made the determination that it *"wasn't any good."* I admire him for that kind of instinctual self-honesty almost as much as I admire the books he deemed to share with us. I've got reams of putrid shite taking up closet space. And while I'm not sure why, at the moment, it's extant, I think it has something to do with a kind of queasy nostalgia I have for the person, the writer, I was when those crippled, doomed works took form. They're some kind of a map I can look back on and see how I got from point A to point B. From time to time I wonder if they might, at some crucial point, offer up a word, a moment, I need. However unlikely, they might yield a functioning lung or kidney at the precise moment I need the organ. There's a terrible novel and dozens of stories I'll certainly destroy, probably sooner rather than later. But it'll take some real fortitude to shred my very first novel. For all its flaws (and they are legion (the arduous, three-year journey of making that book transformed me into a novelist. I have a crystalline memory of the night I finished this book, of stacking those 600 pages and resting them on my desk and looking at this physical manifestation of years of doubt and excitement, of losing my way and discovering, so slowly, my voice. I recall that the manuscript was thicker than my city phone directory. And for a moment that night, I suspended any thoughts of quality, of aesthetic value, and took a rare pleasure in the simple fact of the book's existence. From a very early age, I had been aware that the only thing I wanted to do in my life was write. Staring at that thick block of a manuscript, I felt, for a brief instant, that I'd answered a calling. I know it likely sounds pathetic, but there you are. So it'll take some effort to scratch that one.

What do you wish you'd written? Who do you love, books-wise?

Let me use the standard boilerplate disclaimer favored by every writer who's ever been asked that question: the danger in making such lists is that a). I'll leave out somebody I shouldn't leave out and b). today's list might not be tomorrow's list. Hell, this morning's list might not be tonight's list. (There are writers who effected me deeply, influenced my own growth as a writer, my aesthetic and perhaps my voice, that I no longer reread. I'm done with them.) I'd rather duck the question and say that I read for some ideal combination of voice and vision. That if you speak to me in a seductive voice, from an interesting perspective, I'll listen to any story that you have to tell. That said, it *is* an efficient yardstick of value, isn't it? (which writers cause you to part with cold cash on publication day? Who do you own in hardcover? It's more than likely I'll be in line of the day a new DeLillo or Pynchon hits the shelves. And within the week I'll probably have a new Robert Stone or Paul Auster or Jonathan Carroll or

Steve Erickson. Regarding genre folk, or, rather, folk who, for better or worse, have been labeled "*genre folk*" for so long we pretty much accept the label: I get a rush from the usual suspects (Dan Woodrell, Jerome Charyn, Jim Crumley, James Ellroy, Elmore Leonard, George Pelecanos. I love Thompson and I love Goodis. I love a lot of those Black Lizard guys that Barry Gifford reclaimed for us. I was thrilled to learn of Norton's Old School Books project. I love the possibility of reclamation, of resurrecting writers that escaped us the first time 'round or were forgotten along the way. I can't tell you what a buzz I get when a critic or a publisher or some word-of-mouth movement brings a lost writer back to the surface. A few years back, when I found *Profit and Loss* by C. Gus French, I was just high for a week. Nobody knows French anymore. Not a single book remains in print. I've got a small press interested recently (I've agreed to do the introduction. I'd love to put this fully subversive pulp mythmaker into a few hands again.

The most honest compliment I think a writer can give another writer is "*Goddamn, I wish I'd written that.*" It's a fine child's game. Very likely, the single piece of fiction I most wish I'd written would be Joyce's "*The Dead.*" I wish I'd written *The Trial* and *The Magic Mountain* and *Ulysses* and *Absolom, Absolom* and *On the Road* and *One Hundred Years of Solitude* and *Gravity's Rainbow* and *White Noise*. No big surprises. But it's a game that never ends. If I turn my head at this instant and steal a quick look at my study bookshelves, I'll immediately see dozens of random contemporary novels, mostly American, both genre and mainstream, that I wish I'd written: *Bones of the Moon* by Jonathan Carroll and *Geek Love* by Katherine Dunn and *Misery* by Stephen King and *Easy Travel to Other Planets* by Ted Mooney and *Going After Cacciato* by Tim O'Brien. I close my eyes and take a second look and suddenly there's *Dog Soldier's* and *The Universal Baseball Association*. Carver's *What We talk About* and O'Connor's *Wise Blood* and Roth's *The Ghost Writer* and Didion's *Play It As It Lays*. A third look and there's *Red Harvest* and *Blue Eyes* and *The Last Good Kiss*. You know, how much time do you have?

What are your rules about writing sex?

I'm not one for rules and regs. To me, most of the time, rules and regs are the deathblow, so to say, of the creative impulse. Maybe this sounds simplistic to you but I think the writer should work in a manner that's most natural to him and which most effectively serves his particular story. I don't shy away from sexually explicit passages. I don't find them any easier or harder to write than any other kind of scenes. I do shy away from writers and critics who say *this is the way to handle sexuality in your work*. Legislate the constructions of your own books. If you don't like mine, leave them on the shelf like everyone else.

Can an American writer disregard politics?

The simplest way I can frame a response is also, I suppose, the most

tired. But I honestly think, even in this day and age, maybe more than ever in this day and age, these waning days of the book culture, that writing is, in and of itself, a political act. The very notion that you can transcribe your vision and share it with another is an ardently political notion, suffuse with hope and faith. I disagree, at some fundamental level, with anyone who thinks one can write and refuse any kind of belief in redemption. That's the paradox of the noir form: we write stories of hopelessness, of a perpetual descent into the abyss, and yet, the act of making stories is an act of faith. Inherent in the act is the belief that we're capable of vision, capable of codifying vision, capable of transmitting vision, capable of negotiating the transmission. That's the very reason we feed on stories (they give form to the concerns that have rolled around inside us since the beginning, since we straightened up and got the knuckles off the ground. Stories tweak our perpetual, subconscious ruminations about all the big ticket items. Love and hate and death and God and identity and fear. The greatest bond we have is our eternal need for stories. What platform we use to deliver those stories is another question we could argue about all night in a warm diner. But the need, to me, is one of the chief definitions of the human. One of Philip K. Dick's obsessive themes was *"what is human?"* Often, his answer was *"the capacity for compassion."* A wonderful, problematic answer. I'll stick with my story test. Machines don't need stories. Things without souls do not need stories. Listen, I know what I sound like as I say these things. But when it comes to narrative, I'm a true believer. This is the font where I've drawn meaning throughout my life.

Do films do it for you?

Most of the writers I know both love film, and, to some extent, bemoan the usurping of the narrative tradition by film. But what are you going to do? You're either a novelist or a filmmaker. You want to make films, knock yourself out. Go to film school and claw your way into the industry. But don't ever believe that the stories you tell will be anything but collaborations. I read for individual vision and voice. So far, filmed images can't provide that, can't deliver a fully transforming experience for me, at least not in the way I define it. Perhaps that's a generation problem. But here's one way I think about the difference between the two mediums. When I enter a theater and the lights go down and the film is thrown on the screen, I'm an easy mark to entertain. I've never walked out on a movie and, to the best of my memory, I've only wanted to walk once. But what makes me simultaneously amused and annoyed are those three words that often flash on the screen before or after the title: *"A Film By."* At this point in time, that credit is nothing but a pretension and a conceit. You might have written the screenplay and directed like an iron-fisted dictator. You might have also designed the costumes and built the sets. Maybe you even wrote the score and did the food service tables. But

screw you, pal, it's still a story by you *and* dozens of other people. This simply isn't the case with the average novel. There are obvious exceptions (what Maxwell Perkins did to or for Thomas Wolfe, for example. That's a collaboration. But when I read Kafka, I'm getting an individual nightmare. It's nothing but grace that the nightmare can be shared and universalised. It's grace that, upon receipt, I can take the nightmare and stretch it, warp it, let my own peculiar consciousness make it into something else. But I'm fairly insistent the novel can deliver individual, idiosyncratic vision and, at the present time, film simply cannot.

Despite this, movies are winning. Or maybe they won years ago and we're all still milling around the ring, tallying scorecards. I recall an interview in which Mailer said that he remembers when college students would have fistfights over books. I'm around enough college students to say I can't imagine such a scenario. But I guess I can imagine them coming to blows over a movie.

Maybe the better way to think about the question is to step as far back as possible and gain some perspective. The new forms are already on the road to us. The theorists are already busy at work, aren't they? I love Dennis Miller's line about virtual reality: The day an unemployed ironworker can pay $29.95 to bang Cindy Crawford, it's going to make crack look like candy. It's funny or it's frightening, but it's a dead-on acknowledgment, I think, of what we're sprinting toward.

But ultimately, the mechanism is probably unimportant. I was bemoaning the death of narrative fiction, in, yes, an e mail to Dan Woodrell recently. And I wrote:

"What I wonder is if this is just true for me or for my generation and those that came before it. Maybe we've already bred the next level of 'readers' whose lives, whose consciousness, can be remade by film, by TV, by the virtually real revolution down the road, by the Matrix and Gibson's soap operas to the cortex. I'll be dead and buried by the time that happens, but I feel sometimes like I'm some 19C poet watching folks salivate over the penny dreadfuls."

And Dan wrote back:

"If I am at present the equivalent of a sixteenth century sonneteer, well so what? I've read a few aged sonnets in my day."

And that was exactly what I needed to read. The mechanism is just the vehicle. The truths we need to rehear remain elemental. My sadness at watching the novel die is a personal, emotional reaction. And in this manner, it's also juvenile. As long as we remain human, in the Phildickian sense, there will still be readers and storytellers and they will still intersect at some sacred and beautiful point that will be the story. Even if you or I wouldn't recognise it.

All of my books have arrived in an instant. Someone tells me a story or hands me an artifact, and I realize as she's delivering it to me that it's a gift, it's a fertile ground where a story can grow. My first book, *Box Nine*, arrived on route 146 somewhere outside of Whitensville, Mass. My wife told me a story about working in a post office and finding a box that contained a dead bat. And my alarm went off. My antenna set to quivering. As I listened to her story, dozens of questions occurred to me (*Why do you send somebody a dead bat? What would you do to deserve finding a dead bat in your mailbox? Where do you get a dead bat if you need one?* (then dozens of possible answers occurred to me. So I woke at 5 the next morning and began writing a scene set in a post office late at night. And a mailman was discovering a terrible package. I didn't have a plot. I didn't have my characters. I had that space where I knew plot and characters would grow. Sometimes I tell people that half the process of being a writer is the continual honing of your antenna. That chronic hyper-awareness of the possibility of story in everything around you. The danger in that sensibility, of course, is that your life can be reduced only to fodder for your work.

Your books have a great sense of place...

I've lived my entire life within approximately two square miles. I sometimes think it might be convenient to carry business cards that read *Worcester is not Quinsigamond.* Worcester is, however, the place I know better than any other, with the exception of Quinsigmond. I spent uncountable hours driving around this city with my father. Through my eight-year-old eyes, this rustbelt mill town was a living story. I'm not sure I can say it better than that. All those half-destroyed factories, all those ethnic enclaves, all those rail yards, and scrap lots, and the ruined train station, all those streets that twisted and turned without logic, they all seemed both frightening and enormously intriguing. While to most of my boyhood friends, our town was the definition of a dead end, to me it was the antithesis of the mundane. Now, looking back, it was an amazingly elaborate noir set waiting for a film crew that never arrived. Lots of dark alleys and shadowy warehouses and decayed Victorian manses. But I don't plug the nuts and bolts of my city into my book. Instead, I let my imagination warp the city, enlarge it. I pillage its DNA and radiate it until it glows neon.

You're with HarperCollins in the US?

A timely question given the sacking of the mid-list. I can't say I've had any true nightmares in this regard. My first publisher in the US was Mysterious Press. Good folks who were very nice to me. Sara Ann Freed is a gem. But ultimately, I couldn't seem to write the kinds of books they were best at selling. I'm with HarperCollins now. My UK publisher is Ion Mills at No Exit. I'll tell you, it's a sweet moment when you look at your new publisher's list and find all the books you want to read. For me, it's a sign they *"get"* you. Nice sharing a publisher with Marc Behm and James Sallis and Kem Nunn and Dan Woodrell and Charles Willeford. All writers I respect enormously. Should I stop now, Ion?

The major commercial publishing houses are, by and large, minor subsidiaries of multinational conglomerates. As such, they only exist to turn an adequate profit for the stockholders. Publishers were probably always businesspeople, but in the past, most were, simultaneously, bookpeople. They were in this particular business because they loved writers and writing. That is now a quaint notion, I think. I'm not being dramatic to say that accountants and marketing people decide what books are published today. Books, once the repository of our cultural life, are now thought of no differently than hamburgers. It is not enough that a book earn a profit. It must earn x profit in y time. If it's still under the warming light when the buzzer goes off, send it to the furnace.

This saddens me less as reader than as writer. As a reader, I worry only that I'll have less access to the quirkiest writers because they don't stoke the profit engine efficiently enough. But while that's a bit depressing, I can still go back and read the old oddball visionaries and

As a writer, however, it's a pretty terrifying time to be making new books. But dealing with the reality of the corporate publishing climate, however, has required a renewal of my understanding of the fundamental difference between writing and publishing. Writing (accessing and transcribing that dreamlife (is a deeply personal experience, a meditative plunge into the realm of myth (even if its cheesy myth), by which the writer gains not only some measure of meaning but, sometimes, moments of peace and joy.

Jaysus, it sounds like a lot of pretentious bull, doesn't it, Eve? Can't be helped, I guess. I've never quite been able to follow some of the smartest advice I've ever been given: The wise man says nothing.

As an adolescent wanting desperately to be a writer, I bought fully into the bardic American myth. I just loved the notion of the traveling American writer, read the biographies of London and Kerouac and Hemingway. And as a teen, I was convinced this would be my future: adventuring out into the world, then returning to the monastic desk and working the alchemy by which your life becomes your art. I was young and stupid. Post college, I fully embraced the antithetical notion of craft. I had a Flaubert quote tacked above my desk for years (something to the effect that you should be orderly in your life so you might be wild in your work. You know, Thomas Mann saying writers should dress like bankers. Don't call attention to yourself.

Observe and transcribe. Be a recording machine. Today, I'm pragmatic and, frankly, less interested in the question. Maybe it's a young writer's question. It's so damn hard today just sustaining your own conception of yourself as a working writer, your own conviction, that you need to go with what works, keep your head down and hold tight to your voice.

Next up?

I've been researching a book on the Brazilian *surfistas*, the street kids who surf on the tops of commuter trains. I understand there's been some instances of this here in the UK the past few years as well. It's been a slow process. The book has come to me more fully, in the note-taking stage, before the actual writing, than any other. I'm hoping it comes to fruition. But something new commandeered my attention just weeks ago and it's been coming nonstop and quickly. My guess is that one or the other will force its will in the coming months. And I can only say, may the best book win.

opinion

a personal view
mark timlin

I WAS SLUMPED in front of the TV set early the other Saturday evening, channel surfing through On Digital for anything to escape the dross that masquerades as entertainment on BBC1 and ITV at that time, presented, if that's the word by the likes of Jim Davidson, Chris Tarrant, Noel Edmonds, Lily Savage et al. Suddenly, up around channel thirty or so where the 'gold' stations lurk, as I was dodging between old episodes of *A Touch Of Frost* and *Keeping Up Appe*arances, it suddenly hit me like a bolt out of the blue. The target audience for British TV crime in the late nineties is Hyacinth Bucket. Yes. Old Hyacinth with her airs and graces, crinolined lady hiding the spare toilet roll in the downstairs lavatory and her ilk are the very people who dictate what the rest of us have to watch crimewise. Now bear with me while I elaborate.

Never in the history of human conflict have British TV crime series been in such dire straits. Just check out what has been offered up for our delectation recently. And before you

start, I know not all these are currently being aired, but they're all recent and many are returning to bore the backsides off us this winter. And besides, if they fit my theory I'm running with them. First off there's the aforementioned *Frost* with David Jason, everyone's auntie's favourite TV actor as that jaundiced but lovable DI with his warrant card in one hand and a bacon sarnie in the other. Then there's *The Bill*, which after making something of a comeback with a four-parter where PC Eddie Santini finally got his come-uppance has reverted to the occasional halfway decent episode on a Thursday after the watershed, and loveable old Reg Hollis pottering about in his caravan, or the love lives of the uniformed branch on Tuesdays at eight. But *The Bill* still doesn't ring true. Is it only me, or have you noticed that when anyone gets nicked they always go quietly? Not much reality there. Worse still is *Maisie Raine*, with old pudden' face Pauline Quirk reprising her part in *Birds Of A Feather* which frankly speaks for itself and needs little further criticism from me. Just like *Dalziel And Pascoe*: The moron and the weasel who I don't think could solve the quick crossword in the Sun between them if you gave them the answers. And as for the the weasel's wife... Couldn't she die in a tragic hanging basket accident when one of the silly baskets hangs her?

And they even gave old Hyacinth a series of her own. *Hettie Wainwright Investigates*. Really. The sight of Patricia Routledge rushing around some dreary northern town on her moped trying to solve the mystery of a missing pension book hardly makes me want to set the video. It almost makes one pine for *Anna Lee*. Then of course there's *Inspector Morse*. A cop show for people who really don't like cop shows. How

could John Thaw do it? From playing Regan, the toughest, lariest copper in the Met whose record collection probably contained nothing more intellectual than *Top Of The Pops Vol 7* which he bought because the bird on the cover had big knockers and he quite liked the original of *Barbados* by Typically Tropical that he heard on a pub jukebox once, he now wanders around Oxford behaving like a snobbish prat, listening to bloody opera. But I will admit, if forced, that I've never seen the denouement of even one of his cases. I've seen the beginning of every one broadcast I'm sure, but, like a stiff brandy and a couple of Mogadon, I find *Inspector Morse* a perfect soporific.

Next up is *City Central*. Not bad I suppose. But it's just a soap, more interested in the personal lives of the characters than catching criminals. Just up the road on Merseyside was the location for *Liverpool 1* which again didn't really cut it, although Paul Usher, who played Barry Grant in *Brookside* was pretty good, but would Samantha Janus really be taken seriously as a DC dressing like a hooker?

And hurrah, hurrah, I see in the *Radio Times* that *The Ruth Rendell Mysteries* are back. More good looking home county boys and girls going mental in the Mercs and Beemers. The only mystery to me is why they bother.

But I'm saving the latest and the worst for last. A few weeks ago we were privileged to see the premiere of *Badger*, or Bodger as it's been christened round my house. And a real bodge it is. A mixture of Rolf Harris's *Animal Hospital* and ...well I suppose *Heartbeat* would be the closet if you can imagine anything worse. This series features a wildlife cop unconvincingly played by the Jerome half of Robson and Jerome who surely must have made enough money out of those lousy records to have to sink to this level. But then, thinking of those lousy records I imagine there is no depths he wouldn't sink to. And this one is pretty deep. It's so annoyingly innocuous with its one finger in the ear, Arran sweater electric folk as its background music that it makes me, an animal lover to the core, want to reach for the pump action shotgun and blow all those darling little creatures to a red mist. And we pay a licence fee to make this muck.

We all know that animal husbandry in all its various forms, cooking, DIY and gardening are the staples of mainstream channels right now, and so far two bases have been covered for police series. The execrable *Pie In The Sky* where possibly the fattest serving copper ever, who wouldn't have lasted through one annual medical, ran a restaurant and solved crimes. Unfortunately Richard Griffiths, who appeared to have actually *eaten* all the pies, was so huge that he hardly ever walked, let alone ran after his suspects, and had a terrible job just levering himself out of his car, which left us with probably the most static crime show since *Ironside*. So that only leaves DIY and gardening. An interior decorating cop - now there's an idea, who's called in when someone commits a clashing carpet

What's this doing here? It's an unprincipled plug for Mr Timlin's new book, just £6.99 from Toxic to you guv. Regan 'ud be on to us for corruption like a rat up a drainpipe

and curtains crime. Or possibly a gardening policeman who gets called out when your hardy annuals do a runner *[Amusingly this is the plot of an episode of* Pie In The Sky! *Perhaps you should be* writing *one of these shows, Mark? - Ed]*. Believe me, nowadays anything's possible.

So that leaves only one show that's halfway decent, BBC 2's *Cops*. I can believe that it's a fairly accurate depiction of the police force in general - a bunch of bumbling idiots who couldn't catch a bus. But sadly there's not one member of the cast that I have any sympathy with, so the series as a whole leaves me cold.

Now maybe I live in a golden haze of nostalgia, but does anyone else but me remember *Target, Callan, Special Branch, Hazell, Gangsters, Out*, even the first series of *Minder* before it became *The Arthur Daley Comedy Hour*? This was tough stuff. And even looking at *The Professionals*, risible at the time, you just know that it would never get on TV now in that format, even though there's supposed to be a remake on the blocks. But then there's supposed to be a remake of *The Sweeney* as well, with Dennis Waterman as a Superintendent and Regan gone off to run a trout farm in Scotland. Old trout farm knowing him. But then you just know it's going to be a pale shadow of its former self if it ever gets on the screen. *The Sweeney* was the best TV crime show produced in this country ever, and I'll fight anyone who says different. It's there to see every week night on Granada Plus at nine. And even further back and showing my age now, but there were some tremendous series in the sixties. *The Gold Robbers, Big Breadwinner Hog, Redcap* (Thaw again as a young bruiser) *Public Eye*, and even *Z Cars* and *Softly Softly* in its various formats, although they were admittedly primitive by today's standards. But at least I managed to stay awake throughout. So there you have it, I hate to mention *Hill Street Blues, Homicide, NYPD Blue* and *The Sopranos* in the same breath, but how come the Yanks can keep making quality crime shows for prime time TV and all we can come up with the sort of crap that we do?

THE TIMLIN READING LIST
(There'll be a test later!)

I'm too busy for in depth reviews again, but here's a few books for the summer that have caught my eye recently and I can thoroughly recommend.:

Gideon by Russell Andrews-Little,Brown

Florida Roadkill by Tim Dorsey-Harper Collins

Gone, Baby, Gone by Dennis Lehane-Bantam

The Eye Of The Beholder by Marc Behm-No Exit

The Poker Club by Ed Gorman-CT Publishing

Blood In Brooklyn by Gary Lovisi-The Do Not Press

The Burglar In The Rye by Laurence Block-No Exit

Revenge Of The Cootie Girls by Sparkle Hayter-No Exit

Kissing The Beehive by Jonathan Carroll-Vista

Scorpian Rising by Anthony Frewin-No Exit

Welcome To Paradise by Laurence Shames-Villard (Import)

'Fast, Funny, Terrific' - Ed McBain

The Burglar in the Rye
LAWRENCE BLOCK

Literary agent Anthea Landau, legendary resident of the Paddington Hotel, is auctioning off her personal correspondence from enigmatic writer Gulliver Fairborn. Her famous ex-client, who guards his private life so jealously that he has never been photographed or interviewed, is reportedly outraged by Landau's betrayal - yet can't afford to outbid the collectors who are fighting to get their hands on the letters.

Bernie Rhodenbarr's at the Paddington Hotel to make sure they never do. Gully Fairborn is Bernie's literary idol, so when Fairborn's ex-lover, Alice Cottrell, asks the bookseller-burglar to help her return the letters to their rightful author, Bernie doesn't hesitate. He breaks into Anthea Landua's suite. And finds her...dead.

The police burst in, and Bernie takes a fire escape down to an empty room, where he quietly pockets some nice ruby jewellery. Minutes later, he is under arrest. By the time Bernie is bailed out, his bookstore is visited by a host of mysterious folks, all demanding the letters he doesn't have. That's when Bernie learns that the gems he does have were heisted the night before he stole them. Now, to clear his name and right some terrible wrongs, Bernie must solve a murder or two, track down a rival jewel thief, retrieve the missing letters, find the rubies' rightful owner, and still manage to protect the elusive Gulliver Fairborn...without getting caught.

Available from all good bookshops or by post from No Exit Press, (Dept CT26) 18 Coleswood Rd, Harpenden, Herts, AL5 1EQ (Postage and Packing free) - or buy on the web at www.noexit.co.uk

ISBN:1 901 98260 2   Price: £16.99 Hardback   Publication: June 1999

there is.... *NO EXIT*

pulp fictions

writing in the darkness:
the world of cornell woolrich

eddie duggan

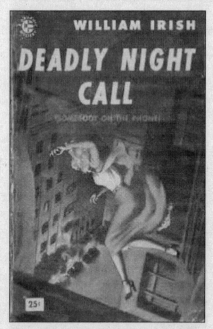

Even today, not every reader of crime and mystery fiction will be familiar with the name Cornell Woolrich, but the chances are many will have seen a film based on one of his novels or short stories, perhaps Alfred Hitchcock's *Rear Window* (1954), based on the 1942 short story 'It Had to be Murder', François Truffaut's *The Bride Wore Black* [*La Mariée était en noir*] (1967), adapted from the novel of the same name, or one of the other numerous adaptations of Woolrich's work. As we shall see, it is not for nothing that Woolrich's work is well known among the cognoscenti of crime fiction and among film makers.

Woolrich's writing deserves to be known by the current generation of readers of crime fiction, not only because his work is significant in itself, but also because of the way in which it has shaped and influenced the dark or *noir* aspect of the crime and mystery drama. Woolrich combines elements of psychological horror with crime writing to produce what we might call the 'psychological suspense thriller'. In his wonderfully entitled study of film noir, *In A Lonely Street*, Frank Krutnik describes Woolrich as 'the prime exponent of the psychological suspense thriller' of the 1940s. Woolrich's work is rightly described as 'noir' or black writing, because the atmosphere of fear, confusion and menace he creates can be sometimes very dark indeed. Woolrich, in Ian Ousby's words, 'put the *noir* in *film noir*'.

A typical Woolrich plot might involve an inexplicably missing person—a wife or husband, say—and the worried remaining partner would be not only unable to trace the missing person, but also unable to convince anyone else the missing person ever really existed. Another typical Woolrichian scenario would be one in which the wife of a wrongly-convicted killer seeks to find the clue or the overlooked scrap of evidence which can prove the loved one's innocence, but must also race against the clock because the wrongly convicted person is sentenced to be executed. Woolrich's world is nothing if not fraught with anxiety and despair.

Frank Krutnik observes that:

"...in 'amnesiac-hero' thrillers the enigma is entwined with a splitting or a break down of unified male identity ... film[s] centred upon amnesiac investigators include ... a significantly large number of Cornell Woolrich adaptations—Street of Chance (1942), The Chase (1946), Black Angel (1947), Fall Guy (1947) and Fear in the Night (1947)." [p. 133].

While Robert Porfirio writes in *The Dark Age of American Film*:

"Woolrich must be considered as comprising the extreme wing of [the hard-boiled tradition's] psychological 'faction' ... his protagonists seldom have their emotions under control ... if they are not unstable to begin with they are rendered thus through the effects of 'dope', amnesia, hypnosis or just plain fear ... Woolrich must be included along with Hammett, Chandler and [James M.] Cain as a major contributor to ... film noir."[pp. 88-89]

Indeed, as Frank Krutnik suggests, Woolrich is "perhaps the most extensively adapted of all the pulp magazine writers (both in cinema and on radio)" [p.41].

Hard-boiled or noir?

Dashiell Hammett, Raymond Chandler and James M. Cain are the leading lights among what used to be called 'the tough guy writers'; this unholy trinity would now be recognised as forming the core of what we might call 'classic' hard-boiled fiction. Sharing some of the hard-boiled sensibilities of these exponents of the 'tough guy' style, but also diverging from them in several important ways, are a

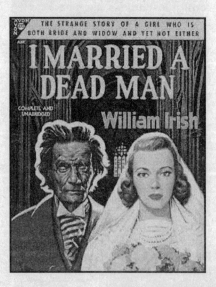

group of writers—I would call them a 'second wave'—that might be identified as 'noir' rather than 'hard-boiled'. Among this second wave one can include Jim Thompson, David Goodis and Cornell Woolrich.

The main difference between the 'classic' hard-boiled writers and the 'noir writers'—although James M. Cain has a foot in each camp—can probably be characterised by two tendencies: a tendency in hardboiled writing to paint a backdrop of institutionalised social corruption; and a tendency in noir writing to focus on personal psychology, whether it is despair, paranoia or some other psychological crisis. The two schools—if we can call these tendencies 'schools'—are by no means mutually exclusive: hard boiled writing can display elements of noir, and noir writing can be hard-boiled.

Institutionalised corruption is taken as given among the hard-boiled school: corrupt institutions (the police force, the judiciary, politicians), and indeed there are several 'bad cop'stories in the Woolrich cannon, just as there are elements of psychological development in the Hammett corpus (the Continental Op stories, for example).

By the same token, there are mean streets in the world of noir, though these streets are peopled by the psychologically insecure: psychological instability is the key characteristic of the protagonists of noir writing, if not the key characteristic of the noir writers themselves (see, for example, *Life's a Bitch: Paranoia and Sexuality in the Novels Of David Goodis* in *Crime Time* 2.1). Paranoid insecurity, doubts and fears about identity, sexuality and personal safety are the key fault-lines of the noir personality.

In Cornell Woolrich's noir world, one routinely finds these traits of despair. The fear expressed in Woolrich's fiction may be one of the ways in which he worked through his own psychological traumas, or Woolrich's writing might be thought of as a kind of social barometer, through which the pressures and tensions of wider cultural fears and anxieties are indicated.

In the post war era, ideas about masculinity had to be re-negotiated as women were reluctantly eased out of their wartime roles and persuaded by various means, including popular novels and films, to give up their newly found independence to return to their former domestic roles. Apart from the 'menace' of the independent woman, post-war America felt particularly at risk from the threat of communism. As America underwent the cultural revolution of McCarthyism, during which time Hollywood sought to 'out' the politically suspect, fears about individuals—or larger social groups—being 'taken over' by sinister unseen forces, sometimes represented as aliens or plants from outer space; or by chemicals, as characters are 'drugged' or otherwise lose control, were prevalent in popular fiction. It should come as no surprise then, that during the nineteen forties and nineteen fifties, at the height of America's cultural and political paranoia, Woolrich was at his productive peak.

In *Pulp Culture*, his study of American popular fiction during the cold war era, Woody Haut comments:

"Unable to maintain sufficient perspec-

tive, Cornell Woolrich would be haunted by his own narratives, from Rear Window to Waltz into Darkness and the notion that urban life—"I think of it as a personal enemy" [Deadline at Dawn]—had become a nightmare. "[H]e could feel hands fumbling around him, lots of hands. They weren't actually touching him; they were touching things that touched him." [The Black Curtain (1941)] ¶ But Woolrich's personal crimes—paranoia, self-neglect, alcoholism—were only against himself. State crimes, in comparison, had become so apparent that even President Eisenhower was forced to focus publicly on one particularly blatant example, the military-industrial complex." [p. 138]

PAPERBACK WRITER

To describe Woolrich's output as 'prolific' would be something of an under-statement: over the course of his writing career, from the late 1920s to the late 1960s, he produced some twenty-seven novels and an almost innumerable number—literally hundreds—of short stories, which have been issued and re-issued under a range of titles, and collected in dozens of compilations. To make things even more complicated, Woolrich revised or re-worked many of his stories, and he wrote under a number of pseudonyms, most notably as William Irish and George Hopley.

The so-called 'black series' of novels is probably Woolrich's best known work under his own name: The Bride Wore Black (1940); The Black Curtain (1941); The Black Alibi (1942); The Black Angel (1943); The Black Path of Fear (1944); and Rendezvous in Black (1948).

Because Woolrich was too prolific for his publisher's liking, he found another publisher, Lippincott, and used the pseudonym William Irish, under which was issued the novels Phantom Lady (1942); Deadline At Dawn (1944); Waltz into Darkness (1946); and I Married A Dead Man (1948) and eleven short story collections. Woolrich also used the nom-de-plume George Hopley for the novels Night Has A Thousand Eyes (1945) and Fright (1950).

POET OF THE SHADOWS

So who was Cornell Woolrich, poet of the shadows, and leading architect of the noir style?

Cornell George Hopley Woolrich was born in New York in 1903. His parents divorced a few years later and the young Woolrich lived with his father, a civil engineer, in Mexico, until moving back to New York as an adolescent to live with his mother and grandfather. According to biographer Francis M. Nevins Jr, Woolrich's formative years were generally disturbed and unhappy.

Woolrich enrolled at New York's Columbia University in 1921 where he spent a relatively undistinguished year until he was taken ill and was laid up for some weeks. It was during this illness—a Rear-Window-like confinement involving a gangrenous foot, according to one version of the story—that Woolrich started writing, producing his first novel, the Fitzgerald-esque Cover Charge, which was published in 1926. The following year a second 'jazz-age' novel, Children of the Ritz, won a college magazine's literary prize which led to Woolrich landing a job as a Hollywood screenwriter; as a result of this early success, Woolrich abandoned his studies at Columbia and did not graduate.

Woolrich moved to Hollywood in 1928, to work under contract to First National Pictures, apparently on the script of *Children of the Ritz*. Whatever Woolrich did during his stint in Hollywood, he received no screen credits under his own name. Interestingly however, during the period when Woolrich was at First National, one William Irish was credited three times—twice for title cards (this was the era of transition from silent to sound film) and once for dialogue: perhaps this was Woolrich's first use of the appellation 'William Irish', the pseudonym under which he would go on to publish four novels and dozens of short stories in the 1940s.

While in Hollywood, Woolrich engaged in what biographer Nevins describes as 'promiscuous and clandestine homosexual activity', which involved cruising the waterfront in a sailor suit. Woolrich also married twenty-year-old Gloria Blackton, daughter of one of the founders of the Vitagraph studio. The marriage—apparently something of a whim, perhaps a cover for Woolrich's homosexuality—did not last. After three months Woolrich left Gloria to return to his mother in New York, with whom he would remain for the next twenty-five years. The unconsummated marriage was later annulled.

Having failed in his attempt to set himself up in Hollywood, Woolrich sought to continue his writing career. Although Woolrich had published six 'jazz-age' novels—concerned with the party-antics and romances of the beau-tiful young things on the fringes of American society—between 1926 and 1932, he was unable to establish himself as a 'serious' writer. Perhaps because the 'jazz-age' novel was dead in the water by the nineteen thirties when the depression had begun to take hold, Woolrich was unable to find a publisher for his seventh novel, *I Love You, Paris*, so he literally threw away the typescript—dumped it in a dustbin—and re-invented himself as a pulp writer.

The pulps provided the Hollywood-reject and failed-novelist with an outlet for his delightfully twisted fiction of coincidence, cruel chance and damnable fortune. Woolrich's work began to appear in *Detective Fiction Weekly* and *Black Mask* during the 1930s under his own name, and under the pseudonyms William Irish and George Hopley. At this stage Woolrich was, in Lee Server's words, 'a broke, despairing recluse, living with his mother at the Hotel Marseilles on 103rd St and Broadway'. Although his writing made him wealthy, Woolrich and his mother lived in a series of seedy hotel rooms, including the squalid Hotel Marseilles apartment building in Harlem, among a group of thieves, prostitutes and lowlifes that would not be out of place in Woolrich's dark fictional world .

In his unfinished autobiography *Blues of A Lifetime* (published posthumously in 1991), Woolrich wrote: 'I had that trapped feeling, like some sort of a poor insect that you've put inside a downturned glass, and it tries to climb up the sides, and it can't, and it can't, and it can't.' Here, in a simple metaphor, directed at himself, Woolrich marvellously captures the essence of despair that would wrack so many of the characters in his novels and stories, alluded to in Frank Krutnik's assertion that 'Woolrich's work contains tortuously elaborate passages of masochistic delirium'. [p. 41]

WOOLRICH'S 'BLACK SERIES' OF NOVELS AND *LA SÉRIE NOIR*

One of the key terms used to describe certain types of crime fiction, and briefly discussed above, is the word 'noir', the French for 'black'—as in black mood, dark atmosphere; dark and doom-laden. The reason the French term 'noir' is used to describe this style is probably because of the series of crime books published in France from the mid-1940s under the series title *Série Noir*, or 'Black Series'.

The French had been deprived of access to American popular culture during the Second World War. Immediately after the war however, in 1945, French publisher Gallimard established the *Série Noir* imprint, edited by Marcel Duhamel (who had, at one time, been Ernest Hemingway's secretary). Among the crime titles published under the *Série Noir* imprint were the works of a number of American 'pulp' writers, including the 'second-wave' noir writers, David Goodis, Jim Thompson and Cornell Woolrich.

This French series is important to crime writing because the critical attention its titles received was quite different from the reception the same works enjoyed in America. While in their native America the works of these 'noir writers' were afforded the status of cultural ephemera—merely cheap, disposable, Lion and Gold Medal paperbacks, packaged in lurid-covers to attract readers to their hopefully equally lurid contents—for French literary critics they were masterful expressions of existential angst. Lee Server notes, for example, that Horace McCoy's *They Shoot Horses, Don't They?* was 'acclaimed by Sartre and Gide' yet remained virtually unknown in America; while Albert Camus acknowledged the influence of James M. Cain's *The Postman Always Rings Twice* on his own *L'Etranger* (*The Stranger*).

The same American titles that were being translated into French for publication under the *Série Noir* imprint were also providing a body of raw material for the Hollywood film studios. When the American films based on these novels became available in France after the war, the direct connection between the American novels published under the *Série Noir* imprint and their adaptation for the American cinema—often by European émigré directors—led French cinema critic Nino Frank to coin the term *films noirs*—literally, 'black films'—in 1946.

Woolrich's biographer, Francis M. Nevins Jr., suggests that the name of Gallimard's *Serie Noir* imprint may have been inspired by Woolrich's own series of 'black' novels.

The first of Woolrich's so-called 'black series' is *The Bride Wore Black* (1940). It is Woolrich's first novel since becoming a 'pulp writer', and marks his entry into the hardback and paperback market, along with other pulp writers who were making the transition about this time, such as Raymond

Chandler, whose first novel, *The Big Sleep* was published in 1939, and Frank Gruber, whose debut novel *The French Key* was published in 1940. Wooolrich dedicated this book to his Remington typewriter.

The Bride Wore Black is a formally structured tale of female vengance. The bride of the title is widowed on her wedding day and swears to avenge her husband's death. Adopting a number of disguises, she insinuates herself into the lives of her various victims. One can remark that the way in which the dangerous female—in the guise of mistress, housekeeper, model—strikes fatally at her unsuspecting male victims captures something of the threat that femininity poses to Woolrich's self-loathing, homosexual recluse, while tapping also into a wider male heterosexual suspicion of female sexuality as the figure of the virgin bride/black widow is condensed into the single, man-killing character, Julie.

The formal, episodic structure of *The Bride Wore Black* divides the book into five sections, each headed with an epigram. Each section consists of three chapters; the first chapter in each section is called 'The Woman' in which the *femme fatale* sets up her victim; the second is named for the victim, in which the assassination is carried out; while in the third, entitled 'Post Mortem', the aftermath of the death is discussed, and a policeman, with the improbably phallic appellation, Wanger, investigates the killings, marking each 'Unsolved'.

The final part of the book is revelatory. Only in the final section does Woolrich allow the reader—and

the characters—full understanding of the events that have happened earlier. While typical Woolrichian laws of probability inform the unfolding of events, the book was well received as a suspenseful thriller by most critics in the American press—one declaring Woolrich to be the literary equivalent of Hitchcock—although the most influential reviews—*The New York Herald Tribune; The Saturday Review of Literature* and the *New York Times Book Review*—found this Woolrichian opus displayed too much 'pulpiness', had an improbable plot, and to be generally 'odd'.

SCREEN AND SCREEN AGAIN

François Truffaut's 1968 film adaptation of *The Bride Wore Black, La Mariée était en noir*, with Jeanne Moreau in the title role, also divided the critics. While *Halliwell's Film & Video Guide* dismisses it as 'uncertain and not very entertaining' and quotes another review which declares it 'a piece of junk', other sources, for example *The Bloomsbury Good Film Guide*, find the film notable for its acting and direction. Also, Nevins cites Donald Petrie's 1970 study of Truffaut, which describes the film as 'a dance in which music and camera combine, the one adapting and suiting itself to the needs of the other.'

Switching the action to Europe, Truffaut also managed to tidy up the narrative by excising most of Woolrich's unlikely elements—along with the character Wanger.

Truffaut filmed another Woolrich novel the following year, *Waltz into Darkness*, which was released as *La Siren du Mississippi* in 1969 (*Mississippi*

Mermaid), starring Catherine Deneuve and Jean-Paul Belmondo. Again, Truffaut transplants the action to Europe and cuts the more improbable elements of Woolrich's original story. As Nevins puts it, Truffaut—the most accessible of the French 'new wave' directors—takes Woolrich's grim world of noir and refracts it through the broader spectrum of his own life-affirming palette.

Perhaps the most widely-known film adaptation of a Woolrich story is Alfred Hitchcock's 1954 voyeur-fest, *Rear Window*, with James Stewart and Grace Kelly.

In Woolrich's original story, first published as *It Had to be Murder* in 1942, but subsequently retitled *Rear Window*, Hal Jeffries is confined to bed with a broken leg. With nothing to relieve his boredom, Jeffries takes to 'spying' on his neighbours in the block of flats facing his window. Subtle clues lead Jeffries to suspect a neighbour, Thorwald, has killed his wife and Jeffries reports this to a policeman friend who, after a brief enquiry, tells Jeffries that all is well. Unsatisfied, Jeffries begins phoning his suspect, and investigates him by proxy, sending his black 'manservant'sam to rifle Thorwald's flat. As Jeffries realises that he is not the only one watching— Thorwald begins watching and ringing him—the suspense builds up until Woolrich releases the tension, delivering the resolution with a characteristic twist.

In Hitchcock's world—in which looking or voyeurism is a key theme— Jeffries', played by James Stewart, neighbourly voyeurism is justified by his being a laid-up press-photographer, and thus surrounded by an array of cameras and lenses. Hitchcock loses the character of Sam and replaces him with a nurse, Stella, played by Thelma Ritter, and Jeffries' girlfriend Lisa Fremont, played by Grace Kelly. Donald Spoto suggests that Hitchcock's *Rear Window* is a complex text about voyeurism, relationships and about film-making, with Jeffries, or 'Jeff', standing in for 'Hitch', as he constructs stories about people and directs his 'crew'. Hitchcock also adds several new neighbours, and uses them to allow Jeffries to muse on a range of possible futures with Lisa. Thus Hitchcock adds a reflective element by making Woolrich's tale of looking-on also function as a story about looking *in*.

In the most recent Woolrich adaptation, director Richard Benjamin has brought *I Married a Dead Man* to the screen in a romantic comedy entitled *Mrs Winterbourne* (1996). However, simply looking at the box of the video in Blockbusters was enough to convince me that I didn't want to know how anyone had been able to get a romantic comedy out of a Woolrich story.

WOOLRICH AND *BLACK MASK*

As well as his notable 'black series', Woolrich can also be included in the so-called '*Black Mask* school', inasmuch as many of his stories were printed in *Black Mask* in the late nineteen-thirties and during the nineteen forties. After *Black Mask* editor Joe 'Cap'shaw was fired in 1936 for refusing to cut writer's rates, Fanny Ellsworth, who has been editing a romance magazine across the corridor, was brought in as new editor. Although she was *Black Mask's* second female editor, her gender was hidden by the use of her initial instead of her forename. After Shaw's sacking, several of his stable of loyal writers (William F. Nolan calls them 'Cap's boys') shunned *Black Mask* and turned instead to rival publications for an outlet for their work. Faced with this exodus, which included Raymond Chandler, Frederick Nebel and Paul Cain, Fanny Ellsworth had recruited a new group of writers by the end of 1937, among them Cornell Woolrich. The effect of this injection of new blood resulted in something of a 'softening' of *Black Mask's* hard-boiled content.

According to Nolan, *"[Woolrich's] detectives were never hard-boiled; they were usually 'little men, trying to do a job within the dark, threatening universe of a big city.'"* [p. 30]

WHAT'S THAT CREAKING? ONLY THE PLOT

In his 1946 essay *Dagger of the Mind*, perhaps the first serious appraisal of Woolrich's work, critic James Sandoe assesses Woolrich's unique ability to combine vivid writing with plotting that sometimes creaked beyond credibility. Sandoe considered Woolrich:

"The most superb and garish literary juggler ... his special capacity has been to perform a series of variations on what will be remembered as the puzzle of the vanishing lady... But while his skill in contriving variations is staggering, his stories are inclined in retrospect to seem more than a little absurd... Woolrich has a facility for catching the reader's attention with a striking situation and then bustling him from shock to shock with a kind of numbing swiftness. The mere facility is only apparent after the last page has been turned and then if one is so unwise as to glance back, the tale itself vanishes into incredibility, very much as Eurydice vanished when Orpheus forsook his vow and turned to look at her before she crossed the threshold of hell.*"

Indeed. However crime-writer and critic Julian Symons looked rather less favourably on Woolrich, declaring:

"His best writing is in the novels he produced at great speed in the forties, including The Bride Wore Black (1940) and one of the Irish books, Phantom Lady (1942), but the melodramatic silliness and sensationalism of many of his plots, and the continuous high-pitched whine of his prose [...] preclude him from serious consideration." [p. 161]

Perhaps the nineteen-nineties reader will need to work a little harder at suspending disbelief when reading Woolrich than when reading some other imaginative works—harder than Symons was prepared to do—but the effort will be well rewarded. For, as Geoffrey O'Brien writes:

"[While] Woolrich had a genius for inventing extraordinary situations (Raymond Chandler called him 'the best idea man') he wrote too often in a bloated purple prose that ... might be tolerable in small doses, but Woolrich writes this way the whole time. Yet through all the crudities of style and excesses of melodrama, something in his work fascinates. He is quite simply the premier paranoid among crime writers. His is the realm of the impossible coincidence, perceived as a cosmic joke at the expense of man." [p. 97]

In Woolrich's 1948 novel *I Married A*

Dead Man (originally a short story, *They Call Me Patrice*, published in a women's magazine in 1946, Woolrich adapted and republished the story as a novel in 1948, under the pseudonym William Irish) the protagonist, Patrice, finds herself about to become a single mother with all the stigma middle America attached to such things in the early post-war era. Attempting to flee from her miserable life, she finds by chance that her circumstances are drastically changed by a freak train accident. In a remarkable case of mistaken identity, Patrice finds herself in a situation that affords her the respectability, security and support she would otherwise have lacked as a single pregnant girl from the wrong side of the tracks. As she settles tentatively into her new life, she begins a relationship that is always haunted by doubt and insecurity. As Woolrich perpetuates twist after twist, Patrice's new life begins to unravel: like one who has attracted the attention of the cruel fates and who becomes their plaything or victim, she is tossed from one awful situation to another.

Seeking to end a marriage amicably in order to build a life with his new love, a man decides to take his wife to dinner and then a show, in an attempt to persuade her to grant a him divorce. Thus begins *Phantom Lady*. However, a row ensues and the reluctant husband strikes off alone, later picking up a female companion for the evening—having agreed to simply keep each other company and to exchange no personal details. Returning home and finding the police waiting to question him as during his absence his wife has been murdered, the protagonist cannot find anyone to back up his story—despite his having being seen by several witnesses, and despite the fact that his anonymous companion was wearing what must surely be the most memorable hat in pulp fiction.

In Cinderella and the Mob (1940) a school-girl is mistaken for a moll after a misdialled call, and finds herself involved in a gangland hit while managing to simultaneously avoid revealing her true identity and avoid understanding the situation in which she is entangled.

However, one doesn't read Woolrich for credible plotting. While most of the stories are well enough written to allow for initial premise—whether it is an unlikely outcome of a marital tiff about a trip to a show; the peculiarly sudden intimacy between complete strangers on a doomed train; a misdialled telephone call; a neighbour seen packing a large trunk just before his wife disappears; a man waiting while his girl delivers a package finds she has disappeared—to carry the story; a series of improbable events tend to unfold: the marital tiff leads to a whole series of unlikely turns; as does the chance meeting on a train; and the misunderstanding on the telephone; the uneven floor; the clippings agency as a front for a spy-ring. It is the whole series of chance events that follow on, one from another, that make the outcome of any Woolrich story one that would be beyond the range of any acturial table.

EASY WRITER
Despite some of the unlikely turns

and coincidences that occur in so many of his stories, there is a certain charm, a knack Woolrich has of engaging the reader and persuading them to not think too hard about so many chance events, that makes the stories so engaging. Not all of the Woolrichian corpus is easy reading, however. One of Woolrich's main faults is his tendency toward stylistic excess. The opposite of the lean, stripped-down prose of Hammett, eight words would never suffice when eight florid paragraphs might be used instead. In his biography of Woolrich, Nevins cites Jerry Palmer, who wrote in *The Literary Review* that *"Woolrich is the best argument yet invented for speed reading: his purple prose is so atrocious that normal word-by-word reading is painful."* However, as Nevins goes on to point out, *"remove the signs of haste and white heat, recast the scene in cool, calm and controlled prose [...] and you will have gutted it."*

Woolrich himself commented on his style with unknowing irony in his autobiography, *Blues of a Lifetime*: he thought his early efforts at writing, those 1920s novels were 'formless', and went on to assert he 'only learned to [write] properly in the 1930s'.

It is difficult to imagine that Woolrich could have lacked self-awareness to such a degree, but perhaps he was as blissfully unaware of the sometimes tortured style in which he wrote, as he may have been unaware of the way in which the tortured life he lived found expression in that prose.

As Gary Indiana put it, *"the novel Cornell Woolrich never wrote concerns a closeted homosexual alcoholic who lives with his mother for 30 years in a fleapit hotel apartment."*

Although Woolrich did live an unhappy life, he managed to live it in a way which found some reward, even if it were only financial. Despite living in a series of seedy hotels rooms and apartments, Woolrich earned a good living from his prolific writing, as well as royalties from paperback sales, numerous reprints fees, film options, and his novels and stories were adapted again and again for the big screen, and for television, and radio.

When Woolrich's mother died in 1957 he did, however, go into a sharp physical and mental decline. Although he moved from Harlem's decrepit Hotel Marseilles to a more upmarket residence in the Hotel Franconia near Central Park, and later to the Sheraton-Russell on Park Avenue, Woolrich was a virtual recluse. Now in his sixties with his eyesight failing, lonely, psychologically wracked by guilt over his homosexuality, tortured by his alcoholism, self doubt, and a diabetic to boot, Woolrich neglected himself to such a degree that he allowed a foot infection to become gangrenous which resulted, early in 1968, in the amputation of a leg.

After the amputation—and a conversion to Catholicism—Woolrich returned to the Sheraton-Russell, confined to wheelchair. Some of the staff there would take Woolrich down to the lobby so he could look out on the passing traffic, thus making the wizened, wheelchair-bound Woolrich into a kind of darker, self-loathing version of the character played by James Stewart in Hitchcock's *Rear Window.*

With the type of closure that is usually only encountered as a literary device, the Woolrich story turns full circle around the oedipally charged foot motif—the writing career that apparently began with a period of confinement attributed to a foot infection ends with an amputation, and the deep Freudian resonance that amputation induces.

Cornell Woolrich survived his mother by only ten years, dying in September 1968, shortly after the release of Truffaut's *The Bride Wore Black*, which he apparently never saw. The wealth which Woolrich had accrued during his lifetime—almost a million dollars—was used, together with his posthumous royalties, to endow a scholarship fund at Columbia University. Again, in a most unlikely turn, the fund does not provide as one might expect, the Cornell Woolrich Scholarship but, ironically, the Claire Woolrich Memorial Scholarship Fund—named in honour of the mother he simultaneously loved and loathed.

WOOLRICH IN PRINT

Woolrich's novels and short stories are re-issued erratically, and are quickly allowed to go out of print. Novels might be found in second-hand book-shops and at car-boot sales; individual short-stories might be found in various compilations, such as *Ellery Queen's Mystery Magazine* and any paperback collections with Alfred Hitchcock's name on the cover. Over the years, many collections of Woolrich's short stories have been published, although some of his stories have never been reprinted in any collection.

The 1971 *Nightwebs* collection is the most substantial posthumously-published collection of stories to date, reprinting sixteen tales in the American edition (but only twelve in the British), while the 1985 compilation *Darkness at Dawn* offers twelve stories. Each has an introduction by the leading authority on Woolrich, biographer and executor of his estate, Francis M. Nevins Jr. There is no short story collection currently in print.

The major novels—some of the 'black series' and some of the titles originally published under the pseudonym William Irish—were issued as Ballantine paperbacks in the 1980s. Several novels are currently available as Penguin paperbacks on the American market, and are available via the Internet from Amazon.com <http://www.amazon.com>. Amazon now has a British subsidiary, Amazon UK, with prices in sterling instead of dollars, and delivery by first class post to UK addresses within days instead of weeks <http://www.amazon.co.uk>.

Penguin have recently issued a collection which is available in both the US and the UK—*The Cornell Woolrich Omnibus*—which contains two William Irish novels, *Waltz Into Darkness* (1947) and *I Married A Dead Man* (1948) together with five of Woolrich's most celebrated short stories (all of which have been adapted by Hitchcock for film or television): *Rear Window, Post Mortem, Three O'Clock, Change of Murder* and *Momentum*.

REFERENCES

Eddie Duggan, 'Life's a Bitch: paranoia and sexuality in the novels of David Goodis' *Crime Time* 2.1 (1998).

Nino Frank, 'A New Kind of Detective Story', *L'Écrán Français* [August 1946] translated by Connor Hartnett and reprinted in William Luhr, ed., *The Maltese Falcon: John Huston, director* (Rutgers University Press: New Brunswick, NJ, 1995).

Woody Haut, *Pulp Culture* (Serpent's Tail: London, 1995).

Gary Indiana, "Man in the Shadows", *VLS* #74 (May, 1989).

Frank Krutnik, *In A Lonely Street: Film noir, genre, masculinity* (Routledge: London, 1991).

David Madden, ed., *Tough Guy Writers of the Thirties* (Southern Illinois University Press: Carbondale, 1968).

Frances M. Nevins Jr, *Cornell Woolrich: First You Dream, Then You Die* (Mysterious Press: New York, 1988).

William F. Nolan, *The Black Mask Boys: Masters in the Hard-Boiled School of Detective Fiction* (William Morrow & Co.: New York, 1985).

Geoffrey O'Brien, *Hardboiled America: The Lurid Paperbacks and the Masters of Noir* expanded edition (Da Capo Press: New York, 1997).

Ian Ousby, *The Crime and Mystery Book* (Thames & Hudson: London, 1997).

Robert Profirio, *The Dark Age of American Film: A Study of the American 'Film Noir' 1940-1960* doctoral dissertation submitted to Yale University, 1979 (Published in facsimile by University Microfilms International, 1982).

James Sandoe, 'Dagger of the Mind' in, *The Art of the Mystery Story* edited by Howard Haycraft (Simon and Schuster: New York, 1946) 250-263.

Lee Server, *Danger is My Business: An Illustrated History of the Fabulous Pulp Magazines* (Chronicle Books: San Francisco, 1993).

Donald Spoto, *The Art of Alfred Hitchcock* (Fourth Estate: London, 1976).

Julian Symons, *Bloody Murder* further revised and updated second edition (London: Pan, 1992).

Cornell Woolrich, *The Cornell Woolrich Omnibus* (Penguin: London, 1998).

bibliography

CORNELL WOOLRICH NOVELS AND SHORT STORIES ON FILM

CORNELL WOOLRICH BIBLIOGRAPHY
<TITLE>, <DATE>, PUBLISHER>

Children of the Ritz, 1927, Boni & Liveright
Manhattan Love Song, 1932, Godwin
'Face Work' , 1937, *Black Mask*
'The Corpse Next Door', 1937, *Detective Fiction Weekly*
'I Wouldn't Be In Your Shoes', 1938, *Detective Fiction Weekly*
'C-Jag', 1940, *Black Mask*
'All at Once, No Alice', 1940, *Argosy*
The Bride Wore Black, 1940, Simon & Schuster
The Black Curtain, 1941, Simon & Schuster
'He Looked Like Murder', 1941, *Detective Fiction Weekly*
'And So to Death', 1941, *Argosy*
Black Alibi, 1942, Simon & Schuster
Phantom Lady [as William Irish], 1942, Lippincott
'Dormant Account', 1942, *Black Mask*
'It Had To Be Murder', 1942, *Dime Detective*
Black Angel, 1943, Doubleday
Deadline at Dawn [as William Irish], 1944, Lippincott
The Black Path of Fear, 1944, Doubleday
Night Has A Thousand Eyes [as George Hopley], 1945, Farrar & Rhinehart
'The Boy Cried Murder', 1947, *Mystery Book Magazine*
Waltz Into Darkness [as William Irish], 1947, Lippincott
I Married A Dead Man [as William Irish], 1948, Lippincott

FILM ADAPTATIONS OF CORNELL WOOLRICH STORIES
<FILM TITLE>, <DATE>, <DIRECTOR>

Children of the Ritz, 1927, John Francis Dillon
Manhattan Love Song, 1934, Leonard Fields
Convicted, 1938, Leon Barsha
Union City, 1979, Mark Reichert
I Wouldn't be in Your Shoes, 1948, William Nigh
Fall Guy, 1947, Reginald LeBorg
The Return of the Whistler, 1948, D. Ross Lederman
La Mariee Etait en Noir (The Bride Wore Black), 1968, Francois Truffaut
Street of Chance, 1942, Jack Hively
The Guilty, 1947, John Reinhardt
Fear in the Night, 1956, Maxwell Shane
Nightmare, 1947, Maxwell Shane
The Leopard Man, 1943, Jacques Tourneur
Phantom Lady, 1944, Robert Siodmak
The Mark of the Whistler, 1944, William Castle
Rear Window, 1954, Alfred Hitchcock
Black Angel, 1946, Roy William Neill
Deadline at Dawn, 1946, Harold Clurman
The Chase, 1946, Arthur Ripley
Night Has A Thousand Eyes, 1948, John Farrow
The Window, 1949, Ted Tetzlaff
The Boy Cried Murder,1966, George Breakston
Cloak and Dagger, 1984 Richard Franklin
La Siren du Mississippi (Mississippi Mermaid), 1969, Francois Truffaut
No Man of Her Own, 1950, Michael Leisen
Mrs Winterbourne, 1996, Richard Benjamin

the two graves of boris vian
paul duncan

PARIS. SUMMER 1946. Jean d'Halluin wanted to launch his new press, Editions du Scorpion, with a bestseller, so he asked his friend Boris Vian if he knew any good hardboiled American writers he could publish. Vian said that he'd just translated a book by Vernon Sullivan, a black American who couldn't get the book published in America because of the racist overtones. The title was *J'irai Cracher Sur Vos Tombes (I Spit On Your Graves)*.

The story is about Lee Anderson, who enters the small town of Buckton, and takes over the management of the local bookstore. To make sure he gets sales, he must use all the sales literature sent by head office (the most salacious titles get the most publicity), he must skim the new books so that he knows what they are about, he must remember the names of everyone in town, and he must go to church.

Making a good living, Lee decides to find out where the local girls hang out. Being, slightly older, blond, muscled, a good dancer, a singer and guitarist, with an ample supply of liquor, he is immediately welcome in the small group. Lee is driven to seek women and to screw them at every opportunity. They are happy to fall into his arms and to take everything he can give.

But Lee is black, a mulatto (in the phrase of the day) who passes for white, and he's seeking revenge on white people for the death of his brother. With this in mind, he finds two rich sisters, and decides he will seduce each in turn, humiliate them, then kill them.

Paris. November 1946. In France, immediately after the war, everything American was great. The film noirs of the war years which had been banned by the Germans, were grabbing the public's attention. Marcel Duhamel started his Serie Noire line of American hardboiled translations at Gallimard. Only not many people seemed to be that interested in Vernon Sullivan. What the book needed was publicity. It got it, in no uncertain terms.

February 1947. Daniel Parker, head of a right-wing moral action group, who was already fighting the "depraved works" of Henry Miller, decided that J'irai Cracher Sur Vos Tombes was equally depraved. Many people had never heard about this depraved work and decided to find out for themselves just how depraved it was.

April 1947. A salesman in Paris went mad and strangled his girlfriend in a hotel room. Beside her lifeless body, he left a copy of the book. He had circled certain passages describing the death of one of the rich sisters by strangulation. It was a scandal. Everyone wanted to know more about the murder, and about the book which inspired it.

Jean d-Halluin printed lots more copies, outselling French favourites Sartre and Camus in 1947, and had sold half a million by 1950. Boris Vian made a lot of money from it too, and some notoriety, because by 1948 it had been revealed that there was no such person as Vernon Sullivan and that Vian was the real author.

Rather than find and translate an American crime thriller, which would have been too much work, Vian had gone on his traditional family holiday to Vendée on August 5th 1946 and, in ten days, had written the book. The American pseudonym had come from Vian's friend Paul Vernon and the jazz pianist Joe Sullivan. The original title was I Dance On Your Graves, but his wife didn't think it was gritty enough, so 'Dance' was changed to 'Spit.' Although Vian had never been to America, he had learnt a lot about racial prejudice and attitudes from black American jazz musicians he played with—Vian was a well-known jazz trumpeter on the Parisian cabaret circuit.

When Vian was brought to court by Daniel Parker for translating "objectionable foreign literature," Vian collaborated with Milton Rosenthal on an English-language version, published by Vendome Press in April 1948, to 'prove' that Vernon Sullivan was real, and deflect attention away from Vian. It didn't work—the cat was out of the bag and, in 1951, Vian was fined one hundred thousand francs.

Boris Vian wrote four other 'translations' of Vernon Sullivan, which didn't have the same impact as the first novel but still sold a fair amount (Much like James Hadley Chase and No Orchids For Miss Blandish). Ironically, it was as a result of I Spit On Your Graves, that he got offered work to do real translations—his first book being The Big Clock by Kenneth Fearing. After that came other crime author translations, including Peter Cheyney, before diversifying with translations of Nelson Algren, A E van Vogt, August Strindberg and, most appropriately, Richard Wright.

Born March 10 1920 near Paris, and

brought up in comfortable surroundings, at the age of twelve Boris Vian contracted rheumatic fever, which left him with a chronic heart condition. He was told that he could die at any time and would certainly not live past the age of forty. Unsurprisingly, this had a profound effect on the way he lived his life, and the subjects he wrote about. Life and death co-existed in his life and work.

Always conscious of the lack of time he had to do anything, Vian threw himself into everything he did. His daytime job was as an engineer. After hearing Duke Ellington's orchestra in Paris, Vian took up the trumpet despite medical advice against it. When he was twenty-two, he was performing with the Claude Abadie orchestra. He worked to all hours.

Vian was a surrealist, a pataphysician, an absurdist. He became the closest French friend of Duke Ellington, Miles Davis and Charlie Parker, and was friends with the leading authors (Jean-Paul Sartre, Simone de Beauvoir) who got his short stories into the influential magazine Temps Moderne.

He wrote two unpublished novels before he got his break with *I Spit On Your Graves*. And after the crime books and translations, his own more personal work, began to appear. Such was his output, that many of these were not published until after his death.

After the publication of what many regard as his best book *L'ecume Des Jours* (published in Eng-lish as *Froth On The Daydream* and *Mood Indigo*) in 1947, Vian gave up the day job and concentrated in writing full-time. *L'ecume Des Jours* is a tragic love story set in a world where figures of speech assume literal reality, and familiar objects fight back surrealistically. Streets are named after jazz figures Sidney Bechet and Louis Armstrong; Colin, the hero, has a *"100,000 doublezoons"* before dinner, Colin and Chloe drink *"pianococktails"* created by a machine which mixes exotic drinks according to the music of Duke Ellington; Chloe becomes fatally stricken when a water-lily grows on her lung. There being no money for a funeral, the undertaker throws her coffin out the window, where it strikes an innocent child and breaks her leg.

He wrote four hundred songs. Dozens of books. Hundreds of articles. Poems. Plays. Libretti for opera. His pseudonyms include Baron Visi, Adolph Schmurz, and Bison Ravi.

In *Papers on Language and Literature,* Jennifer Walters observed that, *"the central theme of Vian's prose work is the way man moves incessantly and irrevocably toward death. His books are liberally bestrewn with corpses of all kinds, and rare is the story which does not end with the death of one or more of the protagonists."*

Vian knew he was going to die, but was going to do what he wanted until that time came. There were no boundaries for him, and his characters reflect this attitude. In *I Spit*

On You Graves, Lee Anderson has no moral compunctions. He screws women and under-age girls. He gets them drunk so that he can screw them. At one stage, he says of Jean Asquith, one of the rich sisters, 'I never had any luck with her. Always sick, either from having drunk too much or screwed too much.'

So what is the point of the book?

Vian wants to shock us, to create a mini-earthquake in our heads. He doesn't hide what people can be like. If you go into a bar, you are going to see a lot of young men and women getting drunk and eyeing each other up, to see who they want to get laid by. Vian shows this. The characters are not worried about this behaviour—it's natural to them. What is shocking is the way Vian writes about it. The language is terse, direct and concise. He doesn't pull punches.

In 1959, a film version of *I Spit On Your Graves* was made, which Vian did not want to be associated with. Watching a preview, as the opening frames flickered on the screen, he commented, *"These guys are supposed to be American? My ass!"* and his heart stopped. He was only thirty-nine. And with him, died Vernon Sullivan.

It is only now, more than fifty years after its first publication, do we get to read *I Spit On Your Graves*. For me, it was a revelation. Perhaps it will be for you as well.

I Spit On Your Graves *by Boris Vian, Tam Tam Books, $17.00, ISBN 0-9662346-0-X*

If you can't find this book, contact the publisher, Tosh Berman, either by e-mail (tosh@loop.com), or by post (Tam Tam Books, 2601 Waverly Drive, Los Angeles, CA 90039-2724, USA).

feature

collecting crime
the thrill of the chase
mike ashley

This is the first in what I hope will be a regular series looking at what's interesting, important and collectible in crime, detective and mystery fiction. I don't mean necessarily what's financially valuable – though when that arises I'll certainly cover it – but more particularly what's crucial to a cornerstone library. Important books, notable authors, key magazines, that kind of thing. In future issues I'd love to cover some of the major authors of the past (such as Christie, Chandler, Gardner) and of the present (Walters, Peters, Rankin). I'd like to look at some of the key themes (impossible crimes, historical mysteries, tv spin-offs) and also some of the crucial magazines (*Black Mask*, *Clues*, *The Shadow*) as well as the most important books.

In fact I'd like you to tell me what you want so I can focus in on what's important to you. Let me know c/o the publisher and we'll take it from there.

But for starters I thought it would be fun to get back to our roots, where it all began, and look

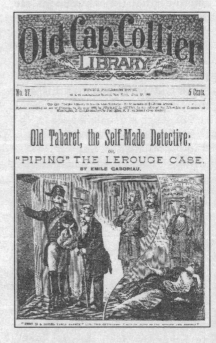

at some of the classic detective stories and novels before Sherlock Holmes set the world alight.

Of course, as with all these things, we can go back to the dawn of time. There are clever little mysteries tucked away in the Bible (or at least in the apocrypha), in the writings of Herodotus and amongst ancient Egyptian papyri, but I don't really want to go back that far. Interesting though these things are, they're a bit remote for me, and I'd rather start at about the same time that literature, as we know it, came into being. If you want to explore some of these really primeval fictions you might want to track down *Classic Crimes in History and Fiction* edited by Peter Haworth (Appleton, 1927). It's been out of print for far too long, but still turns up on the antiquarian circuit. Some of these fossil-tales were also included in *Great Short Stories of Detection, Mystery and Horror* edited by Dorothy L. Sayers (Gollancz, 1928) which is usually easier to find. If these stories prove one thing, they show that solving crimes and mysteries, and the fascination with solving puzzles, has been around as long as civilisation.

Needless to say the French started it all. They started most things literary. Okay, so you can find some detection in Chaucer's *Canterbury Tales* and murder and mystery galore in the plays of Shakespeare and his cohorts, but no real deduction, no applying the mind to solve a mystery. For that you have to turn to François-Marie Arouet (1694-1778), better known as Voltaire. In *Zadig* (1748) he created a philosopher who is a little too clever for his own good. He's so good at describing some lost animals that he's arrested as being the thief and is charged with being a sorcerer. He decides it is *"very dangerous to be over-wise"* and gives up detection. A great shame. Zadig was so nearly the first literary detective.

The fact that uncovering the truth is more trouble than it's worth was also the theme of William Godwin's *Things as They Are; or, The Adventures of Caleb Williams* (Crosby, 1794), better known simply as *Caleb Williams*. It isn't a detective novel, but it is a book about a crime and how its real perpetrator is unmasked. It's Williams who does the investigating only to discover that his master, the honorable and noble Ferdinando Falkland had murdered a local bully. Two innocents were convicted of the crime and hanged. When Falkland realises that Williams knows the truth he has him banished and pursued until he ends up in prison. Although right sort of triumphs in the end, Williams only feels guilty for having ruined his master. At one point Williams confesses, *"My offence had merely been a mistaken thirst of knowledge."* Mistaken or not, it is that thirst of knowledge that has been behind all good detective fiction.

William Godwin (1756-1836) is gradually being forgotten today and is really remembered more for his famous daughter, Mary Shelley, the author of *Frankenstein*. But he was notorious in his day as a political dissenter and intellectual revolutionary, and in certain ways was rather like the non-conformist Sherlock Holmes. The first edition of *Caleb Williams* was almost suppressed because it was issued at the time when government was in fear of revolution in England (following the French Revolution) and any book that was seen as contributing to unrest by challenging the nobility was tantamount to treason. Godwin ended up completely rewriting the book for its second edition in 1796. Needless to say, today both editions are much collected, though not necessarily by the detective devotee. But you'll be lucky to get either edition in good condition for much under £1,000.

William Leggett (1801-1839) is not much known today. A poet and editor, Leggett grew up in the American outback on the prairies in Illinois (before it became a State) and later spent several years in the navy. He wrote up his experiences in *Tales and Sketches by a Country Schoolmaster* (Harper, 1829) and tucked away amongst these memories is a story called *The Rifle*. It had been published earlier in a Christmas giftbook *The Atlantic Souvenir* (Carey, Lea & Carey, 1827) if you want the true first appearance. This little item is really a romance, but it tells of a prairie-man, Jim Buckhorn, who uses his skills and knowledge of rifles to break down another man's alibi and prove the innocence of a young doctor, convicted of murder. It's an intriguing story and a rare early example of logical deduction. It isn't often reprinted, though you'll find it in *The Delights of Deduction* edited by Jacques Barzun (Criterion, 1961). The original *Tales and Sketches*, with its experiences of pioneer life, is very highly collectible today and I've seen copies on offer for $1500 (about £1000).

In the same year that Leggett's book appeared (1829) Robert Peel established London's Metropolitan Police Force. England was a bit late in this respect, since the Bow Street Runners, set up by Henry Fielding in 1749, weren't detectives in the formal sense. France had already had an established police force for some years. Within it they established a special *Brigade de la Sûréte*, which was a bunch of ex-criminals now employed to track down other criminals and spy on the underworld. Head of this unit was François Vidocq (1775-1857), himself a poacher turned gamekeeper, and his story about his life and the establishment of the Brigade was told in *Mémoires de Vidocq* (Tenon, 4 vols, 1828-29). This book, which no doubt embellished the truth with vigorous literary licence was a huge influence on crime fiction over the next fifty years. It was translated into English almost before the ink was dry. An industry erupted, in the English penny dreadfuls, the French sensational literature and the American story papers, of re-telling stories (mostly fabricated) from police sources. Vidocq came to a dubious end when he tried to be both poacher and gamekeeper at the same time. He was dismissed from the force and died in poverty. Honoré de Balzac transformed Vidocq into his own master-thief Vautrin who became head of police in his long-running *Comédie Humaine* during the 1830s.

All of these scattered seeds show that there was much public interest in the activity of police detectives as well as in deductive work in solving crime. It was down to Edgar Allan Poe to bring them all together in *The Murders in the Rue Morgue* (*Graham's Magazine*, April 1841), which introduced his amateur detective Auguste Dupin. The route to this story explains, perhaps, why Poe set his story in Paris rather than in New York. There have been various theories as to Poe's source for Dupin. A friend of Poe's claimed that he had based his detective on Auguste Duponte, a man with impressive powers of reasoning who sometimes helped the French police, whilst the researches of Michael Harrison claimed it was a French nobleman, Charles Dupin, a Baron of the French Empire. In this ground-breaking story, which is also a locked-room mystery, the French police are baffled but by using his powers of deduction, Dupin resolves the remarkable crime.

Poe loved the idea of solving things by deduction. At the time of writing his first Dupin story he had already displayed his own remarkable powers by predicting the ending of Charles Dickens's *Barnaby Rudge* after reading just the first two weekly episodes published in February 1841. Poe returned to what he called his *"tales of ratiocination"* with two more Dupin stories, *The Mystery of Marie Rogêt* (*Snowden's Ladies' Companion*, November/December 1842-February 1843) and *The Purloined Letter* (*The Gift*, 1845 – actually issued December 1844), a fourth detective story, the much overlooked *Thou Art the Man* (*Godey's Lady's Book*, November 1844) and the excellent treasure hunt story, complete with cryptogram, *The Gold Bug* (*The Dollar Newspaper*, 21-28 June 1843). In these five stories Poe covered just about every aspect of the detective art that there is, setting the groundwork for all stories to follow.

They are, of course, easily available in any standard collection of Poe's stories today and in case you think stories over 150 years old will now read archaic, just give them a try, especially *The Purloined Letter*, which remains a masterpiece of its art. Of course the real collector will want original editions. The first book publication of *The Murders in the Rue Morgue* was in one of the most sought after of all Poe volumes, *The Prose Romances of Edgar A. Poe, No.1* (there never was a number 2). It's a small paperbound booklet containing just that story and *The Man That Was Used Up* and was published in Philadelphia by William Graham in the autumn of 1843. Only ten copies are believed to remain and its price in auction is likely to be astronomical. It was valued at $25,000 in 1951 – it would be in the hundreds of thousands today. Alternatively you could try and find the first edition of Poe's *Tales* published by Wiley & Putnam in New York in 1845. This was another paperbound book so copies of the first edition are extremely rare, fetching anything between £12,000 and £15,000. There were later printings with all kind of variant bindings and you can get some good bargains. There's a copy of the clothbound British edition of *Tales*, issued from Wiley & Putnam's London offices in 1845, on the Internet as I write selling for just £1200 – a real bargain – I'd've thought it was worth three times that!

One little known fact is that Poe's *The Purloined Letter* may have appeared in Britain a few days earlier than its American appearance in *Chambers's Edinburgh Journal* for 30 November 1844. It was in this popular weekly magazine that a long forgotten British writer called William Russell began writing a series of stories under the alias 'Waters', purporting to be first-person accounts of a London detective. These first made it into bookform in America as *The Recollections of a Policeman* (Cornish, Lamport, 1852) and later in Britain as *Recollections of a Detective Police-Officer* (J. & C. Brown, 1856). These were immensely popular and highly influential, especially in America, where the image of the detective, especially the private detective, was being further enhanced by the media hype around the first private detective agency established by Allan Pinkerton (1819-1884) – ironically from Scotland – in 1850. Pinkerton became high-profile for his work as a body-guard for the President-elect Abraham Lincoln and was involved in the Secret Service for the North during the American Civil War. Although most of his work involved strikes and labour disputes he delighted in spreading quasi-factual accounts of his exploits and this added a spell of romance over the world of the detective.

The scene now shifts to England and Charles Dickens. Dickens had long been fascinated with the police and had written about them in essays and fictional sketches in his paper *Household Words* during the 1840s. In the intensely interwoven novel *Bleak House* (Bradbury & Evans, 1853), Dickens introduced the first significant police detective in fiction, Inspector Bucket, who helps untangle the mystery. Bucket is a genuine detective who has tremendous experience, knows his territory, understands human nature and observes and considers. And what's more, the criminals know him. There's a history there, not just a character painted onto the page. Bucket (I presume he was not "*Bouquet*") knew his job and did it well. It moved the police detective ahead by a considerable margin. *Bleak House* has always been one of my favourite of Dickens's novels, and last year was brilliantly adapted as a radio play. The book's easy enough to find in modern printings, but the original is increasing in value and will cost you around £300. Better still if you can find the original bound volume of monthly instalments, which contained more illustrations by Phiz, that's worth upwards of £2,000, and I've seen a very fine set complete with original adverts going for $4,800 (about £3,000).

A few years after *Bleak House* Dickens wrote a clever mystery short story, *Hunted Down*. It was specially commissioned by the American story-paper *The New York Ledger*, run by Robert Bonner, who paid Dickens handsomely in advance. It was serialised in three weekly parts from 20 August to 3 September 1859. The story centres upon a girl whose life is insured and then she mysteriously dies. One of the employees of the insurance company, Mr Meltham, looks into her death and tracks down the real criminal. It's a *bona fide* detective story, yet surprisingly little known. If you want to read all of Dickens's excursions into the mysterious then seek out *Hunted Down: The Detective Stories of Charles Dickens*, edited by Peter Haining (Peter Owen, 1996).

Dickens's friend and erstwhile collaborator, Wilkie Collins, also delighted in the detective story. Throughout the 1850s he had written a number of mystery stories, and although they contained no detection, they established a foreboding atmosphere that would develop into the notorious 'sensation' novel of the 1860s. Collins's triumph in this respect was *The Woman in White* (Sampson, Low, 1860). In 1858 Collins had written *Who is the Thief?* (*Atlantic Monthly*, April 1858), which was later incorporated into his novel *The Queen of Hearts* (Hurst & Blackett, 1859) as the episode *The Biter Bit*. It's a fairly light-hearted story telling, by a series of extracts from police memoranda, how the police eventually fathomed out who was the ne'er-do-well. It was another ten years before Collins would produce his masterpiece of detective literature, *The Moonstone* (Tinsley, 1868). It introduces us to Sergeant Cuff who is brought in to find a stolen sacred Indian diamond. Like Dupin and Bucket before him, Cuff is solid, reliable and thorough and though he solves the case, he ensures that the diamond is restored to its rightful home. Cuff is a man of morals. Copies of a first edition of *The Moonstone* are surprisingly easy to find, though not often in immaculate condition since it was much loved by the circulating libraries of the time. If you're lucky you'll get one for about £200.

By this time the detective was popping up all over the place. Mary E. Braddon, the madonna of the yellowback sensation novels had included a detective in her classic melodrama of murder and bigamy, *Lady Audley's Secret* (Tinsley, 1862), one of the most sought after of all Victorian novels. Copies of the first edition just never seem to surface these days, and if one did it would likely to be around £3000 or more. The all-but-unknown William S. Hayward produced, anonymously, *The Experiences of a Lady Detective* (Clarke, 1861) which introduced the first policewoman. It was so popular it spawned a sequel *Revelations of a Lady Detective* (Vickers, 1864). These books are frighteningly rare.

I have not seen them in any recent catalogue or auction and it is possible that all copies of the 1861 edition have long crumbled and vanished. Thomas Bailey Aldrich incorporated a detective short story in his novel *Out of His Head* (Carleton, 1862). His detective is eccentric to the extreme and the story is another early example of a locked-room mystery.

But without doubt the next most important author to enter the plot was the Frenchman Émile Gaboriau (1832-1873). Far too little known today, Gaboriau is remembered in France as the 'father of the *roman policier*' and indeed many believe he can lay claim to having invented the modern detective novel. Directly in the tradition of Vidocq, but further influenced by Poe and probably Eugene Sue (whose *The Mysteries of Paris* had been one of the sensations of 1843), Gaboriau created the police detective Monsieur Lecoq. He appeared in not one but five novels. In the first, *L'Affaire Lerouge* (Dentu, 1866) he takes rather a back seat to the consulting detective Father Tabaret, whose methods Lecoq adopts, but in the later novels he takes centre stage. In fact you can see the character evolve from book to book – *Crime d'Orcival* (Dentu, 1867), *Le Dossier no.113* (Dentu, 1867), *Les Escalves de Paris* (Dentu, 1868) and possibly the best *Monsieur Lecoq* (Dentu, 1869). These books are less easy to find today. The first of them first appeared in an English translation in America as *The Widow Lerouge* (Osgood, 1873)

and that edition fetches well over £100 today. They have all been reprinted over the years but only *Monsieur Lecoq* is currently easy to find in a cheap edition from Dover Books (1975), with an excellent introduction, as one would expect, from E.F. Bleiler.

Bleiler speculates that it was Gaboriau's books, which were rapidly reprinted in dime novel editions in America, that popularised the detective novel form and stimulated the sudden expansion of detective literature across the States. But another factor that contributed to this blossoming of a genre was the success of the dime novel character Old Sleuth. He first appeared in *Old Sleuth, the Detective; or the Bay Ridge Mystery* published in George Munro's *Fireside Companion* in 1872. The Old Sleuth was not a detective in the tradition of Dupin or Lecoq though, like Lecoq (and Holmes after him) he liked to operate in disguise, dressed as a countryman. He seldom solved a crime by deduction – in fact clues had to hit him on the head before he noticed them. Once alerted he preferred fisticuffs to logic and most of his novels usually end with a good scrap. The Old Sleuth stories are well past their sell-by date, despite the part they played in the popularisation of the detective novel, but in their day they were immensely popular and within a few years had more than tripled the circulation of the *Fireside Companion*. It was helped by the fact that the first story had been credited to Tony Pastor who was a theatre manager and popular song writer and who helped create vaudeville. Pastor had no hand in the writing of the stories, but he was a popular character and his name attracted readers. The real author was Harlan P. Halsey (1839-1898) though others soon got in on the act, with stories featuring Old Sleuth and his assistant Badger popping up in several rival publications, including those from George's brother Norman Munro. In the end Halsey had to take recourse to the courts in order to establish his ownership of the character and the right of the original publisher to have sole publication rights. The name Old Sleuth was so popular that it was later adopted as a pseudonym in its own right for scores of dime novel detective stories. Needless to say success bred imitation. In 1877, Norman Munro, the publisher who had first tried to steal Old Sleuth, created his own character, Old Cap Collier for the *Family Story Paper*. It was not quite as successful but still survived for many years.

It was at this same time that Allan Pinkerton began issuing his semi-factual memoirs starting with *The Expressman and the Detective* (Keen, 1874), followed by a dozen or more books over the next ten years, all sensationalising the work of the detective. When Dr Watson observed, in *A Study in Scarlet*, that Sherlock Holmes was well versed in cheap and sensational literature, it was just this kind of material that he meant.

Even more successful, and fated to eclipse his rivals, was Nick Carter. Today the name conjures up the cherubic face of one of the Backstreet Boys, but a hundred years ago Nick Carter was the most popular detective before Sherlock Holmes. He first appeared in the serial *The Old Detective's Pupil; or, The Mysterious Crime of Madison Square* (*New York Weekly*, 18 September to 11 December 1886). The author was the prolific John R. Coryell (1848-1924). Carter would become the template for many later pulp-magazine heroes. He was fit with a finely tuned muscular body, clean living, a master of disguise and had a fund of arcane knowledge. His crime detection begins when his father is murdered and thereafter Carter leads a crusade against crime. Although he has brains he doesn't often use them preferring to battle his way from one scene to the next, or by coming up with some bizarre scheme with his cohort of companions. Although Coryell created the character he only wrote two further novels and then handed the reins over to Frederic Van Dey (1861-1922) who wrote over a thousand adventures. Many of these dime novels are still quite easy to find – at least in the United States — although not in pristine condition. They had their British editions, which are becoming harder to find but can still be picked up for around £10-£15 a copy.

While the dime novel was thrilling thousands, the world of 'Literature' was also exploring the detective novel. Anna Katherine Green

(1846-1935) was the daughter of a leading local attorney in Brooklyn, New York, and his experiences gave her material for what became the first genuine detective novel by a woman writer, *The Leavenworth Case* (Putnam, 1878). I say 'genuine' because Meta Fuller (1831-1886) who wrote dime novels under the alias Seeley Regester had written *The Dead Letter* (Beadle, 1867) which introduces several detectives. However, although the crime is solved by normal means the fact that the plot involves clairvoyance somewhat muddies the waters. *The Leavenworth Case* introduces us to New York police detective Ebenezer Gryce who would feature in ten further novels plus a story collection. Gryce is very matter of fact, friendly and, unlike Nick Carter, not especially fit – in fact he's more like an elderly Frank Cannon. He has no airs or graces and doesn't like pomposity or mixing with the upper echelons of society, which makes some of his investigations difficult. The Gryce stories have dated a little, more in the style of story-telling than in their plots, but they are probably the most important books between Gaboriau's and Sherlock Holmes. The first edition of *The Leavenworth Case* is a much-prized collector's item fetching prices of around £1500, but later printings can be found very easily and there was a good edition from Dover Books in 1981. Green wrote many other detective novels – over twenty – plus scores of short stories. Some of these stories feature Violet Strange, who is from the New York smart set but who secretly becomes a private detective. Some of these stories were later collected as *The Golden Slipper* (Putnam, 1915), but that's beyond our time period.

We're left with just one other major detective novel before Conan Doyle set Holmes and Watson off looking for rooms in *A Study in Scarlet* (*Beeton's Christmas Annual* for 1887). And it's a big one – the most popular detective novel of the century, outselling even Sherlock Holmes — *The Mystery of a Hansom Cab* (Hume, 1886). It was the work of Fergus Hume (1850-1932) who, though born in England, had emigrated with his family back to New Zealand when a child where he later became a barrister. He settled in Melbourne, Australia in 1885. Scouting round for reading matter he was told by a local bookseller that the detective novels of Gaboriau were much in vogue. Upon reading them Hume was fired to produce his own novel and, when no one would publish it, he published *The Mystery of a Hansom Cab* himself. It sold moderately well and attracted interest in England. All rights to the book were bought by an English publisher (which subsequently called itself The Hansom Cab Company) for just £50 and went on to be one of the century's best selling books, selling in the hundreds of thousands. Hume never got another penny out of it, and remained bitter all his life, churning out over a hundred books in the hope of recapturing that magic formula. The story tells of the discovery of a dead body in a hansom cab in Melbourne and of the dogged work by private detective Gorby to discover its identity and the murderer. Things get complicated when another detective, Kilsip, proves that the man charged with the murder is innocent and the whole case is thrown open again. Copies of the English edition are not that difficult to find in one of the many subsequent printings and editions, but the real prize is that privately printed Melbourne edition. Only four copies are known to survive. Find another one and you'll own a fortune.

Surprisingly, unless you're interested in first editions and acquiring all of the above, most of the books I've mentioned can be found in comparatively easy-to-find editions – indeed, quite a few are still in print – and for a moderate outlay you can follow through yourself the forebears of the detective novel.

Considering these forebears it's not surprising that the first appearance of Sherlock Holmes in *A Study in Scarlet* did not cause a huge stir. The book is solidly in the tradition of Poe, Gaboriau and even the dime novels with its episodes in the West. If Doyle had never written another the book it would have remained an interesting curiosity in the annals of an emerging genre. But then came George Newnes and *The Strand Magazine* and a whole new chapter in publishing history and detective fiction began.

And I'll save that for another time. Next issue let's change the scene entirely and consider the prolific Ellery Queen.

Mike Ashley has written and/or compiled nearly 60 books covering a wide range of subjects from science fiction and fantasy to mystery and horror and to ancient history. He has a keen interest in the history and development of genre fiction, particularly in magazines, and has a collection of over 15,000 books and magazines. Amongst his mystery anthologies are The Mammoth Book of Historical Whodunnits, The Mammoth Book of Historical Detectives, Shakespearean Whodunnits, Shakespearean Detectives, Classical Whodunnits, The Mammoth Book of New Sherlock Holmes Adventures *and* Royal Whodunnits—*and he is currently compiling* The Mammoth Book of Impossible Crimes. *He is also working on a biography of Algernon Blackwood.*

a knight to remember
joel meadows

David Mack's Daredevil - it'll ship someday...

NOW THAT KEVIN SMITH'S sporadically published eight issue run on Daredevil has ended, David Mack, of Kabuki fame, has taken over for six issues. It's another interesting choice of creator that will no doubt cement Marvel Knights' reputation as the branch of the Marvel line willing to take chances. Mack was actually contacted by Marvel at the very beginning of the preparations for the imprint:

"When I first heard of what was to become the Marvel Knights, it was long before Daredevil was even mentioned", Mack explains to me from his studio in the centre of America. *" I had just started the new run of Kabuki at Image and Joe Quesada gave me a call to let me know that he was going to be taking over some of the titles at Marvel and he asked me whether there was any character I would be interested in. I could pick a character, get it cleared and write and draw the title. At the time, I knew that it wouldn't be responsible for me to write and draw two books at once. Having said that, it was the dream phone call, to have someone call you up and give you the chance to work on your ideal character. So I told them that I would be interested in doing some covers and that was the extent of the call. Then Joe called back about a week later,*

told me that Kevin Smith would be writing the first run and asked if I would continue it from there, so I agreed. Writing is something that I can do a lot quicker than creating an entire story. So it didn't create a conflict timewise with Kabuki, I was interested in working with Quesada and Palmiotti and I have been a fan of Daredevil since I was young."

Mack is painting the covers over the artwork of Quesada and Palmiotti. Although their styles are very different, he feels that they have merged very smoothly:

"I think that it's blended quite well. Whenever I write for another artist, I always include layouts, which is just my way of communicating what I want on the page to the artist. So Joe took my stick figure layouts and he turned them into these fantastic drawings. But it still has elements of my visual sensibilities too, so to give him the blueprint and then to finalise it made for a very good and seamless blend of what was best from both of us."

The atmosphere of the story is quite different to Kevin Smith's 8 parter and it is the more realistic aspects of the character that appeal to Mack:

"There are threads of Kevin's story that I continue and one that I even resolve but my take on the character and my approach to it is probably quite different from the way that he does it."

It is this down to earth tone that marks it out from the Kevin Smith material:

"The thing that has always appealed to me about Daredevil is that he operates in this realm of Marvel comics that is completely realistic. It works best when he's in Hell's Kitchen and he should be the most different of all the superhero characters. I don't think that I could write a story with Daredevil and Silver Surfer whereas Kevin handled the team up between Daredevil and Doctor Strange very well. Mine definitely brings him back to an urban setting. I know Daredevil mainly from the Frank Miller comics. In fact The Kingpin is a very major player in my story."

Mack felt invigorated by the challenge set by Quesada, who pointed out that Daredevil doesn't really have a rogue's gallery of his own:

"I wanted to bring a couple of new people into the mix who were solely related to Daredevil. I thought that a nice way to segue the introduction of these people was via the Kingpin, who was fairly well-known in Daredevil."

Mack also got a lot of mileage from stripping the characters down to their basics:

"Instead of trying to be grandiose, I really tried to boil the characters down. What really appealed to me about Daredevil, and it can be applied to other characters as well, is that he has taken what is considered a disadvantage and turned it to his advantage. If you have a skewed view, a different way of doing things, you're able to make that take you to a new level. That difference should transcend you rather than condemn you. For me, that's really what one of the major essences of the Daredevil character is about."

Mack, coming from working for Image, seems glad to be working for a company like Marvel and is content to explain the reasons why:

"One of the attractions of doing a story for Marvel Comics is that I'm attracting younger readers than I get on Kabuki and I want to write something that's inspiring, that's entertaining but also educational. You want your hero to be inspirational and you want him to show how you can pull yourself up by your bootstraps. As well as Daredevil, I took a close look at The Kingpin as well. Obviously, although he's a criminal, he had to work to reach his current position. There's never been a definitive Kingpin origin story and while I'm not claiming that mine is exactly that, by default it is because it delves into his past, his childhood and his rise to power."

Moving into specifics, David Mack keeps some aspects of the plot hazy but there are some parts that he's comfortable discussing with us:

"After the Kevin Smith story, in which Foggy has to face consequences, here we see the follow up to those consequences. Foggy and Matt decide to rebuild their law practice. It boils down their friendship and questions what their ideas of law are and what they intend to do with those ideas. Foggy is trying to redeem himself in this story and now you see him trying to make his own way and his mark. It's in a similar position to where things where after the Born Again story but things reverted to normal then whereas that isn't the case here."

Mack has brought in some new figures and one character plays a pivotal role here:

"It really boils down to three major players: Daredevil, The Kingpin and another character called Echo. She is interesting because she develops affiliations with both The Kingpin and Daredevil. Echo's inclusion stems from a conversation that I had with Joe, who said 'Daredevil is all about women and girls'. The two characters are linked through this girl. The affiliation that the Kingpin has is not a romantic one but a familial connection, which make the dynamics very intriguing. The reason why Daredevil can relate to Echo is simple. She also has what some people might call a handicap. Whereas he is cut off from the world as a blind man, she is deaf. So they both experience a sense of isolation. Before Daredevil has spent time

with the Black Widow and they both like to jump around on rooftops but she still can't understand his world completely."

So Mack uses the strengths and weaknesses of the two characters to create an interesting situation:

"While Daredevil can't see, his strength is his hearing, while Echo can't hear but her big trump card is her sight. So what one of the characters has as their strength, the other character has that as their weakness. While this woman isn't a superhero, she does possess certain talents and there is a scene where they're pitted against each other. This is interesting because one can win if they develop the environment that suits their strong point, the other can triumph if the roles are reversed."

Mack also sees the fact that he has to utilise a character who he hasn't created, while reflecting their past and adding something new at the same time as something positive:

"I have written for other people but the challenge here is that I have never written a character that I have not created, so I have had to write a character where you need to respect everything that's been written by other creators whilst incorporating new things. If you don't put something new into the mix then there's no point in doing it."

The fact that the Kevin Smith run came out late meant that Mack had more time to refine his work and this was appreciated by him:

"I'm very happy about the way that things turned out. Although I turned in the complete script at the beginning of May, it meant that I had time to fix things if necessary and fine tune the language."

Finally, Mack has been very happy with the setup on Daredevil and the work that he's done with Quesada and Palmiotti. He feels that it's a suitable introduction to his work for all of the people who've never seen it before:

"When I write and draw comics, I'm going to do something that not so much pushes the envelope of the medium because I don't really acknowledge any envelope but I do try to write and draw in an unconventional way. Working with Quesada has provided a fantastic vehicle to write the way that I do but for him to deliver it in a way that's still accessible to people. It makes the writing far more accessible than if they were to first experience it jumping straight from Iron Man to Kabuki."

Daredevil #9 came out at the end of September. *[Err... no it didn't—Ed]*

...and now, more bloody Batman...

BATMAN ANIMATED BY PAUL DINI AND CHIP KIDD, TITAN BOOKS, A SNIP AT £19.99

As the Batman Animated TV shows are the best adventure based animation to ever be made, it logically follows, as night follows day, that this should be the best book about an animated show to be made, right? *[Only to you, mate, only to you—Ed]* Congratulations! Purchase this book and you will be assaulted with images of rare ferocity and beauty *[What are you on?]* as well as the complete origin story of the most wonderful televisual entertainment! *[We are still talking Batman here, right? Pointy ears, cape, Boy Wonder?—Ed]*.

For long-time fans of the Dark Knight *[Now that's a spelling mistake right there, Mann—Ed]* this is a treat of massive proportions *[Yes, we know all about your 'proportions']*. From the original series all the way up to *Gotham Knights* and *Batman Beyond* this book chronicles the life and animated times of the best costumed crimefighter of all time, not to mention the secret origin of Harley

Grimmer than thou...

Quinn, Hubba, Hubba *[This is a cartoon girl, right?—Ed]*

If you love the Darknight Detective this is for you - tell 'em Peter Mann sent you! *[At the lunatic asylum is that?—Ed]*
Peter Mann

...slimmer than thou...

column

the view from murder one
maxim jakubowski

MAYBE IT'S THE advent of spring, and as men's minds and wandering eyes turn to thoughts of the fairer sex, women on the other hand appear to be turning to crime in a big way. And we males of the species all know to our detriment to what passionately criminal extent women can wreak their obligatory fury! Pride of place in this month's batch of murderous female crime writers is taken by Vicki Hendricks' Iguana Love (Serpent's Tail £8.99), a red-hot tale of Miami vice with more lurid twists than a Florida hurricane. In her first white trash classic novel Miami Purity, Hendricks had dirtied forever our image of the dry-cleaning business; this time around, she applies a sexual twist to her local scuba diving and body building scene with a ferocious, predatory vengeance. With Ramo-

na Romano, her thrill-seeking redhead at the helm, on the prowl for Enzo, the wrong man if ever a man was wrong, Hendricks shatters all conceits of political correctness and presents us with one of the most memorable female noir characters on the make. Intense, sweaty and wonderfully lurid, this is a rollercoaster ride through sin, drugs and sexual action like you've never seen or dreamed of before. And don't even ask what the best use is for a dead iguana, or all about some of the more interesting side effects of steroids on the female anatomy! A guilty pleasure to savour slowly.

Less outrageous but as fast-paced and zany is Jen Banbury's *Like A Hole In The Head* (Indigo £6.99), the uproarious tale of an L.A. slacker which begins in a book shop and soon races all the way to

Vegas and back in a plot reminiscent of classic hardboiled tales a la Hammett and Chandler but brought bang up to date by Banbury's modern vernacular and contemporary mores. Modern screwball noir with a light caper touch and funny as hell on wheels. Nanette, the sax-playing heroine of Charlotte Carter's second thriller *Coq Au Vin* (Serpent's Tail £8.99) is another memorable heroine in this perfect sequel to her debut *Rhode Island Red*. The involuntary black sleuth goes to Paris, a perfect setting for this tale of deceit, love, crime and jazz music amongst expatriates. The love affair between jazz, black musicians and Paris is an eternal story; Carter illuminates it with rare intelligence and a gripping vortex of thrills, feeling and wit. An author for the future.

Lily Pascale is a new female British sleuth with much promise and she appears in journalist Scarlett Thomas's second novel *In Your Face* (Hodder & Stoughton £16.99). Moving between Devon and London, she is a sassy character full of contemporary hipness and uncurbable curiosity which, naturally, draws her to mystery and disappearances like a honey to bee. Classic investigation with the right dash of modernity, this one will grow on you. As elaborate an investigation but with an added gloss of marvellous exoticism is Leslie Forbes' BOMBAY ICE (Phoenix House £6.99), a fascinating tale of wrong doings set in India, in the Bollywood world of local movies, eunuchs, alchemy and corruption. One of the best crime debuts of recent years, this is destined to be a future classic. More traditional is Veronica Stallwood's *The Rainbow Sign* (Headline £17.99), a breakthrough novel by the author of the popular Kate Ivory Oxford-set series. Ghosts of the past are ever close to the surface in this dark, tense psychological thriller of disturbed families and secrets, the pieces of which slowly fit together like an intricate jigsaw puzzle full of human frailties and hopes. A deceptive and atmospheric tale of British crime. Deryn Lake's gaudy, historical adventures of 18th century apothecary John Rawlings continue in *Death In The Peerless Pool* (Hodder & Stoughton £16.99), an effervescent tale that brings the past to life in all its treachery, colourful and lustful vistas and a mischievous sense of gusto. Set in Bath, these new adventures see the blind magistrate at his most Sherlockian and charming. Nice one.

The Sabbathday River by Jean Hanff Korelitz (Macmillan £14.99) returns us to American shores, with a gripping blockbuster of a novel from a novelist previously known for legal thrillers. An edgy tale of a small New Hampshire community changed forever by the passage of crime, this is a heartfelt and suspenseful story of an ordinary woman's resilience in the face of adversity and is no doubt going to make a hell of a movie. Read it now.

The police procedural genre in which cop or cops lead the enquiry is one of crime fiction's most endurable forms, and is often exemplified by Ed McBain's famous 87th Precinct series without which addictive TV series like *Hill Street Blues*, *Homicide* or *Nypd Blue* would never have graced our screens. Craig Holden's *Four Corners Of Night* (Macmillan £9.99) brings a new breath of life to familiar grooves and has the hallmark of a modern classic. Terse, crisscrossed by heartbreaking empathy and pain this is the tale of two cops in a Midwestern city whose lives become intimately tangled up in the disappearance of a local teenage girl. How an unspectacular case, which might not actually involve criminal activity at all, conspires to change the lives of the cops, their families and friendship, and resurrects unwanted ghosts of the past, slowly unfolds in unputdownable manner is what the book is about. But there is more: compassion, anguish like cold sweat and some of the best writing in recent American fiction. Unmissable. The other side of the procedural coin is demonstrated by Kathy Reichs' *Death Du Jour* (Heinemann £10), the sequel to the bestselling *Deja Dead* which introduced readers to Montreal forensic anthropologist Temperance Brennan. Compulsively plotted and full of fascinating minutiae a la Patricia Cornwell but a sad reliance on co-incidence and predictable perils of Pauline-like deadly capers for anybody who befriends the main protagonist, this is a disposable read which sadly required a heavier ed-itorial hand. See it rise up the charts and contradict this reviewer, no doubt! Coincidentally also set in Montreal (a new city of crime?), John Farrow's *City Of Ice* (Century £10) is a gripping thriller in which a local policeman has to unravel a case involving terrorist bombs, the local mob, Russian mafia and American spies. A lethal cocktail against a particularly atmospheric background and with a better sense of place than all of Reichs' laboratory-set sleuthing. Disappearing children, this time, in Manchester launch Val McDermid's *A Place Of Execution* (HarperCollins £16.99), a gut-wrenching tale that spans two decades and brings the resonance of Greek tragedies to England. Psychological suspense that probes, prods and disturbs. A terrific achievement. British author Natasha Cooper breaks ground with a new heroine, Barrister Trish Maguire in *Fault Lines* (Simon & Schuster £16.99), and brings a jaundiced attitude to the prevalence of corruption at the heart of local government. Darkly pessimistic and a cautionary tale of the new Labour years and its endemic problems. Equally bleak, and at times devastating, is Carol Anne Davis'*safe As Houses* (Do-Not Press £7.50), her second Edinburgh-set novel about the evils of everyday life. Women are vanishing from the streets and only one man knows the answers. David is a sadist and has a Secret House where his fantasies become reality. Slowly his wife guesses the horrible truth. Strong stuff than could make even Ruth Rendell or Minette Walters shudder. Recommended. For lighter fare, renew your acquaintance with plucky sculptress Sam Jones in Lauren Henderson's *The Strawberry Tattoo* (Hutchinson £9.99), which takes the smart as nails sleuthette to the Manhattan art world and balances sleuthing with quips, boozy sprees and attitude a go go. A series that sparkles brighter with every new instalment. Anthony Frewin's *Scorpian Rising* (No Exit Press £6.99) retreats from the suffocating ambience of his classic *London Blues*, and harks back to the *Get Carter* gritty tradition of British gangster movies. Great entertainment and you could almost picture the likes of Michael Caine or Bob Hoskins as some of the sharp underworld characters.

Another perfect summer read is Don Winslow's *California Fire And Life* (Century £10), a roller coaster ride hanging on the shirt tails of a fire investigator and his grisly discoveries. American high octane crime doesn't come any faster and better than this. And for exotic delights of the past-is-another-country variety, the best whodunits of the season are both Roman: Lindsey Davis' *One Virgin Too Many* (Century £15.99), in which the crafty Ancient Rome sleuth Marcus Didius Falco gets embroiled with disappearing virgins, cults and the hustle and bustle of local politics. Gently tongue in cheek, this is like Raymond Chandler-lite in togas and a hoot to boot. *Rubicon* by Steven Saylor (Robinson £15.99) is a touch grittier in bringing the darker side of Imperial times to light but no less deft in the adventure stakes and another hit for Gordianus the Finder, a pioneer detective with savvy and determination.

A noted author and anthologist, Maxim Jakubowski is also the proprietor of one of the world's leading crime fiction bookshops, Murder One, in London.

poetry

going straight
bill james

I WEAR head-waiter's tails by choice: these orderly, lickspittle years.
Then, mornings, I take breakfast late
and read the *Mail*. **Last night came lordly**
praise and unextravagant
aggrandisement, in cash and hand to hand;
'Oh, thank you, sir.'

Indigo dreams defoliate
my afternoons: those mid-life blooms
of fright and safety-first slide off.
Pub lunchtime lager works the trick,
plus snorts of anything at home;
a man-sized, gorgeous coma until five;
then think of work.

'No other maitre-d takes care
of us as well as you, Jerome.'
'Oh, thank you, sir.' Their folded, unmissed
tens and twenties glide my way.
This crew have mansions which, ten years ago,
I'd raid and strip with tact when they dined out,
no bulky stuff.

I wear head-waiter's tails by choice:
my rectified, lickspittle times.
Tomorrow, sleeping prim till noon
I'll dream-do crimes. Tonight come lofty praise
and unextravagant
aggrandisement: we're stung for tax on tips;
'Oh, thank you, sir.'

fiction

the poker club
ed gorman

Ed Gorman is one of the founding editors of one of the world's premiere crime fiction magazines—Mystery Scene—and has over thirty novels and countless short stories to his credit. He is acknowledged as the leading exponent of 'dark suspense'— the fusion of noir crime fiction with the sense of unease of horror fiction.

The Poker Club is published by CT Publishing in Hardback at £16.99- see the last page of this excerpt for a special offer

I CAN'T remember now who had the first poker game. But somehow over the past five years it became a ritual that we never missed.

We took turns having the game once a week. Beer and bawdy jokes and straight poker. No wild card games. We hate them.

This was summer, and vacation time, and with Jan and the girls gone, I offered to have the game at my place. With nobody there to supervise, the beer could be laced with a little bourbon, and the jokes could be even bawdier. With the wife and the girls in the house, I'm always at least a little intimidated.

The trouble is, of course, as much fun as I have playing cards, I really start missing Jan and the kids after a few days. Some nights I go in and lie on the girls' beds, the clean scent of their hair still on their pillows. And then I think of how much I love them. And then I feel a tenderness so overwhelming it almost scares me. Then the fun I have at the poker games doesn't seem like so much fun at all.

♠

CURTIS AND BILL came together, bearing gifts, which in this case meant the kind of sexy magazines our wives did not want in the house in case the kids might stumble across them. At least that's what they say. I think they sense, and correctly, that the magazines might give their spouses bad ideas about taking the secretary out for a few after-dinner drinks, or stopping by a singles bar some night.

We got the chips and cards set up at the table, we got the first beers open (Bill chasing a shot of bourbon with his beer), and we started passing the dirty magazines around with tenth grade glee. The magazines compensated, I suppose, for the balding head, the bloating belly, the stooping shoulders. Deep in the heart of every hundred year old man is a horny fourteen-year-old boy.

All this took place, by the way, in the attic. The four of us got to know each other when we moved into what city planners called a 'transitional neighbourhood.' There were some grand old houses that needed a lot of work.

The city designated a ten square block area as one it wanted to restore to shiny new lustre. Jan and I chose a crumbling Victorian. You wouldn't recognise it today. And that includes the attic, which I've turned into a very nice den.

"Pisses me off," Bill Doyle said. "He's always late."

And that was true. Neil Solomon *was* always late. Never by that much but always late nonetheless.

"Just relax," I said. "Drink a beer."

"Yeah," Curtis said. "Or choke your chicken."

"Or," I said, "Squeeze your black-heads."

"Right," Curtis said, his handsome black face grinning. "Or pick your nose and eat the boogers the way you usually do when you think we're not looking."

"You assholes," Bill said. And then started laughing. "You are really a pack of idiots, you know that?"

"Look who's talking," Curtis smiled. "The heavyweight boxing champion of Manor Street."

As a doctor, Bill is a gentle, charming and extremely competent man, the bully side completely hidden.

He once saw my daughter through a really frightening spell of rheumatic fever.

"You have to admit," Bill said. "I've been doing a lot better."

"Yes, he has," Curtis said. "He hasn't punched out a nun for at least two weeks."

Bill could be a crazy sonofabitch, but at least he had the ability to laugh at himself. He was laughing now.

"You jerk-off," he said to Curtis.

Curtis gaped down at one of the dirty magazines open on the poker table and said, "You know, jerking off doesn't sound half-bad right now."

"Hey," I said, snapping my fingers. "I know why Neil's late."

"Yeah, so do I," Bill said. "He's at home swimming in that new fucking pool of his." Neil recently got a bonus that made him the first owner of a full-sized pool in our neighbourhood. "Aaron's the one who should have the pool. He was the swimming star in college."

"Neil's got Patrol tonight," I said.

"Hey, that's right," Curtis said. "Patrol."

"I forgot," Bill said. "For once, I shouldn't be bitching about him, should I?"

Patrol is something we all take seriously in this newly restored 'transitional neighbourhood.' Eight months ago, the burglaries started, and they've gotten pretty bad. My house has been burgled once and vandalised twice. Bill and Curtis have had kerb-sitting cars stolen. Neil's wife Becky was surprised in her own kitchen by a burglar.

The absolute worst incident though happened just four short bloody months ago, a man and wife who'd just moved into the neighbourhood, savagely stabbed to death in their own bed. The police caught the guy a few days later trying to cash some traveller's cheques he'd stolen after killing his prey. He was typical of the kind of man who infested the neighbourhood after sundown: a twentyish junkie stoned to the point of psychosis on various street drugs, and not at all averse to murdering people he envied and despised. He also knew a whole hell of a lot about fooling burglar alarms.

After the murders, there was a neighbourhood meeting and that's when we came up with the Patrol, something somebody'd read about being popular back East. People think that a nice middle-sized American city like ours doesn't have major problems. I invite them to walk many of these streets after dark. They'll quickly be disabused of that notion.

Anyway, the Patrol worked this way: each night, two neighbourhood people got in the family van and patrolled the ten-block area that had been restored. If they saw anything suspicious, they used their cellphones and called the police. The Patrol had on strict rule: you were never to take direct action unless somebody's life was at stake.

Always, always use the cellphone and call the police.

Neil had Patrol tonight. He'd be rolling in here any time now. Patrol was divided into shifts and Neil had the early one.

Bill said, "You hear what Don Evans suggested?"

"About guns?" I said.

"Yeah."

"Makes me a little nervous," I said.

"Me too," Curtis said.

For somebody who'd grown up in the inner city, Curtis was a very polished guy. Whenever he joked that he was the token black, Neil countered that he was the token Jew, just as Bill was the token Catholic, and I was the token WASP. Some might see us as friends of convenience, I suppose, but we all really did like each other, something that was demonstrated when Neil had a cancer scare a few years back. The three of us were in his hospital room twice a day, all eight days running.

"Maybe it's time," Bill said. "The burglars and the muggers and the killers have guns, why shouldn't we?"

"That's why we have cops," I said. "They're the ones who carry the guns."

"People start bringing guns on Patrol," Curtis said, "Somebody innocent is going to get shot."

"So some night one of us here is on Patrol and we see a bad guy and he sees us and before the cops get there the bad guy shoots us?" Bill said. "You don't that's going to happen?"

"It *could* happen," Curtis said. "But I just don't think that justifies carrying guns."

The argument was about to continue when the bell rang downstairs.

"Neil's here," Bill said. "Now we can play some serious cards."

"You've already lost thirty dollars," Curtis reminded him. "I'd say that was pretty serious."

"SORRY I'M LATE," Neil Solomon said after he followed me up to the attic and came inside.

"We already drank all the beer," Bill said.

Neil smiled. "That gut you're putting on, Bill, I can believe it."

Bill always seemed to enjoy being put down by Neil, possibly because most people were a bit intimidated by Bill—that angry Irish edge of his—but Neil didn't seem the least bit afraid of him. And that seemed to amuse Bill all to hell.

"I may have a bigger gut," Bill said, "but I also have a bigger dick."

"His modesty is so becoming" Curtis said.

"That isn't what your wife told me," Neil said. "She said that *I* definitely had a bigger dick."

"Our usual elevated level of conversation," Curtis said, smiling at me.

Neil laughed. Neil is the opposite of beefy, blonde Bill. He's tall, slender, dark, nice looking. In college, he'd been a very good miler.

In the old days—up till two years

ago—Neil had been the clown of the group. He had real wit, and wasn't afraid to be a little foolish in making you laugh.

In the old days.

But three years ago, at an office Christmas party his wife couldn't attend because she was feeling ill, Neil was unfaithful. The receptionist. The first and only time he'd ever strayed.

He got home late, very drunk, to find his wife sitting in the dark smoking a cigarette. She had never smoked in her life.

Her name was Becky and she was very slight and pretty in a warm, earnest way. She told him not to turn on the lights.

She hadn't, she said, wanted to spoil his office party, but she had some news, and it was bad news. She'd been having some troubles the last month and had gone to the doctor. He'd examined her and suggested a biopsy. Later today he'd called her with the results. Uterine cancer. Needed to operate right away. Chemo and radiation to follow.

Five months later, Becky was dead. Neil was left with two things; a beautiful daughter named Rachel and more guilt than any human being could reasonably hope to shoulder.

These days, Neil drank a lot. And you could never guess what he was going to do next. One night I found him smashing his fist again and again into the wall of my garage. He knew he'd broken some knuckles. He was determined to break even more, until I stopped him anyway.

Neil sat down. I got him a beer from the tiny fridge I keep up here, cards were dealt, seven-card stud was played.

Sometimes I wonder how many hours I've spent playing poker in my life. Thousands, probably. And I can't even say I enjoy it exactly. I guess it's the camaraderie. I grew up in a middle-class family of younger sisters, and so I suppose over the years my poker buddies became the brothers I never had.

I lost the first two hands. Even in stud, a pair of eights isn't all that worthy, especially when you're up against savvy players like Bill and Neil. They never lose their tempers or sulk but it's obvious that they play with a lot of intensity.

Curtis said, "How'd Patrol go tonight, Neil?"

"No problems," he said, not taking his eyes off the cards I'd just dealt.

"I still say we should carry guns," Bill said.

"Fucking A we should," Neil said.

"Oh, great," Curtis said. "Another beer commercial cowboy."

"What's that supposed to mean?" Bill said.

"It just means that we should leave the guns to the cops," I said.

"You taking Curtis' side in this?" Neil said.

"Yeah, I guess I am."

"Curtis is full of shit," Bill said. Then he looked at Curtis and smiled. "Nothing personal."

"Right" Curtis said, obviously irritated with Bill's tone.

The battle over guns had been going on in the neighbourhood for the past three months. The sides seemed pretty evenly divided. Because of all the TV coverage violence gets, people are more and more developing a siege mentality.

"Lets jut play cards," I said, "And leave the debate bullshit till later."

WE PLAYED CARDS. In half an hour, I dropped fifteen dollars. It got hot in the attic. We have central air, of course, but in midsummer like this, the attic can still get pretty warn.

The first pit stop came just after ten o'clock, and Neil took it. There was a john on the second floor between bedrooms, another john on the first floor.

Neil said, "The good Doctor Gettesfeld had to give me a finger wave this afternoon, gents, so this may take a while."

"You should trade that prostate of yours in for a new one," Bill said.

"Believe me, I'd like to. I mean, I'm getting tired of bending over and having him put his finger up my ass."

"Aaron and Curtis never get tired of it," Bill said slyly. "They love it when I put my finger up there."

"Another witticism," Curtis said. "How does he keep on doing it folks?"

While Neil was gone the three of us started talking about the Patrol again. Should we go armed or not?

We made the same old arguments. The passion was gone. We were just waiting for Neil to come back and we knew it.

Finally, Bill said, "Let me see some of those magazines again."

"You got some identification?" I said.

"I'll show you some identification," Bill said. "It's about a yard long and it's nice and hard."

Curtis said, "Boy, your nose really *is*

long, isn't it?"

We passed the magazines around.

"Man, I love lesbians," Bill said, as he flipped through the pages.

"I *am* a lesbian," Curtis said. "An honorary one, anyway."

I was just as exultant as they were. The older I got, the more real sex became, maybe because it was the only wild passion I had left in me. Walking down a sunny street, I fell in love a hundred times an hour. I always felt guilty about this, of course. I'd never been unfaithful and hoped I never would be. I'd destroyed a relationship in college by stepping out. She found out and never trusted me again. I just couldn't do that to Jan, not ever. There are some things you can never undo, and cheating on your loved one is one of them.

"You mind if I use the john on the first floor?" Curtis said.

"Yeah, it would really piss me off," I said.

That was the overpolite black man chained inside of Curtis. He never quite took the social liberties the rest of us did. Plantation politics were still a part of him, and it was sad to see. "Captain May I" would always be a sad reactive part of him.

I felt like a jerk for making a joke of it.

"Yes, use the first floor john, Curtis. Take a shower if you want."

"No," he said, "just pissing in your sink will be fine."

After Curtis left, Bill said, "I ride his ass sometimes, don't I?"

"You ride everybody's ass."

"I get to him. I can see it in his eyes."

"So go easier on him."

"Yeah, I suppose I should. There's just something I don't quite like about him. Never have." He looked down at the can of beer he had gripped in his fist. "Maybe I'm a racist."

"Well," I said, not quite knowing what to say. "Maybe you *are* a racist."

He sighed. "I'm going to work on being nicer to Curtis. I really am."

"Good idea," I said. "Curtis is a hell of a nice guy."

The first time I heard it, I thought it was some kind of animal noise from outside, a dog or a cat in some kind of discomfort maybe. Bill, who was still staring at his can of beer, didn't even look up.

But the second time I heard the sound, Bill and I both looked up. And then we heard the exploding sound of breaking glass.

"What the hell was that?" Bill said.

"Let's go find out," I said.

Something was bad wrong. I knew that in a clear, clean way that drained away all my beer fuzziness.

That sound, whatever it was, did not belong in this house.

I thought about the Patrol argument we'd been having. Right now a weapon would feel damned good in my hand.

Just as we reached the bottom of the stairs, we saw Neil coming out of the second floor john. "You hear that?" he said, keeping his voice low.

"We sure as hell did," I said.

"Yeah," Bill said, his face ugly with anger and suspicion. "And now we're going to find out what it is."

But in addition to wariness, there was an excitement in Bill's voice, too.

He loved danger. It was like being a

Big 10 lineman all over again.

He was an odd choice to be a medical man, a healer. There was a lot of hatred in him.

WE REACHED the staircase leading to the first floor. Everything was dark.

Bill reached for the light switch but I brushed his hand away.

My place. My turf. I'd do things my way. I put a sshing finger to my lips and then showed my old Louisville slugger. I led the way downstairs, keeping the bat ready at all times.

"You sonofabitch!"

The voice belonged to Curtis.

More smashing glass.

In the shadowy light from the street, Bill and Neil looked scared.

I hefted the bat some more and then started moving fast to the kitchen.

"Any fucker who lays a hand on Curtis," Bill whispered, "I'm personally going to fucking kill."

I almost smiled, remembering our conversation of a while ago. Maybe it took something like this to make him realise that he really did like Curtis.

Just as we passed through the dining room, I heard something heavy hit the kitchen floor. Something human and heavy.

A moan. A groan. Curtis.

"Cocksucker!" Bill screamed and went running hard into the kitchen, his face hard with rage, his fists tight and club-like.

He was at the back door. White. Tall. Blond shoulder-length hair. Filthy tan T-shirt. Greasy jeans. He had grabbed one of Jan's carving knives from the

huge iron rack that sits atop a butcher block island.

The one curious thing about him was the eyes: there was a malevolent iridescence to the blue pupils, angry almost alien intelligence.

Curtis was sprawled face down on the tile floor. His arms were spread wide on either side of him. He didn't seem to be moving. Chunks and fragments of glass were strewn everywhere across the floor. My uninvited guest had smashed two or three of the colourful pitchers we'd bought in Mexico.

By now, Bill was crouching in front of the burglar.

Neil was ransacking the knife drawer, looking for the biggest blades he could find.

He gave Bill a carving knife, and kept the second one for himself.

Now Neil and Bill were both crouched in front of the guy, ready to spring.

"C'mon, motherfucker," Bill said, "make a move. I'd love to open your fucking throat."

Even though I was still near the kitchen door trying to revive Curtis, I could smell the burglar. Think of a city dump on a boiling July afternoon, that foetid sweet-sour odour. That's what he smelled like even clear across the room.

Curtis moaned, then, and I felt a ridiculous surge of joy. I guess I'd half-suspected he might be dead.

I got him propped up against the wall.

His nose was smashed and it was pretty bloody. There was also a gash above his right eye. He kept touching the right rear side of his head.

I put my hand back there and felt through the damp curly hair a good-sized egg.

Our friend the burglar showed an unmistakable appetite for violence.

I looked back over my shoulder to see how Neil and Bill were doing.

They were still in a standoff situation. Every time they came in close, he raised his knife.

Bill swore every few moments. Neil feigned lunges just about as often. Then Neil's left leg would lash out, trying to catch the burglar in the crotch. But the burglar was quick and the burglar was savvy.

The burglar's face was fascinating in a repellent way. No sign of remorse. No sign even of fear. Just of trapped-animal rage.

He was pissed. He wanted to kill us because we'd had the audacity to catch him.

A noise. The back porch. Somebody tripping over something in the darkness.

The burglar's eyes snapped in the direction of the porch and he then uttered his one and only word, "Run!"

The sonofabitch had brought a friend.

That was when I ran over to the knife drawer, quickly grabbing the longest blade I could find.

I was all reaction now. No thinking whatsoever. I felt the tremendous energy that Bill and Neil always showed whenever they were around violence. No time for fear.

I ran to the back door, ran into the narrow shadowy box that was the porch.

I could still smell last year's Winesap apples, a good clean sweet smell. Jan buys a bushel basket or two of them every autumn then keeps them on the back porch until winter comes. During these months, we eat an awful lot of apple pie.

No one there.

I tried to see through the moonsilver shadows of the backyard. Clothesline. Two-story garage. Line of garbage cans. The kids' swing set.

And then he was there. Peeking around the far corner of the garage. The second burglar.

I burst through the back door, racing after him.

The night air was almost suffocating.

I crept along the length of the garage, keeping to the shadows, waving the knife in front of me. The blade gleamed in the moonlight. I imagined bright red blood along its edge, glistening.

Only now did I feel even a modicum of fear.

What if he had a gun, the second burglar? What if he looked just as crazy as his pal inside? What if he was waiting for me on the other side of the garage, ready to jump me and kill me?

Jan would say I was trying to be as macho as my brother Bob. He was now a detective in St. Louis. He still had ample opportunity to bust heads, and equally ample opportunity to regale us with his war stories at two or three family gatherings a year.

A noise.

I froze in my crouch. I noticed that gleaming edge of the blade was now shaking slightly.

I could picture the bastard only a

few feet away, just on the other side of the garage. Waiting for me.

I almost turned and went back. Almost.

But then I thought of the people who'd been killed and mugged in our little neighbourhood over the past few years.

This bastard and his friends were making a safe, normal life impossible for us and our families.

I got good and pissed and forgot all about going back to the house.

A noise. Again.

The sound of a shoe on gravel.

Wherever he was, he wasn't far away.

I turned back just a moment to the line of four silver garbage cans.

In great vast pantomime, the kind of overplayed movements you see in silent movies, I lifted the lid off one of the cans then carried it back up to the edge of the garage.

I waited, listened.

Despite the seventy-eight degree temperature, I was shivering, sweat beading like ice cubes on my face and arms and back.

I heard bird, dog, train, car. But I did not hear him, even though I suspected he was only a few feet away.

I steadied myself, readied myself.

I would throw the lid into the alley, he would pounce on it and I would jump on him.

Once again I thought of how Jan would react if she knew what I was going to do. She would be scared, and even a little embarrassed, I imagined. My husband, the fourteen-year-old.

I threw the lid the way I would have tossed a Frisbee.

It landed in the middle of the alley, on a mound of tufted weeds and gravel.

Silence, a deep and unnerving silence.

Shadows, shifting shadows that seemed to move and merge and shift again.

I was six-years-old and in my bed and convinced that some monster was in the closet lurking, waiting.

When I finally went to sleep, the monster would come out and soon I would be nothing more than blood dripping from his long and razor-sharp teeth.

Silence.

My trick hadn't worked. He hadn't leapt out in plain sight.

Where was he? What was he waiting for?

I moved two steps closer to the front of the garage. Started to peek around.

And that was when I heard it.

The sound of shoe soles scuffling against the tiles on the garage roof.

By the time I turned around, by the time I looked up, it was too late.

He was already leaping off the roof and landing on me feet first.

I fell to the ground, stunned as my head slammed against the hard earth.

When he dove at me, I got my first glimpse of him, skinny, angular, muscular in a scrawny way. Black T-shirt and jeans. Short dusty blonde hair. Face hidden by dirt and sweat. Angry eyes peering out from a mask of filth.

He threw himself on me, tried to straddle me, meanwhile whipping out a switchblade and snicking it open.

I tried to roll away from him but he had me pinioned tight with iron legs. I saw him raise the knife, moonfire burning silver on its tip, and then somebody shouted "Hey!"

When he saw Neil running toward us, he jumped to his feet and started toward the alley.

"You all right?" Neil said when he reached me.

"Yeah, but he got away."

"You get a look at him?"

"Not much of one."

I was on my feet. My head still hurt from slamming against the ground.

"Cocksuckers," Neil said.

He ran to the alley and looked left then right.

"Bastard's gone," he said when he came back. "You all right?"

"Yeah."

"Anybody call the cops yet?"

We had just reached the porch.

"Nah, Bill and I thought we'd hold off for a while," he said.

"Hold off calling the cops?"

But he didn't have time to answer because just then I heard glass smash to the floor inside, and break in a loud nasty explosion.

BILL STILL had the burglar backed up against the kitchen wall. Every time Bill would lunge for him, the burglar would grab a glass or cup from the sink and hurl it at Bill. Then he'd crouch and sway his long-bladed knife back and forth to keep Bill from coming any closer.

Bill was soaked with sweat. He didn't seem to hear me when I came in. He never took his eyes from the burglar.

I looked at Neil, who anticipated my objection. "Bill's fine. Don't worry about him."

"Where's Curtis?"

"In the john."

"I'll go check on him. Then I'm going to call the cops."

"Your house, Aaron. You can do whatever you like."

"C'mon, motherfucker," Bill said to the burglar. "Give me a reason to cut your fucking throat."

Knife to knife, rage to rage, they hunkered down, glaring at each other.

Curtis was at the sink in the downstairs bathroom. He'd wetted a washcloth and held it to the lump on the back of his head.

I opened the closet, found the flashlight. "Why don't you let me take a look at your eyes?"

"You think maybe I got a concussion?"

"Maybe."

I checked his eyes.

"How do they look?"

"I don't think you've got a concussion. You have a headache?"

"A pisser."

"There's aspirin in the medicine cabinet."

"I know. I already helped myself." Then: "Wouldn't it make more sense for Bill to come check on me since he's a doctor and everything?"

"He's too busy playing gladiator."

He grinned. "You noticed that, huh?"

Then he extended his arm and said, "Look."

His entire arm trembled.

"Scared the shit out of me, man," Curtis said. "I thought I heard something in the kitchen and I went out and flipped on the light and he jumped me. He's got balls, I've got to give him that, breaking in when people are home."

"He probably didn't know anybody was here. We were all up in the attic and there aren't any windows up there. The rest of the house was dark."

He looked in the mirror and smiled at himself. "Thank God I'm still beautiful." Then, "The cops get here yet?"

"We haven't called them yet."

He watched my face in the mirror. "You been talking to Bill?"

"About what?"

He daubed the washcloth over the sore spots on his face. "I tried to call the cops in the kitchen and Bill stopped me."

"He stopped you?"

"Yeah. Came over and took the receiver from me and said he'd call the cops when the time came."

"What the hell's that supposed to mean?"

"I don't know," Curtis said. "But whatever it is, Neil's going along with it. He was the one who sent me into the john. Said he and Bill would handle things."

"Well, I'm going to call the cops and right now."

"Glad you said that. I was getting worried. I mean, you're supposed to call the cops right away after something happens."

I walked to the door. "I'll fix you a drink when we get out there."

"Scotch would be nice."

"Scotch it is," I said. "And the best I've got."

"The week old stuff?"

I laughed. "That's right. The week old stuff."

I was expecting to find Bill still playing gladiator.

But the kitchen was empty.

"What the hell happened to them?" Curtis said.

The first thing I thought of was that the burglar had somehow overpowered them. Dragged them out into the darkness.

But Bill and Neil were big strong guys.

One man dragging them off was unlikely.

"Hey," Curtis said, "listen."

At first, I wasn't sure where the sound of the muffled voices was coming from. In old houses like this, sound sometimes bounces, and you can't quite be sure which room the noise is in.

Curtis walked across the kitchen to the basement door. He silently pointed out the fact that the door was ajar.

He opened it a few inches.

The harsh male voices came clear now.

Bill and Neil cursing at the burglar.

I walked over to the basement door and looked down the steps. They needed a coat of paint.

The basement was our wilderness. We hadn't had the time or money to fly fix it up yet. We were counting on this year's bonus to help us set the basement right. Curtis and I were still junior partners but at our firm that still meant a good bonus.

We went down the steps.

The basement was one big, mostly unused room. There was a washer and dryer in the corner. And stacks of boxes lining three of the walls. Everything that didn't fit into the attic ended up in the basement. The long range plan was to turn it into a family room for the girls. These days it was mostly inhabited by stray waterbugs.

When I reached the bottom step, I saw them. There are four metal posts in the basement, one near each corner.

Then had him lashed to a pole in the east quadrant. His hands tied behind him with a piece of rope they'd found amidst the tools in the west quadrant.

They also had him gagged with what looked like a pillowcase.

His eyes were big and wide. He looked scared. I didn't blame him. I was scared, too.

"What the hell are you guys doing?" I said.

"Just calm down, Papa Bear," Bill said. That was his name for me whenever he wanted to convey to people that I'm this old-fashioned fuddy-duddy. It so happens that Bill is two years older than I am, and this seems to make him feel innately superior.

"Knock off the Papa Bear bullshit," I said. "Did you call the cops?"

"Not yet," Neil said. "Just calm down a little, will you?"

"You haven't called the cops," I said. "You've got some guy tied up and gagged in my basement. You haven't even asked how Curtis here is doing. And you want me to calm down, is that right?"

Bill came up to me, then. There was a pit bull craziness about him now, frantic, uncontrollable, alien.

"We're going to do what the cops *can't* do, man," he said. "We're going to sweat the sonofabitch. We're going to make him tell us who he was with tonight. And then we're going to make him give us the name of every single bad guy who works this neighbourhood. And then we'll turn all the names over to the cops."

"It's just an extension of the Patrol," Neil said. "Just keeping our neighbourhood safe is all."

"You guys are nuts," I said, and turned back toward the steps. "I'm going up to call the cops."

That's when I realised how crazed Bill was.

He grabbed my sleeve so hard that it tore. He said, "We're going to sweat the bastard, Aaron. *Then* we're going to call the cops."

"You tore my fucking sleeve," I said.

We were only inches apart and it was clear that one of us would soon swing at the other.

"I'm sorry about your sleeve."

"This is my fucking house," I said, yelling right into his face. "Do you fucking understand that, Bill? This is my fucking house!"

I hadn't wanted to hit anybody in a long time. Right now I couldn't wait to hit Bill.

That was when Curtis got between us and said, "Let's go upstairs and have a drink on this."

He nodded to the man tied and gagged in the corner. "That asshole's not going any place."

"That's right," Neil said soothingly. "A nice, civilised drink and then some nice, civilised discussion. Okay, you two?"

They got us apart but we still glared at each other like two boxers with a real grudge.

BILL LED the charge getting the kitchen cleaned up. I think he was feeling guilty about our altercation in the basement.

After the kitchen was put back in order, and all the smashed glass swept up with a broom, I broke out four glasses and a bucket of ice, and we all sat in the breakfast nook where we had a clear view of the basement door.

"All right," I said. "Now that we've all calmed down, I want to walk over to that yellow kitchen wall phone and call the police. Any objections?"

"I think blue would look better in here than yellow," Neil said.

"Funny."

They looked more like themselves now, no feral madness on the faces of Bill or Neil. Curtis, who sat next to me, no longer looked frightened or agitated.

It was over.

I got up from the table.

And that was when Neil grabbed my arm.

"I think Bill's right," Neil said. "I think we should spend a little time with our friend before we turn him over to the police."

I shook my head, politely removed his hand from my forearm, and started to stand up again.

"This isn't your decision alone," Bill said.

"Isn't it?" I said. "You want me to show you the mortgage? You want me to show you our homeowners' insurance policy? You want to see the light bill? That's my name on those things, Bill, not yours."

"Yeah, but this also happens to be my neighbourhood, asshole. My wife and my kids live here and I say if we've got a chance to sweat this cocksucker, we should do it."

"When he breaks into your house," I said, "you can do anything you want to with him. In the meantime, I'm calling the cops."

He erupted without warning, coming across the table for me.

I was ready for him, cocking my fist back and starting to bring it down on top of his head.

Curtis grabbed me, and Neil grabbed Bill.

"Hey, for God's sake," Neil said. "We're friends here, all right, you two?"

The breakfast nook has a window where I sometimes sit in the mornings and watch all the backyard animals on sunny days. I saw a mother racoon and four baby racoons one day, marching single file across the grass. My grandparents were the last generation to live on the farm. My father came to town here and ultimately became vice president of a ball bearing company. When I look out this window, I often think of my father. He liked watching animals, too.

I looked back at the table and said, "We're not cops. We're just private citizens. And what we need to do is turn the guy in the basement over to the cops right now."

"You want to bet on how long it'll be before he's back on the street again?" Bill said.

"Hey," Curtis said. "You're the doctor. But we're attorneys. Officers of the court? You know what I'm saying? We've got to turn this guy over to the authorities and right now. Our asses are on the line, man."

"You shouldn't even have tied him up," I said to Bill and Neil.

"Yes, the poor thing," Bill said. "Aren't we just picking on him, though? Maybe you'd like to offer him something to eat."

"Just make sure you serve the right wine with it," Neil said. "I'm sure he's a gourmet."

"Or maybe we could get him a chick," Bill said.

"Yeah, with charlies out to here," Neil said.

I couldn't help it. I smiled. They were being ridiculous and that's just what we needed at the moment. A little bit of ridiculousness.

"I'm sorry I got so pissed," I said to Bill.

And held my hand out.

"Me, too," he said.

"You two want to go somewhere and make out?" Curtis said.

"He always has bad breath," Bill said.

"I just want to ask him one question, Aaron," Neil said. "That's not going to hurt anything is it? Just scare him a little. Ask him the name of the guy who was with him tonight."

I looked at Curtis.

He shrugged. "I guess we could give them a couple of minutes. But you promise you're just going to scare him?"

"Promise," Neil said.

"Absolutely," Bill said.

"Then we call the cops?" I said.

"Then we call the cops," Neil said.

"Okay?" I said to Curtis.

"I guess," he said, still sounding reluctant.

I LED the way down, sneezing as I walked.

There's always a lot of dust floating around in the basement to play hell with my sinuses.

The burglar was his same sullen self, glaring at us as we descended the stairs and then walked over to him.

He smelled of heat and sweat and clinging grime. The long bare arms sticking out of his filthy T-shirt told tattoo tales of writhing snakes and leaping panthers. The arms were joined in the back with the rope. His jaw was still flexed, trying to accommodate the intrusion of the gag.

"Maybe we should castrate him," Bill said.

He angled his face so the burglar couldn't see him wink at me.

Bill walked up to the guy and said, "You like that, scumbag? If we castrated you?"

If the burglar felt any fear, it wasn't evident in his eyes. All you could see there was the usual contempt.

"I'll bet this is the jerk who broke into the Donaldson's house a couple weeks ago," Neil said.

Now he walked up to the guy. But he was more ambitious than Bill had been. Neil spat in the guy's face.

"Hey," I said. "Cool it."

Neil turned and glared at me. "Yeah, I wouldn't want to hurt his fucking feelings, would I?"

I wish I'd paid more attention to Curtis' reluctance. This was a terrible mistake, bringing Neil and Bill back down here.

Then suddenly Neil raised his fist and started to swing on the guy.

All I could do was shove him. That sent his punch angling off to the right, missing our burglar by half a foot.

I was angrier than I should have been, I suppose, but I felt like a betrayed parent. Here my two spoiled brats had promised me to be on good behaviour, and now they chose to break their word.

"You asshole," Neil said, turning back

on me now.

But Curtis was there between us.

"You know what we're doing?" Curtis said. "We're making that jerk-off over there happy. He's gonna have some nice stories to tell his friends in the slammer."

He was right.

The burglar was the one who looked cool and composed right now. We looked like squabbling brats.

As if to confirm this, a certain merriment shone in the burglar's blue eyes.

"Oh, hell, Aaron," Neil said, "Curtis is right."

He put his hand out to shake and then grabbed me and gave me a hug.

"This Patrol shit is making all of us crazy," Bill said. He jabbed a finger in the direction of the burglar. "And it's this motherfucker and his pals who're doing it to us."

"Now I'm going to call the cops," I said.

"Past time, man," Curtis said. "They can pick this asshole up and we'll be done with him."

I could see both Neil and Bill reluctantly going along with the plan now.

And that's when the burglar chose to make his move. As soon as I mentioned cops, he probably reasoned that this was going to be his last chance to do anything.

He waited until our attention was on ourselves and not on him. Then he took off running. We could see that he'd somehow managed to slip the rope.

He went straight for the stairs, angling out around us like a running back seeing daylight. He even stuck his long, tattooed arm out as if he was trying to repel a tackle.

He was at the stairs by the time we

could gather ourselves enough to go after him. But when we moved, we moved fast, and in virtual unison.

Everybody was shouting and cursing.

By the time I got my hand on the cuff of his left leg he was close enough to the basement door to open it.

I yanked hard, and ducked out of the way of his kicking foot. By now I was as crazy as Bill and Neil had been earlier.

There was adrenaline, and great anger.

He wasn't just a burglar, he was all burglars, he was every sonofabitch who meant to do my wife and my kids great harm.

He hadn't had time to take the gag from his mouth.

I grabbed the tail of the gag and yanked on it so hard, he stumbled backwards down three steps.

At first, he kept trying to grab for the door. He even managed briefly to scramble back up two steps.

But I gave another yank on the back of his gag and he came back down right away.

I can't tell you exactly what happened the next half-minute or so.

He around and took a wild swing at me. I grabbed his arm and started hauling him down the steps.

All I wanted to do was get him on the basement floor again, turn him over to the others to watch, while I went upstairs and called the cops.

But somewhere in those few seconds when I was hauling him back down the I heard the edge of the stair meeting the back of his skull.

The others heard it, too.

Their shouts and their curse died in their throats.

When I turned around, I saw the blood coming fast and red from his nose.

The blue eyes no longer held contempt. They were starting to roll up white in the back of his head.

"God," I said. "He's hurt."

"I think he's a lot more than hurt," Bill said.

Bill the doctor.

"Help me get him upstairs," Bill said.

We moved him as gently as possible. I was scared and sick. This was all so crazy. Just a little while ago we'd been scanning sex magazines and playing poker.

By the time we laid him down on the kitchen floor, he started convulsing his body jolting and twitching every thirty seconds or so, as if electricity were being pumped into him.

"Damn," Bill said.

You could smell that the guy had messed himself. Faeces hung sweetsour on the air.

Then Bill was down on the floor next to him, checking eyes and mouth and pulse points in neck and wrist and ankle.

At first I didn't notice that the twitching had stopped. But then the guy stopped moving at all.

I watched his chest, eager to see the subtle rise and fall of his lungs.

There was no rise and fall, subtle or otherwise.

Bill looked up at me and said, "He's dead."

"No way," Curtis said. "No fucking way."

"Hey friend, you're the lawyer, remember?" Bill said. "I'm the doctor. And I say he's dead."

"Dead," Neil said. "Dead."

"I'm calling the cops," I said, and started for the phone.

That's when Neil grabbed my shoulder and spun me around.

"The hell you are" he said. "The hell you are."

I WAS at the hospital the morning my father died. My mother and sister were there, too.

Dad went into post-op and was then brought up and wheeled into his private room. He'd had open heart surgery.

A nurse came in and said we could go in and see him in another twenty minutes or so, after they were finished making him comfortable and everything.

Meanwhile, why didn't we just stay in the waiting room and read some magazines and relax? They'd come and get us when everything was ready.

This was ten years ago but I still remember hearing the 'Code Blue' announced.

I knew instantly that something had gone wrong with my father.

And so did my mother and sister.

My mother got up and started for the door but I stopped her, turned her over to my sister.

"I'll go find out," I said.

I ran down the hall to where I saw two teams of emergency personnel entering a room.

"Please," said a nurse when I tried to get in, "you'll have to stay out for now."

"He's my father," I said.

I think she still wanted to stop me but I pushed past her.

I stood in the corner so I wouldn't get in the way of the hospital people.

They worked fast and hard and you could feel their urgency.

About all I could see of him was half of his face. He looked dead white.

A few minutes later, one of the doctors looked back at me and said, "I'm sorry."

I nodded.

When I got back to the waiting room, I opened my mouth to say something but my mother and sister didn't give me time.

They just held on to me, as if they were drowning and only I could save them.

I let them cry till they were temporarily cried out and then we just sat there, the three of us, in this unfamiliar hospital, in this unfamiliar room, burdened with the unfamiliar knowledge of death and its finality.

No more father.

And we didn't speak, didn't say a word, it must have been fifteen, twenty minutes before one of us spoke.

AND IT was that way tonight, sitting in the breakfast nook, pushing the bottle of scotch back and forth.

Saying absolutely fucking nothing.

None of us knew what to say so we stared out the window or stared into our drinks.

The burglar was across the room. I'd thrown my old bathrobe across him. Blood soaked parts of it now.

After a long while, I said: "I think I'm ready."

"For what?" Curtis said.

"To call the cops."

"Yeah? What're you going to tell them?" Bill said.

"That we caught a burglar and wrestled with him and he accidentally hit his head and killed himself."

"You ever been interrogated?" Curtis said.

"Only that time I killed those three nuns," I said.

"What Curtis is trying to say," Neil said, "is that the cops are going to have a lot of questions."

"About what?" I said.

"About what happened" Curtis said. "You get a good look at his body?"

"What about it?" I said.

"One of you guys hit him pretty hard in the eye. Got the beginning of a shiner."

"So?" I said.

"So?" Bill said, "since the fatal wound is on the back of his head, how do we explain that he got a black eye?"

"Not to mention," Curtis said, "his broken finger."

"He's got a broken finger?" I said.

"Yeah," said Bill the doctor. "I noticed that. I must've busted it when I was tying his wrists together with the rope."

"And," Curtis said, "it's also going to be obvious to the coroner that our pal was dead a long time before we called the cops."

"You guys don't know jack shit about cops," I said. "And neither do I. We're tax attorneys."

"We still know how the system

works," Neil said.

"Enough to know that all of us could be in some deep shit here" Curtis said.

"What the hell're you talking about?" I said.

"What he's talking about," Neil said, "is that Bill here is licenced by the state medical board, and the three of us are licenced by the state legal board. And both of those boards frown on people who practice vigilante justice."

"Vigilante justice?" Bill said. "What the hell're you talking about?"

"Rope burns," Curtis said. "That's the first thing the coroner's going to notice about him. How he was tied up."

"We didn't want him to get away," I said.

"So we tied him to a post in the basement and then beat the shit out of him?" Curtis said.

"We didn't hit him that many times," I said.

"Yeah? How many bruises do you think the coroner's going to find on his body?" Curtis said.

I looked angrily at Bill and Neil. "You two assholes just had to play cowboy, didn't you?"

The phone rang.

We all sat and stared at it as if we weren't quite sure what it was.

Some newfangled contraption.

Sits on your wall and rings like a bell.

"I'll get it," I said.

"Maybe it's his mommy," Neil said, "telling him to come home."

"Funny," Curtis said.

By the time I picked up, the answering machine kicked in. Over my own voice saying wait for the beep and then leave your message, I yelled several times to let the caller know that a living breathing person was actually on the other end of the phone.

"Hi, honey," Jan said.

"Hi, sweetie."

"I'll bet I caught you right in the middle of a poker game, didn't I?"

"Well, sort of."

"Remember our agreement."

"I know. No more than $25."

Because I'd once lost $100 one night and felt totally irresponsible and remorseful for a week after, we agreed that I'd never lose more than $25 in one sitting.

"Listen," I said, "I'm going to take this in the other room, hon. I'll have Curtis hang up when I get in there."

"Great," she said.

I held the phone out to Curtis. He took it.

IN THE darkened living room, I picked up the receiver and said, "I sure miss you guys."

"We miss you, too," Jan said.

Curtis hung up.

"How are the girls?"

"Oh, just having a great time, hon. Mom and Dad are spoiling them as usual. Dad got a new Cadillac—he said that after all his years as District Attorney up here he'd earned it—and they've got their outdoor pool now. So the girls have plenty to do. In fact, they were so tired, they went to bed voluntarily at seven-thirty."

While she was talking, I forced myself to take several deep breaths and to close my eyes while doing so. This helped settle my nerves a little.

"Wow, they must've been."

Pause. "You sound funny."

"I do?"

"Is everything all right there?"

"Is everything all right? What wouldn't be all right?"

"Your voice—you just sound—"

"A little drunk is what I probably sound," I said. "We've been doing our share tonight.

Pause. "Aaron?"

"Yeah?"

"You know our agreement."

"Sure I know our agreement, honey."

"No matter what it is—we tell each other the truth."

"I *am* telling you the truth. Honest."

Two years before I met her, Jan got engaged to one of the campus football heroes. It was the kind of relationship that seemed ideal on the surface—strapping, handsome hero; winsome, bright fiancée. Everybody predicted great lives for them. He'd go on to the pros, she'd be his wife and the mother of his children. Even in our jaded age, a lot of people still like old-fashioned dreams like that.

There was one problem... the hero was a pathological liar. Almost rarely told the truth. The CEO father he boasted about was actually a bus driver in Columbus, Ohio, The manse he claimed to be raised up in turned out to be a shabby apartment house with slashed screens on the windows and dog crap all over the dirt front yard. And all the pro offers he was always talking about... a few halfhearted feelers from the Vikings, who were just doing a little bit of trawling and nothing more serious.

But that wasn't the worst. Oh, no. You might excuse all his fantasies as more than protective coloration—he was poor and she was reasonably wealthy, right? He was ashamed of his background. A lot of people are. So he told a few lies.

Then one day Jan walked into his humid off-campus apartment and found him in bed with her own roomie. It didn't end there. Over the next week, she started asking *all* her close and trusted friends about her fiancée... And all but one of them confessed that they, too, had slept with him.

Devastated, she became a Big 10 version of a nun. She spent her junior year studying... and nothing else. Not a single date. And when she did start going out again, it was with guys she considered 'friends' and not potential suitors.

It only takes once, having your faith in somebody destroyed that way. Jan had never recovered her trust. And even today, it was sometimes a problem. The slightest inconsistency in anything I said made her start wondering if I was lying. Or the slightest mood shift in my voice.

I was hiding something from her. That's what she always thought. I was hiding something.

That's all she'd ever asked of me, really, was to be honest. The night before our wedding, she said, "If you ever lie to me, Aaron, I'll leave you. And I mean it," I gave her my word and for the most part honoured it. Over the years I'd told a few fibs, I suppose, mostly to keep her from worrying about our budget or my health, but I could honestly say that I'd been honest.

Until now.

"How're things at the office?"

"Oh, the usual. We go back to court next week for G & G. That's what I'm mostly spending my time on." G & G was one of our biggest clients, a shipping firm that was suing the federal government for a tax shelter it believed was legal. The trouble with all such suits is that the fed can pretty much decide on a whim—there's always some vague rule in the tax code that covers their ass—what is legal and what is not legal. But if it wasn't for the federal government, half the lawyers in this country would be working at McDonald's.

When I was finished talking, I looked down at the magazine lying next to me on the couch. I had unconsciously ripped off the cover and balled it up.

"Oh, before I forget, the girls asked me to ask you if you'll take them to the new Disney film."

"Sure."

"Dad wanted to take them here. But they said they wanted to wait until you could take them."

I strained to laugh. "Let your Dad take them if he wants to. They always end up going three or four times to Disney films anyway."

"Well, now that you mention it, they do always see Disney films several times, don't they?" Then, softly. "I had a real nice time the night before we left."

"Me, too, sweetheart," I said.

Like too many married couples these days, Jan and I sometimes go two or three days at a time without spending any real time together. Even when we go to bed, it's mostly just to sleep.

But we decided to make the last night before they left very special. It was our tenth anniversary.

We put the girls down at seven o'clock, opened a bottle of champagne, put on some of the old disco records we used to dance to, and then proceeded to neck and giggle our way through the evening. We ended up making love twice that night, something we hadn't done in a long long time, and falling asleep in each other's arms. We'd needed that.

And like Jan, I too kept remembering the best moments of that night.

"I wish you were here right now," she said.

"Me, too."

Then: "You sure everything's all right?"

"Everything's fine. Honest."

"Dad asked if we might stay a few more days. And have you fly up on Friday night."

I liked my in-laws very much. They were good, decent people, and had always been exceptionally kind and open with me. We'd gone through a few family crises together—Jan losing our first baby seven months into her pregnancy, me going through a medical scare when I found a strange bump beneath my elbow—and had become good and true friends.

"The trouble is," I said, "There's just no way I can get away."

"That's what I told them," Jan said. "But it never hurts to ask."

"I sure love you and the girls."

"And we sure love you. Night, hon."

After we hung up, I sat there in the darkness for several minutes.

I could hear the voices coming from the kitchen but they were too far away to be articulate.

I felt safe in the darkness of my comfortable living room, the only illumination being the silver nimbus of streetlight against the pale drawn curtain.

It all seemed kind of funny, kind of harmless actually. Guy breaks in and we play at being vigilantes and then the guy accidentally dies.

The cops would give us some hell, might even ask the district attorney if any charges should be pressed, but a doctor, and three lawyers? No way the district attorney was going to press charges.

I felt much better about the whole thing.

All we had to do was be honest with the police, and they'd gnaw on our asses a little and then let us go.

I went back to the kitchen in an almost gleeful mood. We'd just let our fear and pessimism run away with us.

THE BODY was gone. That was the first thing I noticed.

The second thing I noticed was that both Bill and Neil were holding handguns.

They were standing by the back door.

Curtis was on the floor, wiping up the moisture from the body.

"Where the hell'd the burglar go?" I said.

"Back porch," Neil said. "Bill had a tarpaulin in his trunk. He also had these guns."

He was a strange physician, our good doctor Bill Doyle, far more interested in death than in life.

"What's the tarpaulin for?" I said. "The police'll just make you unwrap him."

Curtis stopped scrubbing and looked up at me. "We've kind've been talking things over, Aaron."

Any lingering euphoria I'd brought with me from the living room was now gone utterly.

"Talking what over?" I said.

Curtis looked at the other two, took a final swipe at the floor then stood up.

"Talking over what we should do with the body," he said. Then: "They're right, Aaron. There's no way we can call the cops now. They'll bring charges for sure. And you know what it's like at our offices. This kind of scandal hits the paper, they'll fire our ass for sure. I've got a huge mortgage, man. I can't afford to be fired."

"Curtis, are you out of your mind?" I said. "Of course we're going to the cops. And of course we're turning over the body. What the hell else would we do with it?"

"Throw it in the river by the little dam," Bill said. "You know, out on old Frazier Road. We've got it all figured out."

I almost smiled.

Four middle-class guys standing in a kitchen filled with all the latest appliances, gimmicks and gizmos—talking about throwing a dead body in a river.

There was something comic about it.

"What happens when it shows up

down river?" I said.

"I checked your garage. You've got six concrete blocks out there," Neil said. "We tie some of them to the body before we throw it in."

They were together now, the three of them, standing in front of the back door.

Three good friends of mine. Men I thought I knew extremely well.

"I hate to spoil your fun, boys," I said, "but right now I'm walking over to that phone and calling the police. And I suggest that you take that body out of that tarpaulin."

I turned and started to the wall phone.

Neil grabbed me.

"Think about it, Aaron. Think of what the media'll do to a story like this. We'll be on the fucking TV news for two or three months. And then there'll be a trial. You realise how many laws we've broken now?"

I shook my head. "Laws you and Bill broke. Not me or Curtis. You two."

"Maybe I should remind you, asshole," Bill said. "You were the one who actually killed him."

"He was trying to escape," I said.

Neil said, "Think of what it'll be like for our kids at school, Aaron. You want to put your little girls through that kind of publicity?"

Neil looked at Bill and said, "And knock off that bullshit about how Aaron killed him. He died accidentally and we're all a part of it. Equally."

"I shouldn't have said that, Aaron," Bill said. "Neil's right and I apologise."

Curtis said, gently, "You know we're right, Aaron. You know we gotta handle it this way now."

"We could go to prison." I heard myself say in a dead voice.

"We could go to prison for what we've done already," Curtis said.

"But a jury—" I started to say.

"A jury?" Bill said. "A jury? God knows what a jury would do to us. You get a lot of poor people on that jury, and they'll just see us as a lot of middle-class bastards trying to get away with killing some poor burglar."

I started to argue but stopped. Bill had a point about juries. God only knew how they'd look at us and our predicament.

I looked longingly over at the phone. Then back at them.

"I'm going to call the police," I said. "And the only way you're going to stop me is to knock me out."

I looked at each one of them.

"You understand?"

They just watched me, silently.

I turned around and walked over to the yellow wall phone.

Funny, it felt as if I was walking a half mile instead of just a few feet.

I was already forming my story in my head.

Had to tie him up so he wouldn't escape. But he got free. And then we had this struggle. And then he accidentally hit his head. Sure. I'm a lawyer. Sure, I know we shouldn't have tied him up. Or struck him. But things just got so crazy —

I lifted the receiver.

Dialled the central number for the police, which was on a small sticker right on the phone.

As the dial tone came on, I looked back at my friends.

Still in front of the door. Still silently

watching me.

To my friends, I said, "I'm doing the right thing, you guys. I really am. I know a good criminal attorney," I said to the three of them. "He'll be able to handle this with no problem. Honest."

Still no answer.

"We throw that guy in the river, we'll never have another good night's sleep. We'll be too scared to sleep."

Then Bill was standing next to me. "Give me the phone, asshole." Just then I heard a male voice on the receiver say, "Hello?"

Bill took the phone from me and said, "I dialled the wrong number. I'm sorry."

Bill hung up the phone.

I leaned forward, pressing my forehead to the wall phone.

There was no way we could innocently characterise what had happened tonight.

Every time we tried to explain ourselves, we'd just get into deeper trouble.

Even if we had a first rate criminal attorney helping us.

I slowly pushed myself away from the wall and turned around to face my friends.

"You want to help us carry him out to your van?" Bill said.

"Yeah," Neil said quietly. "We might as well get it over with."

ED GORMAN

"Gorman is the poet of dark suspense." BLOOMSBURY REVIEW

"Watch Out! Ed Gorman's coming to get you!" CRIME TIME

THE POKER CLUB

The Poker Club *is published in hardback at £16.99 by CT Publishing. You can get it at all good bookshops or order it at the special price of £9.99 by sending your order to CT Publishing, Poker Club Offer, Dept CT26) PO Box 5880, Edgbaston, Birmingham, B16 9BJ (Postage and Packing free)*

fiction

a nameless coffin
gwendoline butler

Gwendoline Butler Is one of the most universally praised of English mystery authors, under both her own name and that of Jennie Melville, and is one of the most borrowed authors in Britain.

A Nameless Coffin is published by CT Publishing at £4.99

WHEN DOES a case begin? When the idea of crime first comes into the criminal's head? Or when the act itself takes place? Or when the police first get to hear about it? Or is it less tangible than that? Is there a subtle shading off, so that ordinary, careless, selfish behaviour slides over the line and becomes anti-social and criminal? Is this why the Devil got his first big casting as the Serpent?

There was a huge new supermarket in the main road in Coffin's manor. Six months ago it had opened on the site of an old cinema. On a corner with a factory and a block of offices opposite and a hospital next door, it was well placed for custom. In fact it was a popular, cheerful place and was soon absorbed as an institution into the life of the neighbourhood. You could park the baby in his pram and drink coffee in the patio on the ground floor. At rush hours there was even a distracted nurse to watch the babies and separate the dogs. There were always dogs, tied to the prams or wandering in and out or anxiously trying to get into the main shop after their owners. A large printed notice declared that Dogs were not Allowed on the Premises, but it was an ineffective prohibition. The store manager used to dream of the coming of a dogs' Pied Piper. His other dream was that he was a dog, and was running round barking and fouling the shop. After nights like these the notices about dogs were always made bigger and more numerous. On this hot day in late April they stood about eighteen inches high and were as thick on the walls as graffiti at Pompeii. But still no one read them.

Most of the shoppers were women, but there were usually a few men and boys among them, looking lost amid their purposeful and pushing sisters. A few of the women were shabbily dressed, but times were prosperous, and the majority wore pretty dresses and smart handbags and shoes.

Between five and five-thirty on that same afternoon about fifty or sixty women with their children, handbags and shopping passed through the cash desks. It was just past the peak hour, and housewives were rushing home to start the evening meal.

About half of these women— twenty-five or twenty-six of them: it was not possible to be precise about the number—discovered when they got home that their handbags were scratched. Some bags were deeply scored, others had received just a tiny little mark, nothing more than a nick. One or two women probably failed to notice that there was anything wrong with their bags at all. The rest blamed their own clumsiness.

None of the women realised that she had been the victim of an attack. Not one knew that she was a *victim*.

It was a horrible summer, day after day of steady heat, which made the pavements livid and dirty. Londoners even began to think wistfully of grey skies and rain. The sales of aspirin and sun-burn lotion went up. Milk turned sour, butter was greasy, and the food in the shops looked dry and stale. The grass in the big parks was brown and trodden into dust. People sat about in their gardens, at the windows, and on the pavements. There was no privacy anywhere.

"We shall have trouble," said John Coffin, Divisional Detective Inspector (hoping for promotion: hadn't he been a good clever boy lately?) for a South London district, gazing out of the window and thinking of the large area he was responsible for, containing houses, shops, factories, docks and one huge comprehensive school.

"I don't know why it hasn't started yet." John Coffin didn't believe in the Devil and the Serpent, but he knew all about crime and a lot about wickedness, and he was learning more every day. He stared at the heat shimmer. "This is the sort of weather the Great Plague must have flourished in," he felt gloomy and unwell himself, and would have liked a good cry, but men weren't allowed to do that sort of thing. Instead he kicked the table and glared at his assistant. "Trouble," muttered Coffin. He looked at the telephone and waited for it to ring.

The telephone was quite silent, as it had been for some time. This was in itself unnerving. "All dead," he muttered. "All dead. Sitting there, hunched over their telephones, all dead." A picture came into his mind of dead people crouched over telephones in rooms all over London.

"Don't you believe it," said his colleague Sergeant Dove, who was not imaginative. Although the sergeant was unimaginative, he was not without the usual burden of introspection and anxiety. Not for nothing was he called Dove. There were swarms of Doves in the district. Many times Coffin had thought that an anthropological survey of his district would make fascinating reading. It was a neighbourhood in which four great family groups still predominated in spite of war, rebuilding and social planning. Nothing any Council planner could do would efface the power of the Stones, the Doves, the Dinebons and the Whitechairs. You still came across these names in every housing list, every school register and every cemetery in the district. They were on both sides of the law, some were honest, some were not. Fred Dove was a policeman. His remote cousins, whom he did not as a matter of fact yet know and who lived down by the docks, were just opening up a line in stolen cars that was shortly going to introduce him to them. There were certain common physical characteristics. The Stones were shortish, solid-boned, but with neat hands and feet; the Doves had poorer physiques, and a tendency to hypochondria (in which Sergeant Fred Dove, not otherwise a typical Dove, shared: he was at this moment wondering if that pain was an ulcer) and were well known to all the local

doctors and hospitals; the Dinebons were large and quiet, so good with their hands that they had once produced the best forger in Europe; and the Whitechairs all had sharp blue eyes and a strong sense of justice which naturally often looked to their friends and neighbours more like a sharp sense of grievance. The Whitechairs marched in protest, went on strike, and organised mutinies as the decades and centuries rolled by. They had been among the Londoners who egged on the Peasants' Revolt in the fourteenth century and enrolled Chartists in the nineteenth. They were often on the losing side but turned out indestructible in the end.

Coffin himself had a streak of Whitechair blood in him. At the moment, oppressed and uneasy, he felt sure there must be a Dove gene or two loose in his blood as well.

"Anyway, we've *got* plenty of trouble," said the sergeant, looking round at the files around him.

"Yes," said Coffin, in a dissatisfied way, as if he wanted more and worse trouble. Then he smiled. "Don't think I'm greedy, Fred." The same Christian names came up time and time again among the Stones, Doves, Dinebons and Whitechairs, and Frederick was far and away the favourite, whether because it had a fine imperial ring to it or because an extremely successful local boxer had been called Fighting Fred Fisher. Coffin was never sure. "I'm not really looking for trouble. I just feel it coming," he settled down to the work on his desk.

Coffin was looking for trouble which carried a gun or killed a child or strangled its wife or burnt down its neighbour's house. His district had had plenty of trouble of this sort over the last decade, but trouble rarely comes wearing the face you expected.

Out in the hot streets, crowded with shoppers and idle walkers escaping from their houses in search of moving air, the knife was already known, had already established its reputation in a quiet undercover way, but no one had thought to mention this to Coffin yet. No one had even told the police.

A long thoroughfare ran through the heart of Coffin's district and went down almost to the river. Half-way along, just where Creevey Buildings stood on the corner of Courcy Street, this road widened enough to contain barrows and street traders. On all weekdays, except Monday, which was a dead day, there were fruit and fish stalls, and at the weekend on Friday and Saturday the fruit stalls were joined by traders in cheap dresses and fabrics, shoes, handbags, stockings and large pale-faced dolls. This bustling energetic market was dominated by a large public house called the Red Bull, hence a trip to the market was known locally as 'going up the Red'. Everyone went up the Red sooner or later. Coffin had done it often himself although as a policeman he was hardly a popular figure there. Changes in social habits, prosperity and the well-designed cheap goods to be bought at the huge chain store just opposite had not really diminished the Red's popularity. The women of the neighbourhood enjoyed picking over the articles laid out on the stalls and bargaining with, and insulting, the traders. Their grandmothers had done it, they had heard their mothers do it and they meant to do it too. The stalls offered good value. They had to; competition was so fierce. Some of the things for sale were stolen property. The police knew it and the shoppers probably knew it. But to buy these things was part of the fun and part of their curious attitude to law and order. A long history of civilised and restrained urban life lay behind them. In spite of all the pressures of disease, poverty and war over the centuries, they had never gone quite so far as to court bloodshed, or shoot anyone at the barricades; and now they queued politely at street corners for buses. But behind this carefully evolved feeling for social justice was a dislike of authority. Coffin realised this as well as anyone, and knew that combined with a real sense of the value of law was a strong desire to put the police in their place. It was often catch as catch can in Courcy Street and Creevey Buildings and among the crowded stalls of 'The Red'.

This partly, but only partly, explained their attitude to the knife.

Out of Creevey Buildings, which was a tall grubby block of flats built in the late nineteenth century by a philanthropist grown rich on the slums around the Tower and river, came a solitary dog. The building was being cleared of its inhabitants. Demolition was due to start next month. Almost everyone had already gone, only one old lady clung on in her rooms on the ground floor with seven empty and derelict floors above her. The local authorities and the police had more than a suspicion that a West Indian family were squatting on the sixth floor and a certainty, so far unproved, that the men who had raided the bank across the road three days ago had used the third floor of the Creevey as their observation post. On the very top floor of all was a tenant who came and went and whom no one so far knew about.

The dog turned the corner and trotted off down Courcy Street. He was living free in the Creevey too but he was a lawless quarrelsome hound who had never had a home and never wanted one. He was off now to steal some food from a steak and sausage shop he knew of in Lower Dock Road. He was limping a little. On his back leg was a long thin scratch which must have been deeper than it looked to impede him so much. It was almost as if he had been slashed by a knife.

The demolition men were in for a shock when they came to knocking down Creevey Buildings. Although the structure looked so derelict, it was really immensely strong, with thick walls and tremendous foundations. Architecturally it was something between a prison and a fortress.

"They say the rats'll swarm out of there when they knock it down," said the newspaper man who sold his papers on the corner opposite.

"Go on," said his customer, who was leaning from her ground-floor window to reach for her paper. The houses faced right on to the road on that side with no front garden and no railings; it had its advantages. "I hope they don't come my way then."

"Oh no, they won't stop here. They'll go straight down to the docks,"

said the newspaper man seriously. "That's where they'll make for."

"With the Pied Piper, I suppose?" said his customer, sceptically.

"They've got a rats' highway through to there," said the old man with a rapt secret look. "They know the way. You won't see them go, though. it'll be at night, with no moon, and the King Rat will lead them."

"I don't know where you get hold of all this rubbish," said the woman, turning round and preparing to draw down her window, "but if you think there's anything in it, you ought to tell the Sanitary Authorities and have them fumigate the building." She shut the window with a bang.

"They could skitter down this road and go straight to the docks and get on a ship and go to the Indies, Scotland or Scandinavia," said the newspaper seller dreamily. He stared down the straight road. Very distantly, he could see the funnel of a ship and the top of a loading crane. He had never been any nearer although he had lived in the district for forty years. He lived and worked and moved in a small area bounded by four roads. Outside them he was a foreigner.

But the idea of the rats had liberated his imagination and set his mind on its wanderings.

"There's boats down there that sail off to Scotland, Iceland and America," he said aloud.

"I've never seen any rats," said the woman, suddenly drawing up her window and popping her head out, "but if it's true, then they ought to burn the place down."

"They'd get out," said the

newspaper man dreamily. "You can't stop a colony of rats. Colony," he said again, as if he liked the word.

"You were going on about the pyramids and the Second Coming last week, now the rats," said the woman angrily, slamming down her window again.

"It's the same thing," he said, with a rattle at her window. "That's what people like you don't understand."

He arranged his papers carefully on her windowsill and left a plate for people to put pennies into. Then he went off down the road to drink some lemonade at a café there.

Between Creevey Buildings and the Red Bull, where the stalls thinned out and finally stopped altogether, was about five hundred feet. Along this short stretch of pavement the crowds were so thick they could hardly move on this hot afternoon. Friday towards five o'clock was always a busy time.

One woman was standing on the edge of the crowd, studying them closely, turning her head this way and that to take everything in. She had bright, slightly protuberant eyes that moved restlessly from person to person as if trying to assess each person's movements. She was thin, almost emaciated, but quite smartly dressed in a cotton dress and white shoes. She had no handbag but she was clutching a bundle of shopping in her arms.

"Not buying anything from the market today, ducks?" called out the nearest salesman.

"I have bought already," she said bleakly, never taking her eyes off the scene in front of her. Her sharp gaze did not miss the figure of the newspaper seller on his way to get his lemonade.

"Old loony," she said spitefully; she was always cuttingly contemptuous of anyone she thought abnormal, not a proper person, as if to emphasise the gap between them. Perhaps because she feared she really fell into the same class with them and there was no gap at all. "*He* couldn't have done it though. Not clever enough. Takes someone sharp to do that to me."

It was her belief that it would take someone very clever indeed to rob her as she had been robbed. Her use of the word sharp was unconsciously significant. A knife had helped to rob her.

She stood there now, studying the crowded street, trying to pick out the person who had taken her bag.

"Because he'll do it again." (If it was a man. It could equally well have been a woman.) "It won't just be me that was robbed of her handbag. He'll try it again and I might catch him at it," her pride demanded that others should suffer too. *She* wasn't going to be the only one caught.

All the time she stood there brooding over what had happened to her, her body was making minute muscular movements as if acting out the scene again. All through her thirty odd years she had fought her own battles and she meant to go on fighting them now. She didn't trust anyone else. "Better lose a character than a pound note," was her cry. Her character had gone long ago. But like a cat she had more than one character to lose: character as a daughter, as a wife, as a mother, as a woman. One by one they had all gone. Now she had nothing left to maintain but her character in her own eyes as a sharp woman.

An hour ago she had started out to buy a new dress in the market, her brown handbag hanging over her arm, a newspaper held in her hand, and wearing dark glasses. Perhaps she shouldn't have worn dark glasses, perhaps it had made all her faculties less keen, made her less aware of the body that brushed against hers and the hands that came too close. She lifted her lips in a thin, tight, sardonic smile.

She had gone into one end of the market with her brown handbag containing over ten pounds and she emerged at the other end with a cheap cotton frock in her arms and with a handle hanging over her wrist.

A sharp knife had cut away her handbag.

She almost thought of the knife as having a separate life of its own.

But she was not going to report the matter to the police. In this behaviour she had good sound reason. Reason of character, reason of circumstances, both weighed with her, and she did not distinguish the two. To her, circumstance *was* character. She was an outsider, she stood a little way from the social group she now surveyed.

"What would the police say to me if I complained of being robbed?" She laughed silently. "Probably tell me I'm fair game," her eyes flickered so hostilely over a passer-by that the woman moved hurriedly away. "I'm not one of *them*, and they know it."

Slowly she walked from end to end of the market ending up not far from Creevey Buildings. The heat did not inconvenience her, she liked it, she was one of the few people out that afternoon who did. The smell of the dusty streets, the heat, even the crowds all had an exotic appeal to her. She was usually happy in this street, like a tourist on Broadway or on the Boulevard Haussmann.

"They can tell lies as well as anyone, can't they? I'll look after myself, thank you."

She looked pugnacious, and you suddenly saw that, cornered, she could be a very ugly customer indeed.

But although she patrolled up and down for some time longer she could see no trace of the bag-snatcher with the knife. Presently even her determination became discouraged, and she turned the corner of Courcy Street, set her face towards the docks and disappeared.

A mean-featured, ferret-faced little woman darted out of the crowd and placed herself against a shop window; she was followed by an older woman moving more slowly because she was heavier and also, burdened with a loaded basket of shopping in each hand.

"Oh, stop panting like that, Mother."

Her mother did not answer at once. Finally after taking several puffing breaths she said in a sort of gust: "You take the bags then."

"I can't, I can't. Oh, I'm in such a state."

"You're a fool, my girl."

"It's too late for that sort of talk, Mother."

Her mother inhaled deeply.

"Pat your pockets to see if it's in one of them."

"I haven't got any pockets. Do talk sense, Mother."

"Pity we never bought that dress we looked at."

"Shut up, Mother."

"At least we'd have had the dress… It must have been when you opened your bag she saw how much money you had there. *That* was your mistake."

"We don't know it was a woman."

"There was only women round us."

"Then perhaps it didn't happen at the stall. How can we know? I looked down and the bag was gone. Cut off," her face was white.

"I told you not to flash that money."

"Oh, come on, Mother. I'll think of something."

Her mother put down the loaded baskets. "No. Let's stay here for a bit."

"Don't get difficult, Mother. I can't stand it if you're going to be difficult."

"I have plenty of friends, dear."

"You *are* being difficult."

"Ten pounds, was it, Doris?"

"Twenty." There was a farmyard resemblance between them, and if Doris looked like a ferret her mother was more like some larger placid creature, say the aurochs, more given to painful and unpleasant ailments like Bang's Disease or the bloat. Oddly enough she was more like a bull than a cow, something like a Dame in a Christmas pantomime.

"We can tell the police," she said, watching her daughter.

"No. I'm not telling them about this money. Jim gave it to me special and he wouldn't want me to go to the police about it."

Their eyes met. They both knew that there were one or two ways in which cash came into Jim's pockets that neither the Income Tax authorities nor his employers the Dock Labour Board knew about. It was warm money that slipped greasily through their hands. Usually they got something for it, but sometimes, as now, it disappeared in a way they could not account for. It certainly wasn't lucky money.

"No, we'd better not say anything. Mum's the word." She was fluent in out-of-date, half jocular slang, leaving the impression that there had once been a world of cheerful, not too scrupulous comrades in which the old woman had moved easily.

So by the time Coffin sat in his room worrying about trouble to come there had already been at least two, and possibly more episodes concerning a knife, of which no one had complained and of which he had heard nothing. But this situation did not last much longer.

At five-thirty on Friday, May 15th, a woman pushing a pram and holding the hand of an older child, suddenly set up a great wailing and crying that her handbag was stolen. Both her children started to cry too. A small crowd soon gathered to help and sympathise. An older woman fetched a policeman.

"What's the matter now?" he said patiently. He too felt the heat and was in the mood to be patient but not energetic.

"I've been robbed. My bag's gone." She was in tears. "And look," she pointed to her coat. "My coat's been cut too." There was a long slash by the pocket.

She had no hesitation in telling him all about it, but she knew so little. She had been occupied with her shopping, the baby in the pram and the other child. She could remember nothing which would cause her to look back and say: Yes, that must have been the moment when it happened.

Within the next half-hour a young girl indignantly reported that her yellow plastic pouch bag had been slashed from her shoulders. The thief had got her week's wages, and, what she valued much more, a signed photograph of John Lennon. She was philosophical about her loss.

"I can get another one, though, I know the way. I'd had it a long while, it was a bit cracked across the nose. Anyway, I think I'd like to move over to The Monsters now." She was a young girl who liked to keep up with the pacemakers in her world. "I've got ten pounds saved up. I'm not worried about the money. I just shan't have to buy my pair of cork-soled clogs this week and perhaps *next* week they won't be all the glass, so I won't have lost anything anyway. Anyway, I reckon it's the biggest glass of all to have your bag snitched," and she danced off. But she was the only one who had any information to offer.

By the early evening of the next day, Saturday, May 16th, some half-dozen similar cases had been reported to Coffin.

And now he *had* a bit of trouble to get on with, Coffin wasn't grateful at all.

"I hate these knife cases," he grumbled. "The knife slips or gets too sharp and what have you got?"

There was still plenty known about the knife and its activities that wasn't getting through to Coffin. Many local people knew, and Coffin didn't, that there were at least two women who had discovered knife marks on their handbags but who for some reason or other still had the bags. They also knew of one woman who had a torn coat and said this had been cut by a knife. The word went round that the criminal was not a professional and probably not a local. Soon it was common talk that crimes of this sort often led to something nastier. People felt as if they had seen the entrance of a new strange character on to their stage. A skittery amateur with quick hands for a knife was not welcomed. In its way the neighbourhood had nerves.

"Six bags and over sixty pounds in two days," said Coffin. (Here he was wrong, of course, in this as in other matters the police information was not complete, the thief had had nearly a hundred pounds.) "Well, there's one thing: if he keeps it up at this rate, we shall soon have him."

But in this too he was quite wrong. There were no more cases next day nor next week and for the moment it looked as though everything was over.

One other incident took place on this hot weekend in May, which was certainly recorded by the constable on the beat which took in Courcy Street and Creevey Buildings, but to which Coffin's attention was not directed.

Late on Saturday night, but still well

before midnight, the constable was stopped by a woman who told him she could hear sounds of fighting in the little alley that ran beside Creevey Buildings back in the direction of the river.

She corrected herself. "Or anyway sounds of shouting. And I heard a woman scream." She had put on her coat and hat to come running out to the police but she was still wearing her bedroom slippers and she was beginning to feel embarrassed by them, and by the policeman's way of seeming reluctant to believe what she said or to take it seriously. Fights were not unknown around here on a Saturday night. "I was just going to bed."

"How long ago was this?"

"Just now. I came straight away. Except for putting on a coat." She stared down at her pink fur slippers: she seemed to have forgotten her summer straw hat with the daisies and roses on top. "Perhaps you ought to call it more like a struggle than a fight," she said in a worried voice, studying his face.

But when the policeman went down Mowbray Alley flashing his light, he could see nothing at all, no signs of a fight or a struggle. Everything was still and empty. Only a cat lurked in the shadows.

The policeman turned back, and put everything down to the imagination of his woman informant.

Perhaps in Creevey Buildings a light flickered high up on the sixth floor as if a candle or a torch had moved there. But there were still secret inhabitants behind that Gothic facade sprung from Jeremy Bentham's 'New Prison' out of *Nightmare Abbey*.

In a small back street about half a mile away from Courcy Street and the Red Bull one old woman, who lived permanently in an invalid chair at the window of her sitting-room, was saying good-bye to another old woman.

"Bye, Lal," said the second old woman, who was as bright and active as a bird. "See you tomorrow."

"Usual time?"

"Usual time."

"I don't know how you can bear to be alone in your house Winnie," said Lal as she watched her friend go. "And your eyesight's getting so bad."

"I don't know how *you* bear the crowd you've got here."

"Ah, but it's company, and I need company."

"Of course you do, Lal. Sorry I spoke."

"Not that I actually see much of them. But I *hear*."

"I should think you could hear that dark chap that has the drum and the electric guitar and the dustbin lid."

"Yes, I do hear him. And the three lads on the floor above. It's company, though."

"You need a woman near you, really," cried Winnie, though conscious as she spoke of the delights of being brisk and energetic and on your own two feet while Lal, who had always been the stronger and the braver, was laid up. Winnie was also thinking of the quiet pleasure of her own tiny house waiting for her. "I mean, just for company."

"I've got you."

"Yes, but I mean at *night*. That's why I've got my lodger."

"Well, let's hope the next one is better than the last one, then," said Lal. "For she was never there, was she?" She was thinking what a fool Winnie was not to know a bad lot when she saw one. Surely that one *was* a bad lot?

"Not much," said Winnie.

"I say, do you think she's…?" And Lal looked down her nose as she hinted.

"Not in my house!" said Winnie sharply. "Goodbye now. See you tomorrow."

"I suppose you *did* give her notice?" said Lal.

"Good-bye," said Winnie.

"Usual time," agreed Lal. "See you tomorrow." But Winnie never came. All next day Lal waited.

She waited and waited, but Winnie never came.

A John Coffin Mystery

GWENDOLINE
BUTLER
A NAMELESS COFFIN

'Butler's imagination could give Patricia Cornwell a run for her money in the unpleasantness stakes…'
CRIME TIME

A Nameless Coffin *is published in paperback at £4.99 by CT Publishing. You can get it at all good bookshops or order it directly for £4.99, Postage and Packing free, from CT Publishing, Dept CT26) PO Box 5880, Edgbaston, Birmingham, B16 9BJ.*

fiction

i spied a pale horse
mark timlin

What can we say about the greatest living English exponent of hardboiled fiction! I Spied A Pale Horse (Toxic, £6.99) is an unputdownable nightmare vision of the millennium from the best-selling author of the Sharman books.

If you think you've seen page-turning, neck-breaking, fast action suspense, chaos and carnage before, forget it. Timlin's just upped the ante!

IT WAS VERY QUIET in the meadow where we were lying. Just the sound of the warm breeze from the west playing through the long grass, a cricket chirping somewhere close, and in the trees to our left, two birds having a territorial argument. It was almost uncanny the way it was now, with no sounds of planes coming down in a landing pattern towards Heathrow or Gatwick, no helicopters following the motorway towards London, no cars, no music or the ambient sound of millions of people trying to live their lives in too close proximity to one another. I doubted now if there were millions of people on the entire planet.

I lay on my back and looked up at the blue bowl that used to be the Suffolk sky, and now was whatever you liked to call it, because counties and countries and territorial borders meant nothing, and watched a pair of butterflies flit from flower to flower. There were more butterflies that summer I swear. Or maybe I'd never taken time to notice them before.

Even Puppy was quiet. She knew the rules. She lay in the grass beside me, her body stretched full out, her tail just twitching occasionally, her head on her paws with an inch of her pink tongue jutting out of her mouth, and her eyes on me all the time. She was the only female I had any relationship with these days and that was the way I liked it.

I reached down with my right hand and placed it on the velvet skin that covered her skull between her ears and she moved her head round so she could lick my wrist.

I looked over towards Ugly. He lay half in and half out of a dry ditch on the other side of the rough track that ran through the meadow. He nodded to me and I nodded back. He was massive, built like the proverbial brick shithouse, and the strongest man I'd ever met. Not for the first time I was glad he was on my side. Once upon a time he must have had a proper name but I didn't know it. Ugly was what he wanted to be called and that was OK by me. He was bloody ugly, that was a fact, but he put it about something shocking.

And then I heard it. The sound we'd been waiting for: the sound of horse's hooves, the creak of harness and the rumble of wooden wheels. I looked over at Ugly again and he nodded for a second time and there was a wolfish grin on his face.

I held the barrel of the pump action shotgun I was carrying in my left hand and waited for the horse and cart to come closer.

I knew exactly what ordnance we were carrying. That was my job. I had a five shot Winchester pump fully loaded with twelve gauge shells, plus another five spare. Under my right arm was a US Army Colt .45 of indetermi-nable age with a full seven shot magazine and one spare clip. Under my left was one of my faithful Glock 17's with a full magazine. The other was in a holster strapped around my waist. Both were fully loaded, but I had no spare ammunition. It was a constant worry. In my boot was a six shot .38 Colt Commando and another twenty shells for it in the pocket of my leather jacket. Ugly had a twelve gauge up and under shotgun with a sawn off barrel and stock. In a bag slung round his neck he carried ten spare cartridges. In his pocket was a Webley .455 revolver load-ed with six bullets and a half box of loose shells. That was our entire arse-nal. But it was enough. For now.

In the late nineties when new hand-gun laws had come into force I knew that almost twenty-six million rounds of ammunition had been destroyed. I wish we had some of those now. Of all the shortages since the Death, ammu-nition for our weapons was the worst. In my dreams I found a stash of full metal jackets hidden somewhere in England. Thousands and thousands of brass cartridges that made my mouth water. And even when I was awake I dreamed of the same thing... Maybe one day.

As the cart drew closer so that I could almost smell the horse's sweat I came suddenly to my feet and saw a lone young man driving the rig. He was no more than twenty with long blonde hair and he wore a denim jack-et over raggedy blue jeans.

Ugly rose beside me and we point-ed our carry weapons at the boy. 'Stand and deliver,' I said. 'Your money or your life.' Just like Dick Turpin in days of old. That's what we are. Highwaymen. It's a growth industry.

'Oh shit,' said the boy as he pulled hard on the reins and reached under his jacket with his right hand.

Ugly shot him in the head, the balls of lead blowing half his skull off his shoulders and he slumped back in the seat of the wagon.

The horse reared at the sound and Ugly reached over, grabbed the bridle and held tightly until it calmed down, speaking softly to the animal all the time. I knew he'd been something of a country boy but he didn't like to talk about it. Didn't like to talk about much. But that was his business. Everyone who'd survived The Death had horror stories. I had my own and I didn't talk about them either.

'I hope that was a gun he was reaching for,' I said when the echoes of the shot had died away and Dobbin stopped pawing the ground. 'Or you've wasted a cartridge.'

'Too bad if it wasn't,' said Ugly. Like I said, I was glad he was on my side.

I walked towards the cart, which was fully loaded at the back, just as we'd hoped, and climbed up next to the driver. He didn't look in too great shape but I was used to dead bodies and I felt under his jacket and came up with a shitty old Sterling .32 automatic in a shoulder holster. Damn. I'd been hoping for a 9mm. I checked the clip in the gun's butt. Six shells. I tossed the pistol to Ugly. 'Yours, I believe,' I said.

Ugly smiled a rare smile and dropped the gun into his bag. I searched the driver but he had no more bullets, just a pack of cigarettes and a lighter, which I kept for myself. Ugly

didn't smoke. None of us would for much longer, but a cigarette is a cigarette is a cigarette.

I jumped down and went to check the load. Puppy joined me. 'Shit,' I said. 'There's brains and all sorts all over this.' I found a rag under the driver's seat and mopped up as best I could. Puppy was licking at some blood on the road and I pushed her away with my boot. 'Don't do that Puppy,' I said. 'It's not nice.'

She stopped. She knew to obey me. That was the rule. My way or on your way.

The flatbed of the cart was stacked with goodies. Crates of wine and beer and scotch. A huge can of petrol which was almost as scarce as ammunition, plastic wrapped cartons of canned food, including enough dog food to keep Puppy happy for a year, unless we humans had to start eating it first, clothes, boots, tools and pots and pans. There was even four hundred Benson & Hedges king sized that brought a smile to my face. They were more precious than gold these days. What I didn't smoke I'd barter. It was a real tinker's wagon. Obviously the boy had been an entrepreneur, venturing into the stench and danger of some town and liberating enough goods to sell from tiny settlement to tiny settlement. It was a shame we'd had to close him down. But that was the breaks.

'You want to go get the truck,' I said to Ugly. 'We'd better split before someone comes along.'

He vanished into the undergrowth and I heard the grind of a starter motor and he forced the Land Rover we were driving through a hedge and on to the track and drove it up tight to the cart.

We siphoned some of the petrol straight into the tank and as always I hoped it hadn't been contaminated which would mean a breakdown and I'd watch as Ugly cleared the fuel lines. We got to work and within minutes we'd transferred the gear from the cart into the back of the truck.

Ugly unharnessed the horse and it wandered further into the meadow and started grazing at the grass. We left the boy where he was and reversed the Land Rover back to the tarmac road and headed Northeast.

After twenty miles or so as the sun started to sink towards the horizon we made camp and Ugly set about preparing some food. I opened a can of the newly liberated dog food and fed Puppy, who after she'd eaten immediately settled down and went to sleep.

After we'd eaten, Ugly and I spread out sleeping bags by the fire and I lit one of the boy's cigarettes.

'Those things'll kill you,' said Ugly.

'That'll be a relief,' I said, and lay back and let my mind wander to different times when everything seemed so settled and my worst fear was lung cancer.

AS FAR AS I CAN WORK IT OUT, and work it out I've tried a million times, it all started when someone exploded a nuclear bomb in the old USSR. To this day no one really knows who, and for sure now, no one ever will. It could've been some crazy old guard Cossack who was fed up with Russia becoming a third world country on a diet of Coca Cola, McDonalds hamburgers and satellite TV. Or maybe it was Saddam Hussein who figured that Boris Yeltsin wasn't giving him the backing he so desperately needed. Or maybe it was just a bomb that blew up by itself. There were a lot of warheads rotting away in Russia in those days. And for certain there still are. Maybe they're popping off now, one by one like a string of firecrackers. We'd never know. That is, we'd never know until our skin started peeling off our faces and all sorts of nasty cancerous growths started appearing on our extremities. That would be funny.

The Death wasn't far behind. And before communications broke down altogether there was a theory that somewhere close to ground zero there was a bacterial weapons dump and a lot of nasty germs were blown up into the stratosphere to drop like the gentle rain from heaven. The quality of mercy is not strained you see.

Or it might just have been that the planet grew tired of us, and shucked most of the human race off like bad skin. Weird things had been happening for years. Global warming, the melting of the ice at the poles, holes in the ozone layer, freak weather conditions. And that was just nature. We humans had been busy having our own *fin-de-siècle* as well. Violence, murder, strange religions, mass suicides, alien sightings, the works. Now I've never been of a green persuasion, but it seemed to me we'd lost touch with our environment. If you treated the planet Earth like a stranger, a piece of rock spinning through space and nothing more, then we were bound to come a cropper. And we had. All we were interested in was getting more money and a better house and a bigger car. But the earth was alive. I could feel it that night as I lay in my sleeping bag with Puppy's head on my chest and Ugly lying on the other side of our camp. I felt it more and more every day. If we'd just given it the respect it deserved maybe we wouldn't have found ourselves in our present position, like the dinosaurs, heading for extinction. And we were. I could feel that too, so it matters little what people like Ugly and me do.

So it's all still a mystery where The Death came from. Ah, but isn't ignorance still bliss? And of course now it's of academic interest only. But at the time the bomb went off. Well, the whole world held its breath for a couple of days in case this was the big one. The one that everyone had been waiting for since the end of World War Two. Armageddon. The end of the world. But the media assured us it was a one-off. A dreadful accident. No problem. Get back to doing the *Sun* bingo and don't worry your pretty little heads, the four horsemen were still in the stable. And like fools we believed them, breathed again, and went back to getting ready for the biggest party in history, The Millennium. The year 2000.

But you see I was interested and I dug a little deeper. And I had an inside track because I was a policeman in those days. Yes. Strange as it may seem by the way I earn a crust these days, I was one of the thin blue line that kept society out of the hands of the vandals. And I wasn't a bad copper. I've seen and known worse. And I was married to the most beautiful woman

in the world. Dominique was her name. Her grandmother had been French and she was named after her. She looked like a black-haired angel and acted like one too, and since the day we'd met I'd never really looked at another woman. We'd met when I'd been a beat copper and she'd been studying to become a medical researcher. I'd never thought I'd had a chance with her, but I persevered and succeeded in winning her heart. Then we had our baby. A little girl named Louisa, which was also from the French. I never cheated on my family, which was unusual for a man in my position. Because when you're a detective inspector in the Metropolitan Police, believe me there are many ways to cheat. Sexually, financially, as many as you can name. But I couldn't be bothered. I had the best at home, why settle for less somewhere else? Not that I didn't go to the odd CID dinner where strippers and lap dancers came out with the brandy and cigars. And sometimes there was lipstick on my collar when I left, but I'd make sure I had a clean shirt in the car and drop the dirty one off at a dry cleaners the next day. On the badness scale of one to ten I didn't reckon that was too awful. Not that it matters now. Not that anything matters now.

Some years before I was transferred to Scotland Yard I'd done a stint with the diplomatic protection squad and I still had a good friend at the Foreign Office. So after all the fuss about the bomb had died down I invited him out for a drink, which turned into dinner and asked him what had really happened.

We met in a dingy little pub off

Whitehall. One of the few in the area that hadn't turned into a tourist trap.

It was hot night on the cusp of August and September and I had come straight from the Yard and was wearing a light summer suit. My contact, a senior undersecretary named Clive Price was sweating in a winter weight pinstripe three-piece when he arrived. I had a pint waiting. 'You're an angel John,' he said as he sank the first inch.

'I've been called many things…'

'Believe me. It's even hotter in the halls of power than it is in here.'

'I can imagine.'

'So what's the interest John?' he asked after he'd lit a cigarette I offered.

'Everyone's interested.'

'Maybe. We've tried to keep the media at bay as much as possible. Didn't want to start a panic.'

'I wonder if this country could panic anymore. We seem to have got more lethargic every year.'

'We thought it was a possibility. We seem now to have a central brain. Located somewhere near the anus. Remember the outpouring of grief over Diana?'

'Of course.'

'You were at the funeral weren't you?'

'I was protecting a foreign dignitary.'

'What from? Elton John's singing? Look I don't want to talk too much in here. Walls have ears. How about dinner? My club's just round the corner.'

I can hardly imagine the existence of gentlemen's clubs now.

'Sounds good,' I said. 'Nursery stodge. Perfect for the weather.'

'Don't you believe it John,' he said.

'We've got a new chef. He's a marvel. I promise he'll whip up something cool and light for us.'

We set off though the boiling streets on the short walk to Clive's club. It was in a massive, grey stone building on the other side of the Mall. Its walls streaked with layers of soot that looked like they'd stood for centuries and would stand for centuries more with no more than a nod to contemporary mores.

'Go on through to the bar,' said Clive when we passed through the massive wooden doors into the reception area. 'I'll sign you in and book a table. A swift one first though. Champagne I think. My usual. Just tell the barman to put it on my bill.'

I did as he said. It was blessedly cool inside the building and I could hear the faint throb of an air conditioning unit beneath my feet. Whatever the club looked like on the outside, inside it was obviously more than ready for the approaching new millennia.

Clive did the necessary with the porter on the desk and followed me through to the bar where the waiter had taken my order. 'Good,' said Clive. 'Might as well fiddle whilst Rome burns.' I felt a chill at his words that had nothing to do with the air conditioning.

We sat at a table and the barman brought over a bottle of Krug and two champagne flutes. He poured, Clive tasted, declared himself satisfied and the barman backed off gracefully.

'Did you mean that?' I asked when we were alone.

'What?'

'The crack about Rome burning.'

'We live in interesting times John,' he said. 'And remember that old Chinese curse?'

'May you live in interesting times,' I said.

'Precisely.'

'So what about this bomb? There's all sorts of stories going round.'

'We don't know,' he said holding out his arms wide, the hand that wasn't holding his glass palm outwards in the oldest way in the world to say 'I'm telling the truth.'

'Why not?'

'Because an area of five square miles just outside Odessa was decimated. Razed to the ground. And bang in the middle was the local radar and Air Traffic Control. We don't know if the bomb was incoming or detonated on the ground.'

'Was it all on its own?'

'Sorry?'

'Was it in a silo or a warehouse or slung under an aircraft? What?'

'We don't know John. All we do know is that at the epicentre of the blast there was a military airfield.'

'What about all those satellites that I've paid for with my tax money over the last ten years? I thought they could pick up a pin dropping in a darkened room.'

He looked embarrassed. 'You know how it is John. Some days nothing goes right. The satellite that keeps an eye on that particular piece of real estate was having problems that day.'

'How about the Yanks? Don't tell me their satellites were having problems too.'

'The *entente cordiale* is not all it could

be at the moment. We're having some local difficulties with our friends in the west. They're playing it close to their chests and keeping all sorts of secrets.'

'How many people died?'

'Once again no real information. The Russkies...' he smiled at the word, '...are being a bit close mouthed. Christ, who can blame them? Imagine if that had happened in Missouri or Montana. Close to the chest wouldn't be in it...'

'Or the South Downs,' I interrupted.

'Don't.'

We finished the bottle of champagne and went into the restaurant where Clive had been right, the food had improved and we enjoyed a light supper gazing at the passers-by with their guidebooks and their backpacks.

'So everything's going to be just fine,' I said to Clive over the pudding course.

'Who knows?' he replied. 'We live in hope.'

But I still remembered what he'd said about Rome burning, and I was reminded when I spoke to him for the last time in early February the next year. He phoned me at home. 'John,' he said. 'Strange things are happening.'

'Like what?' I said.

'People are dying in Africa.'

'So what's new?' I asked. 'People are always dying in Africa.'

'This is different. Maybe you should take Dominique and Louisa out of town for a while.'

'Are you drunk Clive?' I asked.

'Permanently. Just do as I say. Happy New Year by the way. It may be our last.' And he hung up on me. I never spoke to him or saw him again. Sometimes I wonder if he's safe in some bunker somewhere with a bunch of politicos breathing recycled air and waiting for it to be safe enough to come out and form a government. I hope I'm around to see them and use up the last of our ammunition. But more likely he's dead too, like nearly everyone else.

That sticky night last summer after we'd drunk our coffee and brandy I went home by cab to the little house I shared with Dominique and Louisa in Clapham. Things were still so normal then, but somehow I could feel a change coming, like the way you can hear a train if you put your ear to the rails even though it's miles away, and I could do nothing about it.

And I'd been right. The change was to come frighteningly quickly and there were only mere months of the old way left before The Death came and nothing would ever be the same again.

I threw my cigarette into the fire and looked up at the sky. It was so black up there. A black that no one who had lived through the days of electricity had ever seen until The Death came. For the past fifty years or so the sky in this part of the hemisphere had reflected the lights of civilisation and had always had a slight orange glow. But now with electricity gone it was the texture of black velvet only lit by the moon and the stars, which on that night were almost bright enough to read by. And the satellites that I'd talked to Clive Price about were still up there, clearly visible as they sat above us and I wondered if they were still beaming pho-

tographs back down to earth. Photographs that no one would ever see, and I could feel the tears running down my cheeks at the thought of my wife and child, dead all those months since The Death was at its height. I only cry in the dark now so that no one can see. Tears for them, and all the others that have died, and for the way I am now killing the survivors as if there were people to spare.

THE MONTHS AFTER I saw Clive Price went by quickly. It was the autumn and early winter of 1999 and everyone was getting ready for the biggest celebration since time began. That old song by Prince was number one for sixteen weeks and you heard it everywhere you went. A friend of mine owned a penthouse on the Isle of Dogs with a huge terrace overlooking the Millennium Dome that was finally finished that October, and had guaranteed the party to end all parties on New Year's Eve. Dominique and I took Louisa with us. She wanted to stay up and see the million pound firework display that the government had been promising us for months. Louisa was seven years old then, still young enough to believe in Santa Claus, but old enough to participate in the more adult parts of the festivities like going to midnight mass on Christmas Eve and realising what it meant. Dominique and I had spent a fortune on presents and once she was fast asleep after church we piled brightly wrapped parcels around the tree in our living room. That Christmas was one of the best I could ever remember. I was glad that Louisa had died still believing in Santa Claus. It was a small mercy.

The New Year's Eve party was everything that my friend had promised and so were the fireworks. Louisa watched them yawning, but with a look of such joy on her face that I almost wept. Then Dominique and I put her down in our host's bedroom and danced until dawn.

It's one of the best memories that I carry with me now.

But the New Year brought all sorts of strange tidings.

First there was the Millennium bug that had caused such scares for the eighteen months or so before the clock struck twelve on that magical night. According to the media, all sorts of computers were going to crash as the twentieth century became the twenty-first and there'd be no electricity, no gas, no money from the banks, traffic lights wouldn't work and even your CD player would go into free fall and you wouldn't be able to listen to Prince anymore. Which believe me would've been a blessing.

But in fact most things carried on as normal. Except that almost every burglar alarm in London seemed to go off as the laser beam shot from Greenwich Observatory across the river to the dome where the Queen and the Prime Minister were getting stuck into the *gratis* champagne and added a high pitched cacophony to the church bells and car horns and cheers and explosions that welcomed New Year's Day Two Thousand.

But a number of survivalists did take the warnings to heart and stockpiled food and bottled water and batteries and anything else they could think of during that time. Ugly and I have been grateful to them often as we've come across the remains of these caches on our travels.

You see it's an ill wind.

And after Clive Price phoned me with his doom-laden message I started to scan the newspapers every day.

What he'd said was true. People were dying in Africa. And Asia. And no one knew why. And people seemed to care less. There was a strange hangover in the country after the millennium celebrations. There'd been so much talk of new beginnings that the year Two Thousand was an anti climax.

But not for long.

I saw my first victim of The Death in a pub in Marylebone in late February. I'd been giving evidence in a manslaughter case at Marylebone Magistrate's Court that day and went for a pint with the prosecuting barrister when the court was adjourned. It was freezing cold outside, and we were knees in against the open fire in the corner when I noticed a young woman come in with two female friends and go to the bar. She was young and blonde and attractive in a long blue coat. She seemed to have a heavy cold and pulled a handkerchief from the pocket of her coat and blew her nose. But then February is cold and flu season in London.

Then, all of a sudden she went white and sweat broke out on her face like the tide coming in. She held onto the bar with one hand and tried to speak to the friend on her right who was ordering a round of drinks. But all that came out of her mouth was a gout of blood so red that I thought she was vomiting tomato soup and she fell forward, her face smacking against the polished surface of the bar before she crumpled to the floor in a heap.

Both her friends jumped and screamed and I stood up and ran towards them. 'I'm a policeman,' I said. 'Give her some air.' Then to the barman. 'Call an ambulance quickly.'

He stood transfixed and I shouted. 'Call nine-nine-nine NOW.'

He broke out of his trance and reached for the phone as I knelt beside the girl who couldn't have been more than twenty and I felt for her pulse. There was nothing, just the blood still oozing from her mouth and a long string of mucus coming from her nose.

I gave her heart massage and tried to force an air passage but her throat was constricted, and even though I gave her mouth to mouth it was no good.

Later I wondered if mouth to mouth had been such a good idea. But I'm immune to The Death you see. I worked it out roughly that point nought one of the human race are. If I hadn't been, I doubt I'd've lived for the rest of the week.

I was lucky. Or maybe unlucky. I leave you to work that one out for yourself.

The ambulance came about ten minutes later but she was dead. The paramedics took her away and I went back to my drink but couldn't touch it. She wasn't to be the last victim of The Death I was to see by a long way. But I'll always remember her. Someone told me her name was Susan. I never did find out her other name

I SPIED A PALE HORSE is published in paperback at £6.99 by Toxic. You can get it at all good bookshops or order it directly for £6.99, Postage and Packing free, from Toxic, Dept CT26) PO Box 5880, Edgbaston, Birmingham, B16 9BJ.

singleminded
hélène de monaghan

Hélène de Monaghan is one of the leading French authors of crime fiction, and has won many awards for fiction, her plays and her television work. She has been called 'The French Patricia Highsmith'.

Singleminded *is one of the best known crime novels in France, and many critics consider it to be one of the best 'classical' crime novels of all time.*

IT WAS THE DAY before yesterday, while she was extracting a white hair from my head, that I knew she had to die.

Why didn't it click sooner? We all know why: you dream up some nice clean solution to your problems, only to find your 'civilised self' stepping in, aghast.

Civilisation! Some so-called uncivilised people understand that death is the best way to deal with those who get in the way. And as for our own ancestors, well, they knew that a quick nudge to an old one ended his suffering.

But it's not as if Liliane suffers.

No. The little angel radiates health, and when she flashes that beaming grin at me I know she'll live forever unless I put an end to it.

I can't pretend she's been a financial burden. In fact, if we're being honest, I live off her money. Her father was Morel, the shoe manufacturer, and I knew exactly where I was treading when I married her.

I can't even accuse her of infidelity. In five years of marriage I have never had a single reason to feel jealous. She's young, blonde and sexy, but I invite my most captivating friends round to spend whole evenings trying to flirt with her and she won't so much as look at the bait.

Liliane is completely attached to me and tells everyone we meet that her 'Puppy' (which is the pet name she gave me on the first day we met and for which I claim no responsibility) is the light of her life, the apple of her eye, the cream in her coffee.

She will never accept a separation. She is so acquisitive that in her eyes I belong to her as much as her jewels or her furniture. She is the wife of François Lantier and intends to remain so until death us do part.

Which is OK by me, because I'm sick of waiting.

Insurance company statistics tell me that a woman of twenty-eight can expect to die at seventy-eight, by which time she will be visiting me in some nice white loony bin.

I'm not a Moslem; Arab fatalism gives me no consolation. And I'm not the type of sucker who sits around waiting for providence to solve my problems.

I could wait for a wall to fall on her, or a truck to smash her to pieces, or an escaped maniac who could throttle her to death... the world is full of possibilities, all of it wishful thinking.

Since we're being realistic, I'd like to discount the possibility of a heart attack: she's a moderate smoker, hardly drinks, sticks faithfully to a healthy diet, visits health farms and she will never suffer from stress.

And finally, as far as I can see, most of her family live forever and I know she'll outlive me. If I let her.

The mere thought that in two years I could still be facing her across the breakfast table is driving me crazy.

On the morning of my marriage, as I walked out of the church with Liliane on my arm, dazzling and radiant, I had a sudden terrible illumination. I realised I'd made the mistake of my life.

The photographers snapped away, Liliane bubbled over with self-satisfaction and I knew I didn't love her.

I had been blinded by her youth, her beauty, her vitality, as well as her father's generosity in setting up my law practice.

I was a young lawyer, just returned from Algeria, utterly spellbound by her family's money. It would have been impossible to set up an office in Paris without any financial backing. Along with her dowry, Liliane brought me a magnificent, superbly furnished town house on the Avenue d'Lena, plus an authentic Empire desk and some wealthy clients for my practice. I chose luxury instead of happiness.

Five years of marriage have confirmed my worst expectations. Little by little she revealed her true nature: a spoilt child, self-centred and arrogant, with the cold assurance of someone born into money.

She rules our little kingdom like a manicured dictator, decreeing everything, from how I should part my hair to when I must visit the dentist. Our holidays have been planned for the next ten years. Even sex: slotted in just before the late night news.

Her snobbish pseudo-intellectualism on top of her involvement (and mine) in endless Parisian functions would have worn out any man.

Slowly, I began to detest her breath, her smell, her voice, her way of walking, her clothes, how she screams at the maid, her fake laughter, her phoney kindness, her pretentiousness and most of all, her love for me, possessive and oppressive.

And so, for better or for worse, along came Zaza.

If I hadn't met her, my life would have meandered on the same forever. How could I have known, when I hired this myopic assistant, that I'd fall for her like a teenager?

I scarcely noticed her when she started working in the office. She was dowdy and wore thick glasses, and seemed a world apart from the slender Swedes, the buxom Germans or the apple-cheeked Flemish girls I'm usually attracted to. Zaza is tiny, dark and skinny, a country girl. I like sleek women, sophisticated women in couture outfits. Zaza, with her unkempt hair and student clothes, seems never to have heard of designers or hairdressers, let alone facial hair remover. Her wardrobe seems limited to two skirts, two blouses, a red coat and a beret.

She buzzes around the office, joking with my clients, playing tricks on Gilles, my brother-in-law, pulling faces and, worst of all, humming while she rearranges my files. She flits about; I've even caught her dancing in the elevator. In other words, she epitomises everything I usually loathe in a woman.

But I'm madly in love. I don't understand how she did it. One moment I was a free man. Now I'm wrapped around her little finger. What mysterious wiles have transformed polite indifference into unconditional subservience?

How could those twinkling eyes, the echo of her giggling next door, three lines of her illegible handwriting on a file, that ridiculous beret hanging from the rack, become my justification for living?

Simply because she is genuine, alive, funny, gracious, honest. Because I love her and love is mysterious and beyond understanding. My darling Zaza—she would collapse with laughter if I told her I was planning to kill my wife for her.

And in the meantime, she doesn't give a damn for me.

Of course, since I'm neither heartless, nor completely stupid, I didn't reach my conclusion without scanning through several solutions less dangerous for me… and less final for Liliane.

I'm a lawyer. I see couples separating almost every day of the year. Divorce would seem to be the most natural option. But, precisely because I'm a lawyer, I know that it can take years to come through if I can't get a mutual agreement, especially if I don't have any grounds. And I've got to get rid of her right away.

That's my problem. I don't have any grounds. Legally speaking, I'm the happiest husband on the planet. Pick any ten witnesses from a random sample of our friends. They'd all swear my wife is devoted beyond the call of duty, that they've never met such a loving couple, that we're an emblem of nuptial bliss, etcetera, etcetera.

I find it so painful to think of destroying this idyllic image, shattering Liliane's carefully wrought PR. I can't bring myself to hurt her feelings. Killing her is bad enough.

Don't get me wrong; I'm no monster. But, as I hope you've gathered, I'm no sentimental hypocrite either. We watch the death of millions of skeletons in Africa on our TV screens, night after night, without batting an eyelid. Why should anyone really care about Liliane being torn away from her mindless fancyworld? I'll do it quite painlessly.

She's in the prime of her youth. She'll never have to deal with ageing or illness, or the loss of her beloved Mamy, whom we all love dearly. She'll never have to cope with my irredeemable dissatisfaction; she will have eternal peace. Let's face it: I'm doing her a favour.

And it's not as if it's all a bed of roses for me. I'm going to have to handle all the practical side of things, and take all the risks.

I have no delusions; it will be a long way from dream to reality, from the marital bed to the Morel family tomb in Argenton.

Before we begin, I've got to cover my tracks, derail any lead that's going to point to me. The slightest blunder could make her death suspicious, and it would only need some prying cop to sniff out who would profit from the crime.

It must not be me.

Liliane's father died last summer, making her an immensely rich woman. She gobbled up the lot because Mamy foolishly married Daddy with a pre-nuptial settlement which means the old dear gets the corner of some field in Normandy. As for Gilles, Liliane's half brother, he can only sit back and watch the whole cake being forklifted onto her plate. He was a tiny child when his mother hit the jackpot and married again. He was never a real member of the Morel family. The bitter truth is that he'll always be at Liliane's mercy.

Because we don't have any children, when Liliane dies her fortune should revert to Mamy. French law decrees that the surviving spouse gets to inherit only if there is no father or mother or brother or sister or nephew. In other words, you can clean up after some senile partner for years on end and then get nothing for all that slopwork. It just takes some unknown niece to swan in at the last moment for you to lose the lot.

Dogs have more rights. It's enough to put you off marriage.

A few months ago, in order to avert this possible catastrophe, I wheedled Liliane into making out her will in my favour. In return, I mentioned her in mine.

It was like getting water out of a stone. God, the hours of coaxing and cajoling it took to worm it out of her hot little hands.

I hadn't hatched my plan then. I was just thinking of my own security in case she happened to die before me. I never imagined that this prize, which had taken so much to achieve, could ultimately rebound on me, could make me a number one suspect.

So I have to rethink the whole scheme in such a way that I'm no longer Liliane's heir, in case things turn out badly.

But on the other hand, if all goes according to plan and she appears to have died of natural causes, I don't see why I should sacrifice the loot.

I could have torn the new will up, but this would be an act of self-destructive idiocy; who is going to believe that an old lady has murdered her only daughter to inherit her fortune? And besides, I'd lose all the cash.

My infinite acumen tells me that the only thing to do is to convince Liliane to make her will out in favour of someone else, someone who can take my place, if needs be, in the suspects' line-up.

And I reckon young Gilles fits the bill down to a T. He's still a bachelor, in his early thirties, a regular playboy who leads a riotous life crammed full of girls, sports cars and the odd spot of gambling. Perfect! I get Liliane to make out a new will, then keep the precious document secret and produce it only in case of serious danger. It would be a sort of safety net for me.

Then either everything goes to plan and I just tear it up and take full advantage of my rights, or else there's a snag and I produce the second will to get myself out of trouble.

In any case, I'll never be out in the cold. On the day of my marriage, Daddy Morel, respectful of my pride and knowing Liliane must be kept in the style to which she was accustomed, opened a bank account for me, Swiss of course, which contains enough to maintain a small harem for about one hundred years. The apartment was even bought in my name. The old man was shrewd—compensating me in ad-

vance for marrying his daughter.

Come what may, I will prevail.

After an intimate little dinner in an expensive little restaurant, just the way she likes it, we return home, where Liliane does her usual ploy of luxuriating seductively on the bearskin rug, basking herself by the fire. I take advantage of her amorous outburst to slip in a few casual words:

"Do you know, my darling, that bastard Lelong has just inherited a hundred million francs from his wife?"

"So what, baby?"

"It's obscene!"

"What makes you say that?"

"It makes him a money-grabbing posthumous pimp."

"But my Puppy, if something nasty happened to Baby, you would also get all her money. Remember, we also made a will…"

I interrupt.

"And look what I'm doing to that will!"

I point to the fireplace, where an old useless document of mine is scrunched up and burning.

Flabbergasted, Liliane raises her shocked uncomprehending eyes to mine.

"What have you done, Puppy? Why are you doing this terrible thing?"

"That will is evil. It fills me with horror; I feel sick with myself when I think about it. How can I feel any happiness in profiting from your death? It has become intolerable to me, as it would to any man of honour. There can be no discussion. My mind is made up."

"Oh my Puppy, my darling, you are an angel. Only you could have such scruples!"

Liliane loves it. Tears slide out from under her quivering lashes. How right she is!

"Only because I'm inspired by you. Tomorrow you must write another will in someone else's name."

"Oh my sweetheart, if you insist. I shall give everything to a charity for sick animals."

"Are you crazy?"

"What did Puppy say?"

"Er… your father loathed animals. He only liked shooting them. And he always insisted that the money should remain in the family."

"Alright, I'll give everything to darling Mamy."

"At her advanced age? Think of the shock the news might give her. It could be fatal! Have some compassion. And remember, you're sure to outlive her."

"Well then, who?" asks Liliane tersely. She is becoming impatient.

"Gilles, I suppose."

Liliane stands up, amazed. Not a day goes past without me ranting against this nincompoop, whom I'm forced to employ as a partner out of 'family spirit'; more specifically because Mamy insisted, in spite of his incompetence, his deceitfulness, his Godawful laziness and his stutter, which is about as useful for a lawyer as it is for a sports commentator.

Liliane seems gobsmacked. She doesn't know what to say, but that's nothing new.

"Are you serious?"

"Of course. After all, we mustn't forget that he is your brother and your only close family."

"He won't believe it when I tell him!"

"But you won't tell him, will you? You'll tell nobody. It must remain our little secret."

"Why?"

"You know what Gilles is like, my darling. Such a parasite. Always short of money. I can't bear the thought of someone wishing you dead, however unconsciously. You must promise to say nothing."

"Oh my lamb, of course I promise."

And with that she throws herself on top of me. In return for my godlike selflessness, I'm mauled all over. Liliane has always gone a little over the top when she demonstrates her passion.

As I come up for air, I gasp "In any case, my darling, you're going to outlive us all."

Liliane obediently redid her will in Gilles' favour. It is now locked up in my safe and I'm the only one with the key or the combination. And now everything is set. I no longer have any financial interest in the death of my wife. On the contrary. I can easily prove that I was the most pampered spouse in Paris.

"She spoilt me rotten, Officer. Nothing was good enough for her Puppy."

I'm already using the past tense to describe what still exists. It is an auspicious omen for my glorious future.

I'm in the middle of a court hearing. It began at the ungodly hour of 1 p.m., when most civilised people usually choose to eat. But instead of dozing alongside the magistrates, I meditate on my problem.

How can I finish her off?

At some point in their lives, everyone in the world has wanted to kill their wife, their boss, their landlord... But to actually do it, to go through with it, is quite another matter, and few people have got what it takes. Oh they begin alright, and then they start to get a bit reluctant, they hum and haw, they make excuses to themselves and then, inevitably, they give it all up. Then there is much talk about finding some holy interdiction at the bottom of their soul which stayed their hand at the last moment.

Translated, this means they got all coy and were scared of being caught red handed.

But I'm made of sterner stuff. Nothing will dissuade me. I will go through with it and I will come out of the venture without a stain on my reputation because I shall avoid the laughable blunders of amateurs.

For a start, in order to commit the perfect crime, one must avoid the two evils of improvisation and direct action. Improvisation is the trademark of excitable hotheads who like to act before they think. And because they do not bother to use their heads, they will end up losing them. A murder must be planned down to the last detail well in advance. Nothing must be left to chance. Any murderer foolish enough to act on impulse will suffer for it. They will be in the same position as the examination candidate who has never opened his textbook.

Direct action is done by dumdums. Nine times out of ten they leave a trail of clues behind them, leading right to their front door. Because they're always at the scene of their crimes, they have no real alibi, which is a really serious mistake. Furthermore, since they're often killing for the first time, they run a huge risk of botching everything there and then.

You know what I mean. The old sad predictable story. The sticky fingers on the kitchen knife, the footprints in the muddy garden, bloodstained clothes hastily stuffed into the washing machine, the scratches, slashes and bruises inflicted by obstinate victims.

Why don't people learn? Take the strange case of the iron bar. Now, any idea of committing a murder with this old chestnut ought to be instinctively discarded. It implies the twin sins of direct action and improvisation. But day after day, I open my newspaper to find it full of the sob stories of half-wits who continue to use this medieval method, blind to technological advances. This is the twentieth century! If an alien landed in France tomorrow, it could only assume that anyone who wanted to get rid of anyone else automatically stumbled across their mandatory iron bar, as though the country were swarming with them. Personally, I have never come across an iron bar casually lying around but even if they grew in the Place d'Lena, I most certainly would not be using them. I find the method cruel and barbarous on top of being messy.

For the same reason, I exclude

knives, razors or any other sharp instrument which would involve both an appropriate knowledge of human anatomy and a very steady hand, qualities I do not possess. I need not mention the difficulty of finding an alibi even the slowest cop isn't going to swallow some story about how my wife impaled herself while peeling an apple.

We must also eliminate that most orthodox of methods, the sharp blow to the back of the head or between the eyes. It looks simple but it requires split-second timing and accuracy, and I must not overestimate my strength. You wouldn't know it, but sometimes, especially if I'm nervous, I can be really clumsy. And I'm so sentimental that I couldn't bear to catch that look of shocked surprise, her eyes clouding over, tears starting out from under her lashes…

Basically, I'm too tenderhearted. I'm just not capable of actually inflicting damage on her. They say a simple bullet through the heart is the kindest way to go, instantaneous and almost painless, but I've been a lawyer too long to have any illusions about what the cops are going to say when I tell them it was all a fatal accident and I was just cleaning out my gun. Incidentally, I've always wondered if people actually do anything else with their guns apart from clean them and shoot their relations.

No, in order to succeed one must be realistic and that sometimes means recognising that people are not as stupid as one might hope. The cops, the DA and the pathologist are no fools. The slightest error and I'm kaput.

The most important thing to bear in mind, as my Aunt Agatha always used to say, is that one can never really change. I can't wish myself into some callous Kung Fu star with a taste for amateur surgery. I'm a gentleman, and I must use the skills that God gave me. The Lord helps those who help themselves. Violent crime is beneath me. I shall create my crime according to my needs, incorporating my talent and my knowledge, my character, my prudence and my sensitivity.

Already, before I'd even thought of murder, my trusty instincts made me disguise the steady decay of my feelings for Liliane. I remain the most attentive husband. No one in the world, not even Zaza, has the slightest idea of the hopes I'm cherishing in secret.

I must act clandestinely, indirectly. I must stand in the wings, orchestrate it all from the shadows.

To my mind the best possible solution would be for the victim to commit suicide. What posthumous accolades wouldn't I inscribe on Liliane's tombstone if she could just agree to do it herself and retire from the scene gracefully!

Lulled by the drone of the report read by a tired court councillor, I slip into a daydream. I fantasise about a mysteriously grief-stricken Liliane throwing herself onto the subway tracks in front of a horrified mob. How dramatic! But maybe a little complicated… why not just rest her lovely head for a few minutes—I'm told a quarter of an hour is more than sufficient—in the oven, after switching on the gas…

But how can I get her to do it? I know her only too well. She would survive a nuclear war with her lip-gloss intact. The woman is inhuman!

Perhaps I should make it a long-term project: slowly, methodically, insidiously chipping away at her mental state, planting seeds of doubt about her own sanity... I must be going crazy. I might as well try demolishing the Statue of Liberty with a spoon.

No, I don't have the time to wait for Liliane to see the light.

I could make a grand gesture. I could just come out with it, brutally inform her that I have ceased to love her and have a mad passion for Zaza. She would then be desperate, but I know her, there is no way she would do the decent thing. She would just murder my lover and I in a frenzy of rage. Liliane has always lacked class. One can only expect a vulgar reaction from her, and she is much too selfish to even think of doing us a good turn.

However, if I were to die, there is a chance that she might take her own life, that life would seem unbearable to her. It might work, but it entails a certain sacrifice on my part. Still, for a moment, the wonderful image of Liliane, remorseful and in tears, throwing her handcuffed self into my grave as they heap on the clods of earth, seems almost worth that sacrifice...

But a sudden "Sir, you may examine the witness," yanks me out of my coffin. I rise up out of my daydreams: forced back to reality. I discard my Dracula fangs to plead the case of my client, who has been arrested for drink-driving.

Although my plea to the court was not bad, I can remember when I've been more brilliant.

hélène de monaghan

singleminded

"...If you've missed the sharp, ironic wit and style of Patricia Highsmith, meet Hélène de Monaghan, a French writer expert at the sting in the tail (and elsewhere for that matter..)"
—CRIME TIME

Singleminded *is published in paperback at £6.99 by CT Publishing. You can get it at all good bookshops or order it directly for £6.99, Postage and Packing free, from CT Publishing, Dept CT26) PO Box 5880, Edgbaston, Birmingham, B16 9BJ.*

fiction

the long midnight of barney thomson
douglas lindsay

Extract from *The Long Midnight of Barney Thomson by Douglas Lindsay,*
Published by Piatkus Books, Available now, price £6.99

FAITH AND PUBERTY HAVE IT OUT WITH BLISS

The rain streams against the windows. The old wooden frames rattle in the wind, the curtains blow in the chill draught which forces its way into the room. Ghosts and shadows. Outside, the night is cold and bleak and dark, to match Barney's mood as he sits at the dinner table. He pushes the food around his plate, every so often stabbing randomly at a pea or a piece of meat pie, imagining that it is Wullie or Chris. All the while Agnes looks over his shoulder at the television, engrossed in a particularly awful Australian soap opera, taped from earlier in the afternoon. The food grows cold on their plates, as Dr Morrison tells Nurse Bartlett that she will never be able to have children, as a result of the barbecue incident at Tom and Diane's engagement party, and Barney holds forth on what he intends to do to take his revenge upon his colleagues.

'Ah'm gonnae get they bastards if

it's the last thing Ah dae. Ah mean it.'

'Yes, dear.' Agnes's mind is on other things.

'Ah mean, who the hell dae they think they are, eh?' He stabs a finger at her. 'Ah'll tell ye. Naeb'dy, that's who they are. They're naeb'dy. And Ah'm bloody well gonnae get them.'

'Yes, dear.'

There is a mad glint in Barney's eye. The possibilities are endless, the bounds for doing evil and taking his revenge unfettered, limited only by his imagination—a very tight limit, as it happens. He has been thinking it over since the afternoon's humiliation, and the more he dwells upon it, the more he likes the idea of murder.

Murder! Why not? They deserve it. You should never humiliate your colleagues in front of the customers. Isn't that one of the first things they teach you in barber school? But these young ones today. They never even bother with any sort of hairdressing education. Five years of high school learning sociology and taking drugs, and they think they know everything. They lift a pair of scissors and start cutting hair as if they're preparing a bowl of breakfast cereal. It just isn't that simple. It's a skill which needs to be nurtured and cultivated. Like brain surgery, or astrophysics.

The trouble is that they're all bastards, every one of them. Not just Wullie and Chris, but every other cretin who ever lifted a pair of scissors in anger. But not for much longer. It's payback time.

'Whit dae ye think? Stabbin'? Shootin'? Poison even?'

'Yes, dear,' she says, absent-mindedly nodding.

He brightens up. Poison. Brilliant. Agnes was good for bouncing ideas off sometimes. 'Aye, ye're right. Poison's the thing. Ah don't know anythin' about it, but Ah'm sure Ah can find out. Ah'm sure Ah can. Whit dae ye think?'

'Yes, dear.'

'Aye, Ah expect Ah can. It shouldnae be too difficult.' Murderous plans race through his mind, a manic smile slowly wanders across his lips. 'One o' they slow-acting ones, so Ah can stick it in their coffee durin' the day, and they willnae die until much later.' He rubs his hands together. 'Brilliant idea. Bloody brilliant.'

There is some illuminated corner of his mind telling him that he isn't being serious. Not murder. Surely not murder. But it is good to think about it for a while. Thinking about it isn't the same as doing it.

'Yes, dear,' says Agnes. Is Doreen really a lesbian or is she just pretending she loves Epiphany so she can get close to Dr Morrison without Blaize becoming suspicious?

Without any further stabs of conscience, Barney tucks into his pie, chips and peas, all the time plotting his wild revenge. It is sad that it has to come to this, he thinks, but they've brought it upon themselves. Particularly that bastard Wullie.

Another thought occurs. Perhaps he could poison some of those bloody customers as well. They were asking for it, most of them. He gets carried away for a second on a roller coaster of genocide. Calms down. He's Barney Thomson, barber, not Barney Pot, deranged dictator. Still, the thought is there, if it ever becomes necessary. A lot of them deserve it, that's for sure.

His mind begins to wander to a grand vision where he is in the shop with two other barbers, neither of whom anyone will go to, while there sits a great queue of people all waiting for him to cut their hair. He would take three-quarters of an hour over every haircut, and annoy as many of them as possible. Heaven.

He is reluctantly hauled from his dreams by the ringing of the telephone. He stops, a forkful of chips poised on the cusp of his mouth, looks at Agnes. Her eyes remain glued to the television, oblivious to the clatter of the phone. He points the chipped fork.

'You gonnae get that, hen?'

She scowls, answers without removing her eyes from the television. 'Ah cannae. Faith and Puberty are about tae have it out wi' Bliss.'

Executing his trademark eye-rolling and head-shaking routine, he envelops the chips in his mouth, tosses the fork onto the plate, stands up to get the phone, hoping it will be a wrong number.

'Whit?'

'Hello, Barney, it's me.'

Breathes a sigh of relief. It is one of the few people from whom he doesn't mind receiving a call—his drinking and dominoes partner, Bill Taylor. This will be a call to arms.

'Oh, hello, Bill, how ye doin'?'

'No' so bad, no' so bad. And you?'

'Oh, cannae complain, cannae complain.'

They discuss trivialities for a few minutes, such as Bill's brother Eric having told his girlfriend Yvonne that he loves Fiona. Finally, however, Bill gets to the main item on the agenda.

'Fancy goin' out for a few pints the night?' he says.

'Oh, Ah don't know, mate. Ah always go tae see my mother on a Tuesday night, ye know. She'd be a bit upset if Ah didnae go. Ye know whit they're like, eh?'

'Well, how about a couple o' pints before ye go? Ah'll meet you doon the boozer aboot half seven, eh?'

'Aye, awright, that shouldnae be too bad. Can't stay too long though, eh?'

'Aye, aye.'

Barney says his goodbyes, trudges back into the sitting room. Tries to ignore the television while he polishes off his dinner, then slumps into the armchair and falls asleep. He dreams of poison and of long prison sentences and of chain gangs and electric chairs, and then he awakes with a start at just about the time he needs to.

As he leaves the house to go to the pub, the aftermath of dinner remains where it has been for over an hour, while Chastity and Hope attempt to bundle Mercury into the boot of a car, in what he assumes to be an entirely different soap opera from the one he suffered earlier.

'Ah'm goin' tae the boozer, then ma mother's. Awright?'

'Yes, dear.'

'Ah'll be back aboot ten.'

'Yes, dear.'

He waits for some more reaction, waits in vain. Walks out, slamming the door as he goes.

'Aye, well, that's a' very well,' says Bill Taylor, brandishing his pint, 'but who is tae categorise depth? Eh? Everyone's capable o' depth. Nietzsche said, "Some men consider wimmin tae be deep. This is untrue. Wimmin are no' even shallow." Well, tae me that's a load o' crap. Now, Ah'm nae feminist or nothin', Ah'm sure you'll understand, but Ah've got tae say, that even wimmin can say stuff that's deep too. Most o' whit they say's crap now, but it disnae mean they can't come out wi' somethin' intelligent every now and again.'

Barney nods in agreement. 'Ah never realised that ye were a student o' Nietzsche?'

Bill grunts, buries his hand in a bowl of peanuts. 'Ah widnae go that far. Obviously Ah've studied a' the great philosophers, but Ah'm definitely no' a fan o' Nietzsche.'

'Me neither. Typical bloody German. Spent his life writin' about some kind o' master race, tae which he presumably considered himself tae belong, and then he went aff his napper, reverted tae childhood, and spent the last ten years o' his life in an asylum, playing wi' Lego and Scalextric, and pretending tae be a cowboy. Tae be perfectly honest, they nineteenth-century German philosophers get on ma tits.'

Barney wonders about himself sometimes. Why is it that when he sits over a pint and a game of dominoes in the pub he can talk pish with the best of them, but when the chips are down, and he really needs to, there is nothing there? Like the guy who can hole a putt from any part of the green, until someone offers him a fiver to do it.

'My friend, my friend, my friend,' Bill says, his mouth full of peanuts, 'ye dinnae need tae tell me aboot German philosophy. Ah'm as aware as anybody else o' the failings o' German philosophy. An' let's face it, when it comes down tae it, a' German philosophy amounts tae is "if in doubt, invade it". Aye, that's it in a nutshell, so it is.'

'Well, well, Bill, Ah never thought Ah'd hear ye talk like that. Certainly Germany was guilty of horrendous imperialism during the first half o' the twentieth century, but that's no' necessarily indicative of the past two hundred years.'

Barney executes a swift manoeuvre with a double four, lifts his pint.

'Is it no'? Is it no'? That's a load o'shite, so it is, and Ah don't think ye can just dismiss fifty years as no' indicative. Especially when it is,' says Bill.

Barney pauses to take another sip of beer, studies the state of their game of dominoes. It is turning into a bloody tussle, good-natured but life-threatening. He is about to make his next move and expand his thoughts on German imperialism when he pauses briefly to listen to what two young women are saying as they walk past their table.

'…no, no, that's no' right, Senga, so it's no'. Ah'm telling ye, Neptune's the planet that's the furthest fi' the sun at the moment. Awright, Pluto's further away maist o' the time, but Neptune has a circular orbit, while Pluto has an elliptical one, so that for some years at a time, Pluto's orbit takes it nearer tae the sun than Neptune. And that's the case at the…'

The voice is lost in the noise of the

bar as they move away. Barney and Bill look at each other with eyebrows raised.

'Unusual tae find,' says Barney, 'a wummin with so much as an elementary grasp o' astronomy.'

Bill raises his finger, waves it from side to side. 'As a matter o' fact, Ah wis discussing the other day wi' this girl in my work called Loella, the exact...'

'You have a girl in your work called Loella?' asks Barney, with some surprise.

'Aye, aye Ah dae.'

'Oh.'

'And as Ah wis sayin', Loella and I were talking about anti-particles. Ah wis under the impression that a photon had a separate anti-particle, but she says that two gamma rays can combine tae produce a particle-anti-particle pair, and thus the photon is its own anti-particle.'

Barney considers this, while keeping one half of his brain on the game.

'So, whit your sayin' is that the anti-particle o' an electron is a positron, which has the same mass as the electron, but is positively charged?'

Bill thinks about this, slips a two/three neatly into the game. 'Aye, aye, Ah believe so.'

'And a wummin called Loella told you this?'

'Aye, she did.'

The two men jointly shake their heads at the astonishing sagacity displayed by the occasional woman, then return with greater concentration to the game.

They both try to remember what they had been talking about before the interruption, but the subject of German imperialism has escaped them, and Bill is forced to bring up more mundane matters.

'So, how's that barber's shop of yours doing, eh, Barney?' he says, surveying the intricate scene before him, and wondering if he is going to be able to get rid of his double six before it is too late.

Barney shakes his head, rolls his eyes. 'Ye don't want tae know, my friend, you do not want tae know.'

'Is there any trouble?' asks Bill, concern in the voice, although this is principally because he finds himself looking at a mass of twos, threes and fours on the table, and sixes and fives in his hand.

Barney shakes his head, rolls his eyes. 'Ach, it's they two bastards, Wullie and Chris. Ah don't know who they think they are. Keep taking a' my customers. It's gettin' to be a joke.'

Bill nods. In the past, he has been on the receiving end of one of Barney's one-hour-fifteen-minute 'Towering Inferno' haircuts, and in the end was forced to move from the area to avoid subjecting himself to the fickle fate of his friend's scissors. He well understands those in the shop who flock to the other two.

'They're good barbers, Barney.'

Barney stops what he is doing, the words cutting to his very core. Drops his dominoes, places his hands decisively on the table. Fire glints in his eye. A green glint.

'And Ah'm no', is that whit yer saying, Bill? Eh?'

Bill quickly raises his hands in a placatory gesture. 'No, no, Barney, Ah didnae mean it that way, ye know Ah didnae.'

Barney shakes his head. 'Like hell ye didnae. Et tu, Bluto?' he says, getting within inches of quoting Shakespeare.

'Look, Barney, calm down, Ah didnae mean anythin'. Now pick up yer dominoes and get on wi' the game, will ye no'?'

With a grunt, a scowl, a noisy suck of his teeth, Barney slowly lifts his weapons of war and, unhappy that Bill has seen what he holds in his hands, resumes playing.

The game continues for another couple of minutes, before Bill feels confident enough to reintroduce the subject. The quiet chatter of the pub continues around them, broken only by the occasional ejaculation of outrage.

'So, whit's the problem wi' the two o' them, then, Barney?'

Barney grumbles. 'Ach, Ah don't know, Bill. They're just makin' my life a misery. They're two smug bastards the pair o' them. Gettin' on my tits, so they are.'

Barney is distracted, makes a bad play. Doesn't notice, but Bill is watching closely. Bill the Cat. Suddenly, given the opening, he begins to play dynamite dominoes, a man at the pinnacle of his form, making great sweeping moves of brio and verve, which Barney wrongly attributes to him having had a glimpse of his hand.

'So what are you gonnae dae about it?' says Bill, after administering the coup de grâce.

Barney, vanquished in the game, lays down his weapons, places his hands on the table. Looks Bill square in the eye. They have been friends a long time, been through a lot. The Vietnam War, the Falklands conflict, the miners' strike of '83. Not that they'd been to any of them, but they had watched a lot of them on television together. And so Barney feels able to confide the worst excesses of his imagination to Bill.

He leans forward conspiratorially across the table. This is it—a moment to test the bond to its fullest.

'How long have we been friends, Bill?' he asks, voice hushed.

Bill shrugs. 'Oh, Ah don't know. A long time, Barney.' His too is the voice of a conspirator, although he is unaware of why he is whispering.

Barney inches ever closer towards him, his chin ever nearer the table.

'Barney?' asks Bill, before he can say anything else.

'What?'

'Ye're no' gonnae kiss me, are ye?'

Barney shakes his head, rolls his eyes. 'Don't be a bloody mug, ya eejit. Now listen up.' He pauses, hesitating momentarily before the pounce. 'Tell me, Bill, dae ye know anythin' about poison?'

'Poison? Ye mean like for rats, that kind o' thing?'

'Aye,' says Barney, thinking that rats are exactly what it's for.

'Oh, Ah don't know…' says Bill, and then as his rapier mind begins to kick in, and he sees the direction in which Barney is heading, he sits up straight. Looks into the eyes of his friend. 'Ye don't mean…?'

'Aye.'

'Ye've got rats in the shop?'

Barney tuts loudly, goes through his head-shaking routine, slightly lifts his jaw from two inches above the table.

'Naw, naw. It's no' rats Ah want tae poison.' Takes a suspicious look around about him to see if anyone is listening. 'Well, it is rats, but the human kind.'

This takes a minute or two to hit Bill, and when it does it is like an electric shock. As the realisation strikes him there comes a great crash of thunder outside and the windows of the pub shake with the rain and the wind. He stands up quickly, pushing the table away from him, almost sending the drinks to a watery and crashing grave.

This momentarily dramatic display attracts the attention of the rest of the bar, who have, up until now, been sedately watching snooker on the TV. Barney panics, fearing his plan will be discovered before he has even begun its formulation.

'Sit down, Bill, sit down, for God's sake.'

Bill looks down at him, horror etched upon his face for a few seconds, then slowly lowers himself back into the seat. The two men stare at each other, trying to determine exactly what the other is thinking, trying to decide how they can continue the discussion. Bill is clearly not going to be impressed with Barney's idea. Barney wonders if he can talk him into it.

'Look,' he says eventually, attempting to sound hard and businesslike, although Bill knows he is soft, soft as a pillow, 'Ah want tae know if ye can help me or no'.'

The look of horror on Bill's face increases tenfold. 'Commit murder? Is that it? Ye want me tae help ye commit murder?'

Barney looks anxiously around him

to see how many people have noticed Bill's raised voice. Fortunately, the rest of the bar have returned to more mundane interests.

'Look, keep your voice down.'

Bill leans forward, once again regaining the mask of the grand conspirator. 'You cannae seriously be thinkin' o' killin' Chris and Wullie, can ye? They're good lads. For Christ's sake, man, Ah know Wullie's faither.'

Barney shakes his head. He has chosen the wrong man for advice.

'Huh! Good lads my backside. They'll get what's coming tae them.'

'But why?'

Barney thinks about this for a second or two. It is a reasonable enough question, demands a good answer. He fixes his gaze on Bill. 'Because they're asking for it.'

Bill shakes his head. 'Ye're no' makin' any sense, Barney, and whatever ye're planning, Ah don't want any part o' it, dae ye hear me? Keep me out o' it.'

He rises from the table again, starts to put on his coat. Barney feels chastened, looks up anxiously.

'Very well, Bill. Ah'm sorry ye feel that way,' is all he says.

Bill pulls on his cap, nods shortly to Barney as he makes to go.

'We never had this conversation, eh, Bill?' says Barney.

Bill looks him hard in the eye. Is there an implied threat in the voice? If he doesn't help him will he be included in Barney's murderous plans? Another possible victim?—although deep down he cannot believe that Barney is serious. Still waits for him to say that it's all a joke.

'Ah don't know about that, Barney,

Ah really don't know,' he says. Their eyes battle with each other—two weak men—and then he turns and walks from the pub, out into the squalid storm of the night.

WINE-MAKING

Holdall sits looking out of the window. Evening rain spatters against the glass, streetlights illuminate the rain in shades of grey and orange. There is a tangible silence in the room. The silence of a courtroom awaiting a verdict; the silence of a crowd awaiting a putt across the eighteenth green.

The Chief Superintendent reads the latest report on the serial killer investigation, fumbling noiselessly with a pipe. The only light in the room is from the small lamp on the desk, shining down onto the paper which the old man is reading. It casts strange shadows around the room; the old face looks sinister under its curious glare.

Chief Superintendent McMenemy has been on the force for longer than anyone knows, and his presence in the station goes beyond domination. 'M', they call him, and no one is quite sure whether it's a joke or not. There is no Moneypenny, no green baize on the door, but he is a considerable figure. A grumpy old man, much concerned with great matters of state. And perhaps his senior officers like the implication; if he is 'M', then they must be James Bond—although in fact, most of them are 003s, the men who mess up and die in the pre-credit sequence of the movie.

He puts the pipe to his mouth, sucks on it a couple of times while attacking it with a match, eventually manages to get it going. Tosses the box of matches casually onto the table, looks at Holdall. There is nothing to be read in those dark eyes—Holdall shifts uncomfortably in his seat. Long, unnerving silences, another of his trademarks.

Continues to suck quietly on his pipe, finally points it at Holdall.

'Well, one two seven, what have you got to say for yourself?'

Another one of his ridiculous pretensions, thinks Holdall. Referring to everyone on his staff by the last three digits of their staff number. Shows a decent memory, perhaps.

He tries to concentrate on the question. It is a good one. What does he have to say for himself exactly? He can't tell the truth—that he felt like a bloody idiot giving the press conference, and had made something up so that he wouldn't look stupid. Apart from anything else, it is destined to make him look even more stupid when they don't produce the promised serial killer, and he has to explain that one in a press conference.

He looks into the massive black holes of M's eyes, wonders what to say. M grunts, picks up the report so that he can toss it back onto the desk.

'You've got the whole of the country thinking we're just about to collar someone, when as far as I can see we're no nearer making an arrest than we were at the start. What in God's name were you thinking about, man?'

Holdall stares at the floor, tries to pull himself together. Be assertive, for God's sake. The one thing the old man hates is fumbling idiots. He straightens his shoulders, looks him in the eye.

Tries to banish the picture of Mrs Holdall brandishing a frying pan, which has inexplicably just come into his head.

'I thought that maybe we should try and sound positive for once. We've spent two months now coming across as losers, sir. I thought it was about time people started thinking that we've got some balls about us. If we haven't come up with anything in the next few days, we'll have to say that our inquiries in this respect have come to a dead end. But at least we'll look as if we've got some spunk, and that we're putting something into this investigation. Certainly the shit'll be on our shoes the next time someone is murdered, but until then we have to look as if we're getting somewhere.

'We don't know anything about this killer, sir. Why he's doing it, what motivates him, none of that. It could be that he won't kill again. Who knows? Or it could be that we come up with a lead in the next few days. I thought it was about time that we showed some assertiveness.'

He stops, looks into the impassive face, the eyes which haven't moved from Holdall while he talked, the expression of stone. Now M turns his seat round so that it is facing towards the window, and he stares at the night sky, the dull orange reflection in the low clouds. His pipe has gone out, and he once more begins to fumble with the matches.

Holdall waits for the reaction. The fact that he hasn't immediately exploded is a good sign. He had half expected to be out of a job already.

Eventually, after several minutes of working the pipe, followed by ruminative smoking, he turns back to Holdall, holds him in his icy stare. He considers his words carefully; when he speaks, he speaks slowly.

'Well, I'm not sure about this, one two seven, and I'd rather you'd talked to me about it first. But on reflection, perhaps it wasn't too bad a strategy. Of course, if pieces of dismembered body start turning up in the post tomorrow morning, like confetti at a wedding, then we're in trouble.' He stops, points the pipe. 'You're in trouble.'

He swivels the chair back so that he is looking out of the window again, and Holdall is looking at the imperious profile. M toys with his pipe, tapping it on the desk.

'It might be a good idea if you came up with something solid in the next few days, one two seven.'

'Yes, sir.'

He adds nothing to that, and Holdall shifts uncomfortably in his seat, wondering if he has been dismissed. Never rise until you have been told, however, he says to himself.

Finally, M turns and stares at him. There's a look of surprise on his face due to the fact that Holdall is still there.

'That will be all, one two seven, thank you.'

* * *

Mrs Cemolina Thomson is eighty-five, lives alone in a twelfth-floor flat in Springburn. Smokes eighty cigarettes a day, an obscure brand she found during the war, containing more tar than the runways at Heathrow; spends her days watching quiz shows on television. Donald Thomson died when Barney was five years old, and ever since she has attempted to rule the lives of her children. Her eldest son has long since escaped her clutches, leaving Barney to face the brunt of her domineering personality. Her attitudes have not so much progressed with the century through which she has lived, as regressed to some time between the Dark Ages and the creation of the universe. A white, Protestant grandmother with a bad word for everybody.

Barney lets himself into the flat, is immediately struck by a smell so rancid it turns his stomach. His first grotesque thought: perhaps his mother has lain dead in the flat for some days, the smell her decomposing body. He steels himself for the stumble across her rotting flesh, but no, that won't be it. He knows it, as he talked to her the night before. Even his mother's crabbed body would not decompose so quickly—certainly not in the damp chill of Scotland in early March.

The first rooms off the hall are bedrooms, and he looks into those to see if she is there. However, as he nears the kitchen, he realises that this is where the smell most definitely emanates from. Quickens his pace, bursts through the door.

Cemolina stands stirring a huge pot of steaming red liquid, wearing an apron; curlers in her hair. He wonders whether the stench is coming from the pot or from the horrendous stuff women stick in their hair when they do a home perm. Decides it is too bad even for that. Must be the pot.

'Whit the hell are ye daein', Mum? That stuff smells bloody terrible.'

She turns her head, looks at him as if she had known he was standing there. Beads of sweat pepper her face at the effort she is making—haystacks on a ragged hillside. Her face is slightly flushed.

'Hello, Barnabas, how are ye? Nearly finished,' she says, turning back to her strange brew.

Visibly wincing, as he always does at the mention of his name, he walks over beside her, looks down into the pot. It is a deep red, thin liquid, bubbling slightly, close to the boil. Beside it, the stench is almost overwhelming, but Barney does not withdraw; the look of incredulity on his face holding him there as if it might be glue. Aghast.

'Whit on earth are ye making, Mum, for God's sake?'

'Whit does it look like?' she says. Sons should not use such a tone with their mothers.

He stares at it for a while, trying to work it out. Very thin strawberry jam? Jelly, several hours before it has set? Who knows? he thinks. Neither of them would smell like that.

'Ah honestly huvnae the faintest idea. Whit in God's name is it?'

She tuts loudly, bustles some more. 'It's wine, for God's sake, surely ye can see that?'

He stares at it—new understanding, even less comprehension. Maybe that explains the smell, but he knows nothing about wine-making.

'Is this how ye make wine?' he says.

She stops stirring, looks him hard in the eye, lips pursed, hands drawn to her hips. Nostrils flare. He knows the look, having suffered from it for over forty years, and prepares to make his retreat.

'Well, Ah dinnae know about anybody else, but it's how Ah make wine. Now away an' sit down, an' Ah'll be wi' ye in a few minutes.'

He nods meekly, makes his exit, closes the door behind him. Glad to escape the kitchen. Goes into the sitting room and opens up the windows, letting the cold, damp air into the house, clean and refreshing. Stands there for a couple of minutes breathing it in, trying to purge the stench of the kitchen, then withdraws into the room, sits down. Finds the snooker on BBC2, and settles back on the settee.

He doesn't have long to wait before his mother walks into the room, red-stained apron still wrapped around her, a bustle in her step. Tuts loudly when she sees the open windows, closes them noisily, then sits down to light herself a cigarette. Sucks in deeply, two long draws, and with a shock realises that there is snooker on television.

'For God's sake, what are ye watching this rubbish for? *Whose Pants!* is on the other channel,' she says, grabbing the remote control and changing it over.

Barney rolls his eyes, looks at his mother, thinks he might as well not be there. She sits engrossed in the television, while a variety of celebrity undergarments are brought on, and the contestants attempt to identify them from the stains. She has finished her second cigarette by the time the adverts arrive. Lowers the volume, turns to look at her boy.

'Whit are ye making wine for, Mum?'

She shrugs. Not all questions in life have answers, she thinks. 'Ah didnae have enough sugar tae make marmalade,' she says, and pulls hard on her newly lit cigarette. 'So, how are ye? You're lookin' a wee bitty fed up, are ye no'?'

He sits back, stares at the ceiling. Can he talk to his mother?

Probably not. He's never been able to before, so why should he suddenly be able to start now? Mothers aren't for talking to; they're for obeying and running after. At least, that's what his mother is for. Iron hand in iron glove.

'Ach, Ah'm just a bit cheesed aff at work an' a' that, ye know. It's nothin'.'

She draws heavily on the cigarette. 'Oh aye, whit's the problem?'

He tuts, shakes his head. 'Ach, it's they two that Ah work wi', they're really gettin' tae me. Keep taking a' my customers, so they dae. Pain in the arse, tae be quite frank.'

Now Cemolina shakes her head. Lips purse, eyes narrow. Sees conspiracy. Believes Elvis was abducted by aliens on the instructions of the FBI. 'It doesnae surprise me. Yon Chris Porter. He's a Fenian, is he no'? Cannae trust a bloody Tim, that's what Ah always say.'

Barney shakes his head. 'Naw, naw, Mum, the other Yin's just as bad.'

She looks surprised. 'Wullie Henderson? He's a fine lad. Goes tae watch the Rangers every week, does he no'?'

Barney nods. Feels like he's in the lion's den. Even his mother puts great store by football. What is it about a group of men running around like five-year-olds? 'Maybe he does, Mum, but that's no' the point.'

'Oh, aye. Whit is the point, then?'

He shakes his head. 'Ah don't know. They take a' ma customers. Make me look bloody stupid in front o' everyone. They're a' laughin' at me.' Stops when he realises that he sounds like a stroppy child with a major huff on, lip petted, face scowling. Cemolina hasn't noticed. Either that, or she is used to seeing him like this.

'So, whit are ye gonnae dae about it, then?'

He stares at the floor, wonders what to say. Feels he has to obey the golden rule of not confessing murderous intent to your mother— not forgetting the Norman Bates Exception, when you and your mother are the same person—and his villainous ardour has been partly quashed by Bill's horrified reaction to his nefarious scheme. There is little point in talking to her about it. And who is he fooling anyway? He isn't about to kill anybody. He's Barney Thomson, sad pathetic barber from Partick. No killer he.

He shrugs his shoulders, mumbles something about there being nothing he can do. Sounds like a wee boy.

'Why don't you kill them?' she says, drawing hard on her cigarette, as far down as she can get it.

He stares at her, disbelief rampaging unchecked across his face. 'Whit did you say?'

'Kill them. Blow their heids off, if they're that much trouble tae ye. Yer old dad used tae say, "If someone's gettin' on yer tits, kill the bastard, an' they willnae get on yer tits any more".'

Barney looks at her. Staring at a new woman, someone he's never seen before. His mother. His own mother is advising him to kill Wullie and Chris. Stern council. She can't be serious, can she? Was that the kind of thing his father used to say? He remembers him as kind, gentle; distant memories; soft-focus, warm, sunny summer afternoons.

'Dae ye mean that?'

She shrugs, lights up another cigarette. 'Well, Ah don't know if they were his exact words, it's been about forty years after a', but it wis something like that Ah'm sure.'

'Naw, naw, no' that. Dae ye really think that Ah should kill them? Really?'

'Of course Ah dae. If they're upsetting ye that much, do away wi' them. You've been in yon shop a lot longer than they two heid-the-ba's. Ye shouldnae let them push ye aboot. Blow their heids aff.'

A huge grin begins to spread itself across Barney's face. He has found a conspirator. A confidante in the most unlikely of places.

'Ah cannae believe ye're serious.'

'Why no'? They're bastards, are they no'? Ye says so yersel'. Especially yon Fenian, Porter.'

'Wullie's worse.'

She shakes her head, looks sad. 'Ah don't know. A good Protestant lad gone wrong.'

Barney looks upon his mother with wonder. That her mind is now undoubtedly caught in a tangled web of senility is completely lost upon him, so delighted is he to find an enthusiast. He is about to broach the subject of poison when she realises that the adverts have long since finished. Holds up her hand to stop him talking, returns her gaze to the television.

The presenter, an annoying curly-haired man with a thick Yorkshire accent, is holding up a gigantic pair of shorts, festooned with numerous revolting stains. A caption at the bottom of the screen gives a choice of four celebrities. The giggling girl—all lipstick and false breasts for her big TV appearance—partnered by Lionel Blair, presses the buzzer, giggles some more. 'Pavarotti!' she ejaculates, and with a 'Good guess, luv, but not correct this time. A big hand for that try, though, ladies and gentlemen' from the presenter, the audience erupts.

And so the show continues for another ten minutes, before with a 'Thanks for watching, tune in next week for some more pants!', the programme is finished. Cemolina lowers the volume once again, turns back to Barney, the look of the easily satisfied on her face. Barney has been staring blankly at the television, none of it registering, his face a study in concentration.

'So, ye're gonnae blow their heids aff?' she says. Her look gives a stamp of approval.

Barney strokes his chin in murderous contemplation. 'Actually, Ah wis, eh, thinkin' o' poison. Dae ye know anything aboot it?'

Cemolina grabs the arms of the chair, lifts herself up an inch or two. She is a small woman, but still she presents an imposing figure, especially to the weak son.

'Poison!' she shrieks. 'Poison, did Ah hear ye say?' Barney flummoxes about in his seat for a second, a landed fish. Recovers his composure enough to speak, although not enough to stop

himself looking like a flapping haddock.

'Whit's wrang wi' poison'?'

She tut-tuts, shakes her head. 'It's womany for a start. Ye'd huv tae be a big jessie tae want tae poison somebody. Did Ah bring ye up as a girl? Well, did Ah?'

'No, Mum,' he says, sounding dangerously like a six-year-old caught with his finger in the jam jar.

'Naw, ye're right, Ah didnae. Act like a man, for pity's sake. Ye've got tae gie it laldy, Barney, none o' this poison keich. Blow their heids aff. Carpet the floor wi' their brains. Or get a hammer and smash their heids tae smithereens. That's whit tae dae. Beat them tae a pulp. That's whit yer faither would have done. Or kneecap them and...'

'Mum!' There is a growing look of incredulity on his face, horror in his voice. He has long known that everyone has their dark half, but he's never really thought that everyone included his own mother.

Cemolina looks aghast at her son, however. 'Ye want them deid, dae ye no'? Ye says so yersel', so whit are ye blethering aboot?'

'Aye, aye, Ah dae, but something simple. Ah don't like mess, ye know that.'

She screws up her face, waves a desultory hand. 'Well, Ah didnae think ye'd be that much o' a big poof. Ah just thought that if ye were gonnae dae it, ye might as well have some fun while ye're aboot it.'

Barney looks at his mother with some distaste. Maybe she is mad. But then, it was him who was thinking about killing them in the first place. She has merely added some enthusiasm to the project. If she's mad, then he isn't far behind.

'Ach, Ah don't know, Mother. Ah'll huv tae think aboot it. Ah certainly don't think that Ah could go beating anybody's heid tae a pulp.'

She scowls at him, turns her attention back to the television to see which quiz show will be on next.

'Ah can't believe ye're bein' such a big jessie. Yer faither would've been black affrontit, so he wid,' she says, turning the volume back up.

'Yes, Mum,' says Barney.

He can't do it. Not anything violent. He knows he can't. Perhaps, however, he can get someone else to do it for him. A hired hand. There's a thought. Strokes his chin, and as the opening strains of *Give Us a Disease* start up, sinks further into the soft folds of the settee, and loses himself in barbaric contemplations.

A PAIR OF BREASTS

Margaret MacDonald glances up at the television, which has been droning away in the background all morning. They are running over the previous night's football results. She raises her eyebrows. Rangers lost 2-0 at Motherwell. Typical. That was why Reginald was in such a foul mood when he came in last night. And still this morning. Stomping around like a baby who's been woken up too early, and then charging out the door without saying a word to her. God, men are so pathetic.

Her eyes remain on the television, but she isn't watching. She's thinking about Louise, as she has been for the past three days. It isn't like her to just vanish. Nearly twenty now, and there have been plenty of times in the past when she has gone off for the night without letting them know where she is. But three days...

She feels that nervous grip on her stomach, the tightening of the muscles, which she has been experiencing more and more often. Gulps down some tea, tries to put it out of her mind. It's not as if she doesn't have plenty of other things to think about.

The doorbell rings. She jumps. Looks round in shock, into the hall, can just make out the dark grey of a uniform through the frosted glass of the front door. Swallows hard to fight back the first tears of foreboding. It's the police. The police with news about Louise.

The doorbell rings again. Feeling the great weight rested upon her shoulders, she rises slowly from the table, inches her way towards the door. Whatever she is going to find out won't be true until she has opened that door and been informed. Her hand hovers over the key; she wishes she could suspend time; wishes she could stand there for ever, and never have to learn what she is about to be told.

She turns the key, slowly swings the door open, the first tears already beginning to roll down her face.

'Ye awright there, hen, ye're lookin' a bit upset?'

She starts to smile, and then a laugh comes bursting out of her mouth. A big, booming, guttural laugh which she has never heard herself make before. She puts her hand out, touches the arm of the postman.

'I'm sorry, Davey, it's nothing. I thought you were going to be someone else, that's all.'

'Christ, who were ye expectin' wi' a reaction like that? The Pope?'

She laughs again, and for the first time looks past him. It is a dark and murky morning, the rain falling in a relentless drizzle. The winds of the previous day have abated, but still it is horrible, as it has been for weeks.

'God, it's a foul morning to be out, is it not, Davey?'

The postman shrugs and smiles. 'Ah'm no' in it fur the weather, hen.' Rummages inside his bag, pulls out a small parcel. 'Anyway, Ah've got this for ye, an' a few letters. Ah'd better be goin'. Still got bloody miles tae dae yet.'

She takes the parcel and letters from him, looking through them to see if there is one with Louise's handwriting. Looks up to see Davey MacLean already walking down the road, hunched against the rain, the hood of his jacket drawn back over his head.

'Thanks, Davey. I'll see you later.' He responds with a cool hand lifted into the gloom, and—the Steven Seagal of his trade—goes about his business with a certain violent panache.

She closes the door, retreats into the kitchen, shivering at the cold weather. Drops the letters onto the table—nothing from Louise, fights the clawing disappointment—and studies the parcel. She isn't expecting anything, doesn't recognise the handwriting. Studies the postmark. Ayr. Ayr? Who does she know in Ayr?

Then suddenly it's there. A horrible sense of foreboding. A cold hand touching her neck, making the hairs rise; the chill grip on her heart. She lets the package fall from her fingers and land on the table. Her stomach tightens, she begins to feel sick. Walks slowly over to the drawer beside the sink and lifts out a pair of scissors. She starts back to the table, but suddenly the vomit rises in her throat, and she is bent over the sink, retching violently, as the tears begin to stream down her face.

THE ACCIDENTAL BARBER SURGEON

It comes sooner than Holdall could have feared. Every morning he sits in his office waiting for the phone to ring, the angry herald of more news of stray body parts popping through someone's letterbox. Every time the phone rings he assumes the worst, and given what he told the press the evening before, he is even more fearful this particular morning.

However, fate does not even bother to tease him. There is no endless stream of calls concerning more mundane matters, leading up to the dramatic one confirming his worst fears. The dreaded call arrives first, and within three minutes of him sitting at his desk.

A woman in Newton Mearns, a woman with a missing daughter, has received what appears to be two breasts, neatly packed into a small wooden box, that morning. It had been but the thought of two seconds for her to realise that they were more than likely the breasts of her daughter, and that if she is missing her breasts, it's a fair bet that she is in some degree of trouble. And so she had turned up on the doorstep of her local police station hysterical, and who could deny her that—demanding to speak to the bloody idiot who'd been on television the previous night implying that the police had as good as got their man.

The policeman had done his best to calm her down, and then put the call through to Holdall to tell him the grim news. And to ask him what the hell he had meant when he had talked to the press the previous evening.

When the call comes down from MCMenemy's office, Holdall is not the least surprised. Ill becomes those who are summonsed to that office two days running.

The rain is falling in a relentless drizzle against the window of the shop, the skies grey overhead, the clouds low. Every now and again someone bustles past the front, their collar pulled up against the cold wind, a dour expression welded to their face.

The shop is near deserted, as it has been most of the day. Wednesdays are usually slow, and with the cold and miserable weather, today has been even worse. Barney has had to do only two haircuts all day, both of which were ropey; one indeed so bad that he thinks it might lead to retribution. He hadn't liked the way the man had asked Wullie for Barney's address on his way out, and had been surprised that Wullie had claimed ignorance on the matter. Nevertheless, it is a day for keeping his head down.

At three o'clock Wullie offers Chris the chance to go home early, tells Barney that on the next quiet day he can take his turn of an early departure.

After that there are only three more customers, all of whom want Wullie to cut their hair. Barney sits and reads a variety of newspapers, and finally gives in to the boredom and falls asleep, his dreams a web of exotica.

He wakes with a start to slightly raised voices, dragged from a screaming drop down a black, bottomless shaft. Wullie is discussing modern art with his last customer of a dreadful day. Barney stretches, yawns, squints at the clock. Two minutes past five. Time to go. Thank God for that.

He stands and stretches again, busying himself with clearing up, not something that will take very long. Takes his time, however, doing as many unnecessary things as possible, not wishing to leave before Wullie. He listens to the idle chatter from the end of the shop; is not impressed.

'Now sixteenth-century Italian art,' Wullie is saying, as he puts the finishing touches to a dramatic taper at the back of the man's neck, 'there's the thing. It's full o' big fat birds gettin' their kit aff. It disnae matter whit the paintin's about, in every one they always managed tae squeeze in about five or six huge birds, with bloody enormous tits, lying back and showin' their duffs.'

The customer nods his own appreciation of sixteenth-century Italian art as much as he can, given that there is a man with a razor at the back of his neck.

'Ah mean,' Wullie continues, after pausing to pull off some intricate piece of barbery, 'ye've got some paintin' o' a big battle scene or somethin', or a nativity scene for Christ's sake, and they'd still manage tae get in some great lump o' lard, bollock naked, legs a' o'er the place, dangling a pun o' grapes intae the gob o' another suitably compliant naked tart, wi' nipples like corks, and her lips pouting in a flagrantly pseudo-lesbian pose. Ah love it, so Ah dae. It's pure brilliant, so it is.'

'Even so,' says the customer, holding up his finger as Wullie produces a comb to administer the finishing touches, 'Ah still don't think it's a patch on modern art. That's got far more life and soul tae it than a bunch of birds wi' their kit aff.'

Wullie stops combing, looks at the man as if he's mad.

'Yer jokin'. Ah mean, fair enough, if they painted a bit o' paper completely orange, then put a red squiggle in the middle o' it, and called it "a boring lot o' crap that took me two minutes, and isnae worth spit", then that'd be fine. But they don't. They'll dae that, and then call it "Sunrise over Manhattan," or "Three Unconnected Doorways," or "Ah'm a pretentious wank, so you've got tae gie me a million quid", or some shite like that, and get paid millions for it. It's a piece o' bloody nonsense.'

'Naw, naw, ye've got it a' wrang. These things have got a depth and soul tae them, that a lot o' people cannae see. If ye cannae see whit an artist is sayin', then it's because ye're no' in tune wi' the guy. That's hardly his fault.'

Wullie shakes his head as he dusts off the back of the neck.

'Come off it. Any nutter can splash paint ontae somethin' and call it "Moon over Five Women wi' Hysterectomies"—Wullie is indeed a new man—'or something like that. Jings, ma

two-year-old niece could dae it, and Ah bet she widnae get two million quid.'

'Of course no',' says the man, as Wullie removes the cape from around his neck, hands him a towel to apply the finishing touches himself, 'and that's the point. If just any bastard does it, it doesnae mean anythin'. It's got nae meanin'. The artist, however, is expressin' himsel', is lettin' ye see whit's inside him. It means somethin' because it comes fi' within, fi' his soul. That's what gies it heart, and that's why people are willin' tae pay money for it. Artists bare themselves tae the public.'

Wullie thinks about this for a second or two. The man stands, brushes himself down.

'A fine defence o' modern art ye've constructed there,' says Wullie eventually.

'Aye, thanks,' says the customer, fishing in his pockets for the required cash.

'However, it's a complete load o' bollocks.'

The man shakes his head as he produces a five-pound note from his pocket.

'Ye're no' listening tae me, Wullie,' He pauses, stares at the ceiling, tries to think of how he can best get his point across. He is not used to such intellectual debate. Reaching for his jacket, he finds what he is looking for. 'Let's put it this way. If ye're watchin' fitba', right? Let's say some wee bloke playin' for Raith Rovers blooters the ba' fi' forty yards and it flies intae the net. Now, it may seem like a great goal, but let's face it, he probably meant tae pass it tae some eejit out on the wing and mishit it. Whatever, ye know he's bloody lucky. But if Brian Laudrup kicks the ball fi' forty yards and it flies intae the net, ye know he meant it. It's a thing of beauty. It's art. The execution and the outcome are the same, but the intentions were different. That's whit it's a' about. That's the difference.'

He stops on his way to the door, holds out his hands in a gesture of 'there you have it'. Wullie shakes his head.

'Are you sayin' that Brian Laudrup's the same as one o' they eejits who throws a bunch o' paint ontae a picture?' The man shakes his head, laughs, waves a hand at Wullie.

'Ah'll never win. See ye next time, Wullie, eh. See ye, Barney.'

The barbers say their goodbyes, Barney with a grudge—bloody idiot, he thinks—then Wullie turns to start his final clearing up for the day, after fixing the closed sign on the door.

Still shaking his head at the discussion which has just finished, Barney completes the minutiae of clearing his things away. Now that Wullie has finished, he feels free to go. Modern art; naked Italian women; these people don't half talk some amount of shite.

'Can Ah have a word wi' ye, Barney?'

He looks up; Wullie walks towards him. Barney shrugs his acceptance, Wullie sits in the next seat up from his. The usually vacant chair. Barney looks into Wullie's eyes and sits down, feels a tingle at the bottom of his spine. It could be the label on his Marks and Spencer boxer shorts, but he has the feeling that it is something worse than that.

'What is it, Wullie?'

Wullie is staring at the floor. Looks awkward, like a seventeen-year-old boy not wanting to tell his father he's written off his new Frontera San Diego. He struggles with himself, then his eyes briefly flit onto Barney then away again, before he speaks.

'Em, this isnae very easy, Barney. Ah'm no' really sure how tae say this,' he says. Looks anywhere but into Barney's eyes. Barney stares at him, a look of incredulity formulating across his face. He can't be going to say what he thinks he is, can he?

'Em, Ah'm afraid we've hired a new barber, Barney. It's an old friend o' ma dad's who's just moved intae the area. Ye know, ma dad wants tae gie him a job and...'

Barney switches off, knowing what is coming. He can't believe it. Feels a strange twisting in his stomach, a pounding at the back of his head. Cold, wet hands. Thinks: The gutless, gutless coward, making himself out to be merely the messenger of his father's decision, rather than the instrument of it.

How the hell can they let him go? He's the only one in the place who can give a decent haircut. Certainly he's better than these two young idiots, surely everyone can see that? But of course, bloody Wullie will have been telling his father something completely different. Maybe his mother was right—poison wasn't good enough for him; not violent enough.

'...so, ye can work here for another month if ye like, or we'll understand if ye want tae leave now, and we'll keep your wages goin' for the rest o' the month. Ye don't have tae make any decision right now, but if ye could let us know in the next couple o' days, that'd be great.'

Not once has he been able to look Barney in the eye, and now he sits, an attempted look of consolation on his face, eyes rooted to the floor.

Barney is in a daze, a thousand different thoughts barging into each other in his head. Cannot believe it's happened, cannot believe that they have the nerve to do this to him. He is by far the most superior barber of the lot of them. This is ridiculous. His immediate thoughts are of violent retribution. Vicious, angry thoughts involving baseball bats, sledge-hammers and pickaxes.

But he can't show his hand. Not yet. He has to be calm about it. If he is going to avenge this heinous crime, he has to be calculating and cold; has to pick his moment. Cool deliberation away from the scene of the crime is required. And as he sits staring angrily into Wullie's eyes, which remain Sellotaped to the floor, he decides that he will have to stay in the shop, however great the feeling of humiliation, however great his desire to leave.

'Ah'll stay for the month,' he says abruptly.

'What?'

Wullie looks up at him, for the first time, surprised. He hadn't expected an answer so quickly, hadn't expected the one he has been given, and moreover he had been thinking about the phone call to the shop that morning from Serena—the girl from the Montrose. Wondering if that's her real name, anticipating Friday night; vague intimations of guilt.

'Ah'll stay for the month.'

Wullie stares briefly at the floor again. Thinks: Shit. He and his father had assumed that Barney would just take his leave. Hadn't reckoned on an awkward month with Barney still in the shop. He looks up.

'Awright, that'll be great. Ye're sure now?'

'Aye,' says Barney, almost spitting the word out. Manages to contain his wrath. Fingernails dig into palms. Wrath would have to be for later.

'Right, then. That's great, Barney. Ah'll let my dad know.'

That's great, is it? You've just stabbed me up the backside with a red-hot poker, and you think it's great because I accept it. Fucking bastard. Thinks it, doesn't say it.

Wullie attempts another look of consolation, succeeds only in an almost tortoise-like grimace. Goes about his business.

Barney stands up to clear away a couple of things which don't need clearing away. Doesn't want to storm out of the shop immediately, knowing his presence will unsettle Wullie. Doesn't want him to be at ease any earlier than he should be. Although, should he ever be at ease?

As he lifts an unnecessary pair of scissors from his workplace, he realises his hands are shaking. Shit. Doesn't want Wullie to see what effect it is having on him. Steadies himself, lifts a cup to get a drink of water. Fills it at the sink next to his workplace— Scottish tap water, the sweetest-tasting drink; that's what he always thinks; not today, however. But as he raises it in his still-trembling hand, the cup slips free. Strikes the edge of the sink surround and disgorges its contents, some over Barney, mostly over the floor. He mutters a curse to himself. The water runs over the smooth tiles of the floor, a mocking river of humiliation to accompany his disgrace. Mumbling a few other appropriate words which come to mind, he grabs a towel to dry himself off. Wullie looks over at him, starts to walk into the rear of the shop.

'Ah'll get a mop, Barney, and clear it up,' he says.

Like burning someone's house down and then offering to replace the welcome mat, thinks Barney.

'Don't bother, Ah'll dae it in a minute,' he growls at him, but Wullie feels the restlessness of the guilty; scurries off to retrieve the mop anyway. Barney shakes his head, begins to clear away the final few things lying around his work area. He lifts the pair of scissors again and studies them, his eyes drifting to Wullie, his back turned to him in the storeroom at the rear of the shop.

What damage I could do with these, he thinks, but he knows he never will. If he is to avenge this crime, it will have to be by some subtle act of treachery, not a brutal and bloody stabbing.

He still holds the scissors as Wullie emerges from the storeroom with the mop, and walks towards him. Barney purses his lips, tries not to appear too angry.

'Look, Wullie, it's awright. Ah said Ah'd get it, did Ah no'?'

'Ah'll just gie ye a hand, Barney, it's nae bother.'

Fine last words.

Wullie steps forward to start clearing up the water, not noticing it has run so much towards him. His first step is firmly placed into a pool of water lying on a smooth tile; his foot gives way. He attempts to regain his balance, and in doing so falls towards Barney. Barney raises his hands to catch him. Automatic reaction.

Wullie slumps heavily into him and his outstretched hands. Neatly, exactly, with medical precision, the scissors enter through Wullie's stomach and jag up under his ribcage. He rests in Barney's arms for a few seconds, then pulls back to look at him, an expression of stupefied surprise on his face.

He lurches back, blood pouring from the wound, the scissors embedded in his stomach. Falls back against the chair, which topples backwards, allowing him to slump down onto the floor. His back rests against the bottom of the chair, his eyes stare blankly one last time up at Barney, his head falls forward onto his chest.

Barney stares mutely down at the body on the floor, and the pool of blood spreading across the tiles. His face mouths silent words of horror, his voice a hushed croak of wind, and finally, when it finds some substance, it is the weak and desperate voice of the frightened.

'Fuck,' he says.

DOUGLAS LINDSAY

...is a new writer with an original wit and talent. He was born in Scotland in 1964 and wrote this, his debut novel, while living in Senegal—'one of the few countries in the world never to have beaten Scotland at football'.

Douglas Lindsay will appeal to fans of Tom Sharpe, Ben Elton and Christopher Brookmyre, though he brings a unique comic voice of his own to the fiction scene. He has created a truly great character in Barney Thomson, whose adventures are set to continue in Lindsay's second book, *The Cutting Edge of Barney Thomson*, on sale from February 2000.

THE LONG MIDNIGHT OF BARNEY THOMSON

Black humour. Bloody murder. And no kissing.

Barney Thomson's success as a barber is limited. It's not just that he's crap at cutting hair (and he is); it's because he's never had the knack of making small talk with strangers. He hates football for one thing. He hates most people. He hates his colleagues most of all, and the glib confidence with which they can discuss Florence Nightingale's sexuality or the ongoing plight of Partick Thistle. But a serial killer is spreading terror throughout the city. The police are baffled. And for one sad little Glasgow barber, life is about to get seriously strange...

PRAISE FOR DOUGLAS LINDSAY & THE LONG MIDNIGHT OF BARNEY THOMSON:

"Like Irvine Welsh without the drugs...extremely good'
—Daily Mirror
'this chilling black comedy unfolds at dizzying speed...an impressive debut novel'
—Sunday Mirror
'sure-fire top-ten material'
—The Face
'Hair-raising'
—Daily Mail
'Lindsay has succeeded magnificently in putting the lowly barber centre-stage'
—Time Out
'Pitch-black comedy spun from the finest writing. Fantastic plot, unforgettable scenes and plenty of twisted belly laughs'
—New Woman
'Gleefully macabre...hugely enjoyable black burlesque'
—The Scotsman
'Glasgow's answer to Sweeney Todd'
—Arena
'Enjoyable'
—Guardian

THE LONG MIDNIGHT OF BARNEY THOMSON

DOUGLAS LINDSAY

BLACK HUMOUR. BLOODY MURDER. AND NO KISSING.

IF YOU LIKED THE
EXTRACT YOU'LL
LOVE THE BOOK...

OUT NOW IN PAPERBACK

blood red rivers
jean-christopher grange

1

'GA-NA-MOS! GA-NA-MOS!'

Pierre Niémans, fingers clenched round his VHF transmitter, stared down at the crowds streaming home across the concrete terraces of Paris's Parc des Princes. Thousands of fiery skulls, white hats, brightly coloured scarfs, forming a variegated rippling ribbon. An explosion of confetti. Or a legion of demons seen in a haze of LSD. And those three notes, again and again, slow and ear-splitting: 'Ga-na-mos!'

Standing on the roof of the nursery school across the road from the Parc des Princes, the officer was controlling the manoeuvres of the third and fourth brigades of the CRS riot police. The men in dark blue were running below their black helmets, protected by their polycarbonate shields. Standard procedure. Two hundred men stationed at each set of gates and a 'screen' of commandos whose job it was to stop the two teams'supporters from colliding, getting close, or even noticing each other's existence...

On that evening, for the Saragossa vs Arsenal clash, the sole match all year that saw two non-French teams playing against each other in Paris, more than one thousand four hundred policemen and gendarmes had been mobilised. ID checks, body searches, and herding of the forty thousand supporters that had come from the two countries. Superintendent Niémans, his hair cropped, was one of the officers in charge of these manoeuvres. It was not his usual line of business, but he enjoyed this sort of exercise. Pure and total surveillance and confrontation. With neither investigations nor procedures. He relished the absolute lack of accountability. And he loved the military look of this marching army.

The supporters had reached the first floor they could be made out between the concrete fuselage of the construction, just above gates H and G. Niémans looked at his watch. In four minutes' time, they would be outside, spilling across the road. Then would begin the risks of contact, violence, broken ranks. He filled his lungs in one gasp. That October night was seething with tension.

Two minutes. Niémans instinctively turned round and, far away, could see Place de la Porte-de-Saint-Cloud. Completely deserted. Its three fountains soared up in the night, like worried totem poles. All along the avenue, the CRS vans had lined up. In front of them, the men were rolling their shoulder blades, their helmets clipped onto their belts and truncheons slapping against their thighs. The reserve brigades.

The din mounted. The crowd spread out between the iron gratings stuck with spikes. Niémans could not resist smiling. This was what he had come to see. The crowd surged forwards. Trumpets broke through the fracas. A rumbling made every inch of the concrete shake. 'Ga-na-mos! Ga-na-mos!' Niémans pressed the button on his transmitter and spoke to Joachim, the leader of the East Company. 'Niémans here. They're coming out. Push them towards the vans, towards Boulevard Murat, the car parks and the métro.'

From his vantage point, he weighed up the situation. There was practically no risk on this side. The Spanish supporters had won the match, and so were the less dangerous. The English were coming out from the far side, gates A to K, towards the Boulogne stand, the lair of the wild beasts. Niémans would go and see what was going on there, once operations had got well and truly under way.

Suddenly, in the gleam of the street-lights a beer bottle shot high above the crowd. The officer saw a truncheon crack downwards, the compact ranks withdraw, men falling. He screamed into his transmitter: 'Joachim, for fuck's sake, control your men!'

Niémans rushed to the back stairs and ran down all eight flights. When he emerged onto the avenue, two lines of CRS were already pushing forward, set to bring the hooligans under control. Niémans dashed in front of the armed men and waved his arms in long circular motions. The truncheons were just a few feet from his face when Joachim, his head jammed in his helmet, appeared to his right. He raised his visor and glanced furiously at him:

'Jesus Christ, Niémans, are you crazy or what? You're in civvies, you're going to get yourself…'

The officer did not deign to reply.

'What the bloody hell's going on? Control your men, Joachim! Or in three minutes' time we'll have a riot on our hands.'

The chubby red-faced captain panted. His little fin-de-siècle moustache twitched in rhythm to his gasping breath. The radio juddered: 'Ca… Calling all units… Calling all units… The Boulogne turning… Rue du Commandant-Guilbaud… I… We have a problem!' Niémans stared at Joachim as though he alone were responsible for this chaos. His fingers gripped the transmitter: 'Niémans, here. We're on our way.' Then he calmly gave the captain his orders:

'I'll go. Send as many men there as you can. And sort out the situation here.'

Without waiting for an answer, the superintendent ran off to look for the trainee who was acting as his driver. He crossed the square in long strides and, in the distance, noticed that the barmen of the Brasserie des Princes were lowering their iron shutters. The air was racked with tension. He finally spotted the little dark-haired lad in the leather jacket who was hanging around beside the black saloon car. Niémans banged his fist down onto the bonnet and yelled:

'The Boulogne turning, quick!'

The two men leapt simultaneously into the car. Its wheels smoked as it pulled away. The trainee shot round to the left of the stadium so as to reach Gate K as rapidly as possible along a route specially reserved for the security forces. Niémans had a hunch:

'No,' he murmured. 'Go round the other way. Then we'll bump straight into the action.'

The car spun around one hundred and eighty degrees, skidding on the puddles made by the water cannons already set for the counterattack. Then it sped away down Avenue du Parc-des-Princes through a narrow corridor formed by the grey vans of the flying squad. The men in helmets heading the same way made room for it without even glancing at it. The trainee swerved left by Lycée Claude-Bernard then took the roundabout so as to coast along the third side of the stadium. They had just passed by the Auteuil stand.

As soon as Niémans saw the first flurries of gas floating in the air, he knew he had been right: the fighting had already reached Place de l'Europe. The car swept through the white fog and had to brake hard to avoid the first victims, who were in full flight. Battle had been joined in front of the Presidential stand. Men in ties and ladies with jewellery were running, stumbling, tears pouring down their faces. Some of them were looking for a way out onto the streets, while others were climbing back up the steps towards the stadium gates.

Niémans leapt out of the car. On the square, a pitched battle was in progress. The bright colours of the English team and the dark forms of the CRS could just be made out. Some of the latter were crawling on the ground like half-crushed slugs while others, at a distance, were hesitating about whether or not to use their anti-riot guns for fear of injuring their wounded fellow officers.

The superintendent put away his glasses and tied a scarf round his face. He picked the nearest CRS and snatched away his truncheon, at the same time showing his tricolour card. The man was flabbergasted. His breath misted over the translucent visor of his helmet.

Pierre Niémans ran on towards the confrontation. The Arsenal supporters were attacking with their fists, iron bars and steel toecaps, while the CRS hit back and retreated, trying to defend those already laid out on the ground. Bodies gesticulated, faces creased, jawbones hit the asphalt. Batons went up then rained down, juddering under the force of the blows. The officer pushed his way into the scrum.

He struck with his fist, with his truncheon. He knocked down a big lad, then laid straight into him, hitting his ribs, his belly and face. He was suddenly kicked from the right. Screaming, he got to his feet. His baton wrapped itself round his aggressor's throat. His blood boiled in his head, a metallic taste numbed his mouth. His mind was empty. He felt nothing. He was at war and he knew it.

A strange scene suddenly met his eyes. A hundred yards farther off, a man in civvies, who was already in a bad way, was struggling to get out of the clutches of two hooligans. Niémans looked at the supporter's blood-splattered face and the mechanical gestures of the two others, taut with hatred.

One second later and Niémans caught on: under their jackets, the aggressed and the aggressors wore the badges of rival clubs.

A settling of old scores.

By this time, the victim had already got away and had escaped down a side road Rue Nungesser-et-Coli. The two attackers dived after him. Niémans dropped his truncheon, broke through the scrum and followed them.

The race was on.

Down that silent street, Niémans ran, breathing rhythmically, gaining on the two pursuers who were, in turn, gaining on their prey.

They turned right again and had soon reached the Molitor swimming pool, which was entirely walled off. The pair of bastards finally caught up with their victim. Niémans had got as far as Place de la Porte-Molitor, which overlooks the Paris ring road, and could not believe his eyes. One of the attackers had just produced a machete.

In the dim lights of the highway, Niémans could see the blade relentlessly slicing into the man on his knees, who was twitching under the blows. The aggressors lifted up the body and threw it over the railings.

'no!'

The officer yelled and drew his gun at the same instant. He leant on a car, propped his right fist onto his left palm, aimed and held his breath. First shot. Missed. The killer with the machete turned round amazed. Second shot.

Missed again.

Niémans set off again, his gun flat against his thigh in combat posture. He was furious. Without his glasses, he had missed his target twice. Now he, too, was up on the bridge. The man with the machete had already legged it away into the underwood which bordered the ring road. His accomplice stood there, motionless, pale. The policeman rammed the butt of his gun into the man's throat, then dragged him by the hair as far as a road sign. With one hand, he handcuffed him. Only then did he lean down towards the traffic.

The body had fallen down onto the road and several cars had driven over it before a multiple pile-up had brought everything to a halt. A confused crush of vehicles, shattered bodywork... Then the jam broke out into a crazed wailing of horns. In the head-lamps, Niémans could see one of the drivers, who was staggering around near his car, his head in his hands. The superintendent lifted his eyes to stare across the ring road. There was the murderer with his colourful arm band, making his way through the trees. Putting his gun away, Niémans set off again at once.

The killer was now glancing back at him through the branches. The policeman made no attempt to hide. The man must now have realised that he, Superintendent Pierre Niémans, was going to make mincemeat of him. Suddenly, the hooligan leapt over an embankment and vanished. The sound of feet running over gravel gave away the direction of his flight: the Auteuil gardens.

The officer followed, seeing the darkness reflected off the grey rocks of the garden. As he passed by some greenhouses, he spotted a figure climbing a wall. He shot after him and found himself looking down on the tennis courts of Roland-Garros.

The gates were not padlocked. The killer was easily able to move from one court to another. Niémans pulled open a gate, ran across the clay surface and leapt over the net. Fifty yards ahead, the man was already slowing, with obvious signs of fatigue. He managed to get over another net, then clamber up the steps between the stands. Niémans, hardly even tired, smoothly followed him up the stairs. He was just a few feet away from him when, from the top of the stand, a shadow jumped into the void. His prey was now on the roof of a private residence. Then he vanished over the farther side. The superintendent took a run up, then jumped after him. He landed on a platform of gravel. Below were lawns, trees, silence.

Not a trace of the killer.

The officer let himself down and rolled over the damp grass. There were just two possibilities: the house from whose roof he had just leapt down, or a massive wooden structure at the end of the garden. He drew his MR73 and leant his back against the door behind him. It put up no resistance.

The superintendent took a step or two, then stopped in amaze-ment. He was in a hall of marble, overhung by a circular slab of stone engraved with strange letters. A gilded banister rail rose up through the shadows of the upper storeys. In the darkness could be seen imperial red velvet hangings, gleaming hieratic vases... Niémans realised that he was inside an Asian embassy.

A sudden noise came from outside. The killer was inside the other building. The policeman crossed the garden and reached the wooden structure. The door was still swinging on its hinges. A shadow among the shadows, he entered. And the magic grew a shade more tense. It was a stable, divided into carved boxes, occupied by little horses with brush-like manes.

The swishing of tails. Straw fluttering. With his gun in his hand, Pierre Niémans walked on. He passed one box, two, three... A dull thump to his right. He turned. Nothing but the stamp of a hoof. A snarl to his left. He turned once more. Too late. The blade shot down. Niémans got out of its way at the last moment. The machete slid past his shoulder and embedded itself into the rump of a horse. The kick was terrible. The horseshoe flew up into the killer's face. The officer grabbed his chance, threw himself onto the man, turned round his gun and used it as a hammer.

Again and again he hit him, then suddenly stopped and looked down at the hooligan's bloodied features. His bones were sticking up through the shreds of his skin. An eyeball dangled down on a mess of fibres. Still wearing his Arsenal supporter's hat, the murderer was now motionless. Niémans grabbed back hold of his gun, took its blood-stained grip in both hands and rammed its barrel into the man's split mouth. He took off the catch and closed his eyes. He was about to fire when a shrill noise interrupted him. In his pocket, his cell phone was ringing.

2

Three hours later, amid the overly new and excessively symmetric streets that surround Nanterre's Prefecture, a lamp was shining in the building that housed the police headquarters of the Ministry of the Interior. A shard of light, at once diffuse and concentrated, gleamed softly across the surface of the desk belonging to Antoine Rheims, who was sitting in the shadows. In front of him, behind the halo, stood the tall figure of Pierre Niémans. He had just given a terse resumé of his report concerning the chase in Boulogne. Rheims asked him, sceptically:

'How's the man?'

'The Englishman? In a coma. Multiple facial fractures. I've just called the hospital. They're trying to perform a skin graft on his face.'

'And the victim?'

'Crushed by the cars, on the ring road, just by Porte-Molitor.'

'Jesus Christ. Whatever was going on?'

'Hooligans settling an old score. There were some Chelsea fans among the Arsenal supporters. When the fighting started, our two hooligans with the machete sliced up their victim.'

Rheims nodded his head incredulously. After a moment's silence, he went on:

'And what about our friend here? Was it really a horse's hoof that put him in a state like that?'

Niémans did not answer, but turned towards the window. In the chalky moonlight, the strange pastel designs which covered the faades of the neighbouring apartment blocks could be made out: clouds and rainbows drifting above the dark green hills of Nanterre's park. Rheims's voice rose once more:

'I just don't catch on, Pierre. Why do you get yourself into messes like this? You were watching the stadium, that's all, I really...'

His voice faded out. Niémans remained silent.

'You're almost past it,' Rheims went on. 'And out of your depth. Our contract was perfectly clear: no more action, no more violence...'

Niémans turned round and walked over towards his boss.

'Come on, out with it, Antoine. Why did you call me in here, in the middle of the night? You couldn't have known anything about this business when you rang me. So what's up?'

Rheims's shadowy figure did not budge. Broad shoulders, grey curly hair, head like a rock face. The build of a lighthouse keeper. For several years now, the chief superintendent had been running the Central Bureau for the Prevention of Trade in Humans the CBPTH a complicated name for what was, in fact, the head office of the vice squad. Niémans had first met him long before he had become installed behind this particular administrative desk, when they were two swift and efficient cops on the beat. The officer with the crew cut leant down and repeated:

'So, what's up?'

Rheims breathed in deeply:

'There's been a murder.'

'In Paris?'

'No, in Guernon. A small university town in the Isre département, near Grenoble.'

Niémans grabbed a chair and sat down in front of the chief superintendent.

'I'm all ears.'

'The body was discovered early yesterday evening. It had been stuck in between some rocks over a stream which runs along the edge of the campus. Everything points to a psychopath.'

'What information do you have about the corpse? Is it a woman?'

'No, a man. A young lad. The university librarian, apparently. The body was naked. It bears marks of having been tortured: gashes, lacerations, burns .. . He seems also to have been strangled.'

Niémans placed his elbow down on the desk. He fiddled with the ashtray.

'Why are you telling me all this?'

'Because I'm planning on sending you down there.'

'What? Because of a murder? The boys in the local Grenoble brigade will rumble this killer within a week and...'

'Don't kid with me, Pierre. You know only too well that things are never as straightforward as they look. I've spoken to the magistrate. And he wants a specialist brought in.'

'A specialist in what?'

'In murders. And in vice. He suspects a sexual motive. Or something along those lines.'

Niémans stretched his neck towards the lamp and smelt the acrid burning of the halogen.

'You're holding something back, Antoine.'

'The magistrate's Bernard Terpentes.'

An old pal of mine. We're both from the Pyrenees. And, between you and me, he's in a total panic. Plus, he wants to get to the bottom of this as soon as possible. Stop any rumours, the media, all that bullshit. The new academic year starts in a few weeks and we've got to wind things up before then. Get the picture?'

The superintendent stood up and went back to the window. He stared down at the luminous pinpricks of the street-lights and the dark mounds of the park. The violence of the last few hours was still pounding in his temples: the hacking of the machete, the ring road, the chase across Roland-Garros. For the thousandth time, he thought how Rheims's phone call had certainly stopped him from killing someone. He thought about his uncontrollable fits of violence, which blinded his conscience, ripping apart time and space, causing him to commit outrageous acts.

'Well?' Rheims asked.

Niémans turned back and leant on the window frame.

'I haven't been on a case like this for four years now. Why me?'

'I need someone good. And you know that a central office can pick one of its own men and send him anywhere in France.' His huge hands did five-finger exercises in the darkness. 'I'm making the most of my little bit of power.'

The officer smiled behind his iron-rimmed glasses.

'You're releasing the wolf from its cage?'

'Put it that way, if you want. It'll be a breath of fresh air for you. And I'll be doing an old friend a good turn. And, in the mean- time, it'll stop you from beating people up…'

Rheims picked up the gleaming pages of a fax that lay on his desk.

'The gendarmes' first conclusions. So is it yes, or no?'

Niémans went over to the desk and crumpled the roll of paper.

'I'll phone you. To get the news from the hospital.' The superintendent immediately left Rue des Trois-Fontanot and returned home to Rue La-Bruyre in the ninth arrondissement. A huge, almost empty flat, with an old lady's immaculate polished floor. He had a shower, dressed his superficial wounds and examined himself in the mirror. A bony, wrinkled face. A gleaming grey crew cut. Glasses ringed with metal. Niémans smiled at his appearance. He wouldn't have liked to bump into himself down a dark alley.

He stuffed a few clothes into a sports bag, slid a 12-calibre Remington pump-action shotgun in between his shirts and socks, as well as some boxes of cartridges and speedloaders for his Manhurin. Finally, he grabbed his protective bag and folded two winter suits into it, along with a few brightly patterned ties.

On the way to Porte de la Chapelle, Niémans stopped at the all-night McDonald's on Boulevard de Clichy where he rapidly swallowed two quarter pounders with cheese, without taking his eyes off his car, which was double-parked. Three in the morning. In the ghastly neon light a few familiar ghosts were wandering. Blacks in over ample clothes. Prostitutes with long dreadlocks. Druggies, bums, drunks. All of them were a part of his previous existence, on the beat. That world which

Niémans had had to leave for a well paid, respectable desk job. For any other cop, a post in a central office was a promotion. For him, it was being put out to grass plush grass, admittedly, but the move had still morti-fied him. He took another look at the night hawks that surrounded him. These creatures had been the trees of his personal woodland, where he once roamed, in the skin of a hunter.

Niémans drove without stopping, headlights full on, ignoring speed traps and limits. At eight a.m., he took the Grenoble exit on the motorway. He crossed Saint-Martin-d'Hres, Saint-Martin-d'Uriage and headed towards Guernon, at the foot of the Grand Pic de Belledonne. All along the winding road forests of conifers alternated with industrial zones. A slightly morbid atmosphere hung in the air, as always in the countryside when the beauty of the scenery is insufficient to hide its profound loneliness.

The superintendent drove past the first road signs indicating the university. In the distance, the mountain peaks rose up in the misty light of a stormy morning. Coming out of a bend, he glimpsed the university at the bottom of the valley: its large modern buildings, its fluted blocks of concrete, all ringed off by long lawns. It made Niémans think of a sanatorium the size of a town hall.

He turned off the main road and drove down into the valley. To the west, he could see vertical streams running into each other, their silvery current beating against the dark sides of the mountains. He slowed down, and shuddered at the sight of that icy water, plummeting down, obscured by clumps of brushwood, then reappearing again, white and dazzling, before vanishing once more…

Niémans decided to take a short detour. He forked off, drove under a vaulted ceiling of larches and firs, moist from the morning dew, then came across a long plain bordered by lofty black cliffs.

The officer stopped. He got out of his car and grabbed his binoculars. He took a long look at the scenery. The river had disap- peared. Then he realised that when the torrent reached the bottom of the valley it ran on behind the rock face. Gaps in the rock even gave him occasional glimpses of it.

Suddenly he noticed another detail and focused his binoculars on it. No, his eyes had not deceived him. He went back to his car and shot off towards the ravine. In one of the faults in the rock face he had just spotted a fluorescent yellow cordon, of the type used by the gendarmerie: no entry

3

Niémans continued down the fault, which bordered a winding, narrow path. Soon, he had to stop, as it was no longer broad enough for his car. He got out, slipped under the yellow cordon and reached the river.

The flow here came to a halt against a natural dam. The torrent, which Niémans was expecting to see boiling over with foam, had turned into a small, limpid lake. As calm as a face from which every sign of anger had just vanished. Farther on, to his right, it set off once more and presumably flowed through the greyish town which could be seen

in the pit of the valley.

But Niémans came to a sudden stop. To his left, a man was already there, crouched over the water. Instinctively, Niémans raised the velcro cover of his holster. This gesture made his handcuffs clink together slightly. The man turned round and his face broke into a smile immediately.

'What do you think you're doing here?' Niémans asked him point-blank.

Without answering, the stranger smiled again, got to his feet and dusted off his hands. He was young, with fragile features and fair, brush-like hair. A suede jacket and pleated trousers. In a clear voice, he riposted:

'And you?'

This insolence astonished Niémans. He gruffly declared:

'Police. Didn't you see the cordon? I hope for your sake you've got a good reason to be here, because…'

'Eric Joisneau, from the Grenoble brigade. I'm here as a scout. Three more officers will be arriving later today.'

Niémans joined him on the narrow bank.

'Where are the orderlies?' he asked.

'I told them to take a break. For breakfast.' He shrugged carelessly. 'I had work to do here. And I wanted some peace and quiet… Superintendent Niémans.'

The grey-haired officer twitched. The young man went on imperviously:

'I recognised you at once. Pierre Niémans. The ex-star of the anti- terrorist squad. The ex-head of the vice squad. The ex-hunter of killers and dealers. The ex of a lot of things, in fact…'

'Do inspectors always give so much lip these days?'

Joisneau bowed ironically:

'Sorry, superintendent. I was just trying to take the shine off the star. You know you're an idol, don't you? The supercop' all young inspectors dream of becoming. Are you here for the murder?'

'What do you reckon?'

The officer bowed once again.

'It'll be an honour to work with you.'

Niémans looked down at the glittering surface of the smooth waters, which shimmered at his feet, as though crystallised in the morning light. A glow of jade seemed to rise up from the depths.

'So, tell me what you know about this business.'

Joisneau glanced up towards the rock face.

'The body was wedged up there.'

'Up there?' Niémans repeated, staring at the wall of rock, whose sharp contours cast jagged shadows.

'Yes, fifty feet up. The killer stuffed the body into one of the crevices in the rock face. Then manoeuvred it into a weird position.'

'What sort of position?'

Joisneau bent his legs, raised his knees and crossed his arms over his torso.

'The foetal position.'

'Original.'

'Everything's original about this caper.'

'I was told there were wounds and burns,' Niémans went on.

'I haven't seen the body yet. But I have heard that there are multiple traces of torture.'

'Was the victim tortured to death?'

'Nothing is certain for the moment.

There are also deep marks on his throat. Signs of strangulation.'

Niémans turned back towards the little lake. In it, he clearly saw his own reflection cropped head and blue coat.

'What about here? Have you found anything?'

'No. I've been hunting for a clue, a detail, for the last hour. Nothing doing. I reckon the victim wasn't killed here. The murderer just stuffed the body up there.'

'Have you been up inside the crevice?'

'Yes. Nothing to report. The murderer must have climbed up onto the top of the rock face from the other side, then lowered the body down on a rope. He then went down on another rope and wedged his victim inside. It can't have been easy getting him into that dramatic posture. It's all beyond me.'

Niémans looked once more at that ruggedly uneven cliff, stuck with ridges. From where he was standing, it was impossible to gauge the distances, but it looked as if the crevice where the body had been found was halfway up the face, as far from the ground as it was from the top. He spun round.

'Let's go.'

'Where?'

'The hospital. I want to see the body.'

The naked man, uncovered only down to his shoulders, lay on his side on a gleaming table. He was huddled up, as though frightened of being struck in the face by lightning. Shoulders hunched, head down, the body still had its two fists clenched under its chin, between its bent knees. The skin was white, muscles protruding, the epidermis dug with wounds which gave the corpse an almost unbearable reality. The neck bore long lacerations, as though someone had tried to rip open its throat. Puffed up veins stood out in its temples, like swollen streams.

Niémans glanced up at the other men present in the morgue. Bernard Terpentes, the investigating magistrate, spindly with a pencil moustache; Captain Roger Barnes, a colossus, swaying like a merchant ship, who was in charge of the Guernon gendarmerie; René Vermont, another gendarme captain on special mission, a small balding man with a wine-red complexion and bright beady eyes. Joisneau, who was standing back from the rest, looked every inch the zealous student.

'Do we know his ID?' Niémans asked no one in particular.

Barnes took a soldierly step forwards and cleared his throat.

'The victim's name is Rémy Caillois, superintendent. He was twenty-five years of age. He had been chief librarian at the University of Guernon for the last three years. The body was officially identified by his wife, Sophie Caillois, this morning.'

'Had she reported him missing?'

'Yes, yesterday at the end of the afternoon. Her husband had set out the day before on a trek in the mountains, in the direction of the Pointe du Muret. Alone, as he did every weekend. He would sometimes sleep out in one of the refuges. That's why she wasn't worried. Until yesterday afternoon...'

Barnes fell silent. Niémans had just uncovered the corpse.

There was a sort of unspoken horror, a silent scream that stuck in their throats. The victim's abdomen and tho-

rax were riddled with dark wounds of various shapes and depths. Incisions with violet edges, rainbow-coloured burns, black clouds of soot. There were also shallower lesions on the arms and wrists, as though the man had been strapped up with a cable.

'Who found the body?'

'A young woman...' Barnes peered down at his papers, then proceeded. 'Fanny Ferreira. A lecturer at the university.'

'In what circumstances did she find it?'

Barnes cleared his throat once more.

'She's a sportswoman who goes white-water rafting. You know, you descend the rapids on a board, wearing a wetsuit and flippers. It's a highly dangerous sport and...'

'And?'

'She wound up just beyond the natural dam in the river, at the foot of the rock face that borders the campus. When she climbed up onto the parapet, she spotted the body wedged into the cliff.'

'And that's what she told you?'

Barnes looked uncertainly around the room.

'Well, yes, I...'

The superintendent completely uncovered the body. He paced around that livid, hunched-up creature, whose closely cropped scalp stuck out like a stone arrow.

Niémans grabbed the death certificate, which Barnes had handed him. He glanced over the typed text. It had been written by the head of the hospital in person. The doctor made no pronounce- ment concerning the time of death. He simply described the visible wounds and concluded that death had been caused by strangula- tion. For further information, it would be necessary to unfold the body and perform an autopsy.

'When will forensics be here?'

'Any minute now.'

The superintendent approached the victim. He leant down and examined his facial features. He was young, rather handsome, his eyes closed and, most importantly, there was no sign of any blows to the face.

'Has anyone touched his face?'

'No one, superintendent.'

'So his eyes were closed?'

Barnes nodded. With his thumb and index finger, Niémans gently opened one of the victim's eyelids. Then the impossible happened: a gleaming teardrop slowly fell from the right eye. The superintendent started up in disgust. The face was crying.

Niémans scrutinised the others. No one else had noticed this extraordinary detail. He kept his calm and, still out of sight of the others, looked again. What he saw proved that he had not gone mad and that this murder was what every policeman dreads or longs for throughout his career, according to his character. He stood back up and swiftly covered the body once more. Then he whispered to the magistrate:

'Tell us how the investigations are to proceed.'

Bernard Terpentes rose to his full height.

'Well, gentlemen, you understand how this business may turn out to be difficult and… unusual. Which explains why the public prosecutor and I have decided to call in the local Grenoble bri-gade and also the gendarmerie nationale. I have also called in Superintendent Niémans, here present, from Paris. I am sure his name is not unknown to you. The superintendent is currently part of a high-ranking section of the Paris vice squad. For the moment, we know nothing about the motive for this murder, but it may well be a sexual one. And it is clearly the work of a maniac. Niémans's experience will be of great use to us. Which is why I should like him to lead this investigation…'

Barnes agreed with a swift nod of his head, Vermont likewise, but less enthusiastically. As for Joisneau, he answered:

'That's fine as far as I'm concerned. But my fellow officers will soon be here and…'

'I'll put them right,' Terpentes cut in. (He turned towards Niémans.)

'Well, superintendent?'

This carry-on was starting to get on Niémans's nerves. He longed to be out of there, getting on with the investigation and, above all, alone.

'How many men do you have, Captain Barnes?' he asked.

'Eight. No… I mean, nine.'

'Are they used to questioning witnesses, collecting evidence, organising road-blocks?'

'Um, well… that's not the sort of thing we…'

'What about you, Captain Vermont? How many men do you have?'

The gendarme's voice cracked out like a ten-gun salute:

'Twenty. And experienced, all of them. They'll fine-toothcomb the area around where the body was found and…'

'Fine. I suggest that they also question everybody who lives near the roads leading to the river, that they call into service stations, railway stations, houses beside bus stops… Young Caillois sometimes slept in refuges when out trekking. Find them and search them. Maybe he was kidnapped in one.'

Niémans turned towards Barnes.

'Captain, I want you to put out a request for information across the entire region. By noon, I want a complete list of all the area's prowlers, petty crooks, tramps and what have you. I want you to check who's just been released from prison in a two-hundred- mile radius. Thefts of cars and thefts of any kind. I want you to ask questions in hotels and restaurants. Fax them a questionnaire. I want to know the slightest strange occurrence, the slightest suspect arrival, the slightest indication. I also want a list of all the events that have occurred here in Guernon over at least the last twenty years which may or may not have something to do with this business.'

Barnes noted each request on his pad. Niémans turned to Joisneau:

'Get hold of the Special Branch. Ask them for a list of the cults, gurus and other similar loonies in this region.'

Joisneau nodded. Terpentes too, in a sign of superior agreement, as though all these ideas were being plucked straight out of his head.

'That should keep you busy till we get the results of the autopsy,' Niémans concluded. 'I don't need to add that this has got to be kept hush-hush. Not a word to the local press. Not a word to a single soul.'

They parted company on the steps of the University Hospital, striding off through the morning mist. In the shadow of that huge edifice, which looked at least two hundred years old, they got into their cars, heads down, shoulders hunched, without a word or a glance.

The hunt was on.

4

Pierre Niémans and Eric Joisneau went straight to the university, which was on the edge of the town. The superintendent asked the lieutenant to wait for him in the library, in the main building, while he paid a call on the university vice-chancellor, whose office took up the top floor of the administrative block, a hundred yards away.

The officer entered a vast 1970s construction, which had already been renovated, with a lofty ceiling and walls of different pastel colours. On the top floor, in a sort of antechamber occupied by a secretary and her tiny desk, Niémans gave his name and asked to see Monsieur Vincent Luyse. While waiting, he looked at the photo-graphs on the walls, showing triumphant students brandishing cups and medals, on ski slopes or in raging torrents.

A few minutes later, Pierre Niémans was standing in front of the vice- chancellor. A man with wiry hair, a flat nose, and skin the colour of talc. Vincent Luyse's face was a strange mixture of Black African characteristics and anaemic pallor. A few sunbeams shone through the stormy gloom, slicing through the half-light. The vice-chancellor asked the policeman to take a seat, then started nervously massaging his wrists.

'So?' he asked in a dry voice.

'So what?'

'Have you discovered anything?'

Niémans stretched his legs.

'I've just got here, vice-chancellor. I need a little time to settle in. Meanwhile, just answer my questions.'

Luyse stiffened in his chair. His entire office was made of wood, dotted with metallic mobiles reminiscent of flower stalks on a steel planet.

'Have you had any other tricky incidents in your university?' Niémans asked calmly.

'Tricky? No, not at all.'

'No drugs? No thefts? No fights?'

'No.'

'There aren't any gangs, or cliques? No youngsters giving each other funny ideas?'

'I don't understand what you mean.'

'I'm thinking about role-playing. You know, games full of ceremonies and rituals…'

'No. We don't have any of that sort of thing. Our students are a clearheaded bunch.'

Niémans remained silent. The vice-chancellor sized him up: crew cut, big build, grip of an MR73 sticking out of his coat. Luyse wiped his face, then said, as though trying to convince himself:

'I've been told that you are an excellent policeman.'

Niémans responded by staring back at the vice-chancellor. Luyse turned away his eyes and went on:

'Superintendent, all I want is for you to find the murderer as expeditiously as possible. The new academic year is about to begin and…'

'So there are no students on the campus yet?'

'Only a few boarders. They live on the top floor of the main building over there. Then there are also a few lecturers who are preparing their courses.'

'Can I have a list of them?'

'Why…' a hesitation, 'of course…'

'What about Rémy Caillois? What was he like?'

'An extremely discreet librarian. A loner.'

'Was he popular with the students?'

'Yes, yes of course he was.'

'Where did he live? In Guernon?'

'No, here on the campus. With his wife, on the top floor of the main building. Alongside the boarders.'

'Rémy Caillois was twenty-five. That's rather young to be married these days, isn't it?'

'Rémy and Sophie Caillois were both students here. Before that, I believe they met while at the campus school, which is reserved for our lecturers' children. They are… they were childhood sweethearts.'

Niémans got briskly to his feet.

'Most helpful, vice-chancellor. Thank you.'

The superintendent headed off at once, fleeing the smell of fear that pervaded the place.

Books.

Everywhere, in the large university library, numerous racks of books were piled up under the neon lights. Metal shelving holding up veritable walls of perfectly arranged paper. Dark spines. Gold or silver chasing. Labels all of which bore the crest of the University of Guernon. In the middle of the deserted room stood formica-topped tables, divided into small glass carrels. As soon as Niémans had entered the room, he was reminded of a prison visiting-room.

The atmosphere was at once luminous and stuffy, spacious and cramped.

'The best lecturers teach at this university,' Eric Joisneau explained. 'The cream of the south-east of France. Law, economics, literature, psychology, sociology, physics... And especially medicine all the top quacks of Isre teach here and consult at the University Hospital, which is in fact where the old university used to be. The buildings have been entirely renovated. Half the people in the département go there when they're ill and all the mountain dwellers were born in its maternity clinic.'

Niémans listened to him, arms crossed, leaning back onto one of the reading tables.

'Sounds like you know what you're talking about.'

Joisneau picked up a book at random.

'I studied at this university. I started doing law... I wanted to be a lawyer.'

'And you became a policeman?'

The lieutenant looked at Niémans. In the white neon light, his eyes were gleaming.

'When I took my degree, I was suddenly scared that I was going to get shit bored. So I enrolled in the police academy of Toulouse. I reckoned that the police meant an action-packed career, full of risks. A career that would have surprises in store for me...'

'And now you're disappointed?'

The lieutenant put the book back on the shelf. His slight smile faded.

'Not today, I'm not. Definitely not today.' He stared at Niémans. 'That body... How could anybody do that?'

Niémans ducked the question.

'What was the atmosphere like here? Anything special?'

'No. Lots of middle-class kids, full of clichés about life, about politics, about the ideas you were supposed to have... And the children of farmers and workers, too. Even more idealistic. And more aggressive. Anyway, we were all heading for the dole queue, so...'

'There wasn't any funny business? No strange cliques?'

'No. Nothing. Except, that is, there was a sort of university elite. A microcosm made up of the children of the lecturers themselves. Some of them were real high fliers. They won all the prizes every year. Even the sports awards. We were completely left standing.'

Niémans recalled the photographs of champions in the antechamber of Luyse's office. He asked:

'Did these students make up a real clan? Could they all be working together on some sick idea?'

Joisneau burst out laughing.

'What do you mean? A kind of... conspiracy?'

It was Niémans's turn to get up and wander along the book-shelves.

'A librarian is at the centre of a university. An ideal target. Imagine a group of students dabbling in some sort of hocus pocus. A sacrifice, a ritual... When choosing their victim, they could quite easily have thought of Caillois.'

'Then forget about the whiz kids I just mentioned. They were too busy getting firsts in their exams to worry about anything else.'

Niémans walked on between the rows of reddish brown books. Joisneau followed him.

'A librarian,' he resumed, 'is also the person who lends books… Who knows what everybody is reading, what everybody is studying… Maybe he knew something he shouldn't have.'

'You don't kill someone like that for… And what sort of secret reading scheme do you imagine these students had?'

Niémans spun round.

'I don't know. But I mistrust intellectuals.'

'Have you already got an idea? A suspicion?'

'None at all. Right now, anything is possible. A fight. Revenge. Intellectual weirdoes. Or homosexual ones. Or quite simply a prowler, a maniac, who stumbled onto Caillois quite by chance in the mountains.'

The superintendent fingered the spines of the books.

'You see, I'm not biased. But here is where we're going to start. Dig out all the books that could have some bearing on the murder.'

'What sort of bearing?'

Niémans went back down the rows of shelving and emerged into the main reading-room. He headed for the librarian's office, which was situated at the far end, on a raised platform, overlooking the carrels. A computer sat on the desk. Ring-binders lay in the drawers. Niémans patted the dark screen.

'In here there must be a list of all the books that are consulted, or borrowed, every day. I want you to put some of your men on the job. The most bookish ones you can find. Get the boarders to help as well. I want them to pick out all the books that deal with evil, violence, torture and religious sacrifices.

Look through the ethnology titles, for example. I also want them to note down the names of all the students who have regularly consulted this sort of book. And dig me out Caillois's thesis.'

'What about me?'

'You question the boarders. One at a time. They live here night and day, so they must know the university from top to bottom. The habits, the feel of the place, any weird kids… I want to know what the others thought of Caillois. I also want you to find out about his walks in the mountains. Find his fellow hikers. Discover who knew the routes he took. Who could have met him up there…'

Joisneau glanced sceptically at the superintendent. Niémans walked over to him. He was now speaking in whispers:

'I'll tell you what we have on our hands. We have an incredible murder, a pallid, smooth, hunched-up body bearing the traces of unspeakable suffering. The whole thing stinks of craziness. Right now, it's our little secret. We have a few hours, maybe a little longer, to solve this business. After that, the media will get involved, the pressure will build up, and emotions start to run wild. So concen-trate. Dive into the nightmare. Give all you've got. That's how we'll unmask the face of evil.'

The lieutenant looked terrified.

'You really think that, in a few hours, we can…'

'Do you want to work with me, or not?' Niémans butted in. 'Look, this is the way I see things. When a murder has been committed, you have to look at every surrounding detail as though it was a mirror. The body of the victim, the people who knew him, the scene of the crime... Everything reflects the truth, some particular aspect of the murder, see what I mean?'

He tapped the computer screen.

'This screen, for instance. When it's been switched on, it will become the mirror of Rémy Caillois's daily existence. The mirror of his working life, of his thoughts. It will contain elements, reflec- tions that may be of use to us. We have to dive in. Get through to the other side.'

He stood up and opened his arms.

'We're in a hall of mirrors, Joisneau, a labyrinth of reflected images. So take a good look. At everything. Because, somewhere inside one of those mirrors, in a dead angle, the murderer is hiding.'

Joisneau gaped.

'You seem a bit brainy for a man of action...'

The superintendent slapped his chest with the back of his hand.

'This isn't airy-fairy stuff, Joisneau. It's purely practical.'

'And what about you? Who... who are you going to question?'

'Me? I'm going to question our witness, Fanny Ferreira. And then Sophie Caillois, the victim's wife.'

Niémans winked.

'The ladies, Joisneau. That's what I call being purely practical.'   ·

5

Under the dreary sky, the asphalt road snaked across the campus, leading to each of its grey buildings with their blue, rusting windows. Niémans drove slowly he had obtained a map of the university on the way to an isolated gymnasium. He reached another block of fluted concrete, which looked more like a bunker than a sports centre. He got out of his car and breathed deeply. It was drizzling.

He examined the constructions of the campus, situated at a few hundred yards' distance. His parents, too, had been teachers, but in small secondary schools in the suburbs of Lyons. He had practically no memories of them. Family ties had soon seemed to him to be a weakness, a lie. He had rapidly realised that he was going to have to fight alone and, accordingly, the sooner the better. From the age of thirteen, he had asked to be sent to a boarding school. They had not dared refuse this voluntary exile, but he could still remember his mother's sobs from the other side of his bedroom wall: it was a sound in his head and, at the same time, a physical sensation, something damp and warm on his skin. So, he had decamped.

Four years spent boarding. Four years of solitude and physical training, apart from his lessons. All his hopes were then pinned on one target: the army. At seventeen, Pierre Niémans, who had passed his exams with flying colours, went for his three days' induction and asked to join the officers' training school. When the military doctor told him that he had been discharged as unfit and explained the reasons for this decision, Niémans suddenly understood. His anxieties were so manifest that they had betrayed him, despite all his ambition. He realised that his destiny would always be that long, seamless corridor, plastered with blood, where, at the very end, dogs howled in the darkness...

Other adolescents would have given up and quietly listened to the psychiatrists' opinions. Not Pierre Niémans. He persisted, and he began training again, with a redoubled rage and determination. If Pierre could not be a soldier, then he would pick another battle-field: the streets, the anonymous struggle against everyday evil. He would devote all of his strength and his soul to a war with no flags and no glorious deaths. Niémans would become a policeman. With this in mind, he spent months practising the answers to psychiatric tests. He then enrolled in Cannes-Ecluse police academy. And the era of violence began: top marks at target practice. Niémans con- tinued to improve, to grow stronger. He became an outstanding policeman. Tenacious, violent, vicious.

He started working in local police stations then became a sharpshooter in what was to become the Rapid Intervention Unit. Special operations began.

He killed his first man. At that instant, he made a pact with himself and, for the last time, contemplated his own fate. No, he would never be a proud warrior, a valiant army officer. But he would be a restless, obstinate street fighter, who would drown his own fears in the violence and the fury of the concrete jungle.

Niémans took a deep breath of mountain air. He thought about his mother, who had been dead for years. He thought about his past, which now seemed like an endless canyon, and his memories, which had splintered then faded, making a last stand against oblivion.

As though lost in a dream, Niémans suddenly noticed a little dog. The creature was muscular, its short coat glistening in the mist. Its eyes, two drops of opaque lacquer, were staring at the policeman. Waggling its behind, it was approaching. The officer froze. The dog drew ever nearer, just a few steps away. Its moist nose twitched. Then it abruptly started growling. Its eyes shone. It had smelt fear. The fear oozing out of this man.

Niémans was petrified.

His limbs felt as though they had been gripped by a mysteri- ous force. His blood was being sucked away by an invisible siphon, somewhere in his guts. The dog barked, showing its teeth. Niémans understood the process. Fear produced an odour which the dog smelt and which provoked a reaction of dread and hostility. Fear feeding on fear. The dog barked then rolled its neck, grinding its teeth together. The cop drew his gun.

'Clarisse! Clarisse! Come back, Clarisse!'

Niémans re-emerged from his spell in the cooler. Through a red veil, he saw a grey man in a zip-up cardigan. He was approaching rapidly.

'You got a screw loose, or what?'

Niémans mumbled:

'Police. Piss off. And take your mutt with you.'

The man was flabbergasted.

'Jesus Christ, I don't believe this. Come on, Clarisse, come on, little darling...'

Master and hound moved off. Niémans tried to gulp back his saliva. His throat felt harsh, dry as an oven. He shook his head, put his gun away and paced round the building. As he turned left, he forced himself to remember: how long was it now since he had seen his shrink?

Around the second corner of the gymnasium, the superintendent came across the woman.

Fanny Ferreira was standing near an open door and sanding down a red-coloured foam board. The officer imagined that it must be the raft she used to float downstream.

'Good morning,' he said with a bow.

He was back among warmth and assurance.

Fanny raised her eyes. She must have been twenty, at most. Her skin was dark and her hair generously curly, with slight ringlets around her temples and a heavy cascade over her shoulders. Her face was sombre and velvety, but her eyes had a penetrating, almost indecent, clarity.

'I'm Superintendent Pierre Niémans. I'm investigating the murder of Rémy Caillois.'

'Pierre Niémans?' she repeated in astonishment. 'But that's amazing!'

'Sorry?'

She nodded towards a small radio, lying on the ground.

'They were just talking about you on the news. Apparently, you arrested two murderers last night, just near the Parc des Princes. Which is rather good. But they also said that you disfigured one of them. Which is not so good. Are you omnipresent, or what?'

'No, I just drove all night.'

'But why are you here? Aren't our own local cops up to it?'

'Let's just say I'm part of the reinforcements.'

Fanny went back to work she damped down the oblong surface of the board, then pressed a folded sheet of sandpaper onto it with both palms. Her body looked stocky and solid. She was dressed casually neoprene diver's leggings, a sailor's jumper, light-coloured leather boots, which were tightly laced. The veiled light cast a soft rainbow over the entire scene.

'You seem to have got over the shock quickly enough,' Niémans observed.

'What shock?'

'You remember? You discovered a...'

'I'm trying not to think about it.'

'So would you mind talking about it again?'

'That's why you're here, isn't it?'

She was not looking at the policeman. Her hands continued to run up and down the length of the board. Her movements were jerky and brutal.

'In what circumstances did you find the body?'

'Every weekend I go down the rapids...'she pointed at her upturned raft.... 'on one of these things. I'd just finished one of my little trips. Near the campus, there's a rock face, a natural dam, which blocks the current and lets you land easily. I was pulling out my raft when I noticed it...'

'In the rocks?'

'Yup, in the rocks.'

'You're lying. I've been up there. I noticed that there's no room to move back. It's impossible to pick out something in the cliffs, fifty feet up...'

Fanny threw her sheet of sandpaper into a plastic cup, wiped her hands and lit a cigarette. These simple gestures provoked a feeling of violent desire in Niémans.

The young woman exhaled a long

puff of blue smoke.

'The body was in the rock face. But I didn't see it in the rock face.'

'Where, then?'

'I noticed it in the waters of the river. As a reflection. A white blotch on the surface of the lake.'

Niémans's features relaxed.

'That's just what I thought.'

'Is that really important as regards the investigations?'

'No. But I like everything to be clear.'

Niémans paused for a moment, then went on:

'You're a rock climber, aren't you?'

'How did you guess?'

'I don't know… because of the region. And you do look extremely… sporty.'

She turned round and opened her arms towards the mountains, which overlooked the valley. It was the first time she had smiled.

'This is my home turf, superintendent. I know these mountains like the back of my hand, from the Grand Pic de Belledonne to the Grandes Rousses. When I'm not shooting the rapids, I'm climbing the summits.'

'In your opinion, could only a climber have positioned the body in the rock face?'

Fanny became serious once more. She observed the glowing tip of her cigarette.

'No, not necessarily. The rocks almost form a natural staircase. On the other hand, you'd have to be extremely strong to be able to carry the body without losing your balance.'

'One of my inspectors thinks that the killer climbed up from the other side instead, where the slope is less steep,

then lowered the body down on a rope.'

'That would be one hell of a long way round.' she hesitated, then went on. 'In fact, there's a third possibility, quite simple, if you know a little about climbing.'

'Which is?'

Fanny Ferreira stubbed her cigarette out on her heel and threw it away.

'Come with me,'she commanded.

They went inside the gymnasium. In the half-light, Niémans made out a heap of mats, the straight shadows of parallel bars, poles, knotted ropes. As they approached the right-hand wall, Fanny remarked:

'This is my den. No one else comes here during the summer. So I keep my equipment here.'

She lit a stormlight, which hung over a sort of workbench. On it were various instruments, metal parts with a variety of points and blades, casting silvery reflections or sharp glints. Fanny lit another cigarette.

Niémans asked her:

'What's all this?'

'Picks, snaphooks, triangles, safety catches. Climbing equipment.'

'So?'

Fanny exhaled once more, with a sequence of simulated hiccups.

'And so, superintendent, a murderer in possession of this sort of equipment, and who knew how to use it, could quite easily have raised the body up from the river bank.'

Niémans crossed his arms and leant back against the wall. While handling her tools, Fanny kept her cigarette in her mouth. This innocent gesture heightened the policeman's craving. He really did find her extremely attractive.

'As I told you,'she began, 'that part of the rock face has a sort of natural staircase. It would be child's play for someone who knew about climbing, or even trekking for that matter, to climb up first without the body.'

'And then?'

Fanny grabbed a fluorescent green pulley, with a constellation of tiny openings.

'And then you stick that in the rock, just above the crevice.'

'In the rock! But how? With a hammer? That would take ages, wouldn't it?'

Behind her screen of cigarette smoke, she replied:

'You seem to know practically nothing about rock climbing, superintendent.'she seized some threaded pitons from the workbench. 'Here are some spits. Now, with a rock drill like this one'she indicated a sort of black, greasy drill 'you can stick several spits into any sort of rock in a matter of seconds. Then you fix your pulley and all you have to do is haul up the body. It's the technique we use for lifting bags up into difficult or narrow spaces.'

Niémans pouted sceptically.

'I haven't been up there, but I reckon the crevice is extremely narrow. I don't see how the murderer could have crouched inside, then been able to pull up the body with just his arms, and with no pull from his legs. Which takes us back to the same portrait of our killer: a colossus.'

'Who said anything about pulling it up? To raise his victim, all the climber had to do was lower himself down on the other side of the pulley, as a counterweight. The body would then have gone up all on its own.'

The policeman suddenly caught on and smiled at such a simple idea.

'But then the killer would have to be heavier than his victim, wouldn't he?'

'Or the same weight. When you throw yourself down, your weight increases. Once the body had been raised, your murderer could have quickly climbed back up, still using the natural steps, then wedged his victim in that theatrical rock fault.'

The superintendent took another look at the spits, screws and rings that were lying on the workbench. It reminded him of a burglar's set of tools, but a particular sort of burglar someone who breaks through altitudes and gravity.

'How long would all that take?'

'I could do it in less than ten minutes.'

Niémans nodded. The killer's profile was becoming clearer. The two of them went back outside. The sun was filtering through the clouds, shimmering on the mountain peaks. The policeman asked:

'Do you teach at the university?'

'Geology.'

'More exactly?'

'I teach several subjects: rock taxonomy, tectonic displacements and glaciology, too the evolution of glaciers.'

'You look very young.'

'I got my PhD when I was twenty. By then, I was already a junior lecturer. I'm the youngest doctor in France. I'm now twenty- five and a tenured professor.'

'A real university whiz kid.'

'That's right. A whiz kid. Daughter and granddaughter of emeritus professors, here in Guernon.'

'So you're part of the clan?'

'What clan?'

'One of my lieutenants studied at Guernon. He told me how the university has a separate elite, made up of the children of the university lecturers...'

Fanny shook her head maliciously.

'I'd prefer to call it a big family. The children you're talking about grow up in the university, amidst learning and culture. They then get excellent results. Nothing very surprising about that, is there?'

'Even in sporting competitions?'

She raised her eyebrows.

'That comes from the mountain air.'

Niémans pressed on:

'I suppose you knew Rémy Caillois. What was he like?'

Without any hesitation, Fanny replied:

'A loner. Introverted. Sullen, even. But extremely brilliant. Dazzlingly cultivated. There was a rumour going round... that he had read every book in the library.'

'Do you think there was any truth in that?'

'I don't know. But he certainly knew the library well enough. It was his cave, his refuge, his earth.'

'He was very young, too, wasn't he?'

'He grew up in the library. His father was head librarian before him.'

Niémans casually paced forwards.

'I didn't know that. Were the Caillois also part of your big family'?'

'Definitely not. Rémy was even hostile to us. Despite all his culture, he never got the results he was hoping for. I think... or rather, I suppose he was jealous of us.'

'What was his subject?'

'Philosophy, I believe. He was trying to finish his thesis.'

'What was it about?'

'I've no idea.'

The superintendent paused. He looked up at the mountains. Under the increasing glare of the sun, they looked like dazzled giants. Another question:

'Is his father still alive?'

'No. He passed on a few years ago. A climbing accident.'

'There was nothing fishy about it?'

'What are you after? He died in an avalanche. The one on the Grande Lance of Allemond, in '93. You're every inch a cop.'

'So we have two rock-climbing librarians. Father and son. Who both died in the mountains. That is a bit of a coincidence, isn't it?'

'Who said that Rémy was killed in the mountains?'

'True. But he set off on a hike on Saturday morning. He must have been attacked by the killer up there. Perhaps the murderer knew the route he was taking and...'

'Rémy wasn't the sort of person who follows regular routes. Nor one who tells others where he's going. He was very... secretive.'

Niémans nodded his head.

'Thank you, young lady. You know the form if you think of anything that may be of importance, then phone me on one of these numbers.'

Niémans jotted down the numbers of his mobile and of a room which the vice-chancellor had given him at the university he had preferred to set up base inside the university rather than with the gendarmerie. He murmured:

'See you soon.'

The young woman did not look up. The policeman was leaving when she said:

'Can I ask you a question?'

She stared at him with her eyes of crystal. Niémans felt decidedly uneasy. Her irises were too light. They were made of glass, white water, as chilling as frost.

'Fire away,' he replied.

'On the radio, they said… Well, is it true that you were one of the team that killed Jacques Mesrine?'

'I was young then. But it's true. I was there.'

'I was wondering… What does it feel like afterwards?'

'After what?'

'After something like that.'

Niémans moved towards the young woman. Instinctively, she flinched. But, with a touch of arrogance, she bravely looked back at him.

'It will always be a pleasure talking to you, Fanny. But you will never get a word out of me about that. Nor about what I lost that day.'

The questioner lowered her eyes. Softly, she said:

'I see.'

'No, you don't see. Which is just as well for you.'

6

The trickling water dripped onto his back. Niémans had borrowed a pair of hiking boots from the gendarmerie and was now ascending the natural staircase in the rock face, which was a reasonably easy climb. When he reached the height of the crevice, he took a careful look at the narrow opening where the body had been discovered. Then he examined the surrounding rock face. With his hands protected by Gore-Tex gloves he felt for possible traces of spits in the wall.

Holes in the stone.

The wind, laden with drops of icy water, beat against his face. It was a sensation Niémans liked. Despite the circumstances, he had experienced a strong feeling of fulfilment on reaching the lake. Maybe the killer had chosen this site for that very reason: it was a place of calm and serenity, pure and uncluttered. A place where jade waters soothed violent souls.

The superintendent found nothing. He continued his search around the niche: no trace of any spits. He knelt on the ledge and ran his hands over the inner walls of the cavity. Suddenly, his fingers came across an evident opening, right in the middle of the ceiling. He thought fleetingly of Fanny Ferreira. She had been right: the killer, equipped with spits and pulleys, must have hauled up the corpse by using his own body weight. He shoved his arms inside and located three notched, grooved cavities, about eight inches deep, and which formed a triangle the three prints of the spits that had carried the pulleys. The circumstances of the murder were becoming clearer. Rémy Caillois had been set upon while out hiking. The murderer had strapped him up, tortured, mutilated then killed him in those lonely heights, and had then gone back down into the valley with his victim's body. How? Niémans glanced down forty feet below, there where the waters turned into a mirror of lacquer. On the stream. The killer must have descended the river in a canoe or something similar. But why had he gone to such lengths? Why had he not just left the body at the scene of the crime?

The policeman cautiously climbed back down. When on the bank, he removed his gloves, turned his back to the rocks and examined the shadow of the crevice on the perfectly smooth water. The reflection was as steady as a picture. He now felt sure that this place was a sanctuary. Calm and pure. And that was perhaps why the killer had chosen it. In any case, the investigator was now certain about one thing.

His killer was an experienced rock climber. Niémans's saloon car was equipped with a VHF transmitter, but he never used it. No more than he used his cell phone when it came to confidential calls, it being even less secure. For the last few years, he had used a pager, varying from time to time its brand and model. No one else could intercept this form of communication, which necessitated a password. It was a trick he had learnt from Parisian drug dealers, who had immediately caught on to how discreet pagers were. The superintendent had given his number and password to Joisneau, Barnes and Vermont. As he got into his car he took it out of his pocket and switched it on. No messages.

He started his car and drove back to the university.

It was now eleven in the morning. Occasional figures crossed the green esplanade. A few students were running on the track in the stadium, which stood slightly away from the group of concrete blocks.

The officer turned at the crossroads and headed back towards the main building. This immense bunker was eight storeys high and six hundred yards long. He parked and consulted his map. Apart from the library, the huge construction contained the medicine and physics lecture halls. On the upper floors were the rooms set aside for practical work. And on the top floor there were the boarders' rooms. The campus janitor had marked, with a red felt-tip pen, the room occupied by Rémy Caillois and his young wife.

Pierre Niémans walked past the library doors, which were adjacent to the main entrance, and reached the hall: an open-plan construction lit by large bay windows. The walls were decorated with nave frescoes, which shone in the morning sunlight, and the end of the hall, several hundred yards away, vanished into a sort of mineral haze. It was a place of Stalinist dimensions, utterly unlike the pale marble and brown wood of Parisian universities. Or, at least, that was what Niémans supposed. He had never before set foot in a university in Paris or anywhere else.

He climbed up a staircase of suspended marble steps, each block bent into a hairpin and separated by vertical strips. Something the architect had dreamt up, in the same overwhelming style as the rest. Every other neon light was broken, so Niémans crossed regions of utter darkness before emerging into zones of excessive brilliance.

He finally reached a narrow corridor, punctuated by small doors. He wandered down this black shaft here, all the light bulbs had given up the ghost looking for number 34, the Caillois's flat.

The door was ajar.

With two fingers, the policeman pushed the thin piece of plywood open. Silence and half-light welcomed him. Niémans found himself in a little hall. At the end, a stream of light crossed the narrow corridor. It was enough to enable him to make out the frames that hung on the walls. They contained black-and- white photographs, apparently dating from the 1930s or 1940s. Olympic athletes in full flight spiralled into the sky, or dug their heels into the ground, in postures of religious pride. Their faces, figures and positions gave off a sort of worrying perfection, the inhuman purity of statues. Niémans thought of the university architecture. It all fitted together in a rather uneasy way.

Beneath these images, he noticed a portrait of Rémy Caillois and took it down to get a better look. The victim had been a handsome, smiling youth with short hair and drawn features. His eyes shone with an extremely alert sparkle.

'Who are you?'

Niémans turned his head. A female form, draped in a raincoat, stood at the end of the corridor. Still a kid. She, too, could scarcely be twenty-five. Her shoulder-length fair hair framed a thin ravaged face, whose paleness brought out the dark rings around her eyes. Her features were bony, but delicate. This woman's beauty emerged only in moments of crisis, as though it were the echo of a first feeling of uneasiness.

'I'm Superintendent Pierre Niémans,' he announced.

'And you come in like that without knocking?'

'I'm sorry. The door was open. You are Rémy Caillois's wife?'

Her reply was to snatch the portrait out of Niémans's hands and hang it back on the wall. Then, walking back into the room to the left, she took off her raincoat. Niémans had a surreptitious glimpse of a pale emaciated chest in the hanging folds of an ancient pullover. He shuddered.

'Come in,' she said despite herself.

Niémans found himself in a cramped living-room, with a neat austere decor. Modern paintings hung on the walls. Symmetrical lines, distressing colours, incomprehensible stuff. The policeman took no notice. But one detail did strike him: there was a strong chemical smell in the room. A smell of paste. The Caillois must have just redecorated their flat. This detail cut him to the quick. For the first time he shivered at the thought of this couple's ruined hopes, the ashes of happiness that must still be glowing beneath that woman's grief. He adopted a serious tone:

'I've come from Paris, Madame. I was called in by the investi- gating magistrate to help in the enquiries into your husband's sad demise. I . ..'

'Do you have a lead?'

The superintendent stared at her, then suddenly felt like breaking something, a window, anything. This woman was full of grief, but her hatred of the police was even stronger.

'No, we don't. Not for the moment,' he admitted. 'But I'm optimistic that investigations will soon…'

'Ask your questions.'

Niémans sat down on the sofa-bed, opposite the woman who had chosen a small chair in order to keep her distance from him. To save face, he seized a cushion and fiddled with it for a few seconds.

'I've read your statement,' he began. 'And I would just like to get a little additional information. Lots of people go hiking in this region I suppose?'

'What else do you think there is to do in Guernon? Everybody goes walking, or climbing.'

'Did other hikers know the routes Rémy took?'

'No. He never talked about that. He used to go off on ways known only to him.'

'Did he just go walking, or climbing as well?'

'It depended. On Saturday, Rémy set off on foot, at an altitude of less than six thousand feet. He didn't take any equipment with him.'

Niémans paused for a moment before getting to the heart of the matter.

'Did your husband have any enemies?'

'No.'

The ambiguous tone of the answer led him to ask another question, which took even him by surprise:

'Did he have any friends?'

'No. Rémy was a loner.'

'How did he get on with the students who used the library?'

'The only contact he had with them was to give them library tickets.'

'Anything strange happen recently?'

The woman did not answer. Niémans pressed the point:

'Your husband wasn't particularly nervy or tense?'

'No.'

'Tell me about his father's death.'

Sophie Caillois raised her eyes. Her pupils were dull, but her eyelashes and eyebrows were magnificent. She gave a slight shrug of the shoulders. 'He died in an avalanche in 1993. We weren't married at the time. I don't know anything much about all that. What are you trying to get at?'

The police officer remained silent and looked round the little room, with its immaculately arranged furniture. He knew this sort of place off by heart. He realised that he was not alone with Sophie Caillois. Memories of the dead man lingered there, as though his soul were packing its bags somewhere, in the next room. The superintendent pointed at the pictures on the walls.

'Your husband didn't keep any books here?'

'Why would he have done that? He worked all day in the library.'

'Is that where he worked on his thesis?'

The woman nodded curtly. Niémans could not take his eyes off that beautiful, hard face. He was surprised at meeting two such attractive women in less than one hour.

'What was his thesis about?'

'The Olympic games.'

'Hardly an intellectual subject.'

An expression of scorn crossed Sophie Caillois's face.

'His thesis was about the relationship between the sporting event and the sacred. Between the body and the mind. He was studying the myth of the athlon; the first man who made the earth fertile by his own strength, by transcending the limits of his own body.'

'I'm sorry,' Niémans huffed. 'I don't know much about philos-ophy... Does that have something to do with the photographs in the corridor?'

'Yes and no. They're stills taken from a film by Leni Riefenstahl about the 1936 Berlin Olympic games.'

'They're striking images.'

'Rémy said that those Games had revived the profound nature of the Games of Olympus, which was based on the marriage of mind and body, of physical effort and philosophical expression.'

'And in this case, of Nazi ideology, isn't that so?'

'The nature of the thought being expressed didn't matter to my husband. All he was interested in was that fusion of an idea and a force, of thought and action.'

This sort of clap-trap meant nothing to Niémans. The woman leant forward then suddenly spat out:

'Why did they send you here? Why someone like you?'

He ignored the aggressive tone. When questioning, he always used the same cold, inhuman approach, based on intimidation. It is pointless for a policeman and particularly for a policeman with his mug to play at being understanding or at amateur psychology. In a commanding voice, he asked:

'In your opinion, was there any reason for anyone to have it in for your husband?'

'Are you crazy, or what?' she yelled. 'Haven't you seen the body? Don't you realise that it was a maniac who killed my husband? That Rémy was picked up by a loony? A headcase who laid into him, beat him, mutilated him, tortured him to death?'

The policeman took a deep breath. He was thinking of that quiet, un-worldly librarian, and his aggressive wife. A chilling couple. He asked:

'How was your home life?'

'Mind your own fucking business.'

'Answer the question, please.'

'Am I a suspect?'

'You know damn well you're not. So just answer my question.'

The young woman looked daggers at him.

'You want to know how many times a week we fucked?'

Goose-pimples rose over the nape of Niéman's neck.

'Would you co-operate, Madame? I'm only doing my job.'

'Piss off, you fucking pig.'

Her teeth were far from white, but the contours of her lips were ravishingly moving. Niémans stared at that mouth, her pointed cheek bones, her eyebrows, which shed rays across the pallor of her face. What did the tint of her skin, of her eyes matter? All those illusive plays of light and tone? Beauty lay in the lines. The shape. An incorruptible purity. The policeman stayed put.

'Piss off!' the woman screamed.

'One last question. Rémy had always lived at the university. When did he do his military service?'

Sophie Caillois froze, taken aback by this unexpected question. She wrapped her arms around her chest, as though suddenly chilled from the inside.

'He didn't.'

'He was declared unfit?'

The woman's eyes fixed themselves once more on the superintendent.

'What are you after?'

'For what reasons?'

'Psychiatric, I think.'

'He had mental problems?'

'Are you off the last banana boat, or what? Everybody gets dismissed for psychiatric reasons. It doesn't mean a thing. You play up, come out with a load of gibberish, then get dismissed.'

Niémans did not utter a word, but his entire bearing must have expressed deep disapproval. The woman suddenly took in his crew cut, his rigid elegance and his lips arching in a grimace of disgust.

'Jesus Christ, just piss off!'

He got up and murmured:

'So, I'll be going then. But I'd just like you to remember one thing.'

'What's that?' she spat.

'Whether you like it or not, it's people like me who catch murderers. It's people like me who will avenge your husband.'

The woman's features turned to stone for a couple of seconds, then her chin trembled. She collapsed in tears. Niémans turned on his heel.

'I'll get him,' he said.

In the doorway, he punched the wall and called back over his shoulder:

'By Christ, I swear it. I'll get the little fucker who killed your husband.'

Outside, a silvery flash burst in front of his face. Black spots danced beneath his eyelids. Niémans swayed for a few seconds. Then he forced himself to walk calmly to his car, while the dark halos gradually turned into women's faces. Fanny Ferreira, the brunette. And Sophie Caillois, the blonde. Two strong, intelligent, aggressive women. The sort of women this policeman would probably never hold in his arms.

He aimed a violent kick at an ancient metal bin, riveted to a pylon, then instinctively looked at his pager.

The screen was flashing. The forensic pathologist had just finished the autopsy.

7

At dawn that same day, at a distance of two hundred and thirty miles due west, Police Lieutenant Karim Abdouf had just finished reading a criminology thesis about the use of genetic sampling in cases of rape and murder. The six-hundred-page door-stopper had kept him up practically all night. He now looked at the figures on his quartz alarm clock as it rang: 07.00.

Karim sighed, flung the thesis across the floor, then went into the kitchen to make some black tea. He returned to his living-room which was also his dining-room and bedroom and stared out at the shadows through the bay window. Forehead pressed against the pane, he evaluated his chances of being able to conduct a genetic enquiry in the one-horse town to which he had been transferred. They were zero.

The young second-generation Arab looked at the street-lights, which were still nailing down the dark wings of the night. Bitterness knotted his throat. Even when up to his ears in crime, he had always managed to avoid prison. And now, here he was, twenty-nine years old, a cop, and banged up in the lousiest prison of them all: a small provincial town, as boring as shit, in the midst of a rocky plain. A prison with neither walls nor bars. A psychological prison which was gnawing away at his soul.

Karim started daydreaming. He saw himself nicking serial killers, thanks to analyses of DNA and specialised software, just like in American movies. He imagined himself leading a team of scientists who were studying the genetic map of the criminal type. After much research and statistical analysis, the specialists isolated a sort of rupture, a flaw somewhere in the spiral of chromosomes, and identified this split as the key to the criminal mentality. Some time ago, there had already been mention of a double Y chromosome which was supposed to be characteristic of murderers. But this had turned out to be a false lead. Nevertheless, in Karim's daydream, another 'spelling mistake' was located in the set of letters which made up the genetic code. And this discovery had been made thanks to Karim and his relentless arrests. A shudder suddenly ran through him. He knew that if such a 'flaw' existed, then it was also coursing round his veins. The word 'orphan' had never meant much to Karim. You could miss only what you had experienced and he had never had anything which could even remotely be described as a family. His earliest memories were of a patch of lino and a black-and-white tv in the Rue Maurice-Thorez children's home in Nanterre. Karim had grown up in the midst of a colourless, graceless neighbourhood. Detached houses rubbed shoulders with the tower blocks, patches of waste-land gradually turned into housing estates. And he could still remember those games of hide- and-seek with the building sites that were little by little gobbling up the wild nature of his childhood.

Karim was a lost child. Or a foundling. It all depended on which way round

you looked at it. Whichever, he had never known his parents and nothing in the education that he subsequently received had served to remind him of his origins. He could not speak Arabic very well and had only the vaguest knowledge of Islam. The adolescent had rapidly rejected his guardians the carers in the home, whose simplicity and general niceness made him want to puke and had given himself over to the streets.

He had then discovered Nanterre, a limitless territory criss- crossed by broad avenues, dotted with massive housing estates, factories and local government offices, and populated by a sheep- ish crowd dressed in rumpled old clothes and who expected no tomorrows. But degradation shocks only the rich. Karim did not even notice the poverty that characterised the town from the tiniest brick to people's deeply wrinkled faces.

His adolescent memories were happy ones. The time of punk rock, of 'No Future'. Thirteen years old. His first mates. And first dates. Oddly enough, in the loneliness and torments of adolescence, Karim stumbled across a reason to love and to share. After his orphaned childhood, his difficult teenage years gave him a second chance to find himself, open up to others and to the outside world. Even today, Karim could still remember those times with a total clarity. The long hours spent in bars, pushing and shoving over a pinball machine, laughing with his buddies. The endless daydreams, throat in a knot, thinking about a girl he had spotted on the steps at school.

But the suburbs were hiding their

true nature. Abdouf had always known that Nanterre was a sad dead-end place. He now discovered that the streets were violent, even lethal.

One Friday evening, a gang burst into the café of the swimming pool, which was open late. Without a word, they kicked the manager's face in, then bottled him. An old story of refused entry, or a beer not paid for, no one knew any more. And no one had lifted a finger. But the stifled cries of the man beneath the counter became resonant echoes in Karim's nerves. That night, things were explained to him. Names, places, rumours. He got a glimpse of another world, the existence of which he had not even suspected. A world peopled by ultra-violent beings, inaccessible estates, blood-stained cellars. On another occasion, just before a concert on Rue de l'Ancienne Mairie, a fight had turned into a slaughter. The tribes were out once again. Karim had seen lads rolling on the asphalt, their faces split open, and girls hiding under cars, their hair sticky with blood.

As he got older, he no longer recognised his town. A tidal wave was swamping it. Everyone spoke in admiration of Victor, a boy from the Cameroons who jacked up on the roofs of the estate. Of Marcel, a nasty piece of work, with a pock-marked face and a blue beauty spot tattooed on his forehead, like an Indian, who had been condemned several times for beating up cops. Of Jamel and Sad who had held up the Caisse d'Epargne. On his way out of school, Karim would sometimes notice these youths. He was struck by their haughty nobility. They were not vulgar, uneducated or coarse. No, they were aristocratic, elegant, with ardent eyes and studied gestures.

He chose his camp. He started out by stealing car radios, then cars and so became truly financially independent. He hung out with the drugged-out Black, his 'brothers' the bank robbers, and especially Marcel, a footloose, scary and brutal person, who ran wild from dawn to dusk, but who could also distance himself from the suburbs in a way which fascinated Karim. Marcel, a peroxide skinhead, wore fur-lined jackets and listened to Liszt's Hungarian Rhapsodies. He lived in squats and read Blaise Cendrars. He called Nanterre 'the octopus' and, as Karim knew, invented for himself a whole set of excuses and explanations for his future, inevitable fall. Strangely enough, this suburban being revealed to Karim the existence of another life, one beyond the suburbs.

The orphan swore that, one day, he would make it his.

While continuing his thieving, he studied hard at school, which surprised everybody. He took Thai boxing lessons to protect himself from others and from himself, for he was occasionally gripped by uncontrollable fits of violent rage. His destiny had now become a tightrope, along which he walked without losing his balance. Around him, the dark swamps of delinquency and debauchery were swallowing everything up. Karim was seventeen. He was alone again. Silence surrounded him when he walked across the hall of the adolescents' home, or when he had a coffee in the school café, sitting next to the pinball machines. No one dared wind him up. By that stage, he had already been selected for the regional

Thai boxing championships. Everyone knew that Karim Abdouf could break your nose with a flick of his foot and with his hands still flat on the zinc counter. Other stories also went round, about hold-ups, drug deals, epic fights…

Most of these rumours were unfounded, but they meant that Karim was pretty much left alone. He passed his exams with flying colours. He was even congratulated by the headmaster and suddenly realised that this authoritarian man was also frightened of him. The kid enrolled in Nanterre University to study law. At that time, he was stealing two cars a month. Since he knew several fences, he constantly swapped them around. He was certainly the only second- generation Arab on the estate who had never been arrested, or even bothered by the police. And he still had not used drugs, of any sort.

At twenty-one, Karim passed his law degree. What now? Lawyers would not take on a six feet six tall Arab, as slim as a rake, with a goatee, dreadlocks and his ears full of rings, even as a messenger boy. One way or the other, Karim was going to end up on the dole queue and find himself back at square one. Never. So carry on stealing cars? More than anything else, Karim loved those secret hours of the night, the silence of parking lots, the waves of adrenaline that ran through him as he foiled the security systems in BMWs. He realised that he was never going to be able to give up that inscrutable, heightened existence, a tissue of risk and mystery. He also realised that, sooner or later, his luck was going to run out.

It was then that he had a revelation:

he would become a cop. He would then live in that same arcane universe, but sheltered from the laws he despised, and hidden from the country he wanted to spit on. One thing he had never forgotten from his childhood was this: he had no origins, no homeland, no family. He was a law unto himself, and his country was limited to his own breathing space.

After national service, he enrolled as a boarder in the Cannes-Ecluse police academy, near Montereau. It was the first time he had left Nanterre, his manor. His grades were excellent from the start. Karim's intellectual capacities were well above average and, above all, he knew more about delinquent behaviour, gangland law and the suburban life than anybody else. He also turned into a brilliant marksman and his knowledge of unarmed combat deepened. He became a master of té a quintessential form of close combat, bringing together the most dangerous elements of the various martial arts and sports. The other apprentice cops took an instinctive dislike to him. He was an Arab. He was proud. He knew how to fight, and he spoke better French than most of his classmates, who were generally waifs and strays who had joined the police to stay off the dole.

One year later, Karim completed his course by holding down a series of posts as a trainee in various Parisian police stations. Still the same no-man's- land, still the same poverty. But this time in Paris. The young trainee moved into a little bed-sitter in the Abbesses quarter. A little perplexed, he realised that he had made it.

But he had not cut all ties with his

origins. He regularly went back to Nanterre to hear the news. One disaster after another. Victor had been found on the roof of an eighteen-storey building, as crumpled as a witchdoctor's doll, a syringe sticking into his scrotum. OD. Hassan, a massive blond Berber drummer had blown his brains out with a shotgun. The 'brother' bank robbers were doing time in Fleury-Mérogis. And Marcel had become a hopeless junkie.

Karim watched his friends drowning and, with horror, saw the final tidal wave break. aids was now hastening the process of destruction. The hospitals, once full of worn-out workmen and bedridden oldsters, were now filling up with dying kids with black gums, mottled skin and withered bodies. He saw most of his friends go that way. He saw the disease gain in power and size, then ally itself with Hepatitis C and mow down the ranks of his generation. Karim retreated, with fear in his guts.

His town was dying.

In June 1992, he got his badge. And was congratulated by the panel a load of fat bastards with signet rings who filled him full of pity and loathing. But it did call for a celebration. He bought some champagne and headed for Les Fontanelles, Marcel's estate. Still today, he could remember every detail of that late afternoon. He rang the door-bell. Nobody. He asked the kids downstairs, then wandered through the halls of the building, the football fields, the waste tips heaped with old papers… Nobody. He kept on looking until evening. In vain. At ten o'clock, Karim went to Nanterre Hospital's AIDS unit Marcel had been HIV positive for the last two years. He walked through the fumes of ether, past the faces of the sick, and quizzed the doctors. He saw death at work. He contem- plated the terrible progress of the epidemic.

But he did not find Marcel.

Five days later, he heard that the body of his friend had been found in a cellar, his hands fried, his face sliced into ribbons, his nails bored by an electric drill. Marcel had been tortured almost to death, then finished off with a shotgun blast to his throat. The news did not surprise Karim. His friend had been doing too much and watering down the doses he sold. It had only been a question of time. By coincidence, that very day, he received his bright new tricolour inspector's card. That coincidence was, for him, a sign. He retreated into the shadows, thought of Marcel's killers, and grinned. The little fuckers would never have imagined that one of Marcel's mates was a cop. Nor would they have imagined that this cop would have no bones about killing them, both for old times' sake, and from a personal conviction that life just should not be that fucking awful.

Karim started investigating.

Within a few days, he had got the killers' names. They had been seen with Marcel just before the presumed time of the murder. Thierry Kalder, Eric Masuro and Antonio Donato. He felt disappointed. They were three small-time junkies who probably wanted to get Marcel to reveal where he stashed his gear. Karim collected more detailed information: neither Kalder nor Masuro could have tortured Marcel. Not warped enough. Donato was the guilty party. Extorting money with menaces from little kids. Pimp-ing for under-age girls on building sites. Junked out of his mind.

Karim decided that his death alone would assuage his vengeance.

But he had to work quickly. The Nanterre cops who had given him this information were also after the fuckers. Karim plunged into the streets. He was from Nanterre, he knew the estates, he spoke the kids' language. It took him just one day to find the three junkies. They were holed up in a ruined building, close to one of the motorway bridges by Nanterre University. A place wait-ing to be demolished while vibrating from the din of cars shooting past, a few yards from the windows.

He arrived at the wrecked building at noon, ignoring the noise of the traffic and the hot June sun. Children were playing in the dust. They stared at the big guy, with his rasta looks, as he entered the ruins. Karim crossed the hall, full of ripped-open letter boxes, leapt up the stairs four at a time and, through the growling of the cars, distinctly made out the give-away sound of rap. He smilingly recognised A Tribe called Quest, an album he had been listening to for the last few months. He kicked open the door and said simply: 'Police.' A wave of adrenaline burst into his veins. It was the first time he had played at being the fearless cop.

The three men were frozen with astonishment. The flat was full of rubble, the walls had been torn down, pipes stuck out everywhere, a TV sat on a gutted mattress. A spanking-new Sony, obviously stolen the previous night. On the screen, the pale flesh of a porno film. The hi-fi rumbled away in a corner, shaking down dust from the plaster.

Karim felt as if his body had doubled in size and was floating in space. Out of the corner of his eye he saw car radios carelessly heaped up at the far end of the room. He saw torn-open packets of powder on an upturned cardboard box. He saw a pump-action shotgun amid some boxes of cartridges. He immediately picked out Donato, thanks to the photofit portrait he had in his pocket. A pale face with light-blue eyes, protruding bones and scars. Then the other two, hunched up in their efforts to extract themselves from their chemical dreams. Karim still had not drawn his gun.

'Kalder, Masuro, scram!'

The two of them jumped at hearing their names. They dithered, glanced at each other with dilated pupils, then headed for the door. Which left Donato, who was shaking like an insect's wing. He made a rush for the gun. Just as he was about to grab it, Karim crushed his hand and kicked him in the face he was wearing steel-tipped shoes without taking his other foot off the trapped hand. The joints in the arm cracked. Donato screamed hoarsely. The cop seized the man and dragged him over to the ancient mattress. The heavy rhythm of A Tribe called Quest pounded on.

Karim took out his automatic, which he wore in a velcro holster on his left side, and wrapped up his carrying hand in a transpar- ent plastic bag made of a special uninflammable polymer which he had brought with him. He tightened his hold on the diamond-patterned grip. The man looked up at him.

'What… what the fucking hell are you doing?'

Karim loaded a bullet into the cylinder and smiled.

'Cartridge cases, fellow. Ain't you ever seen that on the TV? Never leave cartridge cases lying round…'

'What you after? You a cop? You sure you're a cop?'

Karim nodded to each question, then said:

'I'm here for Marcel.'

'Who?'

The cop saw the incomprehension in the man's eyes. And he realised that this wop couldn't even remember the person he had tortured to death. He realised that, in this junkie's memory, Marcel did not exist, had never existed.

'Tell him you're sorry.'

'Wh… What?'

The sunlight spilled in over Donato's gleaming face. Karim lifted his gun in its plastic envelope.

'Ask Marcel to forgive you!' he panted.

The man understood that he was going to die and roared:

'Sorry! Sorry, Marcel! Fucking Jesus! I'm really really sorry, Marcel! I .. .'

Karim shot him twice in the face.

He got the bullets back out of the burnt fibres of the mattress, stuffed the burning-hot cases into his pocket then left without looking back. He figured that the other two would soon be back with reinforcements. In the entrance hall, he waited for a few minutes then saw Kalder and Masuro legging it his way, accompa-nied by three other zombies. They rushed into the building through the wobbling doors. Before they had had time to react, Karim was in front of them and flattening Kalder against the letter boxes.

He brandished his gun and yelled:

'One word and you're dead. Come looking for me, and you're dead. Top me, you go down for life. I'm a fucking cop, you dick-heads. A cop, got me?'

He threw the man down onto the ground and went out into the sunlight, crushing shards of glass under his feet.

So did Karim bid farewell to Nanterre, the town that had taught him everything. A few weeks later, he phoned the police station on Place de la Boule to ask about their enquiries. He was told what he already knew. Donato had been killed, apparently by two 9mm calibre bullets from an automatic, but they had found neither the bullets nor their cases. As for his two accomplices, they had vanished. As far as the cops were concerned, the case was closed. As far as Karim was concerned, too.

The Arab asked to join the BRI, Quai des Orfvres, a unit specialising in tailing, on-the-spot arrests and 'jumping' known criminals. But his results played against him. They suggested the Sixth Division the anti-terrorist brigade so that he could infiltrate the Islamic fundamentalists in suburban hot spots. Immigrant cops were too rare a commodity to miss out on this chance. He refused. No way was he going to act as a grass, even if it did come to fanatical assassins. Karim wanted to roam through the kingdom of the night, go after killers and face them on their own turf, wander off into that parallel world which was also his own. His refusal was not well received. A few months later, Karim Abdouf, top of his class in the Cannes-Ecluse police academy, and unsuspected killer of a psychopathic junkie, was transferred to Sarzac, in the département of the Lot.

The Lot. A region where the trains did not stop any more. A region where ghost villages sprang up around roads, like stone flowers. A land of caves, where even tourism attracted only troglodytes: gorges, pits, cave paintings... This region was an insult to Karim's personality. He was a second-generation Arab, off the streets, nothing could be stranger to him than this two-bit provincial town.

A dreary daily routine began. Karim had to go through days of tedium, punctuated by menial tasks: writing reports of car accidents, arresting an illicit vendor in a shopping centre, nicking gatecrashers in tourist venues...

So the young Arab started living in his daydreams. He got hold of biographies of great policemen. Whenever he could, he went to the libraries at Figeac or Cahors to pick out newspaper articles dealing with police enquiries, crimes and misdemeanours, anything and everything which reminded him of his true vocation. He also bought old bestsellers, the memoirs of gangsters... He subscribed to the police force's professional press, to magazines specialising in guns, ballistics, new technologies. A sea of paper, into which Karim was slowly sinking.

He lived alone, slept alone, worked alone. At the police station, which must have been one of the smallest in France, he was simultaneously feared and hated. His fellow cops called him 'Cleopatra' because of his locks. Since he did not drink, they thought he was a fundamentalist. And, because he always declined the obligatory stopover

chez Sylvie during their nightly rounds, they imagined he was gay.

Immured in his solitude, Karim ticked off the days, the hours, the seconds. He sometimes spent an entire weekend without saying a word.

That Monday morning, he re-emerged from one of his spates of silence, spent almost entirely in his bed-sitter, apart from a training session in the forest, where he relentlessly practised the murderous gestures of té, before emptying a few magazines into some century-old trees.

His door-bell rang. Instinctively, Karim looked at his watch. 07.45. He opened the latch.

It was Sélier, one of the late-duty officers. He looked wretched. A mixture of worry and fatigue. Karim did not offer him any tea. Nor even a seat. He just said:

'Well?'

The man opened his mouth, but nothing came out. Under his cap, his hair was gluey with greasy sweat. At last, he stammered:

'It's... it's the school. The primary school.'

'What is?'

'Jean-Jaurs School. It was broken into... during the night.'

Karim smiled. The week was getting off to a flying start. Some lay-abouts from a nearby estate must have decided to smash up a school, just for the fun of it.

'Much damage?' Karim asked, while getting dressed.

The uniformed officer grimaced as he saw the clothes Karim was putting on. A sweatshirt, jeans, hooded track-suit top, then a light-brown leather jacket a garbage collector's model from the 1950s. He stammered:

'No. That's just it. It was a professional job...'

Karim was doing up his boots.

'A professional job? What's that supposed to mean?'

'It wasn't kids mucking about... They got into the place with skeleton keys. Took loads of precautions. It was just the head- mistress who noticed something weird. Otherwise...'

The Arab got to his feet.

'What did they steal?'

Sélier panted and slipped his index finger under his collar.

'That's what's even weirder. They didn't steal anything.'

'Really?'

'Really. They just got into a room, then... pfft!... Seem to have left just like that.'

Karim took a brief look at his reflection in the window panes. His locks tumbled down obliquely on either side of his temples, his narrow face was sharpened by his goatee. He adjusted his woolly hat of Jamaican colours and smiled at his image. A devil. A devil sprung out of the Caribbean. He turned towards Sélier:

'So why did you come running after me?'

'Crozier isn't back from his weekend yet. So Dussard and me... We reckoned that you... That you ought to come and see... Karim, I...'

'All right, all right. Let's go.'

fiction

the blue hour
jefferson parker

This is an excerpt from The Blue Hour, *published by HarperCollins in Hardback at £9.99 on the 17th of January 2000*

TWENTY

FREEDOM. VELOCITY. Interstate 5. Windows down, air blasting through the van. Bill felt the rage filling him now, moving throughout his body. Like boiling water removed from the burner, it settled and filled the shape of its container. Bill Wayne, he thought: vessel of retribution, bucket of hate. Witness this.

He found Ronnie's beat up old four door in the Main Place parking lot, near the entrance closest to Goldsmiths Jewelry. So she hadn't lied. All the more reason to get to know her. The mall shops closed at nine tonight, which gave him almost an hour, just right.

So he drove away and into the cluttered construction zone he'd scouted earlier, just .85 miles form the mall according to the can odometer. The mess had something to do with Cal Trans and the I-5. He found the bumpy turnoff and drove along the beaten chain-link fence, past the scaffolding and the watertrucks. The gate was closed but not locked. He drove inside with his headlights off and parked, hidden between two big Cats. He cut the engine and sat there a moment. The moon was just a faint face risen prematurely in the eastern sky. It looked alone and embarrassed. Perfect—just two blocks from a stop for the OCTA bus, which would take him straight into the mall when he was ready.

Bill slipped to the back of the vehicle and opened the toolbox. He wouldn't need Pandora's Box because Ronnie's car was almost certainly too old and cheap to have a comprehensive antitheft alarm wired in. Good. Less to carry, less to depend on. No fuses to slip out of place and end up who-knew-where? That meant he'd only need the knockout cloth in the heavy duty freezer bags, his shopping bag and his trusty Slim Jim. Traveling light.

He got the gas bag out from his instrument kit. It sat atop his surgical "sharps"—the scalpels, dissecting scissors, retractors, forceps, needles and catheters used for the preliminary veinous removal and arterial introduction of fluid.

Holding his breath, he gave the chloroform cloth a heavy fresh dose from the 50mm bottle he'd stolen from the body and paint shop where he'd briefly worked, Saturdays only, over two years ago. He had been a prep man and gofer, tasked sometimes with the unpleasant job of mixing chloroform and alcohol used as a solvent. The liquid was heavy and smelled kind of pleasant, he thought. When he tried it out on a near helpless drunk one night up on Harbour, he had been surprised how quickly it worked.

Bill sealed up the bag very thoroughly and waved his hand in

front of his face before breathing in. It was wonderful stuff—fast acting, quickly metabolized out of the system and only occasionally responsible for heart failure and strokes in people and animals who had breathed a little too much of it.

He slipped the plastic bag inside another one, sealed it, and set the thin package into the shopping bag. The shopping bag was black, large and strong, featuring thick twine handles and the name of the department store in gold script. His book and bedsheet were already in it. New latex gloves too. He added the Slim Jim. It extended a few inches from one end so Bill used the sheet to cover the top of it, disguising it as a mysterious purchase, or perhaps something to return. The sweet ethereal smell of the gas lingered as he went back to the drivers seat.

His last piece of working gear was the micro .32 derringer that he now took from the glove box and slipped into his coat pocket.

Bill always brought reading material for his short bus rides. In this case, *Fodor's Los Angeles*, to suggest he was just visiting. He sat near the front of the bus, on the right side, glancing out the window only occasionally and otherwise engrossed in the book. In fact he was picturing Ronnie: her shapely legs, dark curly hair and high intelligent forehead. Tall and Young. Wouldn't it be something if she'd worn her hair up today?

He disembarked at the north side of the Main Place, then walked around the parking lot to where Ronnie's car was still waiting on the south side.

The light wasn't particularly good

where Ronnie had parked: perfect. He walked past her car and noted it was a Chevrolet. He looked around, saw no one nearby, then went back to the car, set the bag down and acted like he was getting out his keys. Instead he bent down and got the Slim Jim, leaned up close the old sedan and slid the tool down between the window glass and the door. He kept his head up, his eyes alert. It was a matter of feel at this point, and Bill had plenty of that. He'd practiced on hundreds and hundreds or cars so that this part of his job would go smoothly. And it did. On his third pass with the Jim he caught the lock arm and he pulled it up. He heard the tinny report of the lock opening and saw the little black plastic rod stand up inside the glass like a soldier at attention. Then he opened the door, set his bag on the passengers seat, sat down and slammed the door shut.

A moment later he was in the backseat on the driver's side, slumped down and head back like a dozing airline passenger, keeping his eyes on the mall exit.

The black shopping bag with the Fodor's and slim Jim were tucked behind the passenger's seat. The gas bag was on his lap. It was important to have that in a convenient place when you needed it, because if you opened it too soon they might smell something funny and whirl around and ruin the whole capture.

That hadn't happened, yet. The closest was Irene Hulet—his third— who had sneezed one second before he was going to clamp his hand over her mouth and apply the chloroform cloth. That had left him with the cloth already out, spreading its deadly fumes into the closed car.

Luckily, the sneeze had left her without breath for a few nice seconds, as sneezes often do. So by the time she was ready to breathe again, Bill had his left hand tight against her mouth and his right cupping the cloth over her nose. About seven seconds. The reason it worked so well was that people inhaled abruptly and deeply when they were surprised and frightened, then needed to do it again as quickly when they got mostly gas. That, plenty of $CHCl_3$, and a little muscle. It helped if the headrests were solid rather than adjustable, so you could clamp your forearms around each side for purchase as you pulled back.

Bill slid down a little further for comfort , but kept his eyes open. His heart was beating hard and fast. He wanted to hurt someone badly while he felt good. Real good. He was angry, and getting angrier the longer he waited. He could almost smell the anger inside him, like a bad wire smoldering deep within its bundle. He worked his hands into the gloves.

Then he saw Ronnie come through the door.

He melted down into the floor space behind the drivers seat, unlocking the outside gas bag and positioning his thumbs and index fingers on the lips of the inside one. The closing of the car door would be his cue to open it.

He heard her keys in the lock, then the door opening. Her purse clunked to the passengers seat. When he felt her weight settle and heard the door slam he rose behind the seat and clenched his open left hand over her mouth. A split second later his right snugged the damp rag over her nose and Bill pulled back hard, like a rower going for speed.

"Evenin', honey."

Ronnie was a strong one. One. Two. She felt like a big wild animal. Three. Four. But Bill was stronger. This part of it was like a cowboy trying to stay on a bucking bronco. Five, while her feet kicked the pedals and her knees banged the underside of the dash. Six, She dropped the keys. Seven.

Then it was over. He felt her head go loose on her neck and he wrenched her down and to the right, out of sight. He slid up onto the seat, resealing the cloth and tossing it into his shopping bag. Bracing his feet on the front seat he pulled Ronnie toward him like a spider gathering in a huge moth. Head and shoulders. Butt. Legs and feet. One shoe had fallen off somewhere.

She whimpered. The sweet smell of chloroform lingered in the car.

He was breathing hard as he got her laid out across the back and squeezed himself into he front of the car. He pulled the sheet out and covered her, tucking it just under her chin like she was asleep. The keys had landed right in the middle of the floor mat, as if she'd placed them there just for him.

Three minutes later he was slipping the big Chevy in between towering earth movers, up next to his van. The fury was at bay now and he could feel the deeply meaningful sense of affection stirring again down there. He looked out at the moon, then back at the unconscious woman.

He imagined cruising into his garage and having the door shut automatically behind him, then getting things set up. Preparation was sacred. He imagined the candlelit garage with Ronnie on the table and the Porti-Boy pulsing rhythmically as the fluid ran in. He could feel his hands massaging the fluid deep into her thirsty tissues, bringing her body to life again, to a rosy glow that began its bloom at he jugular in her clavicle and spread down, through out her system and finally back to her angelic face. She would bloom beneath his touch like a flower. He could see her eyelids flutter as they awoke tot he fluid of eternity. And he could see himself restored, too, gradually, as he worked the spirit back into Ronnie's tired body. Yes, it slowly would come to him – the feeling worth any price, the feeling that was the spark of his dreams and the flame of his humanity. He would caress her with the expensive essential oils, perfume and dress her in the silk and satin lingerie, dry and style her hair while he grew powerful in his desires. He imagined carrying her upstairs to bed, whispering in her ear. And then he'd really find out how much she wanted him. It was the best thing this short, sad life had to offer, for both of them.

TWENTY-ONE

Hess stood beside Merci near the CAT D6 and looked at the tire tracks left by the vehicle that had carried Veronica "Ronnie" Steven's body into the night.

Kneeling and pointing with his pen, he commented on the tracks of the mismatched tires. They were some of the best tire prints he'd seen at a crime scene because of the soil here in the construction yard—oily, damp and loosely packed.

Hess had been awakened by Merci's call at 6 A.M. He was a little groggy then, nut unfettered by chemotherapy, radiation and the stout scotches he'd drunk before bed. Now his mind felt sharp and clear, though his fingers were oddly heavy, like saps at the end of his hands.

"I hate this man," said Merci, quietly, slowly. " I want to commit mayhem on him."

This was one of the most dismal scenes Hess had ever run across: the big slick of blood that had spread over soil that was already oil stained and packed by heavy machinery; the splash of it against the CAT track; the forlorn Chevrolet with the keys still in the ignition and the purse sitting upright and open on the hood, overflowing with multicolored vitals that spilled out and sent up heat waved from the paint.

Hess had never seen such a gruesome thing. He had stood there for a moment in the early sunlight in disbelief.

Merci had stared in silence with him.

He'd be more likely to send you something UPS.

After that, as always, work to do.

"He must not know," he said. Hess had been wondering if the Purse Snatcher knew about his tires and now had to guess he didn't. Either doesn't know or doesn't care, he thought: and so far he's been very careful. He slipped the pen back in his pocket, his fingers thick and imprecise. He glanced at Merci but she was still looking at the bloody ground.

"Not know how much I hate him?"

"That he's riding on two different tires."

"He'd change them."

"He hasn't."

"He thinks we're as stupid as I feel. I wish I had one of those drinks from dinner right now."

She'd insisted on joining him in Scotch at dinner on Friday. This had not surprised Hess. They had gone to Cancun, a deputy's hangout in Santa Ana. The food was good and cheap and they made the drinks strong if you appreciated them that way. He could feel the disdain when they walked into the place and he knew it was for Merci and not for himself. Kemp was there, unfortunately, with a table of his friends, and the drunken tension in him had leaked into he atmosphere like a gas. It had been too late to back out and go someplace else, so Merci had downed the drinks.

"It wouldn't do you any good, Merci."

"This girl was nineteen years old, Tim. That's just unforgivable. There ought to be special circumstances for victims under twenty-one. You do somebody under twenty-one, any reason, you get the fucking guillotine."

The patrolmen had taped off the scene and kept the construction workers out of the yard as best they could. A foreman had found the car and purse, seen the blood and guts and called it in. He'd heard about he Purse Snatcher, seen Merci on TV, knew what he was looking at. He got her to autograph a piece of paper for his kid.

Hess watched the CSIs working the

purse and the door handles of the car. The hood was smeared and murky where the innards and purse had been. Goddamned flies. He wondered if the Purse Snatcher had picked a woman in an older, alarmless car because Lee LaLonde's electronic override box had lost a fuse in Janet Kane's BMW and failed. Maybe he just like her. Maybe she had her hair up, Two hunts in two weeks.

Building. Growing. Speeding Up.

Would he get his alarm override back to LaLonde for repair?

Hess recalled the statement. LaLonde was selling his inventions at the Marina Park swap meet in Elsinore on a Sunday in late August of last year. A medium height, medium-build male Caucasian, blond/brown, had approached his table. Around thirty years old. "Bill" wore his hair long., Bill asked how LaLonde knew electronics; LaLonde told him of father, schooling, aptitude. Suspect asked if LaLonde knew how to build a small device that would override the alarm system on cars. LaLonde said there were too many combinations on door locks and keyless entry chips to make a universal unlock device feasible – it would be too slow and possibly too large. Suspect then said he didn't care about the locks, he cared about the alarms. LaLonde said that both the lock and the disarm combinations were frequencies digitally registered by a microchip in the keyless entry module – and constantly emitted by the alarm system of a vehicle. He told Bill he could configure a universal override if he had the manufacturers specs on the frequencies. The suspect had shown

him several sheets of paper that "looked like computer print-outs" by nine of the major carmakers, containing the information. Three weeks later, LaLonde had sold Bill a working override device house d in a cell phone body, for $3000 and given Bill back the printouts.

With the fear that Merci had put into LaLonde, Hess bet the young man would call them if his customer contacted him for a repair. Then again, he might not, because the override box could convict them both. Merci had made this clear, that LaLonde was staring at a murder conspiracy rap if he didn't cooperate. It was hard to know which way a person would lean.

LaLonde had sketched his device for them, and Hess now turned to the drawing and noted where the fuse would go.

But you lost it in Janet Kane's car, thought Hess. You opened the cell phone body and the fuse fell out and you didn't notice in the dark.

And the override hasn't worked since. Why open it? Was it failing? Unreliable? Did it open accidentally?

Thus a 1978 Chevrolet Malibu belonging to Veronica Stevens of Orange, California.

Hess could see the wavy-haired, mustached suspect wheeling a vehicle with mismatched tires into his yard in the dark last night, pulling up between the CATs. He know this place because he scouted it early. Ditto the last two places he's used to hide the van and later transfer the woman.

He could see Ronnie Stevens inverted from a rope tied to the top of the CAT's hydraulic blade – about seven feet off the ground. Like the oak branches, strong, but easier to get to.

But, question: How does he get from where he parks to where he hunts?

Hess cursed himself for not thinking of this before. Then he searched his memory for the pertinent distances: between the Jillson abduction site and where her car was found – 5.3 miles. Between the Kane abduction site and where her car was found – 3.3miles. Between the Stevens abduction site – if it was indeed the nearby mall – and where her car was found, well, how far was the mall from here, maybe a mile?

You don't walk five miles unless you have to. Or three. Or even one.

Then how does he get from where he leaves the van or truck or station wagon to where he hunts the women?

A bike? Too clumsy and hard to handle. Hard to stash in the victim's car.

A friend? Hess had hoped that they weren't up against a pair. You didn't see it much in sex crimes, but two were twice as hard to catch, not twice as easy. None of their evidence, until now, had suggested that possibility. For the time being, he let it of.

Hitchhike? Too conspicuous.

Taxi? The same.

The OCTA bus? Well, he thought, check the routes. Should have done that two days ago. Goddamnit, anyway.

Merci was talking to the foreman again. He pointed to the car, the, presumably, to the route he'd driven in.

Hess walked the mismatched tread tracks until they came to an end near Main Street. The ground trembled form the vibrations of the freeway the same way the beach trembled from the waves at the Wedge.

The van had gone right, which was the shortest way back to I-5. This part of Main was light commercial and residential, or had been at tone time. No the buildings were either razed or awaiting demolition to make room for a new bend in the interstate and a fat new on-and-off ramp. Hess trudged back to his car and got out some plastic bags, into which he spooned soil samples from every twenty yards or so of the dirt drive. He spread the samplers against the inside of the bags. He knew that all the various oils and fuels and sand and gravel dropped to the dirt and ground in by construction machinery might help an analyst match up samples taken form the tires of any given van. He wiped his forehead with this shirtsleeve. Give me the truck or the van, he thought. Give me the truck or van with the odd tire.

Back at the Chevy he watched the CSIs dusting the window exteriors. The purse was already gone, bagged up and secure inside the CSI van. Hess stepped over the crime scene tape and looked through the dust on the driver's side window.

"Are you done with the door handle?" he asked.

"Yes, sir, Lieutenant."

"I'm going to open it."

"It's all yours, sir."

Hess swung open the door, bent over and put his hands on his knees, looking in. The interior was alive compared to the Jillson and Kane cars, he thought: recent players; recent events. It was just a feeling. He thought he smelled something sweet and not unpleasant – Ronnie's perfume perhaps. Or maybe a man's cologne. He remembered what Robbie Jillson had told him about smelling his wife's tormentor when he got into her Infiniti a *full day* after she went missing. Ho did he describe it? *Faint. Cologne or aftershave maybe. Real faint. But I smelled him.*

He leaned further in, hoping for a more definitive whiff but getting none. A woman's scent lay underneath it all, he thought, but something else?

A woman's shoe lay on the floor, down by the pedals. It was a black sandal with a thick sole like the young people were earring these days. Hess leaned in and confirmed that the shoe cam up fairly high—above the ankle—and that it fastened with a buckle at the top. The buckle was burst open and the perforated length of leather, bent from hours of use, had sprung free of the broken buckle. He could see her fighting, he looked back toward the headrest of her seat. One long dark hair caught in the stitching of the pad. Because you were being pulled back? Because he's behind you with, what? A cord? A club? Just his strong hands? No chance really, with him coming from behind in the dark. You could have a .45 in your purse but it wouldn't help. It wouldn't help you, anyway. No warning. No purchase. Nothing but your fists and your nails. He could see her unlocking the door, swinging her purse in, dropping herself to the seat and closing the door at the same time. She's just about to put the keys in the ignition when he moves. After the

door closes; before the engine starts. Keys still in her hand.

Keys. We always say to use the keys as a weapon.

Hess saw that they were still in the ignition, a fat bunch and a small flashlight on a ring. The flashlight had a good surface for prints. The Snatcher had touched at least one of those keys, for certain. Hess used his pen and a pocket-knife to guide the ignition key almost free but keep it from falling out. In the smoggy morning light he did not see what he hoped he'd see: darkened blood in the slot and on the teeth of the key. He saw nothing but the clean old metal of well-used metal.

It made him angry and Hess thought, Sonofa*bitch*, I'm going to find you. And if Merci Rayborn takes target practice on your face I might look the other way.

It was easy to get worked up about what had happened to a young woman like this, when you were close enough in time and space to smell her.

Hess backed out gently shut the front door and opened the rear one. There you were, he thought. Your place. Not much room, really.

Hess wondered if he just sat on the seat, unmoving and dressed in dark clothing – maybe a dark ski mask pulled down – and let darkness, reflections on glass and people's general inattentiveness be his cover. Maybe.

You find the woman and you know her car, which means you must have seen her in it. You are on foot now, in the parking lot, where Kamala Peterson first saw you. You walk purposefully and deliberately: a gentleman going to or from the mall, to or from his car. Alert. Observant.

You override her alarm if she has one; jimmy the door lock; get in. You carry the Jim where? Down your pants? In a bag or box? Along with the cell phone override? Along with your choke cord or sap?

You wait in the back; overpower; take the keys and drive away.

Hess tried to picture the Purse Snatcher slugging his victims unconscious with a sap or club. But he couldn't see it happening – the headrests kept getting in the way.

He shut the back door and looked at one of the CSIs. "Do your best."

The CSI nodded. "We've already for a lot of prints, sir. But cars a re traps—you know that. Can I mention something? Did you notice a smell in the car?"

"Yeah, I can't place it."

"I think I can. My cat was operated on a few months ago. They let me watch because the vet's an old family friend. Typically they put the animal under with a ketamine and Valium shot, then keep it down with halothane gas. But last time, my cat got real sick with either the ketamine, the Valium or the halothane. He's old. Almost died. Anyway, they tried chloroform. The vet's an old guy – he used it decades ago and he was good with it. But I got that same smell, sweet and kind of nice, when I opened the door of this car."

It made the kind of sense that sent a little shiver of recognition to Hess's heart.

"It knocked out that cat in about two seconds. And you know how uptight

and nervous a cat at the vet is?"

TWENTY TWO

They found Ronnie Stevens's Santa Ana address and parked right out front. It was a fifties' suburban home in a tract that looked well tended and peaceful. A big acacia tree bloomed purple in the middle of the front yard. An older Chevy – a model once driven by Sheriff Department deputies, Hess noted – sat in the driveway.

"I hate these," Merci said. "Maybe you can do the talking."

Ronnie Steven's mother was tall and dark-haired, an aging beauty, Hess saw. He wondered that a sixty-seven-year-old man with ten-pound fingers would consider a fifty-year-old woman aging. She'd been cleaning the house.

Hess stumbled through his lines as best he could. He felt his face flushing and heard his voice crack as he told her that her daughter was missing and presumed dead. He hated these moments, too: tragedy revealed, and irrefutable evidence of his own failure. Of the failure of his entire profession.

Eve Stevens received the news with a small nod, an uncertain wobble of chin and eyes filling quickly with tears.

"We're going to get this guy, Mrs. Stevens," Merci said.

Eve Stevens excused herself and left the living room. Merci was standing by the cabinet that housed family photographs and mementos. Hess saw the eager shine of trophies and the twinkle of keepsakes.

"Brothers," said Merci. "Baseball and archery. The girl, Veronica, she was a swimmer."

Hess heard a toilet flush. He heard the low keening form the bathroom, then the toilet flush again When Eve returned her face was a sagging mask of tragedy and her eyes looked like they'd been burned.

Eve could only talk about Ronnie for a few minutes. She sobbed steadily the whole time, but Hess was impressed by her courage. Ronnie was a conscientious young woman, had been a good student and reliable worker since she was sixteen. She had graduated from high school a semester early to go full time at he jewelry store. She had no ambitions other than to travel and see some of the world. She saved her money, had a few friends, stayed out late on Fridays and Saturdays. No steady guys. Eve didn't think Ronnie had much interest in drugs, had never found any or seen her intoxicated or overheard her talking about them with friends.

Then she stood and Hess knew the expression on her face.

"May I?" she asked.

"Please."

With this, Hess went to her and hugged her, very lightly, almost formally, and not for very long. He let her break it off when she wanted to.

"Thank you," she said.

Hess just nodded , then handed her the sketch of the Purse Snatcher suspect. He watched her tears hit the paper.

"No. She liked the clean cut type. At least I think she did."

Hess asked if Veronica had remarked anything unusual about a man lately—any man—a stranger, an acquaintance, a customer, a new or old friend.

Eve nodded. "Two nights ago, Thursday, we talked when she came home from work. We talked late. We talked about men, how funny they could act. Because this man had blocked her from getting out of the parking lot, then asked her for a date. Odd."

Merci exhaled with some disgust. "This guy's odd for more reasons than that."

Hess looked at her but it was too late. Rayborn was thick as a post sometimes. "Did she describe him?"

"No."

"He just parked his car right behind her?" he asked, anything to get Merci's last implication out of the air.

"His van. Ronnie said it was a silver panel van."

———

The OCTA bus driver on the Saturday evening route recognized the sketch immediately. It had taken Hess about two minutes and the transit district schedule to see that there were bus routes proximate to all three sites where the cars had been abandoned.

"Last night, late, after eight-thirty," he said. " He got on at Main and 17th, got off at the Main Place Mall. What did he do?"

"We think he killed a woman," said Merci.

The driver looked at Hess, then back at Merci. "He sat on the right, up near the front of the bus. I remember that he wore cologne. Kind of a funny smell. Strong. Had a shopping bag-the ones with the handles on them. He had a book out. *Fodor's Los Angeles.* So I though he was a tourist. Nice clothes, country and western style. Long coat. Mustache and long hair, like the picture. But some guys, they've got this thing about them, you notice it."

"What thing?" asked Hess.

The driver thought for a moment. He was wiry and middle-aged, looked to Hess to be of Latin American blood. "They're fake. They're not real."

"Maybe the mustache is fake," said Merci.

"I didn't notice that," the driver said. " It's more to do with attitude. The whole look. It seemed false. There's something else I noticed about him too. I look at my riders a lot. I talk to them."

" And?" asked Hess.

"He was the kind of guy who is always alone. There's no one in the world you can picture with him. No one to be around him. Just a feeling that's all."

Merci left him her card with her cell and work phones on it, and carefully told the driver how critical it was to call if he ever saw this man again, or remembered anything more about him.

———

At his desk, Hess listened to his messages while Merci showed the Sex Offenders Registry mugs of Pule and Eichrod to Kamala Peterson. It was late Sunday morning by then and headquarters was dead. Hess looked over to see Kamala looking down at a picture on Merci's desk, shaking her head.

Barbara had called to wish him well and tell him it was good to talk to him.

She wanted something, he could tell, but he had no idea what.

Dr. Ramsinghani, the radiation specialist, had called to inquire about his general feeling after the first thoracic scorching. The doctor reminded him that the second treatment would be Monday, same time and place.

Hess listened, wishing that he wasn't the center of his own universe. Like you'd forget a date like that. It would be nice to just blend in and be.

An old contact of his at the DMV had been kind enough to return his call promptly, and with good news: Hess's 1028 request for a list of panel vans registered in Orange County would be coming through by Monday morning. Too bad DMV in California didn't track vehicles by color. How many, he wondered. Two hundred, or fifteen? But how many with mismatched tires? That was the wild card.

Word from Riverside Sheriffs, too: LaLonde surveilled, no unusual activities, would continue another forty-eight hours.

The phone rang. It was Annie Pickering of Arnie's Outdoors, following up on Hess' request of earlier in the week. He was proud to announce that he had found in his computer files just the kind of purchase record that Hess had asked him to find. The talkative Arnie chattered on but finally got out the basic facts: a sale was made in February, the off-season for deer hunting, Hess knew, but the month that Lael Jillson was field dressed off the Ortega. The Arnie's Outdoor's customer had bought a device known as a Deer Sleigh'R, a gambrel for securing game, a hoist for lifting it, two lengths of nylon rope and an electric lantern.

"Can you find the clerk who rang it up?"

"It was Big Matt, here at the Fountain Valley Store. He's here right now if you want to talk to him."

"Give me the fax number there. I'm going to send over a sketch I want him to look at. See if he can put the face with the sale."

Hess took the number and faxed the artists sketch to Big Matt at Arnie's Outdoors in Fountain Valley.

He collected the picture as it groaned haltingly through the fax machine, then looked over at Merci. She was just coming back into the room after escorting Kamala Peterson to the exit, She shook her head disgustedly and came to his desk. She looked around , then leaned forward toward him. He could see the anger on her face, in the hard set of her jaw and in her cold brown eyes.

"Eichrod, Pule and Colesceau all just flunked the Kamal Petersen romantic-vision test. None of them has sad enough eyes. None is Mr. Remorse. She also let it drop that she'd had three margaritas the first time she saw the sonofabitch, up in Brea. When they *communicated unspoken language* with their eyes."

Hess thought about it. "But the bus driver and Lee LaLonde all said the drawing was good. Kamala saw our man, the genuine article, in person. If we haven't shown her his picture yet, then we haven't shown her his picture yet. Maybe we don't have it. Maybe Dalton Page is wrong. Maybe he's

never even had a parking ticket."

Hess's phone rang. He put his finger up to hold Merci in place, then picked it up. Big Matt from Arnie's Outdoors said that the out-of-season purchase was his, he remembered it. It was raining hard that day, and business was slow. But he remembered the buyer because he was dressed up in a kind of gunslingers outfit—vest and long coat—with long blond hair and a mustache, not a typical Arnie's Outdoors customer at all. The buyer looked similar to the guy in the sketch that he was looking at.

"He asked me something odd," Matt said. "He asked me how the gambrel holds the ankles of the deer. I showed him how the hooks go through the ankle tendons. He said he didn't want his deer messed up. I said the gambrel made just a little hole in the ankles. So he asks me if we sell pads to keep that from happening. I said we didn't, nobody cared if the deer had little holes in its ankle because the feet get cut off and thrown away anyhow, You know, unless you're going to save a foot as a trophy or something. He was real certain about not damaging his deer though. So I showed him a cinch gambrel and he bought that."

Hess thought about his. "It's got loops for a cord instead of hooks? The cord cinches over the animals feet?"

"That's right."

He wasn't sure why, but his news didn't surprise him . Maybe something to do with his memories of how difficult a deer hunt could be. He and his father and uncle packing big bucks out of the deep country around Spirit lake. It was hard work. If you were hunting for something else – whatever it might be – you'd protect it as best you could. No holes in the body. It made sense. If the Purse Snatcher used some padding between the gambrel cinch and the flesh, there wouldn't be any bruising or abrasion, either. Especially if he worked fast.

"The Deer Sleigh'R is a carcass sled?"

"Yeah, it's got rope to secure the game on it, then you use the rope to pull it."

Hess tried to picture the Deer Sleigh'R in the back of the Purse Snatcher's silver panel van. "So, there's no wheels on it – it's stiff and flat?"

"It's flat, but it rolls up. That's one of the marketing things they're proud of. You can roll it up like a sleeping bag. Doesn't take up much room. And it's light, too, in case you're packing in."

"No skinning knives, cleaning tools?"

"Nothing like that. Just something to move a body and something to hang it with."

Hess thanked Matt and hung up. He looked at Merci. She was still hovering over his desk. He could see the malice bumping around behind her clear brown eyes.

" A clerk at Arnie's recognized the man in the sketch," he said. " He bought some hunting equipment out of season. February – nine days before Lael Jillson disappeared. Things you move bodies with. Hang them up with. Cash, of course."

The anger and the stubborn resolve were still on her face. "I should have had this picture out there sooner. I should have had this asshole two days ago, when Ronnie Stevens was still

drawing breath."

"You didn't kill Ronnie Stevens. Be kinder to yourself, Rayborn. You're stuck with you for about another fifty years."

A very young uniformed deputy worked his way through the pen toward them, a large cardboard box in his arms. The look on his face said he had interesting bad news.

The deputy nodded at Merci , the at Hess, setting the box down on Hess' desk. His mustache was mostly fuzz.

"Excuse me, sergeant Rayborn, but CalTrans found these on I-5 in Irvine about an hour and a half ago. CHP got the call. I just pulled over because I was driving by, wanted to see what was going on. When I saw these, I thought of you-know-what. They got handles pretty good by the road guys and the patrolmen. But who knows?"

Hess looked down into the box at the three purses.

"One of them must have broken open on the freeway," said the deputy. "The other two, they've got ID, credit cards, personal items. No CDLs. No cash."

Merci looked at the young man.

"Good work, Casik."

"Sergeant, I want to work with you in homicide someday. So I took the liberty of running the two names through our missing persons files. Both of them vanished without leaving any trace we could find. One had car problems on the 55, her car broke down and she apparently went for help. That was twenty-six months ago. The other was shopping at a mall her in Orange County, three months later. Riverside County Sheriffs found her car in Lake Matthews a week after she disappeared. I've got no idea where these purses have been since then, but I've got a hunch."

"I see you do."

"And also, the CalTrans guys shuffled through the purses a little, let some stuff fall out. The they just threw everything in this box. I couldn't help but notice the newspaper clipping you'll find near the top of the black one."

Hess watched Merci use her pen to lift the top of the stiff black purse and he saw folded newsprint. He lifted it out with a couple of paper clips, then set it on the desk and pried it open enough to see inside.

It was an article and photos from the Orange County *Journal*, six days ago, when Hess was brought back to help on the Purse Snatcher case. Mugs of Merci and Hess, standard issue from Press Information, and apparently in the *Journal* photo file. Hess hated it when they ran pictures of him.

In the shots, both his and Merci's eyes were burned out, the paper browned around the holes like a kid's pirate map.

TWENTY-THREE

Hess was still at his desk late that evening, on the phone with the head of the mortuary sciences department of a local college, fishing for something he couldn't articulate yet. Something to do with Deer Sleigh'R, formalin and missing women.

Brighton, who rarely came in on Sundays, appeared in the bullpen and

waved him over. Hess made the appointment with the mortuary sciences director, then hung up and followed Brighton down a short hallway to his office. Brighton waited for him, then shut the door.

"*Three* more?"

"Two look real likely. The third probable."

"He's been at this for two years?"

"Just over. The first went missing twenty-six months ago. Car trouble. The next was last seen, guess where – at all mall."

"Oh, good Christ. No break this morning? Nothing" he pointed to a chair in front of his desk.

"No." Hess sat.

"He's thorough and careful isn't he?"

"I think he's using chloroform to put them out. One of the CSIs recognized the smell from his vet. It makes sense. There's been some struggle in the cars. But not a huge amount. No blood."

"Can Gilliam verify the gas?"

"Not with the blood we've found. Chloroform metabolizes out real quick. But we think he's driving a silver panel van with a set of mismatched tires. It's the best thing we've got."

"Jesus, Tim. *Six.*"

Brighton sat back and crossed his arms. He was a big man with a rural face and a cool intelligence in his eyes. Hess had always liked the way Brighton made ambition for power look easy and natural. He shared the spoils. He wasn't the kind of man always looking around corners at you.

Then again, Hess had little idea what the sheriff did with his spare time, though he did know that like a lot of ranking law enforcement people in

Southern California, Brighton owned a house and property somewhere in Wyoming or Montana. Hess had rarely visited Brighton's home, never dined there or associated with the sheriff outside of department functions, never learned the names of his children. Those intimacies had been shared over decades with more family-orientated men and women on the force – the ones who, like Brighton, had kids to raise. Children and the raising of them seemed to adhere the parents to each other in ways that didn't stick to Hess and his childless marriages, ugly divorces and the long stretches of aloneness that separated them.

Hess was drawn to people more like himself: on the make for something they might understand but often didn't, either recovering from or searching out the next romantic disaster. It always seemed to work out that way, but it was never how he planned it. He saw that you needed to put aside that selfishness if you wanted to fit in with the department pack, otherwise you were perceived as a danger at some point. A family made you understandable, declared your values and your willingness to sacrifice.

Hess hadn't wanted children with Barbara – who was willing – because he was young and hogging his liberties. The world seemed huge then, though his place in it with Barbara – who was insecure and jealous as time went on – seemed constricted. He was stupid to leave her but only realized it later. His guilty conscience had left everything of value to her and to this day he was thankful for that.

He was willing and interested with Lottie when he was in his thirties, but she was young and enjoying her liberties. They drifted away from each other in the classic fashion and parted with minimum drama and no rancor. What amazed Hess more than the divorce was the way a decade could come and go so quickly.

Children hardly seemed to matter until he was halfway through his forties and married to Joanna. Hi parental instincts crept up on him like a big cat: a old but calm desire to guide his blood into the world, to give life, he actually began looking at other people's babies, thinking of names he liked, picturing himself with an infant in his arms. Doted on his nephews and nieces. Thought a lot about his father. And his mother. Something inside him was changing for the good.

Joanna was younger than him by fifteen years, quite beautiful and willing to have a family. These were three of the reasons he married her. Hess suspected a child would help keep them together because they actually shared little in common outside the bed. After five years of trying and failing to conceive, countless consultations and tests, then three increasingly heartbreaking miscarriages, Joanna gave up on doctors, children and Hess. On the dismal March night of his fifty-first birthday, both of them drinking at high velocity, Joanna surprised him with a tearful confession that she was in love with another man. With one of the doctor's who had failed to help her, in fact. It was with extreme and surprising anger that Hess imagined this man with Joanna on his examination table. She said he had his own children and with him she felt less like a failed breeder and more like a successful woman. She took half of everything and dropped all contact with Hess. He rented the room to a young deputy so he could keep the house.

By the time he realized he had pretty much missed his chance to be a father Hess was three times divorced and pushing fifty-three years old. Did everyone know he was a fuck-up? He felt like an ostrich with nowhere to hide his head.

Now, sitting in Chuck Brighton's office, Hess considered all of this to be nothing more than the ancient history of an everyday life. His. And this is where it had led him—semi-retired and sixty-seven years of age, alone again, afflicted by cancer and by treatments for cancer, shadowing a murdering phantom through what could have been one of Hess's golden years. So you don't always get what you want. But grace grows in the cracks sometimes.

You have work to do.

"That must have been bad this morning."

"I've never seen anything quite like it, Bright. I mean, it was so…deliberate. Deliberate an disgusting and just really mean/ All at the same time. This guy's got some snakes in his head."

"He'll make a big mistake. You know that."

"When, is what bothers me."

"Tell me about Rayborn, Tim."

"There's not much to tell. I think she's doing well."

"Good, good. Do you get along with her?"

"She's honest and to the point."

"Like You."

Brighton could be obtuse and Hess figured it was his right.

"What about that sketch of hers?"

Hess shrugged. "The witness needed to be hypnotized. Merci got good results."

Brighton nodded. Old news.

"It was her call, bright. That sketch is getting hits."

"What, the bus driver, that car thief out in Elsinore?"

"And a sporting goods store clerk said it looked like a guy who bought some hunting supplies out of season."

"The question is, why'd she wait so long to get it done – hypnosis or not?"

"Some time to consult with the DA. A day to do the hypnosis and the sketch. She thought it over, wanted to make the right move. More time to get copies, get them out to Press Information."

Hess understood that what kept Merci from acting quickly on the sketch was her doubt about Kamala Petersen's reliability. She'd hesitated on instinct. The margaritas seemed to have justified that doubt, but Hess said nothing. The booze was going to make Merci look bad.

"And Merci paid out of her own pocket for that psychiatrist to hypnotize her didn't she?"

"I really don't know. But she told me she bought some Point Blank body armor with her own money."

"What's wrong with our PACAs? They're rated to threat-level Two-A."

"I guess she thinks they could get her killed."

Brighton raise his eyebrows. "She

lost a potential witness."

"Yeah , she knows that. She knows it was a gamble."

Hess suddenly felt his tiredness slap up against him. It was like a big wave of cold water that sucked the warmth right out of you. It usually happened when he was sitting down. Like Friday, when Merci had to help him out of the chair. Maybe the secret of life was to keep moving. Hop 'til you drop.

"How did she miss those Jim marks on the car windows?"

"Well, they were below the doorframe."

"That's absolutely not what I was asking."

"In that case it was Kemp who missed them."

"I'd taken Kemp off the case by then, Tim. You were on it."

"The damage was done. She couldn't redo every bit of his work. Ike would have found them sooner or later. Or she'd have thought it through and had a look for herself. Really, Bright, that wasn't the kind of thing you'd think of unless you'd run across it before."

Brighton nodded, unconvinced. "It's basic car theft, is what it is."

"Well, she's homicide."

"Maybe that's what worries me. Besides it took you about thirty seconds."

"I'm old."

"Tim , I'd like you to document what you think of her performance on this case so far, just something brief, in writing."

"What about it?"

"How she's handled it – the privately funded hypnosis, not taking the DAs advice about the legal fall out. The car

windows – whose decision it was to remove the glass and have a real thorough, old-fashioned look at it. Just a note for my files, nothing elaborate. A quick and dirty."

Interesting use of words, thought Hess. "I'm sure she'll put all that in her report," he said.

"Her reports are always evasive, partial and uninformative."

"The kind I always wrote."

"Those were different days, Tim. We were small and tight and we hung together. Anyway, I want your angle on it."

"That wasn't exactly in my job description, Bright."

"It is now"

Hess said nothing.

"Is this LaLonde creep a suspect or not?"

"Riverside is watching him for us. So far, nothing unusual. My guts tell me no."

"How did Merci handle him?"

"Well. He built this override device for our man. It works on most car alarms, or so LaLonde says. He can ID our guy if we can deliver him."

"Nice work."

"Rayborn called the shots. I just held up a wall."

"She really carry a switchblade in her purse?"

Hess looked at the sheriff, then slowly shook his head. "I don't know," he said quietly.

"I'd be curious. Look, Tim, I've got some problems here. = Merci's lawsuit accuses Phil of potty-mouth and garb-ass, but it accuses me – between the lines – of looking the other way. In fact, if she wants some kind of monetary damages, she'll eventually have to name the department, and probably me."

"Then she must not want money, Chuck."

"You know me, Tim. I don't look the other way. I've worked hard to make this a good place for men, women, the best sheriff department in the state. Now Merci files this suit out of the blue and three more women have come forward, talking to the press, getting their own suits ready, I assume. One says Kemp raped her. Merci opened the floodgates."

"Damn it, Bright. Maybe you should be glad if she spoke up. If you've got a house to clean, you've got a house to clean."

"And I'll clean it. But I feel like I got a gun to my head. And she never once came to me about any of this."

A long silence then.

"What does she want?" Brighton finally asked.

"How would I know? She hasn't said one word about Phil Kemp to me."

"Find Out."

"That's in my job description now, too?"

"Absolutely. Find out what she wants, Tim. I'll accommodate her if I can get this snowball stopped."

Hess nodded. He felt exhausted.

"Ever heard of a friend of hers named Francisco?"

"She mentioned him."

A long pause then, during which Hess deduced he was supposed to make something of this friend. He sensed the amount of brain power necessary for such a formulation would be a lot more than he wanted to spend.

"McNally told me she'd mentioned a guy, is all. Never introduced them., I'm curious if she might be sleeping with this man."

"I'm not."

"Find out about it and let me know. You can add that and the switchblade to your job description too, if you want to. Help me, Tim. I'm helping you."

Hess looked at him.

Brighton sat back. Hess felt the resentment stirring inside – resentment that his own stupid cigarette addictions had led him to this position, and resentment that Chuck Brighton had allowed peevishness to bloom in his old age. I got cancer and Brighton got petty.

"How are you feeling, Tim?"

"Strong as an ox. A little tired now and then."

"I admire you."

"Thanks."

"And that has nothing to do with feeling sorry for you."

"I hope not", said Hess, but in fact he knew it did, and it broke his heart in a minor way to hear it from an old friend who was ordering him to piss on a fellow deputy half his age.

Hess stood and shook Brighton's hand.

TWENTY FOUR

Merci studied the two missing persons files that Casik has bird-dogged for her, then hovered around the unbelievably slow clerk who processed the purses into evidence. She estimated the guy had an IQ of about 50.

Six, she thought. Six. The idea made

her furious.

By the time she got to the gym she was even more furious. And livid at Kamala for drinking the night in question – then not admitting it until later.

But Merci knew she was primarily angry at herself for nit hurrying up the hypnosis and the release of the sketch. If it had been all over the newspapers and TV two days ago like it should have been, Ronnie Stevens might be working at Goldsmith's today. It was a grinding guilt she felt, tangible, right there in the throat. And now, by the looks of it, three more women had been taken by the Purse Snatcher. *Six.* Time to work off the rage.

The weight room was empty on Sunday. She looked at herself in the mirror when she walked in – face in a scowl, sweats disheveled, arms up, big hands twisting her hair into a wad and applying an elastic band and thought: *Loser. You are a large dark-haired loser who belongs in Traffic.*

She humped the stationary cycle for thirty minutes with the resistance up almost all the way. She was dripping sweat and standing on the pedals to make them move after eight minutes and the final twenty-two were actual torture. Blister time. *Good,* she thought. Let the pain bring the gain. She got off the bike and wobbled to the ab cruncher on legs that felt like petrified wood. Good again: hurt to learn, learn to hurt.

She ran the Nautilus circuit once light and once heavy, resting five seconds between each of the three sets and thirty seconds between each station. Her heart was beating fast and

light as a bird's, fast as that wren's that was blown from its nest in a Santa Ana wind one year. She'd found it in the grass and cradled it home in her hands while its heart beat like some overcharged machine against the inside of her middle finger. The bird had died overnight and Merci prepared a tissue box to bury it, but her mother had flushed it down the toilet. She'd never had luck with animals; her dog had chewed the hair off its own body, her cats ran away, her parakeets died quick; her hamster bit her. Merci catalogued these failures as she struggled on the chin-up bar – twelve more than she could do so she set her sights on fourteen and slid to a gasping heap on the ground after thirteen.

Up, loser. You have work to do.

Time for the free weights. She had just settled under the bench press bare when she heard some commotion near the door. She turned her head to the mirrored wall and watched in the distorting glass as Mike McNally and three of his deputy friends swaggered in, all muscles and mustaches over their necks, smiles merry to the point of insanity. The atmosphere of the room changed instantly. Suddenly she was aware of herself, her body, her clothes, her sweat, what she might look like, what they might do. It was like having 30 percent of your energy sucked down some useless hole. Fucking great.

She did her best to will them out of her universe, turning to look up at the rusted bar above her nose, spreading her hands wide for a pec burn on her beginning weight of eighty pounds, digging the leather palms of her gloves against the worn checkering of the grip.

"Hi, Merci!"

"Hi, guys!"

"Need a spot?"

"Sure don't!"

Then up with it. Ignore them. She liked the feel of the weights balancing above her. She moved her left hand over just a hair to get it right. Then the slow, deliberate motion – all the way down to her chest, then all the way back up again – ten times in all, not super heavy, really, but you could feel eighty pounds when your body weight was one forty. Three sets. Every rep was hotter and slower. Grow to burn, burn to grow.

At one hundred pounds she had to go a bit slower, but she got the ten. She heard the sweat tap-tapping to the plastic bench as she sat there breathing hard and deciding whether to max at one thirty-five or one forty.

She picked the lighter weight to look stronger in front of the men, a decision that angered her. She was saw they were ignoring her but aware of her, too. They laughed suddenly then and two of them glanced over at her. Merci wished she lived on a different planet. She thought again of Phil Kemp's ugly words and his touches and felt like all her strength was about to rush away.

Stay focused. Will away these things.

She heaved up on the bar and ground out five reps before she realized that she wouldn't make ten. Six was a labor. Seven wasn't even up yet when she knew she'd had enough. The sweat popped off her lips as she exhaled. Kind of stuck, actually, not enough gumption to get it back up to safety on the stand, too much pride to set it down on her heaving chest and rest. Mike McNally now appeared in the north quadrant of her defocusing vision, looking down at her, a blond-haired Vikingesque once-upon-a-time boyfriend gritting "One more…one more…one more, Merci" at her until she felt the bare rise magically with his help. Her breathing was fast and short. She felt lungshot. Then she felt the way to her sternum, pause, then halfway up, then a little more than halfway, arms and bar wobbling like crazy now and Mike's lift helping her get it up then suddenly one side shot down and the other shot up and iron crashed with a clang and the bar smacked into her rib cage as the weights slid off and chimes to the floor beneath her head.

She was aware of the three more bodies around her, aware of Mike's cursing them away, telling them she was fine, aware of gripping his hand with hers and rising to a sitting position in the bench. Little lights circled her vision like the starts around a cartoon character hit with a hammer.

"You know the circuits court's going to hear the scent-box case," he was saying.

"That's great, Mike." Merci wasn't positive what century she was in.

" I know its going to be accepted. I know that a hundred years before now they'll be using those boxes in court all the time. A good scent box and a good dog. That's my answer to high-tech crime solving. Plus we're going to patent the thing and make a million. I don't know what I'll name it. Mike's Truth Box or something."

"Hope you're right. Wow."

"Light in the head?"

"Um-hm."

"Lay back."

"No way."

"Well, pass out them."

"I'll lay back."

"Better?"

"Um."

She lay back down on the bench and felt her chest rising fast, her back pressing into the pads, the air rushing in and out. Mike was gone. Just her and the white ceiling and the mirrors in the periphery of her vision and the ringing in her ears. Lots of red.

When her heart rate settled Merci dozed a few minutes. She awoke to the sounds of weights, male voices, the harsh light of the gym in her eyes. She sat up, looked around and yawned. Her muscles felt enlarged and stupid. The pile of spilled weights was still next to her bench.

She worked herself up and collected the weights, walking them one at a time back to the rack and sliding them onto the pegs. Then she lumbered on heavy legs over to the stationary bike and climbed on, setting the resistance lower than the first time, but still pretty darned high.

For just a moment she thought about who she was, and about how strong she was. She remembered the most important thing she had learned in her life thus far: you are powerful and you can make things bend to your will *as long as you try hard enough.*

Your will is the power to move the world.

So she set the resistance even higher than the first time. Effort was how things got moved. Effort was pain. Pain was strength.

She looked at herself in the mirror as she stood on the pedals to get them going. Pale as a sidewalk, she thought, and about as good-looking.

Merci thought of Hess to steady herself—how he might do this, his economy and focus. She liked the way he didn't waste anything. She couldn't forget the look on his face that morning when he'd seen the hood of Ronnie Steven's car. It was the saddest, wisest face she had ever seen. He looked like Lincoln. But he had been diminished by what he had seen. The Purse Snatcher had taken something from him, she thought, and that made her feel angry on Hess's behalf. *For him.* For someone not herself. It was nice to admire someone you didn't want to be.

Thirty minutes on this bike should do it, she thought: burn the foolishness out of my brain and burn the strength into my muscles.

'JEFFERSON PARKER IS
A POWERHOUSE WRITER'
New York Times Book Review

The Blue Hour
JEFFERSON PARKER

www.fireandwater.com
Visit the book lover's website

fiction

stitch

john b spencer

Extract from Stitch *by John B Spencer, Published as a paperback original by The Do-Not Press.*

'YOU THINK, because I have tattoos, wear body jewellery, I should live in a tip?'

'That isn't what I said.'

'It's what you implied.'

Winston's ground floor flat, Carrington Road, North Sheen, fives minutes from the Gloucester House Gate to Richmond Park, Winston jogging five miles most mornings, learnt to hate dogs, some dog walker, distant voice calling to her animal, just before Fido arrived intent on ripping through flesh and bone every fucking time. The flat bought with money his Aunt Anastasia left him a combined living room and bedroom, futon rolled up against one wall, kitchenette beyond a pine shelved divider, extractor above the gas cooker. The walls all painted white with pale grey wood trim and door, light fixtures chrome silver, rush mat flooring, no television, no books, newspapers, magazines no mess.

Aluminium framed album cover on the wall.

Never Mind the Bollocks.

Nothing else.

Winston saying, 'You learn to live without it.'

Sophie saying, 'Without what?'

'The bollocks.'

Wondering if he should tell Sophie about the dog this morning would she scold him like an angry mother? brown cocker spaniel, Winston scooping up the dog without breaking stride, closing its jaws with one hand, the other gripping its ruff, swinging the dog on its own weight, the way you would a chicken, breaking its neck.

Tossing the dead animal into the undergrowth.

Hearing the owner calling, 'Caliban!'

Saying, now, to Sophie, 'Would you call a dog Caliban?'

Sophie saying, 'Caliban was a Shakespearian villain The Tempest. I suppose it would depend on the nature of the dog.'

Winston saying, 'Aren't all dogs the same?'

Then: 'A fucking nuisance?'

Sophie saying, then, about the flat, 'It's so spartan without clutter. The room of an aesthete.'

'Aesthete?'

'Someone who appreciates simplicity like a monk.'

Winston saying, 'Are you always this patronising?'

'I didn't mean'

'You mean ascetic.'

'Oh do I?'

Sophie wearing a navy brushed jersey blouse, the blouse hanging loose over dark chinos, charcoal Mary Jane's with wedge heels. Going for the sophisticated older woman look

The actress, Francesca Annis.

Attractive, but not necessarily available.

Who did she think she was kidding?

Winston reaching forward.

One hand undoing the smoked pearl buttons of her blouse, starting from the bottom. Sophie saying, 'What are you doing?'

Winston saying, 'Take it off.'

Exposing the grey lace bra.

Winston saying, 'And that.'

'I'm self-conscious.'

'You're beautiful.'

Winston dropping to his knees.

Pulling down the chinos.

The matching grey lace panties.

*

Bobby-Boy reversing out of the parking slot, back of Charlie Paul's block, Addison Gardens, right hand pouring blood despite he had one of Charlie's T-shirts wrapped around it, thinking, One of Charlie's T-shirts? Recipe for gangrene, or what? Worried about getting blood all over the interior, not looking where he was going, too pissed off to concentrate on his driving, backing smack! into the milk float. Bobby-Boy thinking, Milk float, for fuck's sake? How many milk floats are there left in London, and I have to back into one of them?

Saying to the milkman, mid-forties, picture of health, sleeves rolled up tight around his biceps macho man, didn't feel the cold: 'Fuck did you come from?'

Checking out the damage.

Saying, 'This, I do not believe.'

Rear off-side wing caved in, indicator and rear light gone, Bobby-Boy looking at a new panel and spray job, could see the mechanic, now, sharp intake of breath, knowing shake of the head, saying, 'It will cost.'

The milkman, all the time in the world, checking the float, the rear platform where the milk crates were stacked, the angular metal corner responsible for the grief to Bobby-Boy's motor, Bobby Boy saying, 'The most exciting thing happened to you all year, right?'

The milkman saying, 'You want to get that looked at.'

Bobby Boy's hand dripping blood on to the pavement.

Then: 'I'll need your particulars.'

Bobby-Boy saying, 'The fuck for? Show me one fucking scratch.'

The milkman saying, 'Nasty knock could be all kinds of problems surface later.'

Then: 'Where there's personal injury involved, the police have to be informed.'

Bobby Boy thinking, All I fucking need.

Not bothering to explain.

Handing the milkman two twenties.

Saying, 'Go away.'

Fifteen minutes earlier, on Charlie Paul's front balcony, Charlie standing in the door in vest and underpants, Bobby-Boy still hungover, each Marlboro Light tasting worse than the one before, thinking, Fuck knows how many nights in a row Charlie had slept in those underpants, didn't bear contemplating, palming Charlie hard

on the shoulder.

Then again.

And again.

Each shove harder than the last.

Saying, 'Fuck you think you're playing at, Charlie?'

Then: 'I ought to bust your fucking face!'

Charlie saying, 'I don't need this, Bobby-Boy.'

Bobby-Boy saying, 'You think I'm fucking blind?'

Then: 'You think I don't know you've been trying to get into Toyah's knickers for fucking years?'

Then: 'Jesus fucking shit!'

Shoving Charlie again.

Charlie saying, 'She called me what was I supposed to do? Tell her to fuck off?'

To the left of the front door, four panelled window with frosted glass, toilet off the front hall. When he was a kid, Bobby-Boy used to stand on the balcony wall in these flats, blow raspberries down the overflow pipe, the noise reverberating in the toilet cistern, scare the shit out of whoever was sitting in there

Bobby-Boy saying, 'Why me, God? What the fuck have I done to deserve this?'

Then: 'Fucking bollocks!'

Punching his fist through the bottom right hand frosted glass panel.

Saying, 'Oh, shit!'

Charlie, looking at Bobby-Boy's hand, blood everywhere, glass shards poking out of the flesh, saying, 'That looks nasty I better run you up the hospital.'

Bobby-Boy saying, 'Go fuck yourself.'

The milkman, now, not taking the two twenties.

Saying, 'Cuts no ice with me, you waving money around.'

Bobby-Boy saying, 'Then, you can go fuck yourself, too.'

The milkman needing to think about that.

Saying, 'Too?'

John B Spencer was born in west London, where he still lives with his wife Lou, and the youngest of their three sons. He is a respected musician, record producer and songwriter and has released a number of CDs.

Published in September 1999, *Stitch* is an atmospheric and gritty tale of lowlifes and those whose lives they touch. It is Spencer's seventh novel and the third in the acclaimed 'London' trilogy, following *Perhaps She'll Die* and *Tooth & Nail*. All are available as paperback originals from The Do-Not Press, as is *Quake City*, a Charley Case adventure set in the Los Angeles of the near-future.

PRAISE FOR JOHN B SPENCER'S 'LONDON' CRIME NOVELS:

'Yet another demonstration that our British crime writers can hold their own with the best of their American counterparts snappy dialogue the pace of a rabbit at a rave. Recommended.'

—*Time Out*

'Spencer updates the noir tradition threats of action that smoulder until you're ready to scream.'

— *Kirkus Reviews*

'Spencer's previous novels have been compared to Elmore Leonard but Spencer has a distinctive voice of his own. The dialogue crackles with electricity and the characters have an energy that leaps off the page. Go out and buy it!'

—*Shots*

oh no, not my baby
russell james

Extract from Oh No, Not My Baby *by Russell James, Published as a paperback original by The Do-Not Press.*

OH NO, NOT MY BABY
(OH NO, NOT MY SWEET BABY)

WHEN ZANE REPLIED, Shiel was peeling potatoes. Zane said, 'I know. You think, I'm a decent guy. I don't want to kill innocent people. It isn't right. You don't feel good about it. You think, Every man's death diminishes me. No man is an island. Don't you?'

Shiel said, 'These are awful potatoes.'

Zane said, 'I can read you like a book.'

Shiel dunked his knife in the water.

Zane said, 'You're having second thoughts. People have to die, Shiel, to make them see the point. Otherwise we're just another lost voice in the wilderness. A dozen lives maybe, to save millions.'

Shiel frowned. 'Half these potatoes are black to the core and the others are pitted with deep eyes. How come they're so different?'

'Different types.'

'They're just rotten potatoes.'

'From different places. Potatoes nowadays come from all over the world. Jersey last week, Egypt this and next week, who knows? It's no surprise they are different.'

'I remember when potatoes were just potatoes.'

*

He had been waiting half an hour. In the car parked outside the yard, Nick blew on his hands. It wasn't really cold but after half an hour in the dark a chill had set in, a cool damp breeze moving across from the Severn estuary. His fingertips were balls of ice. To warm his hands he slid them beneath his thighs. His cheeks were shadows, like craters on the moon. Nick could look haunted at the best of times, and this was by no means the best of times.

Though approaching midnight the plant was still working. From ground floor windows, lights shone across the yard through wraiths of steam. The high wire netting fence made it look like a prison and from what Babette had said, the level of security on the front gate was prison tight. But she was inside. Through the quiet evening air Nick heard humming, occasional clanks, and once or twice the machinery groaned like a truck with a rickety gear. Escape pipes on the wall gave out jets of steam. Ten minutes earlier he had heard a muffled hooter, and two women had come from a side door and stood in the dark to smoke their cigarettes. They wore white overalls and tied-on hats. After they had finished and

gone back, the yard was empty again. Nick wondered whether they had found time to grab a mug of coffee or milky tea before the hooter ended their short break. It sounded a grim way to earn a living.

The humming stopped.

From where he sat in the car it left a silence like dead of night. He could make out fainter sounds now: the squeak and rattle of a metal trolley on a concrete floor; some tinny music, even voices from inside. Somebody shouted something. Someone else called back. The tinny music would be a radio. He heard another shout. Then a bleeper started not loud, but irritating the kind of noise that pricks at your ear and makes you narrow your tired eyes.

Nick exhaled, casting a slight film of mist across the windscreen.

The bleeper changed pitch to become an oscillating howl. He saw someone run out of one side door into another. Two men trotted across the gloomy compound like hospital doctors in trailing white coats. Everyone had to wear overalls. Even Babette had worn one over her red blouson and matching jeans. Another door opened, and a dozen people emerged and stood milling about the yard as if on fire practice. If fire wardens were now going to check everyone off, Babette would be in trouble she wasn't supposed to be there. Perhaps she could hide inside and not come out. It might even help: with everyone out in the yard she could roam around taking photographs. Maybe she had set off the alarm a neat trick.

But they didn't seem to be on fire practice. The staff had drifted out and were now milling around, unsure what to do, while a couple of supervisory types buzzed about as if they had some idea. Nick wiped the side window and squinted through. Though the yard was poorly lit and the small shifting crowd was anonymous he couldn't see Babette among them. She wouldn't be.

He began chewing at his lip. She hadn't explained what she meant to do inside, though how much was there to say? She had the camera, and it wouldn't be hard to find where the carcasses waited to be processed. Starkly lit, no doubt, bodies sprawled across the floor they'd make good photographs.

Babette hadn't worried about the risk. The worst that could happen was she'd be evicted from the premises. The company would not make a song and dance or complain to the police. They'd want the whole affair kept quiet. Their need for privacy would help Babette if she got caught which she wouldn't, she'd assured him. She'd been in there before.

But it was worrying.

The people in the yard seemed uncertain what to do and although sitting in the car left him helpless, he could do nothing else. Babette had told him to come back at half past eleven and wait inside the car ready, if necessary, for a quick getaway.

The bleeper stopped.

It left a slight ringing in his ears, and this time he could hear the voices from the yard. He wound the window down.

It was like a radio in another room. The rolling Bristol accents carried in the night air, but though he could make out some words he couldn't get the full gist of what they said. He'd have to get out. He could stroll across to the wire netting fence but if they saw him outside the fence, nearly twelve o'clock at night, they'd be bound to ask why he was there. Perhaps he could pretend he lived in one of the nearby houses. No. He mustn't draw attention to himself or Babette's car.

He watched the people in the yard. Had something happened in the factory? Was Babette safe?

*

It was when the police arrived he began to worry. First the sickening heave of a distant siren which he tried to tell himself was going somewhere else then the noise grew louder, lights flashed, and a white panda car arrived. As it approached the gate the barrier rose, and the car glided through. Straight to the main door. Straight inside.

It looked bad. If Babette had been caught, there was nothing he could do. He could only stay in the car in case she needed him. He began to wonder if he should back further away. No, the police might be looking around for her confederates, and if they saw his car her car starting up

Please don't let it be Babette. Let it be some kind of fire practice. In that case maybe the police would have to come, as if for a real emergency. But wouldn't there be a fire engine too? He looked at the workers. It wasn't a fire practice.

Another siren. Faster, more urgent. Coming closer.

An ambulance.

Again, the barrier was lifted to let the vehicle speed through. Two men jumped out and rushed inside the building. What had happened? Had Babette been caught? Had she been hurt? Nick knew that whatever was going on had to involve Babette. It was too much of a coincidence that on the very night she slipped inside, another drama made them call the police. And an ambulance.

Another siren now.

People were appearing in the street, drawn from their houses by the sirens and flashing lights. Nothing like an accident on your doorstep to pep up the night. It had to be an accident, didn't it, if there was an ambulance?

Another police car arrived, and went straight in. Nick wondered what would happen if he drove across in Babette's car would they let him through as slickly as they had the others? Don't even think about it.

Yet another police car. Three? This was serious. Nick got out of the car to join the onlookers from surrounding houses. Silence returned. Comparative silence. People chattered in the darkness as if at a theatre before lights dimmed. Inside the compound, small groups of white-coated staff drifted aimlessly low-grade factory staff. Because of their work, he looked for blood stains on their coats, but he couldn't see any.

Beside the fence a woman called to those inside: 'What's happened, darlings? Been an accident?'

No one answered.

'Elsie!' the woman called. 'Someone been hurt?'

From the far side of the compound a thin sliver of a woman wandered over. Her voice was deep a croaky West Country burr. 'Nothing to worry about, no. Well, I'm all right, anyway.'

'Oh, that's all right then,' the woman laughed. 'We can all go back to bed!'

Elsie shrugged. 'Just a practice, I expect.'

'With three police cars?'

Nick had joined them at the fence. He had the kind of face made older women want to mother him, but in the darkness they hardly noticed he was there. Some wore overcoats over pajamas. Elsie's friend outside the wire was fully clothed but slippered. She said, 'Better than working. We can have a fag.'

'Left mine inside, haven't I?'

'Just like you.'

The woman took out a packet and passed a cigarette to Elsie. They both lit up. The night air began to flicker with tiny flares. Other workers came to the fence. No one knew why they had been sent outside.

'Some kind of emergency,' Elsie suggested.

'Someone ate one of your old pies.'

'Not one of us!'

People laughed. Nick glanced back along the front fence to Babette's car, but there was no sign of her. She must be inside.

A factory door opened and the two ambulance men appeared. One was carrying an empty stretcher. As he slid it into the back of the ambulance some of the women in the yard approached to ask a question. Whatever he told them caused a stir. One of the women broke away and scuttled to a colleague to spread the news. No one approached the fence. Nick said, 'Someone's heard something.'

'Can't be much,' a woman said. 'The ambulance is going home.'

The driver had shut the rear door but instead of getting in the cab he and his partner went back towards the factory. Someone called: 'Who was it then anyone we know?'

If the driver replied, Nick didn't hear it. The men disappeared again indoors. Elsie called: 'What's up a false alarm?'

'Bit more than that,' someone called back.

'Oo!' cried Elsie. 'I think I'll stay and finish me fag.'

No one at the fence seemed in a hurry to move away. As they stood chatting, Nick wondered if he looked as conspicuous as he felt. All the others lived in nearby houses. He'd be the only stranger.

The door opened again and a man in a crumpled suit came out with a policewoman. One of the workers groaned. 'Tea break's over.'

The manager ignored the watchers outside the fence. He said, 'Right, everybody, if you'd all come back inside. Please?'

Nick wondered if the manager always looked this grim. The policewoman addressed those outside the fence: 'There's nothing to see, so you might as well go back to bed.'

'I wasn't in bed, darling, I was watching a video,' said Elsie's friend.

'I'm sure that's a lot more interesting than what's happening here.'

'What's is happening?'

'Nothing. You've all got homes to go to.'

She might as well have spoken to the fence.

Inside the compound, the staff wandered back indoors. The policewoman gave a last 'Don't hang around all night,' and turned away.

Someone called, 'Why not? We live here, don't we? We do as we please.'

But the policewoman didn't turn round. As she paced across the compound, she passed Elsie running back to the fence. 'Here,' called Elsie. 'You'll never guess.'

'What?'

Elsie had reached the wire. 'Someone's only fallen in the pulveriser.'

'No!'

Everyone crowded in to her. Everyone except Nick. He stood stock still.

It was several seconds before he made sense of their gabbling voices.

'They think it was an accident.'

'Of course.'

'You'd have to be bloody stupid to fall in that.'

Nick couldn't trust himself to speak. Elsie rushed back across the compound. As she reached the door the ambulance men came out, talking with the policewoman. Nick stared at them, as if by staring hard enough he might hear their words. He felt like a robot whose rusty mechanism had seized up.

*

Slowly, the small crowd began to drift away. The ambulance left, then one of the squad cars, leaving the compound empty of people. The factory doors were closed.

Nick returned to the car and sat inside. There was no reason why the accident should have been to Babette. There was no confirmation that an accident had happened at all. The ambulance had gone and the factory stood locked behind its fence and closed front door. He saw another car arrive, to be let straight through. Management, presumably. Two police cars were still on site, so it didn't seem likely nothing had happened. Perhaps Babette had been caught. Perhaps she had escaped. No: whatever had happened, Nick knew it had to involve Babette. He tried to forget Elsie's words. They were too terrible to contemplate. Babette could have been caught by Security she could have struggled and been hurt She could not have died as Elsie said.

Nick got out of the car. Although he had only been in it ten minutes the night air seemed colder now and damper. No one else was in the street. He walked beside the fence to the security hut at the gate.

'Excuse me for bothering you, but I wondered if there was any news about what happened.'

'What would that be, sir?'

'You know, the accident.'

'Accident?'

'When someone was hurt.'

'Don't know anything about that, sir.'

Nick glanced across the half-lit compound to the unrevealing building. 'I don't want to be a nuisance but I live here. We heard about what happened and if someone's hurt, it could be someone we know.'

'The ambulance has gone now, sir.'

'Look, I'm worried.'

'And why would that be, sir?'

Nick sighed and walked away.

*

It was when the staff were sent home that he knew it was bad. He had been sitting in the cold car for twenty minutes, playing the radio low, when suddenly the factory doors opened and people flowed out across the yard. They no longer wore their white coats. They were dressed for home.

As he ran back to the gate he was joined by people from the houses. When the factory workers came out the gate, Nick feared they might stay shtoom, but they didn't: they talked among themselves and to those waiting. What had happened was too out of the ordinary to be contained. They talked so freely that Nick wondered if they had been briefed on which story to release outside, but he told himself not to be paranoid.

Someone said it was not a member of staff. Someone else said they couldn't be sure. Either way, the factory was shutting down for the night.

'God knows about our wages.'

One of the women shouted back to the man in the security hut: 'I suppose you'll be staying all night?'

'Yeah, but if you don't want to go home I can make room for you in here. I've got it nice and warm.'

'I bet you have.'

They laughed. Nick wanted to hit them. But he asked, 'Is it true did someone really fall into the pulveriser?'

'Seems like it,'someone replied.

'And she's dead? I mean, it was a woman who fell in, wasn't it?'

'Whoever it was, they're going to be dead.'

An older woman added, 'It wasn't staff, don't worry. We're all accounted for.'

The other sniffed. 'Perhaps a tramp, keeping warm.'

'How's a tramp going to get in here?'

The woman nodded at the security man. 'He wouldn't notice anything in trousers. Thinks he's guarding a beach hut, him.'

He leant out of his window: 'You've got a surprise night off your old man still thinks you're working.'

One of the women laughed. 'He'll get a surprise when I turn up.'

'You don't know what you'll find,' another added.

'When the cat's away '

The security guard said, 'If you're looking for a tom cat' .

The woman reached up and prodded him. 'I'd make Kit-e-Kat out of you!'

The others laughed. Nick stood among them as if invisible. Every word was like a whiplash. He saw the policewoman coming across the yard and he tried to read her face.

She said, 'Hurry along now, please. Time we all went home.'

'What happened, Miss?'

Everyone was interested.

She said, 'There's been an accident.'

'We know that, dear. But is someone dead?'

'We're looking into it.'

'Well, either they are dead or they ain't, darling. It can't take much looking into.'

The policewoman paused. 'There does appear to have been a fatality.'

'It wasn't one of us, dear, was it? I mean, we're all right.'

'At this stage we can't say.'

'We're not bloody stupid. We wouldn't go up on that gantry.'

'Not when the machine's working,' another agreed.

One of the women asked, 'Have they got the body out?'

The policewoman shrugged.

The woman said, 'It wouldn't be easy. I mean, if it had slipped right down inside '

'Ugh!' exclaimed a younger woman, laughing nervously.

'Because all the bone and meat is crunched up together. That's the point.'

'Oh, don't,'said someone.

Nick put a hand against the wall. 'Someone fell into the meat pulveriser and '

'Seems that way.'

He shook his head. 'With all the meat?'

'Not just meat, love, is it? It's where they tip the carcasses in.'

He slumped against the wall.

The policewoman asked, 'Do you know someone in there perhaps someone who went inside?'

He opened his mouth but couldn't say a word.

'You don't work here, do you, sir?'

He was feeling faint.

'He don't work here,' someone answered. 'He don't live round here neither, do you, son?'

A large woman asked, 'D'you know something about it, then?'

Nick raised a hand as if to fend off blows. 'No I'm just I'm just passing by.'

The policewoman came closer. 'Could you tell me, sir, what you are doing here?'

'I was just '

He stopped.

'Passing by at this time of night?'

He had to have a drink. Water. He needed water.

'What's your name, sir?'

'I've got to go. It doesn't matter.'

'I think it does, sir. What's your name?'

The group of women was drawing tighter now, and the policewoman was waiting. He said, 'Chance.'

'Chance of what?'

'Mr Chance.'

'Mr?'

'Nick, then. Nick Chance.'

'I see. Do you have some identity?'

'What Why should I produce identity?'

'Do you have identity, Mr ?'

'Chance. No.'

'What's your address?'

'Brendon Road. 30, Brendon Road.'

She was writing it down. 'And where is that exactly in Bristol?'

'Clifton.'

'Then you're some way from home, sir, aren't you?'

He no longer knew what he was

saying. 'No, it's only three or four miles away. I don't know. I mean, have you found a body in there?'

'Whose body might that be, sir?'

'I don't know. But have you got her out?'

'Her, sir? A young lady, do you mean?'

He stared helplessly.

'And what would be the name of this young lady, sir?'

*

Zane said, 'You shouldn't swear so much. It demeans you.'

'Ah, to fuck, you know, that's a load of shit.'

When Shiel looked up, he saw Zane pointing a pistol at his heart. 'Jesus Christ, Zane.'

'I asked you not to swear.'

'But for fuck's sake'

Zane cocked it.

'Put the gun away.'

Zane said, 'You're like all the other heathens: you won't listen, you won't do as you are told. Nowadays no one responds to a polite request. They think they can do anything they like. Regardless.'

He raised the gun till it was pointing at Shiel's face.

'To get what you want, you have to show you mean business.'

'Right. OK, Zane. Just put the gun away.'

Zane smiled. 'You and I mean business.'

RUSSELL JAMES is a British crime-writer known for his hard-hitting, low-life thrillers, mainly set in south-east London, though his latest novel, Oh No, Not My Baby, is set in and around the city of Bristol. He had an author's conventionally unhappy childhood: his father committed suicide, and he was physically abused by relations, before being sent to military boarding schools. Subsequently, he finds himself an observer, a lone wolf.

His previous books include Underground, Daylight, Payback, Slaughter Music and Count Me Out. Oh No, Not My Baby has as its background the meat processing business, incorporating sinister corporate shenanigans, animal rights terrorism and murder.

In a recent interview, he said: 'Most writers don't write crime novels; they write anti-crime novels police procedurals, PI stories and puzzlers. I write crime novels about criminals and victims.'

PRAISE FOR RUSSELL JAMES' WRITING:

'One of Britain's best noir writers.' Andrew Taylor,
—Tangled Web magazine.

'The great unknown talent of British crime fiction.'
—GQ magazine

'Something of a cult He goes looking for trouble where more circumspect writers would back off.'
—Chris Petit, The Times

fiction

taming the alien
ken bruen

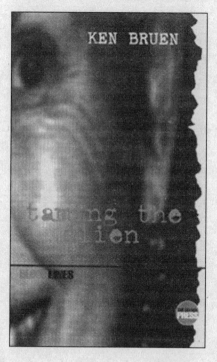

Extract from Taming the Alien *by Ken Bruen (following* A White Arrest *in the 'White' trilogy), Published as a paperback original by The Do-Not Press.*

IF YOU TURNED right on the Clapham Road, you could walk along Lorn to the Brixton side.Few do.

Brant had his new place here. The irony didn't escape him.

Lorn forlorn.

Oh yeah.

Since he'd been knifed in the back, he'd been assigned to desk duty, said: 'Fuck that for a game of soldiers.'

His day off, he'd go to the cemetery, put flowers on PC Tone's grave. Never missed a week. Each time he'd say, 'Sorry son. I didn't watch for you and the fucks killed you for a pair of pants.'

What a slogan Trousers to die for.

The Band Aid couple had gone to ground or Ireland. No proof it was them. Just a hunch. Some day, yeah some day he'd track 'em.

Only Chief Inspector Roberts knew of Brant's hand in the murder of the boy. He wouldn't say owt. Brant's own near death had somehow evened it out for Roberts.

Odd barter but hey, they were cops, not brain surgeons.

Chief Inspector Roberts was ageing

badly. As he shaved, he looked in the mirror, muttered: 'Yer ageing badly.'

Deep creases lined his forehead. The once impressive steel grey hair was snow white and long. Clint Eastwood ridges ran down his cheeks. Even Clint tried to hide them. Wincing is cool sure maybe till yer dodgy forties, but after that it comes across as bowel trouble.

Roberts loved the sun, nay, worshipped it and cricket. Too many summers under long hours of UV rays had wreaked havoc. Worse, melanomas had appeared on his chest and legs. When he'd noticed them he gasped, 'What the bloody hell?'

He knew oh sweet Jesus did he ever that if them suckers turned black, you were fucked. They turned black.

The doctor said, 'I won't beat around the bush.'

Roberts thought: 'Oh, do if necessary, lie to me lie BIG beat long around any bush.'

'It's skin cancer.'

'FUCK!'

After, he thought: 'I took it well.'

Was ill as a pig when he heard about the treatment.

Like this: 'Once a week we'll have radiation.'

'We? You'll be in there with me?'

The doctor gave a tolerant smile, halfways pity to building smirk, continued: 'Let's see how you progress with the 'rad', and if it's not doing the business we'll switch to laser.'

Roberts wanted to shout, 'Beam me up Scottie! Signpost ahead The Twilight Zone.'

He let the doctor wind down. 'Lat-er on, we'll whip some of those growths away. A minor surgical procedure.'

'Minor for you, mate.'

The doctor was finished now, probably get in nine holes before ops, said: 'We'll pencil you in for Mondays, and I'd best prepare you for two after effects:

1. You'll suffer extreme fatigue, so easy does it.

2.It leaves you parched a huge thirst is common.'

He had a mega thirst now.

Right after, he went to the Bricklayers. The barman, a balding git with a pony-tail and stained waistcoat, chirped, 'What will it be, guv?'

'Large Dewars, please.'

'Ice water?'

'What, you don't think I'd have thought of them?'

'Touchy.'

Roberts didn't answer, wondering how the git would respond to rad. As if abbreviation could minimise the trauma. Oh would it were so. Dream on.

Robert's other passion was film noir of the forties and fifties. Hot to trot. Now, as he nursed the scotch, he tried to find a line of comfort from the movies. What he got was Dick Powell in Farewell My Lovely:

I caught the blackjack right behind my ear.

A black pool opened up at my feet. *I dived in.It had no bottom.*

Yeah.

He'd given the git behind the bar a tenner, and now he eyed the change. 'Hey buddy, we're a little light here.'

'Wha'? Oh took one for me. I hate to see anyone drink alone.'

Roberts let it go. Londoners you gotta love them. Bit later the git leans on the bar, asks, 'You like videos?'

'Excuse me?'

'Fillums, mate. Yer latest blockbuster see it tonight in the privacy of yer own gaff. Be like 'aving the West End in yer living room.'

'Pirates, you mean.'

'Whoa, John, keep it down, eh?'

Roberts sighed, laid his warrant card on the counter.

'Whoops'

Roberts put the card away, said, 'I thought in your game you could spot a copper.'

'Usually yeah, but two things threw me.'

'Yeah, what's those then?'

'First, you have manners.'

'And?'

'You actually paid.'

KEN BRUEN hails from the west of Ireland and divides his time between south London and Galway. His past includes drunken brawls in Vietnam, a stretch of four months in a south American gaol, a PhD in metaphysics and four of the most acclaimed crime novels of the decade.

Taming The Alien is the second book in his landmark 'White' trilogy, centred around the exploits of Detective Inspector Roberts and Sergeant Brant of the Metropolitan Police. It follows on from the acclaimed A *White Arrest*, taking the action from south-east London to Ireland and New York.

PRAISE FOR KEN BRUEN'S WRITING:

'If Martin Amis was writing crime novels, this is what he would hope to write.'

—*Books in Ireland*

'The most startling and original crime novel of the decade.'

—*GQ*

'Bruen's ability to keep the reader's interest in an unsympathetic character merits comparisons to Thompson's The Killer Inside Me'

—*Jon L Breen, Ellery Queen Mystery Magazine (review of The Hackman Blues)*

'A very stylish writer. Violence, drugs, double-crosses and emotional betrayal all feature against a background of sleazy London hotels and warehouses, and Bruen keeps the tension agonizingly high throughout. Very, very good.'

—*Tribune Magazine*

BANG! BANG! BOOKCLUB

THE NEW INDEPENDENT BOOKCLUB

fiction

water of death
paul johnston

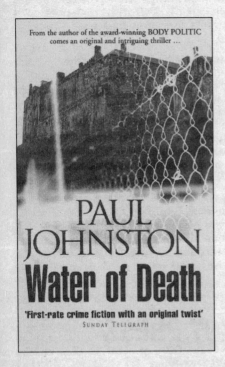

From the author of the award-winning BODY POLITIC comes an original and intriguing thriller ...

PAUL JOHNSTON
Water of Death

'First-rate crime fiction with an original twist'
SUNDAY TELEGRAPH

This is an excerpt from Water of Death, *published in November 1999 by NEL at £5.99*

EDINBURGH, JULY 2025. SWEAT CITY.

When I was a kid before independence, summer was a joke that got about as many laughs as a hospital waiting list. There was the occasional sunny day, but you spent most of the time running from showers of acid rain and the lash of rabid winds. To make things worse, for three weeks the place was overrun by armies of culture victims chasing the hot festival ticket. Now the festival is a year-round event—though a lot of the tourists are only interested in the officially sanctioned marijuana clubs—and "hot" doesn't even begin to describe the state of the weather. Over the last couple of years temperatures have risen by three to four degrees, causing tropical diseases to migrate northwards and bacteria to embark on a major expansion programme. Scientists in the late twentieth century would have got closer to the full horror of the phenomenon if they'd called it "global stewing" except we haven't got enough fresh water to stew anything properly.

What we do have is a cracker of a name for the season between spring and autumn. To everyone's surprise the new-look, user-friendly Council of City Guardians didn't saddle us with an updated designation for the period (think French Revolution, think Thermidor). Our masters were probably too busy discussing initiatives to relieve the tourists of even more cash. As the blazing days and stifling nights dragged by, ordinary citizens gave up distinguishing between the months of June, July and August. And even though the classic *noir* movie hasn't been seen in Edinburgh since the cinemas were closed and television banned by the original Council, people have taken to calling this season the Big Heat. That kills me.

Still, in Sweat City we're really civilises Unlike most states, we've done away with capital punishment and the nuclear switch has been flicked off permanently—the reactors at Torness were recently buried in enough concrete to give a 1990s town planner the ultimate hard on. On the other hand, the Council set up a compulsory lottery last year, turning greed into a virtue and most citizens into deluded fortune-hunters. Deluded, very thirsty fortune-hunters given the water restrictions.

Then some Grade A headbangers came along and raised the temperature even higher than it had been during Big Heat 2024. Giving me a pretty near terminal case of the "Summertime Blues".

CHAPTER ONE

I was lying in the Meadows with a book and a heat-induced headache, making the most of the shade provided by one of the few trees with any leaves left on it. It was five in the afternoon but the sun still had plenty of fire in its belly. The rays glinted off a big hoarding in the middle of the park. It was advertising the lottery. Some poor sod who'd won it was dressed up like John Knox, a bottle of malt whisky poking out of his false beard. "Play Edlott, the Ultimate Lottery, and Anything Goes", the legend said. If you ask me, what goes, what's already gone, is the last of the Council's credibility. There's an elaborate system of prizes ranging from half-decent clothes, to bottles of better-than-average whisky like the one Johnnie the Fox had secreted, to labour exemptions and pensions for life—but only for a few lucky sods. Edinburgh citizens were so starved of material possessions in the first twenty years of the Council that they now reckon Edlott is the knees of a very large Queen Bee. They even willingly accept the value of a ticket being docked from their wage vouchers every week. I think the whole thing sucks but I'm biased. I've never won so much as a tube of extra-strength sun-protection cream.

All round me Edinburgh citizens were lying motionless, their cheeks resting against parched sod that hadn't produced much grass since the Big Heat arrived. I was one of the lucky ones. At least I was wearing a pair of Supply Directorate shades that hadn't fallen to pieces. Yet.

I rolled over and peered at Arthur's Seat through the haze. People say the hill looks like a lion at rest. These days it's certainly the right shade of sandy brown, though the desiccated vegetation on its flanks gives the impression of an erstwhile king of the beasts who's been mauled by a pride of rabid republicans. As it happens, that isn't a bad description of the Enlightenment Party that led Edinburgh into independence in 2004. But things have changed a hell of a lot since then. For a start, like the nerve gas used by demented dictators in the Balkans twenty-plus years ago, you can smell Edinburgh people coming long before you can see or hear them. Water's almost as precious as the revenue from tourists here.

I glanced round at my fellow citizens. If Arthur's Seat is a lion, we must be the pack of ragged hyenas that hangs around it. Everyone was in standard-issue maroon shorts (standard-issue meaning too wide, too long and not anything like cool enough) and off-white T-shirts. Those whose sunglasses have self-destructed wear faded sunhats with a Heart of Midlothian badge on the front. Up until the time of the "iron boyscouts"—the hardline lunatics who ran the Council of City Guardians between 2020 and 2022—only the rank of auxiliaries was entitled to wear the heart insignia, which has nothing to do with the pre-Enlightenment football team The present Council's doing its best to make citizens feel they have the same rights as the uniformed class who carry out the guardians' orders. Except the auxiliaries don't have to wear clowns' outfits.

The hard ground was making my arms stiff. I stretched and made the mistake of breathing in through my nose. It wasn't just that the herd of humanity needed more than the single shower lasting exactly sixty seconds which it gets each week (One of the lottery prizes is a five-minute shower every week for a month.) The still air over the expanse of flat parkland was infused with the reek from the public shithouses that have been set up at the end of every residential street. Since the onset of the Big Heat, citizens have had no running water in their flats. People get by one way or another and the black marketeers do good business in bottles, jars, chamberpots—anything that will hold liquid. But the City Guard has to patrol the queues outside the communal bogs first thing in the morning. It doesn't take long for dozens of desperate citizens to lose their grip and turn on each other.

It was too hot to read. I lay back and let an old blues number run through my mind- No surprises what it was—"Dry Spell Blues". Before I could work out if Son House or Spider Carter was singing, the vocal was blown away by a sudden mechanical roar.

"Turn that rustbucket off, ya shite!" A red-haired kid of about seventeen jumped to his feet and started waving his arms at the driver of a tractor towing a battered water trader. They come daily to refill the drinking-water tanks at every street corner. It stopped about fifty yards away from us.

"Aye, give us a break or I'll give you one," shouted another young guy who obviously fancied himself as a hard man. The pair of them had done everything they could to make their clothes distinctive—they had their T-shirt sleeves folded double and their shorts stained with bleach, pieces of thick rope holding them up. Sweat City chic.

The driver had switched off his engine. Now that he could hear what was being broadcast to him, he didn't look happy. He was pretty musclebound for someone on the diet we get, and the set of his unshaven face suggested he didn't think much of the Council's recent easy-going policies and their effect on the young. "You wee bastards," he yelled waddling towards the kids as quickly as his heavy thighs allowed. "Your heads are going down the pan."

There was a collective intake of breath as the citizens around me sat up and paid attention, grateful for anything that took their minds off the stifling heat. I watched as a woman sitting with a small child near the loudmouthed guys started gathering up her towels and waterbottles nervously.

Our heroes took one look at the big man corning their way, glanced at each other and turned to run. Then the tough guy spotted the woman's handbag. She'd left it lying open on the ground as she leaned over her child.

"Tae fuck wi' the lot o' ye," the kid shouted in the local dialect that the Council outlawed years ago. He bent down to scoop up the bag and sprinted after his pal towards the streets on the far side of the park. "Southside Strollers rule!" he yelled over his shoulder.

The woman shrieked. Her kid joined in. The citizens nearest to them crowded round to help but nobody else moved a muscle. Even the tractor driver had turned to marble. It wouldn't have been the first time they'd seen a bag snatched by the city's new generation of arseholes. It wasn't the first time I'd seen it either. Maybe because I'd once been in the Public Order Directorate, maybe because I was theoretically still a member of the Enlightenment, maybe just because I fancied a run— whatever, I got to my feet and gave what in the City Guard we used to call "chase".

Bad idea.

After fifty yards they were still going away from me, dust rising from their feet and hanging in the air to coat my tongue and eyes. But after a hundred yards, when my lungs were dogging and my legs had decided enough was enough, the little sods had slowed to not much more than a stride: evidence of loading up on illicit ale and black-market grass, I reckoned. Then I cut my speed even more. People who get into those commodities at an early age usually learn how to look after themselves.

They turned to face me and started to laugh in between gasping for breath.

"Hey, look, Tommy, it's the Good fucking Samaritan," the redhead said.

Obviously he'd learned something in school, though the Education Directorate would have preferred something more in line with the Council's atheist principles to have stuck.

Tommy was rifling through the woman's bag, tossing away paper hankies and the Supply Directorate's version of cosmetics and stuffing food and clothing vouchers into his pocket. When he'd finished, he looked up at me and smiled threateningly. The teeth he revealed were uneven and discoloured.

"Get away, ya wanker," he hissed, raising his left fist. It had the letters D-E-A-D tattooed amateurishly on the lower finger joints. I was betting the right one had the word "YOU'RE" on it, spelled wrong. "Come on, Col. We're gone."

He'd got that right. I took my mobile phone from the back pocket of my shorts and called the guard command centre in the castle. As soon as I started to speak, the two of them turned back towards me, their eyes empty and their fists drawn right back.

Like I said—bad idea.

"Are you all right, Quint?"

"What does it look like, Davie?" I took a break from flexing my right wrist and stood up to face the heavily built guard commander who'd just arrived in a Land-Rover and a dust storm.

"Bloody hell, what did you do to those guys?"

I walked over to the bagsnatchers. The carrot-head was leaning forward on both hands, carrying out a detailed examination of what had been his lunch. Tommy the hard man was still on his arse. Unfortunately he'd turned out to have a jaw that really was hard. I had a handkerchief wrapped round my seeping knuckles.

"Where did you learn to fight like that, ya bastard?" he demanded, trying to get to his feet. Then he ran his eye over Davie's uniform. "I might have fuckin' known. You're an Alsatian like him." The city's lowlife refer to the guard as dogs when they're feeling brave.

Davie grabbed the kid's arm and pulled him upright. "What was that, sonny?"

Tommy decided bravery was surplus to requirements. "Nothing," he muttered.

"Nothing what?" Davie shouted into his ear.

"Nothing, Hume 253." Tommy pronounced Davie's barracks number with exaggerated respect, his eyes to the ground.

"That's better, wee man. And for your information, this citizen is not a member of the City Guard."

"He fuckin' puts himself about like one," Tommy said under his breath.

Davie grimed at me. "And there was me thinking you'd forgotten your auxiliary training, Quint."

"Quint?" the boy said with a groan. "Aw, no. You're no' that investigator guy, are you? The one wi' the stupid name?"

Davie found all this highly amusing. "Quintilian Dalrymple?" he asked.

"Aye, the one who's in the paper

every time you bitches cannae do your job."

Too much adulation isn't good for you. "So what are you going to do with this pair of scumbags, Hume 253?" I asked.

Colin the carrot finally managed to get to his feet.

"Cramond Island, I reckon," Davie replied. "The old prison'll be a great place to give them a hiding."

The carrot hit the dust again.

"You cannae do that," Tommy whined "We've got rights. The Council's set up special centres for kids like us."

He was tight. In their desperation to be seen as having citizens' best interests at heart, the latest guardians, or at least a majority of them, haven't only given citizens more personal freedom—apart from anything involving the use of water—and a lottery, but they've organised a social welfare system that treats anyone who steps out of line as an honoured guest. To no one in the guard's surprise, petty crime has risen even faster than the temperature.

"Who are the Southside Strollers?" I asked.

"What's it to you?" Tommy said, giving me the eye.

Davie grabbed his arm and stuck his face up close to the boy's.

"Answer the man, sonny."

"Awright, awright." Tommy had gone floppy again. "It's our gang. We all come from the south side of the city."

"And you spend your time strolling around nicking whatever you can?" I

said.

Tommy shrugged nonchalantly, his eyes lowered.

A couple of auxiliaries from the Welfare Directorate looking desperately eager to please turned up to collect the boys. Colin the carrot was busy holding on to his gut but Tommy flashed a triumphant look at us.

"Just a minute, you," I said, moving over to him I stuck my hand into his pocket and relieved him of the vouchers he'd taken, leaving a streak of blood from my knuckles on his shorts as a souvenir. "Oh, aye, what's this then?"

The pair of them suddenly started examining the ground.

"What do you think, Davie?" I said, opening the scrap of crumpled paper and sniffing the small quantity of dried and shredded leaves.

Davie shook his head. "If it was up to me..."

"But it isn't," the female auxiliary from the Welfare Directorate's Youth Development Department said, stepping forward and looking at the twist of grass. "Underage citizens are our responsibility, not the City Guard's. We'll see they're rehabilitated."

Davie looked at her disbelievingly. Like most of his colleagues, he had serious difficulty in accepting the Council's recent caring policies. Not that he had any choice.

Tommy smirked then bared his teeth at me again. "You're dead, pal."

"Oh, aye, Tommy?" I said "And what does that make you?"

I handed the grass to Davie. We

watched the miscreants get into the Youth Development Department van then I turned back to get my gear.

"The future of the city," Davie said morosely as he caught up with me. "Giving these headbangers special treatment is only going to make them harder to control later. Anyone caught with black-market drugs should be nailed to the floor like in the old days."

"Hand that stuff over for analysis, will you?" We both knew that wouldn't make any difference. The guard's no longer permitted to give underage citizens the third degree so they probably wouldn't find out where the grass came from. I shrugged. "Stupid bastards. I told them to keep their distance but they had to have a go."

Davie laughed. "They weren't the only ones. You sorted them out pretty effectively, Quint."

"I'll probably end up on a charge. Unwarranted force."

"I don't think so. I'll be writing the report, remember."

The citizens under the trees were pretending they'd gone back to sleep. Davie's presence was making them shy. Even in the recently approved informal shirtsleeve order, the grey City Guard uniform isn't the most popular apparel in Edinburgh. The woman came to reclaim her vouchers, flashing me a brief smile of thanks. She probably thought I was an undercover guard operative.

"I'll give you a lift home," Davie said as we headed for his vehicle. "What were you doing here anyway?"

"Trying unsuccessfully to find somewhere cool in this sweat pit to read my book."

"What have you got?" Davie took the volume from under my arm and laughed. *Black and Blue*? Just like the state of your knuckles tomorrow morning."

"Very funny, guardsman."

"Isn't it that book on the proscribed list?" he asked dubiously.

"The Council lifted the ban on pre-Enlightenment Scottish crime fiction at the end of last year. Don't you remember?"

"I just put a stop to crime," he said pointedly. "I don't read stories about it."

"That'll be right. You said something about taking me to my place?"

Davie wrenched open the passenger door of one of the guard's few surviving Land-Rovers. "At your service, sir", he said with fake deference. "Number 13 Gilmore Place it is, sir."

But as things turned out, we didn't make it.

Tollcross is as busy a junction as you get in Edinburgh. A guard vehicle on watch, a couple of Supply Directorate delivery vans, the ubiquitous Water Department tractor and a flurry of citizens on bicycles constitute traffic congestion these days. There was even a Japanese tourist in one of the hire cars provided by an American multinational that the Council did a deal with. He was scratching his head. The lack of other private cars in the streets was obviously worrying him.

"Why were you frying yourself in the Meadows, Quint?" Davie asked. "There are bits of grass around the castle that actually get watered. It's quieter there too."

I looked at the burly figure next to me. He was still wearing the beard that used to be required of male auxiliaries even though the current Council's made it optional. God knows what the temperature was beneath the marred growth.

"Quiet if you don't mind being stared at by sentries," I replied. "Since they moved the auxiliary training camp away from the Meadows, it's become a much more relaxing place."

"Arsehole." Davie was shaking his head. "Anyone would think you hadn't spent ten years as one of us." He laughed. "Till they saw how handy you are with your fists."

My mobile rang before I could tell him how proud I was to have been demoted from the rank of auxiliary.

"Is that you, Dalrymple?"

I let out a groan. I might have known the public order guardian would get his claws into me late on a Friday afternoon. Not that his rank take weekends off.

"Lewis Hamilton," I said. "What a surprise."

"Where are you, man?" he demanded "And don't address me by name." Lewis was one of the old school, a guardian for twenty years. He didn't go along with the new Council's decision allowing citizens to use guardians' names instead of their official titles.

"I'm it Tollcross with Hume 253."

"Distracting my watch commander from his duties again?" Davie had been promoted a few months ago, though that didn't stop him helping me out whenever something interesting came up.

"And the reason for your call is...?" I asked.

"The reason for my call is that the people who run the lottery need your services."

I pointed to Davie to pull to the kerbside. "Don't tell me. They've lost one of their winners again."

"I know, I know, he'll probably turn up drunk in a gutter after a couple of days..."

"With his prizes missing and his new clothes covered in other people's vomit. Jesus, Lewis, can't you find someone else to look for the moron? Like, for instance, a guardsman who started his first tour of duty this morning?"

Hamilton gave what passes for a laugh in his book. "No, Dalrymple. As you know very well, this is a high-priority job. One for the city's freelance chief investigator. After tourists my fellow guardians' favourite human beings are lottery-winners." I knew he had other ideas about that himself. As far as he was concerned, Edlott was yet another disaster perpetrated by the reforming guardians who made up the majority of the current Council. Hamilton particularly despised the culture guardian whose directorate runs the lottery for what he called his "lack of Platonic principles", whatever that means. I don't think he was too keen on his colleague's eye for a quick buck either. The underlying idea of Edlott was to reduce every citizen's voucher entitlement for the price of a few relatively cheap prizes. Still, the public order guardian's aversion to the lottery was nothing compared with the contempt he reserved for the Council members who forced through the measure permitting the supply of marijuana and other soft drugs to tourists. As I saw in the park, foreign visitors weren't the only grass consumers in the city.

"Any chance of you telling Edlott I'm tied up on some major investigation, Lewis? I mean, it's Friday night and the bars are—"

There was a monotonous buzzing in my ear.

"Bollocks!" I shouted into the mouthpiece.

Davie looked at me quizzically. "Bit early to hit a sex show, isn't it?"

I got the missing man's name and address from a new generation auxiliary in the Culture Directorate who oozed bonhomie like a private pension salesman in pre-Enlightenment times.

"Guess what, Davie? We're off to Morningside."

"What?" Davie turned on me with his brow furrowed. "*You're* off to Morningside, you mean."

"Your boss just told me this is a high-priority job. The least you can do is ferry me out."

Davie looked at his watch and gave me a reluctant nod. "Okay, but I'm on duty tonight and I want to eat before that."

"You pamper that belly of yours, Davie."

He gave me a friendly scowl.

We came down to what was called Holy Corner before the Enlightenment. The four churches were turned into auxiliary accommodation blocks soon afterwards. They form part of Napier Barracks, the guard base controlling the city's central southern zone, The checkpoint barrier was quickly raised for us.

"Where to then?" Davie asked.

I looked at the note I'd scribbled. "Millar Crescent. Number 14."

He headed down the main road, the Land-Rover's bodywork juddering as he accelerated. Ahead of us, a thick layer of haze and dust obscured the Pentland Hills and the ravaged areas between us and them. What were once pretty respectable suburbs became the home of streetfighting man in the time leading up to independence. They had only been used again in the last couple of years and the part beyond the heavily fortified city line a few hundred yards further south was still an urban wasteland. It was haunted by black marketeers and the dissidents who've been trying and failing to overturn the Council since it came to power. On this side of the line, the Housing Directorate has settled a lot of the city's problem families into flats that used to be occupied by Edinburgh's blue-rinse and pearl-necklace brigade. The Southside Strollers were the tip of a very large iceberg.

"Ten minutes, Quint," Davie said as he manoeuvred round the water tank and the citizens' bicycle shed at the end of Millar Crescent. "That's all I'm giving you." Then his jaw dropped.

I followed the direction of his gaze. A young woman was on her way into the street entrance of number 14. She was wearing a citizen-issue T-shirt and work trousers that were unusually well pressed despite the spatters of paint on them She also had a mauve chiffon scarf round her neck which had never seen the inside of a Supply Directorate store. She had light brown hair bound up in a tight plait and a self-contained look on her face. Oh, and she was built like the Venus de Milo with a full complement of limbs.

Davie already had his door open. "Well," he said, "make it half an hour."

We climbed the unlit airless stairs to the third floor. The name Kennedy had been carved very skilfully in three-inch-high letters on the surface of a blue door on the right side of the landing. The incisions in the wood looked recent.

"This is the place," I said, raising my hand to knock.

"Where did she go?" Davie asked, looking up and down the stairwell.

"Will you get a grip?" I thumped on the door. "Exert some auxiliary self-control."

"Ah, but we're supposed to come over like human beings these days," he said with a grin.

"Exactly. Like human beings, guardsman. Not like dogs after a..."

Then the door opened very quickly. The woman we'd seen stood looking at us with her eyes wide open and a faint smile on her lips.

"Dogs after a...?" she asked in a deep voice, her dark brown eyes darting between us. A lot of citizens would have made the most of that canine reference in the presence of a guardsman, but there didn't seem to be any irony in her tone.

There was a silence that Davie and I found a lot more awkward than she did.

"Em...I'm looking for Citizen Kennedy," I said, pulling out my notebook and trying to make out my scribble in the dim light. "Citizen Fordyce Kennedy."

"My father," she said simply.

"And you are...?"

She looked at me blankly for a couple of seconds then smiled, this time with a hint of mockery. "I'm his daughter." She hesitated then shrugged "Agnes is my name."

"Right," I said "So is he in?"

"Of course he isn't in," she said, her voice hardening. "That's why we called you." She leaned forward on the balls of her feet and examined my clothes. I breathed in a chemical smell from her. "You are from the guard, aren't you?" Then she turned her eyes on to Davie's uniform. "I can see the big man is."

Something about the way she spoke the last words made Davie, who's never been reticent with women, look away uncomfortably.

"I'm Dalrymple, special investigator," I said. "Call me Quint." I registered the reserve in her eyes. "If you want."

She didn't reply, just looked at me intensely like an artist eyeing up a new model. I resisted the urge to check if my clothes had suddenly become transparent.

"Who's that?" The voice that came from the depths of the flat was faint and uncertain, the accent stronger than the young woman's. "Who's that out there?"

"Is that your mother?" I asked.

"My mother," Agnes Kennedy agreed, nodding slowly. "Her name's Hilda. She's a bit upset. And…and her mind wanders." She looked at me and succeeded in imparting a curious hybrid of appeal and threat. "Be sure you don't upset her." She held her eyes on me for a few moments then turned abruptly and led us down the dimly lit corridor.

"It's the men from the guard, Mother," she said to the thin figure that was leaning against the wall. Then she took her arm and pushed open the door at the far end of the passage. I heard her continue talking in a smooth, low voice, as if she were the parent having to comfort a frightened child. "They're going to find Dad for us…"

Before I got to the door, I heard the sound of curtains being drawn rapidly. I came into the room and blinked in the subdued light, trying to make out the bent woman who stood moving her head from side to side like a lost sheep. She relaxed a bit when Agnes came back from the windows and took her arm.

"You don't like strong sunlight, do you, Mother?" the young woman said "It's all right. Agnes has fixed it for you."

My eyes accustomed themselves to the crepuscular gloom. The women sat down on the sofa, the senior of them looking at her daughter with a confused expression that only gradually faded from her features. Like many Edinburgh citizens, she'd been adversely affected by twenty years of what the Medical Directorate regards as a satisfactory diet. At least there's been a massive reduction in the heart disease resulting from the garbage we used to eat before the Enlightenment. These days people are more likely to die of respiratory failure or skin cancer brought about by the climate change. But this woman looked like she'd been gnawed by mental as well as physical demons.

"How long's your husband been missing, citizen?" Davie asked with customary City Guard forthrightness.

Agnes glared at him angrily then glanced back at her mother, who showed no sign of having heard the question. "Since yesterday morning," Agnes answered.

"Under thirty-six hours?" Davie was unimpressed. "That's not long."

Hilda Kennedy suddenly came to life. She stood up with surprising speed and moved in front of Davie. She stooped and the top of the ragged scarf covering her long grey hair reached not much more than halfway up his chest. "It's maybe not long to you, laddie, but my man's never late for his tea." Then she stepped back, the surge of energy already gone.

I nudged Davie with my elbow. Although the guard usually don't cheek out missing persons for at least three days, lottery-winners are special cases.

"When did he leave the house, Hilda?" I asked.

She inspected me before answering, trying to work out whether to treat me as an auxiliary or an ordinary citizen. My use of her first name seemed to get me off the hook. "First thing in the morning," she said.

Agnes was standing next to her mother now. She took her arm again and tried to make her sit down, but the older woman wasn't having it.

"He went to work?" I continued.

Hilda looked at me like I was a backward child "What work? He won the top prize in the lottery, son."

"It was six weeks ago," Agnes put in. "He was exempted from work for life. Apart from two afternoons and two evenings a week publicity for Edlott."

So the Culture Directorate had chosen Fordyce Kennedy to advertise the lottery like the citizen dressed up as John Knox on the poster I'd seen earlier.

"Which character did he get assigned?" I asked.

"That writer fella," Hilda said. "The one who did *Treasure Island.*"

"Robert Louis Stevenson."

"Aye." She shook her head. "He looked like a right idiot with his false moustache and bloodstained hankie."

I looked round the room in the light that was coming in at the sides of the curtains. The furniture was dark-stained wood, the sideboard, dresser and table beautifully carved They were about as far from the standard citizen-issue sticks as you can get.

"Did your husband make all this?" I asked.

Hilda nodded, smiling unevenly. "Aye, he's a cabinet-maker. Used to make stuff for the tourist hotels till he won the lottery. He did all this in his spare time."

I went over to the dresser and looked at the photographs arrayed on it. There were individual shots of a washed-out man in his fifties, of Agnes and of a sullen young man with hair at what used to be the regulation citizen length of under an inch. There was also a family group. Hilda must have moved when the flash went off, blurring the shot and giving her the look of a corpse that had just jerked up on the sofa. Her daughter had the same faint smile that she'd greeted us with when she opened the door, while the son was frowning. Fordyce Kennedy just looked exhausted. Like many citizens, the family had taken advantage of the Council's loosening of the ruling that banned photos. The original guardians regarded them as socially divisive—they reckoned one of the reasons for the disorder leading to the break-up of the United Kingdom had been the cult of the individual Apparently we can be trusted with a few snapshots now.

"How old's your son?" I asked.

"Allie? He's..." Hilda broke off. She gave an almost imperceptible shake of her head but didn't say anything else.

"Twenty-six," Agnes said, completing the sentence. "A year older than me."

"At work, is he?" Davie asked.

"Him? At work?" Agnes laughed humourlessly. "He spends most of his time with his lunatic friends. Too keen on drinking and messing about."

He wasn't the only young man like that in the city.

"How about you?" I asked Agnes. "What do you do?"

She looked at me coolly like she was wondering whether I was entitled to ask that question. "I'm an interior decorator," she said. That explained the paint on her clothing and the smell of a chemical like turpentine. "I spend most of my free time looking after Mother." She glanced at the woman beside her, who didn't seem to be following the conversation. "She began to lose it last year," Agnes added in a low voice.

"And your father?"

Her eyes flashed at me aggressively. "What about my father?"

I smiled nervously. "Did he have any lunatic friends like your brother?"

"My father doesn't go out much," Agnes said, her eyes fierce. "He's a missing person. He hasn't committed any crime."

"All right," I said quietly. "I wasn't implying anything."

I pulled out my notebook and sat down. You usually run the risk of getting a broken spring up your arse from a Supply Directorate sofa but the lottery-winner must have fixed his.

Hilda Kennedy suddenly twitched her head and looked at me. Maybe she had been following the talk after all. "Fordyce was never the pally sort. He liked to stay in and work wi' the wood." She let out a sudden sob and dropped her chin to her flat chest.

"My father loved his work," Agnes said, stroking her mother's arm.

"So how's he been spending his days since he won the lottery?" I asked.

Hilda looked up again, her eyes taking time to focus on me. "I wish I knew, son. Like I say, he's always back for his tea. But during the day he just disappears. I've asked him what he does but he wouldn't answer. Said something about walking the streets once." She stared at me. "He wasn't happy. They shouldn't have taken his work away." She sobbed again and bent her head.

Agnes looked at Davie and me angrily, her face flushed. "Isn't that enough?" she demanded in a low voice.

"They shouldn't have taken his work away," her mother repeated dolefully.

"Don't worry," I said with as much encouragement as I could muster. "He'll turn up."

"Will he?" Hilda said, suddenly running her eyes on me, her dry lips quivering. "Are you sure, son?"

I avoided her gaze as I made for the door.

"Pretty strange pair," Davie said as we drove back towards the city centre. The sun was blinding where it shone through the gaps between buildings.

"You didn't have to come in with me," I said. "That'll teach you to chase female citizens."

"What do you mean chase?" he said, laughing. "You saw the way she was looking at me."

"Correct me if I'm wrong, guardsman, but don't the City Regulations forbid fraternisation between auxiliaries and citizens under thirty?" Until a few months ago auxiliaries weren't allowed to fraternise with citizens of any age. Another one of the Council's attempts to break down the barriers.

"Aye, I suppose you're right." Davie shot me a suspicious glance. "What are you up to, Quint? Oh, I get it. You reckon that you can have a go at the delectable Agnes on the grounds that you're a demoted rather than a serving auxiliary."

I held my breath as we passed through the cloud of exhaust fumes a guard vehicle had belched out. "Me? Certainly not. I'm already spoken for."

Davie laughed, this time raucously. "Like hell you are."

I let him go on thinking that.

Five minutes later he dropped me at my flat in Gilmore Place.

I pulled the street door open impatiently, wondering if any traces of the perfume I'd got used to over the last couple of weeks would be lingering in the hot air.

They were. I raced up the stairs, opened my door and got an eyeful of the woman I'd been hoping would be there.

That didn't do anything to cool me down at all.

CHAPTER TWO

"Hello, guardian."

The Ice Queen turned and gave me one of the Antarctic glares that led to her nickname. Her short, silver-blonde hair also had something to do with that, as did the high cheekbones and tight lips that were unadorned by make-up. "Where have you been, Quint?" She sounded more like an exasperated schoolmistress than the city's highest-ranking medical officer. "I've been waiting for half an hour."

"Did we have a rendezvous then?" I have a thing about being scolded. Besides, I was parched and I had a nasty feeling I'd forgotten to refill my waterbottles. A quick glance at the collection of empties in the corner of my living room that passes for a kitchen confirmed my fear. I looked at my watch. "Shit."

The medical guardian read my mind. "Missed the street tank?" I nodded. The Water Department locks up drinking supplies at six in the evening to restrict consumption.

"Don't worry," she said, opening her briefcase. "I've got a couple of pints."

I crossed to my sideboard. It was a lot grottier than the one the missing lottery-winner had made for himself but there was something in it I fancied.

"I'm not worried," I said, taking out a bottle of citizen-issue whisky.

The Ice Queen twitched her lips in disapproval as I downed a slug.

"Relax. I'm not planning on offering you any." I breathed in hard as the rough spirit cauterised the inside of my throat. "Jesus, what do they put in this stuff?" I raised my hand. "No, don't tell me." If I'd let her, she'd have provided me with a full chemical analysis. You don't want to give scientists any encouragement. "How about some music?"

"That's not exactly what I came for." The guardian was looking out of the window into the street, her arms stretched out against the frame. The white blouse and grey skirt that female Council members wear during the Big Heat made her look like the strait-laced schoolteacher her voice had suggested. She was of medium height, slim, her body carrying no more weight than the average female citizen's. Then again, her chest was a lot more eye-catching than the average female citizen's so maybe years of a senior auxiliary's diet had some effect. The guardians have always claimed their lifestyle is ascetic but you don't see many signs of malnutrition in their residences in Moray Place.

I was rooting around in my tape collection trying to find something that wasn't the blues—despite the relaxation of regulations, they're still seen as subversive. The trouble is I don't have much apart from the blues. Eventually I put on a Rolling Stones recording from 2001. No one could call that subversive.

"I said that wasn't what I came for," the guardian repeated, moving towards where I was kneeling by my ancient cassette deck.

I turned my head and got a look that didn't originate in the polar regions. In fact, it was positively provocative. Despite the heat, I shivered. A few months ago the Council decided to loosen the rules governing guardians' personal lives. For years they were expected to live on their own in total celibacy. Now they're supposed to show they're ordinary people like the rest of us by getting laid. I still haven't got used to guardians showing their feelings, let alone guardians having sex. Especially not with me.

"Take your hand away, Quint."

That sounded more like what you'd expect a female Council member to say. Then again, it was after midnight, my bedroom was as steamy as the innermost room of a Turkish bath and we'd already made it twice.

I moved my hand from her thigh. "Sorry, Sophia," I said, keeping my eyes on her. It wasn't till we'd spent three nights together that she allowed me to use her name, and she didn't like me using it anywhere other than in bed Although she was still in her thirties, the medical guardian was on the reactionary wing of the Council, like Lewis Hamilton. The idea of ordinary citizens being allowed to address their rulers by first name was about as popular with her as compulsory duty in the coal mines used to be with ordinary citizens until the regulations were changed Sophia had been one of the disciplinarian "Iron boyscouts" who ran the Council before they were discredited. She kept her job because she was so bloody good at it.

"Anyway, you must have had enough of me by now." She was lying on her back, her a= behind her head and her knees apart, trying to cool down. There was a sheen of sweat on her skin. Her small rose-coloured nipples were soft now. She saw the direction of my gaze and covered her breasts With an arm. Being celibate for years had made her modest. Well, most of the time. In bed she combined that modesty with a degree of lasciviousness that wouldn't have been out of place in a nunnery in the days before organised religion went out of fashion.

"It isn't just about sex, you know," I said.

Sophia returned my gaze. "Isn't it?" she asked, her face blank.

Then the hint of a smile creased the corners of her mouth. "Men are such romantics."

"Is that right?" I said sharply, rolling over on to my right side and confronting the heap of dirty clothing that had built up in the corner of my bedroom. I'd managed to miss my session at the wash house last month.

"Don't be childish, Quint," she said, slapping my shoulder lightly. "What are you working on at the moment?"

"The usual. Trying to find the shithead who's g that gang of pickpockets on Princes Street, chasing a Swedish porn dealer who's operating out of Leith. Where are the master criminals, for Christ's sake? Today they got me on to a lottery-winner who's done a bunk. Can't say I blame him."

The Ice Queen let out an impatient sigh. "What are you saying, Quint? Would you prefer us to have trysts at murder scenes and in the mortuary like we used to? I don't approve of all the changes my colleagues in the Council have made but at least we've kept a grip on crime." She shook her head. "Though setting up marijuana clubs for the tourists is asking for trouble."

I knew she and Hamilton had argued hard against that policy. No one bothered to ask me what I thought. I'm a big fan of irony and since the Enlightenment came to power with a mission to root out drugs from the city, the irony quotient in this volte-face is pretty high. But despite an increase in drugs-related petty crime like the one I witnessed in the Meadows, there hasn't been much sign of Edinburgh people wandering around in a grass-induced haze. The fact that citizens have bugger all to trade for dope seemed to regulate demand pretty effectively—there's no cash in the city apart from foreign currency, and the distribution of food and clothing vouchers is closely monitored.

There was a sibilant snore from the far side of the bed. Sophia had fallen asleep as rapidly as usual. Despite, or perhaps because of, the move towards accessibility and openness, the guardians still work ridiculously long hours. At least the daily Council meetings take place at midday now rather than in the evenings, but the medical guardian continues to put in a fifteen-hour day. My experience in the short time she'd been coming to me was that she'd be away to her office in the by five in the morning.

I got up carefully so as not to wake her and went into the living room. My throat was dry but my skin was drenched in sweat. I gulped water from one of Sophia's hordes and sat down gingerly on my sphincter-endangering sofa. Outside, the street was so quiet you could almost hear the tar bubbles popping in the heat. The curfew for citizens has been moved from ten to twelve p.m. but the guard still enforce it rigidly. As usual sleep was as far from me as a cool breeze was from the city.

During the Big Heat my mind likes to pretend it's a nocturnal organism. Just as well. I had a lot to think about. Having sexual relations with Sophia was great, especially as I gave up sex sessions when they became non-compulsory a year back and my body was beginning to suffer serious deprivation. I still dreamed about my ex-lover Katharine Kirkwood and I used to kid myself that we still had some kind of tie, even though she walked away from me in January 2022 and I hadn't seen her since. But I couldn't figure out exactly what Sophia wanted from me. When she first showed up at my door and grabbed the contents of my underpants, I was more surprised than I'd been when the Council opened up its meetings to ordinary citizens. Like I say, the idea of the medical guardian having sex with anyone was pretty weird. Still, I suppose she had urges like everyone else. But why had she chosen me rather than a superfit young guardsman or a high-flying auxiliary? Something told me it was more than

just the use of my genitalia she wanted. When we were together Sophia often asked me what I was working on, as she'd done tonight. Was that simply idle curiosity or was she after something else? Like information she could use against Council members who were more progressive than her?

I took the bottle of whisky into the bedroom and gulped from it as I sat on the bed A stirring came from the other side.

"You should cut down on the spirits, Quint," the Ice Queen said blearily, one eye half open. "They'll poison your system."

I raised the bottle to her and drank again. I've made it a strict rule never to take advice from guardians.

I eventually passed out. I didn't register Sophia leaving and it was eight in the morning before I came round to the racket of clapped-out buses and kids complaining on their way to school. Saturday's a working day in Enlightenment Edinburgh for most citizens, schoolchildren included. They shouldn't complain too much—at least they only have half a day of lessons on Saturdays during the Big Heat. Maybe they were looking forward without enthusiasm to the summer holidays. They last all of two weeks, one of which is spent picking litter from the beaches. At least we still have beaches—unlike the west of Scotland which has been subject to catastrophic flooding because of rising sea levels. Some of the countries that used to send plenty of tourists such as China have gone into subaquatic pursuits in a big way too.

We don't find out much about the rest of the world in our little wire-fenced paradise but news sometimes filters through from tourists and traders. The last I heard, the democratic system in Glasgow was hanging on but had come under heavy pressure from food shortages and organised crime. Most of the other states in Scotland have reverted to anarchy, while what used to be England is going through a modem version of the Dark Ages despite fifteen hours of skull-splitting sunshine every day.

I stumbled through to the living room and discovered that Sophia had left one of her bottles with enough water for me to make a mug of coffee. That commodity used to be harder to find in Edinburgh than silk knickers but the Council recently got into bed with a Swiss food and drink multinational—not that ordinary citizens get anything other than the scrapings from the factory floor. I chewed the end of a three-day-old loaf of bread and had a go at planning the day. What I should have done was try to find a new chain for my wreck of a bicycle, except I didn't fancy queuing for hours at the local Supply Directorate depot. Besides, I told myself, walking is good for you. And the city archive where I needed to go to find the missing lottery-winner's records isn't that far from my flat.

Dragging myself up what is a deceptive gradient on Lauriston Place in the morning sweatbath made me change my mind, It would have been worse on my bike but at least it would have been over quickly. The air was heavy and the stink from the breweries was cut with the acrid ting of sewage coming to the boil in the under-maintained pipes beneath the streets. These days Japanese tourists are told to bring along the little masks they wear in the busy streets back home. Edinburgh citizens haven't been allowed cars for years so there isn't much of a problem with exhaust fumes here. Unfortunately the Council hasn't yet found a way to stop people shitting during the Big Heat. No doubt Sophia's got the Medical Directorate working on that.

Things got a bit better when I reached George IVth Bridge. It's in the central tourist zone, so the pavements are washed down overnight and maroon awnings are hung to keep the sun off the city's honoured paying guests. Further on at the next checkpoint, guard personnel were looking out for ordinary citizens. For all the Council's attempts at openness, the High Street is still off limits unless you have work there. I had a Public Order Directorate authorisation but I wasn't going as far as the barrier. I turned into the archive and felt my body temperature begin to drop immediately in the polished-stone entrance hall Before the Enlightenment the building was the city's central library, but the original Council's policy was to bring books meaning the ones they approved of—closer to citizens, so they increased the number of smaller libraries in residential areas. Which gave them the chance to convert the main library into something they were even keener on—a centralised store containing everything they wanted to know about every citizen, without the citizens being allowed access. It's all on paper, of course. The guardians have always been suspicious of computers, forbidding citizens to possess them and under-using the few they kept for themselves.

"Morning, Citizen Dalrymple."

"Morning, Ray. What's the problem?"

The one-armed auxiliary looked pointedly at the sentry who'd just checked my pass then beckoned me into his office.

"Jackass," he said in a low voice. "You know you should call me Nasmyth 67 in public, Quint." Although the guardians have been encouraging citizens to use their names, auxiliaries are still to be addressed by barracks number—after all, they're the ones who keep control.

"Bugger that," I said. "We served together for years."

"Till you got demoted and I got crippled." Pay looked down at the stump that was protruding from his auxiliary-issue grey shirt. He always rolled the sleeve up as high as he could to make sure everyone got an eyeful.

I held up my right hand with the missing forefinger to remind him we were brothers in arms.

"So what are you after in my house of files this sweaty morning?" He filled a glass of water and handed it to me. During the Big Heat people do that without asking. It suddenly struck me that Agnes Kennedy hadn't given Davie and me a drink yesterday. Maybe she was more wound up about her missing father than I realised.

"There's a lottery-winner who's made a break for freedom," I replied. "Or drunk himself into a stupor somewhere."

"Well, you know your way around." Ray sat down and wrapped his good arm round a heap of folders on his desk.

"Unfortunately. I seem to have spent half my life in here."

Ray looked up and laughed derisively. "You only come for the bogs."

"You noticed? Auxiliary-issue paper, no queues. In fact, now you mention it…"

"Goodbye," he said rapidly.

"I'll see you later. I've got something for you."

"Don't forget to wash your hands."

I raised my fist, this time giving him only the middle finger.

Ahead of me lay what had been the plastered reference room. Its domed ceiling is still visible, but there isn't much else to see apart from stacks and shelves full of grey cardboard folders. Bureaucrat heaven. The people who work in the archive are all auxiliaries. They tend to be specimens whose devotion to the Enlightenment is a lot greater than their physical capabilities. Short-sighted women and puny guys were poring avidly at mounds of files like gold prospectors who'd struck pay in.

"Can I help you?" asked a middle-aged man with pepper-and-salt stubble. It was probably as close as he could get to what used to be the regulation male auxiliary beard.

I declined his offer. The archivists always take a note of the files they bring you, so I collect my own. There's enough surveillance going on in this city without my activities being added to the list. I found Fordyce Bulloch Kennedy's file after a lot of scrabbling and heaving. In the process I inhaled enough dust to clog my bronchial tubes as effectively as a twenty-a-day coffin stick habit—so much for any improvement in my health brought about by the Council's long-standing ban on smoking. I took the thick file to a booth in a corner away from prying eyes and got stuck in.

As usual, most of the documentation was a waste of time annual evaluations of worker competence, personal development statements, lifelong education credits, Platonic philosophy debates attended etc., etc. The original Council was genuinely committed to improving citizens' lives and, more important, citizens' abilities to make more of themselves. Whence the stress on education, the availability of better jobs for those who gained higher qualifications, the chance of roomier accommodation and so on. Even after twenty years no one has much of a problem with those ideals, although these days it's the lottery prizes that provide most of the concrete benefits and very few people win those. You get the impression that the Council, desperate as it is to please the tourists, only goes through the motions with its own Citizens. It's the bureaucracy that's taken charge, a vast, paper-consuming machine that piles tip more and more data and requires a huge staff to satisfy its demands. But I wonder if anyone's life is actually improved by the machine. Most of the files I see are only opened when new pages are inserted No one has the time or inclination to read the contents.

Except in the case of Fordyce Bulloch Kennedy. The consultation sheet stapled to the inside front cover showed that an auxiliary from the Edlott Department of the Culture Directorate had examined the file on 8 June. I checked inside and found that was the day after Fordyce's ticket did the business. Obviously Edlott wanted background information on their latest winner. They'd even taken copies of particular pages, which was interesting because there are hardly any operational photocopiers in the city and auxiliaries are encouraged to make handwritten notes—thus adding to the bureaucracy. Paper in Edinburgh breeds faster than the nuclear reactors that put pockmarks all over the former Soviet Union in the early years of the century. I wrote down the barracks number of the auxiliary who'd been there before me—it was Nasmyth 05.

As for the missing man, he seemed like a pretty average guy—early fifties, highly commended cabinet-maker, no violations of the City Regulations, no contacts with known dissidents or deserters, plenty of Mentioned in Annual Reports for giving voluntary lessons in furniture-making in his spare time. The only black mark was that he was a bit too devoted to his kids—the Council has always discouraged excessive emotional attachment to offspring because they want the city's children to grow up strong and self-reliant. He was also very close to Hilda and had taken what was the risky step back in the early years of the Enlightenment of insisting they continue to live together. The Council then was keen on breaking up what it regarded as the constricting bonds of marriage and encouraging "personal growth". The guardians eventually realised that it was easier to let couples stay together if they wanted to. In general Fordyce Kennedy seemed to be an all-round good citizen. In my experience that's not necessarily a good sign.

I went back to the stacks and pulled the files on his wife and children. As regards the female members of the family, there was nothing out of the ordinary. Hilda had been a cleaner in various tourist hotels until her mental state had begun to deteriorate, while Agnes had trained as a painter and decorator at the Crafts College. Her school records showed that she'd been an average student, one who'd shown no interest in becoming an auxiliary. For the last three months she'd been working in a former school that was being converted into a tourist hostel.

The son Alexander—known as Allie—was a bit more interesting. He'd been a rebel when he was a teenager and had served several spells in the Gulag-like youth detention centres the Council used in the past to sort out nonconformists. He was a postman after that but his recent work records were pretty random. Under previous Councils he'd have been nailed as soon as he missed a day, but things are less strict now and the bureaucracy sometimes doesn't function as effectively as it thinks. I began to wonder what Agnes's older brother was up to. He looked like he might be worth a question or two.

The only other thing that struck me about the family was that the two children were still registered as living with their parents. The Council always encouraged children to move into their own accommodation as soon as they were eighteen in order to break what it regarded as the divisive effects of the family on broader society. Of course, there was never enough decent housing to enable the guardians to insist on the policy for all citizens, but it was still a bit unusual for offspring in their mid-twenties to stay at home. Agnes's excuse was that she was looking after her mother. What was her brother's?

I called the guard command centre in the castle on my mobile and asked the duty watch commander if she'd been informed about the missing lottery-winner. She answered in the affirmative without taking more than a second to think. Lewis Hamilton himself had told her to circulate a description to all barracks. They'd been on the lookout for Fordyce all over the city since last night but there had been no sign of him. I asked her to keep me advised and signed off.

Then I finished taking notes from the folders and replaced them, following my normal practice of omitting my name from the consultation sheets. It keeps people guessing.

On my way out I stopped off at Ray's office. He was deep in his mass of paperwork. I dug into my shoulderbag and tossed over his book.

"Ah, *Black and* Blue," he said, giving it a quick glance. "What did you think?"

"Good, my friend. It was the only one of Ian Rankin's that I hadn't read. A state-of-the-nation novel, no less. I'd almost forgotten that Scotland actually used to be a country."

"Before the robber barons in the Scottish parliament tore each others' throats out and the drugs gangs divided up the territory," Ray said, shaking his head. He sat back in his rickety chair and smoothed the folds of skin on his neck. In the guard he'd been a unit leader renowned for his upper body strength, but since he lost his arm nearly ten years ago he'd turned into a wraith-like figure. His black hair went pure white in the space of a few weeks and the eyes above his grey beard were lustreless. He put his hand on the tattered paperback I'd returned "There was still oil in the North Sea then," he said emptily.

"Not for long there wasn't," I said, catching sight of his fingernails. They were ingrained with dirt that looked a lot more heavy duty than the usual archive dust. "How's the book trade?"

Ray looked up at me sharply and bit his lip. If I didn't know him better, I'd have said he was trafficking more than the odd crime novel "Not so loud, Quint," he said. "That American dealer's still around, I think. Any special requests?"

"Whatever early editions of Chandler he's got. Especially *The Lady In the Lake*. It's my favourite." I smiled. "Cheap early editions, of course."

He nodded. "Aye, of course. What have you got to trade?"

"I still have a couple of EC Bentleys I can live without." I gave him a wave. "See you, pal."

"Don't let them grind you down, Quint."

"You know that's not in my nature, Ray." As I turned to go, I accidentally kicked a book across the ragged carpet on his office floor.

"It doesn't matter," he said quickly. "I'll pick it up later."

"No worries," I said, bending down. I put the copy of Wilfred Owen's collected poems on top of *Black and Blue*. "Ian Rankin and Wilfred Owen. What you might call a strange meeting."

Ray's mouth opened as if he were about to speak then shook his head slowly and went back to his files.

I hit the street and sheltered from the sun under the awning. Opposite stands what used to be the National Library of Scotland and is now the Edinburgh Heritage Centre. For tourists, mind—no locals allowed. A group of Middle Eastern women in long robes and veils had gathered on the pavement. Their guide, an Arabic-speaking female auxiliary dressed up as a society hostess from the time of Sir Walter Scott, was trying hard to whip up interest. No doubt the visitors would just love the exhibition halls stuffed with Council propaganda. The photographs of the riots in 2002, the year before the last election, are apparently a big draw— drug dealers handing out free scores on street corners, policemen being stoned, pub cellars under siege by the mob. No wonder the Enlightenment Party got the biggest majority in British history, then promptly declared independence and left the rest of the UK to mayhem and pillage.

So, I wondered, what to do about Fordyce Bulloch Kennedy? There were several things I wanted to look into. The most obvious was Edlott. He would have a handler in the Culture Directorate, perhaps the one who'd consulted his file, to arrange his appearances as Robert Louis Stevenson and make sure he didn't do anything embarrassing. That auxiliary was probably waiting to he packed off to the border on fatigue duty for not keeping a closer eye on him The Labour Directorate was another possibility. They're forever drafting citizens into emergency squads when pitprops collapse in the mines or workers desert from the city farms. The missing man may have been picked up by mistake, in which case his name should be on a list_ Then there was Fordyce's family. When she was lucid, his wife gave the impression of being worried that he'd disappeared for good but you never know. Most violence is committed by the people closest to the victim, even

in this supposedly crime-free state, and it looked like the son might have been moving in dodgy circles. But there was one possibility I had to rule out before any of those. I turned left and headed towards the checkpoint.

The guardswoman on duty was middle-aged, her fading red hair pulled back in a tight ponytail despite the recent ruling that female auxiliaries don't have to tie their hair down any more. She raised the barrier before I got to it and waved me through, giving me a tight smile. She must have known who I was. Christ, she may have served with me in the guard years ago. Or perhaps it was just that she'd seen my photo in the *Edinburgh Guardian* after one of the big cases.

I walked up to the Lawnmarket and turned left at the gallows where they still put on a. weekly mock hanging for the tourists. A hot wind from the cast gusted up the High Street, filling my eyes with dust. Across the road tourists were panting up the hill but I didn't feel too sorry for them—unlike the locals, they could look forward to air-conditioning in their hotels. A couple of them turned into Deacon Brodie's Marijuana Club. I stood for a moment and watched. Guard personnel dressed in eighteenth-century costume were checking passports, making sure no Edinburgh citizens who'd managed to slip past the checkpoint got into the premises. One of them looked across suspiciously at my faded shorts and crumpled T-shim I stared back then took in the garishly painted building.

Like I said, there's a lot of irony about the way the Council's gone back on its anti-drugs policy. There's also plenty of cynicism. The city's a strictly no smoking zone for the natives on grounds of health but if foreigners want to fill their lungs with the smoke from cigarettes and joints supplied with the guardians' approval, who gives a shit? As long as they pay upfront.

I walked across the suntrap of the esplanade towards the castle gatehouse, ranks of guard vehicles drawn up on both sides. The guard command centre in the old fortifications is about as imposing a place as you can find, even in this spectacular city. It's just a pity that the battered Land-Rovers and rusting pick-ups make the place look like a scrap merchant's yard The only vehicle with any class is a ten-year-old Jeep donated to the Council by a grateful American tourist agency. Somehow it's ended up as Lewis Hamilton's personal transport.

I found the guardian in his quarters in what was once the Governor's House.

"Ah, there you are, Dalrymple," he said, looking up from the neat array of papers on his desk. "I was wondering when you'd show up. I suppose you want to find out if the missing lottery-winner is in my records."

"Well spotted, Lewis." I went over to the leaded windows and ran my eye over the northern suburbs. Across the firth I could just make out the hills of what was Fife in the old days and is now a Scottish version of the Wild West, complete with gunmen on horseback, massacres of the locals and abandoned mining towns—badlands in spades, pardner.

Hamilton joined me. "As much as another month of this bloody heat to go," he said, wiping the sweat from his wrinkled forehead. Although he was in his seventies, the public order guardian still had a firm grip on the City Guard. His beard and hair were almost completely white but his bearing was as military as ever. "Well, I've checked all my Restricted Files. There's no reference to Kennedy..." He broke off and went back to the papers on his desktop. "What the hell was his first name?"

"Fordyce," I said. "Fordyce Bulloch Kennedy."

"Thank you." Hamilton's acknowledgement was curt. He didn't like being helped out, especially by an auxiliary who'd been demoted from his own directorate.

I can never resist having a go at guardians, especially one as thin-skinned as my former boss. "You would tell me if he was one of your undercover operatives, of course."

The guardian's eyes bulged as he glared at me. Finally he managed to spit something out. "I tell you he's not."

"But how do I know you're telling the truth, Lewis?" I asked, prolonging the fun.

"How do you know...?" Hamilton took a couple of deep breaths. Even in these more open times guardians don't like having their veracity impugned, as Councilspeak would have it. Auxiliaries are taught tension control techniques but Lewis was appointed by the first Council and never went through the training programme—unlike me. "You're doing it deliberately, aren't you? Grow up, man."

"Grow up, man," I repeated dubiously. "Bit of an oxymoron, wouldn't you say?"

The desk telephone buzzed, saving me from the guardian's tongue. I watched his expression change as he answered.

"What?" Hamilton bellowed. "Where?" He listened for a couple of seconds. "When?" He listened again. "Any ID?"

Shit. I'd been calculating the odds of him running through the full set of interrogatives beginning with "wh".

"Very well Tell the barracks commander to keep me informed." He slammed the phone down.

"What's going on?" I asked, trying to give the impression of idle curiosity.

"Nothing for you to worry about, Dalrymple," Hamilton said, shuffling files.

Nothing makes me suspicious quicker than a guardian telling, me not to worry. "What is it, Lewis?" I said insistently.

He caught my tone and looked up. "Oh, very well. Body found by the Water of Leith. Sounds like heatstroke or the like."

"Tell me mote," I said, leaning over him.

"Middle-aged male. No identification on the body." The guardian glanced at me then reached over for a buff folder. "Ah, I see what you mean. What age is that missing lottery-winner?"

"Fifty-two."

"You don't think it's him, do you?"

"Only one way to find out, Lewis," I replied, heading for the door. "Call your people and tell them to keep their sticky fingers off the body till we get there."

The latest in books film and sound reviewed by people with time for crime

SAFE AS HOUSES BY CAROL ANNE DAVIS, DO-NOT PRESS, £7.50

David is a sadist who lives a double life. And he knows the reason why women are vanishing from the streets of Edinburgh: His Secret House is the place where he allows his darkest imaginings to achieve hideous life—but his devoted wife Jennifer is beginning to realise the dark undercurrents she is living so close to. This is the menacing psychological territory originally patented by Patricia Highsmith, but more recently colonised by Ruth Rendell and Minette Walters. As in her remarkable *Shrouded,* Davis confronts her jarring material with a clear-eyed and measured authority, allowing a fascinating play of sympathies as her narrative moves towards a grisly climax. As before, her dialogue has the reality of everyday speech (rather than some literary construct), and her new book is almost as unmissable as its predecessor.

Barry Forshaw

JIGSAW BY CAMPBELL ARMSTRONG, DOUBLEDAY, £14.99

One hundred people are killed when a bomb explodes on the London Underground and detective Frank Pagan is brought back from suspension to catch the culprit. Although there are not too many other deaths in this one the clichés pile up at every turn. Pagan the recovering alcoholic, who has lost his wife. The wider myth that people can do their jobs just as well or better after lots of alcohol. The stupid and overbearing Deputy Commissioner who wants regular reports. Stagy conversations, that would be silly in reality (why are they saying this?), to convey information. A powerful, all-seeing, businessman's organisation, with assassins dogging its enemies at every step, that would be invincible if real, but that comes undone for trivial reasons.

Campbell Armstrong is a Scot who lives in Ireland and he seems to take the ex-pats, remote, slightly unfamiliar, outdated and even contemptuous view of the old country. It has been quite a few decades since London was troubled by fog for example. And why the Americanisms 'apartment' for flat; 'elevator' for lift; 'hooker' for prostitute and 'hood' for bonnet?

Armstrong is a popular thriller writer—his books are well borrowed at libraries. Hailed on the jacket as 'the spirit of Jig lives on'—it is a sequel to *Jig*, a book about an IRA terrorist. In what way he manages to live on I will leave for the reader to discover. But it starts annoyingly slowly and it is not until about page 180 that things really get going. Some of the characters are obviously drawn from life—Gurenko is a thinly disguised Boris Yeltsin, one of the terrorists, 'Carlotta', is a female version of 'Carlos the Jackal' and 'the General' appears to be based on Markus Wolff of GDR Intelligence. But 'Stasi' is a western media term—they were actually known as the 'Konsum' or Co-op! But some of the plot turns on incredible points and unlikely coincidences. A high-class call girl accosts Pagan in the street to impart some information. She could not meet him formally because she is being followed. How this is evaded when they do meet is unclear. The police operation generally seems inauthentic and the conclusion more unlikely still. But somehow it sells well.

Mark Campbell

THE EYE OF THE BEHOLDER BY MARC BEHM, NO EXIT PRESS, £6.99

Often called the private eye novel to end all private eye novels, this is quite unique in combining a fascinatingly baffling puzzle and a wonderfully realised love story with a metaphorical descent into the underworld. In just 200 odd pages, Behm covers thirty years and a massive body count as his private eye (a disturbed and sociopathic figure) relentlessly tracks down the bisexual serial murderess whose speciality is disguise. As his protagonist, always referred to as The Eye, follows the killer as she murders her way through a series of moneyed partners, we are taken on a nightmare odyssey through every state in the US to a dark and disturbing climax. One thing is certain: the reader is quite unlikely to encounter anything like this again. This is unquestionably a dazzling one-off.

Judith Gray

THE BEAST MUST DIE BY NICHOLAS BLAKE, PAN £5.99

Pan's Classic Crime series is showcasing some absolutely cherishable titles, some of which have a distinguished reputation that makes one marvel at the fact that they've ever been allowed to go out of print. But are they as good as their reputations, or has memory lent enchantment? This most famous of Poet Laureate's Cecil Day Lewis' thrillers (written under his *nom de plume* of Nicholas Blake) still reads in the 1990s as one of the most compelling crime novels ever written. Famously filmed by Chabrol, the plot involves a detective fiction writer who plots a perfect murder, one that he himself will commit. When a personal tragedy destroys writer Frank Cairnes' life, his tracking down of the man responsible achieves a pathological intensity. But the final confrontation is not what the reader expects. With Blake's famous investigator Nigel Strangeways on hand, the sheer pleasure afforded by this book is guaranteed.

Judith Gray

THE BURGLAR WHO STUDIED SPINOZA BY LAWRENCE BLOCK, NO EXIT PRESS, £5.99

Block remains one of the smoothest operators in the crime writing fraternity, and his regular protagonist Bernie Rhodenbarr one of the most memorably characterised. The fact that Bernie isn't all he should be is one of the charms of a witty and abrasive series, and this time he's after the prized coin collection of a man called Colcannon, confident that his inside information will make collecting the spoils straightforward. The fact that the collection consists of just one coin sounds appealing, but Bernie finds (along with numerous other dangerous complications) that selling the coin is one of his principal problems. Plotting, as always, has the intricacy and precision of the finest Swiss watch, while the pithy first-person narrative allows even the most fastidious reader to be drawn into Bernie's murky world. And the continuing conceit of Bernie's impressive cultural baggage is another element that marks out this delectable series as very different from any of Block's rivals.

Eve Tan Gee

Marc Behm The Eye of the Beholder

EVANS ABOVE BY RHYS BOWEN, ALLISON & BUSBY,. £5. 99.

Journeying to Wales and Scotland has been likened to a walk along a pier—going abroad without getting seasick. A crime story set in North Wales has the advantage of the Welsh dialect and speech rhythm—although the philosopher Sir Walter Raleigh did say *"The Welsh are so damn Welsh it sounds like affectation"*.

Evan Evans is a likeable, well-educated, young police constable in the village of Llanfair (perhaps a subtle allusion to Llanfair ... P ... G., the longest town-name). Missing children, a returned paedophile, two climbers found dead on nearby Snowdon give him the intrigue, crime and pain he thought left behind in the Swansea force. He is intelligent, brave, sensible and ultimately proves his worth in capturing both the rather shadowy multiple murderer (for a third body is found on the mountain), another small girl

missing and a harmless but threatening lunatic.

This first book in Britain has several plus marks and one or two minus. It is written with humour—one lady does even say *"look you"*. There is neat, apt but not overwhelming description of an area which I do know. It is not like some crime books a textbook on mountaineering. Evan is the target of various young women especially the attractive schoolteacher and the pneumatic barmaid. There are cunning red herrings to divert him. There are no tedious love scenes to hold up the smooth action. This first 'tecker by Janet Quin-Harkin writing as a masculine Rhys Bowen (and strangely described as 'him' in the copyright clause) is to establish a repertory company which must mean the peaceful village will have as many crimes as a city as Sherlock Holmes stated. Evans politely takes the schoolteacher through the back door of the Red Dragon

Murder One for all the Pulp Fiction your heart desires.

Murder One where you can find all the Usual Suspects. If it's in Print, in English, we have it. If it's not in Print, we might well have it too. The **ultimate** mystery superstore. **Mail Order** all over the world. **Catalogue** on request.

Visit our spanking new, criminal website at www.murderone.co.uk **and** e-mail:106562.2021 @compuserve.com

Britain's Only Major Mystery Bookstore

71 -73 Charing Cross Rd, London WC2H 0AA, Tel 0171 734 3483 Fax 0171 734 3429

on a Sunday in this wet area as I recall entering an inn on a Sunday in a dry area!

The minus marks can be erased by a trifle more research in Britain or better proof-reading, as current living in San Francisco may explain. For examples, the two first corpses are described as wearing between them, stout boots, running shoes and hundred-pound shoes. Someone asks why Scotland Yard hasn't been called in—which has not happened for years. Evans cautions the murderer making the mistake Agatha Christie made of saying the words could be used against him—oh, no, it couldn't.

Another very good bonus point is that Alison & Busby have dropped the imitation Penguin plain covers in favour of graphic illustrations, which, if you look closely, give a clue to the mystery as did those beautiful Adams covers in paperback for Agatha Christie. The formula for a murder mystery quoted by Haycraft is one-half_Sherlock Holmes, one-quarter P. G. Wodehouse, one-eight sheer adventure and one-eighth anything you know best—Mrs. Quin-Harkin has followed this formula successfully to prove a worthy new recruit to the classic ranks.

John Kennedy Melling

HEARTWOOD BY JAMES LEE BURKE, ORION, £16.99

James Lee Burke is on a roll. *Cimarron Rose* won him the Edgar in 1997. In 1998, he won the CWA/The Macallan Gold Dagger with *Sunset Limited*, no mean feat on a shortlist which included Reginald Hill's *On Beulah Height*. And now in 1999 he has produced *Heartwood*. The first thing to be said is that it is just as good as its immediate predecessors.

In *Heartwood*, Burke returns to the Texas town of Deaf Smith, where passions assume Gothic proportions and life is sometimes lyrical, sometimes nasty but rarely dull. Much of the story is narrated in the first person by his lawyer hero Billy Bob, a former Texas Ranger with a psyche studded with scar tissue. Billy Bob does not have much time for Earl Dietrich. This is partly because Earl is a wealthy sociopath and partly because he's married to Peggy Jean, the woman to whom Billy Bob lost both his virginity and his heart when both they and the world were young. The relationship between the two men rapidly worsens when the Earl frames an impoverished neighbour with the theft of $300,000-worth of bearer bonds and an antique watch from the Alamo.

This is merely the starting point for a richly plotted story with a varied cast including Mexican gangsters, a blind Indian with the second sight, nasty rich kids, prostitutes, a plump and sexy female private eye, a rather nice religious maniac with paedophile tendencies, and a small horde of professional criminals and law-enforcement officials with interchangeable moral codes. Billy Bob is a hero in the classic mould, and at times *"classic"* comes perilously close to formulaic. Like a Swiss Army penknife he is equipped to deal with every eventuality with the possible exception of his own emotional problems. He survives a major beating and a horrendous case of food poisoning with a sprightly resilience Philip Marlowe himself would have envied. Occasionally he recalls Parker's Spenser when he becomes mawkishly sentimental or tiresomely politically correct.

Like those of so many American PI and/or noir protagonists, Billy Bob's cultural roots lie deep in the nineteenth century, in Billy the Kid and Wyatt Earp, in small towns ruled by the silver star and the sixgun. It seems eminently suitable that the book should reach a climax at a contemporary equivalent to the shoot-out at the OK Corral. On screen, Billy Bob

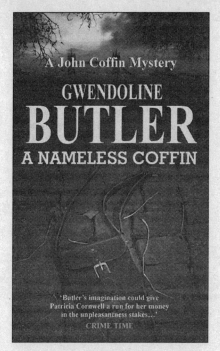

A John Coffin Mystery

GWENDOLINE
BUTLER
A NAMELESS COFFIN

'Butler's imagination could give
Patricia Cornwell a run for her money
in the unpleasantness stakes...'
CRIME TIME

would have made a challenging role for John Wayne.

And yet. The very best crime fiction ends up transcending and sometimes transforming its genre. *Heartwood* comes very close to doing that. As always, Burke writes beautifully, playing on the reader's responses with the skill of the virtuoso he is. The novel is essentially a modern fairytale providing its readers with entertainment and the thrills and spills of an emotional switchback — and also a moral for those who want one. To be human, you feel, is to be dysfunctional, especially if you live in Deaf Smith.

Don't miss this one.

Paul Duncan

A GRAVE COFFIN BY GWENDOLINE BUTLER, HARPERCOLLINS, £15.99

The first pre-requisite a great writer needs is verisimilitude. You must believe in the crime, plotting, characters and venues. You don't need pages of Dickensian description. Everybody believes in P. G. Wodehouse's Jeeves—yet the only descriptions given are *"a darkish respectful sort of johnny"* whose *"head sticks out a bit at the back."* Agatha Christie gave only a slight image of her characters not a pen-portrait. Verisimilitude doesn't mean *"realism."*

The other essential is output—consistency of it, too. The most popular writers are those with the impressive list of titles—Simenon, Christie, Queen, Carr, E. S. Gardner, Creasey—a dozen books doesn't mean you've arrived whatever the paperback sales. Gwendoline Butler qualifies as a great writer from superlative plotting, characterisation, psychology, locales in a steady output now reaching nearly seventy books, each better than the last.

A Grave Coffin has Commander John Coffin faced with two, if not through simultaneous crimes in which failure could bring him down, as happened in real life soon after this current book was printed. He is called on by the Home Office to investigate the collapse through treachery of the small force formed to combat illegal pharmaceutical drug manufacture. We can accept a small force specialised—I know of two forces, one with two officers, the other with three. Someone in his own manor is killing and chopping up small boys, whose families are connected with his own force. Thirdly one of his officers has vanished in shady circumstances. A field day for the gutter press—if he fails. An officer in the specialised force has been found—in five pieces—Mrs. Butler is clinically descriptive. All the other members must be checked, but they are all sound, if with secrets. A Nobel Prize winning professor at Oxford appears. Some small boys know more about the murders but wait to see if the police are clever enough to find out.

Someone attacks Coffin's lovely wife outside their Church tower home—was it the missing officer, presumed dead? A girl's body is dug up—and one of his senior officers reported blown up—for him! The ending has the Margaret Millar trick of three subtle, credible shocks in the last three pages. I had read Gwendoline Butler's books long before I was asked to review for *Crime Time* and I could draw the entire Tower Complex from her descriptions. She has a keen eye—the Coroner *"with unpolished shoes"* bowing to a professional colleague. Like Carr she can make an imaginary City so real that you go to look for it—as I have done. Gwendoline Butler qualifies as a great crime writer—again!

A NAMELESS COFFIN BY GWENDO-LINE BUTLER, CT PUBLISHING, £4. 99.

Gwendoline Butler, for one of the most sophisticated and erudite crime writers, possesses an eerie sense of evil, past, potential and future. In several of her seventy-odd books she describes phenomena we later recognise in life or other fiction.

In this early (1966) book she has a literal epidemic of handbag slashing and stealing which Divisional Detective Inspector John Coffin realises is a sexual symptom, some time before the psychiatrists jumped on this passing bandwagon. The story is divided between his South London manor and a delightful Scottish burgh named Murreinhead, not unlike those adjacent St. Andrews where Mrs. Butler lived with her late Husband Dr. Lionel Butler, the Vice-Principal of that University. The Scottish hero, no plastic James Bond, is a likeable baronet, Sir Giles Almond, a Writer to the Signet (Solicitor to Sassenachs) and Clerk of the Court. What can be the link between the dozens of slashings and murders of two women in London with a missing wom-an, strange court cases, attack on Almond's life and the drey father and son not exactly unsmeared by local crimes in Scotland? The advantage of these two locales enables Butler to cross-cut and edit her scenes in a way worthy of the great Alfred Hitchcock. She has more violence and hatred than most of the so-called hard-boiled writers—and we must not forget hard-boiled eggs often get cracked. Her biting dénouement, which I shall not reveal, is also decades ahead of later television and literary crime-writers. One of the few detective and crime stories you can read more than once—I have and I will!

Ken W. Ferris

RIDING THE SNAKE BY STEPHEN J CANNELL, MICHAEL JOSEPH, £9.99

Robert Ludlum may be read more in France these days than either the UK or America, but his progeny are as healthy as ever. Cannell customises the Ludlum formula with silk-smooth professionalism, and delivers a busy thriller of international intrigue and jaw-crunching action that makes it easy to forgive the less-than-elegant writing. When LA playboy Wheeler Cassidy (past his sell-by date but enjoying life) is obliged to look into the death of his younger brother, he finds himself involved in the same labyrinthine conspiracy that is occupying South Central cop Tanisha Williams. This involves a massively lethal Asian underworld and a criminal conspiracy that reaches to the most rarefied echelons of American government. Cassidy and Williams are serviceably (if conventionally) characterised, the latter's desire to escape from the doldrums of the Asian Crimes Task Force is a solidly-written motivation, and the narrative has the kind of frictionless energy that guarantees the reader's undivided attention.

Barry Forshaw

KILLJOY BY ANN CLEEVES, ALLISON & BUSBY, £4.99.

Newcastle is a City of fascinating contrasts—Hadrian's Wall, theatres, football, Cathedrals and Churches, The Literary & Philosophical Society, corruption scandals, ancient Guilds—and famous crimes. No wonder Ann Cleeves, who lives nearby, has chosen the City for her Inspector Ramsay 'teckers. She combines her knowledge and love of the City with her delineation of her personae, all of whom have flawed characters yet not to such a degree as to make them repellent. More is it perhaps that they carry the seeds of their own destruction within themselves—one man in this book leaving himself like a modern Lear finding everything in which he trusts being torn away by vicious and vengeful Furies.

An amoral teenage girl is found dead in the drama director's car-boot. Her family come from the slums with an anti-police bias running back years. The director and his mistress comprise one thread, her son and his *"friends"* another, a well-meaning Arts Trustee a third, plus a gang of thieves, joy riders and ram raiders the last. Another killing—blackmail—kidnapping—fraud—then Ramsay, who was infatuated with a suspect in the earlier novel, finds one suspect to be his boyhood mistress. The clues lead the reader on, until again like the earlier title, the dénouement in the last lines of the penultimate chapter, swerve violently towards another suspect.

Knowing Newcastle well, I found it fun to endeavour to trace some of her locales. Elego Martin's Dene—Jesmond Dene. Hallowgate—Gallowate—the slum Starling from Elsie perhaps? Otterbridgge—Corbridge? There are one or two aspects left in the air at the end; will the fraudster be prosecuted now? Why was the teenager learning Spanish? Also at least two relevant facts known to the susceptible Ramsay are not disclosed to the reader till the end.

The literary style is convincing, homogenous and fluent and the story reads well.

John Kennedy Melling

GATES OF EDEN BY ETHAN COEN, DOUBLEDAY, £12.99

Better than Ben Elton almost as smart as Woody Allen, Ethan Coen hijacks the celebrity-author, best-seller and takes it on a detour down Mean Street.

We know the brothers Coen from their smartly crafted and eccentrically populated films, each one with a pinch of Hammett here and a dash of Chandler there filtered through the lens of the Steadicam. As the screenwriter of films with such an obvious injection of the literary influence it's no surprise to see Ethan cross the divide from celluloid to print. And from the first paragraph it's obvious that this is a comic author who can cut it with the best of them. *Gates of Eden* is fourteen stories of knockabout farce, adolescent pain and wise guy goombahs all unmistakably inhabiting Planet Coen. If you loved *Raising Arizona* you'll love this. If you got *Miller's Crossing* you'll get this. Purists may find it too cute but this is a brand of knowing that works in context. Stories such as *Fever in the Blood*, *Destiny* and *The Gates of Eden* read like expanded scenes plucked from the centre of a Coen Brothers film. *Johnny Ga-Botz* and *Hector Berlioz, Private Investigator* are throwaway farces straight out of the pages of *Getting Even* except where Woody's wannabe intellectualism crosses Flaubert with The Marx Brothers this is Chandler acted out by the Three Stooges. There is a tenderness in the more personal stories such as *I Killed Phil Shapiro* and a sharply felt poignancy in the vignette of domestic Manhattan *A Morty Story* . At his best he manages to evoke

Raymond Carver in the acutely drawn despair of *The Boys*. But these are the exceptions. The bulk of the stories are cool, razor-slices of genre life. The most comic, *Cosa Minapolidan*, is a wonderful blend of the small-town gothic of *Fargo* and the knowing stereotyping of *Goodfellas* where a trainee mob extortionist is prompted by his partner in the etiquette of verbal threat. The prose throughout is very dialogue driven. Coen can convey the cadence of low-life speech with an authenticity lacking in many genre authors. Despite the eccentricity of the scenarios there is an unselfconscious quality to the writing that sets him apart from the majority of the dilettante celebrity authors. Unsurprising perhaps when you consider the richness of language in the dialogue throughout *Miller's Crossing*. Although the roll call of influences is obvious the stories have a clarity, humour and humanity that is distinctly Coenesque. You get the impression that Ethan had a blast writing this and the enthusiasm is infectious. As Richard Price and Bruce Robinson have shown, writing for screen and writing for print needn't be mutually exclusive. And if Ethan Coen can produce his own personal *Clockers* while still knocking out pearls of cinema like *Fargo* then there's something to look forward to in the new millennium after all.

Mike Paterson

ANGELS FLIGHT BY MICHAEL CONNELLY, ORION, £9.99

When a lawyer, who makes his living suing the Los Angeles Police Department, is found shot dead on the 'Angels Flight' funicular railway suspicion falls on the police themselves. If there ever was a man who had to go down the mean streets although not himself mean, it would be Detective Harry Bosch and he is given the case.

The Police Chief is anxious for the credibility of his department, working in the shadow of the OJ Simpson case — a situation with similarities in London. But this is LA in the 90s and you couldn't be anywhere else. Connelly (interviewed in Crime Time 2.4) a former police reporter for the *Los Angeles Times*, has set new standards for modern realistic mysteries. No surfeit of murders or morbid mania for him to achieve tension and suspense. *"Bosch nodded. He reached over and opened the door. He got out without another word and started back towards his car. He was running before he got there. He didn't know why. There was no hurry. It was no longer raining. He just knew he had to keep moving to keep from screaming."*

Michael Harris, a black man acquitted in the so-called 'Black Warrior' case, where a young white girl, Stacey Kincaid, was abducted and murdered, is widely believed to be guilty within the police force. Questions of miscarriages of justice; wrong verdicts and just who is getting away with what criss-cross through the book. Moral issues and boundaries are raised. Bosch wants to find the killers but sees that that issue has been submerged and side-tracked by others. The case is always in imminent danger of slipping out of Bosch's hands. *"...don't have the time to wait on a warrant. I'm going in. A homicide case is like a shark."* Bosch warns a colleague, *"It's gotta keep moving or it drowns."*

It concludes with sadness and anger in a gripping end that is as far from *"just one thing I don't understand inspector"* as you could get. This is the sixth Harry Bosch and Connelly has also written two non-series books — *The Poet* and *Blood Work* which reminds me I still have some guaranteed good reading ahead.

Martin Spellman
And a second view...

What is it about kiddie-fiddling? Used to be we drew the curtains or gave that sweaty neighbour a sly sideways glance if we saw him washing the car of a Sunday morning. Now it's everywhere. We're all at it, so to speak. You can't turn on the telly or open a book without abused youngsters come tumbling out like so much dirty laundry. Such a to-do for the new taboo.

And it's lazy. *very* lazy. It's all too frequently there just to get a rise, and, regrettably, it works. That's what it does at the heart of Michael Connelly's latest. Kiddie-fiddlers, paedophile web-sites, racial tensions in the City of Angels: all the right buttons to merit himself one of those ugly cardboard standees at airport bookstores.

Hotshot black civil rights lawyer Howard Elias is found gunned down on the eve of a major suit against the LAPD. His client is a man found not guilty in the kidnapping and killing of a 12 year-old white girl. A BLACK man. So light the blue touch paper. Or call Hieronymus 'Harry' Bosch (spiteful parents or smartarse author?), an honest cop adrift on a sea of corruption. Can he find Elias' killer, solve the previous case AND keep the lid on post-Rodney King Los Angeles? Three guesses.

Angels Flight (and yes, the lack of apostrophe does feel somehow wrong) is a well greased machine. It stamps out cookie-cutter characters, inks in a tourist guide view of the city and spews up ribbons of wannabe-tough, information-packed dialogue; exactly what it says on the box. Connelly's prose is adequate to the task but nothing more. And then only chasing bad guys—on the odd occasion he strays in to Bosch's brief, disintegrating marriage (*"'You break my heart, Eleanor. I always hoped that I could make you feel alive again.'"*) the book piles on clichés like Vanessa Feltz piles on the

pounds. He's awful on emotions, can't write women for toffee, and his insights in to the city's complex, seething race relations are tissue thin.

Harrison Ford will play Bosch on film. Figures.

Gerald Houghton

EVERY DEAD THING BY JOHN CONNOLLY, HODDER AND STOUGHTON, £10

This is John Connolly's first novel featuring detective 'Bird' Parker. Hailed on the dust jacket as 'the most terrifying read since *Silence of the Lambs*' this is actually a horror fantasy. There are some parallels with James Patterson's *Kiss the Girls*, published in 1995, in that the 'monster' does not play much part in the story and is revealed very late. Like many 500 pagers it is really two books back-to-back — one about a child murderer and the other about a human vivisectionist.

An FBI man theorises with Bird: *"We were always afraid that one would come who was different from the others, who was motivated by something more than a twisted, frustrated sexuality or wretched sadism. We live in a culture of pain and death, Bird, and most of us go through life without really understanding that. Maybe it was only a matter of time before we produced someone who understood that better than we did, someone who saw the world as just one big altar on which to sacrifice humanity, someone who believed he had to make an example of us all."*

What we have here is a 'super serial killer'— piling body on body and perversity on perversity. There can be no future for the genre in this kind of contest. Actual serial killers like Ed Gein, the model for aspects of *'Silence of the Lambs'*; Jeffrey Dahmer; John Wayne

Gacy and Dennis Nilsen were alienated loners with no normal social life, who committed their murders over a long period. The 'super serial killer' appears to be a socially integrated and connected person whose murders reach massacre level over a short time. If the serial killer here is no more logical than Freddy Krueger, there is still a real writer at work. One can only hope he's more rigorous in future books.

Martin Spellmann

CRIME ZERO BY MICHAEL CORDY, BANTAM PRESS, £10.99

More and more thrillers are being written in what has become a new sub-genre, the tale of a lethal mission in some kind of blighted futuristic society. Ten years ago, these books would have been called SF, but such is the breakdown of barriers in the literary world, that few bother to make the distinction. Cordy's energetic and ambitious novel depicts a world in which violent crime has become a global epidemic, with the US being the fulcrum. Society has given up on everything from the death penalty to liberal reform, but a powerful group of scientists has come up with Project Conscience. And those familiar with Burgess' *Clockwork Orange* will recognise a spin on his concept—this time it's gene (rather than aversion) therapy to treat male criminals and remove their destructive instincts. Criminal psychologist Luke Decker and geneticist Kathy Kerr are opposed to the scheme, but they discover that the ramifications are even more extreme than they suspected. Credible and imaginative, this is a novel that rarely relaxes its grip, even if the desire to keep the reader transfixed has led Cordy into producing some rather breathless prose at times. Nevertheless, despite flaws, a highly effective thriller.

Barry Forshaw

CHRISTENDOM BY NEIL CROSS, JONATHAN CAPE, £10

Former soldier and smuggler Malachi Thorndyke has drifted into alcoholism and is living in the South Australian Reclamation when he is approached by a couple who want him to undertake the most crucial smuggling trip of his life. This will take him to New Jerusalem, capital of the Christian fundamentalist state that America has become. He is to carry a document that will change the course of history. There are thrillers, and then there are literary thrillers. Which category does this one belong to? Cross seems determined to break across every possible genre with this dazzling and elaborate novel. The use of language has real brio, and while the narrative functions as a bizarre hybrid of the thriller and the SF novel, Cross clearly has another agenda: without ever over-stressing his points, he has produced as damning a document on the evils of religious fundamentalism (of any creed) that one is likely to encounter. As in his first, much-acclaimed novel, *Mister In Between*, there is some subtle and arresting writing on offer here, with only the merest missteps.

Barry Forshaw

JOURNEY INTO FEAR BY ERIC AMBLER, PAN, £5.99

There are many neglected authors in the crime and thriller pantheon, but the most shamefully neglected is undoubtedly Eric Ambler. Considered by such masters as Graham Greene and John Le Carré to be the greatest of all English thriller writers, his fall from grace (at least as far as the fact that most of his books are out of print is concerned) is astonishing. Pan, therefore, are to be heartily acclaimed for bringing some of his finest books back into print, embellished with the glowing imprimatur of modern master Robert Harris. The engineer Graham, an Englishman undertaking a terrifying flight across wartime Europe, is the archetypal Ambler hero, an ordinary man attempting to survive in extraordinary circumstances of massive danger and corruption. The modern spy story begins here, with all the comfortable right-wing certainties of an earlier generation of thriller writers seeming remote and implausible. There's no denying that certain elements of Ambler's narratives have dated a trifle, but that shouldn't deter those who've not yet treated themselves to his consummately well-written thrillers.

Barry Forshaw

THE DEVIL'S TEARDROP BY JEFFREY DEAVER, HODDER & STOUGHTON, £10.00

Deaver has proved himself to be one of the most accomplished of current thriller practitioners, and *The Bone Collector* (soon to be filmed) was his breakthrough novel. But his customary protagonist Lincoln Rhyme makes a only a walk-on appearance in this new novel, which is initially less impressive: here FBI forensic document expect Parker Kincaid is caught up in a dizzying narrative that tests both his scientific knowledge and his survival ability. When a man fires a silenced machine gun through a paper bag in a crowded Metro station, this is a prelude to an audacious demand: If the mayor of Washington DC does not pay 20 million dollars, the gunman will strike again. When the brains behind this operation is killed in a hit and run accident, it's up to Kincaid to stop the implacable gunman from killing again and again. Kincaid is not as strikingly characterised as the eccentric Rhyme, but he is a more than a serviceable hero, and the nimble plotting that has served Deaver well in the past is strongly to the fore here. Initial impressions aside, another winner.

Brian Ritterspak

BLOOD RAIN BY MICHAEL DIBDIN, FABER, £16.99

In the desperately overcrowded world of fictional detectives, only the most distinctive have a chance of staying the course. Dibdin's wonderfully characterised Aurelio Zen already has a copper-bottomed following, but it's not just the author's skill in bringing his protagonist to life that makes the series so intoxicating: Dibdin's luminescent abilities in creating for the reader the Italian locations in which his dogged sleuth deals with corruption and bloody murder are every bit as important, and linger in the mind quite as long as the convoluted and thoughtful plots. This time around, Zen is presented with the order that he hoped he would never receive: he is to be posted to Sicily. All the slippery skill and cunning that carried him through the lethal business of the earlier books is called into play in this milieu where the concept of omertà rules supreme. A wagonload of rotting goods parked on a siding at Passo Martino begins a deadly trail that has Zen struggling for his life against the backdrop of the smouldering Mount Etna. In this novel, Dibdin initiates a striking change in his protagonist, one of the many pleasures awaiting the reader.

Barry Forshaw

RESURRECTING SALVADOR BY JEREMY DRONFIELD, HEADLINE, £9.99

Jeremy Dronfield's second novel is a tense, psychological thriller cast in the Barbara Vine vein. Three women meet at the funeral of one of an old friend from college, killed after a fall at the French chateau of the La Simarde family, into which she married. Dronfield deftly blends layers of narrative, short stories, diary entries and even the rather novel inclusion of a computer adventure game to lead the reader through the past of the three women, their dead friend, Lydia, and her husband, Salvador, musical genius and scion of the sinister La Simarde family. Dronfield leads us back through their past relationships at college, and the history of the La Simarde, piling revelation upon revelation until the truth about Salvador and his monstrous mother is seemingly laid bare. Dronfield's skill as a writer is in no doubt, and his prose, although over-written in places and teetering on the brink of pretension, is more than sufficient to explore the past and present psyches of the main characters, and to create a dark, claustrophobic atmosphere. His sense of place when describing college life at Cambridge is faultless, particularly when exploring the intimate geography of the town and colleges, and he shows a remarkable taste for the neo-Gothic, shot through with welcome flashes of humour, in his recreation of the snow-bound, replica French chateau in rural Devon. His characters are also fully-fleshed and relatively sympathetic in their angst and self-doubt, although a touch of parody is occasionally evident here and there. Barring a fairly meaningless sub-plot about wartime French collaborators and the slightly hysterical climax, *Resurrecting Salvador* is an ambitious novel that succeeds very well, and Dronfield a writer to watch.

Dan Staines

EVERYBODY SMOKES IN HELL BY JOHN RIDLEY, BANTAM PRESS, £9.99

Double trouble. Paris Scott, a dreamer who works in a 7/24 store, has a Chaplinesque *City Lights* encounter with pop star Ian Germaine in Hollywood. He walks off with an unpublished tape and Germaine's agent, the worthless Chad Bayless, sends two henchmen after him for it. Meanwhile his flatmate, Buddy, has been involved in lifting a kilo of pure heroin off a dealer, who likewise sends two

of his henchmen after that. Buddy hides the H in the bag with the tape so...

Ridley has been a stand-up comedian, script writer and film director and this is his third novel, after *Stray Dogs* and *Love is a Racket*. Described as a 'funny, fast and angry novel' and written by a black man from Los Angeles, it has parallels with the work of Chester Himes. Himes's wife, Lesley, recounted how Chester used to laugh when typing out his stories. Humour is almost essential when dealing with the low-life, which otherwise seems boring, moronic and pointless. This was a problem in Richard Price's *Clockers* where a lot of time is spent on aimless, hanging out. But Himes had lived the life himself and doubtless saw much more and worse than he could write about. As in *Love is a Racket,* Paris is a loser like Jeffty was. While womanhating would be expected for some of the characters it is a bit too pervasive and Paris might have been exempted. Bachman-Turner Overdrive's *You Ain't Seen Nothing Yet* accompanies the activities of the psycho-killer but perhaps Marley's *No Woman—No Cry* would have been a more appropriate theme. Homosexual desire arises and a hint of lesbianism is included, although that only supports the misogyny.

This is a well paced, funny book. The number of bodies gets top heavy for the plot toward the end but as it is only half serious you don't really mind. The downer is that while Ridley gathers the ingredients for a cracking ending he seems to let them walk out the door when it comes to it—so you are left without the firm punch and closure you might expect.

Martin Spellman

COLD HIT BY LINDA FAIRSTEIN, LITTLE, BROWN, £10.99

With no less than Patricia Cornwell around to add her imprimatur to this thriller, Fairstein starts with an advantage. Does she justify the pat on the back she gets here? When Assistant DA Alexandra Cooper is called to view the body of a young woman whose body has been pulled from the river with her hands and feet tied to a ladder, Cooper is soon in a hunt for a determined killer across a picturesquely realised New York. Fairstein's heroine is a very solid creation, owing not a little to her obvious inspiration Cornwell (hence, no doubt, the latter's nod of approval) and she's as acute at characterising the well-heeled villains of the piece as the dogged NYPD detectives Chapman and Wallace who help Cooper crack the mystery. It's also refreshing to find a clear and mordant intelligence at work behind the kind of narrative that all too often simply offers mindless thrills. New York is conjured up with a freshness that is particularly surprising given the desperate over-familiarity of the city for most thriller readers.

Eve Tan Gee

CITY OF ICE JOHN FARROW, CENTURY, £10

When a bomb explodes in a crowded Montreal street, the victims include both a Mob lawyer and an innocent child. Present, and helpless to prevent the bloodshed, is Emile Cinq-Mars, one of Montreal's most celebrated policemen. When the corpse of a young man is found with a meat hook through his heart and a calling card in English, Cinq-Mars finds that the young man had infiltrated the Mob, and he is drawn back to the bombing. Farrow's massive thriller has the pace of a much slimmer book, and his unyielding protagonist follows a fascinating trail involving the Russian Mafia and an endangered female infiltrator within the organisation. In the final analysis, there are very few new elements in Farrow's well-structured narrative, but the author's in-

telligence and peppy plotting keep the reader comprehensively gripped.

Judith Gray

SCORPIAN RISING BY ANTHONY FREWIN, NO EXIT PRESS, £6.99

The acclaim that greeted Frewin's remarkable *London Blues* took everyone by surprise, and set Frewin (who was also assistant film director to Stanley Kubrick for over 20 years) a daunting task: the follow-up. Within a couple of chapters, it's clear that he's pulled off the same magic as in his last book: plotting that is both delirious and utterly plausible, a sleazy, fetid atmosphere (here, a fading seaside town) and wonderfully unpredictable characters. When leading crime figure Sidney Blattner hears that his innocent brother has been executed in Margate, he sets out (*Get Carter*-style), to find out who the killers were. Two of his aides are murdered, and Vince, Sid's star performer, is sent down to open a very nasty can of worms. Perhaps the bare bones of the plot are warmed-over, but it's what Frewin does with his narrative that is so intoxicating. *London Blues* fans need not hesitate—and, incidentally, the title isn't misspelled.

Brian Ritterspak

RECKLESS HOMICIDE BY IRA GENBERG, NO EXIT PRESS, £5.99

Michael Ashmore is a senior partner at a top law firm. His brother Charlie is a well-respected pilot for a major airline. But when Charlie's daughter dies in a horrible accident, and his wife divorces him, Charlie starts taking barbiturates. One night he loses control of his plane, and Brandon Air Lines sacks him, refusing to accept there was a mechanical fault. Michael succeeds in reinstating him, but then another plane that Charlie is piloting goes down, and this time there are no survivors. In allowing his drug-addicted brother to fly the plane, over a hundred passengers have died, and Michael is charged with, yes, you've guessed it, reckless homicide.

Reckless Homicide is cast In the John Grisham mould from page one, and although the book jacket suggests otherwise, the crash itself is a minor part of the narrative, merely setting up the courtroom battle that will follow. And very much a battle it is, with the wronged lawyer and his (lover) defence attorney fighting against the combined force of a Government that doesn't want to admit liability and a vast corporation that doesn't want to pay out massive compensation.

The courtroom scenes are where the novel really gets into its stride, and Genberg., apparently a prominent trial attorney, amply demonstrates his first-hand experience with legal drama. The cut and thrust of the opposing arguments are deftly handled, and the dialogue is crisp and tense. Which is just as well, because outside the courtroom, Genberg has a problem with believable prose, imbuing every sentence with unnecessary, and sometimes downright ludicrous, embellishment. No simile is left unturned, in his endless quest for ever more purple prose. This is a good one: *"His mouth [forces] his lips slightly upward into the faint smile of a soldier struggling to rally the troops while a fresh wound gushes blood."*

As well as the legal angle, Genberg fills the novel with Christian references, and there is an odd moment when the judge quotes from Leviticus. Michael Ashmore is a Jew, and the plane's fatalities are all black churchgoers attending a Baptist convention. What is to be made of all this I don't know, but at least it adds an extra dimension to the narrative.

So, forget about the...shall we say, enthusiastic prose, and just enjoy the excitement of the courtroom scenes. There are twists and turns aplenty, and a palpable sense of reality in the legal manoeuvring, as each attorney plays to the jury and squeezes the maximum benefit from their witnesses. And while Michael himself is perhaps too squeaky clean to be entirely credible (a *"soft hearted, hard-headed, trial lawyer"* is the book blurb's clichéd description), no doubt you'll be rooting for him in the end. I was.

Brian Ritterspak

MURDER MOST FOUL: THE KILLER AND THE AMERICAN GOTHIC IMAGINATION BY KAREN HALT-TUNEN, HARVARD UNIVERSITY PRESS, £18.50

Murder Most Foul is entertaining and ambitious, continually exuding a confident authority. It also flies in the face of the conventional wisdom which says that Edgar Allan Poe invented detective fiction. The author, Professor Karen Halttunen, traces the style back to the execution sermons of Puritan New England. The words of the preachers who worked at the foot of the gallows were transcribed by the devout and devoured by the curious. By reconstructing the readership for such documents, Halttunen tries to show us where crime fiction began.

For the Puritans, murder was 'merely' everyday sin extended to its logical conclusion. Drinking led to homicide with tragic inevitability. Over time, readers of the sermons got hooked on the mechanics of murder: discovering corpses and culprits, imagining motives. Family sagas proved especially popular. In turn, such morbid preoccupations meant that killers were set up as being a breed apart: the murderer as mental alien. The crime the Puritans viewed as a mortal sin which anyone could commit was gradually reinvented as something only a peculiarly deranged mind could manage. Halttunen shows how professions like medicine and the law all played a role in making the murderer different. Whereas the religious interpretations of murder made everyone a potential killer, the new approach saw the criminal as a separate species. Strangely this was almost the mirror image of the church's approach, in that both seemed to deny choice-making as a human ability.

If we're to understand where crime fiction comes from, we should recognise that its roots were non-literary. That, at least, is Halttunen's provocative argument. Perhaps the book bends the stick too far in this direction: present-day 'true crime' writers and the makers of *Se7en* have probably never heard of the Puritan execution sermon, never mind been inspired by its successors. Nevertheless, she lifts the lid on the fascinating and forgotten world of 18th century New England.

William Field

HANNIBAL BY THOMAS HARRIS, HEINEMANN, £16.99

Any reviewer of Thomas Harris' utterly compelling third book in his sequence featuring the cultured monster Dr Hannibal Lecter has to decide how much to give away of the brilliantly constructed plot: but rest assured that this review will only be indiscreet in its very last sentence. Although not quite the equal of its remarkable predecessors, this is a wonderfully engrossing thriller, with all the elements of the earlier books creatively replayed (Clarice Starling's vulnerability, the mendacity of her FBI superiors, Lecter's Moriarty-like cunning and love of high culture—plus, of course, the grisly violence that is unquestionably not for the squeamish). But in the long gap since the last book, Harris has freshened the brew with some amazing narrative surprises that (with only one or two moments of unfortunate slackening) maintain the iron grip

of the earlier books (even during the long middle section set in a vividly-realised Florence in which Clarice Starling does not appear), and the characters have the solidity of Harris at his best. But (and here's that revelation) many have been—and will be—disquieted by the strangely ambiguous ending in which monstrous evil appears not only to go unpunished but even rewarded. This writer, at least, sees this as a set-up for the final reckoning of a fourth book—which one can only hope will be as unmissable as this.

The Long Wait...has Thomas Harris delivered the Goods?

In the ten or so years that it has taken Thomas Harris to complete the fourth book in what has become his Hannibal Lecter sequence (the cannibalistic doctor being a subsidiary character in the first book, with a smaller part in *Silence of the Lambs* than people remember—his considerable impact enlarges his role retrospectively in the mind), the anticipation built up has been such that the *Evening Standard*'s literary editor called this the most significant sequel since *Paradise Regained*. But the same paper's Christopher Hudson lamented our fascination with such an unspeakable monster, and several reviewers have found the gruesome finale difficult to accept, for a variety of reasons. But for those happy to admit that evil can be utterly fascinating, the praise for the new book was high indeed. *The Observer* called it *"wicked and witty—the novel of the year"*, while Will Self in the *Independent* called it a *"momentous achievement"*. Some writers (notably Joan Smith and Kim Newman) have found the ending unconvincing—but even the book's most hardened detractor could honestly claim they predicted the remarkable narrative conceits Harris springs on the reader. The most common view has been that of the book's supporters—and they have been unstinting in their praise.

Barry Forshaw

IGUANA LOVE BY VICKI HENDRICKS, SERPENT'S TAIL, £8.99 PBK, £15.99 HBK

Noir is a man thing. What I mean is that only men seem to write noir. I do not know why this is. Perhaps men just like to moan a lot more than women, and noir is often just about men moaning about how unfair life is and how evil people are. So, when *Iguana Love* popped through the door, I was suitably intrigued, especially since Hendricks' first novel *Miami Purity* (which I have not read) had many glowing testimonies. This is supposed to be white-trash noir.

Ramona Romano, a nurse, is married to Gary, only she does not love him with that all-enveloping love that excludes her from thinking about fucking other men. He loves her more than she loves him, so she has the power in the relationship. Gary is not enough for her. She wants something else. She wants to feel that all-enveloping love. So Ramona goes down to a club where divers hang out and puts herself about, fucking who she can. She becomes infatuated with the mysterious Enzo, who keeps standing her up because he has 'business' to attend to. In the mean time, she fucks Charlie, who is impotent, so that doesn't work out.

Gary knows what Ramona is up to so, in despair, he kills the neighbour's snake and leaves it in the shower. This is a pretty desperate cry for help if you ask me. Needless to say, cruelty to animals is not tolerated and Gary is thrown out never to see another line of dialogue in the book. To replace Gary, Ramona captures a five foot iguana which is on a tree outside her apartment. Yes, you heard me right—a five foot iguana! She keeps it in her apartment, it does not like her, it stays under the bed, totally still, unblinking. Obvious-ly, this is a symbol, but I am not quite sure what of.

From that moment on, Ramona loses all her inhibitions, maxs out all her credit cards joining the diving club and buying all the gear so that she can be among the men she craves. She is excited by the thought of all the men desiring her. She then fucks her way though a few of them, to revel in their bodies. This is a book about power, and one woman's attempt to get it. Throughout, she is reminded of her puny strength compared to that of the men, because she cannot lift something or she is forced into a situation because of a man's physical strength. In the hands of another writer, the noir aspect of this could be emphasised, and the atmosphere leaden with doom, but Hendricks concentrates on how much fun Ramona has getting laid with lots of different men. The sad thing about Ramona is that she is defined by men—she constantly compares herself to them. She has no identity outside of those reference points. She has no contact with any other women in the book. Perhaps this is an (obscure) comment on how Vicki Hendricks feels as a female noir writer in a male field, or is a general comment on women in society.

What we have here is a competently written book, with some interesting ideas, which do not make a satisfying whole. A far more biting look at the psychology of white-trash can be found in the books of Harry Crews, and for body building in particular look to his novel *Body*.

Paul Duncan

FOUR CORNERS OF NIGHT BY CRAIG HOLDEN, MACMILLAN, £9.99

Nine am in an unnamed Mid West city. Policemen Bank Arbaugh and Mack Steiner have just come off the night shift. But they don't get their breakfasts: over the radio they hear that a teenage girl is missing, and the two men realise that disturbing echoes of the past have reappeared. Seven years before, Bank's own daughter similarly disappeared. Holden is highly skilful at pointing up the parallels between the two cases and characterises his two cops with remarkable psychological concision. His first two novels, *The River Sorrow* and *The Last Sanctuary* had frequent infelicities but demonstrated a growing assurance that is consolidated in this third novel. The revelations that are so effective here are prepared for with subtly and intelligence, although the perspicacious reader may see some of them coming— and a little more work would have remedied this. Nevertheless a solid piece of crime writing.

Judith Gray

MALICE AFORETHOUGHT BY FRANCIS ILES, PAN, £5.99

The rediscovery of this well-loved jewel in the crown of crime novels began with a sympathetic TV adaptation some years ago. But Iles, consummate plot-creator that he is, has nevertheless a writer's tone of voice that can only be present in the novel. This was a book that reinvented the crime novel form. When Dr Bickleigh decides to murder his wife in the small but exclusive Devonshire hamlet of Wyvern's Cross, the (then) radical concept of announcing to the reader the identity of the murderer at the very beginning of the novel created a storm. Amazingly, despite years of imitation, the device still functions as compellingly in the 90s as when the novel was first written. The beleaguered Bickleigh (and his mounting passion for Gwynfryd Rattery) is rightly recognised as one of the best-remembered protagonists of crime fiction, and there are few who will regret reacquainting themselves with this beautifully-crafted piece.

Brian Ritterspak

COLD CUT BY JAMES H JACKSON, HEADLINE, £9.99

The fact that Frederick Forsyth house described James H. Jackson as a young British thriller writer who will go for may not be too persuasive: after all, Forsyth has praised as many tyro writers as has Stephen King. But in this case, he was the right on the button, and the impressive *Dead Headers* is here followed up by a thriller that cunningly utilises Jackson's previous career (as an International Defence and Political Risk Consultant) to produce a novel that has real energy and pace. *Cold Cuts* is a punning title: Russia has long used Siberia as the Soviet Union's unofficial graveyard since the revolution. But when the bodies turning up include some which are mutilated or half-eaten, it's a cue for Colonel Georgi Lazin of Russia's Federal Security Service to be sent East to investigate. Jackson's spin on the Cruz Smith innovation of sympathetic Soviet cop vs. conniving authorities is fresh and invigorating enough to make one forgive the borrowings: as Colonel Lazin becomes aware that his political masters do not necessarily require him to discover the perpetrators of the deaths, a narrative of genuine tension is guaranteed for the reader. And Jackson's conjuring up of his frigid locale will have you pleasurably shivering.

Eve Tan Gee

LOVELY MOVER BY BILL JAMES, PAN, £5.99

If you are one of the many admirers of James' accomplished Harpur and Iles books, this fifteenth entry in the series will be eagerly devoured. Initially, the impression is of one of the lesser H&I narratives: engaging but strangely distanced. James, however, has a strategy—and the precise and geometric plotting slowly builds the novel until it attains the emphatic power of his best books. Dealing with rival drug

"GORMAN'S WRITING IS FAST, CLEAN AND SLEEK AS A BULLET"
- DEAN R KOONTZ

THE LONG MIDNIGHT
by ED GORMAN

A PLACE TO DIE FOR...
Meredith Sawyer had grown up at Dr Richard Candlemas's academy—a place she has spent her life trying to forget. Candlemas was gifted with telekinetic powers and an undeniable brilliance, and so were the special children he recruited.

A MIND TO KILL FOR
Meredith has tried to forget the energies the children unleashed with their minds... and the secrets that had drawn her sister into Candlemas's inner circle of favourites. Now, with her sister long dead, Meredith is a Chicago reporter, with Candlemas's school only a bad memory

A TERROR TO SCREAM FOR
Then police detective Tom Gage investigates the bizarre murder of an academy teacher. His journey into the twisted alleyways of the past leads to the answers Gage needs ... and sweeps Meredith into a vortex of terror. For the truth about Candlemas foretells terrible destruction-and puts Meredith and Gage into a race with death.

syndicates and an elegantly turned-out spy from London (the *"Lovely Mover"* of the title), this one finds DCI Colin Harpur working undercover and playing a dangerous game with the sinister Keith Vine, drug dealer extraordinaire. As always with James, the writing has an elegance and precision that might seem to belong more to the literary novel. But as a thriller writer James is in the very top bracket.

Judith Gray

MOUTH TO MOUTH BY MICHAEL KIMBALL, HEADLINE, £9.99

Because it is set in Maine, Michael Kimball's second thriller will draw comparisons to Stephen King, which is apt because King helped Kimball get started as a novelist. It's also inevitable because *Mouth to Mouth* is structured much like a horror novel, particularly in its slow build-up to the revelation to true evil lurking beneath a seductive surface. But it wouldn't be fair to take the comparison much farther, because Kimball is his own man, and this is an excellent novel.

Kimball seduces his readers via a literal seduction which is the first part of the novel. It begins with the unexpected return of Scott Chambers' nephew Neal, returns to Maine after twelve years to show up at the wedding of Chambers' pregnant teenage daughter Moreen. Neal's arrival distracts Ellen Chambers from her unease at her daughter's marriage to a violent drug dealer, Randy. Neal's return provides a new focus for her life in rural Maine, where her husband's business is failing and her daughters' friends are becoming increasingly dangerous. As Ellen finds herself drawn more and more towards Neal, the past begins to draw itself to the surface, and as the seduction takes place, it becomes evident that it's consequences may be more serious than anyone could imagine.

There are guilty secrets buried all over the Chambers' farm, and revenge is the way they will be re-exposed. Throughout this long scene-setting process, Kimball maintains the book's tension through the give and take of the seduction, which is nowhere near as simple as it may sound. It works primarily because his female point of view is utterly convincing, including a couple of very effective sex scenes written from the female perceptions. The root of horror is internal, and Kimball has found a way of bringing the most powerful of internal feelings to bear in order to create suspense. He tempers this with more bravura writing, in his portrayal of the casual violence and hopeless drug-life of rural Maine, which he does with the same sort of sympathy and menace that Daniel Woodrell has expressed in the Ozarks.

His scene of Randy in the barn, shooting up another teenaged girl at his own wedding, carries exactly the sort of smouldering sexuality and menace to be both alluring and repulsive. It's the sort of thing a generation of American creative writing professors have made their livings doing for the cheap thrilling of a would-be literary audience, but few have done it this well.

In fact, Kimball's writing is so effective that when the story switches gears and becomes more of a suspense thriller, it's something of a let-down, partly because some of these interesting side-plots and characters, like Ray LaFlamme, the local gangster, or Rooftop, local muscle, don't necessarily get their fair share of the spotlight. It also because the physical resolution of the story simply isn't as fascinating as the psychological build-up. It can't be. But that's a price I'm certainly willing to pay. *Mouth toMouth* will please readers across a number of genres, but mostly it will please fans of quality writing.

Michael Carlson

DEATH IN THE PEERLESS POOL BY DERYN LAKE, HODDER & STOUGHTON, £16.99

Lake's earlier outings for John Rawlings and John Fielding, the London magistrate known as the Blind Beak, have achieved a considerable following, not least among fellow crime practitioners such as Lindsey Davis and Jonathan Gash. Her followers will relish this new excursion into a richly created 18th century with Rawlings (her apothecary-come-sleuth) relaxing in the popular swimming baths, the Peerless Pool, when the badly beaten body of a young woman is found. Sent by the Blind Beak to the nearby Saint Luke's asylum for the insane (where Hannah, the victim, was an assistant), Rawlings is soon tracking down a complex web of deception that leads from the elegance of Bath to the darker corners of Paris. As before, Lake ambitiously tackles a massive cast of characters and creates a world of rich and atmospheric as any in historical fiction.

Brian Ritterspak

BLOOD IN BROOKLYN BY GARY LOVISI, THE DO-NOT PRESS, £7.50

Lovisi's reputation as a tough and stylish chronicler of the darker side of urban life was inaugurated with the cracking thriller *Hell Bent on Homicide*. That book functioned both as a loving recreation of the hard-boiled pulps of the 1940s and as a very modern spin on familiar tropes. The new novel introduces the uncompromising Brooklyn private eye Vic Powers whose first person narration gives the book its idiosyncratic power. And when the one constant in Powers' life, his wife, is threatened, he shows that he can be quite as monstrous as the worst of his opponents, including the psychopathic childhood friend who is pursuing him. As before, Lovisi's dialogue burns up the page, and if the Mickey Spillane-style

mindset here is likely to offend readers of liberal sensibilities, the unshockable are in for quite a ride.

Eve Tan Gee

THE KEEPER BY E A MACDONALD, SIMON & SCHUSTER, £16.99

With the collapse of the Soviet Union, it became more and more difficult for thriller writers to use the Russians as the bad guys (although Russian instability, psychotic hardliners and Russian mafiosi are currently providing plenty of material). Still the two key sources of nemesis for thriller writers are a) serial killers and b) religious fundamentalists. MacDonald's assured and gaudy thriller opts for the latter with considerable success. Her intricately plotted narrative follows researcher Jane Carlucci on a trip into the Heart of Darkness, as she investigates cult leader David Norton and his sinister sect, which has been preparing the world for the Second Coming. As Carlucci interpolates a connection between various world disasters (botulism outbreaks, contaminated baby milk) readers won't be surprised by the terminal situations she is soon facing as a controversial document, the Eighth Scroll, begins to play a key role. As with most novels by former journalists, this is much stronger on detail than character, but there's no gainsaying its irresistible pull.

Barry Forshaw

THE BIG BAD CITY BY ED MCBAIN, HODDER AND STOUGHTON, £16.99

A young woman is found strangled in Grover Park, very near the 87th Precinct Station. Initially thought to be a saintly character, engaged in worthwhile work with not an enemy in the world —the route to the motive for her murder is a long one. Sonny Cole, the man who escaped a sentence for the shooting of Detective Steve Carella's father in *Kiss*, published in

1992, resurfaces here on a deadly mission. Also a burglar nick named 'The Cookie Boy' because he leaves homemade, chocolate-chip cookies at his crime scenes, is loose in Isola.

McBain is a known for his deceptively simple, well-constructed books and this is his forty ninth 87th Precinct book with the familiar bunch of detectives, Carella now nearing his 40th birthday; Monroe and Monoghan — the 'M & Ms' from Homicide; Fat Ollie Weeks and a guest appearance by Matthew Hope, the Florida lawyer who features in some of McBain's other books.

Carella reminisces: "... *When we were young. When none of us were married. Remember that bar near the bridge? Just off Culver? All the guys on the squad used to go there and get drunk. Remember? After the big one? Kling was a patrolman back then. Hawes wasn't even on the squad. Remember?"*

"There was a cop named Hernandez I liked a lot," he said. *"He got killed by a cheap thief who holed up in the precinct, remember? Do you remember a cop named Havilland? Roger Havilland? He was worse than Parker. Sometimes I think Parker is Havilland, come back from the dead, Artie, not The Deaf Man. Remember... Jesus, remember the times?..."*

McBain succeeds because he never has too many bodies, characters or subplots for the needs of his story. Neither are they laced with insubstantial Chechen, Medellin or Serbian gangsters to give it a false, contemporary feel. His characters are often memorable, the action is always believable and there is nothing in the narrative that does not move the story forward. Like life not all the ends are tied up but you are guaranteed a satisfying conclusion with the final hundred pages building to climaxes built and foreshadowed earlier in the book.

Martin Spellman

ALIVE & KICKING BY JOHN MILNE, NO EXIT PRESS, £8.99

In 1968, Bermondsey gangster Tommy Slaughter and his driver were ambushed on Croom's Hill, Greenwich. On the orders of Soho denizen and Maltese pimp Mickey De Witt, they died in a hail of bullets. But the murders have resonances in the present, when ex-Metropolitan copper Jenner, now a London private eye, finds himself working for a lawyer on a divorce case. Milne's protagonist was crippled in a terrorist bombing, and his disablement gives him extra problems when the divorce case moves into bloody territory. When De Witt, now in his 60s, gets his eyes shot out in a pub car park, Jenner is a witness. And (as so often in detective novels) the past and the present are on a collision course. Jenner is one of the most masterfully characterised gumshoes in contemporary crime writing, and Milne's authorial voice manages to contain a world of experience, with every aspect of human behaviour as thoroughly explored as in the most respectable of literary novels.

Judith Gray

And another view...

Jimmy Jenner, one-legged ex-cop turned private detective, is a child of Bermondsey, and the Bermondsey of his childhood comes back to haunt him in this novel which manages to combine the Kray-like atmosphere of Sixties London gangland with a modern English take on a dick more spotted than hard-boiled.

This is because, although Milne writes well, he gets bogged down in establishing his mood. A dream-like repetition of scenes is fine: it establishes the past which will figure so meaningfully in Jenner's present, and it also establishes him as a character at loose ends. But occasionally those ends are so loose as to be untied.

When someone takes a shot at Jenner, or at a driver they thought was Jenner, it takes two weeks for *"the penny to drop"*, as he says, and for him to connect it with a murder he happened to witness. It's as if our new motto is *"only disconnect"*.

Similarly, when Jenner recalls his mother, he tells us that she died when he was ten, that she was the kind of woman who let things build up inside her, and that he barely remembers her, all in the space of three paragraphs. You can go too far in bending reality to establish an effect.

Once the story gets going in earnest, however, such bending becomes unnecessary, and the more furiously the plot moves the more interesting the characters become. *"Action is character,"* as F. Scott Fitzgerald said. Milne very cleverly lets Jenner's detective work bring him back closer to his ex-wife; while also using it to allow Jenner to ignore his French girlfriend Amy. If the revelation with young Lochinvar (trust me, the name works) is pretty obvious, his punishment seems, if anything, a bit anglo-centric. The past resolves itself in violence which is left with a certain degree of ambiguity, and we wonder how, even in a fiction Metropolitan Police, it's all going to be sorted out. But it will be worthwhile checking in again with John Milne to find out.

Michael Carlson

SOLO HAND BY BILL MOODY, SLOW DANCER PRESS, £6.99

Evan Horne is a brilliant jazz pianist, but his career is cut short when a car crash rips open his right hand—the solo hand of the title. So what does he do then? Well, in the traditional contrivance of the crime genre, he becomes a detective. A reluctant detective, of course, but actually quite a good one (as in the nature of the genre). He's called in to find the mysterious blackmailer of two music superstars, and get to the bottom (as it were) of some highly incriminating photographs. As he flits between Los Angeles and Las Vegas, Horne uncovers a convoluted plot that takes in stolen ransom money, death threats, and...wait for it...unsold records.

When I began *Solo Hand,* I hoped I would get caught up in the mellowness and melancholy of the jazz world, the cigarette smoke and bluesy bass chords of the late-night Venice jazz clubs. I hoped, indeed, that the author's own experiences as a DJ and jazz drummer would instil the narrative with a genuine sense of veracity. But despite an atmospheric prologue, and the occasional glimpse of musicians in action, Moody's prose is as clinically impersonal as a lab mortician describing an autopsy.

Solo Hand is peopled by a cast of characters who are solely defined by their motivations and their relevance to the plot. Nothing of any substance lies behind their briefly sketched existence (*"a tough, no-nonsense woman"*, *"penetrating eyes that have obviously seen a lot"* and *"an open, friendly face"* are but three examples), and I soon tired of sorting out just which faceless character was which. The only remotely interesting person, a Hollywood record producer, is killed soon after he provides a vital clue to the blackmailer's identity. Perhaps he would have livened up the story too much. And Evan Horne, the hero of the piece, is as one-dimensional as the rest of the characters, with little backstory or decent characterisation to make him stand out. He drifts along with no particular aim in life, no particular cross to bear. His anguish about being out of work—his livelihood probably ruined for ever—is such a watered-down cliché that Moody would have been wiser not to mention it at all.

Apart from the banal characterisation, another problem is the plot. Now, I know not every thriller can have shoot-outs on each page and conspiracy theories to shake the Government to its foundation, but I was expecting something a little more engrossing than record returns as the basis for blackmail. Doing an artiste out of royalty payments may be a topic of concern for accountants and book-keepers, but as the *dénouement* to a crime novel it lacks a certain excitement. Then again, it is at least in keeping with what has gone before.

Solo Hand is apparently one of a series of 'acclaimed' novels. Tony Hillerman even gives a guarded quote on the back cover. But for me, Bill Moody has a long way to go to convince me that he's as competent a writer as he is a jazz musician.

Mark Campbell

WORD MADE FLESH BY JACK O'CONNELL, NO EXIT PRESS £10.00

This is O'Connell's fourth novel set in Quinsigamond, based geographically on the rusting New England mill town of Worcester, Massachusetts, but fictionally more a cross between New York's Lower East Side at the turn of the last century, and the futuristic Los Angeles of *Blade Runner*, at the imagined turn of this one.

Gilrein is a fallen ex-cop, a lowly gypsy hack ever since his wife, also a cop, was killed in an explosion while raiding a terrorist group called The Tung. These are terrorists with a difference: their aim is to overthrow the tyranny of the written word. In the midst of this, Gilren finds himself trapped between searches for two very different types of literature. One is the bizarre testament of Quinsigamond's own Lizzie Borden, EC Brockden, (his name recalling both the early American novelist Brockden Brown and EC horror comics of the 1950s) who carved his wife and children into nothingness when he realised he could no longer speak to them. The other is a manuscript written by a young girl named Alicia, who witnessed the 'erasure; of the Maisel ghetto in old Bohemia: an ethnic cleansing led by a man called The Censor and performed with an horrific machine called a shredder.

This is the last days of the Later Roman Empire brought to nightmarish life, a dark world filled with shadows. Visit the Cabaret Vermin in Ribbentrop Square. Hear Imogene Westwood's *Drunk on India Ink* played over and over on Canal Zone radio. Watch police stage gladiatorial fights to the death. In his epigraph, O'Connell quotes Paul Auster *"The fall of man is the fall of language."* That may make O'Connell language's Lucifer, because he sure writes the hell out of Auster. Ever since he won an open competition for crime novels with his first, *Box Nine*, he's used the framework of crime to create darker and denser realities with each book. He's gone beyond hard-boiled, to petrified.

Reviewers love making O'Connell comparisons: Pynchon, DeLillo, Kafka, Hammett, Borges, Calvino, Chandler, *Zap Comix*. Think of Auster and add eyes and heart and teeth.

Recalling Gertrude Stein's Oakland (*"there's no* there") one character describes Quinsigamond as *"a burg too intensely* there *for its own good."* So too *Word Made Flesh:* The head of Quinsigamond's police Eschatology Squad, for whom Gilrein's wife died, is the Inspector, Emil Lacazze. She described his writing as *"petulant, esoteric, pun-laden, self-serving, bursting with neologism and the sense of the author's uncontainable ego."* A fair description of O'Connell himself, one of the best and most challenging writers in America today.

Michael Carlson

SMALL VICES BY ROBERT PARKER, NO EXIT PRESS, £5.99

After a period in which the master of modern-day Chandleresque prose gave every impression of coasting on autopilot, it's heartening to report that Parker continues to find his best form again—and this lively outing is something like his vintage style. Spenser is hired to break the frame on Ellis Alves, *"a bad kid from the hood with a long record"*—but did he really murder Melissa Henderson, a white student from the fragrant groves of Pemberton College?

Dialogue crackles in best Parker style, and the badinage between Spenser and longtime associate Hawk has a freshness that wipes way the memory of the recent workaday books. Other characters, too, leap off the page, and one can only say (with gratitude): welcome back, Bob.

Brian Ritterspak

A FIRING OFFENCE BY GEORGE P. PELECANOS, SERPENT'S TAIL, £5.99

One part Willeford, one part Woodrell, one part, well, whoever fits the bill (it's the bit with all the plot at the very end; after we've had our fun), *A Firing Offence* is more—much more—than just the sum of its parts.

Washington D.C. *"A city where the only common community interest was to get safely through another day."* Mid-80s. Thirtysomething Nick Stefanos works advertising paste-ups for Nutty Nathan's: blow-out sales and shady deals. Swap the strap-lines. Oh yes. Then he gets this call from the grandfather of a kid he befriended at work. Jimmy Pence's gone missing. Sure, he shaved his head and hung with that punk crowd, but that doesn't MEAN he'd go missing. And he kissed grandpappy at the door that last time. So, can Nick help? Being buddies and all, and being as how Jimmy and Nick are—were—alike: speed metal, rec-drugs, rebel-boy shit.

That's your plot. Which is perfunctory. As Pelecanos well knows. Because almost as soon as it's introduced, he forgets about it. Much of the first third of *A Firing Offence* is about drinking and drugs and BB guns and casual abuse in the electrical retail trade. Honest. The spiralling madness of wild days and crazy nights on the floor, selling you—us—what we don't need. Sound dull? It's (pardon me) electrifying, gill-packed with the coal-hearted misanthropy of Charles Willeford on a bad, black day. *That* good. Daniel Woodrell we think of when Nick and his buddy take off for a brief sojourn in country. Highways, bars and beers. Slack, loose, all but pointless—and absolutely riveting.

Getting the idea yet? Pelecanos keeps plot afloat only long enough to get us aboard the boat. It's the bait, not the hook. Which is why the book's at its slackest—that's slack like a taut fishing-line is slack—at the end, when he suddenly realises he ought to tie something up. So he wastes half a dozen bad guys and gives Nick a reason to go on. All's fair.

No, forget that and just know Pelecanos is *great*. There's some sly politics, some smart action stuff, his writing tight, full of personality but never showy. And, like prime-rib Willeford, his audacity can fair take your breath away. Great because any book where the lead listens to Public Enemy, Billy Bragg and Pere Ubu can't be all bad, right? Right. And if nothing else it'll make you think twice about shopping in Dixons ever again.

Gerald Houghton

BLUEBOTTLE BY JAMES SALLIS, NO EXIT PRESS, £6.99

Reading James Sallis's latest novel about Lew Griffin, New Orleans PI, you could be forgiven for thinking that detectives have come a long way since the wise-cracking, tough-talking days of the pulp, given Griffin's apparent addiction to quotation and literary allusion. However, some of Griffin's more hallucinatory musings are extremely fitting, as the novel's superb opening chapters find Griffin, blinded from trauma, drifting in and out of consciousness as ER staff around him try to save him from a life-threatening gunshot wound. The first half of the book passes in a slight blur, as Griffin slowly recuperates and tries to fill in the missing gaps in his memory, namely exactly why he was shot after leaving a nightclub with a white woman, dredging up links to Neo-nazis and a missing novelist, which he finally determines investigate as he recovers. Sallis' intention seems to be to illustrate the meaningless of unfulfilled narrative, but the occasional lack of coherence may be accepted, since Sallis is a superb stylist; his evocation of New Orleans is second to none, his characters broadly sympathetic and his dialogue crisp and believable. I'd be interested to read some of Sallis' earlier novel, just as long as someone can assure me he limits himself to just one quotation of a modern French philosopher per chapter.

Dan Staines

EASY MONEY BY JENNY SILER, ORION, £5 99

This is the account of an ex-junkie young woman, courier for crooks, who is hired to take across America a computer disk, which she says could have been posted—about all I can state with certitude, as this is an extremely convoluted story.

I don't think there are any good guys in the entire book, unless the ex-CIA operative murdered in the first few pages is one. The CIA is either to blame, or is not to blame, for what happened to the rebel Viet Cong (known as VC in Vietnam), and

if not, then the American Army is to blame, or maybe not to blame, either. When she gets to Florida, she sinks the disk in the sea, which has a faint echo of the end of *The Maltese Falcon*, but makes the whole operation a waste of time.

The courier takes as much punishment from the ungodly as Marlowe or Dick Tracy. She packs three guns, one strapped to her ankle (echoes of the Saint's ivory-handled knife), and one like Modesty Blaise in her bra—which must mean a very small gun or a very large bra. Despite the batterings, she shews a masochistic streak in her dealings with her crook lover-boss. Finally, she routs single-handed a gang of four, led by yet another ex-CIA operative.

Her car journey across America has the nightmarish quality of Alice in Wonderland or Dorothy Gale on the Yellow Brick Road to Oz. She meets an ex-soldier transvestite, known as 'she' who lives with a prostitute, also apparently a 'she'. She gatecrashes an all-male wedding, with a fat man in a dress describing 'himself' as *"the mother of the bride."* The one integrated character is a woman charter ferry pilot who helps her escape to a new life abroad. Lively stuff, but I did wonder if this was written with one eye on television adaptation, and if the girl is meant to be a parody of James Bond.

John Kennedy Melling

NIGHTS IN WHITE SATIN BY MICHELLE SPRING, ORION BOOKS, £9. 99.

This is a book of startling contrast and contradictions. Set in Cambridge University, with detailed, and over-long, descriptions of colleges, functions and personae, yet the University is subtly blamed for what occurs. There is a distinct bias against men, yet the two main female characters are distinctly flawed. None of the leading players commands any sym-

pathy—and the first main murder does not take place until page 110 out of 310 pages.

The missing girl in white satin, sounding innocent and happy, proves to have the morals of an alley-cat and a weird naive outlook. She thinks dabbling in prostitution should not make any difference to her romance with an upper-class undergraduate (Can you imagine her at her first Hunt Ball?). The sleuth, Dr. Laura Principal, often using the ungrammatical Ms , varies from the abrasive to literally crawling to her business-partner-lover when she thinks he is ditching her—mind you, she does tidy the woman Detective Inspector's hair for her—she was one of her past students. The descriptions of Cambridge are graphic, and the minor characters treated sympathetically, but the last few pages are in a rush which leaves various problems unsolved.

John Kennedy Melling

A MAZE OF MURDERS BY RODERIC JEFFRIES, ALISON & BUSBY, £5. 99

The author is famed as the son of the great Bruce Graeme, who carried on his father's epoch-making Blackshirt series. This current title has the Spanish Inspector Alvarez as sleuth, a steady, likeable, plodding detective, with problems with his superior and susceptibility to the women suspects. The story is set in the author's Mallorca, and the first two deaths are of those typical British visitors on the 'sun, sex, sand and sangria' type of holiday and their female pick-ups. Attention turns to wealthy ex-pats, and soon a third body is found in the sea. Alvarez journeys to Paris, to unravel a strange case of mistaken identity, and finally solves the case. At this point I tried what the late Sir Alfred Hitchcock knew as the *"icebox syndrome."* You see a film, TV production, or play, or read a novel and you are staggered by the dramatic finale. Then, a

little later, as you raid the icebox, you start to consider the denouement rather more calmly, and here the rather rushed last three pages leave you with several queries such as, will the killer be charged? And the helper? Just what were the motives for all the deaths? As the French say, it makes you furiously to think.

The greatest mystery is the copyright page. Roderic Jeffries does write under several pseudonyms, and it is this name for the copyright—but it says the Wodehouse-ian Brian Battison is identified as author! Curioser and Curioser, said the White Rabbit.

John Kennedy Melling

THE DEVIL IN DISGUISE BY MARTIN EDWARDS, NEW ENGLISH LIBRARY, £5. 99

Martin Edwards is himself a lawyer so we expect the legal business and characters to be described accurately and with sufficient interest to capture non-legal readers, and this he does with great precision. His down-at-heel Liverpool solicitor is called in to see just what may be wrong with a long-established artistic family foundation. The strange death of the Chairman of the Trust, followed by the murder of another Trustee lead on to a violent finale with yet another death, by which time Devlin has found all the Board to have very unsavoury secrets, with one exception. The twists get more complicated, but Edwards always keeps the explanations easy to follow, and his descriptions of the City and its various haunts from an exclusive gentlemens' Club to a Labour Party headquarters convincing and amusing. Strangely yet again this is a novel with a lot happening in the last few pages which leaves unanswered questions—is the killer to be punished? What will happen to the false, contrived claim against the Trust? Will all the details come out at the trial?

I am not sure why Devlin is treated as so nondescript—a reference to his Marks and Spencer suit and Hush Puppies when he visits the Club for a Trustee meeting is louche, not only for the wrong shoes but M & S sell their mens'suits made from the same factories as the great Italian designers—perhaps Devlin's platonic women friends don't like to tidy him up?

John Kennedy Melling

A SIMPLE PLAN, SCOTT SMITH, DOUBLEDAY, £9.99

A bit like *Treasure of the Sierra Madre* with snow and 100-dollar bills rather than sand and gold dust, and now released as a film, this begins with the discovery of $4.4 million by brothers Hank and Jacob and Jacob's friend Lou. They originally agree that Hank will hold the money for six months but trouble soon starts.

Hank's wife Sarah has the ludicrous idea of putting some of the money back! One totally unnecessary death follows — beginning a spiral of killing that eventually consumes almost everyone in the book. The plot is not credible or convincing because of the basic lack of adequate causes and reasons for the actions. When anything is possible a book takes a fantasy quality. Adequate motives would have given it the realistic bite that most mystery readers expect. As it is many may feel irritated by the nagging question 'why are they doing this?'

Intended perhaps as a tale of greed and mistrust it assumes the attitude of middle-class manners and selfishness. Hank and Sarah decide what is good for everyone else — Jacob has to leave, Lou can't have his share, Jacob is a bed wetter and, worse still, poor. His cleanliness leaves much to be desired and he won't get a job. Dear me, these working class types — they won't work and they smell as well! No one would disagree that Jacob and Lou are losers but they could

have been more convincingly drawn as characters.

After a while body starts to pile upon body to keep the story going but as the characters are so thin you can't care about these people. The paradox is that mysteries must hold concern and respect for human life or it has no effect when it has an expendable quality. I have not seen the film — I hope it is better. The book, though, does have many admirers—I'm just not one.

Martin Spellman

COPS AND OTHER ROBBERS BY I K WATSON, FOURTH ESTATE, £5.99

I picked this one up with apprehension—are we tired of police procedurals? Not if they have the energy and idiosyncratic detail that Watson specialises in. Even the now over-exposed plot devices (including a hunt for a paedophile) are handled with a commanding freshness, and it's axiomatic that writers as talented as Watson can shuffle warmed-over ingredients to produce something rich and strange. Watson is also good at dealing with the disillusionment involved in the day to day life of a copper, and DI Rick Cole is a trenchant hero, even if his drinking is another one of those over-familiar touches. The plotting is bracingly original, and this deserves to do every bit as well as Watson's earlier books.

Barry Forshaw

TROUBLED WATERS BY CAROLYN WHEAT, NO EXIT PRESS, £5.99

Wheat has always specialised in the careful delineation of character, perfectly dovetailed with plots of intelligence and complexity, best exemplified in such books as *Fresh Kills* and *Dead Man's Thoughts*. In this latest outing, she takes her Brooklyn lawyer Cass Jameson on the most challenging case of her career when she is forced to defend her brother against a murder charge. This takes Wheat's doughty heroine back to her past in which she and her brother were jailed for their attempts to protest social injustice. And the death of a Federal Agent, plus the appearance of her brother's fugitive girlfriend give Cass what looks like an unsolvable case. As well as fashioning her cleverly constructed plot, Wheat is just as fascinating in dealing with Cass' relationship with her brother, who appears unwilling to do what he must to save himself, and the author freights some pertinent social issues into a distinctive and highly readable thriller.

Eve Tan Gee

RECHERCHÉ BY JIM WILLIAMS, SCRIBNER, £16.99

"If it weren't for Harry Haze, this would be a boring story" begins Jim William's follow-up to his well-received novel, *Scherzo*. Well, in a sense I agree. Without the *Zelig*-like influence of Haze on the narrative, the novel would be a lot shorter and a lot simpler, but it would at least be intelligible and half-satisfying, if not exactly exciting. With the addition ofHaze it merely becomes irritating.

Recherché is ostensibly about middle-aged lawyer John Harper who leaves his wife for his secretary and flees to a small village in France. There he attempts to regain his lost youth—his secretary, Lucy, is twenty years his junior. All is going as well as could be expected until they bump into a shambolic old man called Harry Haze who has an amazing expanding carpet-bag. From it he produces an array of bizarre artefacts that 'prove' beyond doubt that he has been a Nazi war criminal, a stand-up comedian, a murderer, and—first and foremost—a vampire.

Novels like *Recherché* are hard to classify. Is it crime, or magic realism?

Farce or horror? Is it *"a brilliantly conceived web of allusion and illusion"* (as the press release puts it) or a pretentious mishmash of comedy and introspection that uses the conventions of the crime genre as metaphor for something completely different? At the end of the day, should I be reviewing this for Crime Time or for the Times Literary Supplement? And the answer is: it's not really well-written enough to be a literary success, nor is it exciting or clever enough to make a good crime story.

Recherché is really two stories. Harry Haze's recollections—in the form of self-contained tales—are given chapters to themselves, and rarely, if ever, advance the main narrative. One senses that Jim Williams so enjoyed crafting these meandering Monty Python/Spike Milligan-style interludes that he forgot about the plot completely. These tales could have been pruned, or even cut, without any loss to the narrative. One interminable tale—something to do with Adolf Hitler escaping to America—is even composed in cod-Shakespearean verse! For a page or two it is slightly amusing, but then the joke wears thin. Indeed, most of Harry Haze's stories, even the character himself, could be seen as a joke at the reader's expense, and as with all jokes that go on too long, the effect becomes wearying.

I was reminded at times of John Fowles' *The Magus*, another story that mixes fantasy with reality. But *The Magus* was written by an extraordinarily talented writer with an uncanny grasp of language and imagery, and with the best will in the world, *Recherché* is not in the same league. For his next book, Jim Williams should give up trying to be a literary post modernist, and either write a comedy or a crime novel. It's obvious that he can't do both.

Mark Campbell

A LITTLE DEATH BY LAURA WILSON, ORION, £6.99

A Little Death presents the reader with a triple murder on page two, and then leaves no room for speculation: one of the three must have shot the others and then committed suicide, we are told quite firmly. It is a testament to Laura Wilson's story-telling skills that she not only keeps our interest, but winds up the intrigue so that this book is difficult to put down.

The narrative unfolds through the alternating perspectives of the main protagonists Georgina, Edmund and the admirable Ada, each voice possessing its own distinct and distinctive qualities. A childhood death is responsible for their ruined lives and doomed prospects, and what unfolds is a tale of sacrifice and selfishness, isolation and missed opportunities. Written in a deceptively sedate style it nevertheless had me galloping through the pages to see what the characters would get up to in the next chapter.

A Little Death provides a strong sense of time and place, it is understated, witty and sharply observed, building a multi-layered, seductive and spell-binding mystery.

Margaret Murphy

A SMALL DEATH IN LISBON BY ROBERT WILSON, HARPERCOLLINS, £16.99

Wilson's considerable reputation continues to grow from book to book, with this latest offering well up-to-par.

1941. Europe cowers under the dark clouds of war, and Lisbon is one of the world's tensest cities. Klaus Felsen, a reluctant member of the SS, finds himself drawn into a savage battle in the mountains for a vital element in Hitler's Blitzkrieg. In modern-day Lisbon Inspector Zé Coelho is an outsider in the cliquish world of the Policia Judiciaria. Investigating the death of a young girl, he suddenly finds himself deep in the events of 50 years ago, with ramifications for the Portuguese Revolution which is hardly a generation old. Wilson has carved out a niche for himself as a remarkable writer of atmospheric, colourful thrillers written in a striking literary style. Here again he echoes his forebears Greene and Ambler in a complex and powerfully characterised story that builds inexorably to a breathtaking climax.

Barry Forshaw

CALIFORNIA FIRE & LIFE BY DON WINSLOW CENTURY, £10.00

Jack Wade is a top claims investigator for the eponymous insurance company.

His speciality is fire investigation, and he understands fire. Fire has become his life; fire and surfing.

Once Wade was the top arson investigator for the Orange County Sheriffs Department. He could smell arson. But he roughed up a torch and planted evidence, in order to protect an eye witness whose life would be worthless if he actually was forced to testify. It cost him his job, his girlfriend, a Latina cop called Letitia, and his self-respect.

Then Billy Hayes, known as 'Goddamn' Billy, brought him back with this insurance job. So when Jack investigates a routine house fire which appears to be the result of a drunk woman's smoking in bed, it should be open and shut. Except that Jack's arson nose tells him it isn't. That the woman's husband is a Russian mobster, and her half-sister turns out to be his ex-girlfriend simply drags Jack deeper into a battle he has no chance of winning.

Don Winslow is an interesting writer. This story is told in flashback, and in clipped, fast-moving prose that reminds the reader of nothing so much as flames crackling to a start in a big fire. He uses

the technical background of fire itself and of arson to build the suspense and to bring the reader into his own sort of investigation. And he uses the whole California ethos of real estate and insurance scamming to draw a not so pretty picture of LaLa Land which leaves Jack, as the Dana Point surfer, exposed in more ways than one.

If anything, the strands of the story wind up being too complex, and the conspiracies too complicated, to allow the sort of resolution Winslow offers. The relationship between Wade and Hayes has clever echoes of that between Neff and Keyes in *Double Indemnity*, which suggests at least some of the twists. But by the time we finish we have Vietnamese gangs, Russian Mafia, KGB, and just plain American crooks all out on the road looking for money and revenge, and as the bodies stack up one wonders why the key clue which Wade needed, which seemed obvious at the time, went overlooked for so long.

This is quibbling. Winslow has produced an engrossing book whose pace keeps you moving with it, and whose characterisations are drawn effectively and compactly. No mere flash in the pan, this one.

Michael Carlson

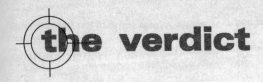

crime and history
gwendoline butler

While writing her own highly acclaimed crime novels for HarperCollins, Macmillan and CT Publishing, we're glad to say that Gwendoline Butler takes time out to take her regular look at recent historical crime novels for CT…

IT SEEMS AS WELL to begin this article by reviewing a book on women in crime: *A Career in Crime*, edited by Helen Windrath and published by The Women's Press, paperback. This is a collection of essays by women crime writers on how, and why, and with what success they have written crime books. The list of contributors is impressive, containing names such as Val McDermid, Marcia Muller, and Stella Duffy amongst others.

Let me say at once that I enjoyed reading it. Being a woman crime writer myself I was looking forward to a keyhole view into my contemporary professional's lives. Working lives, but I found I got their private lives as well, and the answer is that you cannot separate the two.

Each writer described her own life which they mined, more or less consciously for plots, characters and atmospheres. I was uneasy at first, until I was forced to realise that this was what I did myself as indeed I suppose all writers do.

Characters, plotting, all were discussed, but what I noticed too was that not one of these writers mentioned the pleasure of writing sentences, the actual bedrock of a book. Did style not matter at all? Interestingly, only one writer, Abigail Padgett, spoke of creating an atmosphere of suspense and fear. Anne Wilson dwelt on a sense of place which I too consider vital.

I found each article worth reading, but I felt they told me more about the women writers (more perhaps than they guessed) than how to write crime fiction. It seemed to be a kind of therapy for them, which perhaps, all writing is.

What healing the writing of historical crime offers to writer and readers, I am not sure. Periods differ in their popularity: the Middle Ages (by which I mean anything from Harold and Canute to the Tudors) are very popular: the Crusades, the Plague, Leprosy all attract interest.

Anything Roman reads well, perhaps because there are plenty of records in good translations to aid the writer. Egypt gets sparser attention from writers, perhaps because of their highly stylised pictorial representation of themselves, which makes us hard to identify with them. (Cleopatra excepted of course but she was Hellenic anyway) Further back still, the Babylonians and the Hittites, from whom our culture descends however reluctant we are to see it, remain an unmined field.

Blood On the Borders, by Judith Cook, Headline. This story is set in the late Sixteenth century with Dr Simon Forman as the hero. He is an attractive figure, a medical man, with a distinguished set of patients, a man who may even have treated Shakespeare. This a robust and entertaining mystery story. Some readers of historical fiction enjoy the appearance of real characters from the past, others can't abide it. This is a book in which real characters abound from Robert Cecil to Christopher Marlowe, all so interesting that it would have been a pity not to have met them.

Squire Throwleigh's Heir by Micheal Jecks, Hardback, Headline. A very well told story with a violent yet convincing plot. Jecks succeeds in writing both a book which smells of the Middle Ages and yet is a detective story. No mean feat. Perhaps that whiff of the past is derived more from Powicke and Tout and Plucknett than the Plea Rolls themselves but yet there is

a feeling of them too. That said, it is also the kind of tale that Chaucer might have written, even to the irony at the end.

Falconer And The Great Beast, by Ian Morson, Vista.

This is an altogether darker tale. Set in Oxford in the late thirteenth century with the arrival of a group of Tartars, a race known for their fierce aggression. It is an enjoyable story though, with Master Falconer making an interesting detective.

In Pursuit Of A Proper Sinner. Elizabeth George, Hodder and Stoughton. This, of course, is not a historical novel but a detective story in the grand tradition such as no one else is writing now, with an aristocratic detective who has a manservant. Impossible not to draw a comparison between DI Thomas Linley and Lord Peter Wimsey. Here it must be said that Lord Peter is the more convincing aristocrat of the two: he speaks better English to begin with and appears better educated.

This book is densely plotted which makes it a hard read on occasion. That said, I must also say that I enjoyed reading it as a magnificent fable.

A Walk Through The Fire, by Marcia Muller, The Women's Press. A contemporary novel as with Elizabeth George's but a very different kind of book. To begin with the investigator is a private detective, and a woman at that, Sharon McCone, no one could be less like Lord Linley. She works with a computer, to begin with, and it goes wrong which makes her like the rest of us. If Lord Linley did have a computer it would always behave.

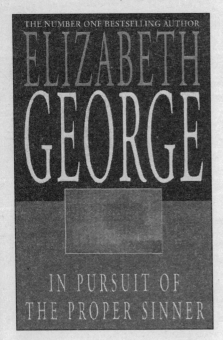

THE NUMBER ONE BESTSELLING AUTHOR

ELIZABETH GEORGE

IN PURSUIT OF THE PROPER SINNER

This is an adventure story with a touch of sex more than a straight detective story but not the less enjoyable for all that. Sharon is called to Hawaii to help a filmmaker who is being threatened with death. Marcia Muller writes with conviction and energy. The action crackles along and so does the dialogue. These two books: the Muller and the George ought to be read one after another, they make a good, contrasting pair. Both being very well written, and carefully plotted, and both with a strong sense of place.

Finally, as I began with the sagas of women crime writers, let me end with a real life detective story.

Anybody's Nightmare by Angela and Tim Devlin, Taverner Publications, The authors call it The Sheila Bowler Story, The introduction to this book is written by Francis Gibb, legal correspondent to The Times and Tim Devlin is the son of Sir Patrick Devlin, a very distinguished lawyer indeed.

This carefully researched and well written piece demands equally careful reading. It tells the story of Sheila Bowler and her elderly and invalid aunt who was believed to be helpless and unable to walk unaided. Yet she got to a river and there drowned. Sheila was accused to leading her aunt to the River Brede there to let her drown. Or help her, even. But she always protested her innocence which many people, the Devlins included, believed in. In spite of this, Sheila was given a prison sentence, This is the story of how the two Devlins, who believed in her innocence, worked to free her. It is both interesting and exciting how they struggled to find out what could have happened and then had to fight to convince the judicial powers. Everyone who is interested in criminal cases ought to read this book.

As a crime writer myself I think it is time the genre was taken seriously. It can be a kind of therapy.

Who was it wrote that the reader, sunk in fantasy can experience under the guidance of the author, all the aberrations of the moral world and yet come back safely out the other side, back to the world where there are still rules.

Unreason can be folded away, punishment enjoyed and dangerous fears worked out? All as Coleridge said, without ministering an impulse to action.

'A pure pulp vision, closer to Spillane than Chandler. His books are bloody romances of the south London badlands'

—John Williams The Face

QUICK BEFORE THEY CATCH US!
MARK TIMLIN

The New Sharman Novel

Quick before they catch us
MARK TIMLIN

FAMILY TROUBLE! Growing old quietly was never really an option for Nick Sharman. When he takes on a job for a prosperous Manchester businessman looking for his runaway teenage daughter, Meena, he should perhaps have known better. He finds himself in a race against time to save the girl from the kind of trouble that gives families a bad name. Trying to do the right thing, Nick swaps sides and ends up starring in his own version of a Straw Dogs shoot out with family and friends, where nobody comes out the winner.

'Full of cars, girls, guns, strung out along the high sierras of Brixton and Battersea, the Elephant and the North Peckham Estate, all those jewels in the crown they call Sarf London"

—Arena

'Once again the man Timlin pulls a cracker from his bottomless bloodstained sack'

—Loaded

the verdict

natasha cooper on...

CT prides itself on the number of top crimewriters who are happy to write for these pages – and we've just added a new scalp. The wonderful Natasha Cooper, regularly to be found as reviewee at the back of CT for her HarperCollins Trish Maguire crime treats joins our reviewing staff to look at **The Sword Cabinet by Robert Edric•(Anchor) and The Death Pit by Tony Strong (Doubleday), along with another view of Val McDermid's A Place of Execution (HarperCollins).**

THE NOVELS BY Edric and Strong could stand as an example of the difference between literary and commercial fiction. Both are about the investigation of old crimes and the difficulty of seeing through deliberately engineered illusion. But one demands efforts from the reader and repays them with a sinewy kind of pleasure; the other lays everything out on a plate and offers rather less satisfaction. Robert Edrich's *The Sword Cabinet* makes no concessions to speed of narrative or likeable characters, and it forces the reader to work hard to pick out what is happening from the fractured sequences of three separate stories. There is Mitchell trying to escape his current financial and legal difficulties, while forcing his reluctant girlfriend to pretend she is being pierced with swords he

thrusts into her stage coffin; there is his search for the truth about his mother, one time assistant to Morgan King, the greatest escapologist since Houdini; and there is Morgan himself, developing an act even Houdini refused to attempt and trying to talk his way out of the clutches of the police, who believe he is a serial killer. The stories meet and split and meet again, held together only by Mitchell's urge to make sense of the past and whatever glue the reader's own imagination can supply. The rewards come from the clear austerity of the prose, the utterly believable (if squalid) characters, and the satisfying mixture of real and metaphorical escapology and illusion. *The Sword Cabinet* is an impressive if uncomfortable novel.

In contrast, Tony Strong's *The Death Pit* whips along at a smart pace and leaves nothing to the imagination. The story is driven by Terry Williams, a lesbian academic, who is in Scotland on the trail of material about Catherine McCulloch, who was burned as a witch in the seventeenth century, and is now thought to have been a lesbian herself. Terry's search involves her with a coven of new age witches, a hellfire Presbyterian, a man who is setting up a torture museum as a draw for tourists, and a pig farm owned by an attractive young woman, in whose death pit are found the body of a recently killed woman and several older corpses of babies. The academic quest is interesting and Terry's eventual discoveries underline the absurdity of modern preoccupations with sexuality, but there are problems with both the modern killings and the central character. While the motive for the murders is just about credible, the inclinations of the killer are put down to a genetic inheritance that does not convince, any more than Terry's personality convinces. There is a fashion for male novelists to write in the voice of a woman and some do it better than others; there are problems here, but otherwise it's an interesting crime novel.

And so to *A Place of Execution* by Val McDermid (HarperCollins). Abduction and murder of children feature in the work of many different crimewriters. Some use them to shock; others to call out readers' deepest sympathy; still others, perhaps, as a way of fending off the dreadful reality. Val McDermid's angle is especially interesting. The first two thirds of her novel is written in the form of a journalist's account of a 1960s abduction case. At a time when the Moors Murderers were active not far away, thirteen-year-old Alison Carter went missing from her home in Scardale, an isolated village in the Derbyshire Peak District. Eventually a man was hanged for the crime. The victim's family, friends and neighbours, as well as DI George Bennett, the chief investigating police officer, have all talked to the journalist, Catherine Heathcote, which allows her to reproduce their dialogue and remembered emotions as well as her own analysis of what must have happened. This is a clever device because it allows Val McDermid to play games with the reader and present the appalling story with a journalist's detachment, besides injecting occasional reminders of life in the 1960s in a way that would be heavy-handed in an ordinary novel. In the final third of the book she reverts to her own voice to tell the story of what is happening to Catherine and the survivors of the case in the late 1990s. The style relaxes and the emotions intensify because they are given to the reader direct instead of being filtered through the mind of the journalist. She first became involved when she met Bennett's son, Paul, a press officer with the EU in Brussels, who is engaged to a woman whose sister lives in Scardale. Revisiting the case with Catherine forces Bennett to reassess his whole working life and most of his relationships. It also enables McDermid to show how much has changed since the early 1960s.

The relationship between Bennett and his wife was almost one of master and servant, although it is clear that he loved her inordinately. His son's dealings with his fiancée are quite different: she is his equal in every way. Similarly the women of Scardale endured lives of domestic drudgery with no thought of finding personal fulfilment, but now Catherine, whose class and upbringing mirrored those of Alison Carter, is an independent journalist travelling the world. As the 1990's story opens out it is clear that George's wife and the women of Scardale had their own ways of exercising power, as people must if they are to survive, but they were covert. Greater equality has meant a more open society, as well as a fairer one, but as the final, agonising twist in Alison Carter's story is revealed, it is clear that there are still limits to the honesty that can be endured. In this way, *A Place of Execution* becomes not only a gripping crime thriller but also a novel with a great deal to say about who we are and how we become so and why it matters.

the verdict

the crime time panel

CT's editor Barry Forshaw (overworked— and doesn't everyone hear about it) chooses to disagree with three of the magazine's key reviewers (the opinionated Eve Tan Gee, the over-enthusiastic Judith Gray and the dour Brian Ritterspak) on just about every crime novel that the quartet have jointly read. Whose side are you on?

BF: Well, I suppose we'd better get one book out of the way first—but let's make it brief, as it's going to be discussed ad nauseam. And I reckon it's necessary to say that readers who've not yet tackled *Hannibal* (Heinemann) should skip the next remarks. Brian, what did you make of it?

BR: Utterly wonderful: Harris has re-jigged the formula so successfully that you hardly notice the familiar elements falling into place. And that ending!

ETG: Yes, that ending: utterly ridiculous! Did you really buy what Harris was doing there, Brian? The only good thing about it is that, while the rest of the book read like a movie treatment, it's hard to imagine Anthony Hopkins slurping down brains while Jodie Foster has one breast hanging out.

JG: Oh, come on, Eve—there are plenty of very fresh concepts in there. And the whole Florence section is a tour de force, isn't it?

ETG: I can't believe it! You all like it!

What about you, Barry?

BF: With reservations. There are some delicious conceits—I just found myself thinking that I trust the fourth part will give Lecter more of a hard time. I was uncomfortable with him not getting even a toe nibbled by those pigs. Anyway, that's enough *Hannibal*. What did we all make of Faye Sultan's *Help Line* (Fourth Estate)?

JG: I enjoyed this. I'm a bit sick of intelligent, liberal, female protagonists, but Sultan's very good on the psychopathology.

ETG: Yes, I agree. I liked her *Over the Line* more, but this was very smoothly written.

BR: Didn't get round to this one, sorry.

BF: I've read several novels that were similar recently, but it was a very assured piece. Now we had quite a batch from Allison & Busby to get through. Should we just pick our favourites? I was very glad to see Peter Lovesey's *Wobble to Death* back in print—I live quite near Islington's Agricultural Hall and often think of that book when I pass it.

BR: Yes, I'd never read it before, although I know its reputation. Isn't the Agricultural Hall now the Business Design Centre?

JG: Yes, it's sort of *They Shoot Horses,*

Don't They? investigated in the Agi Hall by a Holmesian copper. Gripping stuff.

ETG: I liked Ann Cleeves'm*urder in My Back Yard*. She doesn't sustain the opening momentum, but Ramsay is a solid protagonist and the plotting was very skilful. If we're still on Allison & Busby favourites, I liked Bartholomew Gill's *The Death of Love* and—what was that Spanish book?

JG: *The Crimson Twins* by Pavón—yes, beautifully written. I'm an Ed Gorman fan, and I liked *Murder in the Wings*—good old-fashioned whodunnit, less grue than other Gorman books.

BF: Brian, any favourites here?

BR: Well, A&B's *Parker Omnibus Volume 2* is sui generis, isn't it? How did you feel things like *The Split* read these days, Barry? I still find them satisfyingly lean and mean.

BF: As sharp as ever. I remember I once complained to Westlake that I had trouble with the amorality of the Stark books.

JG: What did he say?

BF: He said he liked to upset liberals like me! A&B have got some good things coming—I know not everyone likes June Thomson's Sherlock Holmes books, but I'm a real fan. OK, on to Arrow. Eve, what did you think of Candace Robb's *A Gift of Sanctuary*?

ETG: Well, I'm an Owen Archer sucker—what is this, the fifth or sixth? Drop me in Fourteenth Century York, and I'm as happy as Margaret Thatcher at a Pinochet tea party.

BR: The Robb was a bit formulaic, didn't you think? But I liked Richard Doyle's *Executive Action*, and I suppose that was as formulaic as you could get—fun though. I didn't have much time for Ri-

chard North Patterson's *No Safe Place*, did you, Judith?

JG: Was that the one about the younger brother of an assassinated presidential aspirant?

BF: Yes, being stalked by an abortion fanatic who wants to kill him. Standard stuff, I thought, but very capably written. Anti-abortion fanatics might join Islamic militants as the new-all-purpose bogeymen of the modern thriller—this is the third I've encountered in a novel. If we're doing this alphabetically, I liked two books from Anchor: D J Taylor's *Trespass*—a really haunting piece—and *The Sword Cabinet* by Robert Edric.

ETG: Yes, the Edric was something special, wasn't it. He's won all kinds of prizes—the James Tait Black Prize and so on. I liked the Taylor, too—very atmospheric.

BF: Have you noticed, Eve, how the use of language has become crucial to the crime novel these days?—I mean the tone of voice used in the sassy contemporary novel. Did you read Dennis Lehane's *Gone, Baby, Gone* (Bantam)?

BR: Yes, but- if I can butt in, Eve—I thought that Chandleresque prose was a bit warmed-over. I liked his last book better. Was that called *Sacred*?

ETG: Well, on the subject of tone of voice, I thought Eric Miles Williamson's *East Bay Grease* (Bloomsbury) has a very distinctive edge—as that's next on my list of Bs. Nicely realised anti-hero, and a good enough book to make you put up with the publisher's boasting about the ludicrous number of jobs Williamson has had. Don't they realise we're bored by that? I liked another Bloomsbury book—Patricia Melo's *In Praise of Lies*: Dostoyevsky with a Latin sensibility.

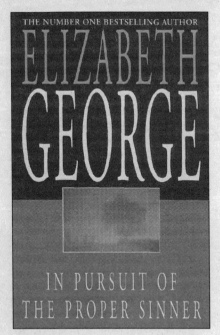

THE NUMBER ONE BESTSELLING AUTHOR

ELIZABETH GEORGE

IN PURSUIT OF
THE PROPER SINNER

BF: OK: Century. I was impressed with John Farrow's *City of Ice*, but I thought Donald James' *The Fortune Teller* was serviceable, no more. He can do much more accomplished work.

ETG: I thought exactly the reverse— I found the Donald James a quantum leap in terms of technique over his earlier books.

BF: Alright, books we disliked. Judith?

JG: Well, I didn't have much time for Victor Davis' *Getting Away With It* (Gollancz). Can writers still be cloning Forsyth in the 90s?

BR: You want to know what I hated? That adaptation of an Agatha Christie play—*The Unexpected Guest* (HarperCollins). I'm a Christie fan, if push comes to shove, but her plays... My God! And Charles Osborne's adaptation was leaden.

ETG: Well I hated about half of the books we're discussing. The level of ambition, let alone the level of achievement was so modest.

BR: Oh, come on, Eve. There were some great things in this batch. I loved those two Prion re-issues: Dalton Trumbo's *Johnny Got His Gun* and Moravia's *The Conformist*—two copper-bottomed classics, although I suppose Judith is going to say that the Moravia was better in the original Italian. And both of the Penguin books we looked at were wonderful: Nicci French's *The Safe House* and Richard Montanari's *The Violent Hour*—a great revenge thriller. Oh yes, I liked that other Nicci French too: *Killing Me Softly* (Michael Joseph).

JG: Yes, I thought the Nicci French was a casebook example of how the psychological thriller should be written. And incidentally, Brian, I've only read one Moravia in Italian—it wasn't *The Conformist*. I can't remember what it was, but I wasn't converted. And I know probably none of you liked Mike Ashley's *Royal Whodunnits* (Robinson), but I found that a delightful collection.

ETG: I agree. I probably wouldn't have picked it up if it didn't have Mike Ashley's name on, but I was pleasantly surprised. And if we've alphabetically jumped to Robinson, I thought Steven Saylor's *Rubicon* was well up to par. Still prefer Lindsey Davis' Roman sleuth, but there's not much in it.

BR: Well, if we're talking about historical crime, I think Michael Pearce's Egyptian series has been really consistent. And *Death of an Effendi* (HarperCollins) has a wonderful Edwardian feel.

BF: OK, we're running out of time. Let's pick a few favourites. I'll take an editor's prerogative and start: I'm sure we all liked Val McDermid's *Star Struck* (HarperCollins) which is in paperback now, did we? And Barbara Rogan's *Suspicion* (also HarperCollins). From Headline, I was very taken with Ann Granger's *Running Scared*—very difficult to bring off yet another young female investigator, but she manages it. Eve?

ETG: Of the Headline batch, I liked that debut novel by Michael Blaine, *Whiteouts*—a very striking study of psychological disintegration. And Irene Lin-Chandler's *Hour of the Tigress*—perfectly realised Chinese milieu. I'm a big fan of Anne Perry too, although I didn't think *Bedford Square* was among her best.

BR: Still on Headline, are we? I thought Martha Grimes' *Biting the Moon* was a very accomplished piece, but what about *In Pursuit of the Proper Sinner* (Hodder) by Elizabeth George?—now there's real professionalism. Have you ever seen the Peak District so vividly used as a locale? And I found Clive Egleton's *Dead Reckoning* (also Hodder) masterly—although I wish he could have avoided such a clichéd title. Why do so many authors re-cycle titles?

JG: How many titles can there be? Chas Brenchley is always value for money, and *Shelter* (Hodder) was Chaz pretty well at the top of his form. And I can't leave out Lauren Henderson: *The Strawberry Tattoo* (Hutchinson) wasn't vintage Henderson but more than good enough to be going on with. And who was that author who got short-listed for the Poe and Agatha Awards, Barry?

BF: Deborah Crombie, *Kissed a Sad Goodbye* (Macmillan). Good use of the Blitz as the source of the mystery. Okay, the coffee's finished. Shall we call it

a....yes, Eve?

ETG: Can I put in two more favourites? *Four to Score* by Janet Evanovich and the great Minette's *The Breaker* (Pan)? And that's it, I promise.

JG: Well, if Eve can get away with a few extras, I'll be damned if I'll miss out a selection from the smaller presses: Serpent's Tail had a winner, I thought, in *Left for Dead* by Diane Langford. And I thought that No Exit title, *Shut Up and Deal* by Jesse May was one of the great gambling books—real Walter Tevis territory. And Joe Quirk's *The Ultimate Rush* (also No Exit): self-consciously hip, maybe, but a wonderful read.

BF: Right, that's enough. But we didn't all read every book, did we? Should we aim for that next time? You've got your goodie bags of new crime thrillers: get to it!

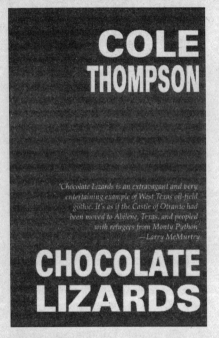

film

true clint
michael carlson

TRUE CRIME
Directed by Clint Eastwood
Screenplay by Larry Gross, Paul Brick-man and Stephen Schiff, based on the novel by Andrew Klavan, with Eastwood, James Woods, Isaiah Washington, Denis Leary, Diane Venora

IN *UNFORGIVEN* Clint Eastwood went back and revisited, if not rewrote, the past thirty years of westerns, and it was invigorating. If *True Crime* appears to do much the same thing with thrillers, it's only because most of it is so famil-iar. Working with such derivitive mate-rial, Eastwood's direction, which builds things gradually in visual layers, simply gets lost. When the key piece of evi-dence is finally revealed (so late to do nothing to convince us of Clint's char-acter's ability as an investigative jour-nalist) it is done so in a shot so tele-graphed it might as well have a silent movie caption attached.

I wonder if the crime film is really what Clint was interested in here: he's been there and done that. The only times the movie really comes to life are in the newsroom scenes, in the office politick-ing of Denis Leary and in the wonderful editorial role, right out of *The Front Page*, reserved for James Woods. It's as if the generation gap between that film and *All The Presidents Men* and the 1990s has been laid out before us,

with Clint playing both Woodward *and* Bernistein trapped out of time.

But that makes his character, Ev Ev-erett, into another problem, not least because he's about 15 years too old as he's played by Clint. His affairs are un-convincing, his romancing less so. His problems with wife and child seem more like father with daughter and grandchild, and really, the marital cli-ches don't really seem to work. It's hard to escape cliché throughout this film. It's never unwatchable, but it's rarely very satisfying.

THE CORRUPTOR

Directed by James Foley, Written by Robert Pucci, with Chow Yun Fat, Mark Wahlberg, Ric Young, Kim Chan, Paul Ben-Victor

James Foley is a reasonable choice of action director to bring Chow Yun Fat to a wider public, but *The Corruptor* isn't necessarily the best vehicle for that. As an action film it boasts a complicated plot, as a tightly plotted thriller it boasts a lot of action. But what this is really about is immigration: the Chow Yun Fat story as microcosm for assimilation into the American dream. Hence the music we hear every time there's a scene of Chinese illegals could be as much Irish as Oriental. The Chinese gangs may be indistinguishable in action from American gangs, but the Chinese cops are very much distinguishable from their occidental counterparts.

Chow himself is given a role full of shadows and contradictions, which sometimes strains against the limitations of the buddy-buddy cliches audiences have come to expect. But when the other buddy is Marky Mark, those cliches take on entendres of their own. If Foley is aware of Fat's Hong Kong roots, he's even more aware of a former gay icon. The scene of Mark sucking a long-neck bottle, and wiggling away in his tight jeans, T-shirt and key-ring play not very subtly on this, but also on the conventions of police partner pals.

Lost in all this is that balance between action and suspense, which is a shame, because there is enough depth untouched here to form the basis of a classic crime movie. Instead, we get a strangely overblown reliance on Brian Cox as Mark's father to provide further motivation, when very little more is actually necessary.

A CIVIL ACTION

Directed by Steven Zaillian
Screenplay by Zaillian based on the book by Jonathan Harr, with John Travolta, Robert Duvall, James Gandolfini, William H Macy, John Lithgow, Dan Hedaya

John Travolta does a nice job of catching the essence of lawyer Jan Schlictman, the high-powered legal trickster who gets so caught up in a case that he loses almost everything, if not his basic character. Travolta's conversion is done with delicacy; he still retains the ego to miss the chance to make a favourable settlement, and if he seems a little too good to be true at film's end, we can cut his character a little slack.

On the other hand, Robert Duvall's excellent portrayal of Schlictman's main opponent, Jerome Facher, while fascinating in its catching of the details of a man subsumed in the mechanics of winning the corporate law battle, misses the main point of the book. Harr shows quite clearly how Facher's victory in the civil suit was the result of his (illegally) withholding important evidence from the plaintiffs during the discovery process.

He was aided in getting away with this by the sometimes bizarre rulings of his law-school colleague, Judge Skinner, who protected Facher from facing the blame just as he had protected his case during the trial.

This change is certainly not Duvall's fault, because it's obvious the screenplay has no interest in examining any flaws in the legal system. It leaves the "few bad apples" syndrome to industry, and not even to the corporations, necessarily, but to the original tannery owner, played by Dan Hedaya as a cartoon villain.

Which is a shame because this a movie with a lot of subtle nuance, beautifully shot for emotional expression by Conrad Hall. Jonathan Harr's book was very much a crime story: in this film it's reduced to a battle of lawyers, where the eccentric wins and the converted crusader finds happiness in an office next to a barber shop.

film

kubrick's eyes
paul duncan

"There's no sacrifice too great for a chance at immortality." In A Lonely Place (1950, directed by Nicholas Ray)

As soon as news came in that Stanley Kubrick had died in his sleep, everyone was there to praise him. He was a grandmaster, a titan, the last of the great old-time directors. This is true, but it makes him sound as though he belonged to an earlier era, which, when you watch his films, is obviously untrue. Kubrick's work, like all masterpieces, have a timeless quality. His vision is so complete, the detail so meticulous, that you believe you are in the three-dimensional space displayed on a two-dimensional screen.

I was walking around a Robert Capa exhibition recently. Capa was a war photographer who made his name with stunning pictures of the Spanish Civil War, and became one of the founders of the world-famous Magnum photo agency. He's come into vogue recently (although he never really went out of vogue) because his blurred pictures of the D-Day landings on Omaha Beach were the inspiration for the filming style of Spielberg's *Saving Private Ryan*. (Ironically, the blurring was a complete accident. Capa was known for his pin-sharp photos but, when his rolls of film were being developed in the Time building in London, the technician made a mistake and all but eleven photos were unusable, and those eleven had all been blurred in the process.) The reason I mention Capa is that as I stood in front of the photos—whether it was

From '2001' to 'A Clockwork Orange'

The Startling Vision of STANLEY KUBRICK

Matisse bent at 90 degrees drawing giant sketches with a long stick, or Chinese children frantically involved in a snowball fight amidst the Japanese invasion, or the grieving widows of Italian fighters, or American GIs talking to English kids—they were so perfectly framed and realised, that I was there, and it was happening to me now. They were no longer images—they were experiences.

In our daily lives, we are constantly surrounded by diverse images. Where once the written word was king, now images have taken their place. The spoken word is

subservient to a series of moving images. But the power of the image has been diluted from overuse. Here then, is Kubrick, who started as a photographer for *Look* magazine (straight from school, aged 17), who told stories through his images, who meticulously collected images for his movies, so that when that image moves, it moves from one perfectly framed and realised image to another. Now that Kubrick is dead, we will no longer see the world through his eyes, except for one last film, *Eyes Wide Shut*.

The subjects of Kubrick's films have always been difficult to predict, the director using genre subject matter to explore his own concerns.

He has directed four anti-war films *Fear And Desire* (1953), *Paths Of Glory* (1957, book by Humphrey Cobb), *Dr. Strangelove* (1964, book Red Alert by Peter George) and *Full Metal Jacket* (1987). *Fear And Desire*, which Kubrick produced, edited, and served as director of photography, was made for only $100,000, and is little-seen today, mainly because there is only one known print in existence, and it's in private hands. Supposed to be badly-made and pretentious, it's probably just as well. *Paths Of Glory*, starring Kirk Douglas, is gutwrenching—based on a true incident, it shows how soldiers are unjustly killed by their superiors because of ambition, pride and snobbery. Many regard this as Kubrick's best. *Dr. Strangelove* is well, unique. A cold war black comedy which everybody took seriously, it depicts the madness of war. *Full Metal Jacket* deals with the dehumanisation of soldiers so that society allows them to kill. Some can take it, some can't.

Early on, there were a couple of crime films: *Killer's Kiss* (1955) and *The Killing* (1956). The former has some bad acting bolstered with some great directing. The later was the breakthrough movie. Famed for its racetrack robbery depicted in chopped-up timing , later used by Tarantino to great effect, people credit Kubrick with the technique when, in fact, it is in Lionel White's source novel *Clean Break*. A great crime movie about the fallibility of man.

After some writing on *One-Eyed Jacks*, eventually directed by Marlon Brando, Kubrick took over from Anthony Mann on *Spartacus* (1960, book by Howard Fast). At the time, the most expensive film ever made, it won Kubrick many admirers because of the stunning photography perfectly combined with intimate acting. I rushed to my local multiplex when it was re-released and was knocked out seeing the movie on the big screen—pity I was the only one there.

And then, some decidedly different approaches to cinema. *2001: A Space Odyssey* (1968, story by Arthur C Clarke) is full of optimism, showing how man has used tools to extend his physical reach, but needs a little help to advance onto the next stage of evolution. *A Clockwork Orange* (1971, book by Anthony Burgess) uses a futuristic setting to explore attitudes to violence, and who takes responsibility for it. *The Shining* (1980, book by Stephen King) uses the horror genre to explore the creative urge subsumed by sloth and other pleasures of the flesh.

Most of Kubrick's films show his characters in relation to, and their interaction with, their environment. It is this 'coldness' to people which has been a sticking point with some critics. (Some people even make the mistake of assuming that because Kubrick shows 'cold' people, then Kubrick too must be cold, which is a ridiculous notion. If you follow that argument, then Scorsese, Tarantino and DePalma must be killing people all the time.) Kubrick examined the 'hotter' human emotions in the love stories of *Lolita* (1962, book by Vladimir Nabokov) and *Barry Lyndon* (1975, book by William Makepeace Thackeray). And this strand is followed with *Eyes Wide Shut*.

After the release of war film *Full Metal Jacket* in 1987, Kubrick worked on several projects. For many years, Kubrick was building a story called *AI*, which stands for Artificial Intelligence. An epic science fiction story, based on Brian Aldiss'short story *Supertoys Last All Summer Long*, he shelved it in 1991 because the effects needed at the most basic level could not be put on the screen.

Kubrick moved on to *Aryan Papers*. Set in World War Two, it was about a Jewish boy and his aunt trying to survive in Nazi-occupied Poland by passing as Aryan. Based on Louis Begley's first novel *Wartime Lies*, it was to star Joseph Mazzello (the kid from *Jurassic Park*) and rumour had it that anyone from Julia Roberts and Uma Thurman to Jodie Foster were to play the aunt. Location scouts were sent to Poland, Hungary, and Slovakia where the production was to be based. A 100 day shoot was to begin in the summer of 1993 for a Christmas 1994 release, but Kubrick decided not to make it because the subject was too similar to Steven Spielberg's *Schindler's List*.

Spielberg's other movie that year, *Jurassic Park*, gave Kubrick the confidence that perhaps the special effects he wanted for *AI* could now be achieved. Set in a future where many of the world's cities are under water (the ice-caps have melted due to the greenhouse effect) and robots perform most daily tasks, the focus is on a robot-like boy who wants to become a human being. Kubrick talked of it being a modern *Pinocchio*.

After investigating further with special effects companies ILM and Digital Domain, in December 1995 it was announced that *AI* was in the final stages of set design and special-effects development but, while he was waiting, Kubrick would make a small film...*Eyes Wide Shut*.

Kubrick, like Hitchcock, always preferred using source novels and interpreting them in his own unique way. In this case, *Eyes Wide Shut* is based on Arthur Schnitzler's 1926 German novella *Traumnovelle*, published in English as *Rhapsody: A Dream Novel*. (Schnitzler's well-known play *La Ronde* was the source of David Hare's recent London and Broadway stage hit, *The Blue Room*—starring Nicole Kidman.) It's a film Kubrick has had in his head for some time. In the early 1980s, when interviewed by Michel Ciment, Kubrick commented, *"It's a difficult book to describe—what good book isn't? It explores the sexual ambivalence of a happy marriage and tries to equate the importance of sexual dreams and might-have-beens with reality. All of Schnitzler's work is psychologically brilliant..."*

The book is set in 20s Vienna, and concerns the marriage crisis of Doctor Fridolin and his wife Albertine. On the surface, everything is fine and dandy, but whilst holidaying in Denmark both are attracted to other people, and upon their return the marriage is failing because both are still fantasising about might have been.

Dr Fridolin is called out, but he finds his patient dead. The patient's daughter tells him that she is in love with him, but before anything can happen her fiancée arrives. That night, Fridolin meets his friend, a pianist, who says he is sometimes hired to play blindfolded in a villa. Intrigued Fridolin follows his friend to the villa, and sees fully dressed men dancing with naked women who hide their identity behind a mask. When Fridolin is discovered, the rules of the group decree that a woman is 'sacrificed.'

Arriving home, Fridolin is told by Albertine of her strange and cruel dreams with a man like the one she fancied in Denmark. When Dr Fridolin learns in a newspaper report of a baroness'suicide, he thinks it's the woman from the villa. When he tells his wife of his adventures, they are reconciled.

Kubrick to Ciment again, *"The book opposes the real adventures of a husband and the fantasy adventures of his wife, and asks the question: is there a serious difference between dreaming a sexual adventure, and actually having one?"*

In the past, Kubrick has remained close to the plots of his source novels, and this is no exception.

In 1972 Frederic Raphael, a damn fine English writer and Oscar-winner for his screenplay for *Darling* (1965, directed by John Schlesinger), wrote the script for what is now known as *Eyes Wide Shut*. *Who Were You With Last Night?*, supposedly a novelisation of the screenplay he'd written for Kubrick was published the same year. For whatever reason, the film was shelved in favour of *Barry Lyndon*.

Filming finally began November 4 1996. As usual, Kubrick worked on the script, rewriting scenes each day, so it's a pretty good bet that the details of the script have changed, although the plot seems fairly intact. The setting has changed from 1920s Vienna to modern New York at Christmas. The central characters are a married couple, played by Tom Cruise and Nicole Kidman. Tom plays Dr Bill Harford, and he embarks on an odyssey of fantasies involving sex, drugs and masks.

All the filming took place in England, so Manhattan street scenes and interiors were built in Pinewood Studios. London locations like Hatton Garden and Worship Street were dressed to look like New York. Some scenes were also filmed at Hamley's toy store in Regent Street. The climactic masked-ball and orgy took place at Elveden Hall near Bury St Edmunds, and Highclere Castle near Newbury. The stately home Luton Hoo was used for the first party scene. Knowing of Kubrick's reputa-

tion for working through the night, Luton Hoo insisted filming should stop at midnight.

As well as box-office faves Cruise and Kidman, thesps Harvey Keitel and Jennifer Jason Leigh were hired at the beginning of the shoot. However, Harvey Keitel, who played Ziegler, left after six months without commenting why. (Speculation: Some reports say he cited the usual *"artistic differences,"* whereas others pointed out Keitel is known for walking off the set while working with meticulous directors, notably being replaced on Francis Ford Coppola's *Apocalypse Now*. Or perhaps he'd already contracted to do another film.) Keitel was replaced by film director Sydney Pollack (*They Shoot Horses Don't They?*, *Three Days Of The Condor* etc.) who was so brilliant acting in Woody Allen's *Husbands And Wives*. A new actor = reshoots. So, all the scenes of Keitel with lots of extras, filmed in Luton Hoo in November 1996 had to be refilmed in May 1997 with Sydney Pollack, whom Kubrick called *"a genius."* Jennifer Jason Leigh played the woman who comes onto Cruise, Todd Field a jazz musician, and 14 year-old Leelee Sobieski as a girl who comes on to Cruise.

I've used the word 'meticulous' a few times when describing Kubrick's working method. For example, he had a road on a set re-tarmaced because it didn't look old enough. He even made Tom Cruise walk through a door 95 times—watching the video playback, Kubrick looked up at Cruise and said, *"Hey, Tom, stick with me, I'll make you a star."*

The shoot was originally set for 13 weeks, with a budget of $40 million. Supposedly the longest shoot in modern film history, it officially ended on January 31 1998. That's almost 15 months, although there were eight weeks of vacation within that period. Cruise on Kubrick: *"He worked seven days a week. I got faxes from him at three in the morning with scenes."*

I would guess, and this is pure speculation on my part, that Kubrick learnt how to tell the story as he went along, that he discovered each shot through the re-takes and, when he understood it, moved on to the next shot. The reason I say this is because Kubrick was self-taught—his father gave him his first camera aged 12, he learnt photography, he learnt to make films by making them. Each of his films show a love of learning, of pushing back the boundaries. Cruise again: *"Suddenly, he'll say something to you, or you'll see how he creates a shot, and you realise this man is different, this man is profound. And it seems without effort. You come out of this experience and realise the possibilities of film, the possibilities of how to communicate ideas and concepts in a way that you never thought."*

Then came news that Kubrick wanted to reshoot Leigh's scenes with Cruise. However, by this time, Leigh had already started in the lead role of David Cronenberg's *eXistenZ*, so she was replaced by Swedish actress Marie Richardson (*The Best Intentions*). So Tom Cruise flew back to England to redo his scenes with Richardson in April and May of 1998. Then the announcement that Thomas Gibson, star of TV sitcom *Dharma And Greg*, plays Richardson's fiancé, and principle photography ended in June 1998.

So, filming eventually stretched to 18 months, and the budget went up to $60 million. For all the flak Kubrick gets for being slow, that's pretty cheap for a Tom Cruise movie nowadays.

Kubrick went into the editing suite and did his stuff, whilst the newspaper people did theirs and speculated and rumoured to their hearts content. As is usual with big-budget/event movies, cast and crew were strictly forbidden (by a punishable contract) to discuss any aspect of the project. This, of course, fuels more speculation and rumour, which leads to great opening weekend box office. Kubrick was one of those rare directors, both commercial AND artistic.

On March 2 1999, Cruise and Kidman, as well as Warner Brothers chairmen Terry Semel and Robert Daly saw the final cut in New York which ran to 2 hours and 19 minutes. Normally Kubrick showed final cut in London, but Kidman was ill and had temporarily withdrawn from *The Blue Room* on Broadway, so Kubrick's assistant flew a print over there, showed it (making the projectionist turn away), and flew it back to the UK, all on the same day. Everybody was happy with it. Except for adding the titles and some fine tuning of sound and colour quality, *Eyes Wide Shut* was complete.

On March 6 1999, Terry Semel talked with Kubrick concerning the marketing campaign and small additions to the score, which is mostly classical music. Kubrick was very excited by the positive response to the screening, and told Julian Senior, his closest colleague at Warner Brothers' London office, Eyes Wide Shut is *"my best film ever."*

On Sunday, March 7 1999, Kubrick died in his sleep from a massive heart attack. He was 70, was one of the world's most respected directors, and received numerous tributes. Kubrick's power and mystique in the industry was without equal: Warner Brothers gave him the money and Kubrick took 40 per cent of the profits. In death, his search for privacy, the control he exerted within the film industry, the loyalty he demanded (and got) from his troops, became even more alluring a story. No doubt, in due course, at the appropriate moment, suitable and considered memoirs will be written and published. Or maybe not.

On March 10 1999, a 90 second clip from *Eyes Wide Shut*, specially prepared by Kubrick, was shown to US cinema owners at the ShoWest convention in Las Vegas.

According to Kubrick's personal wishes, the clip was at the same time given to TV broadcast stations all over the world via satellite by Kubrick's company Hobby Prod. The trailer shows Tom Cruise and Nicole Kidman naked, embracing each other in front of a mirror, with Chris Isaak singing *Baby Done A Bad, Bad Thing* in the background. The reaction of the cinema owners? Stunned silence. Carlos Walther, manager of General Cinemas in Mexico, said, *"It seems like kind of an erotic film, but I don't have any idea what it will be like,"* whereas an anonymous exhibitor from Minnesota said, *"It's garbage. You don't have to understand stuff like that."*

The sexual nature of the film bothered the film business community. Explicit sex in major American film means a NC-17 rating and no money at the box office, even with Tom Cruise and Nicole Kidman fronting it. To avoid the NC-17 rating in America the orgy scene was partially censored with the placement of computer-generated objects and characters in front of the more sexually explicit details. The European theatrical release remains uncut.

If you were to believe the hype, it would seem that Kubrick had finally done what he told the late Terry Southern back in the 1960s after they'd watched a couple of porno films. *"Wouldn't it be interesting,"* Kubrick said to Southern, *"if an artist were to do this with beautiful, first-rate actors and good equipment?"*

This, of course, is all bullshit. *Eyes Wide Shut* is the work of a mature artist who is still probing the human psyche to find out how it works. You can see for yourself with *Eyes Wide Shut*. It's the last time you'll see the world through Kubrick's eyes.

Paul Duncan has written books on Stanley Kubrick and Alfred Hitchcock, published by Pocket Essentials (www.pocketessentials.com), on sale now from all good booksellers.

BOOKS ON KUBRICK

Stanley Kubrick by Vincent LoBrutto, UK, Faber and Faber, 1998, Paperback, 589 pages, £14.99, ISBN 0571193935, US: Da Capo Press, 1999, Paperback, 606 pages, $17.95, ISBN 0306809060

The best of the Kubrick biographies around at the moment. LoBrutto has interviewed friends, family and colleagues, as well as done his research, and has found that there is very little to find. Workmanlike, he takes us through the films, and the people involved, giving very little insight into the subtext of the films, but explaining how the films were financed, written, filmed and received by the critics. He pays close attention to the technical innovations—perhaps we hear a little too much about focal lengths and lens. It tells you how Kubrick got to be respected in the film-making community. Buy for the basic information.

The Cinema Of Stanley Kubrick by Norman Kagan, UK: Roundhouse Publishing, 1997, Paperback, 264 pages, £10.99, ISBN 1857100263, US: Continuum, 1997, Paperback, 264 pages, $18.95, ISBN 0826404227

There is much to like in this film-by-film analysis but, equally, there is much wrong. Kagan consistently misnames characters and facts from the movies, which is most annoying. For example, when explaining *Spartacus* he thinks that Batiatus and Marcellus are one and the same person. On the other hand, he also rigorously analyses the films in a manner which I haven't seen elsewhere. But then he is sometimes too rigid and tries to make some films fit his pre-ordained view. On the plus side, there are well-chosen quotes from reviews. So, all-in-all a mixed bag, but a bag worth rooting through for the odd gem here and there.

Stanley Kubrick Directs by Alexander Walker, Sybil Taylor, Ulrich Ruchti, UK:

Weidenfeld, Hardcover, 368 pages, £25.00, ISBN 0297824031, US: W W Norton, Hardcover, 368 pages, $35.00, ISBN 039304601X

This is an updated edition of the 1971 original, which was the first book of critical appreciation about Kubrick. Walker is very lucid and interesting all the way through—the attraction here is that Walker takes us through the scenes, frame by frame, cut by cut—there are over 350 black and white film stills. So, equally interesting for those who have or haven't seen the films in question. Walker is in the privileged position of being well-liked by Kubrick, who gave him access and interviews. The book also features interviews people Kubrick worked with, as well as commentary on his films and the ideas behind them.

Stanley Kubrick by Michel Ciment, Collins, 1983, Paperback, 238 pages

A unique book, made in collaboration with Kubrick, containing three interviews (on *A Clockwork Orange*, *Barry Lyndon* and *The Shining*), plus interviews with some of Kubrick's collaborators. Ciment contributes some perceptive essays and notes. There are great photos, many of which were selected by Kubrick who made frame enlargements from the original film. Highly recommended. The big problem is that it is out of print.

Stanley Kubrick by John Baxter, UK: HarperCollins, Paperback, 416 pages, £9.99, ISBN 0006384455, US: Carroll & Graf, Paperback, 384 pages, $13.95, ISBN 0786704853

Perspectives On Stanley Kubrick by Mario Falsetto (Editor), US: Macmillan, Hardcover, $55.00, ISBN 0816119910

A compilation of writings about Kubrick's films covers *Killer's Kiss* to *Full Metal Jacket*, includes an article by Kubrick, and a piece by Anthony Burgess on Kubrick's adaptation of *A Clockwork Orange*.

Eyes Wide Open: A Memoir Of Stanley Kubrick by Frederic Raphael, UK: Orion, Hardcover, 186 pages, £12.99, ISBN 0752818686, US: Ballantine Books, Trade Paperback, $12.00, ISBN 0345437764

Frederic Raphael first met Stanley Kubrick in the early 1970s. This is an account of their long conversations as the screenplay of *Eyes Wide Shut* was written. The book takes a cinematic form: the prose is intercut with 'clips' in the style of a film script.

The Making Of Kubrick's 2001 by Jerome Agel, Signet, Paperback, 368 pages, 1970

Wow! If you ever find this, pick it up and just delve straight in. It contains a 96 page photo insert retelling the *2001* story with comments/notes, interviews with everybody. Reprints news, articles, reviews, includes Kubrick's *Playboy* interview. You must have it.

The Lost Worlds Of 2001 by Arthur C Clarke, Sidgwick and Jackson, Paperback, 240 pages, 1974

This time we hear about *2001* from Arthur C Clarke's point of view. Unlike other books, which try to unlock the enigma of a man called Kubrick, Clarke treats Kubrick as a fellow traveller on the road to discovery. Clarke's measured tones and erudite discourses on the ideas behind the film can lead one to much thought on the subject.

...and JASON STARR looks at Kubrick's last film...

It would be almost impossible for any movie to live up to the enormous hype that preceded the U.S. release of *Eyes Wide Shut*. Even before Stanley Kubrick's sudden death, rumors swirled about problems on the set of the extremely lengthy production, and after the release date was pushed back several times, the movie was already destined to be one of the most eagerly anticipated movies of 1999. Kubrick's death only upped expectations for the film. Now the public was not only expected a good film, but the crowning achievement in the career of one of the century's greatest directors. While *Eyes Wide Shut* is not a masterpiece, it may be one of Kubrick's finest accomplishments that, despite such impossibly high expectations, the film does not disappoint.

Set in New York (but filmed mostly in London) and loosely based on a semi-obscure Austrian novel *Traumnovelle* by Arthur Schnitzler, the plot concerns the marriage Dr. Bill Harford and Alice Harford, superbly acted by Tom Cruise and Nicole Kidman. After a dinner party where Cruise and Kidman flirt with other people, Kidman suspects that Cruise had an affair. Seeking a kind of sexual revenge, Kidman plays a head game with Cruise, confessing to an erotic fantasy. Oddly affected by Kidman's confession, Cruise embarks on a night-long sexual Odyssey, that brings him in near-contact with a string of beautiful women, and ultimately places his life in jeopardy a mysterious orgy.

If taken on face value, Cruise's extreme reaction to Kidman's rather harmless fantasy—and thus the impetuous for the movie's entire plot—is not very believable. But this dream-like *"irrational irrationality"* is exactly what Kubrick is striving for, and which is what makes the film so successful. *Eyes Wide Shut* is a sexual frustration dream on celluloid. The movie evolves at an unpredictable pace, yet maintains a certain dream-like logic and clarity. It is only if the viewer pulls back from the action that the absurdity of the plot is revealed, yet thanks to Kubrick's skilled direction this never happens. The film is over three hours long, but there is never a dull moment thanks to cleverly strung together scenes and gripping noirish cinematography. The London/New York setting adds to a vision of a world where everything is not exactly as it seems.

Typical of a male fantasy dream, as Cruise descends into a Manhattan night in search of sexual revenge, beautiful, available women are in abundance. It seems like around every corner there are stunning streetwalkers or the daughter of shop owner with the unbridled libido of Bond girls. The run-on joke is the movie is that each encounter with a woman leads tantalizingly close to a sex scene, but in each case something happens to prevent it. This clever technique creates an increasing sense of frustration and feeds the suspense.

The movie's major sequence is the now famous orgy sequence. While advance hype on the film suggested that this would the most sex-packed mainstream movie ever, don't get your hopes up. While there is a lot of nudity in the film, it is nothing that will shock a hardened nineties filmgoer.

The orgy sequence is extremely weird and filmed and leads to an intriguing mystery that Cruise spends the rest of the movie trying to solve.

Without Kidman and Cruise's star power, the film probably wouldn't be as good as it is. After a few forgettable attempts, the married stars final achieve on-screen chemistry. Cruise—who is in almost every scene of the film—gives a sturdy performance and Kidman gives her best performance since *To Die For*. In a supporting role, Sidney Pollack play a great sleazeball. Some of the film's points about the effect of the female libido on a man's psyche are a bit dated, but in the end this minor flaw seems unimportant. *Eyes Wide Shut* may not be Kubrick's best film, but it is one of the best films of 1999.

Jason Starr is the author of Cold Caller *and* Nothing Personal, *published by No Exit Press*

a chalk outline of crime film

mike paterson

Do you pick your feet, Poughkeepsie?
The 1970s saw a decade of kid directors slipping into Hollywood as the new producers and executives held open the doors. After 'Easy Rider', 'Midnight Cowboy' and 'Mash' there was a brief period of freedom in which the film school punks and the TV documentary-unit graduates took on the mantle of artists and created a body of work unprecedented before or since in mainstream cinema. Before *Star Wars* rewrote the rule book the story of this decade is of the glowing halo surrounding six years of film making from *The French Connection* and *Get Carter* in 1971 to *Taxi Driver* in 1976 by way of *The Godfather* I & II, *Chinatown*, *Dog Day Afternoon*, *Badlands*, *Serpico*, *The Offence*, *Mean Streets*, *The Long Goodbye*, *Thunderbolt & Lightfoot*, *The Taking of Pelham 123* and many others. If ever there was a golden age this was it.

Similarly a fresh generation of actors inspired by Clift and Brando rather than Wayne and Cooper and schooled in the Strasberg method elbowed aside the prettier and safer studio-contracted starlets. The rough-hewn authenticity of the B Movie icons was being reflected in this intake of talent. For every John Ireland, Richard Conte and Sterling Hayden there was now a

Gene Hackman in The French Connection

Michael J Pollard, a Tony LoBianco, and an M Emmet Walsh. Goodbye Doris Day, hello Faye Dunaway. As if charged into action it also resulted in overlooked hired-hand directors fashioning their best work. Don Siegel, after years in the B underworld, tore a strip through the box office with the *Dirty Harry* films and Sidney Lumet, quietly and consistently, worked into the Nineties gathering classics along the way. But this was the decade of kids. TV and repertory cinema had allowed a generation to pick over the minutiae of scenes, the nuance of lighting and the power of editing. Their minds were awash with montage and homage. They'd seen the Bs, the Italian realist movement, German expressionism and the French New Wave and they wanted in on the action.

The first true classic of the decade was a film of confused plot, shaky camerawork and unsympathetic characters yet *The French Connection* had enough dirty panache to win five Oscars and elevate Gene Hackman to the status of a great. Hackman's Popeye Doyle (based on real-life narc cop, Eddie Egan) is no clean-cut hero. He's violent and boorish with the blunt energy and single-mindedness of a an obsessed man. This is a blue collar working Joe who's seen a world of stake-outs and shake-downs. Director William Friedkin (another former TV drone) shot the Brooklyn streets like a hit and run driver filling the screen with washed-out, dull colours and shaky camera long-shots. There's an authenticity to the dialogue and an almost improvisational feel that gives the police procedure a truth that was lacking in any previous film. Pauline Kael called it *"an aggravated case of New York"*. The film is one long chase; smugglers and police endlessly circle one another, Doyle and his partner slowly move in on their under-observation suspects, a dance of slow pursuit runs in and out of the subway and most thrillingly (and famously) a car hurtles through on-coming traffic in parallel to a runaway elevated train. Hackman maintains the momentum throughout with a performance of manic energy. His snapped entreaty to his petty collars, *"D'ya pick your feet Poughkeepsie?"* is never explained.

By 1970 Martin Scorsese and Francis Coppola had long since graduated from the New York University Film School and UCLA respectively. Scorsese had made some grant-aided shorts, worked in Roger Corman's talent pool and edited the *Woodstock* movie. By the turn of the decade the elements of his Italian Catholic heritage and the film infused into his head would come together to formulate a new school of intense personal drama that would reach a peak by 1990 with the seminal *Goodfellas*. Coppola had, like Scorsese, worked through the Roger Corman school of schlock and by 1970 had directed three films and won an Oscar for his screenplay of *Patton*. By contrast, at the age of 31, he had hit the ground running.

The Godfather trilogy has become an opera cycle of cinema. Already its status in the history of film is that of a Cosi Fan Tutti or a Magic Flute. Its magnificent myth is one of simple indicators essaying epic themes. It is the story of the corruption of power and the ambivalent family moral code. It is the story of migrant poverty becoming ruthless capitalist success. It is how a classic Hollywood genre and a dynasty of acting invented a masterpiece. So much of *The Godfather* is now part of common currency that there is a universal familiarity with the dialogue, the musical refrain and the characters. Yet in 1970 Paramount Pictures, despite the frantic bidding war for the rights, had unambitious expectations for an overpriced gangster film from a pulp Airport best-seller. Like the disparate elements in the story, the characters involved in the making of the film came together in a clashing fusion at odds with the stateliness of the end product; Robert Evan's preening producer, Mario Puzo the failed gambler, Nino Rota Fellini's in-house composer, Coppola the grand young director chosen for his authentic heritage after Peckinpah had been rejected and Arthur Penn, Peter Yates and Elia Kazan had turned it down and a cast of actors largely immune to the demands of the box office.

The producers fought for Brando who they felt would provide an effective short-cut as an iconic centre with skilled character actors slotting into stereotyped roles around him. Even more effective and risky was the casting of Al Pacino as the young idealist at odds with the mob ethos but eventually seduced into its darkness. Blending epic elements of Shakespearean import with intimate family drama Coppola succeeded in creating a perfectly realised world of the machinations of organised crime in 1940s New York in a way only an idealistic megalomaniac could. There is a music in the names (Clemenza, Luca Brasi, Sollozzo, Tessio) and a grand sweep in the familiar set-pieces, many structured around formal family occasions, that is magnificently expanded in the 1974 sequel. The two films were box-office blockbusters, created stars out of Pacino, De Niro and James Caan, elevated Coppola's name to above-the-title status and helped set up today's industry of cash-making event films. Popular cinema could now say it had a genuine work of art.

Pacino, with his Cagney intensity and fresh-faced cool established, went on to star in two of Sydney Lumet's great real-life based crime films of the decade. Serpico (1973), from the book by Peter Maas, is the account of NY cop Frank Serpico's journey from idealistic cadet to hated crusader against police corruption. Lumet shows a hip, cynical flip to an America in a time of confusion, where heroes and villains both hold centre stage in Vietnam, the Whitehouse and US society. Dog Day Afternoon (1975) shows Pacino (reunited with John Cazale from The Godfather), increasingly manic as the temperature rises and his control slips, as a desperate loser stuck in a failing bank hold-up. Under the glare of the live TV cameras and the gathering New York crowd he goes from villain to anti-hero to despised gay to sympathetic underdog in the course of the day. Lumet choreographs the chaos and contrivance with a feel for the horror of the power of the media and the effects of social change on urban living. As a director of intense emotion, weaving narrative strands and soliciting outstanding performances, Lumet is peerless in the world of crime film. The Offence (1973) is Sean Connery's finest hour as the policeman fighting his revulsion over a suspected child molester and the feelings that they share. In between odd projects Lumet has always returned to form with his stories of police procedure, corruption and culture. As the two unheralded triumphs of his later career Prince of the City (1981) and Q & A (1990) stand out as mature character pieces of complicated ethics and driven motivation featuring two of the great faces of American character acting, Jerry Orbach and Nick Nolte.

New York has always staked a claim as being the romantic urban home of Panavision crime but contrasting the unexpected location with the expected criminals has provided some classic exceptions. With Get Carter (1971) writer Ted Lewis and director Mike Hodges isolated a lone man in an environment of seediness and industrial decay to create a simple mythic story that resonates today with a timeless, efficient cool. Britain had attempted such stories before but never had the style to bring it off. After Performance and the legacy of TV documentary it was more natural to depict a uniquely British flavour and culture in the arena of guns, revenge and corruption. Not until The Long Good Friday in 1981 blended director John MacKenzie's authentic sense of urban hoodlum pulp with Bob Hoskin's street-wise bruiser would British cinema see something as great. With a London at the fulcrum of change between recession blight and cash-rich dockland development, playwright Barrie Keefe caught the tone of the times with stunning accuracy.

Also removed from the darkness of New

York were the sun-sheared open streets and fields of 1930's Los Angeles which were the setting for one of the great takes by an outsider on American culture; *Chinatown* (1974). Using the era but discarding the stereotypes Roman Polanski's *Chinatown* was a nostalgia-free, private-eye film with a bright new sheen. Free of the clichés of the noir loner and viewing a world without the filter of modern cynicism the characters are able to experience the ingredients of classic Chandler and Hammett with full, unblinking force. Robert Towne's screenplay twists, turns, confuses and amuses but always within its own logic. Jack Nicholson hits the perfect tone as Jake Gittes and John Huston chills as the rapacious patriarch. Contrastingly, Robert Altman's *The Long Goodbye* (1973) took a hip spin on 1940s noir. As private eye Philip Marlowe, Elliot Gould is a laconic, semi-stoned dude of an anachronism. With a witty style, amusing score and some inspired performances (especially Mark Rydell and Sterling Hayden) it skips along the precipice of spoof. By the 1970s and 1980s noir had become the genre of parody. Only by working through the demons of cliché through films such as *Dead Men Don't Wear Plaid*, *Married to the Mob* and, indirectly, *Blade Runner* (1982) could noir reinvent itself for the modern age.

The scar tissue left by *Bonnie & Clyde* in the 1960s was being opened up by a new breed of violent films in the 1970s. Protest, war and terrorism were on TV and silencers, Magnums and blood-splattering special effects were ruling film. From the crass (Peckinpah's *Straw Dogs*) to the sublime (*Dirty Harry*) film makers were taking every opportunity to use advances in special effects technology to show the aesthetic of arterial blood in full flow. As an indicator of society crime film was always at the forefront. As Watergate bled into the American consciousness a distrust of government led to a slew of conspiracy films in the 1970s.

From *The Parallax View* (1974) and *Three Days of the Condor* (1975) to the immaculately insane *Winter Kills* (1979) the lone good guy pursued by the shadowy assassin has been a rich vein in a time of paranoia. As the ultimate, pure look into the mind of madness at this time' *Taxi Driver'* (1976) stands out as a defining moment.

It is a film that is marginal in terms of the crime genre but pivotal as an indicator of the psychological mechanics of the motivations for crime. As films split into camps that led on one path to heist films and the other to crazed killing sprees Scorsese's film and to an extent Terence Malick's *Badlands* (1974) are exemplars of authenticity. De Niro's Travis Bickle is a man slowly turned insane by the alienating nightmare of New York City and a society that rejects the outsider. The image of the blood-cleansed Travis at the end, finger to the head in a gun salute and crazed smile on his face, is a visceral warning of the future. A generation of madness is coming of age.

In a more elegiac form, *Badlands* also acts as a warning. Through beautiful cinematography and haunting music the acts of banal violence perpetrated by the bored young couple, seeking to escape their stultified lives, become almost heroic. Martin Sheen and Sissy Spacek's romantic killers, fuelled by images of James Dean and teen magazines, were based on the real-life original spree-killers, Charles Starkweather and Carol Ann Fugate whose exploits elevated them to the status of folk heroes. As a vision of how guns become the solution to an empty life in a morally confused age they set a template to film makers looking to mirror a violent society.

The raised fist of Black Power had a gun put in it by the Blaxploitation genre.

At its best—*Shaft* (1971), *Sweet Sweetback's Baadasssss Song* (1971) and *Superfly* (1972)—it was a genre that reflected the black experience in America in the context of simple, B movie melodrama. Although only partially empowering in terms of control it had a slow-burn influence to crime film.

After the seismic shift in film that was *Star Wars* things mutated. Cinema became a corporate entity with enormous sums of money running on the success of the biggest releases. Crime film took cover under the blanket of the independent film circuit with relatively low budgets and almost B Movie low risk. Into the 1980s the rise of the home video market had an immediate effect. This was the decade of Palace Pictures. Their influence in nurturing talent turned the tide for the genre. Art direction, rapid editing and an ironic glee for knowing parody elbowed aside more mature works. Style was beginning to take over from substance. With a primary-coloured neon wash *Diva* (1982) came out of France like a catwalk model. Chic, funny, stylish and full of character it was a film that set the tone for the decade. Jean-Jacques Beneix' film typifies the video age where hyperactive camerawork keeps an attention-span deficient audience satisfied and a slick package of sex, violence, chase sequences and lurid colour fill the senses. In Hollywood Brian De Palma was in his element as he reworked as many Hitchcock set-pieces as possible within the framework of his movies. *Dressed to Kill* (1980), *Blow Out* (1981), the gloriously mad *Scarface* (1987) and *The Untouchables* (1987) are all expertly crafted works of entertainment filled with the nods and winks to the history of cinema which fill film today.

But there were many mainstream films which had a maturity beyond the reach of those television commercial-trained and music video-schooled directors of the time. *Body Heat* (1981) had Kathleen Turner as the ultimate in femme fatales in a sexually-charged reprise of *Double Indemnity*. *Cutter*s Way' (1981) showed Jeff Bridges as one of the most under-rated actors of his age. *Thief* (1981) announced Michael Mann

as an auteur of the genre. *The Black Marble* (1980)—with a wonderful neurotic performance by Harry Dean Stanton—was another quiet gem from Harold Becker who would later team up with poet of street dialogue, Richard Price for Al Pacinos return to form in *Sea Of Love* (1989).*Once Upon A Time In America* (1984) attempted to copy the epic formula of *The Godfather* Part II but succeeded only through the combination of performance (De Niro and the great James Woods) and technical style. *Prizzi's Honour* (1985) was a dark satire on the Mafia myth. *The Hit* (1984) was Stephen Frears' razor sharp story of gangster retirement and revenge. *Cop* (1987) injected some James Ellroy sleaze into James Woods' character in a rare film by James B Harris, Kubrick's former production partner. *Blood Simple* (1984) blazed the names of Joel and Ethan Coen onto the big screen as the masters of reinterpretation and reinvention of a tired genre.

At the head of the queue to the door marked weird was David Lynch. With *Blue Velvet* (1987) he created a film of such startling originality of vision that it stands as one of crime film's paradigms. His America is one of 1950s archetypes supercharged into a modern nightmare. His is a Normal Rockwell vision gone wrong. He described *Blue Velvet* as *"the Hardy Boys go to hell."* Lynch has the ability, like few directors, to create a world that is utterly his own. With *Blue Velvet* he created a fairy tale of fear surrounding the descent into an underworld of kidnapping, violence, psychosis and perverted sex by a naïve innocent acting as a cipher for a nostalgic age that never was. By deploying a range of cinematic techniques from aural textures, parodic music and dialogue to surreal expressionist style Lynch collects a multitude of symbolic elements to create a cohesive narrative entertainment. In Dennis Hopper's Frank Booth it provides a cinematic electric shock of insanity. Similarly in *Wild at*

Heart (1990) his take on an Elvis road movie becomes a darkly witty battering ram of a film. In *Lost Highway* (1997) he reached strangely disturbing heights in the depiction of internal madness through a confusing noir narrative. We can only imagine what wonderful magic he would have spun if his original desire to film Thomas Harris' *Red Dragon* had been realised.

Looking at crime film now the perception of this decade could be said to be one of serial killers and Quentin Tarantino. Certainly the Tarantino effect has looped the genre around itself several times over. His recycling of images from his video store days combined with the prevailing culture hit a nerve that many see as being the spirit of the age. His instant legend has made him an Orson Welles of splatter and the ripple effect of his style (pop-culture riffs, blatant stealing from classic films, clever use of narrative structure, killer soundtracks) has been seismic. Oliver Stone attempted some reflected glory with the amphetamine, eye-slamming, pure cinematic experience that is Natural Born Killers but along the way seemed to miss the point. At the heart of it, *Reservoir Dogs* (1992), *Pulp Fiction* (1994) and *Jackie Brown* (1998) are all great films. Hats off.

The serial killer genre reached the 1990s with John McNaughton's graphic, gruesome and stark *Henry; Portrait of a Serial Killer* (1990). But with *Silence Of The Lambs* in 1991 every element that makes an instant classic came together. In Hannibal Lector fiction has one of its great monsters. While Michael Manns *Manhunter* (1986) was a more stylised work with Brian Cox's Lector more at the periphery, Anthony Hopkins takes centre stage in a performance of coiled, animal evil.

This decade has seen an explosion of talent in terms of crime film. Hong Kong is producing films of the quality of *Chunking Express* as well as their own brand of pulp. In the last few years the roll call of films of quality, intelligence and style includes *Clockers, Miami Blues, Miller's Crossing, Fargo, Deep Cover, One False Move, King of New York, The Player, Things to do in Denver When You're Dead, Heat, LA Confidential, The Grifters, Red Rock West, The Last Seduction* (with a definitive noir performance by Linda Fiorentino), *The Usual Suspects* and at the very top of the tree (and most influential of all) *Goodfellas*. It is the coda to *The Godfather*, the underside of that world. These made guys are the footsoldiers of the mob aspiring to the culture of criminal success with an arrogant swagger and a cocaine mania. Scorsese films them with the vigour and style of a big screen musical, revelling in the intimidating elegance of the times and not flinching from showing the reality of their sudden flashes of horrific violence.

At the cusp of the new century the visual image of crime never stands still. We see infra red images of car-jackers, joy-riders, looters and video courtroom testimony of celebrities auditioning for the world. Things are getting confusing. The real beneficiary of this culture is television. With its quick turnaround the TV movie and ongoing series can incorporate the here and now much more readily than film where the shelf-life of news currency is short. In retrospect it is television of the last two decades (and with the exception of Cracker, American television) that has risen to command the most consistent respect in the genre. From *Hill Street Blues* to *NYPD Blue* to *Homicide* to *The Sopranos* production values, writing talent, acting prowess and 24 episode runs give the ability to run the richest of story arcs that are beyond the two hour film.

In the 1990s the crime film has become the cinema's conscience. Where incoherent multiplex fodder congeals on the screen the crime film has become the refuge of intelligent, popular cinema. It is filling in the gaps.

Do you find me funny? Funny how?

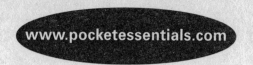

Alfred Hitchcock

by Paul Duncan

Everything you need to know about Hitchcock in one essential guide

ISBN: 1903047-00-5 Price : £2.99 Paperback

Who was Hitchcock? A fat git who played practical jokes on people? A control freak who humiliated others to make himself look better? A little boy afraid of the dark? One of the greatest storytellers of the century? He was all of this and more - 20 years after his death, he is still a household name, most people in the Western world have seen his films and he popularised the action movie format we see every week on the cinema screen. He was both a great artist and dynamite at the box office.

What's in it? As well as an introductory essay, each of Hitchcock's films is reviewed and analysed. In addition, the effect he has had on the industry is explained - virtually every big action movie of the past three decades has been influenced by his work. Not only that, but there's a handy reference section listing all the far weightier (and more expensive) books about Hitchcock.

An exciting new series of Info Books

Pocket Essentials is a new series for the MTV generation brought up in the three-minute culture. Short, snappy text. Easy to read. Riveting. Enthusiastic. Fresh. Juicy. Packed with crunchy goodness, backed up with opinion, crammed with information, this is the first step into the world of films.

Available at all good (and some not so good...) bookstores at £2.99 each, order online at **www.pocketessentials.com**, or send a cheque to: **pocketessentials (Dept CT26), 18 Coleswood Rd, Harpenden, Herts, AL5 1EQ.** Please make cheques payable to 'Oldcastle Books'. 50p Postage and Packing for each book

film

action man
the films of don siegel
charles waring

At present, everyone seems intent on looking back to the past rather than forward to the future. Although the glossy Sunday supplements and influential style magazines will, no doubt, offer some kind of vague prognosis about future trends and the stars of tomorrow, for the most part they are preoccupied with the artistic achievements of the current epoch. Such is the extent of this retrospection that you get the feeling that maybe, just maybe, the world is really coming to an apocalyptic end at the close of 1999.

But so far, lists rather than the bombs of Armageddon are being dropped on us. The public have been bombarded by list upon list of things ranging from the trivial to the profound, from the greatest pop records ever made to the most significant books of all time. Curiously, the majority of listed items usually have their origins in the twentieth century which somewhat puts paid to the idea of a bona fide millennium chart.

Cinema, as one of this century's most exciting and potent artforms, has not been neglected by those indefatigable anoraks who compile those sometimes intriguing but mostly frustrating listings. But, in a poll of the top film directors of all time, the odds are against you finding Don Siegel's name. In fact, you're not likely to find Siegel listed in any pantheon devoted to the directorial

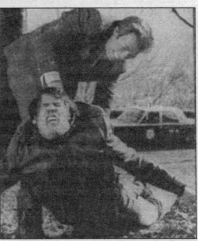

Clint Eastwood and Don Stroud in Coogan's Bluff

legends of Hollywood. And yet, Siegel, while not acknowledged as a master of his art in the way that say geniuses like Hitchcock, Scorsese or Spielberg have been, was in many ways much more than just the merely technically competent film maker described by some critics.

It is a widely held view that tough, hard-boiled action movies were Siegel's forte. This would probably be a fair assessment of Siegel's measure as a director: indeed, that's what he seemed to excel at, but Siegel, himself, didn't view his aptitude towards the action genre as a wholly natural pre-disposition. Rather, he perceived it as something that was foisted upon him by the studio heads and because he happened to do it well, Siegel felt he wasn't considered for other, more meaningful projects. In fact, towards the end of his lengthy career, Siegel, with the brutal candour he often evinced, seemed to genuinely rue his being pigeon-holed as an action director:" I was forced into the action mould because of a series of circumstances over which I had no control and I had to go with it because there was nothing else around…by the time the Committee had noticed me, they couldn't see me do anything but action. I can't rewrite my past, which, all things considered, wasn't bad but I haven't had the options I might have wanted."

One of the options that Siegel never seemed to have was a decent-sized budget for his films. Many of his movies he shot on a shoestring, using his technical background as a special effects man to help conceal the lack of investment. Even Siegel's reputation as a man who could shoot a picture under-budget and under-schedule did not help procure him the big star-studded movies. He worked miracles considering the often meagre resources at his disposal. Only towards the end of his career (after he had hooked up with the highly bankable Clint Eastwood) was Siegel given the opportunity to make big money pictures. Even so, Siegel's name didn't last very long on Hollywood's A list of directors. Not long after the phenomenally successful Dirty Harry, Siegel was still banging heads with studio bosses over what he could and could not do.

Sadly, Siegel may have felt a profound chagrin at his inability to make more varied and perhaps cerebral pictures but he was, without a doubt, one of the best directors of hard-hitting crime movies. It is for this reason that CT salutes the work and life of one of Hollywood's unsung heroes, Don Siegel.

"I realised this was a man who could do an awful lot with very little" Clint Eastwood on Don Siegel

Don Siegel cut a distinctive figure in Hollywood. With his jet-black hair, tanned complexion, and short, athletic stature, the film director's looks may have appeared to some observers as resembling those of an archetypal Italian waiter. His penchant for sporting a well-groomed moustache only seemed to deepen this impression. What added to the sartorial singularity of Siegel's appearance was his predilection for wearing natty headgear on the set (rarely was he to be seen without a hat).

Strangely, though, his autobiography, fascinating as it is, is conspicuously lacking in details related to the director's family background and the kind of life he led before he went to work in the film industry. What we do know is that he was born Donald Siegel in Chicago, Illinois on October 26th, 1912. Siegel tells the reader nothing of his family's financial or social situation except that his father was that very rare-breed of professional musician, a virtuoso mandolin player. Reading between the lines, one has to assume that the Siegel family were fairly affluent because Siegel Jnr received education at some of New York's finest public schools and was sufficiently gifted academically to take up a place at Jesus College, Cambridge here in England. He also attended the prestigious Beaux Arts in Paris before returning to England to enrol at The Royal Academy Of Dramatic Arts. Siegel's intention at this time was to become an actor but at the age of twenty, a change in his father's financial fortunes abruptly curtailed his education and European travels, prompting him to become a merchant seaman and work his way round the world back to America.

After 6 years away in Europe, Siegel eventually landed back on American soil when he arrived at Los Angeles in 1934 with no money but a distinctly sophisticated, cosmopolitan air about him. He knew nothing about films or film-making but applied for a job at Warner Brothers. He was granted an interview with Hollywood producer, Hal Wallis, simply on the grounds that Siegel was following the recommendation of his 'Uncle Jack.' Many people at Warners, perhaps including Wallis himself, assumed Siegel was referring to the studio head, Jack Warner, who they believed, erroneously, to be his uncle (in fact, later on, Siegel started a rumour, which many also believed, that he was Warner's illegitimate son!). As nepotism was rife in tinsel town at that time (and probably still is!) Siegel's brazen bluff paid off and he got a job as an humble film librarian. In his revealing 1991 autobiography, *A Siegel Film*, Siegel offered this advice to aspiring film-makers: *"If you don't have an Uncle Jack, invent one. Don't hesitate to bluff or lie. The moguls or lesser fry do the same."*

Siegel's naiveté concerning the film industry was epitomised by his expectations that the film library would be filled with *"thousands of books, periodicals, magazines of all sizes and shapes, crammed with knowledge, technical data and stories galore."* He was in for a nasty shock. To the 22-year-old Siegel's incredulity and disappointment, the library contained none of these things, merely a myriad reels of film. Basically, Siegel was no more than a glorified errand boy, running here and there with cans of film at the behest of editors and projectionists. Certainly at this time, Siegel had no great aspirations to be a filmmaker and could often be found dozing-off in the studio's projection rooms.

However, after a few months at Warners, a genuine interest in film-making began to stir within Siegel. His curiosity was particularly aroused by watching the 'dailies' (nowadays often referred to as 'rushes'- the first print of a day's shooting when the film is returned from the processing laboratories). Siegel's fascination with the creative process of film-making fanned his ambition and prompted his promotion to the cutting room where he learned not only about the mechanical job of splicing film together but also about the more artistic task of editing. Following a somewhat unsuccessful spell in the editorial department (he was described by his boss as *"the worst assistant I've ever worked with"*), Siegel moved on to special effects. Siegel's first task was to learn how to shoot 'inserts'— these were usually close-up shots inserted into a dramatic scene which gave the audience a closer view of what a character was doing or seeing: inserts often depicted images like an article in a newspaper or a hand writing a letter. Amazingly and despite his patent lack of experience, Siegel was given his own crew comprised of a camera operator, an assistant cameraman, a grip and an electrician.

He soon got the hang of making inserts and developed into a competent and imaginative insert director although it was during this stage of his career that he began to lock horns with both his immediate superiors and those in the upper echelons of the Hollywood hierarchy. Siegel's conflict with the industry's money men and business suits would continue throughout his career. In Hollywood, money called the shots and Siegel, despite his desire to be free of artistic constraints, had to comply, albeit rarely without a fight!

From inserts, Siegel graduated to the montage department, where celluloid images are superimposed upon one another, often symbolically and in an impressionistic way using short dissolve shots to either establish a setting, visually describe a situation, develop the story or background or simply bridge a time gap. Classic usages of montage techniques can be seen in Sergei Eisenstein's *The Battleship Potemkin* and Orson Welles' *Citizen Kane*. It was a technique that required a great deal of thought and skill but Siegel was equal to the task, his creative juices stimulated by the challenge. In fact, Siegel soon earned himself a reputation as a particularly imaginative montage maker, providing inventive sequences for directors like Raoul Walsh (in particular *The Roaring Twenties*). By this time, Siegel was already taking charge of second unit work, undertaking the direction of action sequences while the main director worked elsewhere on another sequence of the film. Siegel also directed sequences in movies by Michael Curtiz (*Yankee Doodle Dandy* with James Cagney and *Mission To Moscow*) and Howard Hawks (*To Have And Have Not*, starring Humphrey Bogart with Lauren Bacall in her screen debut). Siegel's big break came when Vincent Sherman, who was then directing *Flight From Destiny*, was taken ill and unable to continue shooting. Siegel was asked to step in and although later confessed that he had no idea of how to approach certain scenes, managed, somehow (with the help of the actor, Thomas Mitchell, who had worked with John Ford and generously shared his knowledge with Siegel) to do a satisfactory job.

Those who had worked under Siegel's second-unit directorship, particularly the actors Walter Huston (in *Mission To Moscow*) and the corpulent Sydney Greenstreet (in *Passage To Marseilles*), sang his praises to Jack 'J.L.' Warner, urging the truculent movie-mogul to provide an opportunity for Siegel to direct on his own. Warner— who regarded all thespians as 'shit'- was reluctant to hand Siegel a break on a mere actor's recommendation. The two didn't get on and were often at loggerheads over movie matters although Siegel wasn't in the least intimidated by Warner's belligerent, megalomaniac attitude. Inevitably, though, Warner recognised Siegel's talent and offered him a *Casablanca*-style picture called *The Conspirators* starring the Austrian sex-siren Hedy Lamarr and produced by Hal Wallis. Unfortunately, Siegel's elation was tainted by his disgust at Warner's proposed contract which would tie him to the company for seven years. Siegel would be obligated to direct any picture the company chose with the consequence that a couple of bad movies on his part could effectively end his career not only at Warners but anywhere else too. Although it was an opportunity to direct, Siegel was adamant that the contract's terms were grossly unfair. He proposed a shorter, two-year contract and offered to direct on the same salary he was getting for his special effects duties. This resulted in a somewhat heated altercation with Jack Warner who leapt out from behind his desk declaring to Siegel *"I'm going to kick the shit out of you!"* On hearing Siegel calmly utter the words *"J.L., you couldn't kick the shit out of anyone,"* caution quickly dampened the movie mogul's ardour to cause bodily harm. Not accustomed to such insolent bravado in his presence, Warner prudently retreated but vowed to suspend Siegel from his duties immediately. This suspension was initially set to last three months, in which time (and without pay), Siegel brushed-up on his tennis skills. When his three month suspension had elapsed, he returned to the studio. But after completing a day's work, Siegel discovered that he was to be laid-off for an additional three months. Warner wanted to puncture Siegel's morale and bring him obsequiously into line. When the six month suspension finally ended, Siegel was assigned to the film which he had hoped would represent his directorial debut. *The Conspirators*, however, had a new director (the Romanian, Jean Negulesco), with Siegel relegated to assistant director. He may have been humiliated by Warner's tactics but Siegel's spirit remained indomitable and it pleased him greatly that the film turned out to be a complete and utter financial and artistic failure.

Eventually, Warner, who seemed to admire Siegel's feisty recalcitrance and respect the fact that, unlike everyone else, he wasn't a mere sycophant in his presence, asked the young director to direct a short for the company. 'Shorts' were films that usually ran for about 33 minutes duration (or 3000 feet of celluloid) and often preceded feature films in cinema programmes during the 1930s and 40s. Their demise was precipitated by the advent of double features and the fact that they proved economically unviable.

Surprisingly, Siegel was given a lot of creative latitude by Warner and endeavoured to engender an idea that the self-opinionated movie-mogul would flat-out refuse: *"I came up with an idea that I was sure Warner would hate. A modern parable about the birth of Christ—Star In The Night. I figured Warner, who was Jewish, would turn it down. To my surprise and dismay, he okayed the project."*

Ironically, Warner loved the picture while Siegel detested it, regarding it as too maudlin and saccharine for his personal taste. However, it also found instant favour with the Hollywood's prestigious American Academy of Motion Picture Arts and Sciences, who bestowed upon it an Academy Award for the best two-reel short film of 1945.

The film's success prompted Warner to demand another short a year later. Siegel believed his new idea would be unceremoniously repudiated by Warner as too offensive—it was a proposed documentary entitled *Hitler Lives* using montages created from old stock footage of goose-stepping Nazis. To Siegel's utter disbelief and chagrin, it too won an Oscar (for best two-reel documentary short) and Jack Warner even went so far as to take credit for its conception!

The first full-length feature film that Don Siegel got to direct was *The Verdict* in 1946 with Sydney Greenstreet and Peter Lorre. The film was essentially a crime-thriller set in the Victorian era. It was not the sort of material that Siegel truly wanted to direct but because he was under contract at Warners he had no real option but to make the picture. By his own admission, Siegel found *The Verdict* excruciatingly boring. Jack Warner viewed the completed film in his private screening room and declared that Sydney Greenstreet could not be given the role of a murderer and had the ending changed to an ambivalent one which only hinted (by dint of visual clues and an unsubtle musical cue) that Greenstreet might be the guilty party. Despite his own poor assessment of the value of *The Verdict*, Siegel strongly objected to Warner's interference but had to comply to the mogul's imperious dictates.

It was three years before Siegel sat in the coveted director's chair again. By this time his contract with Warners had expired. After 14 years service, Siegel was told in no uncertain terms that the company was not going to renew his contract. This brought a mixture of relief and apprehension for the director who knew that in Hollywood, the grass is not always greener on the other side of the fence.

During his tenure at Warners, Siegel had been solicited by none other than the then RKO head-honcho and eccentric billionaire Howard Hughes. Hughes had sought Siegel's directorial intervention in an to attempt to salvage and right the manifold wrongs on his catastrophic movie Vendetta. As Siegel had unceremoniously turned down the offer of helping Hughes in his hour of need, he was flabbergasted when the movie-mogul insisted on hiring him for RKO's *The Big Steal* (1949), starring Robert Mitchum as an army officer who is framed for a payroll heist and chases the real thief across Mexico pursued by the police.

In the 1950s, Siegel directed thirteen movies, mostly action-orientated and concerned with crimes of one sort or another. They included a western, *The Duel At Silver Creek*, (1952) starring Audie Murphy, an espionage yarn, *No Time For Flowers*, (1952), *Count The Hours* a suspense drama about a wrongly convicted man and *China Venture* (1953) a war movie whose main focus was capturing a Japanese general from the Chinese jungle. Basically, these were all B movies, customarily shot in black and white because of the film's small budgets. Resources and name-actors were limited but the dependable Siegel made the best of the situation and usually made something watchable out of his material.

In 1954, however, Siegel made a film that made others take notice of his blossoming film-making skills. That film was *Riot In Cell Block 11*, a grim but gritty, believable and compassionate prison drama with a strong moral conscience. It caused controversy not only because of its realistic subject matter but because of its tense, claustrophobic, edge-of-the-seat direction and graphic violence (though admittedly very tame by today's lurid standards!).

The success of 'Riot' propelled Siegel to even greater things, albeit in low-budget, B movie terms. Perhaps the greatest science-fiction B movie of all was Siegel's *Invasion Of The Body Snatchers* which first hit the silver screen in 1956. It was an intelligent, subtle and well-orchestrated drama focusing on 1950's American paranoia. Its subject: alien invasion. This seminal SF tale spawned many ghastly imitations and even two Hollywood remakes. But none have bettered it. More crime thrillers followed in the late 50s: films like the highly-regarded gangster biopic, *Baby Face Nelson* (1957), *The Gun Runners* (1958), *The Lineup* (1958) (based on a popular TV detective series) and *Edge Of Eternity* (1959) about the discovery of murders related to the disputed ownership of a mine. This was

the first film that Siegel helped to produce. It was a significant step for the director and allowed him more artistic autonomy. Indeed, as will be seen later, his most satisfactory movies were ones that he, himself, produced.

The sixties began with Siegel directing none-other-than Elvis 'The Pelvis' Presley in a tale of an Indian half-breed during the time of the American Civil war. That was *Flaming Star*. It was followed by a war movie with Steve McQueen, *Hell Is For Heroes* (1962) which again exploited Siegel's flair for action sequences. Although Siegel's minimalist, crisply edited style had taken him out of B movies, the really big pictures still eluded him. In fact, one of Siegel's most popular films (at least among his cult following), *The Killers*, dating from 1964, was originally intended for television as the first two-hour made for TV feature. The censors, however, thought it too violent for the small screen. Consequently, it was given a cinema release and fared well with both pundits and punters.

Television, in fact, was a medium that Siegel worked in quite frequently during the late 50s and early 60s. In addition to *The Killers*, he shot two other two-hour features for TV, both of which ended up in the cinema: The Hanged Man (1964) and Stranger On The Run (1967). Among the shows he directed for TV were episodes from the cult cop show, *The Lineup*, a couple of episodes of *The Twilight Zone* and pilot for *The Legend Of Jesse James* series in 1966. He even directed a single episode of the popular Lloyd Bridges show.

If *The Killers* was a landmark film for Siegel, the tough cop thriller, *Madigan*, starring Richard Widmark in the title role, four years later in 1968, cemented the director's reputation as a master of all things hard-boiled.

In the same year, Siegel teamed up for the first time with Clint Eastwood, just back from Italy and making movies with the legendary Italian director, Sergio Leone. Eastwood was looking for a suitable vehicle to introduce him to American audiences. He chose *Coogan's Bluff*, a story about a macho, no-nonsense Arizona sheriff who ventures to the Big Apple to pick up a fugitive. Siegel and Eastwood not only formed a productive, mutually rewarding creative partnership but also established a lasting friendship. Their special relationship would result in four more pictures together, including *Two Mules For Sister Sara* (1970), *The Beguiled* (1970) and, of course, the rogue-cop classic, *Dirty Harry* (1971).

Dirty Harry proved to be Siegel's most successful film. It also sparked much controversy, particularly with the divided critics, some of whom viewed the film as espousing fascist views and right-wing politics. That same year, Siegel made his acting debut (as the bartender Murphy) in Eastwood's acclaimed directorial debut, *Play Misty For Me*.

The seventies witnessed Siegel shooting yet more taut, fast-paced action movies. The cult-classic, *Charley Varrick*, with Walter Matthau as a small-time bank robber who outwits the mob was released in 1973 followed by the appearance of the somewhat more flaccid thriller in the form of The Black Windmill with Michael Caine (1974). In 1976, Siegel, who at 64 was by this time regarded as a veteran, directed one of the best westerns of that era. *The Shootist* starred another movie veteran, John Wayne, in his last role. Shortly afterwards, Siegel made the spy film *Telefon* with the brawn-over-brain action-hero, Charles Bronson, in the lead role. Ironically, Siegel returned to the screen as a performer in the first remake of a film he had brought to the big screen twenty or so years earlier: *Invasion Of The Body Snatchers*. One year after, in 1979, Siegel joined forces with Clint Eastwood again for *Escape From Alcatraz*. It was the last film they made

together. By this time, Eastwood's achievements as an actor and, more significantly, director, were now eclipsing those of his former tutor and mentor. Siegel's declining fortunes and waning powers were no more evident than in 1980's *Rough Cut*, a leaden, heavy-handed attempt at a lightweight comedy-thriller with Burt Reynolds and David Niven. The critics were even more savage with the Bette Midler starring-vehicle, *Jinxed!*, two years later. Siegel, himself, was singularly unimpressed and didn't mince his words about the quality of this execrable film: *"Jinxed stinks!"* Significantly, it turned out to be his last film although he would make a cameo appearance as himself in Jon Landis' 1985 off-beat comedy-thriller, *Into The Night*, along with other illustrious Hollywood directors Jonathan Demme, Lawrence Kasdan and David Cronenberg.

Before Don Siegel died in 1991 at the age of 79, he had compiled a collection of movie memoirs which was eventually published as *A Siegel Film: An Autobiography* by Faber and Faber in 1993. It is one of the most riotously humorous and riveting books of Hollywood reminiscences ever published and provides a good insight into not only Siegel's character and temperament but the strange practices that are commonplace in Hollywood even today.

In that laconic, self-effacing way that became a Siegel trademark, the director once dismissed his work as being of little lasting value: *"most of my pictures, I'm sorry to say, are about nothing. Because I'm a whore. I work for money. It's the American way."*

And yet, ironically, it was the quintessential American flavour of Siegel's energetic direction that won the plaudits from many European critics, particularly in France, where his work remains highly-regarded.

By far the greatest tribute to Siegel's

work and ability came from his former protégé, Clint Eastwood, when he was interviewed in the 1970s by his then biographer Stuart Kaminsky. Eastwood often cites Siegel's influence on his own considerable directorial work and here gave a glowing testimonial of his former mentor's talent:

"I like his attack on directing...he never gets bogged down, even in disaster. I think he's fantastic. We have worked a lot together, and probably will in the future. I feel he's an enormously talented guy who has been deprived of notoriety he probably should have had much earlier because Hollywood was going through a stage where the awards went to the big pictures and the guys who knew how to spend a lot of money. As a result, guys who got a lot of pictures with a lot of effort and a little money weren't glorified. So Don had to wait years until he could get to do films with fairly good budgets. He's the kind of director there's not enough of."

For most of his long career, Don Siegel struggled to make decent films out of limited resources. There is strong evidence to suggest that his Hollywood career was probably hampered by his unbridled contempt for the film industry's shakers and movers, the producers and moneymen. But in Siegel's formative years as a filmmaker, the so-called suits all kow-towed to studio bosses like Jack Warner and Louis B. Meyer. If Siegel resented interference from tyrannical figures like Warner with his sycophantic minions (*"the largest club at Warners: the Agreers"*) then the changes in Hollywood from the 1950s onwards provided an even more frustrating scenario: although less colourful characters had wrestled Hollywood out of the hands of the despots, the grey men in grey suits, the lawyers and accountants, established a new hegemony in tinsel town. These were the men who now decided what got made and what

didn't. Money talked in Hollywood and if you didn't listen or speak its language you were history. So Siegel hung in there, battling to get films made and hustling for finance.

But as he later found out, though, an increased budget didn't necessarily mean more artistic freedom. In a famous exchange with the French director, Jean-Luc Godard, Siegel said he envied Godard his freedom. Godard's retort was *"You have something I want—money."*

Filmmaking is a curious marriage of art and commerce in which the latter usually has the upper hand. Significantly, it was in all probability economic factors which helped shape Don Siegel's distinctive style. He was so accustomed to impecunious production budgets that he was forced to become somewhat parsimonious in terms of how many takes he took of a particular scene. For Siegel, less was more. He always prepared well in advance with his camera set-ups and preferred to go with the spontaneity of first takes. Some directors would execute many repeated takes as a kind of insurance policy covering all possible contingencies. Siegel, however, preferred not to waste time and money reshaping the film in the editing room but was prepared to take risks and follow his instinct. As Clint Eastwood once noted, *"He's willing to take a lot of chances that way."* Eastwood admired Siegel's ability to know exactly what emotion or meaning he wanted to extract from a scene and how to get it as quickly and effectively as possible. Siegel's pacy and precise minimalist style didn't waste precious film on needless repetition and so not only prevented boredom from seeping onto the set but more importantly, kept costs down. Eastwood equated Siegel's skill with that of *"the really great directors of the old days, like John Ford, Howard Hawks or Hitchcock. They knew in advance what they wanted."*

tv crime

the sopranos
charles waring

Organised crime in the guise of the Mafia is as all-American as Coca-Cola and Pecan pie. Certainly, no one will doubt that the mob's place of origin and spiritual home is Sicily, but ever since boatloads of Italian immigrants set foot on the land of opportunity, the transplanted Cosa Nostra culture has thrived and weaved itself into the very fabric of American life.

Indeed, the Mafia has achieved almost institution-like status in the public consciousness. This may largely be due to Marlon Brando, who stuffed cotton wool into his cheeks and created the role of Don Corleone in Francis Ford Coppola's big screen adaptation of Mario Puzo's *The Godfather* epic almost 30 years ago. The extent of the Mafia's influence upon contemporary US life has also been documented more recently in graphic wise-guy films like Goodfellas and Casino by Italian-American director, Martin Scorsese. Finally, the small screen has received an arresting slice of contemporary mob life in the shape of HBO's magnificent 13 part Mafia soap-opera, *The Sopranos*, shown on Channel 4.

The Sopranos was first screened on British terrestrial TV in July this year and found instant favour with both critics and viewers (although it's fair to say that Channel 4 have probably received numerous complaints about the show's graphic vi-

olence and colourful language). Unsurprisingly, this ground-breaking series has already garnered sixteen Emmy nominations in the US. It's not hard to see why.

From its opening titles, where slick editing depicts Tony Soprano's drive through genuine New Jersey locations accompanied by an evocative and very apposite soundtrack (*Woke Up This Morning And Got Myself A Gun* by the Alabama 3), *The Sopranos* conveys quality television entertainment. But as well as looking good, this series oozes substance, wit and intelligence.

MOB LIFE CRISIS

As a drama, *The Sopranos*, makes us an offer we can't refuse. It tells the engaging story of mob boss, Anthony ('Tony' or 'T' to his familiars) Soprano, a forty-something, seemingly happily married father of two with a thinning thatch and an expanding girth. We are introduced to Tony at a critical and traumatic time in his life. He has been experiencing panic attacks which either leave him gasping for breath or else collapsing in a state of unconsciousness. A mob leader has to display strength and inspire confidence so should any of Tony's Mafia family discover his predicament, he could suffer from a permanent blackout!

Tony's response to this situation is an unusual one and demonstrates that even the mob with its long and archaic traditions moves with the times: he turns to a shrink, Dr. Jennifer Melfi, whose cathartic psychotherapy sessions function as a valuable confessional conduit for the beleaguered mobster. He never actually spells out to his therapist the exact nature of his occupation but she's sufficiently perceptive to read between the lines. Although Tony finds the Mafiosi code of silence a frustrating impediment, by embarking on therapy, he is endangering the lives of both himself and Dr. Melfi.

MARRIED TO THE MOB

Tony's situation is much more than just your average mid-life crisis. The main source of his trials and tribulations is family life. Tony, however, belongs to two families and both come with onerous duties, responsibilities and obligations. *The Sopranos* depicts an incestuous kind of bigamy: not only is Tony married to Carmela but he's also inextricably bound by deeper ties to his all-male adopted family, the mob.

It's this friction between the polarity of both families and their two opposing worlds that creates the show's dramatic tension. The great irony is that Tony has more problems coping with his genetic family than the nefarious antics of his business associates, though the combination of domestic issues and business ones have explosive repercussions for his health. This results in a Prozac prescription, with Tony downing the little white pills like M&Ms.

MOTHER KNOWS BEST

At the heart of Tony's domestic troubles is his demanding, difficult mother, Livia. She's the bane of his life. He tries to be a dutiful son but his mother's attitude puts a strain on his filial piety. She's a morose, cantankerous elderly widow full of self-pity and obsessed with the prospect of her own death. After living on her own for a long time, a series of disasters (she set fire to her kitchen and ran over one of her friends in a car) prompt Tony to persuade her that it's time she moved to a retirement home. Tony, of course, can't resort to his habitual Mafia methods of persuasion on his own mother— while he will quite happily strangle a mob informer (or 'rat') without compunction, members of Tony's own family require a more subtle approach. Subtlety, though, is beyond Tony's scope, as Dr. Melfi will testify: in one episode, Tony's crush for his psychotherapist results in him wanting to know more about her. Instead of directly asking her, like any 'normal' person, Tony gets to 'know' the good doctor by having her followed until he is familiar with the intimate details of her life. Furthermore, when Dr.Melfi describes the problems she is experiencing with her ailing car, Tony's response is to send some hoods out in the dead of night to steal the vehicle, fix it and then return it before morning breaks!

Try as he might, Tony just can't seem to do the right thing.

TROUBLE AT HOME

In relation to his close-knit Mafia family, Tony enforces the law remorselessly with swift punitive action. However, laying down the rules for his blood relatives is a far harder task. His son, Anthony Junior, for example, boosts the sacramental wine from the school chapel which results in disciplinary action both at school (suspension) and at home (as well as being grounded, Anthony Jnr is banned from using the Nintendo!). But Tony has difficulty enforcing it. After all, he was no angel himself as a juvenile. More significantly, he suspects that his children now know that he's a gangster. If so, then his actions will stink of hypocrisy. And Tony is an honourable man even if he is a mobfather. This is just one of the many dilemmas that push him to the brink of a breakdown and a bottle of Prozac. Only the consulting couch of Dr. Jennifer Melfi offers some form of sanctuary.

THERAPY

Therapy is supposed to iron out the creases in Tony's life but his confessions and the cosy professional intimacy he enjoys with the serene Dr. Melfi lead to further complications. He starts having mildly erotic dreams about her and half way through the series boldly announces that he loves her, which, to his dismay, she shrugs off with professional insouciance. To make matters worse, Tony discovers that the Prozac he's been shovelling down his throat to ease anxiety has weakened his sexual libido—even Tony's mistress is surprised by his wish to talk rather than cut straight to the action. To be honest, she's rather give head than get inside Tony's head!

THE BACKGROUND

The Sopranos is the brainchild of writer/director/producer, David Chase, a seasoned Emmy award-winning writer who also contributed to critically-lauded shows like The Rockford Files starring James Garner in the 70s and more recently, the offbeat Alaskan series Northern Exposure And I'll Fly Away, a civil rights drama set in the 60s. Chase, who is an Italian-American himself, was raised in New Jersey (where the series is set and filmed) and weaned on a diet of hard-boiled gangster movies. Consequently, Chase attempts to bring an authenticity and sense of verisimilitude to The Sopranos that is too often all too lacking in TV crime shows.

WHY IS THE SOPRANOS SO DAMNED GOOD?

The Sopranos is compulsive viewing because it works well on many different levels. The show's seamless blend of action, mood, emotion and pithy dialogue, seasoned with choice expletives, of course, is profoundly arresting: wry, ironical humour counterpoints moments of genuine pathos while scenes of graphic violence are juxtaposed with instances of domestic tenderness and sensitivity. David Chase and his crew have worked very skilfully at presenting a flawless drama. It's sharp and incisive but never too slick. Above all, the quality of script writing is exemplary. The dialogue crackles with authentic New Jersey patois while the vivid characters have prodigious life and substance: from the major starring roles down to minor, bit parts, each personality is fully-rounded, three-dimensional and totally believable. The Sopranos offers the potent kind of material that actors love getting their teeth into. James Gandolfini (who starred in True Romance, Get Shorty and Joel Schumacher's recent, controversial 8mm, among other things), gives a towering, charismatic performance as Tony Soprano. What makes Tony Soprano memorable is the pathos inherent in his situation: beneath

the callous mob exterior lies a soft un-
derbelly. It is this aspect of vulnerability
that endears the viewer to the Mafia capo.
Over the duration of thirteen gripping
episodes, we not only intimately ac-
quaint ourselves with Tony and both his
motley crews, but grow to care for them
too!

I LAUGHED UNTIL I DIED

There's an absurd, almost surreal element in *The Sopranos*, but it is this rare
quality that makes it true to life. There's a
moment in one episode where a truck
driver whose vehicle is hijacked is accidentally killed when a hoodlum drops
his gun. It's reminiscent of a scene in
Tarantino's *Pulp Fiction*, which elicits in
the viewer not only a moment of jaw-
dropping shock but also a wry chuckle at
the comic absurdity of it all. There's a
similar absurdity in Tony's interest in the
welfare of a pair of ducks that come to
the family's swimming pool. You wonder at the contradictions and vagaries in
the human condition that the programme
throws up for our contemplation: there's
big Tony, a ruthless bear of a man who
will (and does!) kill his enemies with his
bare hands if need be and there he is
worrying about a couple of wildfowl!
Despite the ruthless and brutal mores of
mob life, the viewer sees that Tony is not
a total monster but has a redeeming compassionate side to his personality. This
ambivalence creates a disquieting moral dilemma for the viewer.

THE SOPRANOS AS THE SIMPSONS?

The Sopranos achieves a near-perfect
balance between the domestic, human
side of Mafia life and its brutal business
practices. The balance between sardonic humour and hard-hitting, visceral drama is also spot-on. The series is in essence a tragi-comedy. Some observers
have perceived *The Sopranos* as a real

life version of America's most notorious
dysfunctional family, *The Simpsons*. It's
an intriguing comparison.

Although the show pays homage to
the great gangster movies of old, it is
also deeply satirical and pokes fun at
Mafia mythology. One of the show's most
mordant ironies is the fact that Tony's
crew quote passages from The Godfather as if it were some kind of holy scrip-
ture: Italian-American gangster movies
while attempting to reflect mob life have
actually contributed to the perpetuation
of Mafia mythology. Even more significantly, *The Sopranos* also breaks the
stereotyped moulds of gangster life. Can
you imagine Don Corleone consulting a
therapist?

THE SOPRANO FAMILY

TONY SOPRANO
(JAMES GANDOLFINI)
The only son of
racketeer Johnny Boy
Soprano, Tony is the
head-honcho of the New
Jersey Mob, assuming
the role of 'capo' after the death from
cancer of Jackie Aprile (although Tony's
Uncle Junior is installed as head of the
firm, little does he know that he's nothing
more than a puppet). Tony claims his
occupation is in *"waste disposal
management"* but curiously, he spends
most of his time either at a salubrious
strip joint called the Bada Bing, a
butcher's shop called The Pork Store or
the Centanni Meat market where he holds
council with his crew. He also services a
fiery young Russian mistress on his
'fuckpad,' a boat called the Stugats. At
other times, Tony can be found at his
mother's house (where he's often seen
kicking his car before leaving!). Tony is
the overlord of the underworld. He's a
likeable character but is a cold-blooded
killer when he needs to be. Sometimes,

the duties of moblife impinge too closely on his domestic responsibilities, causing immense stress: whilst taking Meadow on a tour of colleges in Maine, Tony spots an mafia informer and is compelled by mob law to dispatch the rat (which he does with a piece of rope). Meadow realises her father seems disturbed and flustered by something but has no clue that he's committed murder in such close proximity to her.

CARMELA SOPRANO (EDIE FALCO)

She's blonde, brash, a devout Catholic and obsessed with interior decorating. Carmela's been happily married to Tony for 18 years and has two teenaged children: a daughter, Meadow, and a pubescent son, Anthony Junior. Tony doesn't have a monopoly on stress—despite the designer clothes, a flash Mercedes and glitzy manicures, it's hard being married to a mobster. When Tony's away (often in the arms of his mistress), she watches movies on the DVD and shares pizza with a trendy young Catholic priest, Father Philip Intintola, who often comes over and administers Holy Communion at the Soprano residence.

LIVIA SOPRANO (NANCY MARCHAND)

Wretched, miserable and intent on giving her only son a mammoth guilt complex, the irascible Livia, at 70 years-of-age, is the quintessential Mafia matriarch. She has made a saint of her dead husband, Tony's father, and confides in her brother-in-law, the old-school hood, Junior Soprano. Her erratic and increasingly eccentric behaviour suggests impending dementia and forces

Tony and Carmela to relocate her from her own home to a plush retirement community, Green Grove.

MEADOW SOPRANO (JAMIE-LYN SIGLER)

As Tony and Carmela's daughter, Meadow is a model student who also excels at playing soccer and sings soprano in the school choir (the only kind of 'singing' that goes unpunished in a Mafia family!). She's the apple of Tony's eye but her advancing maturity and nascent womanliness (she's 16) disconcerts her father. Tony becomes apoplectic when he discovers she's tried speed (he's unaware that one of his crew also supplied it!).

ANTHONY SOPRANO JNR. (ROBERT ILER)

Like most suburban adolescents, young Anthony (pronounced with a soft 't') has his cerebral cortex hardwired into his Nintendo console and is not averse to downloading porn from the net. He realises his father's 'connected' when a school adversary uncharacteristically backs out of a fist-fight (his curiosity as to his father's occupation is also aroused when he spots 'Feds' jotting down number plates at Jackie Aprile's funeral). Commits a cardinal sin by stealing the sacramental wine!

JUNIOR SOPRANO/ AKA CORRADO ENRICO SOPRANO (DOMINIC CHIANESE)

Bespectacled and always seen sporting a flat cap, the hawkish

Junior, is the older brother of Tony's father, Johnny Boy Soprano. He bonded with Tony at an early age by taking him to ball games. But Junior's volatility and absence of both discretion and wisdom is always upsetting other people (and more often than not, it's Tony who has to step into the dispute as peacemaker). Armed with traditional mob values, Junior is particularly wary of the ambitious young hoodlums trying to work their way up through the ranks. Unbeknownst to Junior, who's only a figure-head, the real power is wielded by his nephew, Tony. When the truth finally dawns on old Junior the 'merda' literally hits the fan!

CHRISTOPHER MOLTISANI (MICHAEL IMPERIOLI)

The son of Carmella's cousin, good-looking, twenty-something Chris is an ambitious, over-zealous but immature member of the Soprano crew. His one aim in life is to be a 'made' guy but he's always blowing his chances by doing dumb things. Tony is attached to the kid but is frequently angered by Chris's impetuous behaviour and potentially hazardous antics (he begins writing a screenplay about mob life and also shoots a toe off the proprietor of a cake shop when he doesn't get served promptly!).

KEY CHARACTERS

PUSSY BOMPENSIERO /AKA BIG PUSSY (VINCENT PASTORE)

Described by Tony Soprano as a 'stone gangster,' the corpulent, cigar-chomping figure of Big Pussy eats and drinks well but plays rough. He grew up with Tony and is one of the crew's main men.

SILVIO DANTE (STEVEN VAN ZANDT)

Smartly-attired member of Tony's crew with slicked-back hair who happens to own one of Tony's main hangouts, the Bada Bing strip club.

PAULIE WALNUTS (TONY SIRICO)

A bona-fide hardnut. He is enraged by what he sees as the *"rape of Italian culture"*—he fervently believes the mob should be gathering royalties from anyone in business who sells Pizza or cappuccino!

DETECTIVE VIN MAKAZIAN (JOHN HEARD)

A bent New Jersey cop who's on Tony Soprano's payroll because of excessive drinking, gambling debts and two extortionate alimonies. He does surveillance (at Tony's behest) on Dr. Melfi and in his eagerness to please ends up hospitalising her boyfriend.

HESH RABKIN (JERRY ADLER)

Hesh was a record producer who was in on payola scams in the 50s. He's Jewish but is a trusted and well-respected member of Tony's clan (he counselled Tony's pop), although because he's not Italian, Hesh can't be inducted into the mob and become a 'made' guy. Tony helps Hesh out when a truculent rapper tries to muscle in on the music publishing scene.

DR.JENNIFER MELFI (LORRAINE BRACCHO)

Dr. Melfi is herself from Italian-American stock and is aware of the implications of her professional relationship with a mobster like Tony Soprano. She's acts as Tony's confessor and is unfazed by the don's connections and displays even more equanimity when he declares that he's in love with her!

THE MOBSPEAK LEXICON:

(FROM *THE SOPRANOS* WEBSITE):

borgata: an organised crime Family

capo: the Family member who leads a crew; short for capodecina

captain: a capo

clip: to murder; also whack, hit, pop, burn, put a contract out

code of silence: not ratting on your colleagues once you've been pinched—no longer a strong virtue in organised crime families!

confirm: to be made; see made guy

consigliere: the Family advisor, who is always consulted before decisions are made

crank: speed; in particular, crystal meth

crew: the group of soldiers under the capo's command

cugine: a young soldier striving to be made

don: the head of the family; see boss

eat alone: to keep for one's self; to be greedy

family: an organised crime clan

G: a grand; a thousand dollars; also see large

garbage business: euphemism for organised crime

Golden Age: the days before RICO

goomah: a Mafia mistress; also comare

heavy: packed, carrying a weapon

hit: to murder

juice: the interest paid to a loan shark for the loan; see vig

lam: to lay down, go into hiding

large: a thousand, a grand, a G

made guy: an indoctrinated member of the Family

mock execution: to whip someone into shape by frightening the shit out of them!

mattresses: going to, taking it to, or hitting the: going to war with a rival clan or Family

message job: placing the bullet in someone's body such that a specific message is sent to that person's crew or family

mob: a single organised crime family; OR all organised crime families together

mobbed up: connected to the mob

Omert : to take a vow of silence, punishable by death if not upheld

rat: one who snitches or squeals after being pinched

RICO: Racketeer Influenced and Corrupt Organisations Act. Passed in 1970 to aid the government in clamping down on organised crime activities, its scope has since broadened to prosecute insider traders and anti-abortion protesters.

shake down: to blackmail or try to extort money from someone; also to scare someone

shy: the interest charged on loans by loansharks

shylock business: the business of loansharking

soldier: the bottom-level member of an organised crime Family, as in 'footsoldiers'

This Thing Of Ours: a mob family or the entire mob

through the eye: a message job through the eye to say *"We're watching you!"*

through the mouth: a message job through the mouth to indicate that someone WAS a rat

underboss: the second in command to the boss

vig: the interest paid to a loanshark for the loan. Abbreviation of vigorish; see also juice

waste management business: euphemism for organised crime

whack: to murder

wiseguy: a made guy

A second series of *The Sopranos* is already under production and starts screening in the USA on January 16th next year with Channel Four likely to follow suit next summer. Let's hope that the show's dramatic potency is not diluted by an over-reliance on stale formulas. Fingers crossed!

* If, perchance, you missed this wonderful series, episodes are now available to purchase on video. Unless you live in the US (sorry!).

* For the web-surfers out there in CT land, check out *The Sopranos'* informative website: http://hbo.com/sopranos/

FORTHCOMING ATTRACTIONS

In the early 1960s, she played Emma Peel, the leather-bound, karate-kicking female sidekick of the suave John Steed in *The Avengers*. These days, however, Diana Rigg, is considered a grand dame of the British theatre and as such plays roles that require a little more gravitas.

In the New Year, Rigg returns in less provocative attire to the small screen as Mrs. Adela Bradley, a chic, drawing-room sleuth in *The Mrs.Bradley Mysteries* with Neil Dudgeon (George Moody, her chauffeur and confidante) and Peter Davidson (Inspector Christmas) assisting. A favourable critical response to last summer's Mrs. Bradley feature has prompted the BBC to commission a new series of films which follow the exploits of the eponymous heroine. The series was inspired by the novels of Gladys Mitchell and is set in the 1920s. In each film, Mrs. Bradley, an affluent, upper-class, amateur detective and a fervent disciple of Freud's pyscho-analytical doctrines, investigates a series of brutal and perplexing murders. In contrast with other whodunits, the show's protagonist, Mrs. Bradley, occasionally plays directly to the camera, addressing the audience with witty asides. Although a transmission date is yet to be confirmed, *The Mrs. Bradley Mysteries* will probably be screened in the early part of the New Year.

Also figuring strongly in the Beeb's New Year plans is *The Wyvern Mystery*, a one-off thriller based on a novel by the cult 19th century horror writer, J.S. Le Faun . Set at the beginning of the last century, *The Wyvern Mystery* stars Derek Jacobi (*I Claudius, Cadfael*) as a nefarious squire who has lustful designs on an orphaned girl he brought up—it also transpires that he was responsible for the death of the girl's father. The heroine is played by *Tank Girl* star, Australian actress, Naomi Watts in her British TV debut. Sinister intrigue, horror and a spine-chilling finale ensue.

Not to be outdone by the Beeb's devotion to high-quality crime drama, ITV have commissioned two feature-length Poirot movies from Carnival Films. After a five-year hiatus, David Suchet reprises his role as Agatha Christie's meticulous Belgian detective, Hercule Poirot.

Supporting Suchet is his stalwart team comprised of Philip Jackson (Chief Inspector Japp), Hugh Fraser (Captain Hastings) and Pauline Moran (Miss Lemon). In the first film, *The Murder Of Roger Ackroyd*, we find the man with the 'little grey cells' enjoying retirement and cultivating marrows in the countryside. Poirot's retirement is put on hold when the slaying of a local business man arouses his suspicions.

In the second Poirot feature, *Lord Edgware Dies*, we discover that country life did not agree with the Belgian detective, who has since returned to residence at London's Whitehaven Mansions. It's worth noting that Suchet co-starred in a 1985 film version of this Christie tale (retitled *Thirteen At Dinner*), playing Inspector Japp opposite Peter Ustinov's masterly portrayal of the famous detective. Suchet later confessed that it represented the worst performance of his career and prompted him to contemplate how different it would be if he could play Poirot himself. Well, the rest, as they say, is history.

There's a possibility that ITV will screen the first of these films over the Christmas period with the other following in the New Year.

...and finally
john kennedy melling

GOLDEN DISTAFF

Numerically, male sleuths outnumbered the fair sex in the Golden Era. Equally many of the men were unmistakably characters, with charisma, as we didn't say then. There were Toffs, the Wimseys, Vances, Saints, Queens, Norman Conquests, all in the era of "silly assery". Then the police detectives - Freeman Wills Crofts (1879-1957) with Inspector French from 1925: G D H. and M Cole (1889-1959) and (1893-1980) brought in the heavier Superintendent Wilson in 1923: and Dame Agatha Christie (1890-1976) invented Superintendent Battle that same year. The intellectuals like Dr. Priestley who first appeared in that same year again (a good vintage) from John Rhode (1884-1965). What of the distaff side? Indeed they, too, all seemed to qualify as characters. One of the first, and London based, was Lady Molly Of Scotland Yard , whose cases in short stories appeared in 1910 from Baroness Orczy (1865-1947). She spends five years whilst proving her husband's innocence. Baroness Orczy also pro-duced another female Watson, but unlike Lady Molly the case solver, her short stories first appeared five years earlier from The Old Man in the Corner whose cases ended in 1925 (yet again); he used to meet story-teller Polly Burton in the tea shop in Norfolk Street (you won't find it now). Of his thirty eight cases, twelve became short films in 1924. Let's look in alphabetical order at some female sleuths. Nurse Hilda Adams (Mary Roberts Rinehart, 1876-1958), nicknamed "Miss Pinkerton" and very like her creator, first appeared as such in 1932 and for the next ten years. A film of that title in 1932 from First National/Warner starred Joan Blondell, 66 minutes, black and white, then was remade in 1946 by Warner, as The Nurse's Secret, starring Les Patrick, who will be remembered as Sam Spade's secretary in the great The Maltese Falcon. In complete contrast comes Dame Beatrice Aidela Lestrange Bradley, the Home Office psychologist, described as looking like a lizard or snake, with an electric cackle. Gladys Mitchell (1901-

1983) introduced her in 1929 in *Speedy Death* and her final novel was in 1984, *The Crosier Pharaohs*. Patricia Craig, who with Mary Cadogan wrote the excellent history *The Lady Investigates*, shewed me her complete shelf of charmingly signed Bradley novels. Unconventional eccentric, a law unto herself, and a great problem solver. In different mould is Miss Climpson, the secretarial agent who helps Lord Peter Wimsey, first in *Unnatural Death*, 1927, then in *Strong Poison*, three years later. She lives in London, knows Bloomsbury well, and is the invention of Dorothy L. Sayers (1893-1957). Some of Wimsey's fatuous humour rubs off on. In Washington, D. C., lives Mrs. Grace Latham, attractive if slightly annoying widow, friend of the patient Colonel John Primrose, the official investigator devised by Leslie Ford (Zenith Ford (Zenith Brown, 1898-1983), in a series starting with *Ill Met By Midnight*. Latham is slightly of the Had I But Known or Gothic School. Dame Agatha Christie based Miss Jane Marple on her own grandmother, and though Joan Hickson would be a natural choice for the role, as she proved on BBC-TV - much unlike Dame Margaret Rutherford's more blancmange approach in four films. She first appeared in *The Murder At The Vicarage* in 1930, and lasted till 1976. This first novel varied greatly from the TV production and from the West End play which ran for years, as I know because I saw the latter at least seven times, especially when my friend Barbara Miller, who suggested the title of *Murder Done To Death* for my recent book, was playing in it. Miss Marple, with china blue eyes and white hair compares village sins with murder motives successfully. Incidentally St. Mary Mead is in Kent in *The Mystery Of The Blue Train*, but switched Westwards soon after. Miss Palmyre Pym was created by Nigel Morland, the criminologist (1905-1986) and her titles started with *The Phantom Gunman* in 1935, lasting through over twenty novels until 1961. One alleged American authority wrote that she appeared in some half-dozen novels! I have always admired her car, with its specially strengthened bumpers marked Jump Or Die. A delightful 65 minute black-and-white film was made in Britain in 1939 with the redoubtable Mary Clare in grey costume trouncing the ungodly. Patricia Wentworth (1878-1961) devised Miss Maud Silver in 1926 in *Grey Mask*, and the former governess and spinster was still solving the crime of *The Girl In The Cellar* in 1961. Fond of knitting, like Miss Marple, but unlike her, Maudie is a professional investigator, whose clients can be friends or strangers. Finally retired headmistress Miss Hildegarde Withers was created by film scriptwriter (Falcon, Bulldog Drummond) Stuart Palmer (1905-1968) in 1932 in *The Penguin Pool Murder*, and the series lasted till 1969; she was based on his own father and on his high school English teacher. She helps successfully Inspector Oscar Piper of NYPD solve his cases. Edna May Oliver played her in three PKO films from 1932, then Helen Broderick, and finally Zasu Pitts, in the last two. Elegant, wisecracking Eve Arden portrayed her on TV. So, these ladies couldn't be more different, but they are all unforgettable, indelible and fascinating as they make the Golden Age even more glistening!

FACE TO FACE WITH F. A.C.E

Another valuable contact when Gwendoline Butler and I visited New York's Police was Frank Domingo, one of the finest forensic artists in America if not world-wide. We rang him from Delmonico's, and we took him, in his car, to lunch in a very soignée fish restaurant in the Fulton Fish Market. After taking us to a large crime bookshop nearby he drove us to the John Day College of Criminal Justice in Tenth Avenue (happy echoes of Slaughter On) to meet the Editor of Law Enforcement News, the attractive and talented Marie Simonetti Rosen. Frank's last fifteen years till 1993 in NYPD was as a Composite Artist, Detective. Then he set up his won Studio and Business in Malverne, NY, as F. A. C. E. , the acronym for Forensic Art Counselling Enterprises. His amazing work outside police art include the facial reproduction of the British Honduras "Crystal Skull", the facial recreation of Alexander the Great, from terra cotta fragments and, above all, his recreation of the Sphinx in Egypt, proving it to be thousands of years older than previously thought. A composite artist's work is not confined to preparing a likeness of a perp from the witness(es) description, or putting the face on to a skull. He must be able to age a face to shew what it would be like some years later; if a victim hasn't photographed his valuable, and now stolen antiques, he must be able to produce an identifiable likeness - or even the image of a complete person seen by a witness. Sometimes he may have to depict a perp's visage from the memories of more than one witness - and without prompting them, or letting them prompt each other. (I remember a crime film in the 1940's where the artist carefully draws a face from the witness's description , only to find it ended up as that comedy actor, playing the cop, Allen Jenkins!) Weapons, tattoos, vehicles, clothing, all must be within his artistic skills. Furthermore, he must have a friendly, encouraging personality, be adept in psychology and coping with a witness under stress, e.g. a rape victim, or unable to express himself very coherently, over-anxious to help, or intimidated by being in a police office. Was the perp at the head of a staircase? if so, foreshortening will occur, or parallax. Frank Domingo proved an eminently knowledgeable, precisely-spoken and most amiable professional, from whom we learnt a lot in a few hours and who has done much to bring the skills of the composite artist as a valuable adjunct to the investigator.

UPLIFT FOR A VAULT

The recent Little, Brown party in Crime In Store was both elegant and sophisticated in the organisation. *The Vault* is the title of Peter Lovesey's latest book from that publishing house. There were only two speeches, both neat, crisp, short and eminently audible none in all parts of the shop which was closed for the occasion. Rosalie Macfarlane from the company introduced Peter, and he explained with his strong sense of humour twenty one was a lucky number for him - it is his 21st. book, on January 21st., and he has just been sold to his 21st. country, and so on. The guest list was a microcosm of the genre. The women writers included Gwendoline Butler, perhaps our best-dressed scribe, and ex-policewoman Joan Lock, escorted by her attentive and witty husband. The authors were headed by debonair New Yorker Otto Penzler, Donald Rumbelow and Harry Keating. Editors were represented by Hilary Hale, one of the best of that ilk. A few of the most enthusiastic fan-readers also attended, all looked after by affable manager Geoffrey Bailey.

CONGRATULATIONS

A most useful reference book over the years has been *The Lady Investigates*, (mentioned earlier), a comprehensive survey of lady detectives by Mary Cadogan and Patricia Craig. These two have collaborated on other books, notably *You're A Brick, Angela*, the history of girls' literature, and have each written their own differing books. Patricia Craig, edits anthologies as well, including the volume of Detective Stories. Mary has another unusual interest in that she edits the useful monthly Story Paper Collectors Digest. Her big news is that the Digest celebrates its Golden Jubilee this year and it seems to be the only such magazine that has stayed on its own strict unbroken course all its life. It covers detective fiction, with essays on the canon of Sexton Blake. In the October issue is a piece refuting that the Blake stories contained no highly educated females, citing Yvonne Cartier, another on the Nelson Lee Library, and a third about the detective Up-To-You Pilkington in Comic Cuts Congratulations to Mary Cadogan and if you're interested in her private, non-profit making magazine contact her at 46, Overbury Avenue, Beckenham, Kent, BR3 6PY.

John Kennedy Melling is a critic, public speaker, and all round good chap, whose book Murder Done To Death *(Scarecrow Press) is required reading for lovers of the parody and pastiche in detective fiction.*

back issues

Crime Time 1 Our debut issue contains interviews with John Harvey, Martina Cole, Derek Raymond, Andrew Klavan (*True Crime*). Plus, features on *Cracker*, Colin Wilson, Griff, Dannie M Martin, and our notorious reviews section.

Crime Time 2 Sorry, sold out.

Crime Time 3 We interview Robert Rodriguez (*Desperado*) and Michael Mann (*Heat*), investigate the transvestite hitman fiction of Ed Wood Jr, talk the talk with Elizabeth George, Elliott Leyton, and Lawrence Block, give the low-down on German crime fiction, and feature an article by Booker prize nominee Julian Rathbone.

Crime Time 4 'The Violence Issue' Reservoir Dog, ex-con and writer Edward Bunker tells us how it is, Ben Elton takes the piss out of it, Joe Eszterhas exploits it, Morgan Freeman abhors it. Plus *Mission: Impossible*, *Heaven's Prisoners* (Phil Joanou), *Curdled*, Kinky Friedman, *The Bill* and *The Verdict*!.

Crime Time 5 Female Trouble! Interviews with Patricia Cornwell, Michael Dibdin, James Sallis and William Gibson. *Feisty Femmes And Two- Fisted Totty* gives the lowdown on women PIs, Ed Gorman talks about Gold Medal books of the Fifties, Hong Kong filmmakers Wong Kar-Wai & Christopher Doyle discuss *Fallen Angels*, and Michael Mann (*Heat*) is examined.

Crime Time 6 The Mean Streets issue contains interviews with writers James Ellroy, Gwendoline Butler, Sara Paretsky and Joseph Hansen, and film directors George Sluizer and Andrew Davis. Articles include Post-War Paperback Art, Batman, Crime Time:The Movie, and Steve Holland's excellent Pulp Fictions.

Crime Time 7 Val McDermid, Hong Kong Cinema, Phillip Margolin, Molly Brown, Ian Rankin, Michael Connelly, Daniel Woodrell and a cast of 1000s in this special 96 page issue!

Crime Time 8 Fantastic! Homicide, Faye and Jonathan Kellerman, Mark Timlin, Anthony Frewin, Gerald Kersh, Gwendoline Butler, Chandler on Celluloid, James Sallis on Chester Himes, The Payback Press and the biggest review section yet!

Crime Time 9 We *Got Carter*, with *Get Carter!* director Mike Hodges writing about making the film and Paul Duncan profiling the man who wrote *Jack's Return Home*. This plus scads of good stuff and the inimitable review section...

Crime Time 10 *Sin City*, Ed Gorman interviewed, Lawrence Block in the Library, Stella Duffy, Lauren Henderson, Sean Hughes, Denise Danks, Jerome Charyn and a cast of squillions...

Crime Time 11 Shut It!!! *The Sweeney* cover feature with those cheeky chappies Regan and Carter, Colin Dexter, Sparkle Hayter, David Williams, Gary Phillips, Janwillem Van De Wetering and the Great Grandam of kid's crime Enid Blyton.

Crime Time 12 The Last Time! (In floppy format anyway!) Joe R Lansdale, Simon Brett, Jay Russell, Steve Lopez,

James Patterson, *Black Mask* magazine and the late Derek Raymond on Ted Lewis.

Crime Time 2.1 We re-invent ourselves in shorter, thicker trade paperback format, with interviews with features and fiction including James Sallis, Mark Timlin, Gwendoline Butler, Colin Dexter, Alan Moore, Jerry Sykes, Edward Bunker and more! 288 pages of sheer crime pleasure

Crime Time 2.2 Ed McBain, Mark Timlin, Steve Aylett, Fred Willard, Gary Phillips, Jason Starr, Russell James, Neil Jordan, Stuart Dawson, Paul Duncan and a host of others make this the most enjoyable 288 pages since the last issue of *Crime Time.*

Crime Time 2.3: Loads of stuff, just take our word for it. Oh, OK. Reg Hill, John Milne, Sharky the Sharkdog (just checking to see you're awake), Mark Timlin, Simon Clark. Much too much to list here. An aardvark to you, guv.

Crime Time 2.4 Sipowicz speaks as we interview Denis Franz from *NYPD Blue* and present a full epsiode guide to the series. Featured Authors include Caroline Graham, Robert ?Goddard, Michael Connelly, Paul Doherty and a cast of thousands...

Crime Time 2.5: Can Mel Gibson fill the shoes of Lee Marvin (answer: No) in the remake of *Point Blank*? Nick Blincoe, Jerry Raine, Alison Joseph, Val McDermid, Ron Ellis and others round the excitement off.

Each issue up till number 12 is £3.00 post paid in the UK (please add £3.00 p&p per order overseas and Southern Ireland). Issues 2.1 onwards are £5.00 each. Make cheques payable to 'Crime Time' and send your orders to: **Back Issues (Dept CT26) Crime Time, 18 Coleswood Rd, Harpenden, Herts AL5 1EQ.**